BRO

to

Beautiful

Jake Lynch

ISBN 979-8-9893828-1-1 (paperback)
ISBN 979-8-9893828-0-4 (hardcover)

Printed in the United States of America

To all those who are struggling
and trying to find hope.

Foreword

This book is not meant for everyone. This book is meant for those who feel like loners and losers. For the people who feel stuck and aren't doing too well right now. If you are looking for a happy, chill, entertaining story to read, then I suggest you go do something else. This will not be a light-hearted read. For this book is not meant for the winners, it's meant for the losers.

A fair warning, this book will draw out the darkest moments of your life. It will deal with issues you would probably want to have buried and be able to simply forget about. However, if you want to find hope in this dark, cruel world, then keep on reading. Trust me, there is a reason for all of this.

So, to my fellow compatriots out there, I wish you good luck, and I hope you enjoy my story.

The Dream

"Life without purpose is unbearable."

—Krystal Henninger

Wind flapping through her hair, the cold rooftop concrete beneath her feet swam with activity. Her shoes were dirty, her dress fluttering in the wind as she stared toward the city before her. The night sky and lights made the city look like the circulatory system of a living organism, as the lights pulsed and flickered, the streets of cars calmed and stopped before running on again.

She stood there, her body trembling. The wind blew her hair wildly as she stared out feeling empty and broken, having nothing to live for. Tears streaked down her face in strong twin rivers as she tried to keep it in. She tried to hold back the scream for as long as she possibly could, but the emotion in her heart kept building and building. There was no sound as she stood on the rooftop alone and screamed.

PART ONE

Suffering

CHAPTER 1

A Day in The Life

"What is the point of living if it is only endless suffering?"

—Krystal Henninger

She slowly opened her eyes, revealing a stark white ceiling as her vision cleared. She took her time, having no desire or care to rush. She took in a breath, letting the air fill her lungs and for a moment she thought, *It's gone. It's finally gone.* Her thoughts betrayed her as the emptiness and depression came back as strongly as they did the night before, maybe more. The gaping hole inside her chest pulsed and expanded, sucking portions of the air from her lungs. She immediately felt exhausted. Her arms and legs were heavy, her brain and mind yearning for the day to already be over. She moved her arm and laid it in the center of her chest, digging her fingertips gently into her skin, attempting to reach down into that gaping hole inside her and rip it out. But there was no hole. Not physically at least. And yet, she still dug her fingertips in as much as she could until she could bear the pain no longer, removing her hand from her sternum and lying it flat against the bed.

Her head turned slowly, without enthusiasm or endeavor, and glanced over at the phone on the table next to her. She picked it up and checked the time, 5:43am, at least fifteen minutes before her alarm would go off. She wanted to groan, to complain about waking up too early but there were no words. She just sighed and moved on. She laid back in her bed in silence, staring at the ceiling for another few minutes. She took in slow, deep breaths, hoping the oxygen would relieve her and give her energy, but there was none to be found. She was as tired as when she went to bed the night before. She let out a slow exhale and leaned forward, her legs and lower body still covered with the bed sheets. She stared down at her lap. Her mind and soul with no motivation whatsoever to get out of bed. There was no hope. No reason to breathe. She wanted to check her phone again, but she knew it hadn't even been one minute. Every breath was a struggle. A fight to survive. But for what? Why did she go on living? Why was she living at all? She remained still and stared down at her lap.

Kill yourself. The girl felt her body slowly tense as she felt a stab of disappointment in her heart. *No, not again. Not now.* But her thoughts ran rampant. She rolled up into a ball, ignoring the fatigue, and clamped her hands over her ears, a vain attempt to block out the suicidal thoughts from entering her mind.

You should kill yourself . . .

Why don't you kill yourself . . .

Isn't there something better to this life than suffering?

Why do you go on living, huh?

What terrified her most of all, was how the thoughts were spoken in her own voice, playing through her head. It was not the sound of a creepy stranger or devil with a pitchfork playing tricks in her head. It was her own voice she was hearing. That made it even more vivid. Hearing your own self telling you to kill yourself.

Don't think about it. Don't think about it. Just think about something else. But fighting it only made it worse. The suicidal thoughts ran rampant inside her mind, draining what little energy she had left before leaving her an empty wreck on her bed. The thoughts subsided for a time, and she was left with a sense of gloom floating over her, with the belief that things wouldn't get better, that she was *trapped.*

The girl reached for her phone and checked the time. 5:47am. Only four minutes had passed and she was already done with the day. She clicked the phone off and stared at the screen reflection of herself, looking deeply into her eyes. Her midnight purple eyes stared back, watching just how lifeless they were. Eyes with no hope. She thought, *I have no hope. No reason to get out of bed. Why do I bother to keep on breathing? Why?* Then she thought, *I'm a loser. I don't have any friends. No reason to feel loved.* She wanted to cry, to wrap her arms around herself and tell herself that it would be alright, but she was too tired to lift her arms. Exhausted, she dropped her phone and stared at the ceiling in dread, wishing for the day to already be over.

She opened her door and headed toward the kitchen. The girl stepped into the stark white kitchen with the black granite countertop with the stove in the center and other materials spread across it. Next to the kitchen was the living room, containing a table, a tv, and a tanned sofa. She glanced over at the kitchen table and found a plate of cold eggs and bacon wrapped under some plastic. A note written on it, saying, *Hope you have a wonderful day today sweetie! Love mom.*

The girl wanted to smile but she didn't share her mom's enthusiasm for what the day would bring. She knew exactly what was going to happen today. She put down the note, unwrapped the plate, and heated up the food in the microwave. Everything felt gray, like there was a trench coat of gloom hovering over her. She sat down with the steaming plate of food before her, tried to smell the food, to feel hungry. She hadn't felt like eating for a while now, but she forced herself to pick up the fork and take a bite.

It was difficult. Simply raising the fork and forcing herself to chew was torture in itself. She didn't even taste the egg in her mouth. She swallowed and took a sip of water. She felt the dead silence of the morning with nothing but herself and her thoughts. She stabbed her fork into another piece of food, hoping the sweet taste of bacon would fill her soul with a little happiness . . . it didn't. She looked around and felt nothing but the emptiness of the apartment around her. Dread filling every cell in her body.

The bus came to a halt as the dreary sight of the school filled her vision. She raised her head and felt her guard go up as she stared at the buildings in front of her. She couldn't help but feel the sense that she was trapped somehow. Like a convict knowingly going back to prison against their will. The girl stared with saddened reluctance, breathing a deep breath, and sighed. *Here we go again.*

The girl stepped down from the bus onto the concrete ground. She took her first steps, looking up at the ocean of gray in front of her. Her feet moved on automatic, heading toward her locker as always.

She finished her errand at her locker and headed toward her usual spot in the main courtyard of school. The courtyard was the heart of the school, as all students needed to pass through it to get to their classes. The girl's bench was perched along the side of the courtyard with a pleasant view of the rest of the area. She found her usual white bench covered in bird dung and laid her backpack down on the side, avoiding the bird droppings, and waited. The girl watched as groups of students began flowing into the courtyard. Gradually, the cliques began to form into neat circles as she watched them develop one by one, watching silently from a distance.

A fancy blue Porsche pulled up and parked in the front lot, and out stepped the beautiful Kristina Walker. She had a sleek figure and was tall for a girl. Kristina was easily a head taller than her but emanated true beauty with her pale white skin combined with her gorgeous black hair down her back. The girl thought Kristina even looked like her too, aside from the lustrous clothing she wore. People from all around drew their sights toward Kristina Walker, the famous actress in their hometown. Every day, like clockwork, she came up to the front of the school dressed in beautiful fashion and addressed the crowd with enthusiasm. The girl's interest quickly died as she shifted her attention elsewhere.

She watched as more and more people funneled into the courtyard and the cliques began to complete their circles. Across the way were the most popular people in school, with Summer McAdams as the head of the group and by far the most confident out of all of them, followed by her best friend Amber Cutthrose, accompanied by Jonathan Newhart, Cassie Newman, Luiz Patron, Jaime Fisher, and a dozen more people. Even the teachers were fond of them and gave the group a lot of praise. For some reason unknown to her, the girl had always wanted to be one of them. She was conscious of the idea of popular kids, but there was something about this group that made her want to be friends with them. Was it the happiness they seemed to exude? The seemingly carefree life they had? She didn't know.

She watched from her bench with saddened interest as the clique engaged with each other. Summer had just arrived and was given a warm greeting from everyone in the group. The girl couldn't help but compare herself. Imagining herself being greeted by a large group of people who were happy to have her there. The idea seemed so unreal, so distant, so imaginary, like it was only a pipedream, one that may never come true. The girl's heart was heavy and she felt it drop, tugging at her, depressing her mood. *I wish I could have something like that.* Instantly, she felt self-conscious about just how alone she really was. It felt like there was a distance between herself and everyone around her, even the people passing by. She felt like a ghost, that no matter what she did, nobody would see her. It felt as if the whole world had slowed down, and she could do nothing but suffer all alone. A prisoner of her own misery.

She heard thick boots clambering by; the girl shifted her attention and saw one of her old classmates from elementary school, Andrew Holcomb, heading her way. He sat next to her all throughout third, fourth, and fifth grade, and was dressed in his typical military outfit, or mostly it was just a camouflaged shirt with a military backpack. But nonetheless, he was heading her way. The girl tried to feel some sense of joy at the sight of her old classmate but felt only a lingering sense of disappointment. She hadn't talked to him in years, so maybe seeing him would raise her spirits a bit. She paused and felt the words lodged in her throat. Andrew came closer and was now walking right in front of her, when the girl stood up, looked directly at him, and waved well within his line of sight in an attempt to get his attention. She expected Andrew to stop and notice her, but he kept on walking like she didn't exist. Her faked cheerfulness died quickly, letting her hand drop and a sense of betrayal tear her heart. She sat back down on her bench and wrapped her arms around her knees.

Maybe he didn't see me? But she knew the truth.

Yes, he did.

The girl felt self-conscious again, watching now as all the cliques around the school courtyard fully developed. There were at least a dozen groups spread throughout the courtyard, all of them contagious with laughter and high smiles. The growing chatter filled the din of the courtyard as the school slowly came to life like a sleeping beast awaking from its slumber. The girl could do nothing but merely stare at the backs of every single clique around her. Everywhere she looked, there was another group of people standing or sitting in a perfect circle, with their backs all facing her. She couldn't help but feel shut off and distant from the sight of their backs, all of them telling her, "Go away!" The pain in her chest was so strong her heart almost choked. The emptiness and gloom encompassing her, suffocating her soul and draining all hope, leaving only the husk of shell she was. Her gaze drifted from left to right across the courtyard, and everywhere she looked, there was another clique, and with every clique, she felt even more isolated from them. She compared herself again, feeling self-conscious with every glance, sitting alone on her white bench with no one to talk to, no one to sit with, no one to share how their weekend was with her. She was completely and utterly alone.

She crumpled into a ball again. *I'm a loser. Just a loner who doesn't have any friends. I don't deserve to live.* Now that was a thought the girl did not contest. She could feel that was truly how she thought of herself. Her head naturally lowered to the ground, staring with dead eyes at the black gum-ridden spots on the concrete slabs beneath her.

Three hundred eighty-seven, she thought. *Three hundred eighty-seven.* The school bell rang, it was time to go to class.

The teacher finished writing, Y=MX+B, on the board and said, "Can anyone tell me what this is?" He pointed the dry eraser at the "b" and waited for the class to answer his question. The room was dead silent. The girl sat at her desk near the far back. The air in the room was so dry and uncomfortable that any motion was immediately noticed. She kept her right hand planted firmly on the desk as the teacher scanned the class, waiting for an answer. The girl bit her tongue and kept her head down. *Please, someone answer.*

The teacher grew suspicious and asked, "Can anyone tell me what's the square root of sixteen?" Again, the whole class remained silent. Of course, the answer was four, but the girl wasn't going to say it. She knew the answer, but she didn't want to say it out of fear of being seen and heard by everyone in the room. She secretly checked the room, with the expectation that someone would answer. That someone brave would raise their hand and answer the question. But no one did. Even if someone did speak up, they would leave the comfort of their seat and have thirty people staring at them, expecting them to get the right answer. And if they got the wrong answer, they would have to suffer the humiliation of answering the question wrong in front of the entire class. So naturally, they all sat there quietly and hoped someone *else* would answer the question.

After what felt like ten years had passed, the teacher finally said, "Four! The answer is four."

Please, the girl thought. *Let this end.* The teacher reluctantly gave up, turning his back to the class, and went back to giving his lesson. The entire class stopped holding its breath and relaxed for a minute. The girl exhaled, relieved it was over, then she looked at the clock and let out a silent groan. *Only an hour and thirty-eight minutes left.* She sighed and leaned her cheek against her fist. She took her eyes off the clock and tried to focus again on the teacher as he finished the lesson.

You should kill yourself!

The girl flinched but fought hard to not freak out. It took every ounce of willpower she had to keep herself from screaming. She tried again to pay attention to the teacher, but the words echoed in her mind on repeat.

Why don't you kill yourself?

You should kill yourself.

Come on, you should just do it. Do it right here and now.

No one will miss you.

She quietly leaned her head into her arms and surreptitiously put her hands over her ears. Hoping it would somehow block out the awful, intrusive thoughts that took over her brain like parasites, each one more intense than the last.

I don't want to think these thoughts. I don't want to think about this. But the suicidal thoughts kept raging in her mind while the dead silence of the classroom was undisturbed.

You should kill yourself.

Please, I don't want to think these thoughts.

You should kill yourself. Make all the pain go away.

The sound of her own voice in her head made her body tense and begin to shake, but she held herself together so as not to disrupt anyone around her. She cupped her hands over her ears and thought, *Someone please, save me! Please! Someone save me!* Her eyes peered through the cracks in her arms at people around her in class, but no one seemed to notice her suffering. Not one person seemed to notice how close she was to having a breakdown in the middle of class. They were all in their own worlds, oblivious to the pain around them. Her pain. But she couldn't freak out, that would only make her stand out even more and that would cause people to not like her. They would think she's a freak and wouldn't want to hang out with her. So, what options did she have left? Suck it up and be quiet. Because that's just the way things are in this school. The silent agenda, the unwritten rules of society. And so, the girl looked back up at the clock, wishing the long arm would hurry up and complete its hour.

She blinked a few times to prevent her eyes from drying out, leaning forward on her desk, taking her hands from her ears and laying her head in her arms like a pillow. She peeked in the corner of her eye and saw Summer McAdams sitting on the far-right side of the classroom, looking cheerful and energetic as ever. The girl could also see Amber Cutthrose sitting next to Summer. The two of them sneaking text messages with each other, doing their best to keep their laughter contained.

The girl yearned; *I wish I could be part of that. To have that comradery with someone. To laugh and share life with people over the simplest of things.* She felt a stab of pain inside her chest. The emptiness within her soul grew deeper every day, having grown from the size of a drop of water, now to the size of the Pacific Ocean. The stress and power it had over her drained her willpower and left her exhausted. She wasn't sure how much more of this she could take.

It was accompanied by a thought, *There's got to be more to life than this.* This time she didn't fight this thought; she didn't entertain it either. She just sat there, feeling her soul ache from the emptiness within. The girl stuck out her tongue and could have sworn she tasted blood in the air. The mixture of iron and salt on the edge of her tongue.

She felt a tingle in her nose, arched her head back and sneezed like a gunshot, "ACHOO!" nearly giving the person next to her a heart attack. She wiped her nose and continued watching the teacher while the class remained silent. A moment later, Summer McAdams sneezed from across the way, and suddenly an uproar of "Bless you" erupted from the entire class. Summer thanked them, turning on the cute act then went back to texting Amber. Even the teacher had said a "Bless you."

The girl's brow lowered into a straight line mixed with curiosity after watching Summer. Then the girl's nose tingled again, and she braced herself as she fired off another round. "ACHOO!" The girl wiped her nose and looked around, but no one in the class bothered to say, "Bless you." Not a single person. Even the teacher didn't say anything and continued his lecture. The girl's jaw dropped slightly in astonishment as she searched the room from left to right for someone to look her way and address her disappointment, but no one bothered to look.

She felt even more alone now. Like she didn't exist. Like she was invisible. Her nose tickled again, and this time she tried with all her might to prevent the sneeze, but she couldn't hold it back. Her lungs filled up and she let out another round into her arms, expecting someone to say something after she had just sneezed for a third time, but again, the class remained dead silent. The girl felt a mixture of both astonishment and betrayal. *Why on earth hasn't anyone said, "Bless you?"*

Then Summer reared up for another sneeze and she let out the tiniest achoo, as soft as a baby bird chirping, and was met with an applause of "Bless you" from the entire class. Summer put her hands to her heart as if she had won an Oscar and said, "Thank you, thank you, you guys are too kind," then went back to texting Amber.

The girl could not believe her eyes. The complete and utter disrespect her classmates had shown toward her compared to Summer was astounding. She expected at least one person to say bless you when she herself had sneezed *three times!* But that wasn't the answer she received. The girl wiped off her sleeve and lowered her head back into her arms, leaving her left with a sense of betrayal lingering in her heart. It was like everyone in the class had just told her, *"You don't matter!"* The weight of worthlessness began to crush the girl's heart from both the outside and within. Only deepening the empty pit inside her heart where she desperately wished happiness and peace would grow. The emptiness aching in her heart and loneliness pounced upon her like intense water pressure within the depths of the ocean. The girl felt her soul reach out for help. Hoping to find healing from someone around her, but she found none. Tears began to well up in her eyes, but she blinked them back. *Why?* she thought. *Why is this happening to me?* but she received no answer. She was alone.

The teacher finished the lecture and handed out a piece of paper to the class and said, "Now that the lecture is over, we're going to use the rest of the class to work on this assignment in groups. So, if everyone would group together you can complete this assignment together or work on it on your own if you'd wish."

The moment the teacher had relinquished control; the entire class immediately began to shuffle their desks around like a strategic assault. People shifted desks around into tables, laughter and conversation burst forward like a spring of water from underground. Everyone had shifted toward the right side of the classroom where Summer McAdams was the epicenter of all the activity. Leaving the girl alone on her side of the room. She looked over at the seven people all sitting around Summer's table while the rest of the class huddled up into their own groups, watching them play games on their phones and take pictures for their social media accounts, ignoring the assignment the teacher gave them. The girl watched all the groups get together and wished someone would ask her to join their group, but no one did. She inched her desk closer to one of the table groups nearby, looking around the classroom for available spots, but there was not a single desk or table nearby that had an opening. She didn't exist to a single one of them, she knew that well.

She looked at all the tables in the class; all of them had their backs to her. It was like she was homeless or clique-less, socially speaking, and it was too awkward to stand out and ask someone to join their group. Doing so would make both parties feel uncomfortable. So, the girl accepted she would be working alone. It didn't bother her too much actually. She preferred working alone because most people in groups didn't take the assignments seriously, and she had a goal-driven mentality to get her work done as quickly and as effectively as possible. A hard work ethic she had inherited from her mom. As a result, she relinquished herself to finishing her work alone . . . as always.

She was halfway finished with the assignment, breezing through the questions like a knife through butter when her mind heard, *You should kill yourself.*

STOP IT! I don't want to think these thoughts. I don't want them. She cupped her hands over her ears, hoping the thoughts would go away, but they continued to play in her mind on repeat. She was trapped, like a prisoner sentenced to life. No end. No white light at the end of the tunnel.

The suicidal thoughts weren't going to let her off easily. *Then do it! Make it all end! You will die and then it will be all over!*

STOP IT! I CAN'T TAKE THIS ANYMORE! Her conscience retorted.

She was already so tired from the mental fatigue that she had forgotten all about the assignment in front of her. She was shaking a bit by the time she glanced around and saw that no one had noticed her freak out. No one at all. Everyone's backs were facing her, and the girl was left in the background, feeling the distance between her and her classmates grow farther and farther apart. Not even the teacher noticed. The girl's heart ached again and this time she didn't even want to cry. She just stared down at her assignment with lifeless eyes and finished her work, wishing for the clock to move faster.

∽

The girl looked at the clock. The long hand stuck in the same minute. *Only three more minutes left.* She could tell other people were thinking the same thing because the sound of backpacks unzipping gradually filled the room. She slowly began putting her own stuff away and the sound of packing grew louder in the classroom. Following the motions of the class, everyone suddenly packed up as quickly as possible. The teacher had given up on trying to stop the class from packing up early and said, "Don't forget about Winter Formal coming up this Saturday! I hope you all have fun." The bell rang and all the students erupted out of their seats and charged for the door like a bull run. Third period ended and the girl hurried through the crowds of students scurrying from the buildings all going in separate directions like schools of fish in the ocean.

The sun shined down brightly on the girl, her black hair trailing down her back as she put her hand to her forehead to block out the sun. She looked up at the sky, an ocean of blue glaring down at her. Disappointed, she thought, *I wish it would rain more.* She knew that most people living in her hometown enjoyed the constant sunny weather, but she genuinely enjoyed the rain. There was a sort of refreshment that came with it that brought out the happiness inside her. When it was sunny like this all the time, she felt like she was going to dry up like a fish out of water. Everyone else couped up inside, unable to cheerfully go about their lives the way she could only daydream of. In some way, it gave her a small sense of solidarity.

Her head naturally looked down at the concrete, letting her black hair fall over her face, covering the front of her eyes as her feet moved on autopilot through the crowd. She stopped by her locker and finished putting her remaining books away then closed it.

The entire school was active as students made their way toward their cliques to sit with during lunch. The girl glanced around and noticed the circles forming up. Cliques and other clusters gathered around the edges of buildings and alongside the lockers as well, offering a haven to high schoolers yearning for a place of belonging. But for those on the outside like her, it was a constant reminder of how utterly alone she was. She could again see the backs of all the people sitting in their cliques, hanging out and chatting, laughing, and enjoying their high school experience. The girl yearned for that, wanted to be a part of that, to have a community to belong to and feel valued in. The problem was getting into a clique; you couldn't simply ask to join a clique, because that would be too uncomfortable and out of the ordinary. You must naturally be part of one from the beginning, because if you ask to join one, or don't know someone on the inside, then it is awkward for the asking party to join. It's easier to avoid the awkwardness altogether.

Lunchtime had begun, and the girl pressed her way through the heavy metal doors that led toward the main school courtyard. She found her plain white bench on the side of the courtyard, in plain view across from Summer's group. The bench was laid against a pillar connecting to the main tent, or the White Mountain, as some people called it.

The girl's black jeans and black long-sleeved sweater baked in the sun as she sat in her usual position on her white bench outside and ate her lunch alone.

She waited a couple minutes and saw Summer's group walking down from the student admin building. She tried to act normal and pretend she wasn't expecting them, but as they were approaching, she raised her hand and tried to wave at them. She was dead in their sights, with no feasible way they could have missed her waving at them, but they walked right by her like she wasn't even there.

It wasn't the first time the girl sat on her white bench and watched Summer's group from afar. She had been watching them for some time. For the past year and a half, she sat on this white bench, watching this group of awesome people hang out in front of her. She always wondered what it was like to be included, to feel like she belonged somewhere, and to have a solid group of friends to just laugh and hang out with. It's hard when you don't have friends growing up, feeling left out on the streets like you're worthless and don't matter. It's not like she hadn't thought about going up and asking if she could sit with them, in fact, she thought about it every day for the past year and a half and hadn't done anything about it. It was just too awkward.

Well, what about today? Huh? Why not make that happen today? she thought. The girl shrugged her shoulders, *Why not?* and stood up from her bench and measured the distance growing between the group and herself across the courtyard. She felt like she was about to walk through the valley of the shadow of death. She could feel the urge to sit back down. Her willpower flexed to its maximum just to keep herself standing. She took her first step, but gravity became a thousand times heavier. She took her second step and could sense the discomfort lingering in the air, with the faint scent of blood and iron.

She felt she was walking against an invisible forcefield targeting her heart and soul. Every cell in her body was telling her to stop and sit back down on her bench where it was safe and comfortable, where she was in *control*. The girl got halfway across the courtyard, approaching a small mound of grass then stopped. Her feet planted and would not move. It felt like gravity was pulling harder on her legs, preventing her from moving. Her motivation and willpower vanished, and she thought, *I can't do this*, then turned around and went back to her bench. It felt easier to come back to her bench, but it was always so difficult to venture out into the unknown. Why is that? Why is it so hard to go outside of our comfort zone and do something different?

She scolded herself, *Dang it! Why can't you just do it! Why can't you just go over there and say hi to them?* She sat back down on her bench and watched Summer's group hang out and laugh in the distance. The girl leaned back. *I've got to get over there. I've got to try to say hi.* She built up her resolve, the amount was less this time than before, and felt the distance between herself and Summer's group widen. It felt like the ground itself grew longer and more dreadful the more she looked at it. The girl took a couple deep breaths, built up her willpower once again, and pushed back onto her feet. Immediately her legs felt heavy, like someone had strapped jugs of water to them. Fatigue and discomfort encroached on her body, yearning for her to sit back on her bench the moment she stood up from it. Her heart was pounding inside of her. She took another step, using every bit of willpower she had to simply take a step. She willed her next foot forward, hoping the journey would get better, but it didn't. Every step she took got harder and harder, and with every step, the girl grew more and more self-conscious. Each stride she took was more agonizing than the last.

Walking towards a different destination, toward a different group of people was out of her normal schedule. The awkwardness in the air was potent and powerful. It was like a warm perfume, potent and relaxing that made the body soft and fatigued. Like sitting in a sauna or a warm room that made you want to lie down and sleep, causing the body and soul to yearn for comfort instead of the awkwardness of standing out. The girl felt her willpower dwindling with every passing second and she knew she wasn't going to last much longer. The closer she got, the more uncomfortable she felt. It was torture.

The girl was a few feet away and saw Summer and her friends finish eating their food and were now standing up, talking to each other. Huddled together in a group with their backs turned toward the rest of the school. The girl felt her heart gripped by fear as every cell in her body screamed at her to go back to her bench. Even her conscience wanted her to go back.

No, no, you should go sit back down. It's safer there. We don't have to endure this needless pain. Just sit back down and be comfortable again.

But she planted her feet, knowing they would walk back to the safety of her bench if she let them. She made it all the way now and stood directly behind Summer, tasting blood in the air, listening to Summer talk; clueless to the girl behind her.

Standing next to Summer was Amber Cutthrose, wearing a brown autumn-colored shirt with her amber-colored hair, while Summer was dressed in a gorgeous white and yellow dress, perfectly complimenting her luscious blonde hair. If anyone stood out in the group it was Summer, not just because of her blonde hair, but also because of her personality. Summer exuded a confidence that drew people toward her. Now, just remember, this is high school. Many people are still learning to feel "comfortable" with themselves, and to have as much confidence as Summer did that early on was a huge plus. Most people Summer's age didn't have that kind of confidence.

The loner girl couldn't even feel confident about herself to say she was attractive. She didn't wear makeup, she didn't brush her hair that often, and she only wore black clothes every day, not because she was poor, but because she didn't have an interest in fashion to begin with, unlike most girls. But Summer was like a bright sunflower. Everyone seemed to like her because of her striking personality while portraying more confidence than anyone around.

The girl stared at Summer's back, the lingering question on her mind. *"May I join you?"* But fear of standing out gripped the girl like a snake and pulled her down to the center of the earth. She immediately felt so self-conscious, a spread of goosebumps shivered through her skin as she couldn't take being outside her comfort zone for so long. Nobody in the group around

Summer seemed to notice the girl, not even Summer, but she couldn't help but feel like she didn't belong here.

The girl watched and waited, hoping that Summer or any of her friends would notice her standing directly behind them. She could hear some of the dialogue going on inside their circle. She had never been so close before. But the discomfort of where she stood, was too much for her. The awkwardness permeated her heart, soul, and entire being. *I can't take this! I can't do it. I can't do it!*

Of course, you can't. What kind of person like you could do something so amazing?

She gave in to the temptation, turned her feet, and started walking back to her bench in defeat. *Dang it . . . why can't I do it? Why is it so hard?* The discomfort faded as she returned to her bench, but the loneliness returned the moment she sat back down. Watching just how happy Summer and her friends were from across the way. Would she ever have that?

The girl's heart ached as she tried not to compare herself to Summer and her friends, but she couldn't help but look around and see all the cliques in the courtyard having a good time. She finished the rest of her lunch and felt bored. Taking another glance around the courtyard and felt the need to do . . . something. So she got up from her bench and started walking. No direction, no place to go, just walking. It's not like she didn't want to sit down, but she couldn't sit and feel depressed all day while watching everyone else have a good time. She felt a massive disconnect with every person around her as her heart yearned for someone to talk to; someone to connect with. It was a fickle matter, but it made all the difference. *Why do we need to be social?* she thought. Even she would admit there were some days when she preferred to do her work alone, but that's just because she was an introvert. At the end of the day, everyone needs friends. *Humans . . .* she thought. *Can't live with them, can't live without them. Funny right?*

The girl had finished her fourth loop around the school, witnessing the same scenery over and over: The flagpole, the outer portable classrooms, the basketball courts, the student courtyard, the lockers, over and over, feeling the depression weigh heavily on her body like she was draped in a thick trench coat of sorrow. It drained the happiness and hope from her heart as her eyes hung half open, her head naturally looking at the ground.

Every day she walked around this school, waiting . . . waiting for something to happen. For something to change in her life. So what does she do? She walks. She walks and walks and walks. Going nowhere, with no purpose, no hope, and no place to belong. Breathing but not alive. Like a walking corpse.

Her dreary eyes squinted slightly from how bright it was outside. The reflections from all the cars out front stung her eyes, but she was too sad and unmotivated to cover them. She simply closed her eyes and stood there feeling empty and alone. She took a deep breath, *If I can just get home, then I'll feel better.* The eagerness in her heart warmed to a slow boil as she couldn't wait to get out of this prison and relax at home with her mom.

The girl waited at the front of the school. The days ended like they always did. With all the students rushing to their cars, eager to get out of this social prison, while the girl waited for the bus. She saw the big yellow bus decelerate in front of the school, the brakes screeching to a halt. The girl tensed from the piercing sound as the door swung open with a strong whisp. The girl got onto the bus and looked around for a seat. She managed to find a seat near the end of the bus and waited, staring out into the blur of the roadside as the bus accelerated forward, taking her home.

The girl exhaled and felt her defenses lower as she opened the door to her apartment. She put away her keys, investigated the dreary, dusty apartment, and flicked on the light. The tense white light from the doorway revealed a living room and a small kitchen, along with two separate bedrooms. It wasn't much, but it was enough to make a middle-class girl feel at home. She tossed her backpack onto the tan couch and took in the feel of the apartment.

It was lifeless and empty. The whole apartment was like a museum with all the lights turned off. Of course, there wasn't anything fancy inside. It was all her mom could manage being a single parent raising a child, but it was enough. She couldn't imagine living in a huge mansion or house with ten children running around. The thought of having a larger family warmed the girl's heart for a moment. She imagined young children running around the apartment to take care of, with her as the older sister in charge. She didn't know why, but that thought seemed to brighten her day a little. But like all great things, it came to an end. The imagery faded and the silence filled the room again as she was left with nothing but the emptiness of her home.

❧

The pot of pasta boiled beneath her. The girl inhaled the smell of salt and garlic as the pasta bubbled. The door opened, and the girl's mom stepped in. Her heart lifted and her day grew slightly brighter. Her mom raised her hand, revealing eyes heavy from lack of sleep and physical fatigue. The girl's mom exhaled and said, "Hey sweetie pie!"

"Hi, Mom," she said, her voice coarse and unused.

She finished preparing the pasta and pulled out the marinara sauce. Mom pulled up a chair and took a seat at the table, putting her hand to her forehead, attempting to catch her breath. The girl poured the rest of the pasta into two bowls, sprinkled some shredded cheese over them, and walked them over to the dinner table. The girl gave her mom a bowl and a utensil and took a seat across from her. Mom lifted her hand from her face and smiled at the sight of warm food being delivered. Mom sat there breathing heavily for a moment before reaching for her fork and slowly taking a bite out of the pasta. Her mom looked satisfied for a moment, feeling some of her energy return to her body, and said, "I've missed your cooking sweetheart." The girl wanted to smile but there was nothing there. Her blank face stared back at her mom with eyes ladened with sadness. Her gaze was directed half toward the table and the other half at her mom. Mom took another stab of food, now with more energy in her voice, and asked, "So how was school today, Krystal?"

Krystal shied away for a moment, but since she was at home speaking with her mom, the only person close to her, she felt a little more open to talk than at school. Krystal answered plainly, "It was fine." But it was not fine. Her day was a living hell.

Mom picked up the hint and asked, "Anything in particular happen today?" Krystal stared at her food, thinking of what to say. Mom waited for Krystal to answer but she said nothing. Mom grew concerned and asked, "Are you okay sweetie?"

Krystal answered honestly, "No . . ." raising her head, giving Mom her full attention. "I'm not." Krystal took a breath and gathered the words. "Mom . . ." her voice desperate and low. "I'm not doing too well . . ." Krystal was on her last legs. It was an admittance of defeat. Her mother's heart cringed with worry at the sound of her daughter choking up from the difficulties of school bearing down on her. There was a pause, Mom giving Krystal her full attention. Krystal waited for Mom to say something, something to cheer her up, but Mom said nothing and let her speak. Krystal searched for the right words, tears filling her eyes, but she held them back, fighting to get the words out of her throat. "Mom . . . I can't keep going . . . I don't know . . . I don't know what it is . . . I don't know what's wrong with me, but I can't keep living like this. I feel stuck. Stuck in this dreadful cycle every day, and I need some relief. I want to feel better, but I don't know how."

Krystal's voice choked from the tears that wanted to come out. Krystal built up the words that she needed to get out. She wanted desperately to be freed, once and for all. The silence of the room bore down on her. Krystal pushed the words through her throat and whimpered, "I want to die . . ." The room fell silent. "I want to kill myself and be over with it." Krystal's face was now desperate, watching her mom, waiting for her next move as her mom pushed her chair away, and walked over toward her.

Mom put her arms around Krystal, allowing her warmth to comfort her, knowing that her mom was here for her. Krystal relaxed from her mom's comforting presence and whimpered as her mom stroked her head and whispered to her, "It's gonna be okay sweetie. It's gonna be okay."

"When?" Krystal weakly retorted.

"I don't know. I don't know." Krystal and her mom fell silent. They held each other there for as long as they wanted. Krystal managed to calm down and was now exhausted. Mom slowly released Krystal from her arms. Krystal looked up and saw her mom's fatigue. She was just as fatigued herself, if not more, noticing the lines under her mom's eyes from sleep deprivation and overwork. Krystal lowered her eyes to the ground, pushed her chair out, and whispered, "Thanks, Mom. I'm gonna go to bed now."

"Okay . . . I love you sweetie pie."

"I love you too Mom," while her mom watched with saddened eyes and a heavy heart, feeling the guilt and helplessness from watching her daughter suffer.

Krystal closed the door behind her and stared into the dark room. It was just as dark as the rest of the apartment, and it always felt lifeless. Maybe it mirrored her soul in that way. The moonlight gleamed through the square window above her table, with her desktop computer there and the rest of her schoolwork laid out. Stacks of fantasy and sci-fi novels lay sprawled all over the place. A lonesome guitar sat in the corner. Krystal stood in the doorway watching the light from the kitchen reveal small details amidst the darkness. There was no motion, no activity, not even the thrum of the air conditioning in here. Krystal didn't bother to turn on a light, there was enough from the moon to cover that.

Krystal walked over to the whiteboard hanging on the wall next to her bed. She unclipped the head of a dry eraser marker and wrote, "387." Krystal clicked the cap back on the marker and sat upright on her bed staring at the number and the title above it.

# of Days I've Wanted to Kill Myself
387

She glared back at the number. No thoughts were in her mind as she stared blankly at the board.

Krystal lay flat on her bed and stared at the ceiling. She lay her hand gently on the center of her chest. The pain aching at a singular point, concentrated in the center of her soul, yearning for something, but what? What was it that her soul was searching for? She inhaled a sharp breath, hoping the oxygen would fill the emptiness inside, but it didn't. She felt her lungs expand but the hole itself did not fill. *How do I fill this emptiness inside?*

Krystal thought about what tomorrow would look like and how the image was the same. It would look like today, and the same the next day, and the next day, and the next day, until she graduated high school. But that was years away, and Krystal wasn't sure she'd be able to survive that long. She rubbed the center of her chest one more time, trying to dig deep down into that cavity within her soul, "Maybe tomorrow will be better? Maybe the emptiness will be gone by the time I wake up?" she whispered, closing her eyes.

It won't.

CHAPTER 2

Another Day In Hell

"Humans are social creatures. We need community and a place to belong to. But what happens when that basic need goes unfulfilled?"

—JL

Her eyes slowly opened; Krystal remembered everything the night before from the moment she closed her eyes. *"Maybe tomorrow will be better?"* Krystal checked her physical body, everything felt fine. She didn't feel anything. Nothing was in her chest. No emptiness—

The moment she thought of it, the emptiness and loneliness came back like an older brother pouncing on you unannounced in the morning. (Trust me I know. I have an older brother and he loves doing it . . . Then again, I've done it to my younger brother too, so the tradition goes on hehe.)

Dang it, Krystal thought. The void in her soul came back and expanded into the depths of her being. Krystal lay on her bed in the same position as when she had fallen asleep. Her eyes met the same white ceiling, her room still dark since the sun had not yet risen. Her arms and legs lay comfortably where they were, but they were already fatigued. Tired, just like her aching soul. Krystal tried to send messages for her arms and legs to move but they refused to comply. She wasn't surprised. She could feel the depression and fatigue coursing through her veins like thick oil, weighing her down. She tried to move but couldn't. The thought of school and what today looked like sprouted in her mind.

She didn't want to go to school again. She wanted to stay here. Images of yesterday and days prior played through her mind and the thought did not excite her. It was a never-ending cycle that she couldn't seem to escape.

Krystal took a deep breath and felt the air pressing into her lungs. Her chest expanded and so did the void within her. *It's still there.* Krystal immediately wanted this day to be over. To be able to fast forward to where she could just lie down in bed at the end of the day and die.

She tried to encourage herself with cheerful thoughts such as: *Don't worry. It will get better*, but she didn't believe that for a second. Her conscience told her that things would get better, but her heart, soul, and subconscious felt otherwise.

You should just kill yourself.

The first batch of the day. Krystal felt a trench coat of sadness loom over her again. "Why can't I just be happy?" she whispered, trying to lift her arms and body from the bed but failing. She had no energy for it. She could barely breathe. Krystal hadn't even got out of bed, and she was already defeated.

Her eyes stared at the ceiling, unblinking and lifeless, "I have no hope . . . Why can't I just be happy?" She paused and took another breath, letting the words flow, "I wake up, I go to school, I get ostracized, I come home, I do my homework, I go to bed, and do it again tomorrow . . ." Krystal let the thought trail off and echo on repeat in her mind. *What else for me is there?* She thought of Mom's encouragement last night. It was nice but it wasn't practical. People can still feel discouraged even when there are others to support them. Then a thought dropped into her mind, *Would anybody even notice if I was gone?* Krystal imagined her mom standing there on a rainy day as the only person at her own funeral. Krystal tried to brush off the thought, but it wouldn't budge. The image was too clear, and it lodged deeply within her mind like a rock.

The world would be better off without me. I'm just a burden to everyone. Krystal imagined the world without her for a split second. A school with one less student. And a mom with one less burden.

No! It wouldn't be like that. Krystal shifted her attention and looked at the time, 5:36am, and glanced back at the ceiling. *It's time to get up.* However, her body was already exhausted; she was breathing heavily like she had just run a marathon, but the day hadn't even started yet, as she muttered under her breath, "Just kill me."

✍

"Are you ready for Winter Formal?"

"Heck yes I am girl! Do you already have a dress picked out?"

Rachel squealed with excitement. "It took me forever to pick one out, but I settled on the cutest thing in the world!" Krystal listened and observed as the girl named Rachel pulled out her phone and showed a picture of her Winter Formal dress to her friend sitting across from her. The classroom had settled into quiet chaos. Mixtures of students doing either nothing or working on their homework. The square room bristled with activity, the brown dull walls plastered with math symbols and old sayings. The din of the classroom was moderate, only one notch below noticeable from the teacher. All the desks turned into tables aside from a few strays, and the smell of dust and boredom lingered in the air.

Krystal had settled on doing nothing for a change, and nothing meant eavesdropping because it was the only interesting thing she did to get some small form of entertainment. Krystal leaned over on her desk, pretending to be asleep as she peeped through a small crack in her arms to eavesdrop on the two girls sitting next to her.

The second girl put her hand to her mouth in awe of the photo. "Awww! Rachel, you look amazing in that dress!"

Rachel nodded. "I can't wait to take this to Winter Formal. Speaking of which. Do you have a date yet Dorothy?"

Dorothy shook her head, "No. I don't think so, but I think I'll just go stag with you guys."

"You have a point. We'll have more fun that way." Both girls nodded and giggled. Krystal watched more carefully, envious of their laughter and smiles. Wishing she could have that for herself, she took her eyes off the two girls and thought to herself. *Winter Formal huh?* It would be a pleasant change of scenery from the monotonous purgatory that is her life. Then the follow-up problem arrived. *But who would I go with? Forget about the prospect of having a date, I have never had a date in my life to any of the school dances.*

Krystal deflated and felt her self-esteem drop, *I'm not pretty enough to get a date.* She sighed, slouching into her arms. She thought of the girl called Dorothy talking about going with her friends. *Maybe it's not such a bad idea.* Very quickly the idea of not having a group of friends stopped her thought process. *But it wouldn't be fun without people to go with.* So, Krystal pushed the thought aside and continued with her day, eavesdropping on the next group of people who looked somewhat interesting.

"So how was school today?" Mom asked.

Krystal toyed with the chicken nested on her fork then took a bite. "It was fine." Her voice was still coarse and unused. "Nothing happened today," as usual. But Krystal didn't stop there like she normally did. She took a breath and held it, wondering what to say. Was there something she wanted to talk about? Krystal pondered for a moment and then said, "I heard some people talking about Winter Formal today."

Mom sat across from her at the dinner table chewing her food, "Hmmm?" She looked Krystal's way, Krystal noticing the excitement in her hum.

Krystal poked at her food, avoiding her gaze. "I've never been to one, or any of the school dances."

Mom took another bite, "Are you interested in going?"

Krystal idly toyed with her food again, "I don't know. I don't really know how to feel about it." Krystal kept her eyes on her food, knowing her mom wanted to meet her gaze.

Mom took a sip of water and said, "I think you should go."

Krystal raised her head like a canine hearing a low-frequency pitch, "Really?" allowing hope in her words.

Mom nodded. "I think it's a great idea. You'll get to hang out with everyone at school and there are only so many school dances you'll get to go to in your life."

Krystal lowered her head again. "I guess you have a point," retreating to her depressive glare at her food.

Mom raised an eyebrow and mentioned, "We could get you a nice dress. Maybe take pictures beforehand."

Krystal raised her eyes to Mom again. "I would like that." Mom glanced at the clock and said, "We have some time today. We could go right now?"

Krystal swallowed her food, "Right now?"

Mom spread a thin smile and nodded kindly, "Yes, right now." Krystal pondered it for a minute. The brash and sudden change of plans made her feel uncomfortable. Venturing into the unknown from her normal schedule scared her, but she trusted Mom and said, "Okay."

Mom stood up, grabbed her purse, swung it over her shoulders, and said, "Let's get you ready for Formal sweetie."

Krystal stared in the mirror, watching the reflection in the glass stare back at her. She noticed, *Her eyes . . . they look so sad.* The girl in the mirror stared back at her, wearing a black dress and black gloves that stretched down her forearms. The girl in the mirror didn't look like her. Krystal tried to feel comfortable in the dress but couldn't. She wasn't used to wearing very fashionable things most girls her age liked to wear. She never had piercings, never wore jewelry, and never put on makeup. Even her hair was brushed and looked smoother. Krystal was insistent against wearing makeup for the dance but gave in after hearing Mom mention how there's only so many times that she'll get to see her daughter in a dress. Mom won the argument and supported Krystal's new dress as well as the other commodities.

Krystal could tell her mom wanted what was best for her, so she played along. But the girl in the mirror still looked like a total stranger to her. Like it wasn't who she truly was. Krystal didn't like the girl in the mirror and thought, *I'm a loser.*

Mom called, "Krystal it's time to go."

"Coming," she called. Krystal took one last look at the girl in the mirror and then took a deep breath. *Maybe you'll have some fun tonight?* She doubted that very much. Krystal left her bathroom and headed towards the front door to their apartment. She opened the door and stood out on the balcony walkway, looking out to a semi-cloudy sky and a weakening sun hidden behind some hills. Krystal looked down to the right where she found her mom standing at the bottom of the stairs next to the car with a phone in her hand and an expression of eagerness on her face.

Mom put a hand to her mouth and gasped, "Oh sweetie. You look amazing." Krystal tried to smile but failed. She tried to look as appealing as possible, not wanting to disappoint all her mom's hard work for her.

Out of shyness Krystal's left hand grabbed her right elbow and let the arm hang limp, "Thanks, Mom." Feeling extremely uncomfortable; still not used to her own skin yet.

"Look here. Smile." Mom hoisted up the phone for a picture. Krystal tried to pose and smile but couldn't. Mom took the picture and looked at it. Krystal noticed her mom paused for a brief moment, then lifted a cheerful smile, "That's a great picture sweetie."

Krystal knew it was a lie. She knew her mom was trying to be supportive, but Krystal understood her mom's feelings better than she knew. She understood how her mom worked so hard to feed and support Krystal; to give her the best life possible, but Krystal felt so depressed, it was next to impossible to find happiness in anything these days.

Krystal wanted to be happy, but it was weighed down by the collection of perpetual sadness, emptiness, and loneliness. It wasn't like Krystal was different. She was a regular girl who's had some hard times. Mom raised the phone again for another photo, Krystal tried harder to smile but felt extreme difficulty as gravity pulled her cheeks down. It's not like she didn't want to smile, but the tugging at her heart from faking it was too much to bear, even for a picture. So Krystal didn't smile. She didn't have the energy or the motivation anymore.

Mom took a few more pictures; Krystal went along, playing dress-up model, and actually had a little fun. Mom took some great photos and said, "Okay. It's time to go to the Evergardens."

The Evergardens, a small but relatively secluded park with fine scenery for pictures and couples to hang out. It lay on a hill close to the school, so even if someone lived around here, they would only have to walk a short distance in order to get to school. Krystal sat in the passenger seat and stared out at the Evergardens, now jam-packed with a hundred people or more. Cars were parked all along the street as groups of high schoolers exited like celebrities while the parents led the way as their kids' personal chaperones. Everyone was looking their best for their Winter Formal pictures, wearing dresses and suits they would only wear for such an occasion, knowing they would look back on this time through the pictures they had taken. Krystal stared through the glass and observed all the activity. People all around, looking for nice spots to take photos with their friends and dates. Groups of high schoolers ranging from seven to nine people were spread out through the Evergardens. Boys dressed handsomely in their suits and girls dressed beautifully in their dresses, taking pictures with one another. The car pulled to a stop and Mom put the car in park, "Here we are sweetie. You ready to take some more pictures?"

Krystal glanced at her mom and said in monotone, "Sure." There was neither hope nor joy, only a neutral expression. She dared to allow herself to hope.

"Great!" Mom got out of the car in excitement, her phone ready for some more photos of her little girl and nice scenery. Krystal took one last glance through the glass and exhaled. *Here we go*, then opened the door. The din of the crowd surrounded her. All sorts of activity and groups shifting around, some of them even jumping for their photos. The activity was a little overwhelming to Krystal. With so many people around with no order to them, it was close to becoming a frenzy. Krystal put her hand to her elbow. She instantly felt uncomfortable, wanting to go home, to be away from all the commotion. A small sense of doom nudged Krystal's heart, *I have a bad feeling about this.*

Mom stepped in front, leading the way, "Come on sweetie, let's get some more cute pictures of you." Krystal followed as ordered, and wondered, *Am I really cute?* She thought about it for a moment. *I doubt that,* yet she wanted it to be true anyway. *I would like to feel cute, at least for a little while.* Krystal followed Mom, now standing near the edge of the crowd. It was like staring from the outside into a storm, with no sense of order or direction as people were shuffling around trying to get their perfect photos. Krystal wanted nothing more than to disappear from this moment.

Mom led the way and brought Krystal over to a nearby oak tree. Mom pointed, "Here, stand right here and lean against this tree." Krystal obeyed, getting into position, but when she stood next to the tree, all she wanted to do was hide behind it. Krystal forced herself to stand out in front of the camera while trying to pose for the photo. She had stopped trying to smile a while ago and now just wanted the photos to be over with. Mom snapped the photo and said, "That's a good one. Let's go—" Mom's phone vibrated, Krystal watched her wield it to her ear, the idea already forming in Krystal's mind. *Please don't be what I think it is . . .* Mom put the phone down and hung up, disappointment struck her face as she let the phone dangle in her hand. Mom looked at Krystal, who already knew what she was going to say, but Mom said it anyway, "I have to go in for work. They're short-staffed tonight and there's been an uptake in drunk driving." Krystal nodded. She knew the drill . . . understood the value of her mom's job. She didn't want her mom to leave but understood as well that her Mom needed to pay the bills and raise a daughter at the same time. So the least Krystal could do was give Mom her blessing.

Krystal said, "You can go Mom. I'll be fine."

Mom looked both relieved and disappointed. She pointed toward the car, "Do you want me to drop you off at the dance?" That question took Krystal a minute to answer. Her gaze drifted toward the crowd on her right, managing to pick out a few people she recognized in the swarm. Krystal looked out past the greenery toward her high school below then back at her mom, a bit indecisive but said, "I think I'm gonna stay."

"You sure?" Mom asked cautiously.

"Maybe," Krystal replied. She was still a bit indecisive about the whole scenario, but she was also bored of simply going home and feeling depressed all the time. She wanted to mix things up a little. After all, what was the worst that could happen? Surely this dance couldn't be so bad.

Mom nodded, feeling a little proud of Krystal, and said, "Okay, but if you ever want to go home, don't hesitate to call me. I'll come get you as soon as I can."

Krystal nodded, "Thanks Mom." Krystal would remember that, in case things went sour, but for the time being, she was feeling a little optimistic. She saw people that she knew in the crowd, so maybe it wouldn't turn out so bad after all; reinforcing her initial hope. Krystal glanced at her mom one last time and said, "Okay, I'll stay then," sounding more resolute in her voice than her prior answer.

Mom nodded back, "Okay. I'll see you later tonight sweetie."

"See ya Mom." And then, without turning back, Krystal's mom was gone. Off with the wind as they say, and Krystal immediately experienced a feeling of loneliness. She wasn't used to being away from her mom except at school, but here things were different. Krystal was left with a lingering sense of dread. The hope she had felt earlier faded and was now left with a giant crowd of people swarming around her and the fleeting prospect of having a good night.

Krystal had no choice but to enter the crowd since there was nothing to do for an hour but take pictures. Doubt crept into her mind as she faced the giant crowd of people in front of her, like staring at a living beast, hoping it wouldn't bite her. Reluctant, Krystal stepped into the fray and was quickly surrounded by a flurry of energy and excitement from all the people around her. Krystal kept her arms close, grabbing her right elbow, leaving the arm limp, feeling uncomfortable being surrounded by so many people.

Krystal looked around, hoping to find familiar faces, and found she was able to identify a few. There was Andrew McCarthy, Taylor Williams, Matthew Mateen, Cynthia Longhorn, and a series of other people she knew from her classes. Most of the people were dates from other schools, while others from Krystal's school were grouped into their own social cliques. Krystal couldn't help but feel like she was at school just dressed differently. Krystal could identify at least a dozen cliques surrounding her, all in separate locations, with no one venturing away from the safety of their own circle. Meanwhile, Krystal was on the outside, feeling like a homeless person stuck in a city.

She suddenly found herself standing next to her old classmate Andrew again. He was dressed nicely in a white tuxedo, looking well-shaven for a young man, shoulder to shoulder with the rest of his military buddies for a photo. Krystal waited for the photo to end, then tried to approach Andrew. She pulled her phone out and held it in front of her, but the awkwardness of talking to people suddenly hit her.

Krystal came up right behind Andrew and felt the words lock inside her throat as she stared at Andrew's back. He was easily a head taller than her and was busy talking to his friends while she stood silently behind him. Krystal fought to get the words out of her mouth, but the idea of nudging Andrew terrified her. For Krystal, it was not normal to go up to someone she didn't talk to and ask to take a picture with them. The fear of standing out overpowered her, causing her to retreat and hide among the crowd. Krystal watched Andrew from afar and thought, *This shouldn't be that hard. I should just go up and say hi. It's not that difficult.* She tried again, taking a few steps toward Andrew, holding her phone out in front of her with the camera ready, and planted her feet behind Andrew as he talked among his service buddies, but the words lodged in her throat. Krystal fought to get them out, but the discomfort of standing out gripped her heart and screamed for her to go back to where she was before and abandon the whole endeavor. Krystal tried to fight the feelings. To tell herself that it would be all right if she asked him. But the awkwardness prevented her from saying anything, so she backed off and would try again another time.

Krystal cursed herself. *Why can't you do it! Why can't you just say hi to somebody?* But Krystal knew just as well as any other high schooler, it was uncomfortable to talk to people who weren't your friends. Simply talking to anybody outside your friend group would instantly cause you to stand out, and that was a discomfort most high schoolers feared. So generally, they stayed within the confines of their clique, leaving the clique-less people out on their own, literally.

Krystal gripped her right elbow and felt self-conscious of her loneliness again. The chaos around her was drowning her in sorrow as she wandered helplessly, wondering where to go or what to do. A sense of boredom mixed with emptiness dawned on her and she instantly wanted to call her mom and go home. But it would be awkward to call her mom right after she left. Krystal decided to stick it out a while longer until her mom could come back and get her.

She felt like a lost child, surrounded by crowds of people who all knew where to go and what to do, while Krystal had no direction and was left in the cold. Krystal covered her shoulders with her arms. She wasn't used to exposing so much skin, as her typical outfits were mostly long-sleeved shirts and pants, never revealing much skin to begin with.

Krystal noticed another person she knew, Grace Friar. She was another classmate from middle school but had gone to another high school. Krystal moved through the crowd toward Grace, consciously trying not to touch anyone out of fear of making them uncomfortable. But to Krystal's own surprise, Grace was making her way in Krystal's general direction too. Krystal stopped where she was, raised a hand, and attempted to wave at her, failing to smile in the process, but Grace walked right past Krystal like she wasn't even there. Heading off to join her own group of friends in the parking lot. Krystal felt her self-worth plummet at the sight of her middle school classmates ignoring her. *Am I really that despicable?*

The same process happened over and over for the next hour as Krystal went from person to person, attempting to get a picture with them, only to have them ignore her. Krystal gave up on trying to take a picture with most people and went on searching for Summer's group instead. To her luck, she found Summer and her friends on the far side of the Evergardens, where it was more remote to take pictures. There were about eight to ten people in Summer's group. All of them dressed nicely and with their dates. Krystal's heart yearned for companionship, to have a group of friends like that whom you can dress up and take pictures with. Krystal wanted nothing more in the world. To simply . . . *belong.* Krystal edged her way toward Summer's group, eager to get away from the massive crowd.

Suddenly, Summer brought herself forward among her friends and shouted, "Let's all take a group picture together!" She wielded a Nikon camera around her neck and ran straight towards Krystal. Krystal's heart began thumping immediately at the sight, *Oh my gosh! Is this really happening! Does she actually see me? Or even better yet, is she going to ask me to be in a picture with her?!*

Summer came up and handed Krystal the camera. Krystal held the Nikon camera, looking at it perplexed, unsure what to do. She looked up to hear Summer say, "Hey, could you take a picture for us?" Krystal's heart sank, killing what hope she had left. She nodded timidly as Summer and her friends huddled together for the picture. Before Krystal could snap the photo, Summer drastically turned and shouted toward the crowd, "If anyone wants to join us for a group photo, they can come in right now!" The air shifted as more and more people began pouring into the group photo with Summer and her friends, like air sucked into a tornado. Krystal watched hopelessly as more and more people lined up into the shot. Her heart was wounded before, but now it was on the verge of death. Suddenly, thirty people were all lined up together, all eager to take a picture with Summer.

Krystal buried her sadness, holding the Nikon camera, and said, "Say 'cheese.'"

Everyone in the photo shouted, "CHEESE!"

Krystal snapped a couple photos and checked the camera. When she saw how happy everyone looked, she sadly whispered, "That actually looks pretty good," striving to hide her sadness behind the dam of emotions building within her.

Summer came over and snatched the camera back from Krystal to check the photos. "OHHH! That looks so good! Don't you think guys?"

Everyone came up and crowded around the camera to get a look. To all their enjoyment, they said:

"That looks so good!"

"I can't believe it turned out so well!"

"That's a good one, that's for sure."

Then they all noticed how much Summer stuck out and began complimenting her, "Yeah Summer, you look the best!"

"I couldn't imagine a better photo with you in it."

More and more people added on, "You look so beautiful Summer!"

"You're such a star Summer! You should be a model!"

Krystal watched them discuss the photos right in front of her. She couldn't help but think of those photos. How happy everyone looked, how awful it made her feel. The emptiness and loneliness came crashing down on her. She tried hard not to cry and held back the tears, but it was the sense of betrayal and loneliness that just made her feel . . . *worthless.*

The crowd thinned out after a couple minutes, as Krystal was left with just Summer's group of friends standing there. She sensed an opportunity arising as the group dwindled to go take pictures somewhere else and only Summer was left standing looking down at her phone. Krystal saw her chance and took her approach. *This is it*, she thought. *This is my chance to get a picture with her.*

The fear of coming up to Summer gripped Krystal. She felt self-conscious again, like someone was watching her, and wanted to back away. The fear was paralyzing but the thought of failing to talk to Summer back at school ran through Krystal's mind. *No. I'm not going to let it happen again.* Krystal pulled her phone out and held it there like it was a gentle baby in her fingers. She flipped the phone to the camera setting and took her first steps toward Summer.

Summer was still busy checking her phone, admiring the awesome photos taken, not showing any sign of having noticed Krystal. Krystal took that in stride and tried to use it to boost her confidence. *Just a little closer, maybe then she'll notice me.* Krystal was now only a few feet in front of Summer, well enough within her line of sight. It was just the two of them, standing among the grass in the Evergardens. This was finally her chance. She started to feel anxious, she'd never done something like this before, to go out on a limb and *actually* try to talk to someone, let alone Summer.

Krystal's heart was thumping hard in her chest. She waved to try and get Summer's attention, but Summer's eyes never lifted from her phone. Krystal waved a little harder, trying not to be overt about her intentions, but Summer never looked up. Krystal took a step closer and was now standing directly in front of Summer. The fear and anticipation inside Krystal's heart were screaming for her to run away in terror. The awkward silence of it all made Krystal feel exposed. Summer lifted her eyes, and said, "Oh? You want to take a photo together?" Krystal's heart leaped with happiness. The happiness of simply being *noticed* brought so much joy to her heart. Krystal reared her lips to speak, but Summer walked right past her and spoke to someone else.

Krystal stood there, blank, and stared. Completely dumbstruck. She was standing right in front of Summer and yet Summer still didn't notice her. Krystal felt a stab of pain and betrayal in her heart. The sorrow and depression weighed down on her, but worst of all, she felt *worthless*. Like a piece of forgotten trash picked up on some random weekday, tossed into a landfill never to be thought of again.

Krystal turned and watched Summer vanish back into the chaos of the crowd. Krystal wanted to be mad but couldn't. All she felt now was sorrow. Her body started to tremble. Krystal fought to keep herself under control but was failing. Her heart screamed from the pain within. The emptiness aching and expanding within her soul, draining any sense of hope and happiness. The loneliness from around her wounded her heart. The sadness and reality of being purely and utterly . . . alone.

Krystal had never felt more invisible in her entire life. Like she could have a seizure in the middle of a crowd, and no one would notice. Everyone else was busy running off getting the best pictures of their lives, while Krystal stood there, her face and mind blank, frozen, unable to think; all she could do was exist, like she was an outsider that no one wanted, that she should just go away and die. Those thoughts were like arrows wounding her heart and soul, piercing deeper and deeper. The crowd became a blur and Krystal was ready to give up. Her mind went blank, and so, she just . . . walked away. Her feet moved automatically. Krystal pulled out her phone and dialed her mom's number. The phone rang a couple times before Mom picked up and said, "Hello?"

"Mom." The sorrow leaked out of her voice, more than Krystal had wanted.

She could tell something was wrong as her mom spoke with immediate concern and worry, "What is it, sweetie?"

The tears choked in Krystal's mouth. Krystal gagged, her throat thick with moisture, "I want to go home." The tears pushed beyond Krystal's will, begging to be free. Flowing down her cheeks. Krystal wanted nothing more than to be away from here. To be at home sitting on her couch with her mom. Her cheeks grew hot, and her nostrils filled with mucus as she snorted to keep her tears contained. The words faltering out in desperation, "I wanna die . . ."

Mom responded instantly, "I'm on my way," her voice more resolute. Krystal could hear the determination in her mom's voice. A nurse on a mission as they say. Krystal hung up the phone and walked down the street where an intersection connected to the main roads of Marbury and Addison Blvd. The intersection was filled with cars on all four sides as families were eager to get pictures of their kids in their formal attire before heading to the local dance. Krystal walked down the hill on the sidewalk and waited by the intersection, watching people pass her by like a ghost, not one person noticing how unhappy she looked.

Krystal breathed hard to catch her breath and maintain her composure. The last thing she wanted was to break down in the middle of a crowd and have them videotape her crying. A thought entered her mind for a moment, *Maybe I'll finally get noticed?* But then her logic kicked back in. *Yeah no, that's not going to be the kind of reaction you want.*

Krystal stood at the curb, waiting for half an hour when she finally received a text from her mom saying she was five minutes out. Krystal clicked her phone off and waited. Cars were roaring up and down the intersection. Krystal could feel the kinetic energy of the cars as they whisked by her. The thought of going home, watching a movie, and drinking some hot chocolate, filled Krystal's mind. The items of escape she needed. Krystal kept checking the street, looking across the street where her mom's bright red Nissan Altima would come from. The anticipation within her heart grew like a ray of hope inside her chest. It could have been a great night, but that's not how it turned out. What Krystal got was an evening of buildup followed by constant disappointment. How awful . . . maybe she'd look back at this day and laugh . . . maybe.

Krystal looked up for the hundredth time and could finally see her mom waiting on the opposite side of the four-way intersection waving back at her through the windshield. Relief encompassed Krystal like a shower as she looked forward to being at home and watching movies all night with Mom.

The expectation for a green light was beginning to eat Krystal from within. Her body began to bob up and down, begging for the light to turn green. Krystal had never wanted to go home so badly in her life. Then the light turned green, and she watched her mom's car pull forward and cross the intersection, only to see a pickup truck slam sixty-five miles an hour into the driver's side of her mom's red Nissan Altima. Krystal's eyes went wide with horror and stared, the world going silent. Krystal felt what was left of her soul shatter. Her thoughts running on repeat, *I'm going home. I'm going home. I'm going—*

〜

"Did you hear about the car accident near the Evergardens the night of the dance?"

"Like totally. I heard about that and was like, 'Oh my gosh that is like so awful.'" Krystal sat at her desk overhearing everything. Everyone was talking about the car accident the night of Winter Formal, but the sad reality of it all was that nobody knew it was Krystal's mom. As a result, everyone just passed her by like nothing had ever happened.

The days following the accident were complete and utter hell. Krystal's guardian, Aunt Sarah, came down to care for her and was now living in Krystal's apartment, but she worked the same night shift as her mom, so she was never present at home.

Krystal hung her head forward, staring down with dead eyes at her desk. Seeing nothing. Being nothing. Her entire world had been shattered. Disbelief and shock were still fresh in her mind, repeating the same emotion she felt the moment she lost her mom. There was nothing left for her. The one person on this earth who cared about her unconditionally was now gone. If things were bad before, they didn't compare to how bleak things felt for Krystal now.

Meanwhile, everyone in school went on with business as usual. The smiles, the laughter. The complete distance from every soul around her. It seemed unreal. Krystal was completely and utterly alone, watching the world spin around her like nothing happened.

CHAPTER 3

Life and Death

*"Without hope, for what is there to live? Without
a purpose, why continue breathing?"*

—Krystal Henninger

Krystal opened the door to her apartment, the sharp white light beaming on the rest of the apartment like an interrogation room. Doubt crept into her heart. Her thoughts flooded with memories of sitting with Mom on the couch watching the Bachelor, complaining about how she hated the show while she secretly loved the experience. Mom's soft, joyful laughter echoed in Krystal's mind as she surveyed the empty apartment. Overlooking the empty chairs and dinner table. The couch lifeless; the kitchen without a soul. Krystal felt just how empty the apartment was. There was no life here. No joy. Only pain.

Krystal spotted a note left on the kitchen table from Aunt Sarah:

Dinner is in the fridge. I'll be out for the night shift again.
—Aunt Sarah

She put down the card and walked over to the kitchen, eyes dead with sorrow. Krystal pulled the largest kitchen knife from its covering and headed over to her room. Krystal closed the door, locking it. She slowly aimed the knife at her left wrist, pressing the gentle steel against her skin, the cool metal felt unmalicious and oddly inviting. It was as if the metal felt accompanied to her skin and her skin vice versa. An odd thought to have before you're about to die.

Should I really do this? Should I really end my own life?

The voices in her head grew louder and louder with every pressing thought. *Kill yourself! Kill yourself! Do it! End the pain! End it all!* Krystal tensed up and clenched her teeth as the thoughts screamed in her mind.

Mom is gone! And there is no bringing her back!

Tomorrow will just be more of the same! More pain, more suffering!

If I cut my wrist, then it will all be over . . . right? The voices screamed so loud in her mind that Krystal felt a window would shatter.

I can't take it anymore! I can't take it anymore! Krystal felt so many emotions she didn't know how to react. Fear, heartache, sorrow, depression, suicidal thoughts, anger, all raging through her mind like a hurricane. Her head was on fire, her heart thumping so hard in her chest. Her breath was hot with moisture as tears coursed down her face. She gripped the knife harder in her right hand, shaking the knife in place against her wrist.

Do it!

Please you can get better tomorrow!

You won't make it to tomorrow!

You'll die a loser and a loner!

Mom was in that accident because of you!

I am merely a burden. I don't deserve to live.

"SHUT UP!" Krystal yelled at the top of her lungs, but they wouldn't stop. Krystal just wanted it to end. She wanted the voices to stop and for everyone to be quiet. She didn't care if she was going to heaven or hell if she died. She assumed she was just going to heaven, right? If there was one? She didn't care anymore, she just wanted to be done with it. In her mixture of sorrow and pain, Krystal put the knife against her wrist, the metal pressing against her skin. Tears flowed, her heart and mind filled with pain. She couldn't take it anymore. Krystal braced herself; her mind screaming.

Don't do it! Don't do it! Tensing the grip on the knife handle.

Please, SOMEONE SAVE ME!

God, please! If you're real, then please SAVE ME!

But the voices kept coming, screaming louder now, shouting at maximum capacity.

DO IT! DO IT! DO IT! JUST DIE ALREADY!

Her soul screaming! *SOMEONE SAVE ME!*

And in one motion . . . she sliced the knife against her wrist.

Everything went silent. It was quieter than she had expected. For a moment, she felt nothing. There was no pain or feeling. Then suddenly, an intense pain shot from her wrist, and blood spurted out onto the wooden floor. Krystal dropped the knife and gripped her left arm so tight she felt her whole hand would fall off. She wanted to throw up, gagging from the gushing blood.

Krystal stared at her hand in horror, watching the life drain out of her. Her senses dulled. Fatigue gripped her mind and body as she felt weak. Krystal let go of her hand, letting it dangle and bleed onto the floor under her. Her legs gave out and she fell flat on her back, into a puddle of her own blood. The blood was so dark, so red, so . . . warm. Krystal hadn't felt this warm in a long time. It was strange. *Is this what death is like?* Krystal felt her vision begin to fade as she stared at the white ceiling above her. Krystal laid her head back into the growing pool of red, her hair now soaking in her own blood.

Is this it? Is this the end of my story? Knowing these would be her last moments, she mustered the last of her strength and said, "I still . . . feel . . . empty." Her eyes closed, disappointment filling her heart. The emptiness remained, even to her dying breath. This is the end. And in the end, she lost.

PART TWO

The Truth

CHAPTER 4

A Stranger's Kindness

"Everyone hits a low point in their life.
The question is, will you get back up?"

—JL

Krystal's eyes slowly opened. Her mind blank, and her lungs taking in a weak breath she didn't expect to receive. *Is this what heaven is like?* The warmth beneath her body was gone, but the puddle remained.

Krystal gave a weak groan. She attempted to lift herself up from the floor slowly but failed. She laid back down and felt a sharp pain in her wrist. Lying on the floor, she turned her head, the pool of blood still visible beneath her, trying to twist her arm to check her wound, but gravity pulled down on her weakened body, causing her to take deep, gasping breaths. She took her time, but eventually, Krystal managed to turn her arm, finding a massive two-inch wound across her left wrist. Krystal tried to ponder what exactly happened, but her mind was foggy and her body too weak from blood loss.

"Did . . ." Speaking took all her energy. Her body felt slow, her breathing shallow, like she was digging deep into her lungs but was only receiving twenty percent of the air in her lungs. *Did I . . . do it right?* Krystal was ready to faint again. Her mind was hazy, but she couldn't remember if she slid the knife correctly across her wrist or not. It was hard to remember. Either way, her wrist was in a lot of pain. She looked around and saw that she was covered head to toe in blood. She was so weakened that she didn't have energy to freak out. Hunger came like an angry roommate and the light from the window gleamed down on her like an alcoholic waking up from a hangover. Krystal tried to ease herself up again but failed. She lay there, not keeping track of the time, staring at the ceiling, imagining she was in her bed. She wanted to lift her other hand and lay it on her chest, but she was too weak to move. Krystal did a mental check on her heart and soul, and to her disappointment, she still felt the emptiness inside. She could feel it every time she took a breath. Nothing had changed, even when she tried to kill herself.

It's still there.

Krystal was too weak to be surprised by anything. Krystal made the effort to look at her wrist again. "Why . . ." Saying that one word took the breath completely out of her, but it needed to be said. She took a moment to catch her breath, breathing hard and long, until she had some semblance of energy. *Why . . . am I not dead?* The pain felt like someone slid a buzz saw through her arm. She could still see drips of blood leaking from her wrist. The wound hadn't been sealed.

Krystal lay there for hours, waiting to regain her strength. Eventually, Krystal felt some strength return and managed to ease herself up, taking her time slowly, not aiming to aggravate the wound in her arm, feeling the blood in her hair drip from its ends. Her clothes, soaked to the bone in red. The first thing she wanted was . . . some fo—

Why get up?

Krystal sighed in disappointment. If she had tears, she would have cried. *Can't I get a break?* But part of her found the thought logical in a way.

Why should I get up? If I lie here, then I will eventually die. So what's the point? Krystal held onto her breathing. Hoping it would regain some of the strength she lost. But part of her still wanted to lie there and die. She didn't know what to do. Whether to live or to die, it was her choice. And last night, she had chosen to die. But what about today?

Despite her pain, she chose to live, not knowing why. Krystal managed to crawl into the kitchen at a granny's pace and found her mom's first aid kit. She cleaned and wrapped the wound in bandages, familiar with medical techniques since her mom was a nurse. But the question still lingered in her mind, *Why am I not dead?*

Her gaze drifted back toward her room, where the trail of blood followed her into the kitchen. *I should . . . clean that up.* Krystal grabbed a rag, crawled back to her room, and, very slowly, began wiping up the pooled blood. She wrung out the towel into a nearby bowl, watching the velvet blood mix with the water. Her very life essence poured out before her. Then the thought struck her. *I almost died.* But she wasn't horrified like she thought she would be. She wanted to but couldn't. It felt too casual. Just another day in the life for her. But the wound remained, and it was still a problem. Krystal continued wiping, not caring about what day it was or what time. None of that mattered. She didn't care if the police busted in right now and dragged her to an asylum. Krystal made another long, slow wipe with the blood-soaked towel. *Huh . . . it's funny . . . I'm cleaning up my own murder scene. And the killer is . . . me.*

Krystal finished soaking up the rest of the blood, but there were portions where the blood had stained the ground that she couldn't remove. Afterward, Krystal showered, put on some clean clothes, and rebandaged her wrist, the blood already soaking into the bandages. Her wrist still hurt beyond imagination and Krystal's next thought was . . . *Hospital. Yeah . . . hospital.* So, she picked up her phone and dialed 911.

Krystal lay in her hospital bed. The white sheets covered her body, allowing her to stare into oblivion at the ceiling above. It was one of her best hobbies, staring. She often wondered how long she could stare at something without blinking. She had gotten rather good at it too, but her tear ducts suffered because of it. But that didn't matter, there were no tears left to shed. The doctor had written Krystal off as suicidal, (big surprise), so that would mean she would have to go through a week of therapy at a counseling clinic to help her with her "suicidal tendencies." Krystal hated that. She wasn't schizophrenic, she knew she wasn't crazy. She was just a normal girl who was suffering. Krystal glanced at the wound on her left wrist and the results begged to differ. She lay her head back on the pillow and continued to stare into the ceiling while the IV in her right arm gave her blood.

It's funny, she thought. *I tried to kill myself and it didn't solve any of my problems.* She thought back to last night. The screaming in her mind, all the voices, the pressure, the knife, the weakness, and then . . . the silence, as she lay on the floor in a pool of her own blood, feeling emptier than she'd ever felt in her life. Suicide didn't change anything, but the voices were still there. She was still breathing, but she wasn't alive either.

I have no hope . . . She lay there feeling fatigued. All the physical traumas took a toll on her body so she spent most of the day lying in bed, waiting to heal physically so that other people could tell her to "get better" and then she could go back to her normal empty life of being a loser at school.

Krystal sighed, *That sounds like hell to me. So, I'm not too eager to get back to the real world.*

Krystal heard a birthday party from across the hall for one of the patients. Someone had brought brownies from the food court and was handing them out. Krystal wanted one but couldn't ask for it. She wasn't part of that group; she just wanted a brownie. She took her eyes off the birthday party and went back to zoning out at the ceiling for half an hour. She had nothing but time anyway. She glanced at her bandaged left wrist. Couldn't even see the skin because it was so wrapped up. Her left hand looked like a ball of tightly wrapped cotton. They had a nurse check up on her, to make sure she didn't do anything . . . drastic. But Krystal didn't have strength for anything drastic, let alone to breathe. She made her attempt and was now too tired to do anything. The strength would come . . . as she fell asleep.

The smell of something sweet filled the air. Krystal opened her eyes and followed the scent to find a steaming brownie sitting on the tray next to her bed. Even after a full night of sleep, Krystal was still fatigued. She felt as though she had just fought a champion fighter, every inch of her body ached with a soreness Krystal had never experienced before. It wasn't just the physical injury that was draining her. It was the emotional and spiritual fatigue inside. Krystal looked at the steaming brownie and felt her mouth salivate. Without thinking she reached over with her left hand, a mistake she regretted instantly, grunting as the intense pain shot up her left arm. Krystal tensed then leaned back, correcting her mistake, and using her right hand this time to grab the plate.

Krystal took the warm brownie, put it to her lips, and took a bite. It wasn't the best brownie in the world, but in her current state, it tasted like heaven. She could tell it was one of the cheap brownies they offered in the hospital, but she didn't care, at least it made her feel better. She could feel a little energy coming back to her after she ate the brownie, enjoying how much better it tasted warm than cold. Krystal finished the rest of the brownie, then laid back in her bed and instantly fell asleep. Maybe she would have a sweet dream of a distant land where none of her pain and suffering took residence, she could only hope.

◇

She awoke hours later, deep in the night. The activity in the hospital earlier was replaced by its melancholy boredom. Krystal welcomed the calm, welcomed the silence it brought. Life was too hectic to be loud all the time, so she welcomed the silence when it came. She just wished she could have that peace in her own mind. To be able to lift the suicidal pressures off her heart and ease the thoughts in her mind. Still, though . . . she wondered who it was that left her that brownie.

The rest of the hospital was quiet when Krystal heard a mop out in the hallway. She didn't bother to look; the splashing of a wet mop grew louder and louder. She didn't care if anyone was passing by. She was too tired to worry about anything. She couldn't muster the energy to care if she tried, and she certainly didn't feel like trying anymore. What was the point?

Inside her room, the lights were off, with only the moonlight glimmering through the shaded window. Krystal felt herself drifting again, but the sound of the mop grew louder, drawing her focus back to reality until a shaded figure finally entered the room and paused. Krystal just closed her eyes and hoped they would go away. For a long moment, there was no movement, no sound coming from inside the room.

That snapped Krystal's conscience awake, as the sudden lack of activity made her curious. She kept her eyes closed, but her mind was alert. Was the person gone? Did they leave already? Krystal remained still, hoping to find her answer soon. She heard some movement in the room. Then heard a tray being placed next to her. Krystal's curiosity was getting the better of her and she wanted to snap her eyes wide awake and startle this person in her room, but she was still too weak to do that. So she waited. Waited for the figure to finish their business and leave the room.

When it was quiet enough, Krystal surreptitiously slid open one eye and glanced over at the tray table next to her bed. There was another brownie, a box of apple juice, a sandwich, and a bottle of water. Krystal opened her eyes to find the shaded figure quietly walking out the door.

Krystal tried to lean upright, bringing the tray closer to her bed with her good hand. She took the sandwich out from the wrapper and took a bite.

It was dry, so she washed it down with a little water. She ate silently in the moonlight, feeling her strength slowly returning. It had to be well past midnight, but she didn't care. She could feel her strength returning with every passing bite. She downed the rest of the sweet apple juice, finished off the brownie, and lay back in her bed with a full stomach. Feeling more refreshed as the food brought more relief to her already hurting body. And then, she fell asleep again.

Another couple hours passed of blissful sleep. Sleep that Krystal had not experienced in a long time. It was the deep REM sleep that she loved so much. There were no nightmares, no memories of the hard world outside her mind, only rest. Rest she hadn't expected to receive. Krystal awoke slowly, taking her time, her body feeling well-rested after so long. That restful feeling you get after waking from a deep and long-needed nap. The pale moonlight gleamed through the window, bringing a gentle glow into the room. Krystal leaned forward, able to feel some strength return to her body. She heard a mop passing down the hall and glanced over at the doorway, hearing it get closer, each sploosh closer than the last. She was still too tired to anticipate anything, so she just waited for whoever was going to pass from across the door. A figure appeared, a man, who looked well into his seventies, wearing a gray jacket, was mopping the floor. He moved like a young man, but his hands were so worn from obvious years of wear and tear. Krystal recognized him as the figure who had delivered the food earlier.

The man turned into her room and quickly began working on the floor, making sure no spot was left untouched. She could tell he had done this a thousand times before. She slowly turned her head and faced the direction of the man, his back facing her. She was suddenly out of breath, feeling the remainder of her strength slip away. Her stomach rose and deflated, breathing heavily under the white sheets. The man turned and saw her gazing at him. He paused, looking at Krystal with a hint of compassion, as if he understood. Then he asked with genuine concern, "Are you okay?"

Twin tears immediately flowed down her cheeks. Krystal's heart flushed with relief. It had been so long since someone had actually *seen* her. The feeling of some stranger noticing her in pain and asking about it brought her more joy than she could have ever imagined. Instantly relief poured into Krystal's soul like life-giving water, filling the rest of her being. She could feel it washing over her like parched soil finally receiving rain. Krystal started whimpering, unable to hide herself. Then she felt her strength return and was able to whisper, "No. No I'm not."

The man leaned against his mop. "What's wrong?" he asked. His voice was so gentle and soothing, revealing elements of compassion within them. The pure relief of someone asking her a question was too much to take. Krystal wondered when the last time was that someone other than her mom had asked her a question. It had been so long she had forgotten. Krystal felt the dam of emotions that had been building within her for years begin to burst. Krystal lifted her wounded hand up. The stranger saw her gesture and asked, "What happened?"

Krystal glanced at her arm, her mind slowly becoming more alert. It had been so long since she'd spoken to anybody that the yearning for conversation made Krystal want to explode. A part of her didn't want to talk, yet at the same time, she felt like she needed to talk to someone about what had happened. Krystal was a little short on talking partners, so she would take what she could get. And right now, it was this Janitor standing in the room.

Part of Krystal felt scared, but that fear evaporated because of the fatigue from her injury and the overall exhaustion from her emotions and suicidal tendencies. In everyday life Krystal wouldn't talk to anybody about this, but she was so low right now that she needed to talk to *anybody*. So, she figured, *Why not? I've got nothing else to lose. I'm dead already.* Krystal brought the words to her lips and said frankly, "I tried to kill myself."

She expected the man to react with astonishment, almost defensively, to tell her that she shouldn't do that or even think of that idea and that it is an awful thing to even think of something so horrid . . . but he didn't. He just stood there, unfazed by the dramatic confession of horror. He leaned in and said, "Tell me more." Krystal was stunned. She did not expect him to say that, yet there was an odd relief in her opening up to him. There was something comfortable about this man that made her want to keep talking. But it was also combined with her breakdown the day before and the total emptiness and unhappiness raging in her soul right now, that made her somewhat comfortable talking to a stranger.

Krystal took a deep breath before starting. Where would she even begin with such a story? She had no idea. So she just went with the first words that came to her lips, "All my life I've been a loser. I haven't had any friends or anyone to speak with. I typically sit by myself at lunch and spend my time walking around campus wishing something would change. I see kids at my school and how popular they are. I often wonder how different I would be if I were one of them, but that's not how it went down."

She paused, "For so long I have lived with this growing sense of emptiness, watching it drain my soul, sucking away all my hope and happiness, leaving me bored and unfulfilled. Knowing nothing would fill it, causing me to believe that I have no reason to live." She turned to the Janitor, "On top of that, I've struggled with suicidal thoughts every day, trying to fend them off, trying to get myself to believe that I have a purpose in this world, that I have a reason to live, but no matter how many times I've tried to convince myself, nothing worked. I've been on medication, gone to counseling, read the self-help books, and still nothing . . . nothing works."

She trailed off and paused. Expecting the Janitor to say something but, surprisingly, he remained silent. The patient expression on his face showed he wasn't going to say a word, no matter how long it took. He was going to wait for her to get it all out, allowing her to speak, a privilege Krystal hadn't felt in a while. It brought more healing to her soul than she'd felt in a while, more so than the pills or the counseling she's had; just having someone to listen to brought immense relief to her heart. Yet it still fully didn't take the problems away.

"I've always felt like a burden, especially to my mom. I saw her every day when she came home from the hospital, working extra hours to take care of me." Krystal took a breath. "Fast forward to last week, when I was taking pictures for Winter Formal before the dance, I watched my mom get hit by a green pickup-truck going sixty-five miles an hour—" Krystal caught herself reliving the memories. Even though she was weak, the memories were still just as clear as ever. Memories that would haunt her for the rest of her life if she allowed them to.

Krystal slowly forced herself to come to grips with reality, "And now I don't even have her anymore . . ." Krystal choked, looking down, "So when she got hit by that truck, something inside me shattered." She shook her head, "I lost everything . . . I have no reason to live anymore." Her words choking on her tears as the dam was ready to burst. Krystal sucked in a breath, "And so, last night I took a knife . . ." the words growing heavy, "and I . . ." choking, "I slit my own wrist and tried to take my own life." Krystal broke down.

The dam burst, throwing her free hand to her face as she cried, now fully understanding what she just did. The effect of it all hitting her like a sledgehammer. Krystal didn't care if the man was watching, she just needed to cry. Needed to get it all out now before she went insane again. The whole time the man was quiet, watching Krystal cry in front of him without interrupting.

"I watched myself bleed out on the floor, lying in a pool of my own blood, as the life drained from my body." She looked at the Janitor with a hard glare, "And you know what I felt?" He didn't answer. "Nothing. I felt nothing. No happiness, no satisfaction. I felt no different from before I slashed my wrist open. And I still feel unhappy. I am still unfulfilled . . . So I woke up and cleaned up my own crime scene." Krystal took in a breath, wiping the tears from her face and chuckled sorrowfully, "And so, here I am. A loner schoolgirl, with no friends, no mom, and no hope, dealing with the hardships of life." She felt a sense of shame shadow her. Hearing aloud what she had done to herself, how awful it truly was. "Just a soulless person, sleeping in this bed, hoping to get 'better.'" Krystal took a breath, wanting to get it all out, to leave no thought unsaid. "I'm just a broken and empty person. A hallow shell of a human being. No happiness, no life. I may be breathing but I'm not alive. My heart may be beating but I don't feel its warmth. I'm just a dead man walking. A living corpse, with no reason to live."

She glanced at the Janitor, only to find the man silently crying. Tears streaked down both sides of his worn face after hearing her story. Krystal wanted to be surprised, but she was too weak to even do that. Krystal waited until the man wiped the tears from his face as he said, "I'm so sorry." He broke down weeping again and took a seat. Covering his face with his arm. Krystal wanted to cry but she had exercised all her tears. Watching him weep, something inside her wanted to reach out to this man and say it was going to be alright, but she didn't. She just lay there, watching this stranger weep for her after hearing her tragic life story. Then again though, if Krystal heard her own life story from someone else, she would weep too.

Krystal took her eyes off the weeping stranger and stared at the ceiling again, stonehearted. "It's okay. I'm not dead yet."

The man wiped the tears from his face, "I'm glad you're not." That caught Krystal's attention. *He's glad? How could he be glad for a total stranger?* But Krystal didn't have the energy, nor wanted to get angry at the only person who had shown her kindness. Krystal realized that this total stranger was weeping *for* her. Not many people would have done that, let alone taken time out of their day to hear someone talk about their recent suicidal attempt, and yet here was this man who had brought her a brownie, and *listened* to what Krystal had to say.

Krystal felt the weight of opening up lift from her heart. Of course, the emptiness was still there but she at least felt a little better. The man finished his crying and wiped his face, saying, "That's terrible. I'm so sorry for what you've gone through. I can imagine it has been difficult."

"It has been difficult," Krystal said in agreement. "It's been so difficult that I can barely get out of bed in the morning."

Krystal saw the man nodding, "That's tough."

Krystal exhaled. "So that's it. That's what's been on my mind lately, or life, lately." The man regained his composure, nodding. Krystal nodded as well, and said, "Thank you . . . for listening to me. It's . . . it's been a while . . . since I've talked to someone . . ."

"Any time," the Janitor replied, "And thank you for indulging yourself to me. It has been really nice listening to you."

Krystal couldn't explain it, but she felt a sudden sense of joy emanating from this man. There was something about him that just made her feel . . . happier. Krystal replied, "Thank you again for listening . . . I really do appreciate that."

The man put his hand to his heart, then asked her, "May I pray for you?" Krystal wasn't sure how to respond to that question. She wasn't at all familiar with religion or anything, but she figured nothing was wrong with it, so it wouldn't hurt.

She said sure and the Janitor bowed his head and threaded his hands together, Krystal subconsciously closed her eyes and followed along, "God . . . this girl is hurting. She is in deep, deep, pain . . . but God, please give . . ." the man trailed off and asked, "What is your name?"

Krystal was uncomfortable giving her full name to a stranger, so she decided to meet him halfway. "Krystal," she said.

"Please give Krystal the hope to live. Please show her that her pain will one day end. Please come into her life and comfort her and let her know that this pain will not last forever. Please strengthen her against the suicidal thoughts, and Lord may you fill her with Your Spirit, and show her the path to life again. I pray all this in Jesus' name, amen."

Krystal opened her eyes, feeling no different than before she entered the prayer, but she did find that prayer unusual. At least it was a gesture to help, however small it was. Then the Janitor stood up and took that as his cue to leave. He stopped at the doorway and said, "I'm glad to have met you, Krystal. I have great hope for someone like you."

"I have great hope for someone like you." Those words rung true in Krystal's being. It was like those words were an arrow that struck the very heart of her being. Giving Krystal a sense of encouragement she had never known. No one had ever said that to her before. She instantly felt warm in the presence of this man, causing a final pair of tears to streak down her face.

There was something about this man that made him different from others. Something that made him . . . shine. Krystal couldn't put her finger on it, but she knew she wanted it, whatever *it* was. She said with ghastly reverence, "Thank you."

The Janitor bowed his head slightly, putting his hand to his chest, "It was my pleasure." Then he turned, and like a gust of wind, he was gone.

CHAPTER 5

Questions

"What makes a person kind when people are naturally selfish? What causes someone to care for others when it wouldn't benefit themselves?"

—Krystal Henninger

The next few nights were nothing but repetition. Krystal had regained most of her strength and because of that, was sent over to a nearby mental health clinic, and she hated it instantly.

Krystal would lie in bed in her free time, regaining her strength, and then go to some counseling classes, where a woman named Karen McKarthy would talk to her about her "problems" and tell her how to "fix" them. Krystal hated talking to Karen simply because she was the worst counselor in all of history. Karen was the one counselor who actually talked more than the patient. Telling Krystal all about her awesome life of going to Hawaii and how much fun she had in high school. Frankly, Krystal was sick of it and just wanted to be out of this looney house and away from her.

Krystal lay on her bed with her arms behind her head, staring at the ceiling. Her arm had healed enough to where she didn't have to worry about it, but it still bled every now and then. There was something different in the air and Krystal could tell. It all happened because she met that Janitor the other night. When he gave her that brownie and listened to her, it relaxed her. Krystal hadn't felt relaxed in a long time, especially after talking to someone who genuinely wanted to listen to her. It just felt so good, so good to be honest for a change and talk to someone and have them talk to you, giving you their full attention. Krystal wished it was like that at school, but she didn't want to think about that right now, not even for a second.

Krystal lay in her bed in her dorm room, pondering the encounter, pondering the kind man she had met. *What was it about him that made him . . . shine so much?* Krystal wrestled the question over and over, finding no answer. At least she felt better physically, but she still had questions. Questions about that man. Where he came from and what he was all about. Why did he pray for her and what was it about him that made him so . . . *different.*

Krystal recalled the exact words he said, *"I have great hope for someone like you."* They were simple words to say, but they had a ripple effect on Krystal's heart. It was like those very words coming out of his mouth gave her the encouragement she had been yearning to hear for so long. And it was the man's generosity, going out of his way to bring a lonesome patient dinner, that made it more impactful.

He must have noticed I didn't eat the whole day . . . that must be why he brought me the food but . . . that's not the main issue. The fact is . . . he noticed *me . . .* She paused, letting that thought linger in her mind. *He noticed me, unlike everyone else . . . why? Why did he take interest in me when no one else would?* The thought that he was a creep did cross her mind, but Krystal knew that wasn't the case. She could tell just by the man's body language that he wasn't a loon. He wasn't a predator of helpless girls; he was a genuine and kind man.

But I don't understand why he was so kind? Why did he stay and listen to me when he had work to do?

All her questions were left unanswered. She didn't have enough material to work with to come to a solution, but one thing was for sure. It did get her thinking. Krystal lowered her left arm and stared at the bandage, thinking about the wound, but also the Janitor's kindness. *What makes a person kind when people are naturally selfish? What causes someone to care for others when it wouldn't benefit them?* Again, no answer.

Krystal looked at her wound again, "I should be dead . . . why am I not dead?" And almost as if on cue, a quiet thought dropped in her mind. *What's the purpose of life?* She paused, feeling the question ripple through her like a drop of water in a pond. Every cell in her body was calm, as she remembered the question. The strange thing about it was it wasn't her own thought. It was coming from something else. Coming from a gentle, peaceful voice in the back of her mind.

Krystal shifted her position in her bed and heard, "Hey could you stop shuffling?" Krystal lifted her head to find a girl with brunette-blonde hair lying in a bed a few feet from her. They had moved Krystal in with a roommate a couple days ago, and for the most part, Krystal and the girl hadn't talked. The past couple days Krystal's mind has been so racked with questions that she felt the need to ask somebody about it.

Krystal whispered, "I'm sorry."

The girl lifted herself from her sheets and glared at Krystal. "You should be."

Krystal wasn't in the mood to get in a fight in the middle of the night, so she let it pass. Lying back down in her bed, hoping that tomorrow would be better.

It won't.

~

"Mmkay. Now I'm going to take you through some breathing techniques. Mmkay." Her counselor and group leader, Karen, was now in charge of over a dozen girls all struggling with suicide and mental illness. It was one of those hospital clinics that provided room and board for its patients, but prevented them from having anything at all that would cause self-harm. And for right now, it was Krystal and Karen, in a one-on-one session, while Krystal sat in her green chair, uninterested, loathing every minute of this therapy session. Karen smiled and said, "Now close your eyes and do as I do."

Karen inhaled, breathing in deeply like she was enjoying "the spirit of the universe" soak into her. Krystal saw the hidden joy from the exercise on Karen's face. The sight of her counselor acting like a high school cheer leader turned Krystal off on every wavelength. She didn't want to sit here and have a charismatic person tell her to be happy. Krystal leaned back in her chair, unmotivated to try these "breathing techniques" that are supposed to help her.

Krystal reluctantly complied, closing her eyes, hearing Karen say, "Now I want you to picture a river, and let that river flow down and down." Karen tried to let the silence infuse into Krystal. Krystal could feel it too, but it wasn't making her feel any better. Karen spoke again, "Now let's focus on our breathing. Taking a deep breath in, holding it for ten seconds, then breathing out for another ten seconds." They repeated the process for five whole minutes. Krystal was trying to picture the river in her mind, but she could feel herself rebelling against these practices. *What is this supposed to do with the emptiness I feel inside?* Krystal did a mental check and could still feel the emptiness within her. The aching hole drained her happiness and energy, leaving only boredom and pain. She may have recovered physically, but the pain and emotional turmoil were still there. Krystal tried to focus on the river, but it wasn't helping. She gave up and opened her eyes. Karen noticed and said, "Is something wrong Krystal?" Krystal stared at her in quiet hatred. *You have no idea how I'm truly feeling do you?*

The next forty-five minutes they did the same stupid breathing techniques over and over. Krystal continued to try and picture that stupid imaginary river that would somehow "help" her. But it didn't. She left the session, feeling emptier and more frustrated than she had before.

Well, that was a waste of freaking time.

Krystal stormed out of the counselor's room furious and headed straight back to her dorm. *That was the dumbest therapy session in the world.* The sun had set an hour ago and the darkness of the dorm room was oddly comforting. It was fine, Krystal didn't want to see the hideous green walls and the wooden frames of the beds. It felt like an old dorm room from the eighties, even the blinds on the window were from back then and the carpet was a hideous gray, starchy and uncomfortable. Krystal got into her bed when she heard, "Counseling didn't go well?"

Krystal shifted her gaze toward the bed next to her. The brunette-blonde girl from before lay hidden within her white hospital sheets, revealing only her glossy blue eyes. Krystal replied, "Yeah . . . you could call it that."

"Eh don't let it get to you. That woman doesn't know a thing." For once Krystal had to agree with her. Krystal glanced at the girl, who shifted onto her side revealing a white shirt with black overalls. The girl was clearly younger than Krystal, but she sounded older, more experienced in the clinic setting. She had to be no older than twelve years old and Krystal couldn't tell whether that was a good thing or not.

Krystal had regained most of her physical strength, but she still felt sluggish in her movements. She may have regained her body, but she hadn't regained her soul. She stared passively at the girl and replied, "What do you know?" Krystal never intended it to come out harsh, but it did.

"Oh, I've been here a couple times," the girl replied sarcastically.

Krystal felt the following question linger on her heart, "What happened?"

The girl sighed, then sat upright, revealing portions of her arms and neck. Krystal could barely tell in the darkness but there was enough moonlight to point out the scars. "This one right here was from cutting myself last year. This one right here was from a failed hanging two years ago. This one right here was another attempt to slit my wrists, and so on." Krystal wasn't surprised. She was so dead inside that reacting wasn't part of her facial vocabulary anymore.

The girl asked the question back, "And you? How are you here?" Krystal simply raised her arm and made a single slicing motion. The girl nodded. "Ah I see. You slit your wrists like me."

Now it was Krystal's turn to speak. "But I'm . . . still alive . . . for some reason."

"Why *are* you alive?" she asked.

Krystal shook her head. She didn't have the answer to that question. She had thought she knew where the artery was in her wrist, mostly because her mom was a nurse and had taught Krystal some medical practices. But the very fact gave her pause. *Why am I alive? How could I have missed the artery? Or did something else happen?* Krystal glanced at her bandaged arm then returned her gaze toward the girl. She shrugged her shoulders, "I don't know." Then without thinking Krystal asked, "Why do we die?" more to herself than to the girl.

The girl laid back in her bed, staring up at the white ceiling, and without hesitation replied, "Why do we *live?*"

That question made Krystal ponder. *"Why do we live?" That's a good point actually. What is the point of living if we are just meant to suffer?*

Krystal replied, "I don't know. I don't have the answers to any of these questions."

"I wouldn't worry about it."

"Why not?"

"Because I don't have the answers either." Krystal found that answer dissatisfactory. She had wanted the girl to say something, anything, or at least attempt to answer the question, but Krystal knew she was asking too much from a girl who looked to be twelve. Heck, Krystal was still in high school herself and she didn't have the answer. The silence between them gave a casual understanding that the conversation was over. The girl pulled her sheets over her, "I think I'm going to bed now."

Krystal faintly whispered, "Okay." But she did not close her eyes. She only stared at the ceiling, pondering everything from how she got here to why she got here. Allowing the darkness to slowly overtake her as she drifted to sleep.

∽

"Everyone take your seats."

Krystal pulled a silver chair and sat in the circle surrounded by twelve other girls who were just like her. Although Krystal felt like she stuck out like a sore thumb dressed in all black. They sat in a small auditorium inside the clinic, feeling more like they were in a church setting than a clinic. The air was dusty and old. Krystal could tell just by feeling it that the air was dead and there was no activity aside from them.

Karen instructed, "Now . . . who would like to go first?" only to find everyone avoiding eye contact. It was their weekly discussion, where everyone would "open up" and talk about the problems they were dealing with. It was a load of bull because nobody wanted to participate. Nobody wanted to share their deepest darkest horrors with a bunch of strangers. It was like taking you to church and forcing you to confess your sins in front of the whole congregation. Krystal wasn't sure if Karen was completely oblivious to the fact or was just plain stupid. Karen gestured a hand to the girl next to Krystal. "Susie, would you like to go first?" Susie shook her head. Karen took the hint and moved on. "How about you Micah?" Micah didn't say anything and just twirled her hair, hoping to outlast the awkwardness lingering in the room. Karen gestured to herself and said, "I'll go first then."

Oh gosh, here we go, Krystal thought. Bracing herself ready for another salvo of monotony as she slumped into her chair.

"I'll start with how I've always wanted to be a counselor and lead into that. Is that alright? Mmkay." Karen received looks of insouciance. No one cared, why should they be concerned with how Karen wanted to be a counselor and try to "help" girls like them? She was basically calling them broken because she was so perfect. Karen started up again. "I always wanted to be a counselor since I was fifteen years old. I would always love to give my friends advice and they would think I'm the greatest . . ." Krystal zoned out, successfully losing herself in her own thoughts. It was a way of fast forwarding through the day, a technique Krystal had learned after years of sitting in class.

Karen finished with how great her origin story was, then gestured out a hand, "Would anyone else like to share how they tried to kill themselves?" The burden to speak cast upon the rest of the group.

Krystal's eyes glared at Karen, who sat there with a smile on her face like she was a wealthy princess staring at a group of filthy commoners. Krystal felt a fire begin to light within her, growing larger and larger with every passing moment. Krystal's lungs inhaling deeper now, exhaling sharp breaths as if she were ready to go to war.

Karen tried to put more emphasis on it. "It's okay to share you guys. Mmkay." She threw her hands into a wide circular motion, closing her arms like she was hugging a bear and said, "This is where the heeeaaaling begins." That statement irked Krystal even more. The tiny campfire within Krystal was now a raging house fire and continued to grow.

The silence in the room was pure torture; no one else wanted to share. Krystal thought, *Someone please go. This is killing me.* But everyone kept their mouths shut.

Krystal's wrist began to throb as a small drop of blood seeped through the bandages and fell onto her shoe. Krystal covered her wrist with her free hand and crossed her arms. It's a good thing black hides stains in clothing.

Karen restarted, "There's nothing wrong with opening up you guys. It was like this for me when I tried out cheerleading for the spot of head captain. It helps to open u—"

"Oh my gosh SHUT UP!" Krystal interrupted. Karen seemed taken back for a bit but then recomposed herself with a wide smile. Krystal hated that smile and felt like she was going to explode just from looking at this woman. Krystal thought, *Does she have to be so happy all the time!*

Krystal spoke sternly, "Let me ask you a question *Doc* . . . were you *popular* growing up?"

Karen's smile turned into an unwanted grin filled with guilty admission. Happily, reluctant to answer, she said, "I was . . . kind of the president of my school for three years." Chuckling in happy embarrassment.

"Figured," Krystal said heartlessly. "You don't come across as the *silent type.*"

Karen happily and nervously looked around with a grin on her face, still holding onto that happy look, like she was guilty for being awesome and said, "No, I wouldn't say that I am."

"No . . . you wouldn't." Krystal angrily agreed. "Cause you just *loooove* the spotlight, don't you?" Her words were shooting through Karen's act.

"I wouldn't say that." Karen replied, but her eyes and smile disagreed. The corners of Karen's lips broke into a creepy smile.

Krystal did not react well to that response. The fire building within her grew so hot she thought she was going to melt if she kept it in any longer. "Here's another question. Have you ever felt like a loser?" Karen's smile faded like water down the drain. Krystal hit the nail on the head, "That answers that question." Krystal thought she should stop but she didn't. "Here's another one." Everyone braced themselves, even Karen. "Do you know how to cure this emptiness that I feel inside?" Krystal pointed to her chest, "To be able to feel whole and complete? To have happiness and hope?"

Karen said nothing. Krystal twisted the knife deeper. "Didn't think so." Krystal glanced around the entire circle. People's expressions hadn't changed much but Krystal did have their attention now. Krystal decided to end this once and for all. "So how in the world can you lecture us about how to be happy and find hope, when you yourself aren't happy? How can you tell us there is hope when you can't even cure this emptiness I feel?" Krystal pointed her finger to her sternum and pressed down hard. "Because I have this deep gaping hole within myself and it's yearning for . . . *something*! But you can't even tell me what that is."

Karen faintly tried to reply, "Well, there's drugs for tha—"

"The drugs *don't work!*" Krystal retorted. She got up from her chair. Her whole body felt on fire, hot with rage, and she wasn't going to let anyone stop her. "The drugs eventually wear off and I end up feeling emptier afterwards. You can teach me yoga, or meditation, or have me do a sport or give me friends and a family, but in the end, I would *still* feel this emptiness inside. So tell me *Doc* . . . what do I do to fill this hole in my heart? What do I fill this intangible ache within myself with when nothing physical seems to do the job? What advice can you give me that's actually *helpful* in any regard!

"Because my unhappiness comes from both the ostracism in high school and the emptiness and loneliness I deal with every *minute* of my life. And you sit there telling me about how "awesome" your life is. You don't know me. You don't know any of us," Krystal gestured toward the rest of the group. "You're the popular girl in school trying to tell all the losers how to be happy." Krystal followed up with another question. "Tell me, do you have a family and a lot of friends who will be there for you when you're down in the dumps?"

Karen was starting to feel ashamed with the expected answer, "Yes," she admitted, "I have a lot of friends and family I stay connected with."

Krystal pointed to herself, "Well I *don't!* I don't have any of that!" Karen stared at Krystal in horror, but Krystal didn't care. She simply did not care anymore. "Now unless you have something genuinely *useful* to offer me, then you can just piss off."

Krystal sat back in her chair with her arms crossed; the room was dead silent. Krystal could feel her arm beginning to bleed through the bandages as everyone stared at her with mixed reactions. Krystal glanced around the circle and said sarcastically, "Oh I'm done by the way." Then leaned back into her chair, checking the clock for how much time they had left.

Krystal lay in her bed frustrated. Today's counseling session was not the best with Karen. While Krystal verbally pummeled her into a corner, she still felt like she hadn't found answers to any of her questions. She was tired of being in this clinic, was tired of the prescriptions that never worked, she was tired of being tired. She wanted out. She wanted to find some happiness for a change. To feel better for once in her life. She was fed up with this dragging feeling. The constant weight of the world pressing down on her chest like a giant slab of concrete. She wasn't sure how much more of that pressure she could take until she finally snapped. Or had she already and this is what was left? Permanent misery.

Krystal lay in her bed, the darkness surrounding her like a weighted blanket while she thought of the Janitor again. Pondering the man's kindness and character. *Why does he keep coming back to my mind? And what was it about him that made me feel like he was so different?* She thought about it and remembered a new detail. *He prayed for me. Yeah, that's right. He prayed for me . . . why? What did that do? It's not like I believe in God or anything.*

Then the thought clicked, and her frame of thinking changed. *God? What does God have to do with anything?* She briefly remembered praying to God the night she tried to kill herself, how desperate she prayed for God to save her. *Now that I think of it, why did I pray that?* She tried to answer her own question but didn't have the materials. She was left empty handed by her own thought process. *This is getting annoying.* Krystal readjusted in bed and stopped moving, glancing over at the girl resting sideways on her bed across from her. Krystal debated whether to ask her a question. It wasn't a good time to ask so late in the night, but Krystal had nothing but time these days. Krystal leaned over to the side of her bed and whispered, "Hey, you awake?"

The girl groaned, "No" then shifted onto her back.

Krystal asked, "Can I ask you a question?"

The girl sighed, "I'm already awake, so you might as well ask."

Krystal paused for a moment, knowing she was about to take a leap of faith asking this question, but she knew she had to ask it. "Do you believe in God?"

The girl took a moment to answer then shifted onto her side facing Krystal, "My whole family is Christian, so I guess, yes." Krystal could sense a hint of bitterness in there.

"You don't sound too convinced."

The girl sighed, "I was raised Christian, but I never really followed any of that stuff."

"But do you believe in an afterlife?" Krystal insisted.

"Vaguely."

That wasn't what Krystal was expecting but still she didn't react. Right now, she was just asking questions and she wanted to hear what other people thought on this matter. "What do you mean?"

The girl sat upright, "I don't know. I never really considered any of that stuff. I kind of put it aside and decided I would worry about it when I was like eighty or something?"

Krystal wasn't sure how to react to that answer. "Well, what happens when you're eighty and you're nearing your death bed?"

"I mean, I figured I would go to heaven or something. Or I would just see black for the rest of my life . . . after death of course."

"But are you sure about that?" Krystal asked. Her curiosity continued to pique, she didn't mean to pry, but she couldn't help herself.

The girl raised her voice in a fit of rage, suddenly losing her patience, "Why are you so interested in this stuff all of a sudden?" Her words were starting to appear more hostile the more Krystal engaged into the topic.

The girl shot Krystal a death stare, Krystal matched it with her own and said, "You tend to think things differently once you tried to kill yourself."

Krystal could tell the girl was at the end of her patience, responding to

Krystal like she was a hostile witness in a courtroom, "I don't have any of the answers to your questions!"

"Why?" Krystal asked honestly.

The girl yelled, "Because I don't want to talk about it! Most people don't enjoy talking about this type of stuff!"

Krystal remained quiet, yet unmoved. She found that curious though. *Why does she not want to talk about it?* (She felt like Donkey talking to Shrek.) Krystal aimed to ask another question, but she knew aggravating the girl further would get her nowhere. "Sorry," said Krystal, deflating the situation with her calm words. Feeling defeated, Krystal decided maybe she should drop the subject altogether.

The girl wanted to be mad, but Krystal's lack of hostility forced her to drop her own. The girl shook her head, annoyed, but said more graciously, "Look. If you're looking for answers, try to go to church or something."

"Church?" Krystal found that idea very peculiar.

"YES CHURCH!" the girl yelled. She was out of patience. Krystal did not move. She wasn't afraid of the girl yelling at her. The girl could yell as much as she wanted, and Krystal still wouldn't break face. She was too dead inside to care. The girl looked away and threw her pillow over her head, "I'm done with this conversation." Krystal wanted to ask more but she knew their discussion was over. At least Krystal *has had* a conversation with someone these days. Nevertheless, it left Krystal with more questions than before.

Krystal lay back in her bed and whispered, "Church huh?" She suddenly thought of the Janitor again. The idea still bugging her conscience. *Why was he so kind? What made him shine so much?* She didn't have the answer, but the idea of that man's kindness made Krystal want to know more. What made him care for someone like her, when no one bothered to even look at her throughout her normal life? What made him so different? And whatever it was, she wanted it. But she didn't know where to start. All she had were questions. Questions, she hoped would take her somewhere.

Krystal's time at the hospital clinic had ended after about a week of counseling and group therapy classes, accompanied with a strong prescription of meds for her depression. Krystal wasn't too happy about the medication. She knew they just wore off eventually and the emptiness and depression remained. But at least they helped in the short term. Still, it wasn't a real solution. And she needed to find one or else . . . she might kill herself again, and next time, she might not fail. That simply couldn't be an option, at least at the very depth of her soul, she didn't want it to be.

Something was different after Krystal's suicidal experience though, and she recognized that. There was something about it, something in the air, which caused her to search for . . . something. She wasn't sure what it was, but it was out there, she knew it had something to do with the Janitor she'd encountered. But what was it? What was it about him that made him so special? And why were all these questions about life hitting her now? Why hadn't she thought about these tough questions like, "Why do we live? How did we get here? Is there an afterlife?" until after she had tried to commit suicide? Krystal figured that coming so close to death had caused her to start asking the challenging questions in life. Questions she had no answers to.

Krystal's arm was still wrapped in bandages, but people didn't notice. She was still as invisible as ever. Except this time, she was on a quest. A quest for answers. Answers, she was hoping to find, and soon.

CHAPTER 6

Searching

"What happens to us after we die?"

—JL

She could tell from the moment she stepped foot on the school grounds, she wanted to be anywhere but here. Not only did Krystal have to catch up on all the schoolwork she missed, but the average lifestyle of her school hadn't skipped a beat. Krystal could feel the familiar sense of sorrow and loneliness strike her the moment she arrived at school. She had gone to her classes and back to her locker, and every, single, thing, was, the same. Only she didn't have her mom.

It was shocking how constant everything was. Everything was the same in her schedule. She went to class, listened to the teacher, did her work alone, then she'd walk to her locker during lunch and sit back down on her white bench. Krystal's dead eyes were shocked at how nothing had changed. Not a single moment in her average life had changed since she came back from the hospital or after her mom was hit by that truck. Not a single aspect of her schedule was different. Not even her teachers noticed. It was like life was on repeat. The same day played over and over like Groundhog Day, only Krystal was stuck in the living hell of being lonely at school with no friends, struggling with suicidal thoughts every day. Life goes on, as they say, but they didn't mention that life sweeps the hard parts under the rug and continues regardless. What happens then?

People hadn't bothered themselves to ask about the bandage around Krystal's arm. There were times when she would sit with a group during class and not a single person would notice the bandages on her left wrist. Things just continued as usual, and that was what made it so horrible. It showed Krystal just how terrible something in her life could go, and not a single person would notice it. She could die for all she cared, and no one would notice that she was missing from class. They probably didn't even know her name, despite sitting with these same classmates for years. People she had grown up with since preschool. It was all too much to bear, and Krystal couldn't continue performing the same melancholy tasks as before she slit her wrist open. Something had to change, or else she was just going to kill herself again.

People weren't talking about the car accident at the Winter Formal anymore. That was outdated and nothing would change that. Krystal wanted to feel mad about everything but couldn't. She was too empty inside to care anymore, the little bits in her heart that had the capacity to care died when she saw her mom in that wreck. Krystal sat on her white bench in the middle of the school courtyard and hated being back. Krystal sat on her bench, eyes wide and empty from how normal things were, thinking. *No, I've got to do something different. I've got to do things some other way. Something that will help me. But what?*

The questions from the hospital arose within her mind. *What happens to us after we die?* Krystal leaned back in her chair, stumped. She didn't know.

Huh. What does happen to us when we die? She thought back to her encounter with the brunette-blonde girl in the hospital. Remembering how she didn't have the answers. *Maybe, I need to ask an adult about this?* Krystal thought. *They would know more about it than that girl in the hospital.* Krystal wondered if she would get the same result. Either way, she didn't know that many adults to talk to other than Aunt Sarah, and she wasn't going to get home until she finished her evening shift at the hospital. *Just like Mom. They're two peas in the same pod.* Krystal wished the Janitor were around. She wanted to ask him more questions, but she knew he was gone. A figure she wouldn't see again for some time, possibly ever. So she was left to ponder her options. *I can ask some random adult, like a teacher, I could ask a counselor but that didn't go well, or . . . I could look it up myself?* Krystal thought about it for a moment and then realized she could just look the question up on her phone.

Without thinking, Krystal took out her phone and typed in the phrase, *"What happens to us when we die?"* and clicked enter. Multiple articles came up, all of them different. Krystal searched the articles, checking mostly the first recommendations that came up from her search. Most of them were not helpful. Krystal kept scrolling through her phone, getting increasingly frustrated with the lack of legitimate answers. Most were just articles talking about how the human body decomposes shortly after death, while other articles told her to look within herself for the answer. She found it to be a bunch of bull.

Krystal clicked on a new article without looking at the title. *This is the last one or else I'm giving up.* Krystal started reading and the first thing she read was, *"What happens to us when we die?"* piquing her interest. Krystal kept scrolling, mostly skimming through a majority of the article idly, not absorbing what it was saying when suddenly something caught her eye, something she recognized. Krystal read:

> *"For God so loved the world, that He gave His only Son, so that everyone who believes in Him will not perish, but have eternal life."*
> —John 3:16 (NASB)

"People all over the world are wondering . . . what happens to us after we die? A majority of religions in the world believe in a heaven and a hell but do we really know what happens to us after death? To know what comes after death is an important gambit. Not only does it answer an important question in life, but it settles an area of doubt.

But what truly happens to us after we die? Well . . . Jesus Christ teaches that whoever believes in him shall not perish but have eternal life.

Have you asked yourself that question? Have you settled the reality that you are one day going to die? What comes next? What happens after we breathe our last? These are many questions that can be answered if you ask God to come into your life. Jesus Christ promises eternal life to all who believe in Him.

For if you claim to know what comes after death, may I ask you this . . . are you willing to bet your eternity on it? Because what if you're wrong? What if there really is a heaven and a hell? If so, which one would you go to?"

Krystal found herself intrigued by the article. It drew her in enticingly, there was something about that John 3:16 verse that clicked with her, yet she didn't know why.

Krystal clicked out of the article and pondered. *Huh . . . Jesus Christ huh . . . what does He have to do with death? And what about that verse, John 3:16. Why is that so important?* Krystal didn't have the answer to her question, but one thing was for sure. She was intrigued and wanted to find out why.

Jesus Christ . . . isn't that guy part of Christianity or something?

For some reason, her mind drew again to the Janitor, accompanied by the smell of a warm, steaming brownie. It took Krystal back to the hospital room and savored the flavor of the warm brownie. *Perhaps that Janitor had something to do with this?* Again, Krystal wasn't sure. She had too many questions and no answers, and she was getting tired of not knowing. There was a building urge in her heart, a weight to ask someone about it. She couldn't simply stay where she was and live in the gloomy hell that was her everyday life. She had to do something.

Strangely enough, Krystal stood up from her white bench and felt like walking like she always did toward the cafeteria. She soon found rows of tables spread out with colors and borders erected between them, activity buzzing through the line of tables as the spring semester clubs were getting started. Krystal wasn't overly excited at the sight of all the club activity in front of her, but her legs were moving on their own and she had nothing better to do, so she walked into the crowd of people, all of them bustling around, holding up signs, screaming, "Come join us! We need members!"

Krystal went from table to table, checking out their clubs. There was the biology club, the chemistry club, the anime club, the baseball club, the football club, cheerleading club, etc.

The activity around was beginning to wear Krystal down. She came up to a final club that said, "Cookies for Christ." Krystal cocked her head to the side, *That's odd. I literally just thought about Jesus for the first time less than twenty minutes ago. Plus, I didn't know they had a Christian club here on campus.*

The thought of the girl in the clinic flashed in her mind, *"Go to church!"* Krystal pondered for a moment. *Is this what she was talking about? I don't really know anything about church.*

A woman who looked about twenty-four with blue eyes, blonde hair, and jean overalls greeted her, "Hello." Krystal didn't notice and continued staring at the main sign on the table. Krystal shifted her gaze down to the plate of cookies on the side. The blonde woman gestured her hand, "Would you like one?" Her voice was gentle and welcoming.

It took Krystal a long moment to realize the woman was actually talking to her. Krystal paused and stared at the woman. Making sure she was the actual target of her question. After an awkward silence, Krystal lightened a bit, checked over her shoulder to ensure no one was around her, then pointed to herself.

The woman nodded patiently, "Yes you, feel free to take one," gesturing to the cookies on the table. Krystal's eyes slowly went from the woman to the cookies, then back to the woman. Krystal was more surprised that this blonde woman actually *saw* her. Krystal said nothing, picked up an Oreo cookie, and took a bite. The woman asked, "What's your name?" Krystal froze. She wasn't used to hearing that question. To be honest, she still wasn't used to people talking to her in general.

Krystal swallowed and said timidly, "What?"

"What's your name?" The woman asked for a second time. Krystal paused again, still holding the half-eaten cookie in her hand, her mind searching for an answer but unable to find one. The blonde woman stood there, waiting patiently for Krystal to speak.

Krystal took a second to bring herself back to reality. "My name is . . . Krystal." It came out more awkward than she'd intended. Krystal cleared her throat, realizing she was looking at the ground the whole time, "My name is Krystal." That was better, but her voice was still low like she was whispering in a library. She couldn't find it in herself to look the woman in the eye.

The woman tilted her head slightly, not from curiosity but more out of adoration. "It's nice to meet you Krystal," gesturing to herself, "I'm Carmen."

"Nice . . . to meet you." Krystal looked down at the table, unsure of what to say next. After her mom's accident, and Krystal nearly killing herself, her interactions with people were limited to Aunt Sarah and . . . well, herself. Plus, being back at school brought back old habits, and those were hard to break. As a result, talking had become much more difficult for Krystal lately. She found herself becoming more of a recluse with each passing day.

Krystal searched for an answer, anything to say, but her mind went blank.

Krystal shook her head and said, "I . . . I'm sorry . . . I'm not . . . particularly good at this."

Carmen raised a hand to calm her, "It's perfectly fine." Carmen chuckled. "You're not the first person to come up here feeling awkward." Krystal said nothing and watched Carmen with her blank stare. Carmen put her hand over her heart and said, "Trust me, I know high school can be awkward. So don't worry. You're not unusual."

Krystal said nothing. She wasn't sure whether to take that as a compliment or if it meant something else. Carmen could have phrased it better, but it was their first meeting, and to Krystal it felt awful.

Krystal pointed to the table. Carmen followed the gesture and said, "Yes, would you like to know more about the club?" Krystal nodded innocently. Carmen smiled, "We are a Christian club that meets up for a Bible study every Wednesday night at 7pm." Carmen handed Krystal a paper containing the information for the next Bible study. Krystal looked up from the pamphlet and into Carmen's eyes. Strange, there was something familiar in her eyes. Like there was some presence about Carmen that made her feel familiar to Krystal, but where did she recognize it?

Carmen said. "Kay, I'll see you there." Krystal took that as her cue to leave. Krystal turned away and continued walking through the maze of club tables surrounding her. None of them piquing her interest anymore. There was something new that unfolded, Krystal held out the piece of paper, checking the address for the Bible study.

She wanted to chuckle but didn't.

You've gotta be kidding me . . . It's only a block away from my apartment.

⁊

Krystal clutched the paper in her hands like it was her green card into America. Krystal stood on the front porch. The large wooden door staring her down like she was about to enter a dungeon in a castle (or a horse stable, either one works). Krystal raised her hand to knock, but she pulled it back. *This . . . is going to be uncomfortable.* Krystal knocked on the door twice, and thought, *They probably didn't hear it.* The door swung open quicker than she anticipated, and Carmen stood there wearing overalls, "You made it!" Her voice was both cheerful and welcoming. Carmen opened the door all the way, "Come on in." Krystal stepped in through the door, her left hand automatically clutching her right elbow. Her eyes fell to the ground as she stepped on the wooden floor and saw a brown staircase to her right. The house had a white outline to it with family pictures displayed all over the walls.

Krystal felt an eerie presence walking through the house. It felt as if there was a "distance" between something in this house. She always felt uncomfortable being around new people or in new situations, and now, all Krystal wanted to do was go home. Either watching tv or doing homework, both of those sounded like much better alternatives to her right now. Her heart yearned for comfort; however, she knew the feeling was false, and yet she still yearned for it anyway. Krystal loathed being out of her comfort zone that she had spent years carefully crafting for herself. *It's strange. The more I try to connect with people, the more I want to be away from them. It's funny, the prison of loneliness. You yearn to connect with people, yet you want to be comfortable and stay away from them.* (That's what life calls a paradox . . . or is it irony? Whatever works for you.)

Krystal kept looking around the house and noticed a family photo of Carmen in slacks with a younger boy with brown hair. It was a typical family photo, photoshopped into black and white with them standing around some beach, wearing white clothing with the wind blowing. A third girl stood to the right of the boy, she looked to be about ten or eleven-years old. Krystal's voice went mute, so she pointed to the photo and looked at Carmen.

"Oh that?" said Carmen. Krystal nodded. "That was a family picture a couple years ago." Carmen pointed to the other characters. That's my younger brother Jaime, and that's my younger sister Ca—" Carmen shut off. Inhaling slowly, then exhaled, recomposing herself. Krystal wondered what struck Carmen suddenly, but she kept her reaction to herself. Carmen noticed Krystal's silence and decided to change the subject, "Would you like something to eat or drink?"

Krystal nodded and began following Carmen when the garage door opened and out stepped the same boy from the picture, only looking a little older. He had those strong water polo shoulders but still looked thin. He was taller than Krystal by a head and had nice short brown hair. He walked through the garage door with momentum in his step, like he had somewhere to be and didn't want to say. Carmen greeted him with a "Hey Jaime! How was your day?"

"Fine," he said flatly, passing his sister and heading straight up the stairs.

Not the kind of warm greeting you would expect from a sibling. Krystal saw Carmen gaze off into the stairway her brother disappeared into. Krystal sensed Carmen was disappointed. Carmen shrugged it off and turned back to Krystal. Carmen noticed Krystal's eyes shift from her to the stairwell. Carmen understood the reference and said cheerfully, "He's not in a good mood today."

Krystal made no gesture to the weak pun, when the front door flew open and a beautiful blonde girl with energy equal to the sun, walked in shouting, "We finally made it!" Summer walked through the front door followed by two other girls. Summer was no doubt beautiful and had this sort of eminence or magnetism that pulsed throughout the room. Summer and her group of friends walked past Krystal like a street pole and hugged Carmen. Krystal couldn't help but feel a stab of pain from that.

You're still a loser.

You're right about that.

Stop it!

Krystal didn't notice she was looking down, gazing at her black shoes while everyone exchanged greetings. Carmen gestured a hand towards Krystal, "Everyone, this is Krystal, she's new to our group."

Summer was the first to come up to Krystal, grabbing her hand with such enthusiasm and shaking it so hard Krystal thought her arm was going to fall off. Summer spoke so fast Krystal did not know how to react, "It's so nice to meet you! I am so glad you are here! I like your clothing, all black, it's so . . . so . . . you know what I mean, like I like to wear black sometimes but I'm more of a yellow-colored girl or like a sunflower." Summer's enthusiasm was so overwhelming it felt like Krystal was staring at the sun. She could only nod cautiously.

Carmen gestured a hand to a girl with light blonde hair, "This is Cassie Newman."

Summer interrupted Carmen and pointed to the shorter girl with amber, red hair next to Cassie, "And this is Amber Cutthrose."

Krystal waved a hand but remained silent.

Carmen ignored the interruption and gestured toward the outside patio, "Shall we head outside to the patio?"

Summer exploded with energy, throwing her hands in the air, calling out, "YAAAAASSSSSS!" Summer turned to the rest of the group, and said, "Let's go learn about JESUS!" then turned and led the group out through the glass door onto the patio outside.

They all took their seats, finding anything from a concrete slab to an actual chair to sit as Carmen pulled out a small notebook and said, "Everybody please flip to the book of Mark 5:21." Krystal found an actual chair to sit in, but it was a tall chair compared to the rest. Luckily, there was another chair that Carmen sat in, making Krystal not feel as alone and on a pedestal. Everyone pulled out their Bibles or went on their phones while Krystal sat there motionless, not knowing what was going on. Carmen noticed Krystal's dilemma and gave Krystal her own Bible.

Krystal nodded in appreciation while Carmen switched to the Bible app on her phone. Krystal had no idea what kind of book she was holding. It was a leather cased book with gold lining on the pages. Krystal had never held a Bible before. It was oddly attractive in a way. She opened it and flipped through the pages, feeling the slick paper slide beneath her fingers. There was something satisfying about flicking through the pages.

Krystal had no idea where to go, let alone recognize the names of the books. There were all sorts of weird names such as Malachi and Hosea, but then there were more common names like James and John. Krystal was still trying to find where the book of Mark was, but her fears were confirmed when Carmen spoke up, "Alright, can somebody please read Mark 5:21–24."

Summer raised her hand like an overly eager child in a classroom. "Can I read?"

Carmen nodded, "Yes, you can read first."

Summer started flipping through the pages, paused, readjusted herself and took a deep breath, but to everyone's disappointment she continued flipping through the pages for another minute; the whole group watching in silence. Summer raised a finger, "Wait hold on, I've almost got it," more flipping. The whisp of her pages begged to differ. Krystal took the opportunity to try and find the right page but was just as confused as Summer. Carmen noticed Krystal's dilemma and helped her find the right page. Krystal bowed her head in appreciation while the whole group waited another long minute, staring at Summer with silent expectation. Thirty seconds passed in what felt like the longest thirty seconds of Krystal's life, and yet Summer still didn't have the right page.

Carmen asked cautiously, "Would you want somebody else t—"

"No no, I almost got it." Summer interrupted insistently, still flipping. The anticipation in the air driving Krystal mad until Summer finally planted her finger and said, "Ah-ha! Here it is."

Krystal exhaled a breath of relief. *Finally.*

Summer blinked a couple times and looked up, "What were the verses again?"

Krystal turned to stone. *Is she being serious right now?*

"Verses twenty-one to twenty-four." Carmen repeated, maintaining a welcoming and gentle voice.

Summer planted her finger and finally read,

> *Jesus got into the boat again and went back to the other side of the lake, where a large crowd gathered around him on the shore. Then a leader of the local synagogue, whose name was Jairus, arrived. When he saw Jesus, he fell at his feet, pleading fervently with him. "My little daughter is dying," he said. "Please come and lay your hands on her; heal her so she can live."*
>
> *Jesus went with him, and all the people followed, crowding around him.*
> —MARK 5:21–24 (NLT)

Carmen chimed on cue, "Alright, now flip to Mark 5:35–43." Pages flipped; Krystal did her best but was having difficulty keeping up. Carmen's eyes swept the group and asked, "Does anyone have the next verse?"

No one raised their hands. Deep down part of Krystal wanted to read, but she instantly felt uncomfortable at the idea of reading aloud in front of a group of strangers, especially Summer. Krystal locked her tongue within the confines of her mouth like a convict in prison and waited for somebody else to read. After a few seconds of awkward silence, Cassie reluctantly raised her hand. Carmen gave Cassie the gesture to begin, so she raised her Bible and said, "You have hear—"

"Can I read this one too?!" All eyes shot toward Summer.

Carmen was a bit taken back and stammered, "Uhh, Cassie already has the verse."

But Summer was persistent like a puppy, "But I really want to read it!"

Carmen checked with Cassie, "Uhh Cassie?"

Cassie hesitated then backed off, "It's fine," she said. But Krystal noticed a hint of submission in there.

Summer pointed her finger and read:

> *While he was still speaking to her, messengers arrived from the home of Jairus, the leader of the synagogue. They told him, "Your daughter is dead. There's no use troubling the Teacher now."*
>
> *But Jesus overheard them and said to Jairus, "Don't be afraid. Just have faith."*
>
> *Then Jesus stopped the crowd and wouldn't let anyone go with him except Peter, James, and John (the brother of James). When they came to the home of the synagogue leader, Jesus saw much commotion and weeping and wailing. He went inside and asked, "Why all this commotion and weeping? The child isn't dead; she's only asleep."*
>
> *The crowd laughed at him. But he made them all leave, and he took the girl's father and mother and his three disciples into the room where the girl was lying. Holding her hand, he said to her, "Talitha koum," which means "Little girl, get up!" And the girl, who was twelve years old, immediately stood up and walked around! They were overwhelmed and totally amazed. Jesus gave them strict orders not to tell anyone what had happened, and then he told them to give her something to eat.*
> —MARK 5:35–43 (NLT)

Summer finished reading and Carmen chimed in. "Well done, Summer." Carmen turned back to the group. Carmen asked, "So what are the takeaways from this kind of story?" Carmen waited as the group nervously avoided eye contact, so Carmen decided to answer for them. "Alright, we have a little girl in this story and a synagogue leader. The girl was supposedly dead, and the synagogue leader wanted Jesus to come and heal her."

Carmen pointed to her phone, "Notice how in verse thirty-six, Jesus says, 'Don't be afraid. Just have faith.' That's because sometimes all that's required for a miracle is a little faith. Jesus wanted the synagogue leader to have faith in him, in that he would heal his daughter and as a result, the girl awoke and instantly walked around." Carmen checked the circle for understanding. She got a few nods back, just out of pure habit rather than actual understanding.

Krystal was busy leering at the phrase, *"Don't be afraid. Just have faith."* That part stuck out to her for some reason while Carmen picked up the discussion again.

Carmen said, "So how did thi—"

Summer cut in again, "That reminds me of this one time of when I had a puppy, and I totally thought the puppy had died, you know, because he wasn't moving. And so, I called 911 to come on over to help me with my dog, you know, since my parents weren't around, but it turned out the puppy was just sleeping, and I could have just petted the dog to make sure he was okay." The group stared at Summer in silence, Krystal watching Summer in mild puzzlement.

Krystal thought, *What is she talking about?*

Amber chimed in, "That was such a good story."

Then Cassie jumped in, "Yeah it was a great story."

Krystal frowned. Not the kind of reaction she was expecting, and certainly not with any common sense either. Krystal lowered her brow and wondered, *How is that a good story?* Krystal could see all the eyes of the other girls centered on Summer, like she was a magnet for attention. Krystal understood the scene and leaned back in her chair.

Carmen felt stymied again but tried to play off Summer's interruption (key word: "tried"). "Okay, yeah let's roll with that." Carmen turned to Summer, "You wanted to make sure the puppy was okay, so you went to a higher power, the police, to make sure the puppy was okay. Well done." Krystal knew that was a horrible example, but she could tell Carmen was trying to make the most out of the situation.

Summer nodded her head with enthusiasm as if she had just won the Nobel Prize. Krystal stared at Summer bemused and annoyed, but deep down, part of Krystal still thought Summer was cool. It was almost uncontrollable, there was a certain magnetism towards Summer. The kind of confidence that most kids Krystal's age lacked, so they centered themselves around people who did have the confidence, hoping it would rub off on them.

Carmen sat back in her seat; Krystal could sense Carmen's frustration as she tried to hide her emotions. Carmen said, "The main point of the message is that when things seem hopeless, we should put our hope and our trust in Jesus."

Summer opened her mouth and started speaking again. "Oh my gosh! This reminds me of this one time . . ." Krystal leaned back in her chair. *Here we go again.* For the next forty-five minutes Summer began to tell story after story. Giving no break in the conversation. All of it sounded interesting at first, until Krystal realized how little common-sense Summer had after the first thirty seconds. None of her stories ever had any relevance to what Carmen was talking about, but her posse cheered her on, nonetheless.

Eventually Carmen checked her phone and stood up, "Alllright guys. I think that's enough discussion for the night. The next Bible study will be next week at the same time and location. I hope to see you there." Amber, Cassie, Summer, Carmen, and Krystal all stood up, stretching their legs.

Summer said, "That's okay, the girls and I have to get going anyway."

Carmen nodded then led the way back into the house, sliding the glass door open for everyone to follow. Krystal spotted activity in the kitchen as she passed by, noticing two adults, most likely Carmen's parents, busy making dinner. Krystal took a moment to glance at them then resumed following the group on their way out. Carmen opened the front door for Summer and her friends as they walked out, then called out, "I hope to see you guys soon!"

"Of course, we will!" Summer shouted back.

Amber said, "You'll see us again Carmen."

"Bye!" Cassie said.

Carmen closed the door behind her and let out an exasperated exhale. Carmen looked up at Krystal, reading the question in her mind, "Yeah . . . it's usually like that." Krystal stared impassively and gave no reaction. Just ample acceptance.

The smell of salt filled the air as both Carmen and Krystal could feel their mouths salivate in response. Carmen looked over toward the kitchen then back at Krystal and said, "Would you like to stay for dinner? My parents get home later so we normally have dinner after the Bible study." Krystal stood there unsure of what to do. Her instincts told her to go home, but part of her simply couldn't decide. Deep down she wanted to stay and have an actual chance to connect with Carmen, something she hadn't truly done with anyone other than her mom. Carmen invited Krystal and walked back to the kitchen. Krystal decided to follow along and went after Carmen, slowly making their way towards the delicious scent.

Inside the kitchen were Carmen's parents preparing dinner. Mrs. Fisher, a middle-aged woman with a slight roundness to her, wearing an autumn brown apron fitted the description of a perfect motherly character, was finishing the final touches to the lamb while Mr. Fisher, a tall masculine man with a strong build and black beard, was busy dicing up cucumbers, lettuce, and tomatoes into a bowl. The sight made Krystal salivate. She didn't realize how hungry she was until she felt the gaping hole in her stomach come alive with a powerful rumble.

Carmen stepped forward and introduced Krystal. "Mom, Dad, this is a friend of mine. She's new to our Bible study." Mrs. Fisher put down her work and walked over toward Krystal extending her arms out and gave Krystal the widest hug in the world. Krystal was surprised by the sudden familiarity but didn't reject it either. The warmth of Mrs. Fisher enveloping Krystal brought a comfort she hadn't felt in a while. It sort of reminded Krystal of her own mom. That warm, comforting presence melting the icicle around Krystal's heart with Mrs. Fisher's physical touch. Krystal's blank expression softened a bit as Mrs. Fisher pulled back, gripped Krystal by the shoulders and said, "Let me get a good look at you sweetie." Sizing Krystal up like she was a little child, "Oh you look adorable!" Krystal wasn't sure how to react to the comment. Mrs. Fisher kinda reminded Krystal of Mrs. Weasley from Harry Potter but more modern, not as overweight but still bearing a nice motherly roundness to her. "Oh George, doesn't she look adorable!"

Mr. Fisher had put down his utensils and extended a large hand out towards her. Krystal took the hand, finding his hand to be three times larger than her own. The man had the build of a lumberjack and dressed like one too. His skin was rough, but his hand was gentle. Krystal enjoyed the handshake more than the hug. Mr. Fisher towered over Krystal, like a giant in the woods and spoke in a dark manly voice, "It's nice to meet you." Krystal nodded in return, finishing the handshake.

Mrs. Fisher stepped aside, clapping her hands together, looking at Krystal like she was the cutest thing in the world, "And what is your name sweetie?" Krystal stared at them for a long moment, her entire body frozen, as if she received the words a few seconds late. Krystal didn't even realize she was looking down and fought hard to force the words to her lips and whispered, "Krystal." It came out rough and unclear.

Mrs. Fisher leaned in closer, "I'm sorry?"

Krystal spoke a bit louder, but the words were still faint like a whisper. "Krystal."

Mrs. Fisher snapped her spine straight and cupped her hands, "It's wonderful to meet you, Krystal!" All this excitement in one night made Krystal extremely uncomfortable. She wanted to go home and finish her homework. Socializing with these people made her want to retreat into her shell. However, she knew it would be rude to leave after just meeting Carmen's family, so Krystal played along. The three of them were being so kind to her after all, a kindness she hadn't experienced from strangers before. Mrs. Fisher went back behind the countertop and finished lathering the lamb with sauce. She looked to Carmen, "Carmen could you get your younger brother down here?"

"Sure thing." Carmen jogged up the stairs and vanished, leaving Krystal alone with the parents. Krystal stood there, unsure of what to do. She looked around the kitchen and living room when Mrs. Fisher asked Krystal, "Would you like some water?" but Krystal didn't think she was speaking to her. Krystal's eyes were staring down at her shoes when Mrs. Fisher politely asked again, "Krystal?" Krystal broke her stare and realized Mrs. Fisher had asked her something. Mrs. Fisher leaned in, "Would you like some water?" Krystal nodded cautiously and remained silent. Either way, Mrs. Fisher seemed delighted with her response.

She went to grab Krystal a cup of water when both Carmen and Jaime came down the stairs. Jaime, who seemed a bit reluctant, stopped on the stairwell and gave Krystal a puzzling accusatory look. The kind of face that said, *"Who are you and why are you still here?"*

Krystal got the message, shooting back an uninterested scowl. Her eyes deadpan; her glare strong. The room felt both silent and loud as the two of them glared at each other. Krystal grew tired of the game and broke contact first, not because she lost but because she didn't care to compete with the guy.

Carmen walked over and set up the utensils on the wooden dinner table, seating about five people in total. Everyone took their seats while Mrs. Fisher laid plates and dished out the food while Mr. Fisher followed suit with the vegetables. Once finished, the parents sat at each end of the table while

Carmen sat across from Krystal, leaving Krystal sitting next to Jaime. Krystal stared at the steaming plate of food before her. Able to smell barbeque sauce on the lamb as well as the balsamic vinaigrette on the vegetables. Her mind began to drift as she stared at the food.

What do you think you're doing? You don't deserve this. You don't deserve any of this.

Krystal winced. Why did that thought cross her mind? Krystal shrugged it off and snapped back to reality with everyone looking at her. Krystal was a bit confused, Mrs. Fisher looked as if she was going to say something, but Jaime whispered to Krystal, "We're going to say grace."

Krystal nodded. Everyone threaded their hands together and closed their eyes. The whole family started voicing the Lord's prayer in unison, "Our Father, who art in Heaven, hallowed be thy name . . ."

Krystal wasn't entirely sure how the process worked, so she sat there and watched in silence. She noticed Jaime's head wasn't bowed in prayer like the rest of his family, his eyes glancing briefly in Krystal's direction then back down at his food. *Why isn't he praying?* She wondered. When they all finished, it came a time for people to voice their prayers to the group, Krystal could feel a sense of awkwardness linger in the room. The moment to pray to God in front of everyone else was upon them, even with everyone's eyes closed it was still uncomfortable. After a couple seconds of awkward silence, Mrs. Fisher said, "Thank you for a great day and thank you for bringing Krystal here with us."

Everyone said, "Amen" and opened their eyes.

The motion to start eating was given and everyone dug into their plates. Krystal followed suit, trying not to look too out of place, but her movements were slow, as she wasn't as eager to eat as everyone else was. Krystal noticed Jaime expressed the same kind of sentiment, although it was more out of angered disinterest rather than hunger. Mrs. Fisher finished eating a slice of lamb and said, "So Krystal . . . tell us about yourself." Krystal paused and felt instantly self-conscious as all eyes were on her, except for Jaime. Krystal swallowed her food and tried to find the right words to say but nothing came to mind. Krystal's mouth opened slightly, as if rehearsing the words she was going to say, but she changed her mind and didn't say them. She succumbed to her failure and whispered, "I . . . I don't know." It was an awkward response but who could blame her.

Jaime spoke while still staring down at the lamb he was cutting, "You're supposed to answer the question moron."

Carmen yelled, "Jaime!" Mr. Fisher lifted a hand to calm her.

Then Mr. Fisher turned to Jaime, gave him a stern look. Jaime briefly exchanged looks with his dad and backed off. "Sorry," he said. It sounded half-genuine, but it was still rude. Jaime resumed cutting his lamb and let the spotlight shift back on Krystal.

Mrs. Fisher tried again to foster the conversation. "Is there anything you like to do for fun Krystal?" Krystal shook her head. Mrs. Fisher felt dead-pan again and switched gears. "Tell us about your family." Krystal froze, her mind going to a different place, reliving memories. She didn't look up and stared forward at the center of the table in silence. Mrs. Fisher clarified, "Tell us about your parents. What does your dad do? What does your mom do?"

Krystal said plainly, "I never knew my dad." The clatter of silverware stopped. Only Jaime kept cutting his meat. The other half of the surprise was how blunt Krystal was about something so deep that it caught the entire family off guard.

Mrs. Fisher tried to recover the conversation, "Well what about your mom?"

Krystal answered the same way, "She got hit by a truck." The room was dead quiet. Even Jaime had stopped cutting his food and simply stared at his plate. You could hear a pin drop the room was so quiet. The whole room seemed to just . . . stop. Krystal could feel everyone's gaze on her again. Krystal sighed, lowering her gaze toward the steaming food beneath her. "I'm sorry . . . I'm . . . I'm not good . . . at . . . talking."

Mrs. Fisher replied with compassion, "It's okay, take your time."

Krystal whispered, "Thank you," and resumed eating.

Jaime chimed in again, poking his lamb with his fork, "You really should work on that. You won't have any friends if you don't talk."

"Jaime!" Carmen cut in again. This time her face was bright red with anger. "That's enough."

Krystal looked at Jaime in the corner of her eye with both disinterest and hardened sorrow. Jaime turned and met her gaze as she said timidly, "I don't have any friends." Jaime's expression weakened so he backed off. Mr. Fisher was glaring at Jaime in soft hurt. Jaime saw the look on his dad's face and deflated. Jaime put his fork and knife down and stood up from the table.

"I'm going to bed." Jaime left the table and headed upstairs.

Carmen watched him head upstairs, then turned back to Krystal, "I'm sorry. He's not himself lately."

Krystal said, "It's fine," and resumed her eating. The rest of the family followed suit and they ate in silence for a few more minutes. Krystal stabbed her fork into the lamb and found the taste to be absolutely delicious. It was the first time she had eaten with somebody in a while.

Carmen swallowed a bite of lamb, eager to change the subject, "So, blessings and bummers?"

Mrs. Fisher said, "Ohhh I'll go first! The blessing is, I made a new friend at work. It turns out my co-worker Stacy just moved into her new apartment last week and they needed help, so I went to help her out this week."

"That was very nice of you honey," said Mr. Fisher.

Mrs. Fisher pondered for a moment and said, "Other than that, nothing really negative has happened this week. What about you Carmen?"

Carmen replied, "We set up our table for our club Bible study and we got Krystal to come," gesturing at Krystal. Krystal didn't look up and continued eating. "Bummer was, we didn't have a very big turnout, but that's okay because that means we will have a more intimate group this year."

Mrs. Fisher turned to her husband, "And you honey?"

Mr. Fisher put down his fork and knife, "We had some guys get laid off this week so that was a bummer. They were some good guys too. I'll miss them. Blessing . . . uhhh well the food tonight was really good sweetie, and our pastor is hosting a greeting party after the service this Sunday."

"Right after church?" asked Carmen.

"Uh-huh," said Mr. Fisher.

"Alllright. Sounds like fun." Carmen looked across the table at Krystal and said, "You're welcome to join us, Krystal." Krystal looked up from her food and pondered the invitation. She thought about her schedule and what she would be doing on Sunday.

The only thing I have planned is to try and not to kill myself. So, I'm free. Krystal swallowed. *It's church huh . . . I don't really know about it or what the scene is like. Then again, It's not like I'll be doing anything important that day.* The idea of church lingered in her mind. The brunette-blonde girl from the clinic flashed in her conscience, telling her to go to church. For some reason, Krystal couldn't shake the feeling. It came now and again throughout her day, pressing her heart once more. The fear of the unknown weighed on Krystal's mind. She had no idea what the church scene was like or who would be there. It could very well end up being like she was at school and getting ostracized again. Krystal weighed the options, but her time ran out as she gazed back at Carmen with contemplative eyes. Then nodded her head. She didn't know why she did, but she was genuinely curious to see what that girl from the hospital was talking about. Maybe she'll find some answers there.

Carmen seemed delighted, as were her parents. Mr. Fisher smiled and then got up to take everyone's plates. Carmen clapped her hands together like Mrs. Fisher and said, "Great! We'll pick you up around 10:15am on Sunday."

Krystal replied faintly, "Okay."

Carmen stood up from her chair and asked, "Just one question. Where do you live?"

"Down the street."

CHAPTER 7

Emptiness

*"Have you ever felt empty? Like there was a gaping hole in
the center of your chest and nothing could fill it?"*

—JL

Krystal let out a yawn and hesitated to knock on the mahogany brown
door. She knew the Fishers said they would come get her, but she only lived a
block away so she decided to just meet them at their house. She glanced at the
bandage on her left arm. The wound still hadn't healed in the recent weeks
since she exited the hospital. That worried her. Wounds typically healed with
time but for Krystal the wound had barely healed at all. It bled every now
and then, and that part of her worried her the most, since her arm could leak
at any time, even during church. She didn't want anyone to notice a wound
that was obviously self-inflicted, and the last people she wanted to notice
were church folk.

Krystal hesitated to raise her hand. Part of her thought she should call
the whole thing off and just go home. She could do it, she assured herself.
She lived only a block away. But Krystal was also curious, she had questions
and perhaps she would find some answers by going to church, not that she
expected to find any. She didn't even know where the church was, let alone
what the people were like. For all she knew, she was on her way to go join a
cult. That made her nervous thinking about being around people who were
always so "nice," but she had nothing better to do on her Sunday morning, so
she raised her hand and gave a gentle knock on the door. She heard footsteps
and was not surprised to see Carmen answer.

"Krystal! Hey! Good to see you. We are coming out now, wait on the driveway and we'll hop in the car and go." Krystal obeyed and walked out onto the driveway. The garage door opened, finding the Fisher's dressed in semi-formal clothing. The typical polo shirt and nice dress did well enough. Krystal's heart clenched. She'd realized her first mistake: dress code. She would stick out like a sore thumb given her black outfit, until Carmen came outside dressed in her typical blue overalls and white shirt. That brought some relief to Krystal, knowing she wasn't alone. Mr. and Mrs. Fisher came out and went to the driver and passenger seat of their Range Rover while Carmen opened the side door and hopped in. Krystal looked around and noticed Jaime wasn't with them. Krystal pondered for a moment but was interrupted when Carmen opened the door for her. She took her seat, and they loaded up and headed off to church.

The car pulled to a stop, and they unclicked their seat belts. Krystal followed suit and exited the car, finding herself standing before a single-story building with a triangular roof and a white chimney that stretched up with a metal cross standing on top of it. People were crowding the side of the building like a clotted vein. Krystal gripped her right elbow with her left hand. Her blood pumped faster at the idea of going into a crowded building. Krystal felt uncomfortable being around this many people again. Not since the photo shoot at the Evergardens. Not since going back to school after her . . . accident.

The Fishers led the way and Krystal followed. The air outside was dusty and cool, with people chatting around the entrance of the building. Krystal felt skeptical going up to these people. She had never believed in God, and she never gave any thought to going to church before, so she went in with the belief that these people were low-key a cult. Krystal entered the doorway as people stood by the entrance greeting others.

"Good morning!" was sent out to everyone who walked through the doors. Krystal blended with the Fishers and walked into the building, unsure of whether the greeters at the door saw her. Either way, she didn't care. Krystal stepped inside and found herself in a hallway filled with people. There was chatter all around, happy smiles, and the constant smell of coffee. The scent of hazelnut in the morning pleased Krystal's nostrils even though she didn't drink coffee. It gave her a comforting feeling, and she slowly became more at ease.

Krystal followed Carmen into an auditorium with a stage at the end and chairs filling the rest of the room. There was some musical equipment set up on stage and Krystal wondered what that was for. The night before, Krystal tried to picture what a church looked like. She imagined a tall cathedral with a priest dressed in robes, but none of those images met her expectations. This church building was simplistic, almost had sort of a modern feel to it. Krystal looked around, finding wooden columns spread diagonally along the sides of the auditorium. The room looked to sit about a hundred people. Maybe two hundred if they stretched it. Most of the people were still in the hallway or were outside talking. Those that weren't outside were at the coffee stand off to the side where people flocked like moths to a flame. Carmen and her parents went to grab some coffee, but Krystal stood where she was, taking in the sight of the church auditorium.

I have no idea what is going on or what these people are all about.

Krystal felt warm liquid on her left arm. The bandages under her sleeve turning red and damp. Krystal grasped her arm and checked if anyone was looking. *Oh no*, she thought. Speeding to find the nearest restroom. Krystal pushed her way through a wooden door out the auditorium into an empty bathroom with two stalls. She unwrapped her bandages and revealed the open wound in her wrist. It still looked as fresh as when she first cut it. There was no crustation or any improvement in her skin. The wound simply hadn't healed. Terror began to grip Krystal as her pulse quickened, causing more blood to ooze from her arm. Krystal put her wrist under the sink and attempted to wash the blood away. The pain in her wrist made her forearm tighten. She grabbed some paper towels and tried to clean the blood off. *That's why you wear black, so no one can see the blood.* Krystal wiped her arm and took out some extra bandages she kept on her. She wrapped the bandage neatly around her wound and made it inconspicuous enough once she rolled her sleeves up.

Now to get rid of the bandage. Krystal checked around for a garbage can, but before she could throw away the bloody bandage, one of the stalls opened and a young woman looking to be in her late twenties with tattoos sleeving down both her arms, walked out. She had short black hair and stepped next to Krystal to wash her hands. Krystal tried not to look the woman in the eye and threw the bloody bandage into the garbage can, but she wasn't sure if the woman noticed. Maybe the woman just pretended to not see it or she never saw it in the first place, either way, Krystal didn't want to be there any longer than she had to be.

The auditorium was packed when Krystal returned. A band had taken the stage and were playing some music Krystal had never heard before. *I thought there would be some choir singing today, not a full-on band.* Krystal searched for Carmen and the Fishers and found them sitting on the left side in the middle of the auditorium. Krystal eased through the crowd and found an open chair next to Carmen and her parents.

She wasn't sure what she was supposed to do, so Krystal reverted to her usual habit of standing still and being quiet. Krystal looked at the Fishers, noticing an empty seat next to them. *Why is Jaime not with them?* Krystal wanted to ask, but that was for another time. She surveyed the crowd and saw what kind of people were here at this event. To her surprise Krystal found Summer sitting across the room with someone else, noticing how enthusiastic Summer was singing the songs. Everyone else in the room was either mouthing the words or trying to follow suit with the same passion as they sang songs about this guy named "Jesus."

Krystal felt uncomfortable standing amongst these people, all of whom had their attention focused on the stage as the band played song after song with the audience casually singing along. There were some massive screens displayed on the left and right side of the stage, showing the lyrics to the songs. Krystal didn't understand the words or what they were talking about, so she stayed silent and waited for the singing to end.

Krystal gazed amongst the crowd and noticed there weren't many young people in the church. Most of the people were either middle-aged or newly-wed couples holding their young children. There were only a few teenagers and young adults, aside from Summer and Carmen. But there looked to be only a handful of people as young as Krystal.

The singing finished half an hour later and Krystal was glad to finally be able to sit down. The band exited the stage and a man walked on who looked to be in his mid-thirties with a checkered shirt and glasses.

The Preacher stepped onto the stage and stood in front of a podium. He put down a Bible, smiled and said, "It's lovely to see everyone here this morning. We have a great sermon laid out for you. Or . . . at least that *was* the plan for this weekend." The Preacher raised his hands in happy defense, "Don't worry I'll give the regular sermon next week. I'm sure I'll see you here next week." The crowd chuckled.

The Preacher lowered his hands, "Normally my friends I would give you a sermon based on the series we were going through, but I had been getting this feeling from the Holy Spirit that I needed to preach a different message this week." The Preacher stepped away from his podium, "These days we are surrounded by technology and information, that it is easy to forget the basics. It is easy to forget *why* we believe."

Krystal slumped down in her chair, feeling like she was back in class listening to a teacher give another lecture, only it was with a larger crowd of people and some people were taking notes. Krystal's eyes were suddenly very heavy. With the comfort of the chair and the lecture going on, Krystal was bound to fall asleep anytime soon. *What should I expect for my first time at church?* But it was strange. Krystal had felt wide awake before she came here, and now she felt ready to take a nap. What gives?

The Preacher paused for effect, "Now . . . I'd like to ask you a question." He carefully laid both arms on the sides of the podium and spoke softly, "Have you ever felt a sense of emptiness in your heart? Have you ever wondered whether there may be more to life than this?" Krystal's eyes snapped open, her sleepiness vanished, as she focused on the Preacher with all her intent. The Preacher put his hand to his chest and said, "There is a God-shaped hole within every human heart." He gestured his hand toward the crowd, "You've felt it, I've felt it. Everyone feels it. There is not a single person on this planet who has lived that hasn't experienced this emptiness within." The Preacher looked straight in Krystal's direction. Krystal couldn't help but feel like he was speaking directly to her, like she was the only one in the room. Krystal's body went into fight or flight mode, ready to storm out of the room, but the fear of making a scene planted her firmly where she was sitting.

The Preacher backed away from his podium and began pacing around the stage, "So what do we do to fill this hole in our heart? How do we fill this void, this . . . this . . . gaping hole within ourselves that sucks away our happiness?" Krystal leaned forward with interest. Now he was speaking her language. The Preacher threw his arms in the air, "What do we do? What do we do to fill the hole in our lives?" He began listing off his fingers. "We could try to fill that hole with friends and family, but friends and family don't last forever. We could try to fill that hole with sex and drugs, but those are only short-term pleasures. They aren't enough to fill that hole in our lives, and that hole keeps getting bigger and bigger, no matter how we try to fill it.

"Then there is the matter of purpose. For what purpose are we human beings existing on this earth? Ask yourself . . . why are you here on this earth? Why are you breathing this very moment at this very time on this very day? Why are you existing in this world at all?" He pushed up his glasses, out of habit.

The Preacher continued, "There are some people who walk through this life with no hope . . . They don't know who or what they are. Why they exist in this world. In fact, most people just *exist*. They aren't *living*. You could be alive but feel dead at the same time. You could be breathing but not living. Some people are just drifting through life like a walking corpse. They aren't truly living. They aren't happy. So what is it then? What is that thing that we need to fill this hole in the center of our being?"

Krystal leaned in closer, *I've never heard anybody ask these kinds of questions before. And he's speaking the exact same questions that I'm going through* . . . Krystal leaned on the edge of her seat with thirsty intrigue. She subconsciously put her hand on her sternum, rubbing the exact spot where the hole remained. She didn't even notice until a few seconds after her hand was on her chest.

The Preacher spoke softly, "My friends, I'll tell you . . ." He paused. "That hole in your life is your soul calling out to God. And the only way, the *only way*, to fill that hole . . . is to accept Jesus Christ into our hearts." He backed away from his podium and started pacing again, "You could try to fill that emptiness with material things. You could try to fill it with the pleasures of this world, but those things are only temporary. They will not give you an everlasting and perpetual fix." The Preacher pinched his index and thumb together, "But if you want to find lasting fulfillment for that gaping hole and to truly live life, then keep listening . . ." The Preacher spread his arms, "If you don't believe me, then *test me*!" The words echoed off the walls. He spoke softly, "Test me . . . I dare you. Find me something that will give you more purpose and more hope than Jesus Christ. Find me something that will fill that never-ending vacuum within our hearts. For Jesus offers this hope to you, not for a price, but as a free gift. There is no other way to find fulfillment than through Jesus Christ."

Krystal sat there in awe. She had no idea what to think of this man or what the rest of his church thought either. But the words he spoke with such authority and love behind them . . . it reminded Krystal of . . . the *Janitor*. Krystal thought, *This Preacher, he has the same "glow" as the Janitor. That same kind of joy he had. But what is it? And . . . who is Jesus?* The Preacher returned to his podium and said, "My friends, I do hope you go home and think about these things, for if you truly seek God with all your heart . . . you will find Him." The Preacher paused, searching his audience, "Grace and peace."

"Grace and peace," replied the audience. Then just like that, the show was over, and everyone was back to socializing and chit chat. Krystal sat there stunned. She had just seen something momentous yet couldn't understand it. She sat there, trying to ponder what just happened, but one thing was sure. Krystal had a question on her mind . . . *Who is Jesus?*

> "Does kindness come naturally, or does it take effort?"
> —JL

Carmen leaned over and whispered, "Hey." Krystal met her eyes but didn't say anything. "We are going to chit chat for a bit then we'll leave. That okay?" Krystal nodded and Carmen went to socialize with the other church people while Mr. and Mrs. Fisher kept to their own business, sipping coffee, and hanging out. Krystal took the opportunity to go to the bathroom; this time she actually had to go because she had been holding her bladder the entire sermon. Krystal finished her business then stood out in the hallway. There were some people chatting, all of them seeming happy. Krystal ignored their cheerfulness and went to find Carmen. Krystal still wasn't comfortable being around this many people and she wanted nothing more than to go home. But she did have new questions. Questions she hoped would be answered.

Krystal walked down the hallway when she came across a shelf full of books. Some of the objects said "free" while others had price tags. Krystal gazed at the shelf, skimming the titles. Most of them looked like self-help books or religious books about Christianity. One book caught her eye. It was a black hardcover with gold lining, making the book appear more like a treasure. Krystal couldn't tell why, but something drew her to this book. She took the book from the shelf and opened it to the first page. The paper felt slick and thin beneath her fingers. That odd "thirst" to the style of paper made her want to keep flicking through the pages. She flipped through the book until she found a story called Genesis, and read:

"In the beginning God created the heavens and the earth."

Krystal paused after reading that first sentence. Oddly enough she wanted to read more. It felt like something was . . . calling to her, but the voice was so soft and gentle, wishing for her to buy this book. It wasn't a forceful thought though. It felt more peaceful, giving her freewill in the decision rather than the pressure (or temptation) to do something. Krystal closed the Bible and flipped to the back, looking for a price tag. It said "$1." Krystal sighed.

I don't have a dollar, she thought. Out of habit she stuck her hand in her pocket, and her eyes suddenly lit up. She pulled her hand slowly from her pocket and in it was a single dollar. She stared at it for a long minute, both amazed and petrified at what had just happened. Krystal took deep breaths to calm herself down.

It's okay. It's okay. It's just a coincidence. It's just a coincidence. But her heart felt otherwise.

There's no way I carry cash in my pocket. I don't even have my wallet on me!

Krystal was too flustered with her own reasoning to conclude, so she took the dollar and laid it on the shelf. Krystal took the Bible and backed away in fearful reverence. She stared at the dollar sitting on the shelf and backed away, then turned towards the exit. *That . . . was creepy.* Krystal couldn't help but wonder if she would return to this strange place, they called church. Well one thing was for sure, it had been an interesting morning.

Krystal headed toward the exit and found Carmen and her parents standing there chatting with the Preacher. Mrs. Fisher noticed Krystal and turned, "And this is Krystal, she's new."

The Preacher turned and extended his hand out toward Krystal. "It's nice to meet you, Krystal." He said smiling. Krystal said nothing and shook his hand. She wasn't sure how to react to the Preacher, but she knew he had a certain aura to him. One that was gentle yet authoritative.

Mrs. Fisher chimed in, "She doesn't talk much." That was the understatement of the century. The mere presence of four people all looking at Krystal, let alone the main Preacher of the church, caused Krystal so much discomfort she thought her heart was going to stop.

Wouldn't be a change of pace though.

Mr. Fisher extended his hand out to the Preacher, "Always good to see you, but we need to head out now."

The Preacher responded, "I understand." He turned to Krystal, "It was a pleasure getting to know you." He turned to the Fishers, "Have a lovely Sunday."

"You too," Mr. Fisher replied, and just like that, they all left the church building. Opening the car door, Mr. Fisher said, "Who's hungry?"

"I'm hungry," said Carmen.

"I can eat," said Mrs. Fisher.

Mrs. Fisher turned to Krystal, "Would you like to join us for lunch?" Krystal wasn't sure how to answer. She wasn't sure if it was okay to go to lunch with them. She didn't want to trouble these people any longer, or be a burden to them, but she was hungry now that they mentioned it. She caved in by nodding her head. One nod was all it took for Mrs. Fisher to turn round and said, "Alllright. Let's get some food." Krystal couldn't help but look at Carmen and thought, *Like mother, like daughter*, as they stepped in the car and headed out for brunch.

They came up to a bagel shop and Krystal couldn't help but take in the sight. It looked more like a café than a bagel shop, but maybe that was the intended design. The title of the shop said, *"Noir."* Krystal was the last to enter the shop as Mr. Fisher held the glass door open for her and his family. Carmen was first in line, then her mom, Mr. Fisher, and Krystal. All over the cafe people were eating specialized egg sandwiches in a formal way that made Krystal feel like she was eating peasant food in a noble manner. She had never been taken out to a place with strangers before, let alone people she'd just met earlier this week, but at least it was better than sitting at home feeling bored about what she was going to do with her life.

Krystal stood in the back of the line and could smell the scent of eggs and French toast in the air. The constant commotion from behind the countertop, where more delicate orders were being prepared, the slicing of spatulas, and the grilling of grease flooded Krystal's senses. The smell of food activated her salivatory glands and caused her stomach to contract. She was hungry alright, but how was she going to pay for the food? She didn't have a job and she couldn't exactly ask Aunt Sarah for money until she got home so . . . what? Krystal stood in front of Mr. Fisher, knowing she had no money to pay for her own food, even after she checked then double checked her pockets for any remnant money.

Carmen went forward and ordered, as did Mrs. Fisher. Krystal hadn't even looked at the menu yet. *I'll just get nothing*, she thought. *I don't want to trouble these nice people any more than I already have.* Mr. Fisher went up and ordered, then looked over his shoulder at Krystal and asked, "What would you like Krystal?" Krystal shook her head, but Mr. Fisher saw the hungry look in her eyes. He turned to the cashier, "And can I get a breakfast burrito for her please."

Krystal glanced up at Mr. Fisher in small surprise. The blank stare of hers, showing a ray of light for a change, as her curiosity grew. Mr. Fisher finished ordering and handed the cashier his card. The cashier gave him a receipt and told him it would be a few minutes. Mr. Fisher turned and headed toward the table where Carmen and Mrs. Fisher sat. Krystal followed and asked, "Why did . . . you do that?"

Mr. Fisher calmly stopped halfway, "Do what?"

Krystal hinted over toward the cashier, "Why . . . why were you . . . so kind to me?"

Mr. Fisher squatted down to her level and said calmly, "I was kind, because God was kind to us first." Krystal couldn't help but stare at the man in awe. There was something different about Mr. Fisher and the rest of his family . . . just like that Janitor she'd met. But what was it about them that made them so different? Why did they all . . . *glow*? Krystal didn't have an answer, but one thing was for sure, she was hungry.

They sat down at an open table and a couple minutes later the waiter brought them their food. *This café works fast*, Krystal thought. The waiter brought Krystal a large burrito on a plate. Krystal stared at the burrito steaming in front of her. She looked up at Mr. Fisher who had his hands together, as did Carmen and Mrs. Fisher. They said a quick prayer then dug in. Krystal still waited, then Mr. Fisher caught her gaze and said, "Go ahead."

Krystal cautiously picked up the burrito, feeling its warm texture on her fingers. She took a bite and tasted onions, diced peppers, salt, pepper, sausage, and egg, mixed together with cheese and salsa. The flurry of flavor in her mouth was a joy beyond imagining. Krystal felt a wave of goosebumps flutter over her body. It was the most delicious thing she'd ever tasted. She looked up with a full mouth, chewing as she checked the Fishers and their food. Mr. Fisher caught her gaze and could almost see a smile break on her face, but Krystal contained the joy and hid the possibility of a smile. But Mr. Fisher could read the thought on her saddened face, *Thank you.*

CHAPTER 8

Genesis

"Can something come from nothing?"

—JL

Krystal lay in her bed, letting the darkness envelop her. The moon was hidden and only black gave way outside her window. The night was still, as if time had stopped. She checked the time on her phone, 11:43pm. It had been a few days since Krystal had been to church and the entire time her mind was racked with more questions. Questions she wished would go away, yet a part of her knew they were valid. Krystal stared at the ceiling idly with no expression. She hadn't moved for a solid hour, but sleep would not be granted to her tonight, so she stayed awake, staring at the white ceiling in contemplation.

Who is Jesus and why should I care? She wanted to dismiss the thought, but it was persistent in her mind like a rock in a river.

She thought back to the service with the Preacher and his words: *"the only way to fill that hole . . . is to accept Jesus Christ into our hearts."* Krystal felt skeptical, but she didn't have a reason to argue why.

But what was that Preacher talking about? How did he know about the hole in my heart in the first place? Krystal couldn't help but wonder if the Preacher's words were actually true. She felt a magnetism toward them for some reason. Some force telling her that this is the right path. She pushed those thoughts away and went on to another topic.

Then comes the dollar. The one dollar in my pocket. Krystal felt her right thigh where her pocket would be. *Where did that money even come from? I don't even carry cash on me, so how did it get there?*

Maybe Aunt Sarah was doing your laundry and she accidentally put it there?

That doesn't sound like it would happen. It's not like I found the dollar on the street or anything. It was in my pocket, and I never carry cash in my pocket.

Come on, how can you confirm that?

I don't know. You tell me.

That's what I'm asking you.

Krystal gave up, "This is pointless."

Her thoughts ran back to Mr. Fisher buying her lunch. Those words he said to her, implanted in the back of her mind whether she liked it or not: *"I was kind, because God was kind to us first."*

Krystal thought, *He genuinely believes there's a God in this world huh? But then why would Mr. Fisher be generous to me? Being generous doesn't benefit the person buying the food, it only increases their expenses. Unless he was trying to curry favor with me, but what do I have to give? It's not like I have anything to offer.*

Maybe he's trying to convert you?

That could be . . . it is a probable cause for people who are in a cult.

But that idea didn't sit right with her. It plagued her heart with doubt. *Those words he said to me, "because God was kind to us first." Why would he say that? What does that gain him?* Subconsciously her mind drifted back to the Janitor and his kindness he'd shown her. *They're all the same. They all have the same . . . "glow" about them, but I don't know what it is.*

Krystal took a breath, and asked the true question on her mind, "Is there really a God?" Krystal shifted her head and glanced over at her nightstand, the Bible she had bought at the church lay there, silently calling to her. Without thinking, she reached over and grabbed it, turning on her light and getting comfortable in bed. She centered the Bible on her stomach and opened the hardcover, reading the opening page "Addressed to: _____" Krystal felt the urge to fill her name there, so she took a pen and filled her name in. "Addressed to: <u>Krystal Henninger</u>."

She flipped to the next page. There were some portions labeling the history of the Old Testament and how it connects with the New Testament, some of them dating back thousands of years.

"Hmm . . . Old and New Testament. I've never heard of that before." Krystal tried to think of a time when she and Mom had talked about the

Bible or God, but she couldn't remember. The topic of God was not common between them, so Krystal had never given it much thought. Krystal flipped to the first book called Genesis. Krystal readjusted her position and began reading aloud:

GENESIS 1
The Account of Creation

In the beginning God created the heavens and the earth. The earth was formless and empty, and darkness covered the deep waters. And the Spirit of God was hovering over the surface of the waters.

Then God said, "Let there be light," and there was light. And God saw that the light was good. Then he separated the light from the darkness. God called the light "day" and the darkness "night."

And evening passed and morning came, marking the first day.
—GENESIS 1:1–5 (NLT)

Krystal stopped, "First day? First day of what?" and kept on reading.

Then God said, "Let lights appear in the sky to separate the day from the night. Let them mark off the seasons, days, and years. Let these lights in the sky shine down on the earth." And that is what happened. God made two great lights—the larger one to govern the day, and the smaller one to govern the night. He also made the stars. God set these lights in the sky to light the earth, to govern the day and night, and to separate the light from the darkness. And God saw that it was good.

And evening passed and morning came, marking the fourth day.
—GENESIS 1:14–19 (NLT)

. . .

Then God said, "Let us make human beings in our image, to be like us. They will reign over the fish in the sea, the birds in the sky, the livestock, all the wild animals on the earth, and the small animals that scurry along the ground."

> *So God created human beings in his own image.*
> *In the image of God he created them;*
> *male and female he created them."*
> —GENESIS 1:26–27 (NLT)

Krystal frowned, "God created male and female?" shaking her head, "This book just gets weirder and weirder." Yet, when she said that, the thought entered her mind, *God created male and female? How does that work?* Krystal saw there were other passages ahead and decided she'd had her fill. It wasn't exactly like reading a book for entertainment. Krystal closed the Bible and put it on her nightstand and resumed her casual stare at the ceiling.

Did God really create the world? In the Bible it said God created the heavens and the earth? Well, did He? But then why would I believe in a God who would let so many horrible things happen to me?

Krystal paused. *I don't know. Those are questions I don't have the answers to.* Krystal was beginning to grow frustrated with her lack of answers. She was tired of not knowing. She wanted to know more. She glanced over at her Bible again, watching it sit there idly. Almost as though it was inviting her to read it more. Krystal ignored the invitation and looked at the ceiling, but her will faltered and she snuck another glance, as if checking if it moved.

It was still there, so Krystal resumed staring at the ceiling in contemplation. *What do they know, those Christians? They could be just believing in some false lie that was made up by some ridiculous person thousands of years ago.*

A gentle voice in the back of her mind creeped in again. *But what if it's true?* The thought echoed throughout her being like a ripple in a pond. Her mind drifted back to what the Preacher said the other day.

"For if you truly seek God with all your heart . . . you will find Him"

Krystal thought about that sentence. *Seek Him with all my heart?* Krystal got up and sat on the side of her bed. She put her hands together in prayer and was unsure how to proceed. "Uhh okay, God . . . if you're real . . . then please show yourself to me?" She suddenly felt very stupid. She had never prayed before, so she didn't know how it worked.

Look at me, I'm talking to thin air right now. One could hardly call that a prayer.

Krystal quietly lashed back at herself like a rebellious teenager grumbling to an adult, "At least it *was* a prayer." Krystal surprised herself. "Did I just pray?" Krystal shook her head. *What is happening to me? I'm turning religious and I'm not even trying.* She looked at the Bible again, like it was calling to her, but it wasn't pressuring her either. Krystal's boredom joined the fun and added some extra incentive. Krystal craned her head back in annoyance, "I don't have anything better to do."

She scooted over on her bed and grabbed the Bible again, getting back into her reading position, opening to her bookmark in Genesis chapter 2. She read:

GENESIS 2

Then the LORD God formed the man from the dust of the ground. He breathed the breath of life into the man's nostrils, and the man became a living person.

Then the LORD God planted a garden in Eden in the east, and there he placed the man he had made. The LORD God made all sorts of trees grow up from the ground—trees that were beautiful and that produced delicious fruit. In the middle of the garden he placed the tree of life and the tree of the knowledge of good and evil.
—GENESIS 2:7–9 (NLT)

. . .

The LORD God placed the man in the Garden of Eden to tend and watch over it. But the LORD God warned him, "You may freely eat the fruit of every tree in the garden—except the tree of the knowledge of good and evil. If you eat its fruit, you are sure to die."

Then the LORD God said, "It is not good for the man to be alone. I will make a helper who is just right for him."
—GENESIS 2:15–18 (NLT)

. . .

So the LORD God caused the man to fall into a deep sleep. While the man slept, the LORD God took out one of the man's ribs and closed up the opening. Then the LORD God made a woman from the rib, and he brought her to the man.

"At last!" the man exclaimed.

"This one is bone from my bone,
and flesh from my flesh!

She will be called 'woman,'
because she was taken from 'man.'"

This explains why a man leaves his father and mother and
is joined to his wife, and the two are united into one.

Now the man and his wife were both naked, but they felt no shame.
—Genesis 2:21–25 (NLT)

Krystal frowned, "Wait what? They're naked?" Against her will, Krystal's mind thought back to sex ed class in early middle school. The thought of naked people gave her shivers. She clasped her clothing and covered herself with her arms. The idea of roaming about naked would be the most uncomfortable thing in the world.

The tiny voice said, *"But why is that?"*

Krystal was puzzled by the question. *I don't know . . . Why* do *we wear clothes?* Krystal felt she was about to answer when the question took root. She got up from her bed and began pacing around with her hand to her chin. *Hmm, why do we wear clothes?*

It was a bit awkward to think about this late at night but at the same time the question had a sense of logic to it. It was a question Krystal had never thought of before. She was pretty conservative about showing any skin at all. Most of her clothing was long black pants and long-sleeved shirts, never revealing much skin to begin with. But the question began to dive deeper. *Well . . . why is it uncomfortable for people to walk out naked in public. I mean sure, there are some people in the world who do that, but then the police would come and arrest them for public nudity. So why do we wear clothes in the first place?*

This time Krystal wasn't frustrated with the lack of an answer. In fact, she felt like she was onto something for once. Like she was a bloodhound who had caught the scent of something and wanted to find out what it was. Krystal turned and looked at the Bible again. That same attraction calling out to her.

What the heck is going on? It was like she had to know what happened next, so she picked up the Bible and kept reading.

GENESIS 3
The Man and Woman Sin

The serpent was the shrewdest of all the wild animals
*the L*ORD *God had made. One day he asked the woman,*
"Did God really say you must not eat the fruit
from any of the trees in the garden?"

"Of course we may eat fruit from the trees in the garden," the
woman replied. "It's only the fruit from the tree in the middle
of the garden that we are not allowed to eat. God said, 'You
must not eat it or even touch it; if you do, you will die.'"

"You won't die!" the serpent replied to the woman. "God
knows that your eyes will be opened as soon as you eat it,
and you will be like God, knowing both good and evil."

The woman was convinced. She saw that the tree was beautiful
and its fruit looked delicious, and she wanted the wisdom it would
give her. So she took some of the fruit and ate it. Then she gave
some to her husband, who was with her, and he ate it, too. At that
moment their eyes were opened, and they suddenly felt shame at their
nakedness. So they sewed fig leaves together to cover themselves."
—G*ENESIS* 3:1–7 (NLT)

Krystal said, "Huh. That's interesting." Feeling both disgusted and intrigued. She read on.

When the cool evening breezes were blowing, the man and
*his wife heard the L*ORD *God walking about in the garden.*
*So they hid from the L*ORD *God among the trees. Then*
*the L*ORD *God called to the man, "Where are you?"*

He replied, "I heard you walking in the garden, so
I hid. I was afraid because I was naked."

*"Who told you that you were naked?" the Lord God asked. "Have
you eaten from the tree whose fruit I commanded you not to eat?"*

*The man replied, "It was the woman you gave
me who gave me the fruit, and I ate it."*

Then the Lord God asked the woman, "What have you done?"

"The serpent deceived me," she replied. "That's why I ate it."
—Genesis 3:8–13 (NLT)

. . .

*Then he said to the woman,
"I will sharpen the pain of your pregnancy,
and in pain you will give birth.
And you will desire to control your husband,
but he will rule over you."
And to the man he said,
"Since you listened to your wife and ate from the tree
whose fruit I commanded you not to eat,
the ground is cursed because of you.
All your life you will struggle to scratch a living from it.
It will grow thorns and thistles for you,
though you will eat of its grains.
By the sweat of your brow
will you have food to eat
until you return to the ground
from which you were made.
For you were made from dust,
and to dust you will return."*
—Genesis 3:16–19 (NLT)

. . .

Paradise Lost: God's Judgment

*Then the man—Adam—named his wife Eve, because she
would be the mother of all who live. And the Lord God
made clothing from animal skins for Adam and his wife.*

Then the LORD God said, "Look, the human beings have become
like us, knowing both good and evil. What if they reach out, take
fruit from the tree of life, and eat it? Then they will live forever!" So
the LORD God banished them from the Garden of Eden, and he sent
Adam out to cultivate the ground from which he had been made.
After sending them out, the LORD God stationed mighty cherubim
to the east of the Garden of Eden. And he placed a flaming sword
that flashed back and forth to guard the way to the tree of life.

Krystal could feel the slumber encroaching upon her eyelids. It was getting late, and she had too much on her mind. Feeling a headache from her tiring eyes creep up, she closed the Bible and lay it back on the side of her nightstand. It still called out to her, but only mildly, like it was an invitation without any guilt attached to it. The idea of the story floated in her head as she rolled up in her bed sheets, listing off the main ideas from the passage.

So God created the heavens and the earth? God created the universe in seven days. God created male and female, Adam and Even ate the forbidden fruit and were cast out of the Garden of Eden, and realized they are naked.

Krystal took a calm breath, "That was a lot." She had no idea how to unpack all of it, but even when she thought it was a fictional story, there was something about it that lingered in her mind. *I mean sure, it's an interesting story but how do we really know if any of that is true? We can't. Right?* Krystal suddenly felt doubt creep into her heart.

The gentle voice spoke again, *But what if it's real?*

"What if it's real?" Krystal whispered doubtfully. She tried to imagine what she would do if that story were real and came up blank.

Her thoughts drifted back to the Preacher the other day, *"the only way to fill that hole . . . is to accept Jesus Christ into our hearts."*

Krystal thought, *What if that Preacher was on to something? What if he's right? What if this hole I'm feeling really is my heart calling out to God?* Krystal shook her head. *Listen to yourself. You're going to believe some religious nut you met only a few days ago?*

Krystal's conscience retorted; *I don't see you producing any ideas! Because the way we're going, we're going to end up killing ourselves again. And I won't miss next time.*

Krystal was tired of bickering with herself. She felt slumber envelope her as the warmth of the bed sheets relaxed her body, causing her eyes to feel heavy. She still felt empty, but she was searching, and that gave her some relief.

Maybe tomorrow will be better . . .
I doubt that.

CHAPTER 9

How Do You Know It's Real?

"You must determine for yourself whether Christianity is true or not. Because if it's not true, then it's the greatest lie in all of history, but if it is true . . . then it's the greatest truth of all time."

—Dana Romero

"We are going to have so much FUUUUNNNNN!" Tonight, Carmen's Bible study was doing something different from their casual Bible reading. They were going to church to listen to a guest speaker. Krystal wasn't all too excited. She still wasn't sure why she even bothered coming to these Bible studies in the first place. It still seemed mundane to her in the moment.

Krystal sat in the back of the car, watching Carmen's brother Jaime in the driver's seat, Summer in the passenger's, and Amber in the seat next to Krystal. Krystal glanced at Jaime in the driver's seat. The guy did not look happy, especially with Summer fawning over herself in the passenger seat. Every couple of seconds, Summer would turn around and lean over, holding her phone out to show Amber and Jaime some new pictures on social media, but she never bothered to show Krystal. This left Krystal feeling like she was still the odd one out of the group, the outcast.

Krystal let it go but still felt some irritation. Why would you not show the person behind you the photo you took after you just showed everyone else? Krystal wanted to see it, not because she was interested but to feel included.

Summer showed Jaime a new picture on her phone. Jaime took a quick glance then resumed his watchful eyes back to the road. Summer asked, "Sooooo, whatdoya think?"

Jaime replied in monotone, "It looks fine" then went back to driving. Krystal watched his lips, as he grumbled under his breath, "Why'd I have to get sucked into this?" Summer didn't hear the comment and Amber was too busy focusing on Summer's next picture to notice. But Krystal found that intriguing.

He doesn't seem to be in a good mood. In fact, I haven't seen him in a good mood once. I wonder what's been bothering him lately? Krystal had only been to the Fisher's house a couple of times, but every time she was there, she saw Jaime ignore his family and head upstairs. And when he was downstairs he didn't talk to anyone and only looked at his phone. Meanwhile, Carmen was busy with work tonight, so it was up to Jaime to drive the group to church. Krystal could tell Jaime was not happy about that, but he obeyed his parents, only to grumble about it in the car. Krystal put the inquiry out of her mind and decided to let the guy be. It was already uncomfortable enough with Summer in the car, but at least there was some noise and chatter though. It would have been dead quiet if Summer weren't there, so maybe that was a good thing.

Jaime pulled the car up to the church and said, "This is your stop. Carmen will come by at the end of the session to pick you up."

"Thanks Jaime!" Summer leaned over the passenger seat and gave Jaime a hug. Jaime didn't reciprocate as Summer forced her arms around the guy. Jaime looked awkward receiving the hug, but mostly because he wasn't in the mood for it. Krystal saw the unhappy expression. He looked like he wanted to be alone, like he needed to fume about something but couldn't let out. Krystal took that as her cue to exit the car. She got the feeling she didn't want to see this guy mad for some reason.

Krystal stepped out and glanced at the church. It looked different at night. The darkness added a new shade and the dull orange light from the street poles offered a damp amber coloring to the area. Summer and Amber exited the car as Amber said, "Do you think they'll have food here?"

Summer clasped her hands together as if she were praying like an innocent little girl, "Oh I hope so. They should have food for us because God always provides." Krystal glanced at Summer and tried not to roll her eyes.

They headed up the walkway and approached the open entrance doors. Krystal paused and glanced at the church before entering. She inhaled. *Here we go again. Why I keep coming back here I do not know.* Krystal turned and watched Jaime put the car in reverse and disappear into the night, going opposite the direction from where his home was located. *Where is he going?* she thought.

Krystal turned and headed inside, finding a circle of chairs sitting in the main auditorium. Usually there would be chairs set up in rows for the audience to sit, but the main area was cleared out so the chairs could circle up into smaller groups. In the center was a thin woman with short black hair, wearing a black top and had tattoo sleeves down her arms. Krystal couldn't tell if this woman was older than she looked. But if she had to guess, this woman was either in her late twenties or early thirties. (But don't ever guess a woman's age. For you guys, just round down.) The woman smiled, a little contrast from all the tattoos on her arms. "Good evening and welcome." She stood up from her chair. Oddly cheerful for someone who looked like she was part of a biker gang, but still thin enough to look innocent and good looking.

Images of sitting with Karen and the discussion groups in the clinic flashed in Krystal's mind. *Oh great . . . it's going to be just like discussion group with Karen.* The thought of Krystal sitting in a circle while Summer talked the entire time bereaved her. *It better not come to that or else I'll just leave. Even if I have to walk.* Not like she had a ride to get back anyway.

Amber and Summer were getting busy giggling on their phones when the woman greeted them. The woman came up to Summer first and said, "Hi how are you?"

Summer looked up from her phone, "Oh! It's so nice to meet you!" Summer pointed to herself, "I'm Summer," gesturing to her right, "and this is Amber." Krystal waited for Summer to introduce her, but Summer never mentioned her name.

The woman held out her hand to Summer and said, "I'm Dana Romero it's nice to meet you." Dana had a calm, controlled manner of speaking and with enough energy to sound pleasant and welcoming. A bit contrasting with her looks, but it was starting to grow on Krystal. Dana and Summer shook hands, then Dana turned toward Krystal, "Who's this?"

Summer turned, "This is—"

"—Krystal. Her name is Krystal," Amber cut in.

Krystal found that a bit curious why Amber answered for Summer, but she let it slide. Dana shifted her attention toward Krystal and said, "Carmen isn't here tonight, so she asked me to lead the group. I'll be giving you all my personal story and then we can talk and hang out afterwards. Sound good?"

Summer yelled out, "I think it's GREAT!" Her enthusiasm pulsing like a star in the night. It almost made Dana jump.

Amber stepped forward. "Hey is there some food here? I'm kinda hungry since it's getting late."

Dana gestured toward one of the nearby tables, "There's some snacks over there if you're hungry. Feel free to help yourselves." Summer and Amber both took off like a bunch of toddlers looking to play with a new toy. Krystal remained stationary, not because she was hungry, but because she couldn't match that kind of energy from both Summer and Amber, leaving Dana and Krystal alone with each other.

Krystal felt the awkward silence roll in, not knowing what to say. Dana looked at Krystal, "Aren't you hungry?" Krystal said nothing. She looked over at the snack table and then back at Dana, nodding her head. Dana said, "I'm sorry, I know I probably already introduced myself. I'm Dana." For a moment Krystal merely looked, then she took the hand and shook it. The woman had a lot of calluses on her hand, as well as a strong grip, yet she was awfully thin and cute for someone her age. Dana asked, "Is this your first time here?" It took Krystal time to register the question. She was too stunned to understand.

Is she actually trying to have a conversation with me? Krystal wasn't used to talking. While hanging around with Summer at the Bible studies, Krystal practically didn't talk at all, and for most of her time at school she didn't talk to anyone, so talking had become difficult lately. All Krystal did was nod.

Oddly enough, Dana didn't seem uncomfortable with Krystal's lack of expression. "Sweet. We're glad to have you here." Dana spread her arms out, gesturing to the empty church as a whole. Krystal was unimpressed, yet oddly comfortable, at least for getting this far into the conversation. Dana asked, "What year are you in school?"

Krystal knew she had to talk now, so she fought to get the words out, having them come out like a toddler not knowing how to burp. "Sophomore," she said.

Dana pulled up a seat and relaxed in her chair, leaning one arm on a nearby table, "Gee, it's been a while since I've been in school."

Krystal felt the opening in the conversation. "How . . . old are you?"

Dana wasn't offended by the question at all, if anything, she welcomed the inquiry. "I like to test people on that." She put her fist under her chin, acting cute, "Guess how old I am?" Krystal held two fingers up, making her other hand make an "O" shape. Dana said, "Twenty," Krystal shifted her hands to the number seven, "Seven."

Dana was cheerfully surprised. "Wow, that's dead on the money. You've got a keen eye." Krystal said nothing about the comment. Dana gestured to the seat next to her, "You wanna sit? The Bible study won't start for another five minutes." Krystal glanced over at Summer and Amber, the two of them giggling on their phones, pacing around the room as if they were on some sort of treasure hunt for some game on their phones. Krystal pulled up a chair and sat down. She pulled out her Bible from her bag and held it in her lap. Dana said, "That's a nice Bible that you have there."

"Thank you," Krystal whispered, looking away timidly.

"It looks brand new. Where'd you get it?" Krystal pointed down. Dana said, "Here?" Krystal nodded.

Dana seems friendly, Krystal thought. *She at least talks to me more than other people do.* Krystal found relief in that. It was nice to have someone ask her questions for once, even if she was replying in sentences shorter than a small text message.

Summer and Amber came back from their mini treasure hunt game within the church walls. "This place has got some good treasure!" said Summer.

Amber said, "Yeah, I found some nice gems for sure. I'll be sure to sell these later to defend my fortress."

Dana said, "I used to play that treasure hunting game for a little while, I got bored of it. I didn't have enough people who played with me."

"You can play with us!" said Summer.

"No thanks. I've had my take at the game, now it's time to move on. We can get the Bible study ready now." They all took their seats as Dana shifted to the center of the semi-circle. Dana pulled out a piece of white paper and unfolded it, while Summer and Amber sat across from Krystal. Krystal tried not to take offense from that, but come on, it felt like they were deliberately avoiding her. Krystal shrugged it off despite feeling a stab of pain in her chest.

You know they don't like you.

Stop it. I don't want to hear from you right now.

Why do you bother going to this church anyway? It's not like it's going to change anything in your life.

I don't know why I'm here. I'm curious.

Why not go home . . . and kill yourself?

Krystal flinched but luckily no one saw it. Dana was still getting her notes ready while Amber and Summer were too busy whispering to each other.

Please . . . not now. I don't want to do this now.

You have no choice. I will come back no matter what.

No!

Dana finished unfolding her notes and said, "Here we go, we can get started now on the Bible study . . ." Krystal got comfortable in her chair.

Here we go . . . this is going to take a while.

"And that is how I got delayed a year in getting my driver's license." Amber cracked up as Summer finished her story. The Bible study hadn't been a Bible study at all. The entire time Summer had been interrupting Dana's message and telling stories about her own life, but Krystal had heard a majority of the stories back at the Fisher's house, so Summer was sometimes re-telling the same stories. Krystal stared into oblivion, the only way for her to cope with Summer's excessive talking amongst the group. Amber chimed in a time or two but not even Summer would let Dana finish her message. The night was all about Summer. Krystal felt bitterness grip her heart as a small flame birthed in the depths of her heart. The flame continued to grow the longer Summer spoke. The fire grew and grew, causing Krystal's heart to beat faster, and as a result, her bandages began to ebb once again. Krystal noticed the bandages changing color and calmed herself down. *Breathe. She's almost done . . . I hope.*

Krystal couldn't help but sneak a look at her phone to check the time. She tried to be surreptitious, and it worked. But that's because neither Dana nor Amber were paying attention to Krystal anyway, and Summer was too busy telling her stories to notice anything around her. Krystal checked her phone. 8:47pm. *We've been here for an hour and thirty minutes.* Krystal still held her Bible in her lap and realized she hadn't opened it. She was getting annoyed with the constant discussion and watching Summer talk. Krystal used the only card she had in her book and got up to go to the bathroom. Dana caught a glimpse of Krystal leaving the room, glancing down at her arm, and could have sworn she saw something. Summer hadn't noticed a thing and Amber was too involved in talking with Summer that neither of them noticed Krystal leave.

Krystal pushed through the wooden doors to the bathroom and turned on the sink. Washing her hands, Krystal checked how the bandages were holding up. Slightly red but not enough to change them. *Good enough*, she thought. Krystal rolled her sleeve up and turned off the sink. She dried her hands and stepped back out into the auditorium.

Summer and Amber weren't in their seats. Krystal figured they were off somewhere having the time of their lives, meanwhile Krystal found Dana sitting at one of the tables, fiddling with a water bottle between her fingers. Krystal felt more comfortable now that Summer and Amber were gone. It was only Dana left, and she looked a bit disappointed. Krystal tried to imagine if the water bottle were a beer and the scene clicked too perfectly. *I see.* Dana released her fingers from the bottle and let it shuffle back to its stationary position on the table.

Dana saw Krystal approach and said, "Welcome back." Krystal said nothing. Dana exhaled and put her arms on her lap, looking down at the floor, "You know . . . I'm a bit disappointed that tonight didn't go as planned." Krystal said nothing and observed Dana with blank eyes. Dana continued, "I was hoping to get into this message. It was a good message too, but you know how it is these days with high schoolers."

That seemed to resonate with Krystal for some reason, and for once, she agreed with her. Krystal felt her expressionless face shift as she magnetically looked down at her feet and whispered, "I do." Dana quickly looked up at Krystal, surprised that she talked. Dana smiled and said, "You don't talk much, do you?" It wasn't an accusatory tone; it was gentler and accepting. Krystal went back to her mute demeanor. Dana gestured to an open chair. "Wanna sit?" Krystal recalled sitting in the semi-circle the whole night and how her butt was sore, but after stretching her legs she was feeling better now that Summer was gone. Krystal took a seat and the two of them sat there in silence, not knowing what to do. Krystal felt the awkwardness linger in the air, trying to find something to say, but nothing came to mind. Krystal's eyes sized up Dana's appearance. Her eyes drifted down toward Dana's tattoos on her arms, finding a dark T-shaped figure on her forearm. Krystal opened her mouth to say something, but the words never came, so she pointed at Dana's arm. Dana got the reference, "Oh this?" She pointed, "I got that a while ago. Maybe seven years ago."

Krystal felt the question jump in her throat and back down her lungs.

She knew she had to say something or else her message would never get across and her questions would never be answered. Krystal clenched her teeth and forced the words to her throat. "What . . ." her lips shut again; the weight of gravity felt ten times stronger as her mouth went numb.

What are you doing? Why are you bothering to ask this woman about her tattoos? That's rude! Krystal disregarded her thoughts, raised her index finger, and wheezed out, "What . . . does that mean?" pointing to the cross on her arm.

Dana raised her arm to look at the cross and said, "The cross? Oh, it's a symbol of the Resurrection." Krystal stared in blank confusion. The kind of confusion you get when a teacher is giving you a lecture and the students pretend to understand when in reality, they lost track of the lesson forty-five minutes ago. Krystal went mute but she tried to display the follow up question on her face. Dana understood the expression, "It is a sign of Jesus Christ dying on the cross and being raised three days later."

Krystal shook her head slowly, urging the words to come out, "What's that?"

Dana seemed delighted at the question. "It's when Jesus Christ willingly died on the cross for our sins so that we can all go to heaven." Krystal had never felt more bewildered in her entire life.

I have no idea who or what this woman is talking about. Dana gestured her hands out, as if that would help her explain things. It wouldn't.

"Back two thousand years ago, Jesus Christ died on the cross so that we all could go to heaven, not just the Jews." Krystal tried not to look puzzled, but she couldn't hide her expression. Dana saw that she was losing Krystal, so she tried to simplify it. It was difficult because Dana could tell Krystal had never heard the story before. "Basically, Jesus Christ is the Son of God, and because Adam and Eve sinned in the Garden of Eden, Jesus died on the cross to pay for our sins so that we could enjoy eternal life in heaven." Krystal blinked in confusion. Clearly the explanation was not getting through to her . . . also, Krystal was hesitant to believe anything this woman told her.

"What makes you think this is all real?" was the question Krystal wanted to ask. She felt the words bulge within her throat. Krystal genuinely wanted to talk to someone about the questions she had, and this was an excellent opportunity, she just had to take the initiative for once. Krystal could feel the risk, the fear gripping her heart. *What if she doesn't react well to it? What if*

she thinks I'm a freak or we get stuck in another forty-five-minute conversation?
Yet the burden of not asking dragged Krystal's heart down like a rock underwater, back into the depths of her empty soul. The only way to release this
kind of pressure was to be open and honest, and that terrified her. Krystal
tensed the muscles in her sternum and forced the breath out, "What . . ."
Dana glanced up like a deer caught in headlights, "What makes you . . . think
it's real?"

Now that was a question Dana was not expecting to hear tonight, but
it was not unwelcome. Dana took a moment to collect herself and figure out
how to properly answer the question. Dana pointed to her arm, "You see
these tattoos?" Krystal nodded. "All of these represent the struggles I've gone
through." She pointed to a raging bear drinking furiously out of a waterfall.
"This one was added when I got out of rehab. I was a raging alcoholic for
a long time." Krystal tried to picture Dana looking depressed with a beer
bottle in her hand and the picture fit too well. Dana pointed to another tattoo, this one of a raging liver with pulsing muscles on it, "This one was when
I was in the hospital after my liver gave out and I almost died of alcohol
poisoning one night."

Dana rolled up her shirt, exposing her lower belly. "These, are from
every bad day I had in high school." Krystal wanted to be shocked, but the
expression wouldn't come. She was so desensitized after her own near-death
experience that hardly anything ever shocked her anymore, so she just sat
there unfazed, gazing across Dana's lower stomach where dozens of cuts lay.
Krystal covered her wrist with her hand, remembering the night where it all
happened.

"What . . . happened?" Krystal asked cautiously.

Dana stared at the floor for a minute and said, "School was tough,"
her voice faltering. Krystal could feel the weight of the emotion behind her
words; could sense the pain leaking the more Dana spoke. "I turned to alcohol when I was fifteen and I didn't stop." Dana took a quick breath and let
out a sharp exhale, as if irritated somehow. "I went deeper and deeper down
the rabbit hole, trying to forget the pain I felt." Dana lifted her hand and
planted it right on her sternum, in the same spot where Krystal lay her hand.
Krystal instantly felt her own heart cry out, as if Dana had activated the emptiness with Krystal's heart. Dana shook her head, "I wanted to forget . . . to
be able to feel good for a change, but the more I tried to satisfy this emptiness

within me, this 'hole in my heart,' the more I sought alcohol to fix it." Dana looked out toward the giant wooden cross on the stage. "I was getting out of control. Going deeper and deeper into my addiction. I was going to parties, getting crazier at every event, wanting more, trying to fill this hole within me." Dana stopped as if she hit a roadblock within herself. Dana looked at Krystal, "Then one night I drank so much I ended up in the hospital again."

Sounds familiar, Krystal thought, more on the hospital note than the drinking part.

"I knew I needed to make a change, but I didn't know how. While I was in the hospital, I had a friend of mine invite me to church. She told me they had a group of people to help deal with my drinking problem. So I started going, hating it at first, but then they started talking, and eventually I accepted Jesus into my life." Dana looked straight at Krystal, "I was able to overcome my drinking problem, but more than that . . ." she paused, leaning closer to Krystal, "I felt *whole.*" Dana leaned back in her chair. "For the first time in my life, I felt complete. I was happy. I was able to deal with my drinking problem and I'm now seven years sober." She pointed to her arm again, "And this cross here, it reminds me of just how much Jesus saved me. How I couldn't save myself. Without Jesus I would have died from alcohol poisoning. The fact that I'm still alive today, is a miracle."

Krystal objected. "But . . . what makes you so sure . . . that this is the right . . . thing?"

Dana replied, "I can't give you a better answer than this . . . I was dead, now I'm alive. I was empty, now I am whole. I was ashamed, now I am forgiven. You can choose whether or not to believe me, but I can tell you are going through almost the exact same thing I was going through. For nothing in this world will ever fill that hole in your heart except for Jesus Christ. And Krystal, you are not alone. There are many other people in this world struggling with what you are going through. You are not a freak or some defective person to be cast aside. I can see you are someone who is hurting, who is actively seeking the truth. I can already tell that you are hot on the trails. So keep searching and you will find God." Dana paused and pointed at Krystal, "You must determine for yourself whether Christianity is true or not. Because if it's not true, then it's the greatest lie in all of history, but if it *is* true . . . then it's the greatest truth of all time."

Krystal's mouth hung half-open. She wasn't sure what to say. This woman had just opened up to her and challenged Krystal to prove her religion wrong. There was something about Dana that Krystal couldn't quite understand. A kind of assurance that Krystal did not have; a joy Krystal wanted but could never find.

What is with these people? They're so confident in what they believe. I'm not even sure if they've done the research themselves to prove whether their religion is fake or not.

Krystal didn't show it, but she was mildly surprised by Dana's story. *How does an alcoholic suddenly turn sober? She could have willed herself to become sober, and some people do that, but most people still struggle with it to this day.* Krystal would have never guessed this woman had those kinds of struggles before.

Without thinking, Krystal began unwrapping the bandage on her left arm. Almost like a sign of good faith between them. Krystal had never shown her wound to anyone before, so the element of fear struck Krystal after she had finished unwrapping the last strand. Dana leaned closer and with one look, instantly started crying. The sight of the two-inch wound across her left wrist was more horrifying than Dana imagined. Meanwhile, Krystal was casual about it and rewrapped her wound. *I certainly did not expect that kind of reaction,* she thought. Dana's sudden change in emotions caught Krystal off guard. She tried to cheer Dana up with some weak taps of assurance on the shoulder, but they did not stop Dana crying. Dana faced Krystal with eyes red and makeup smeared. "I'm so sorry for what happened to you."

Those words shot through Krystal's soul like an arrow piercing the armor around her soul. Feelings of life poured out from Dana and into Krystal with her honesty and how genuine she was. Krystal wanted to cry too, but she held the tears back. Krystal inhaled and took a breath, calming herself. Dana did the same and the two of them chuckled. Krystal chuckled for a split second and then stopped, letting the silence fill the gap between them. Dana finished wiping her face and managed to calm down. "Well . . . that was enough for one night. What do you say I treat you all to some ice cream?"

Krystal didn't react, "Why?" but there was a hint of curiosity.

Dana answered, "Because God loved us first." Krystal wanted to react, but the words were too much of a coincidence to ignore. *That's just like what Mr. Fisher said.* Dana left the room to get Summer and Amber, leaving Krystal to her own thoughts.

I can't understand these people or what they're talking about. But for some reason, they have a happiness about them that I want. I just don't know how to get it.

Her thoughts interjected. *But that would mean joining a cult.*

Krystal fought back, *Is it a cult? Are you sure? Like Dana said earlier, "What if it's real?" Huh? What then?* Krystal thought back to Dana statement, *"You must determine for yourself whether Christianity is true or not. Because if it's not true, then it's the greatest lie in all of history, but if it's true . . . then it's the greatest truth of all time."* Dana came back into the room with Summer and Amber trailing behind her.

"Come on," Dana called, and nudged her head like an adventurer, "we've got some ice cream to slay."

✍

Krystal stared at the selection of ice cream spread before her. There were so many options Krystal couldn't decide. Hazelnut coffee, pistachio, cookies 'n cream, rainbow sherbet, the whole shebang. Krystal raised her head to Dana, as she said, "Get as much as you like. It's on me tonight."

Krystal was stunned. "But why?" she asked, "I don't . . . deserve it."

Dana replied, "It's not about whether you deserve it or not. That's the beauty of *grace*. It is a gift given to you regardless of whether you deserve it or not. That's the whole point of it being a gift." Dana looked back at the assortment of flavors, "So get as much as you like, and I will pay for it." Dana looked at Krystal like she was her younger sister. Krystal looked at Dana like a cautious child silently asking if it was alright, then pointed hesitantly toward the sherbet ice cream. The worker behind the stand said, "How many scoops would you like?" Krystal looked at Dana who gave her nothing but a nod of approval, then Krystal raised two fingers. The worker said, "Two scoops? You got it," and went to make her ice cream. Krystal watched as Summer and Amber roared in excitement and instantly began ordering flavors left and right. Dana's expression of joy shifted to horror, "Oh no . . . what have I done?"

The worker handed Krystal her ice cream and she took a lick, feeling the sugar rush over her tongue, the tart flavor overwhelming her taste buds. Dana saw her reaction and chuckled while Krystal stared at her ice cream like it was a lost treasure, enjoying how delicious it was.

CHAPTER 10

Aging and The Rainbow

"Have you ever wondered why we only live to be around a hundred years old? Why not more? Why not less? Why is one hundred the average number for us to live and die?"

—JL

Krystal lay in her bed pondering. Thinking about everything that's happened so far. The kindness from the Janitor, the kindness of the Fishers, and Dana's generosity. All of them didn't have an ulterior motive, they weren't lying. Krystal could tell they were being genuine, and yet, they all looked so happy. It all started with that Janitor giving her that brownie. How delicious that thing tasted, and the relief she felt knowing someone had *seen* her and took the time to care for her when no one else would.

She thought back to what Dana had said about Christianity. *"If it's not true, then it's the greatest lie in all of history, but if it's true . . . then it's the greatest truth of all time."*

Krystal spoke, "But how do I know if it's real or not?" keeping her voice quiet to not rouse Aunt Sarah's attention. Krystal sat up; her head magnetically drawn toward the Bible on her nightstand. Without thinking she took the Bible and opened back up to where she was in Genesis chapter five. She read:

> *"This is the written account of the descendants of Adam. When God created human beings, he made them to be like himself."*
> —GENESIS 5:1 (NLT)

Krystal scoffed, *Huh, okay . . .*

*"He created them male and female, and he
blessed them and called them 'human.'"*

When Adam was 130 years old,—"
—Genesis 5:2–3 (NLT)

Krystal stopped and frowned. *One hundred thirty years old? That's
impossible.* She let it slide but it still nagged at her as curious and continued.

*"—he became the father of a son who was just like him—in
his very image. He named his son Seth. After the birth of
Seth, Adam lived another 800 years, and he had other sons
and daughters. Adam lived 930 years, and then he died."*
—Genesis 5:3–5 (NLT)

Krystal was surprised but she didn't have the emotional capacity to show
it. "Nine hundred and thirty years? How could someone live that long?"
Krystal continued.

*"When Seth was 105 years old, he became the father of Enosh. After
the birth of Enosh, Seth lived another 807 years, and he had other
sons and daughters. Seth lived 912 years, and then he died."*
—Genesis 5:6–8 (NLT)

Krystal lowered the Bible aside and sat there perplexed. "How on earth
can someone live that long?" The thought ate at her. *I've never heard of someone living over a hundred years old before. Is that really how old people used to
live?* No answer, so she read on to chapter six.

*Then the people began to multiply on the earth, and daughters were
born to them. The sons of God saw the beautiful women and took any
they wanted as their wives. Then the Lord said, "My Spirit will not
put up with humans for such a long time, for they are only mortal flesh.
In the future, their normal lifespan will be no more than 120 years."*
—Genesis 6:1–3 (NLT)

Krystal shook her head in casual disbelief. "First clothes, now age. How much more complicated can this get?" But a new question entered her mind. *Why do we live to only be around a hundred years old?* Krystal lowered the Bible and wondered.

"Huh. Why *do* we only live to be around a hundred years old?" She paused and let the question sink in, feeling as if the answer was right there, right in front of her, yet she couldn't fully grasp it. Krystal glanced at the Bible. *Is that really why we live to only be a hundred years old?* (One hundred and twenty, if you want to be literally accurate.) She tried to think of examples of people living longer than a hundred and a few cases came up. A majority of people live up to be around eighty these days, some get on to ninety and only a few get to be a hundred but that's it. Few people can really surpass being one hundred and twenty. Krystal remembered reading an article about a woman who was one hundred and five years old and how that blew her mind, but now the bar had been raised to nine hundred! "How can someone live that long?"

Maybe humans were different back then and were able to live longer?

But then why do we only live to be a hundred? Her thoughts dragged back to the verse she just read. Her thoughts answering before she could reason against it. *Because God made us live to only be a hundred years old.*

She shook her head. *No way. No way. There has to be another explanation.*

But what then? Regardless of whether we could try to live past a hundred, why do we still only live to be a hundred? Why don't we live longer? Or die sooner? Her questions were left unanswered and not fulfilled. Krystal felt this curiosity was actually getting her somewhere, better than her life before where she had no questions whatsoever. Now it felt like she was on to something. Like she was being led somewhere, where she would find her answers. Krystal flipped the page and read the next passage title. *Noah and the Ark.*

"Hmm, why does that title feel familiar?"

Why does this stuff feel familiar at all? I didn't even know about this stuff before and yet I have even heard the story about Noah and the Ark from somewhere. Krystal couldn't shake the nagging feeling in her heart that all of this meant something, like they were pieces of a puzzle, she just didn't know how they all fit together, or piecing together a crime scene with the evidence you've got, while trying to determine who the suspect is. Krystal skimmed the story of Noah, mumbling as she went, "So we've got God, Noah is a good guy, God tells Noah to build an Ark, God floods the earth, the flood subsides, blah blah blah blah blah . . ." She came to a passage in chapter nine after the flood had subsided and Noah and his sons left the Ark.

> *Then God told Noah and his sons, "I hereby confirm my covenant with you and your descendants, and with all the animals that were on the boat with you—the birds, the livestock, and all the wild animals—every living creature on earth. Yes, I am confirming my covenant with you. Never again will floodwaters kill all living creatures; never again will a flood destroy the earth."*
>
> *Then God said, "I am giving you a sign of my covenant with you and with all living creatures, for all generations to come. I have placed my rainbow in the clouds. It is the sign of my covenant with you and with all the earth. When I send clouds over the earth, the rainbow will appear in the clouds, and I will remember my covenant with you and with all living creatures. Never again will the floodwaters destroy all life. When I see the rainbow in the clouds, I will remember the eternal covenant between God and every living creature on earth." Then God said to Noah, "Yes, this rainbow is the sign of the covenant I am confirming with all the creatures on earth."*
> —GENESIS 9:8–17 (NLT)

Krystal lowered the Bible and craned her head back in one swift motion. She cocked one eyebrow, "So the rainbow is a sign from God?" She wanted to ask, *How does that work?* but she knew she wouldn't get an answer. She slunk back against the wall, feeling her conscience drift slowly into slumber. *It doesn't rain enough here anyway. I can't remember the last time I saw a rainbow.* Krystal paused, contemplating the passage. Reasoning with it almost. *But what if it's true? What if the rainbow really is sent by God?* She leaned her head back against the wall, looking up at the ceiling. "I would really like to see that. It's been a while since it rained here, and I like the rain. I feel more at home in it." It had been a dry season and there hadn't been so much as an inch of rain the entire year, or the years prior. Krystal's eyes slowly drifted to sleep as she whispered, "I would like to see that. Just once . . ."

CHAPTER 11

Masterpiece

"What is your true value?"

—JL

Krystal waited outside, the frigid air sharp against her cheeks, her eyes feeling the dry air piercing her irises, her hands held close, wrapped tightly within the confines of her black jacket. Krystal pulled out her phone and looked at the time, 10:24am. Krystal stuffed her phone back in her pocket and waited. The world was quiet this Sunday morning. The lack of activity outside made everything feel calm and more enjoyable. Krystal waited a few more minutes out front before the Fisher's Range Rover picked her up. Mr. and Mrs. Fisher were sitting in the front while Carmen sat on the left-hand side of the Range Rover with an open seat for Krystal next to her. Krystal stepped in and took her seat.

"Good morning, Krystal," said Mrs. Fisher, "Did you sleep well?"

Krystal nodded. She had been up since seven in the morning, not of her own accord but simply because her body had naturally woken up since then, so she lay in her bed, waiting for time to go by. Krystal closed the door as the car pulled forward. She finished putting on her seat belt when she glanced around the cabin, noticing how unnaturally quiet it was with the Fishers this morning. Krystal checked the empty seat next to her, and the question that had been lingering on her mind for some time bubbled up to the surface of her lips. Krystal hesitated but she felt the urge to ask the question. Krystal shifted her head toward Carmen and asked, "Where's . . . Jaime?"

Carmen paused for a quarter of a second before she looked at Krystal and said, "He doesn't want to come with us." Krystal figured that was the answer. She had noticed Jaime never hung around his family since Krystal had met them. She wondered sometimes if that was normal for a family. Maybe he was going through a phase or something, but Krystal noticed there was a common theme to Jaime's disappearances. Most of them occurred whenever they were going to church or whenever Carmen held the weekly Bible study at their home. Either way, Krystal hardly saw Jaime. He always seemed closed off, like he was thinking of something else and wanted to be alone.

That sounds familiar. Krystal could easily picture herself acting like that in her apartment. That's what happens when school is tough, and you don't fit in. It makes life a living hell. Krystal relinquished her curiosity and abandoned the conversation all together. She didn't want to dive into another family's problems when it wasn't her business, but it was becoming a growing concern with how distant Jaime was from his own family. There would be times when Carmen wouldn't see Jaime for days. The most she would get would be him passing in the garage and that was it. Other than that, Krystal only saw Jaime when he was on his phone, always scrolling through something. She often wondered what it was, but that was for another time.

They took their seats in church as the crowd settled for the upcoming service. The band stepped on stage and began to sing. Krystal looked around while they were singing their worship songs. She had spotted Dana across the way, sitting with Summer. The two of them seemed cheerful, but it was hard to tell with the crowd blocking a majority of Krystal's view. Krystal had hoped Dana or someone from across the way would notice her, but no one looked. Krystal tried to ignore it and continued watching the singing take place. She did notice a majority of the people in the church were afraid of singing. It certainly wasn't one of those churches where people were dancing in front of a crowd praising Jesus for all that He's done. It was the opposite. Here, people were afraid of singing too loud, for then people would notice their singing and they would stand out amongst the crowd. Krystal felt it herself, although she didn't sing with them, she did find it peculiar. *Even here, in church, people are afraid to stand out sometimes.* Not that everyone was out of the singing game. There were a few characters singing louder who didn't care. Krystal shied away from pulling any stunts like that for the rest of her life, but she did appreciate their boldness.

The singing ended and Krystal was finally able to sit down with Carmen and her parents next to her. Krystal got comfortable in her seat and instantly felt the morning drowsiness hit her. Her eyelids bobbed up and down, trying to not fall asleep. *That's strange timing for me to get drowsy all of a sudden.* Krystal readjusted her position hoping it would awaken her, but it didn't help. *Whatever. I'll just tough it out unless I fall asleep, then that wouldn't be so bad either.*

The Preacher stepped onto the stage, put his coffee down on the side of the podium and said, "Hi friends." The crowd replied with "hello" and yawned. The Preacher stuck his hands in his pockets, "Still waking up this morning?" The crowd chuckled in agreement. The Preacher smiled, "We are so grateful to have you here. I hope you all got plenty of rest. It is Sunday after all. The day of rest. Anybody?" The crowd chuckled again. The Preacher, enjoying his own dry comedy, continued. "I want to start us off with a question."

Krystal inhaled through her nose and sighed with a lack of surprise. *The same catchphrase every time huh. Okay.*

The Preacher lifted a finger to his chin, "Tell me, what are we?"

Krystal still sat slugging down in her chair. *He certainly knows how to hook an audience.*

The Preacher pushed his glasses closer to his face. "Are we just random bags of flesh that have developed over time? Are we just empty specks of dust floating on an empty piece of rock surrounded by hundreds and thousands of galaxies in an ever-expanding universe? Or are we something more. More than simply dust. More than this flesh and bones we call a body." Krystal felt some of the sleepiness vanish, her interest growing.

"Or how about another question." He paused. "How valuable are we?" The audience fell silent like a submarine crew. Krystal leaned on the edge of her seat. "What is our value? What do we base it on?" The Preacher stepped away from his podium and began his usual pacing around the stage. "Do we base it off our net-worth? How much money we make or how useful we are? Do we base our value off what other people think of us? But then we have to go back to the question of 'what are we?' If life is simply a battle for survival, then wouldn't all human life be meaningless if we are just empty specks of dust on this lonely planet? Are we just empty bags of flesh roaming this earth trying to get rich and have a lot of kids?" He repeated the question. "What *are* we?"

The Preacher returned to his podium and leaned forward with intensity. "I'll tell you what "the world" thinks about you. "The world" tells you that you are *nothing*. "The world" tells you that you are *worthless*. You may have even been told by your parents that you were an *accident*. That they never intended to have you in the first place." All of Krystal's drowsiness vanished as her eyes became laser-focused on the Preacher. He straightened his back and took a breath, as if he were about to cry, calmed himself, and spoke softly, "My friends, this is *not true*." Krystal felt those words gently tap against her soul, sending ripples through her whole body, stirring the dam of emotions held deep within. The Preacher lifted his hand up and placed the other upon his chest. "In order to find out our true worth, we have to look to the One who created us." He looked down at his Bible, "In the book of Genesis 1:26–27 it says,

> *Then God said, "Let us make human beings in our image, to be like us. They will reign over the fish in the sea, the birds in the sky, the livestock, all the wild animals on the earth, and the small animals that scurry along the ground."*
>
> *So God created human beings in his own image. In the image of God he created them; male and female he created them.*
> —GENESIS 1:26–27 (NLT)

The Preacher paused, then raised his voice, "The God of all creation! Decided to make *you*! In *His* image." Pause. "My friends, do you know what this means? It means that no matter what anyone tells you, *you matter.* You are not worthless. You are priceless! For God made you in His image and He loves you like there were only one of you!"

Krystal's heart stopped. *I have value?* she thought, unable to believe the words she just heard. She didn't feel valuable. She felt the emotions hidden begin to rise to the surface as the Preacher went on, "It is the reason we are different from animals. While animals are made *by* God, they were not made in His image, and still, what does God say? In the book of Matthew 6:26, Jesus says,

> *"Look at the birds. They don't plant or harvest or store*
> *food in barns, for your heavenly Father feeds them. And*
> *aren't you far more valuable to him than they are?"*
> —MATTHEW 6:26 (NLT)

The Preacher looked up from his Bible. "My friends, out of all of God's creation, He calls you the greatest. And He loves us and wants to bring us into His own family." The Preacher looked down again, "In the book of Ephesians 1:4–5 the Bible says,

> *"Even before he made the world, God loved us and chose us in Christ*
> *to be holy and without fault in his eyes. God decided in advance to*
> *adopt us into his own family by bringing us to himself through Jesus*
> *Christ. This is what he wanted to do, and it gave him great pleasure."*
> —EPHESIANS 1:4–5 (NLT)

The Preacher lowered his Bible and said, "My friends, this verse right here, explains the very purpose for why we exist." He pointed and requoted verse five, "God decided *in advance* to adopt us into his own family by bringing us to himself through Jesus Christ. This is what he wanted to do, and it gave him great pleasure." The Preacher looked up from his Bible, "If you want to know why you exist, it is because God wanted a family." The Preacher leaned over his podium and lowered his tone, "Which means, God wanted *you* in His family."

God wanted me in His family? Krystal thought. Her heart rate increased and the dam behind her heart was stirring. The words firing like arrows of truth, striking her soul, wanting to let all her emotions out like criminals from a prison. Krystal's mind flashed back to slicing her wrist. The sharp pain shooting through her left arm. Krystal bit her tongue and held her breath, preventing a scream.

Stop. Please. I can't take much more of this! she thought, but part of her wanted the Preacher to keep going. To keep telling Krystal that she did had value in this world. That she could change and be better. Krystal tried to keep her body from shaking, but Carmen noticed and whispered, "Are you alright?"

"No" was all Krystal managed to say without breaking down, even then she faltered in her speech. Carmen extended her arm around Krystal and pulled her close. Krystal's eyes widened in surprise, but she welcomed the hug, feeling Carmen's presence warm her soul with healing she never knew existed. Her soul was in turmoil as this Preacher peeled away the scabs on her heart.

Krystal lifted her eyes back to the Preacher as he said, "God wanted you in His family so much, that before all of time, He planned to have you exist." The Preacher looked at his Bible, "In Jeremiah 1:5 God says,

"I knew you before I formed you in your mother's womb.
Before you were born I set you apart
and appointed you as my prophet to the nations."
—JEREMIAH 1:5 (NLT)

The Preacher said, "In Psalms, chapter 139:13–16, King David writes,

"You made all the delicate, inner parts of my body
and knit me together in my mother's womb.
Thank you for making me so wonderfully complex!
Your workmanship is marvelous—how well I know it.
You watched me as I was being formed in utter seclusion,
as I was woven together in the dark of the womb.
You saw me before I was born.
Every day of my life was recorded in your book.
Every moment was laid out
before a single day had passed."
—PSALM 139:13–16 (NLT)

The Preacher lifted his eyes and looked at the crowd. "My friends, God planned you even when the world didn't. People may tell you that you are an accident but my friends, *You are not an accident!*" The whole room fell silent. Krystal could feel her emotions stirring like a whirlwind at a hundred miles an hour. Tears fighting to the surface as Krystal held her breath and fought them off. The words breaking through all her defenses, ready to unleash the dam of emotions held within her.

The Preacher looked at the silent crowd from left to right, "You are *not* an accident. No matter what the world may tell you, no matter whether your parents wanted you or not. You are not an accident. In fact, God goes even further to tell us that we are the most valuable thing to Him. That we are his 'masterpiece.'" The Preacher looked at his Bible, "In the book of Ephesians 2:10 it says,

> *"For we are God's masterpiece. He has created us anew in Christ Jesus, so we can do the good things he planned for us long ago."*
> —EPHESIANS 2:10 (NLT)

The Preacher slowly raised his head from the passage, speaking softly, "My friends, we are God's *masterpiece!* God looks at the world as if there were only one of us and loves us that way and more. He calls us His masterpiece. That means, you are not a mistake. You are not a broken piece of garbage tossed aside and left alone. You are not the worthless person who people say you are. No. You are a Mona Lisa. You are the greatest thing in all of God's creation." The Preacher leaned over his podium, hovering over it like a spaceship. "You. Are. His. *Masterpiece.* That means, every part about you was made for a purpose. Your personality, your physical body, your interests, your passions, as well as what experiences you would go through in life. God planned it all and He calls you, His Masterpiece." Krystal covered her face with her arm, weeping quietly into the cotton of her sleeves.

The Preacher straightened his back and said, "My friends, if there is one thing that I want you to leave with today, it is this." He lowered his voice and spoke softly, like a father speaking tenderly to a child, "You are not an accident. You are not worthless." He paused to let the words sink in. "You have *value* in this world. Even when nobody else says you do. For you . . . are God's Masterpiece." The Preacher paused for the final time, "I'm going to leave you with that today, and I hope you can remember, and understand, just how much God loves you."

The Preacher threaded his hands together, "Will you pray with me?" He bowed his head and closed his eyes. "Father . . . I know I have done wrong. I know I don't deserve any of Your love. But God, You call me Your masterpiece. You carefully made me before time began, before I took my first breath, You loved me. I want to say thank you. Thank you for making me and loving me. Thank you for giving me value and purpose in this world. Now, for all those who are feeling unworthy and worthless, may You show them just how much You love them. For even the sparrows have worth, but how much more do You love us compared to them. I pray all of this in Jesus' name, amen."

Krystal whimpered, "Amen" under her breath as she broke down completely and gripped Carmen's shoulders, crying as quietly as she could into her sweater. Krystal couldn't contain it any longer. All the years of suffering and pain, everything she held deep within her, now came rushing to the surface, hearing the words of comfort she desired her entire life, finally coming into the light. The only thing that was ringing through her mind was the Preachers words, *"You are not an accident."* Over and over, playing on repeat, soothing her heart and soul. Melting the ice around her heart, allowing the healing to come. And for the first time, Krystal believed, *I am not an accident. I am not an accident.* Simply hearing those words brought Krystal more relief than she's felt in her entire life. And, just maybe, she felt that tomorrow would be okay. That things would be better.

Maybe.

CHAPTER 12

Reflection

"What would happen if there really is a God?"

—Krystal Henninger

Krystal sat on the edge of her bed, thinking about the church service this morning. She took note of her breathing, how fatigued she was from the emptiness inside and the emotional stress from earlier. The service had brought out some raw emotions, and she hadn't been prepared to cope with them in the middle of a Sunday service.

"What happened?" she whispered, her mind eagerly trying to solve this puzzle. "Why did I break down during the service?"

You know the answer to that.

Krystal sighed and sat upright, facing the truth, "That was the first time someone said I wasn't an accident. That I had value. That I'm not a worthless piece of trash." Thinking about those words brought tears immediately to her eyes. Krystal broke down and whimpered. *Why? I don't get it. What does any of this have to do with me? I don't understand half of what they are saying or even what this church is about, but yet, it still has an impact on me, like it did today . . . Why?* Krystal felt the void within her pulse and ached even stronger now. Like it was reaching out toward something. Krystal wiped one eye, *Is what they say actually true? Is there really a God in this world who cares about me?*

A thought dropped in her mind. *What would happen if there really is a God?*

Then I would have value. I wouldn't be just a worthless speck of dust roaming the earth.

Kinda like what you were already doing?

Yeah.

Krystal paused. *Am I actually agreeing with myself?* She could feel the questions paving the road for her, but the thoughts asking these questions came from another source. They weren't malicious as her own thoughts were. They were gentle, like a flower petal in the wind.

But her thoughts betrayed her once more.

Do you really think someone like you could be loved? After what you did? You deserve to die! Krystal put her hand to her head, her forehead pulsing in pain. *Do you think that by going to some church you will be forgiven for what you did? Those people are just trying to trick you so you could join their fancy cult.*

Krystal tried to fight back. *But what if it's real? What if what they are saying is true? What then?*

Do you think that will really make it all better? No, you are going to suffer for the rest of your life!

Krystal slid down from her bed onto the floor with both hands on her head as she shriveled into a ball.

In desperation she whispered, "God please help me." The words struggling through her moist throat. She felt exhausted, like she just ran a marathon. Krystal shook her head. "I can't do this on my own. I'm going to drown. Drown in my own depression." Krystal never felt so helpless in her life. Here she was, a normal girl living in a wealthy society, yet she was as powerless as someone fighting a chronic disease. Feeling it eat her from within until there was nothing left. Could she make it? Could she pull through if there was an end to it? Only time would tell. Krystal craned her head back and felt pale. Her eyes glancing around the room for no apparent reason. Her breathing was heavy, and she felt like she was going to pass out. And that's exactly what she did. She passed out. Slipping away into one of the only reliefs she got from her pain, sleep.

CHAPTER 13

Who is Jesus?

"What is the greatest news you've ever heard in your life?"

—JL

Krystal sat in the car, her eye shifting next to her at the empty seat. *Where is Jaime? Why is he never here?* Krystal didn't know why she noticed him when he was missing but the rest of the Fishers seemed acclimated to Jaime's absence. The car drove in silence this morning. Krystal had been reading up on the Old Testament. Going through the journeys of Abraham to the Promised Land, the Exodus of Moses, and the trial of David and Goliath. All ancient time stuff that happened thousands of years ago. Surprisingly, Krystal felt a little eager to get to church this morning, as she wanted to hear more of what the Preacher had to say. She had never been alive with such curiosity before, wondering and worrying, about what message the man will say today. *Every time I go into that place, my soul gets rocked. Now I'm almost expecting it to happen again.* Her soul felt more exposed for some reason, like it was lacking the armor she had grown so accustomed to wearing. It made Krystal wonder what it was that made that Preacher . . .

Different?

Yeah. She agreed. *Just like the Janitor, and Dana, and the Fishers. There's something different about them.*

The car reared to a stop and the church came into view in Krystal's window. The crowd seemed less intimidating, but Krystal hadn't bothered to talk to anyone. She snuck a look at Carmen as she unbuckled her seatbelt. *At least I feel comfortable around Carmen. She seems genuine.* Krystal was still growing accustomed to the church setting all together. Her feelings hadn't been settled on whether Christianity was all a hoax or not. But she kept coming back. Why? She didn't know that herself. She just did.

I don't have all the answers, and I don't know why I keep coming back but . . . I still feel like I'm on the right track.

Her thoughts retorted, *But what is the right track?* Krystal didn't bother to answer the question. She didn't know and she was getting tired of giving that same answer.

They stepped out into the heat. Krystal felt the blazing sun fry her skin the moment she stepped out of the air-conditioned car. Her mouth instantly felt parched, and she wanted to drink some water. They all walked eagerly into the church building and took their seats after grabbing some water. The auditorium looked the same, the casual crowd still mobbing over the coffee stand while Summer sat on the opposite side of the church. Krystal thought for a moment about going up to her and saying hi, they did go to the same Bible study every week. Krystal had been hanging around Summer a lot recently but the thing that still puzzled her was why Summer never talked to her when they were at school. Strange.

The band took the stage and played their usual worship songs. Krystal for once mouthed the words but never sang. Still too uncomfortable. The Fishers stood next to Krystal, and Krystal still wondered where Jaime was, even though it was not her business. *Maybe that's just the norm with them. Don't ask questions. Don't pry into their personal life.* The worship songs ended, and the Preacher took the stage, once again wearing the same checkered shirt just a different color. *Honestly, this guy needs to get a better wardrobe.*

You're one to talk. Krystal did not deny that retort. All the clothing she wore was black and that was enough for her to feel content. She never shared that same sense of shopping other girls her age felt.

The Preacher took the stage and planted his coffee mug on the edge of the podium.

I hope that doesn't spill mid-speech, that would be funny. Now that she thought it Krystal half-expected it to happen. She was just waiting for the man's hand to spread out and smack the coffee all over the stage. Krystal almost laughed, almost.

The Preacher glanced out among the audience for a full minute and said nothing. His face looked determined, yet he held it back. Like there was something big he needed to tell the audience. He smiled, "Hi friends." The crowd relaxed and murmured back. He raised his index finger, "I want to start us off with a question."

As you always do.

The Preacher stared at the crowd for a brief moment, his words soft yet powerful, "Who is Jesus?" He paused to let the question sink in. Krystal felt the words reverberate off the walls and pass over her like a gust of wind, making her skin crawl.

We just started and he's already got me on the edge of my seat.

The Preacher flung his arms out, "Why should we care?" He shook his head, "How can we even know about a man who lived so long ago? So I say it again, Who is Jesus?" The crowd was silent, on the edge of their seats like he was about to give them the secret to eternal life.

The Preacher pressed his glasses closer to his face and said, "Well . . . some say Jesus was just a teacher. Was He just a teacher? Some say He was a revolutionary. Was He a revolutionary? He never led a military revolution that overthrew Rome. Then there were some that said He was a mad man. That He was deliberately evil. Was He? Then there were those who said that He was a prophet. Was He a prophet? Or maybe He was just a fraud. Some guy lying about his own made-up religion and was later killed by the authorities." The Preacher paused and leaned in closer to the podium. "And then there were those who claimed that He was the Son of God. *Was He?*" The Preacher threw his arms up in exasperation. "Who was He?" The Preacher stopped. The words echoed off the walls like sonar. Krystal was on the edge of her seat, eager for the Preacher to answer the question.

The Preacher stepped back from his podium and asked, "Why is it that we are still talking about Jesus? Why is it so many people feel so undecided about Him? If you read His skills on paper, He was just a rabbi, a Hebrew teacher at the time. He never traveled more than a hundred miles. He never had a formal education like we do today. He only lived thirty-three years and yet *two thousand years* later, people are *still* talking about Jesus. Why? Why can't we escape Him?"

The Preacher leaned closer to the podium and spoke softly, "My friends, the reason why Jesus is so important is because He is the Son of God." The Preacher paused. "He is the Son of God who came down to die for our sins on the cross so that we may be holy and live eternal life with God in heaven." The Preacher held out his arm, "As I have said in my prior sermons, in the story of Adam & Eve, how they took the Forbidden Fruit and ate it, and because of their sin, death entered the world and we were separated from God, because He is holy, and we are not . . . We committed a wrong against God and that is why we feel that emptiness in our heart calling out to God."

The Preacher looked up, "You see, even while we were still broken. God still loved us." He lowered his gaze and stared toward the crowd. "Tell me, is there a single person alive who is perfect? Is there anyone at all who has not made a mistake? Raise your hand." No one raised a hand. Krystal saw someone lift their hand and then stop. "If any one of you raised your hands, then congratulations you are no longer perfect. Welcome to the human race." The crowd chuckled. "You see, there is not a single person alive who has not done something wrong. In Romans 3:23 it says,"

"for all have sinned, and fall short of the glory of God;"
—ROMANS 3:23 (ASV)

The Preacher pushed up his glasses. "You see we all have fallen short of God's standard. We all have sinned against Him. It's exactly why we feel guilty when we do something wrong. But that begs a better question." The Preacher extended his arms out. "Why is it wrong to rape a woman or to steal from your neighbor? Why is it wrong to molest a child or to murder a person?" Krystal sat up straight in her chair, with her eyes still laser-focused.

The Preacher reiterated the question. "Why is it so wrong to do these things? I'll tell you. It is because inside every human being, there is a sense of morality that God puts in us, and we have that sense of morality because we were made in the image of God. For God is a righteous God. He put this sense of morality in us to understand what is right and what is wrong." The Preacher raised his arms and let them fall in exaggeration. "So what do we do then with this guilt that we accumulate from all our sinful actions? How do we lift this invisible burden from our hearts?" He pushed up his glasses, "We could use drugs to try and dull the feelings we're experiencing, but drugs only last for so long. We could try to forget the wrong we've done in the past but the past never forgets us. We could try to reconcile with the person whom we wronged, but what happens if you murder someone, and you can't get their forgiveness? Or a better question. How do you forgive yourself?"

The Preacher slowed his tone, speaking more empathetically. "Some of you have been struggling for a long time. You feel as though you're stuck in a pit, with no one who can get you out of it. You have tried and tried but no matter how hard you attempt to get out of that pit, you sink deeper and deeper into darkness." The Preacher took a breath. "My friends, you are not alone." He paused. "You are not the only person going through these problems. Every person in the world has struggled with that emptiness inside at some point or another." Krystal clasped her hands on her seat, pondering the Preacher's words.

I'm not the only person going through this? She couldn't believe it. It was like her entire world had changed.

The Preacher took a sip of coffee from his mug, "But God in His love, already had a plan to get us back, even when He knew we would fall away. In Romans 5:8 it says,

> *"But God showed his great love for us by sending*
> *Christ to die for us while we were still sinners."*
> —ROMANS 5:8 (NLT)

The Preacher looked up, "Just like in a court of law, there has to be some penalty for breaking the law. And what is the penalty for committing sin? The penalty is death and separation from God. Well, what does that mean? I'll tell you: Hell." The Preacher pointed to his Bible, "Yet here we have God saying that He is going to take away all our sins and forgive us and make us right with him. Yet how does God do that? How does God pay for all of our sins?" The Preacher paused and lowered the tone of his voice, "By sending His Son, Jesus Christ to die on the cross." The Preacher paused. "God wanted to make us right with Him and give us eternal life despite all our sins against Him." The Preacher raised his arms wide, "We don't deserve it! We don't deserve to be forgiven! We don't deserve to go to heaven! For all have sinned and gone against Christ. Yet, God still looks at us with compassion and says, *'You are worth it!'*"

Krystal's eyes have never been so laser focused on a person in her life, staring at this man in awe. Those last words struck Krystal's core as her heart raced faster, pounding within her. It was like the words activated something within her, something alive and growing.

"You see, back in ancient times, in order to be forgiven for a sin, one must pay tribute with the sacrifice of an animal. It is the same way a court system works where a criminal receives punishment for committing a crime. For God is holy and we are not." The Preacher lowered his head in submission. "But God did not want to leave us that way. He could have left us to our punishment . . . He could have abandoned us to our fate. Consider it the equivalent of being convicted for a crime that you committed, only to have someone walk into the courtroom and say, 'I will take their place, let them go free.'"

The Preacher clicked his glasses, "Jesus willingly went into a Roman crucifixion to set you free." He paused, then spoke somberly, "Do you know what happens in a Roman crucifixion?" The Preacher stretched his arms as wide as he could and said, "You are laid out on a rugged, wooden cross, and have nails hammered through your hands and feet." Krystal gasped. The Preacher lowered his arms and pointed to his open palm. "Imagine a nail the size of a cigar hammered through your hands and feet, impaling you to a cross so you cannot move. Then you are hoisted up until you slowly run out of energy and suffocate to death." The Preacher pushed his glasses up again, "But Jesus did not only take the physical punishment of being nailed to the cross, but He also endured *all the sins of the world!*" The Preacher paused. "Jesus Christ took on all the sins of the world! The sins of the past, the present, and the ones in the future you haven't committed yet. He took them all and became the holy, living sacrifice so that we may be right with God. Think of it this way, God is our judge, and we are all guilty of sin by nature, with the wages of sin being death. Yet Jesus paid our fines when He shed His blood on the cross for us, so that we can be free of the punishment of death and have eternal life so long as we accept Him into our hearts and believe in Him with true faith."

The Preacher paused again, "My friends, Jesus Christ did not have to go to the cross. He did not have to become a human being and live on this earth to die a criminal's death. He could have left us to our fate in Hell, yet He willingly went to the cross to die for our sake. And because of that, He wiped away all our sins from all of existence, and now, we are clean as we were in the Garden of Eden."

The Preacher extended his arms out again, reaching wide, saying, "When Jesus Christ, the One and only Son of God, hung on that cross, it was God saying to the whole world, *'I love you.'*" The words echoed through the room. Krystal felt the words encompass her heart, sending waves of relief over her aching body. Feeling the love that she yearned for her entire life.

The Preacher took a breath, speaking with more authority, "And not only that, but Jesus Christ *rose from the dead!* He didn't just die; He rose from the dead three days later on Easter. That is why we celebrate Easter to this day. Because of the Resurrection of Christ."

The Preacher stepped away, "But then why would God do this? Why would Jesus willingly go to the cross to die for our sake? I'll tell you; it is because God *loves us.* In Ephesians 3:18 it says,

> *"And may you have the power to understand, as all God's people*
> *should, how wide, how long, how high, and how deep his love is."*
> —EPHESIANS 3:18 (NLT)

The Preacher looked up and said, "God loved us so much, that He wanted to bring us back to Him, and He did so, by sending His One and only Begotten Son, Jesus Christ to die for us." The Preacher gestured his hand out toward the crowd, "All of you have heard of the famous verse, John 3:16?"

Krystal's eyes widened. *Even I know that verse.* Krystal was astounded with the credibility coming from this man standing before her. *Where does he get his authority?* Krystal had to fight hard to keep herself composed, but again, she found herself weeping into Carmen's arms.

The Preacher said, "It says here in the King James Version of the Bible,

> *"For God so loved the world, that he gave his only begotten Son, that*
> *whosoever believeth in him should not perish, but have everlasting life."*
> —JOHN 3:16 (KJV)

"You see my friends; death is not the end. It is only a passing point. For all men die." The Preacher paused to take a breath. He had been going on a roll and it was time to wind down. "Now that we are forgiven, we can come back to God as we were in the beginning before the Fall of Adam and Eve. In Romans chapter 3:24–25 it says,

> *"and all are justified freely by his grace through the redemption that came by Christ Jesus. God presented Christ as a sacrifice of atonement, through the shedding of his blood—to be received by faith. He did this to demonstrate his righteousness, because in his forbearance he had left the sins committed beforehand unpunished—"*
> —ROMANS 3:24–25 (NIV)

"My friends, this is why Jesus is so important. His birth is the very reason we celebrate Christmas. The word Christmas itself has 'Christ' in it. To answer the question, 'What is the true meaning of Christmas?' I will tell you; it is to celebrate the birth of Jesus Christ, the Messiah, into the world. And because of that celebration, time was split into BC and AD. You can look at a calendar today and check what happened two thousand years ago. And so, when Jesus Christ died on the cross and rose again three days later, He wiped away all our sin and made us holy with God again."

The Preacher raised his head. "God promises to fill our hearts with His Spirit and to give us everlasting life if we just believe in Jesus Christ as our Lord and Savior and follow Him. I'm not talking about some human who walked the earth. I'm talking about the Son of God. The living Deity throughout all of history, who died and raised from the dead for you, so that you could be part of God's family. He's not some false idol. Not some made-up religion. He is the truth, for Jesus said, 'I am the Way the Truth and the Life.'"

The Preacher lowered his tone and spoke softly, "Some of you are very weary right now. You have been in the dark for so long and are looking for rest. Some people don't even feel anything anymore, they've been hurt so much for so long that they've given up on life. You feel like you aren't living, that you're just a walking corpse; you're breathing but you're not alive." The Preacher put his hand to his heart, "Personally I too have struggled with finding hope in this life. I have had my fair share of struggling to get out of bed in the morning . . . But I tell you this, *your pain will not last.*" Silence. "It is okay to not be okay. There's nothing wrong with that. My friends, I'm here to tell you that there is hope in this world, and His name is *Jesus Christ*. The hope He brings will not let you down. He will not leave you empty-handed. This hope will change your life for the better. You will feel whole, complete, joyful, and hopeful, and be filled with a new life once you live in the grace of Jesus Christ."

The Preacher pushed up his glasses, "So ask yourselves this, who is Jesus, and I'll tell you friends, He is the Son of God, the Immanuel, the First and the Last, the Everlasting and Almighty God. Jesus Christ died for you, because God loves you and calls you, His masterpiece. He wants to give you eternal life and to have you with Him in heaven. So when you ask yourself, 'Am I deserving of such a love?' The answer is no. We don't deserve it, but that's the amazing thing about grace, because with grace it doesn't matter whether we deserve it or not. God gives it to us as a gift regardless. Not as a requirement. Not as a set of rules to follow or traditions to uphold, but because God gives it to us freely out of love. That's how much God loves us."

The Preacher pushed his glasses one last time, "So when you leave today, I want you to remember all that God has done for you. How He created you because He wanted you. How Jesus died for you because He loves you, and how God has great plans for your life, even when you don't think He does . . ." The Preacher tapped his index finger to his temple, "Think about that as you're having your coffee. Think about that as you go out to lunch right now, because I know you're all hungry and thinking about food at this point in the message," the crowd laughed, Krystal couldn't help but laugh with them, "Think about that as you go to bed and know that *you are loved!* The world may say you are worthless, but God says you are *priceless!* Will you pray with me?" He threaded his hands together and bowed his head. The crowd followed suit, as did Krystal.

"If you want to accept Jesus into your heart, will you pray this prayer with me . . ." He took a breath and spoke softly, as if admitting something to an old friend. "Father . . . I'm tired of living this empty life. I'm tired of feeling unfulfilled. Jesus Christ, I believe that You came down to save me. Please forgive me for all the wrong I've done. I know I don't deserve Your mercy. I know I am a broken person. Jesus will You please come into my heart and fill me with Your Holy Spirit. You are the Son of God and I believe that You died on the cross for me. Thank you for rising from the dead so that I may live with you for eternity in heaven. In the name of Jesus Christ I pray, amen."

"Amen" echoed the crowd, and slowly the auditorium came to life. Krystal mumbled the prayer but didn't say them aloud, yet something deep in her soul was touched. As if a new path had been laid out for her.

The Preacher lifted his eyes, "If you prayed that prayer for the first time could we welcome you to the family of God." The whole crowd applauded. Krystal clapped along. She didn't fully pray it, she was still having a tough time keeping up with her mind wandering during the prayer, but she could feel the exhilaration and celebration in the room. She could sense the joy in the air and felt it permeate her own soul. So she clapped too, and she didn't know why.

The Preacher waited for the applause to end, "Well, I will see you next week my friends. Grace and peace."

"Grace and peace," mumbled the crowd, and like that, the sermon was over. Krystal just sat there, staring off into space. She did not know what to say or how to react. There was so much to take in, so much to process but she didn't know where to start.

She felt her stomach growl as her mind clouded, and looked over as Carmen asked, "Wanna get some food?"

Without hesitation, Krystal said, "Yeah."

The food had helped. Krystal sat outside at a table with Carmen, eating a delicious sandwich. They had gone home after the service and dropped Carmen's parents off, but Krystal and Carmen still wanted to get some food so they went out to a nearby sandwich shop. Krystal wanted to get away from the church scene since her mind was too overloaded to process all the information. She tried to remember. The memory felt like a blur for some reason. She needed more time to relax before she could continue. Either way, she still felt she needed some clarity.

Krystal finished munching on her sandwich and watched Carmen in front of her, debating what she should do next. The weight of her need to ask someone about the sermon was building, and Krystal felt comfortable asking Carmen about it. Carmen was her Bible study leader, so she should be able to talk freely about this with her. Krystal swallowed her food and felt the fear trying to prevent her from speaking, but she pushed past the fear and said, "So . . ."

Carmen stopped eating; surprised by the fact that Krystal had initiated a conversation. Krystal saw Carmen's surprise as her opportunity to ask before Carmen could say something. Krystal built up the courage to ask her, knowing it was just one on one and not like speaking to a whole crowd of people. "That sermon..." Carmen waited, both stunned and curious. Krystal looked up from the table and into Carmen's eyes. "I have . . . some questions."

Carmen swallowed her food and waited for Krystal to say something, but she didn't. Therefore, Carmen took that as her cue to speak. "About what?"

Krystal lowered her eyes back to the table, feeling slightly embarrassed. The sheer act of speaking to Carmen lowered her self-confidence dramatically. "Well...what did...what did he mean...when he said Jesus...died for us and rose again?"

Carmen took a breath and braced herself. She scooted her chair in, put her elbows on the table, and said, "For full context, back then, and I mean, back two thousand years ago, Jesus was born in a manger on Christmas day, that's why we celebrate Christmas. Jesus was the prophesied Messiah that was to come through the nation of Israel, descendants of Abraham and the current Jewish people we know today. Back when the Roman Empire ruled most of the world, Jesus started His ministry. Preaching and teaching all throughout the country of Israel." Carmen gestured to Krystal, "You can look it up, it's a real country. But getting back to the point. Since we were separated from God because of our sin, Jesus came into the world to fix that. As a result, people conspired against Jesus to have Him crucified, you know, the process where Roman soldiers hammer giant nails into your hands and feet so that you're stuck to a cross until you suffocate and die." Carmen expected Krystal to react in horror, but she didn't. That was almost as much of a surprise to Carmen as it should have been to Krystal. Carmen continued, "Since we have gone astray from God, we are the ones who deserved to be nailed to that cross. We deserve to go to Hell because we have sinned, but Jesus took that punishment for us and took away all our sins. Then, He raised Himself from the dead three days later, hence the holiday Easter.

"And so now, we can have a clear conscience, we can be forgiven, we don't have to go to Hell and more importantly, we can have eternal life with God in heaven. That means no more pain, no more suffering, no more crying. All of those things don't exist in heaven. We can have all that if we simply believe in Jesus Christ as our Savior and follow His ways. That's it. That's the Resurrection in a nutshell."

Now it was Krystal's turn to ask. She lowered her eyes to the table, "Did . . . did he . . . did he really . . . do that for me?"

Carmen nodded once and slowly, "Yes." Her voice and expression were so genuine, there was no way she was lying. Krystal could tell she was telling the truth. Krystal had gotten her answers, and that was that.

"Okay," was all Krystal said, as their joyful lunch came to an end.

CHAPTER 14

The Bleeding Woman

"If you declare with your mouth, 'Jesus is Lord,' and believe in your heart that God raised him from the dead, you will be saved."

—Romans 10:9 (NIV), The Apostle Paul

Silence befell the room like a coat of mist. Permeating everything around her. Not even a cricket sounded outside. Only the sound of silence, the deep ringing in her ears, remained. Krystal sat on the edge of her bed, palms up, staring blankly into nothing. Her thoughts elsewhere. Drifting in the world of her conscience. Krystal shifted her attention toward the window, revealing an empty night sky with no stars, not even a cloud. Krystal brought her attention away from the window and back to her lap. Thoughts of the church service and what the Preacher said were circling in her mind. One thought managed to fall into the storm, *I wish it would rain . . . it's been too long since it rained.* It had been so dry lately. The only time Krystal felt cool was when she was traveling with the Fishers to go to church in the morning in their air-conditioned car. The rest of the day had been a scorcher, not a cloud to accompany it.

Krystal sighed, bringing her thoughts to the matter at hand. "What do I do?" Krystal held her arms out, palms up. "I can't go back to living as I was . . . I'll die. But if I accept this new religion, then I could be following a cult." Krystal lowered her head even further. *But it doesn't feel like a cult.* She thought of Dana. How genuine and kind she was, along with all the pain she carried. Krystal shook the thought off and lowered her head.

She paused. Waiting for what she was going to say next. The question building without her trying. "Is there really a God?" Her thoughts dragged back to the Preacher speaking about time. How BC and AD were split because of Jesus. "What happened two thousand years ago? Did Jesus Christ really exist? Did He really die on the cross, for me?" The void within her pinged like a ripple in water. Her eyes glanced at her sternum. She felt her body wane. Growing fatigued from the constant emotional stress, suddenly out of breath.

But is what that Preacher said really true? Can I fill this void within me just by believing in Jesus Christ?

The verse, John 3:16 played in her mind.

"For God so loved the world, that he gave his only begotten Son, that whosoever believeth in him should not perish, but have everlasting life.
—JOHN 3:16 (KJV)

Krystal wanted to brush the thought off, but her energy was gone. She didn't have much to begin with so it's not like she could do anything about it. Besides, she wasn't in the mood to get in a fight with her own thoughts again. Her suicidal thoughts had not gone away the past couple of months. It was getting tough again. In a few weeks, Krystal might even pull the plug again. It's not like she had anything to live for anyway. But thinking that caused a sense of conflict within her.

I do have something to live for.
Like what?
. . . Jesus.
You really buy into that crap? You know it's a cult, right?
I don't think so. I don't think it is. At least not from what I've seen.
They're all just liars. Why should you believe anything that they say?
Because . . . I don't have anywhere else to go. The facts, the questions they bring up, it all strikes me as curious. That just maybe, it's true. Maybe Jesus did die on the cross for me. Maybe that hole in me can be filled.
You are nothing!
NO! I am a masterpiece! Krystal's body tensed as if she had just screamed. Krystal began to whimper, slugging down off her bed, crumpling into the fetal position. *I am loved. I am not a nobody. I'm tired of you telling me that I'm a loser. I'm tired of everyone telling me I'm an accident or that I should just die. I'm tired of it!* Krystal looked up at the ceiling, as if there were an open

sky above her and said, "God, please . . . if you're real. Please give me a sign. I need to know that this whole thing is not just a hoax. I need to know." She lowered her head and suddenly grew extremely fatigued, as she fell on the floor and blacked out.

∽

Her eyes awoke from her heavy slumber with intense pain in her left arm. The bandages bleeding through once again. Krystal realized she'd fallen asleep on top of her wounded arm. The warmth of the blood oozing out from the bandages comforted her for a second. Krystal's mind was fuzzy, unsure what time it was or how late in the night she'd fallen asleep. She didn't want to move, but the pain in her wrist forced her to get up and go to the bathroom. Blood dripped from the bandages, leaving a small trail across the floor.

Krystal stepped into the bathroom and unwrapped the bandages around her left arm. It was painful to move her left wrist as the tendons still hadn't healed yet. She finished unwrapping the bandage to reveal the large cut across her wrist. It hadn't healed at all since Krystal's "accident." Krystal cleaned the wound and put on a new bandage, wiping the blood off the floor. Her eyes magnetically drifting toward her nightstand where her Bible lay. The words playing in her mind, *"If you truly seek God with all your heart, you will find Him."*

Krystal slugged over and grabbed the Bible and sat on the floor against her bed. The bed sheets provided a cushion as she sat. She held the Bible in her hands, the wound in her left arm still hurting, but not as much anymore. *I wish I wouldn't look at it anymore. All it does is remind me of what I've done.* Krystal brought her attention back to the Bible. She opened the Bible and scrolled randomly until she stopped in a book called Mark, starting on Mark 5:21.

> *"Jesus got into the boat again and went back to the other side of the lake, where a large crowd gathered around him on the shore."*
> —MARK 5:21 (NLT)

Krystal snorted. *Huh, more about this Jesus person.* She continued.

> *"Then a leader of the local synagogue, whose name was Jairus, arrived. When he saw Jesus, he fell at his feet, pleading fervently*

143

*with him. "My little daughter is dying," he said. "Please come
and lay your hands on her; heal her so she can live."*
—MARK 5:22–23 (NLT)

Krystal said, "This is the same passage I read the first time I was at
Carmen's Bible study." But there was more to the passage that she hadn't
read. So she continued reading.

*Jesus went with him, and all the people followed, crowding around
him. A woman in the crowd had suffered for twelve years with constant
bleeding. She had suffered a great deal from many doctors, and over
the years she had spent everything she had to pay them, but she had
gotten no better. In fact, she had gotten worse. She had heard about
Jesus, so she came up behind him through the crowd and touched
his robe. For she thought to herself, "If I can just touch his robe, I
will be healed." Immediately the bleeding stopped, and she could
feel in her body that she had been healed of her terrible condition.*

*Jesus realized at once that healing power had gone out from him, so
he turned around in the crowd and asked, "Who touched my robe?"*

*His disciples said to him, "Look at this crowd pressing
around you. How can you ask, 'Who touched me?'"*

*But he kept on looking around to see who had done it. Then the
frightened woman, trembling at the realization of what had
happened to her, came and fell to her knees in front of him and
told him what she had done. And he said to her, "Daughter, your
faith has made you well. Go in peace. Your suffering is over."*
—MARK 5:21–34 (NLT)

Krystal lifted her eyes, awe-struck. The words echoed through her heart
and soul as if they were spoken directly to her. For a moment, Krystal forgot
where she was. She recounted the final sentences.

*"Daughter, your faith has made you well. Go
in peace. Your suffering is over."*

Krystal glanced down at the notes beneath the passage and read,

"This woman was most likely suffering from an incurable condition that caused constant bleeding, which prevented her from having social contact with anyone. For years, this woman suffered isolation and constant bleeding, but her faith in Jesus allowed her to be fully and completely healed. It is only faith that releases God's healing power. Move beyond curiosity. Reach out to Christ in faith. That touch will change you forever."

Krystal stopped reading, lifting her head up as the realization finally hit her. Her mouth open, the words coming slowly to her lips.

"I am the bleeding woman." Krystal looked down at her wound, then back to the ceiling. Krystal tried to catch her breath. "I have been alone, for so many years. And I've never had anyone help me. But then this man, this . . . Jesus Christ healed this woman, a woman who went through exactly what I'm suffering from, if not more. And if Jesus can heal her, then He can heal me too." Krystal shifted onto her knees in the middle of her room. She threaded her hands, feeling uncomfortable with the motion. Instead of lowering her head, she raised her eyes to God and said, "God . . ." Pausing. She didn't know what to say. "God . . . just like this woman, I am broken. I need help." Krystal lowered her head, letting the tears come out. "I can't save myself," choking on her own words, "but I believe You can." Krystal took a few breaths. Her heart ready to take a leap of faith. "Jesus, I believe that You are the Son of God. Please forgive me for trying to take my own life and for all the wrong I've done." The tears came down like rivers, "I don't deserve to go to Heaven. I don't deserve to have a good life . . . I'm ashamed of what I did. I am broken . . . so broken and empty inside that I don't know what to do with myself . . ." Krystal raised her head once more to heaven, "Jesus, I believe you are the Messiah. I believe in You. Please come into my life and change me." She lowered her head and unthreaded her hands. And before she could do anything, she fell asleep.

She awoke, slowly, from her deep, long sleep. Her eyelids heavy, yearning for more rest. Feeling her mind gradually awaken. Krystal lay flat on the floor facing the ceiling, with her left arm down and her right arm on her chest.

Her breathing was slow and steady, taking long breaths after a healthy rest. Her eyes took in the sight of her room, the white ceiling the same as before, yet different somehow. She turned at a snail's pace, finding her body in the same position the night she tried to take her own life. Only this time, there was no pool of blood beneath her. Her right hand was placed upon her chest where the emptiness lay, but felt nothing there. Krystal's mind slowly realized as her eyes welled up into tears, only this time it was with tears of joy. Krystal gasped and took a deep breath, letting the air fill her lungs, feeling refreshment and relief wash over her. Then she said words she never thought she would say. "It's gone," she whispered. "It's over . . . it's over . . ." The sense of dread that had encompassed her for years was now gone. The heavy trench coat she carried with her was no more. Her shoulders felt lighter and her soul felt . . . *whole.*

Krystal threaded her hands together in prayer, whispering with joyful desperation, "Thank you God . . . Thank you." Remembering the bleeding woman from the Bible and the One who had healed her. Krystal unthreaded her hands and rubbed her forehead with her left arm. She froze. Then she turned her arm slowly and found the wound on her left wrist was fully healed. The bandages were not even on her arm. They had vanished completely. What was an open wound before was now a two-inch scar across her wrist, fully healed but still very noticeable. It was ugly but Krystal disregarded the massive scar left on her arm and was more glad to see the wound fully healed. The bleeding had stopped, and the words from the passage she read last night sounded in her mind.

> *"Daughter, your faith has made you well. Go*
> *in peace. Your suffering is over."*

Krystal put her hand to her head and smiled, truly smiled. "God really is real," she whispered, filled with joy from the miracle that had taken place. The sound of tapping against the window grew louder as rain drops fell by the thousands outside. Krystal saw the raindrops and didn't hesitate. She jumped up, having more energy than she ever imagined she had. Never in the years that passed had she felt this alive.

Krystal stormed out her door and ran outside. Watching the rain pour all around her. Letting the joyful water encompass her and fill her with its comforting presence. Krystal twirled in the street like a dancer, with arms raised high, soaking in the amazing feeling of being alive! Letting the rain drench her hair, clothes, and even her soul, as the emptiness was gone, and now only hope and joy remained.

Krystal lifted her eyes and couldn't believe the sight, laughing, "Aww come on. Now You're just showing off!" Lifting her eyes to see the most beautiful rainbow she'd ever seen.

PART THREE

Friendship

CHAPTER 15

New Beginnings

"Anyone who belongs to Christ has become a new person.
The old life is gone; a new life has begun!"

—2 Corinthians 5:17 (NLT), The Apostle Paul

Krystal knocked on the Fisher's front door and waited. She couldn't hold it in any longer. She had to tell someone about this, to ask someone who was already a Christian what this was all about. The door opened and luckily it was just the person she wanted to see. Carmen stood in the doorway, half-asleep, "Good morning," she yawned.

Krystal still felt the fear of speaking to others, but this time it was faint, weaker almost, and her enthusiasm was brimming, at least for her standards. Carmen was more surprised with how joyful Krystal looked. She was *smiling*. The girl was actually smiling for once. That shocked Carmen. She hadn't seen any other expression on Krystal's face other than sorrow and a blank stare. Now she was seeing a whole new side to this girl standing in front of her. Carmen waited as Krystal said, "Hey . . . can I come in?" The rain from outside poured. Carmen glanced outside at the heavy rain, now pounding the street, then glanced at Krystal. She was drenched to the bone, but Krystal didn't seem to mind, not even as much as a flicker from how drenched she was. Carmen nodded and opened the door. Krystal took the moment to wipe her feet on their door mat, then stepped inside. Without asking questions Carmen got a few towels and handed them to Krystal.

"Oh thanks," Krystal said. Carmen closed the laundry room door but still had her eyes on Krystal. Almost like she was seeing something she didn't quite believe yet. She was almost suspicious of it. Krystal wiped herself down until she was dry and wrapped herself with the towels, "I need to ask you something."

Carmen gestured toward the living room couch. "Have a seat." They sat down and Krystal glanced around the house, finding it both quiet and empty for once. The rain outside added a touch of laziness to the home, and that relaxed Krystal. Carmen took a seat, "So what's up?" Krystal's energy defused but only a bit.

She collected herself, wondering where to even begin. She said, "I gave my life to Christ last night."

Carmen was stunned. For months Carmen had no idea what Krystal was even thinking and now she lands this on her. Regardless, it was good news to hear. Carmen didn't know how to react at first. She shook herself out of her daze, "Really?" Krystal nodded happily. Carmen slowly realized it, "Congratulations!" and gave Krystal a hug. Krystal returned it with equal joy. The warmth of another person was so comforting to Krystal's soul it felt incredible. Truly incredible. She hadn't felt like this for as long as she could remember.

They pulled apart and Krystal said, "Thank you." Carmen didn't know where to begin, but before she could ask her questions, Krystal had a question of her own. "Which is why I came here." Carmen braced herself as this sounded like the conversation was about to turn down a road. Krystal took a breath, her enthusiasm dimming to her regular levels of expression, "What now?" There was a pause between them. "What do I do now?"

Carmen certainly wasn't ready for this kind of question so early in the morning and on her day off either, but things change, and the day is never boring if you look at it that way. Carmen took a moment to comprehend the question and formulate her answer. Carmen straightened her back, raised her index finger, and said, "Start with loving your neighbor as yourself and then second, continue reading your Bible. The rest will come."

Krystal replied, "Okay," but this time with more hope in her words than the last time they spoke. Carmen remembered seeing this girl the first time she came to her house, looking so gloomy and sad, now had a spark in her eyes. A spark Carmen hoped would continue to grow. Carmen raised the right corner of her lip and said, "Good luck. I'll be praying for you." Krystal calmed now and looked more determined; a new path lay before her. Krystal nodded and said, "Thanks. I'll do that."

CHAPTER 16

Valuing Others

*"Don't look out only for your own interests,
but take an interest in others, too."*

—Philippians 2:4 (NLT), THE APOSTLE PAUL

It was weird. It was *really* weird. Krystal sat at her normal desk at school and could tell things were different. She still didn't understand the whole Jesus thing, but she did understand one thing, her mind was unusually quiet today. The new school year had started as Krystal went through her normal classes, and sat at her normal lonely spots, and yet for some reason she felt . . . hopeful. The day somehow felt brighter despite the constant rain outside. Krystal didn't mind the rain. In fact, she loved it. It was where she felt the most at home. Too bad she lived in a state where it only rained two weeks out of the year. Regardless, Krystal had gone through a majority of her day, and she never once had a suicidal thought bother her conscience. It was strange, it was quiet, and a tad bit . . . uncomfortable. Krystal lowered her head into her arms, pondering her feelings.

It's odd. I feel . . . good, for once, and yet there is part of me that misses the pain. Almost like it was . . . comfortable? Krystal shook her head. *No, it was more like I had gotten used to it. I had grown familiar with my pain, that now it almost feels alien to me to live without it.*

Krystal lifted her scarred left hand and placed it over her heart, right where the emptiness used to be, but no longer. Krystal soaked in this feeling of being whole and took a breath. *It feels so nice to feel complete. It feels so wonderful to feel . . . whole, for once.* Krystal closed her eyes and basked in this feeling, in the ability to find hope throughout the day. To know that the nightmare was over, and she had made it to the dawn. Krystal felt relief rush over her body, covering her with goosebumps as the rush went up her spine and then over her shoulders, causing her body, muscles, even her soul, to relax. Having nothing to worry about.

So what do I do now?

She remembered Carmen's words.

"Start with loving your neighbor as yourself and then second, continue reading your Bible. The rest will come."

At least she keeps the instructions simple, Krystal thought.

The bell rang and the class bolted out of their seats while Krystal remained. She took her time, going at her own pace. Krystal basked in the feeling of how quiet her mind was. She was deeply appreciative of having her thoughts silent for once and her heart settled. Krystal exited the class and merged into the flow of traffic as hundreds of students poured out from their classrooms, all following the single exit to the school courtyard.

Amidst the crowd Krystal saw Jaime passing by, looking down at his phone. Krystal didn't know why she had noticed him. Usually, she didn't pay attention to anyone at school, only now, for some reason, she noticed something about Jaime that just stuck out to her. Krystal followed him at a distance. She wasn't concerned about losing him, he wasn't exactly her target anyway.

Jaime continued staring at his phone as he exited the hallway and stepped out into the school courtyard. Krystal followed behind him but not so close. She didn't know why she was following him; she just did. She rounded a corner and stopped, watching Jaime's body language as he vanished amongst the crowd.

That was interesting.

Krystal couldn't put her finger on it, but there was something about Jaime that seemed . . . *familiar.* Krystal gave up on the thought and decided it was time to head back to her normal routine. Krystal walked over to her bird covered white bench and sighed, *That hasn't changed.* Krystal took her seat and began eating her lunch. She stared out at all the same cliques and friend groups around the courtyard, but something was different. Something in the way she looked at people was different; and now some characters she hadn't noticed before were now coming into perspective. It was hard to explain but one of those characters was Jaime. Krystal spotted Jaime again as he came out from the lunch line and headed toward his usual friend group. He didn't have his phone out since his hands were holding his plated lunch, but something looked off about him. Krystal couldn't put her finger on it, she just knew something was wrong. Something in the way he walked, in the way he carried himself, in the way he lowered his head.

Just like I do.

Krystal didn't know why she hadn't paid attention to Jaime before. So why now? Why was she just noticing him?

Krystal observed Jaime as he passed Summer's group and headed off toward a group of guys who looked to be water polo players. Krystal's thoughts drifted to Summer for a second and wondered why Summer hadn't invited Krystal to sit with her group yet. They had already spent time together every Wednesday for the entire summer, so there was no reason why Summer shouldn't have invited her to her group. But then again, Krystal hadn't asked to join Summer's group either so that could be why.

Krystal could see Amber, Cassie, and of course, Summer, at the center of the circle. That sight didn't change much and so Krystal took her attention off Summer and focused back on Jaime. She watched him from afar as his blank frown quickly changed and he was suddenly smiling amongst friends. *Well Jaime has always been popular in school, that hasn't changed much.* She watched closer and after a couple minutes realized Jaime's smile had fully disappeared, and the guy was looking back at his phone. Krystal leaned forward; *I wonder what he's looking at.* The entire time Jaime never took his eyes off his phone. He never once talked to his friends. Krystal didn't think he was looking at a video, although she had no proof of that, but it didn't seem like he was on social media either, because he wasn't scrolling through anything. It was hard to tell but Jaime was staring at something. Krystal threaded her hands together and placed her elbows on her knees.

She said to herself, "I don't know why . . . but there's something about him." Krystal observed him for a few more minutes before Jaime got up and left his group of water polo friends. Jaime rounded the corner and disappeared. Krystal found that curious and sat there disappointed for some unknown reason. She wanted to talk to him, even though talking to a stranger would be the scariest thing in the world for her to do. So she let Jaime vanish behind the corner, still staring at his phone.

✺

Krystal sat on her bedroom floor with her knees bent and hands threaded. She closed her eyes and prayed,

"God . . . I'm not really sure how to ask this or what the process is for prayer but . . ." Krystal opened her eyes and looked out toward the glowing moon in the night sky. *"Please . . . give me a friend. Please give me a friend . . . I don't want to be alone anymore."* She lifted her head up higher, "Please," she whispered, "could you give me a friend?" Feeling the still air carry the silence as the moon rose higher into the night.

✺

"My friends, do you believe that you were put on this planet to live for yourself?" The Preacher took a breath while Krystal scribbled vigorously in her notes to keep up. "The Bible says in Leviticus 19:18,

> *"Do not seek revenge or bear a grudge against a fellow Israelite*
> *but love your neighbor as yourself. I am the Lord."*
> —LEVITICUS 19:18 (NLT)

"And in the Gospel of Matthew it says,"

> *Jesus replied, "'You must love the Lord your God with*
> *all your heart, all your soul, and all your mind.' This is*
> *the first and greatest commandment. A second is equally*
> *important: 'Love your neighbor as yourself.'"*
> —MATTHEW 22:37–39 (NLT)

The Preacher looked up from his Bible, "You see, the greatest thing you can do for another person is to love them as you would yourself. Think about how you would want to be treated by your peers. Would you want them to be rude to you? No. In the same way, we must love on them the way God loves us. By giving mercy when we don't deserve it and loving our enemies. In the same way, we are to love our neighbors as if they were ourselves." The Preacher flipped to another marked portion in his Bible, "In Philippians 2:3, it says,

"Don't be selfish; don't try to impress others. Be humble,
thinking of others as better than yourselves."
—Philippians 2:3 (NLT)

"*Think* about the people around you and look at them with humility. Don't think of yourselves as better than they are, instead, look at them with value and reverence. Think of others as better than you, not in the sense where you put yourself down, but think of them as more important than yourself, the way Jesus did, where you value others above yourself. Look at them, and love on them the way Jesus did for us. Without judgment or assumptions, but with love. But not only that, the Bible says we must take an interest in others as well. In Philippians 2:4 it says,

"Don't look out only for your own interests,
but take an interest in others, too."
—Philippians 2:4 (NLT)

The Preacher lifted his eyes from his Bible and said, "We must take an interest in others too. Tell me, when was the last time you took time out of your day to think about someone else? To call someone and check how they are doing. Christ wants us to be aware of the needs of others just as much as our own needs. So do not focus only on your needs but learn to think about others and what's going on in their lives."

Krystal finished scribbling her notes. The notebook Carmen had bought for Krystal was coming in handy. Krystal was using every line of it. She paid more attention in church lately, taking important notes.

Krystal finished writing down the last verse the Preacher said. *Philippians 2:3–4 huh? That's a good passage.* Krystal closed her notebook; she got what she needed. Now came the hard part. Applying it.

CHAPTER 17

Shadow By The Fire

"You never really know what other people are thinking.
What kind of pain they are currently going through."

—JL

Summer hollered, "Are you guys ready?!"

"YEAH!" The group of girls all raised their arms in excitement, everyone but Krystal. Krystal only held her arm up halfway. Clearly not sharing the same enthusiasm with the group. The idea of a sleepover at a house down the street from her wasn't so much a golden opportunity as it looked. Krystal gave up and sighed. At least it was Friday night, and they could all sleep-in tomorrow. Krystal remembered the invitation from Carmen, how shocking it was to hear at first. Krystal wasn't used to receiving invitations from anyone, so the idea scared her.

Krystal stood amongst Carmen, Summer, Cassie, Amber, and another girl with long brown hair that Krystal didn't recognize, as they sat around the living room of the Fisher's house. They were all in their pajamas, ready for their late-night sleepover. Krystal had to admit, she felt a bit childish doing something like this, but it was one of their "required" Bible study nights. Krystal knew it was entirely Carmen's idea, but she didn't want to shoot it down and be the Debbie-downer in the group, even though she knew she already was.

They all sat around the multiple couches in the living room. The tan and brown leather couches complimenting the room well. Krystal sat on her own couch while all the other girls, aside for Carmen, sat on the same couch as Summer. Krystal couldn't help but feel a little alienated with four people sitting across from her and none of them sitting next to her. Krystal's spiritual high had dissipated as the weeks went on, as she settled back down to her old, reserved self, despite there being some minor changes, she was still shy with a lot of people aside from those she's close to, but that was the effect of years of isolation and loneliness. Even here, amongst girls who all go to the same Bible study, Krystal couldn't help but feel like the outlier in the group.

The night went on and Krystal hadn't moved from her couch except to grab something to drink every now and then. They just stayed up and talked. Well, Summer mostly talked, all the time. Summer would be in the middle of a forty-five-minute-long story and then Amber would jump in and start telling a story of her own. Krystal's eyes drifted off. Concentration was growing increasingly difficult with every passing second. *I wish we would do something other than just . . . talk.* Krystal hadn't muttered a word the whole night. Whenever she tried to jump in on the conversation, Summer would cut her off mid-sentence and start up again. Krystal sighed and let the girl talk. Struggling to stay awake with the boring conversation.

Summer spoke, "And so, this one time, I went down on the side of this cliff so I could take a picture, and I like, went down without a rope or any experience with rock-climbing whatsoever and I like, held myself with one hand on like the side of the ledge and then the dirt where my hand held almost gave way and I like almost died. But I got like the best social media photo you'll like ever see. Cool right?" Summer finished and Krystal craned her head back in apathy.

That was the dumbest story I have ever heard. But her thoughts were refuted when she heard one girl say, "That was a remarkable story! You truly are a wonderful and amazing human being!"

Cassie joined in on the compliments, "Yeah you were so brave! I could never do something like that!"

Then Amber joined in, "Oh yeah, that's our Summer for you." The cheers and congratulations went on and on. Krystal wanted to be mad but a part of her wanted to join in on the compliments too, at least to be part of the group. But she knew that wouldn't be the case. Summer basked in the compliments and for a second there was a brief pause in the conversation. A point where nobody said anything. Krystal thought of this as an opportunity to say something, but her mind went blank.

What would I say? She thought for a moment. There was a story of when

Krystal and her mom went out camping and they thought they were being haunted by the forest around them. *Yeah, I'll say that.* Krystal fought to get the words to her lips. Using the split-second opportunity to say something, despite how difficult it was to talk at all.

"I . . . uhhh went camp—"

Summer cut her off, "And so this other time I like, went out and got like attacked by a dog, because I wanted to pet the dog, even though the dog was foaming in the mouth and had rabies, and I like totally needed like my rabies shot, and so I like ended up in the hospital . . ."

Krystal sat across from Summer, both hurt from the interruption and bitter from the story Summer replaced her own with. *Why is that story relevant? There wasn't even a question asked. You just spoke that out of the blue.* Krystal still wanted to join in on the conversation as people were jumping back and forth.

Cassie chimed in, "I'm so sorry that that dog hurt you. Did you end up helping the dog? Was the dog okay? I know a person like you would help that dog."

Summer crossed her arms together against her chest like an X, deeply touched. "Yes, I like, helped the dog. After I got out of the ER from almost dying, I saw the dog again later and then tried to give it a hug again and I like almost got bit a second time, but we like called Animal Control and they like took the dog away after the second encounter."

Probably to get put down, Krystal thought. *You weren't worried that you almost died?* Krystal couldn't understand what she was listening to. Whether this girl Summer was making up these stories or was just so big an airhead that she had no regard for her own safety. Krystal couldn't understand whether that was a good trait to have or not. A part of her did want that trait, but then Krystal thought of her own "accident" and decided to drop the subject.

I know. I'll try talking about my mom since she was a nurse . . . The thought stymied her, and her mood darkened. *Maybe you don't.*

Krystal nodded. *Yeah. Don't.* She tried to cheer herself up and plan to say something else while the conversation in front of her raged on like a tornado, always trying to break in and go with the flow. They were talking about childhood pets now, and Krystal didn't have anything to say to that. She had produced the camping idea but had nothing else to say about any other topic. Some of the girls even talked about sports for a while, girls like Amber at least.

Amber was clearly the tomboy out of all of them and she seemed to enjoy it. Krystal wasn't like Amber. She didn't share the same knowledge about sports or fashion sense as the others. It was another topic Krystal couldn't relate to.

Krystal yawned and eased down on her couch and watched the show unfold with more of Summer talking as usual. Krystal tuned out the conversation, her eyes shifting position, looking at the glass toward the backyard patio, into the night, closing her eyes before she fell asleep. Krystal awoke to find the living room in total darkness; aside from the moonlight creating small glints of detail, there wasn't much to go off of or let alone see. If Krystal weren't careful, she would easily smack her foot or knee into the nearest furniture. The entire sleepover had taken its toll as slumber finally claimed everyone in the group. Krystal leaned forward and rubbed her eyes; she had no idea what time it was, but she knew it was late in the night. Her eyes shifted toward the glass door leading to the outdoor patio. Krystal could see orange lighting coming from outside and wondered, *What is that?* She glanced around at the sleeping bodies around her. Everyone was accounted for, so who was out there this late at night? Krystal rose and stepped cautiously, tip-toeing her way over the sleeping bodies. She opened the glass door and followed the glow to the side of the yard, coming up to the concrete wall. Krystal found a large fake rock to hoist herself up and gazed over the wall to see a communal firepit nearby. The orange and red flames flickered in the pit, as the cool wind outside fluttered and kicked the flames like a flag. There were some chairs around the pit, but all were empty . . . all but one.

She peered closely, trying to figure out the identity of the shaded person. It took a couple seconds until Krystal realized it was Jaime, sitting out there alone. He seemed to be focusing on the flames like they were a living television set. Krystal could see Jaime's conscience was present in the moment yet deep in thought. As if something was weighing on his mind. For a guy so popular Krystal wasn't used to seeing him like this. A warm presence pulsed within her heart. It wasn't harmful or pressuring her. It was gentle, like a warm sunrise in her heart. Gently urging her to go up to him and say something. Krystal held her ground but continued to observe Jaime stare into the fire. What was he looking for? What was he hoping to find in those flames? Krystal let the idea fade. *Maybe he's not looking at all, maybe he's . . .* Krystal shrugged off the idea. She had no idea what was going on in his mind or what he was going through but she could tell something was wrong. No one just wakes up in the middle of the night and simply stares into a fire for no reason.

Krystal watched him for a few minutes, as he showed no sign of change. He simply stared into the fire, blinking every now and then, remaining completely still. Krystal checked behind her to make sure no one else saw her. All the other bodies were right where they belonged. Krystal looked back at Jaime one last time, wondering what was going through his mind and felt empathy for him. She didn't even know what it was, she just felt bad for the guy. Krystal lowered herself from the rock and made her way back inside. She tiptoed around the bodies and crawled back onto her makeshift bed on the couch. She got comfortable and then stared into the darkness.

He's got that stare about him. That look. I don't even know why I noticed it. I didn't notice it before so why am I noticing it now? Krystal felt the warm presence inside her dwindle. The warm presence within her, the "Holy Spirit," as they called it in church, filled the void where her emptiness used to be, flickered away yet left an impression on her heart. She thought about it before the heaviness of her eyes took over and her mind drifted back to sleep.

CHAPTER 18

Jaime Fisher

"There is always someone hurting around you. Whether they are smiling or not, someone is hurting inside."

—JL

He got out of class in a fury of anger. Jaime fought to keep his emotions contained like a bomb about to explode. He clenched his fist, gripping his backpack strap. *That teacher is so annoying! Completely oblivious to the atmosphere of the room. Can't he tell that no one wants to ask a question? Is it that hard to figure out?* Jaime stormed out of the classroom and headed toward his locker, quickly finding himself surrounded by the entire school hastily leaving their classrooms in mass exodus. Everyone was trying to go and sit with their friends at lunch. Jaime scoffed, *Give me a break.* He stepped out into the sun and looked up at the sky. He stared up for a few seconds, glaring angrily as if he knew someone was up there. He took his sights off the sky and managed to calm down a bit once he got to his locker. He twisted the dial and got his lunch, slamming the locker with half-strength. The locker made a loud wham, but it was nothing unusual compared to the din of the crowd that surrounded the courtyards of the school.

Jaime made his way through the outer courtyard, watching as groups of friends and cliques spread around the sides like cholesterol clumped together in an artery. The new school year had started, and Jaime tried to imagine what change had occurred. *Nothing's changed here. It's still all the same as last year, and the year before.* Jaime exited the hallway, pushing through the heavy metal doors, feeling the sun beat down on his short brown hair. He entered the courtyard and spotted his water polo buddies. Taking a breath, *If I get over there, then maybe things will feel better.* Jaime started walking and was greeted with, "HEY JAIME!" Jaime turned and found Summer and her friends chilling out by some benches by the drama department entrance. Summer was waving him over. Jaime approached the group, as Summer said, "Hey Jaime! It's good to see you."

"It's good to see you too," Jaime replied courteously. He felt some enthusiasm infuse with his speech, making his voice sound better.

Summer asked, "Wanna like sit with us for a bit?" Jaime gripped his backpack strap tighter. Not sure whether he should accept or decline. Then everyone in the group chimed in:

"You've gotta come."

"It won't be the same without you."

"Come on man."

Jaime thought it over and decided to give them a couple minutes, hoping someone would notice. Jaime said, "Alright alright, I'll sit with you." Sounding happier than he actually was. Summer cheered and everyone followed.

Summer gestured him to sit next to her, "Oh you can like, sit right here!" Jaime followed her gesture and took a seat. He was good friends with some of the people in Summer's group, so it wasn't that bad. Jaime started working away at his lunch, watching the conversation continue without his intervention.

Summer started again. "Oh my gosh, so like this one time, I was out with my dad and we were like hunting for ducks and so I like, wanted to go to the bathroom and when I went, I found this nice looking mushroom on the tree bark next to me and I like totally remembered reading somewhere that mushrooms are good for you, and so I like ate the mushrooms bare and I like ended up having to go to the hospital because those mushrooms were poisonous, and I like almost died." There were wows and wonders shared among the group. Jaime didn't bother with the conversation and continued eating his food in silence.

The conversation went on for a few more minutes. Summer scooted a couple inches closer, turned to Jaime and asked, "How's like, water polo going?"

Jaime looked at her briefly then turned away. "It's fine," he said sternly, not hiding the detest in his voice. Summer either didn't notice or backed off from the attempted conversation. The rest of the group asked a few more questions but Jaime only gave them shallow answers. He didn't want to talk about anything, yet he secretly wanted to talk about everything. He didn't want to be rude, but he didn't want to deal with small-talk either. Jaime finished the remaining questions and sat back, looking somber. Jaime couldn't tell whether they noticed the look on his face or were completely oblivious to how he felt. The look on his face showed he was having a bad day, like all the other days. Jaime quickly grew sick of the conversation and needed to get away. He got up, taking the remainder of his lunch with him.

Summer was the first to notice, "Where you going?"

Jaime said, "I'm going to head over and join my water polo buddies. They've been waiting for me too long." The whole group aww'd in disappointment. "I'll be back another time," he said.

He turned his back to them and heard Summer call out, "Okay, see you soon!" Jaime walked away, a little eager to get away for some reason. He spent the last ten minutes eating his lunch, listening to a bunch of stories he didn't care about; now he headed over and saw his group of water polo buddies come more into view. Some guys shifted and turned their heads, smiles grinning wide. The lot of them greeted, "Heyyyyyyy!" Jaime smiled, raised his hands to calm them, but his buddy Luiz Patron stood up and started clapping slowly, emphasizing each clap, then picked up the pace, as did the rest of his buddies, until all of them were clapping in full applause to the entrance of Jaime Fisher. Jaime shook his head, grinning from the unwanted welcome as he entered the circle, feeling pats around his back. His thoughts were pushed away for the moment, and he was now in the presence of some of his closest high school buddies, throwing punches and receiving some, all in good fun.

One of the guys started yelling, "SPEECH! SPEECH! SPEECH!" as the others all joined in, "SPEECH! SPEECH! SPEECH!" One of them pretended to hand Jaime a fake microphone and Jaime couldn't help but play along.

Jaime took the imaginary mic and said, "I'd like to thank all you guys for your hard work. We would have never made it this far without you, and I do my best and give all I can for this team." (That was surprisingly good for someone improvising off the top of one's head huh?) The group was impressed and laughed it off. All of them getting along just nicely like old football buddies. Jaime took his seat, feeling a bit better now that he was among friends. *At least these guys get me.* But the high didn't last. Gradually, the entrance wore off and Jaime was back to feeling his bitter self again. Jaime didn't hide his emotions as his smile and happiness faded away. He was left with a sullen expression, a sight that warned people to stay away yet yearned for attention. They all took their seats on their corner next to the English building and continued on with the normal chatter. Some of them went on their phones minding their own business while others engaged in conversation about the most random of topics. Jaime simmered back into his sullen glare as he leaned back against the school building.

A few guys asked him how he was doing, Jaime answered sternly, "I'm fine," but he was not fine. Jaime felt a sting of guilt for not telling them, but the memories came rushing back, bringing him down into the darkness. In a way, he wanted all his friends to ask him what was wrong, but they would never understand. It hurt, but Jaime refused to talk about it.

Jaime tuned out the conversation and pulled out his phone, raising the invisible barrier that implied: *"Do Not Disturb"* to everyone who dared talk to him. He scrolled through his phone, looking at something he knew he shouldn't. It was painful and he wanted to look away, but part of him refused to take his eyes off the screen. Every now and then Jaime casually checked the faces of his buddies, and all of them seemed pretty happy. Jaime felt the atmosphere of the group and it made him want to feel happy too, but he refused to partake in it, causing this deep sense of anger directed at all his friends.

Lucky you. You all get to have a good time.

Jaime lowered his head and looked away.

It's not like they would understand anyway.

He didn't hide his anger, but Jaime knew getting mad at his friends for being happy was not the right thing to do. He sighed, leaned back against the wall, and stared out amongst the courtyard.

As people were passing by, Jaime found his eyes trailing them with curiosity. Every person had a story. So where was everyone going? Jaime's eyes followed from person to person, everyone who was passing by the building corner, as he quickly grew bored, until he recognized someone he knew. Jaime realized it was the girl from Carmen's Bible study. Jaime took note of her dresswear, *Hmm, all black huh? Get a wardrobe,* as she passed by and vanished behind the corner. Jaime relaxed a little, forgetting about the girl, letting his mind wander while his buddies lived their happy lives in front of him. A couple minutes later Jaime resumed his people watching, only to find the girl in black walking by again, going the same direction she did before. Jaime straightened up and lowered his brow. Observing the girl's movements as she passed by and vanished again. He found that a bit odd and tried to forget it.

Jaime leaned back, trying to relax, but now he was on guard. Jaime watched attentively as the crowd passed by, and to his lack of surprise, the girl showed up again, going in the same direction as last time. *Okay, what is with this chick? Is she making a loop or something?* Jaime checked the time on his phone, there was still some time left during lunch, so why was this girl walking so much? Didn't she have somewhere to be or people to sit with?

Jaime watched her vanish behind the corner again and waited. Waiting to see her come out on the other side. Jaime checked the time and waited a few more minutes. Surprise, surprise, there she was, walking around the cafeteria building coming towards Jaime's group of friends again. Jaime found that peculiar. *What is this like her fourth loop or something? Where is she going?* Jaime's eyes shifted to her legs, her all black pants not showing an ounce of skin, hiding any sense of attraction. He watched more closely, trying to analyze her body language.

Huh, that's weird. She's not moving that fast, and her movements are sluggish. The girl rounded the corner and vanished again. Leaving Jaime with one more question in his day.

Okay, that was weird. The bell rang a few minutes later and Jaime said his goodbyes to his buddies. His thoughts dragged back down to the pit where the pain awaited. Jaime grimaced as he walked to his next class. *Don't go back there, don't let your mind wander back there.* The hatred and bitterness increasing the closer his mind drifted to that abandoned corner in his conscience. *Don't think about it. Don't think about her. Don't think about her!* But it was too late. Memories came rushing back to his mind. Times of immense joy, and the pain that came after. His heart swelled with anger.

Why? Why! Jaime tensed up, trying to keep himself under control. *I don't want to think about YOU. Just get out of my life! You're not real!* All the while, Jaime walked by his classmates, watching them smile and laugh. The world goes on, as they say.

∽

Ahhh the benefits of being out of college while living at home. Carmen lay on her family's couch reading a magazine for a change. She was tired of looking at her phone, browsing through all the housing images of people, like her parents, who decided to buy their own real estate and renovate their houses. Carmen flipped through the pages, finding pictures of happy-looking families, the kind of picture-perfect photos that showed just how happy everyone in the family was. Carmen couldn't help but smile at the images, then her smile quickly died when she thought of her own family. *I wish things could go back to the way they were.*

The sound of sizzling filled the kitchen. The sweet aroma of diced sausages and seasoned cauliflower filled the air, making Carmen salivate. She could not wait for dinner to be ready. Carmen put the magazine down and asked, "Mom, how much longer until dinner's ready?" Mrs. Fisher was busy dicing up the rest of the cauliflower.

"Just a couple more minutes, then we will be ready."

"Alright," Carmen said, returning to her magazine. The garage door sounded and in walked Mr. Fisher. Carmen lowered her magazine again, "Hey Dad!"

Mr. Fisher walked in with a bit of sweat on his brow but a genial attitude for a guy his size, "Hey Carmen!" Carmen watched as her tired dad trudged along. *Seriously, every time Dad walks in, I swear he looks like a real-life lumberjack. It's the checkered shirts and overalls that sell the look, plus the black beard and the hefty build to the guy. No wonder Mom fell for him.*

But he didn't walk over and give Mom a kiss, a greeting that should have ensued. Instead Mr. Fisher walked straight to the dinner table and sat down. He leaned over and asked, "How much more time honey?"

Mrs. Fisher was slightly annoyed by the question, and answered, "A few more minutes hon. Keep your patience."

"I will honey," he replied.

Carmen went back to reading her magazine when the garage sounded again. That could only mean one thing. Carmen lowered her magazine and watched Jaime enter the house. Carmen got up and called out, "Welcome home Jaime!"

But Jaime walked right past her and muttered, "Yeah."

Mrs. Fisher called out, "Dinner will be ready in a few minutes Jaime."

Jaime called back, "I'm fine," then vanished upstairs. Carmen heard a thump as his door slammed shut. A shot of disappointment struck Carmen. *It's been a while since he's talked with us. I hope he's okay.* Carmen's eyes looked up toward Jaime's room, *What's going on in your mind Jaime?* Her heart wanted to reach out and comfort him, but Jaime wouldn't let her in. He wouldn't let any of his family in. Carmen glanced over toward the kitchen and saw her mom doing the same thing. Wondering the same thing she was, while Mr. Fisher was staring at the table, sulking in the absence of his son. Carmen could see it all. The memories of what had been, lingering on all of them. Carmen glanced at the stairs, her heart begging, *Jaime please . . . come back to us.*

CHAPTER 19

Loving Your Neighbor

*"What does it mean to love your neighbor as yourself? It
means you put yourself in another person's shoes and think
from their perspective. You ask yourself, 'If I were them, how
would I want to be treated?' and then act accordingly."*

—JL

Krystal raised her fist, hesitant to knock. This part always felt uncomfortable no matter how many times she did it. She threw her hand down against the wooden door, knocking harder than she intended and then pulled back and knocked too light. The door swung open as she finished, and Carmen stood there excited. "Glad to have ya!" Stepping aside, allowing Krystal to walk in. Krystal stepped inside and saw that Summer and Amber were already here, sitting around the living room, hanging out. Krystal had brought her Bible study notebook and was ready for another evening session, only this time, the Bible study was inside and not out on the outdoor patio. Krystal glanced through the glass doors leading to the backyard. Her mind thought of Jaime sitting at the firepit by himself late that night. She dismissed the thought and went to join the circle.

A few other people had joined the session tonight, most of them were from Summer's group at school, and once again, strangers surrounded Krystal. She found an open seat on a couch and watched the group talk. Summer led the conversation as always, "And like this one time I was so thirsty that I found this pool of water that looked totally like disgusting, and so I like, drank some of the water and I ended up getting a bacterial infection from drinking the water and ended up in the ER."

Krystal thought, *How many times has this girl ended up in the ER? I honestly can't tell whether she's telling the truth or is making this all up? Because there's no way she's doing this without knowing the consequences . . . right?* Krystal felt her doubts creep in. She nearly smacked her forehead.

One of the guys cut Summer off and said, "That reminds me of when I was out snowboarding with my family. I hit a tree and nearly split my head open." An idea struck Krystal after hearing that. *I have a story related to that.* Krystal felt her heart glow, feeling like she had something to say for once. This was her chance to be a part of the conversation. To have that comradery that everyone longed for. Krystal built up the words in her head, prepping what she was going to say. *I'll talk about how Mom used to treat a patient who was involved in a snowboarding accident.* Krystal let the guy finish and waited for her turn in the conversation.

The guy said, "So yeah, I was going down this major black diamond and I couldn't stop myself from tumbling down, and the next thing I knew I hit the tree head on and nearly split my head open. It was a fourteen-hour surgery, but they put me back together again and now I'm all good."

Krystal waited, feeling the conversation come to an end, and felt this was her chance to say something. Her time to finally speak. Krystal built the words up in her throat, ready to give her small speech, and opened her mouth, "So my mom one ti—"

Summer cut her off, "Oh my gosh! That's awful. That's like, a totally horrible crash you had. That reminds me of a time when I was riding my bike . . ."

Krystal backed off, *Okay, I'll try another time and wait for a break in the conversation.* Krystal had to wait another twenty minutes before Summer finally finished her latest story.

Summer continued, "And that was like, a totally tragic point of when I peed my pants in fifth grade." Summer stopped and took a breath. Krystal woke up from her boredom and quickly realized the opportunity she was presented with. She had been planning what she was going to say but Summer had started a new story and trailed off into something completely different.

I was going to talk about my mom being a nurse but now I don't feel like it's appropriate for the conversation. It seems we are talking about childhood memories in elementary school now. Krystal thought about some of her childhood memories, her face darkened, remembering how even back then she didn't have any friends. It was painful for Krystal to go back to that place and reminisce about those awful times. Krystal remembered playing tetherball with herself every day in elementary school. Never having the enthusiasm to play hopscotch with the other girls or even to play with dolls for that matter. She simply played tetherball by herself. Sometimes she had fun, but the fun would only last for so long. Krystal wanted to smile but the other memories of elementary school engulfed the brief moment of joy with reality. It was tough, even back then. Krystal deflated and became depressed. *I never was enthusiastic. I never had the drive to be competitive in sports. I just watched people. That's all I did, from my time in elementary school to . . . now.*

Krystal thought of something to say from elementary school, remembering the time when they played a game of capture the flag for the first time. Krystal nodded. *I'll talk about that.*

She waited for Summer to finish, "And that like goes to show like that I should like have never like peed my pants back in elementary school." Summer took a breath. Krystal saw the brief pause in the conversation.

This is it. This is my chance.

Krystal spoke, "Back in elementary sch—"

But Summer started up again, "That like reminds me of another time of when . . ." Krystal clamped her mouth shut, both disappointed and slightly offended.

Did she do that on purpose? Krystal's suspicions were raised. She wasn't sure.

Carmen entered the room and called out, "Alright! We about ready to start the Bible study tonight?"

Summer turned and exclaimed, "Yeah we are!" Raising her arm in the air, everyone in the group following her example shouted. "YEAH!"

Krystal never raised her arm but was at least ready to get the Bible study on. She heard a door close and footsteps coming down the stairs. Krystal looked over her shoulder and saw Jaime coming down. Carmen said, "Hey Jaime, you wanna join us tonight?"

Jaime didn't even look at Carmen, opening the fridge, grabbing a cannister of juice, then walked back up to his room. A silence crept into the room like a mist after the door slammed, leaving Carmen to try to pick up the pieces before people noticed her reaction. But Krystal saw the impact across Carmen's face, the disappointment clear as day, vanished right before she picked up her smile and said, "Alright then, let's get started!" Krystal watched Carmen with concern. Feeling a part of her heart sink with empathy.

I'm sorry Carmen. Krystal turned her head and thought about going up to Jaime's room and asking if he was okay, but the fear gripped her, and she decided now was not the time. Krystal turned back, as Carmen said, "Now let's get this Bible study started, let's flip to . . ."

ᔕᔦ

Carmen said, "Alright guys I think that's enough for tonight. Next week we'll cover Jesus talking to the woman at the well, so bring your Bibles this time." The group paid no heed to Carmen's announcement and the chatter dragged on. They did not get through the Bible study. Summer began talking after the first passage and the rest of the group chimed in on the conversation. Soon enough the Bible study had evolved into another hang out session with Krystal sitting on the couch bored and Carmen failing to regain control of the group.

Krystal looked around for something to do when she noticed Carmen picking up empty snacks and bringing them over to the kitchen. Krystal saw the trash lying about and glanced at Carmen, thinking, *"Love your neighbor as yourself."*

The thought rung in her mind as Krystal thought, *If I were Carmen, then I would want somebody to help me with picking up the trash.* So Krystal reached over and picked up the nearest empty bag of chips and began collecting the rest. Krystal gave up on trying to be a part of the group conversation and was now in full cleaning mode.

Krystal walked on over with two arms full of trash and dumped them in Carmen's trash can. Carmen was taken back for a moment. Surprised at the sight of Krystal helping her clean up. Carmen spoke softly, "Thank you, Krystal." Krystal raised her head like a deer in headlights. She wasn't used to having someone call her name except her mom or Aunt Sarah. Krystal felt a bullet of compassion smack her heart, cracking the armor. Carmen saw the crack and gave a soft smile. Krystal wanted to smile but there wasn't enough joy in her heart yet to create a real one. She may have become a Christian recently, but her spiritual high had ended months ago. She was back to her normal, saddened self, but with more purpose in her step. But at least she didn't try to kill herself anymore. She had a will to live at the very least.

An idea struck Krystal while she had Carmen all to herself. Krystal stood there, holding her right elbow with her left hand. The fear and tension was so uncomfortable it made Krystal want to run for her life. But the love of Jesus compelled her to ask, so Krystal opened her mouth and asked, "Hey..." Carmen stopped what she was doing and gave Krystal her full attention, Krystal checked from side to side as if searching for the right words to say. "Could I... if you don't mind..." Krystal glancing away from Carmen's gaze, "Could I maybe have... Jaime's phone number?" Pause. Krystal's heart tensed up so hard she thought it was going to snap in half. It was the most uncomfortable thing she'd ever said.

Krystal looked up, expecting Carmen to take a while to process what she'd just asked. But Carmen responded instantly, "Yeah sure," like it was no big deal.

Krystal's impassive eyes widened a bit. "Okay..." Her heart tightened like an anaconda. Krystal held out her phone and Carmen pulled hers out as well.

Carmen said, "You can have my phone number too, in case you need to contact me."

Krystal froze like a statue. *Not what I intended but I'll take it, nonetheless.*

Carmen finished typing, "That is mine, and this... is Jaime's." Carmen handed Krystal her phone back and let her see Jaime's contact info.

Krystal asked, "Is it... okay for you to... give me your brother's... number without... his permission?"

Carmen shrugged her shoulders and said, "He can take it up with me if he has a problem. I have Older Sibling Rights. He'll be fine. Besides, I don't think it'll cause any harm," Carmen winked at Krystal. Krystal gave no reaction.

Now what is that supposed to mean? Krystal thought.

Carmen grinned, "I'll see ya around Krystal, and thanks for helping clean up," then left the kitchen.

Krystal took that as her cue to leave also, walking to the front door, this time saying "Goodbye" to the whole group, expecting someone to say something back, but no one noticed. Krystal felt the sadness surround her again. She sighed. *They still don't see me.* Krystal closed the door behind her and walked back to her apartment.

Krystal pulled out Jaime's contact info on her phone, the name Jaime Fisher splayed across the center. Without looking up, Krystal thought to herself, *It's the first time I've gotten a guy's phone number... now what?*

Krystal gripped the phone in her hand like a grenade without the pin, pacing around her room like a cat. The cool night air fluttered through the window. Krystal stared at the phone with Jaime's contact info on display. The green messaging icon staring at her. Krystal grunted. *I have mixed feelings about this.* She lowered the phone and continued pacing. *On the one side, I could text him and ask him how he's doing, but then it might look like I like him, which I don't. On the flip side, I don't text him and leave things as they are.* She put her hand to her chin. *Hmmm, it feels more comfortable to choose the latter but . . .* Krystal looked at her phone and laid it face up on her desk. She took a couple steps back and tried to make up her mind. Krystal tensed up, rubbing her head like she was ready to explode. *All I have to do is text him. That's it. How hard could it be?* Krystal reached over and picked up the phone, then put it down immediately. She picked it up again and put it down a second time.

Growing frustrated, Krystal swiped the phone from the desk and tried to force herself to tap into the messaging app, getting all the way to Jaime's contact info, and then put the phone down a third time. She clenched her fists. *This is ridiculous! All I have to do is text him. Seriously how hard could it be?*

Krystal glared at the phone on the desk and felt it mocking her. Just sitting there with its smug face laughing at her. *I seriously can't text the guy?* She lingered over the phone, staring at the blank screen, feeling torn about what to do next. *It feels like all the forces in the world don't want me to text this guy. So why on earth is it so darn uncomfortable?*

Maybe it's because you've never texted a guy before.

Krystal straightened her back and frowned. *Oh, give me a break. This has nothing to do with that.*

Oh really? So why haven't you texted him yet?

Krystal felt her anger flare up. *Don't give me that. You're just as frustrated as I am.*

So text him.

Krystal rolled her hands through her hair. *I can't believe I'm getting mad at myself!* Krystal took one last look at the phone, then gave up and left the room.

"I'm going for a walk."

She never texted him.

CHAPTER 20

Making New Friends

"You want a close friend; be the close friend."

—Carmen Fisher

Jaime sat at the edge of the circle, his back against the building, looking out amongst his friends at lunch. All of them were not talking to each other today, all of their heads were looking down at their phones, minding their own business, eating their food. The conversations today were dry and there wasn't much to go off of. There were times like these where Jaime wondered whether these people were his real friends or not. Did they really connect with each other or are they just a bunch of people who banded together and called each other "friends"? Jaime took his eyes off the group and wondered, feeling the sour look on his face come back. His mind drifting back.

No! Don't think of that! Think of something else. Don't think of—
Too late. *DANG IT! I TOLD YOU NOT TO THINK OF IT!* Jaime finished punishing himself and checked to see if his friends noticed. Not a single one of them noticed his debacle. Jaime sighed and tried to compose himself. He didn't go looking for attention, but it had been so long now that Jaime was beginning to wonder if his friends even cared at all.

Do they even know? Do they even care? They haven't bothered to ask me since it happened. Then again, it was unreasonable to expect other people to know what problem is going on in your head, but Jaime had a justifiable reason for his friends to ask. And only asking them about it would be begging for attention. Jaime didn't want that. He wanted someone who truly and genuinely cared. Someone who noticed when he was having a bad day and asked about it and *listened*. Jaime eased his back against the concrete building, looking around at all the people in school. *They don't get it. They don't understand the kind of pain I'm in because they're all too busy going about their usual lives.* Jaime felt the bitterness grow. He forced himself not to look up. Feeling the idea sprout in his mind.

No! I'm not doing that.

Jaime shifted his gaze back toward his "friends" and shook his head. *You know what? I've had enough.* Jaime got up, took his backpack, and left without a word. Some people called out to him, but he didn't bother to answer. None of them genuinely cared anyway. And so, Jaime walked just wanting to get away. He counted the minutes for when he would be home . . .

Only a few more hours.

⌇

"I need . . . your help." Krystal looked up from the coffee table at Carmen, sitting there all dressed nicely in her fall clothing. Krystal took her eyes off Carmen's nice dresswear, as Carmen welcomed the question.

"What do you need help with?"

Krystal waited a few seconds to gather the words then realized it felt odd to be the one initiating the conversation for once. The two of them met in a coffee shop called Half & Half close to the school. Krystal sighed, "I . . . don't know . . . I've been . . . having trouble . . . fitting in . . . with the group." She shook her head slowly. "It's hard . . . making friends."

Carmen nodded, as if she were agreeing wholeheartedly with what Krystal was saying. Nodding and making the expression, *"I hear ya sister."* Carmen waited for Krystal to finish, but Krystal was done quicker than she realized. Carmen saw the moment was hers and said, "So what do you want advice about?"

"Well . . ." Krystal fought to keep the words in her throat. "How . . . do you be . . . someone's . . . friend?" Krystal leaned back and took a sip from the carmel macchiato Carmen bought for her. "I've been . . . trying . . . real hard to . . . fit in and . . . get along with . . . people. But . . . how do you . . . become someone's friend? Also . . . if you couldn't tell . . . I have difficulty . . . talking to . . . people."

Carmen hummed in agreement. Krystal raised her eyes to Carmen's. Carmen pondered for a long minute, twisting her mouth in thought. "Hmmm . . . that's a tough one."

Krystal felt the need to go on, "And . . . I've been praying . . . and . . . praying . . . for a friend . . . for so long now . . . I . . . I just don't know . . . how to do that."

Carmen thought hard on this, knowing what she said would be important for Krystal in the days to come. Carmen took a sip from her own coffee, enjoying the sweet mint flavor. Carmen spoke solemnly, "Friendships are hard. They are difficult to describe, and they are harder to explain." Carmen shook her head and looked out the glass window. The clatter of pots and spinning machines filled the din of the coffee house. The smell of coffee beans and card transactions filled the background. Carmen tuned all that out and returned her gaze to Krystal. "There are some people whom you connect with really well and some people you can't help but butt heads with. Either way, everyone is different, individually speaking. You have some people who are extremely outgoing and extraverted, while you have other people who are more reserved and introverted. That doesn't make either side bad, they are simply different parts of our individual personalities." Carmen crossed her arms. "You don't need much to start a friendship. Sometimes friendships can occur without having uttered a single word. Sometimes you don't talk with your friends but do stuff with them instead. While in other cases, sometimes all you do is talk when you hang out." Carmen shrugged her shoulders. "There are four levels of friendship," Carmen said, holding up four fingers. "The first is acquaintances. These are people you know of but don't really talk to that much. You might see them around at work or school, or you might be friends with their friends, but you don't have a deep connection with them."

Carmen continued, "The next level is friends. These are people you spend more time with and have a closer relationship with. You might hang out with them a few times and get to know each other more personally than an acquaintance, but that is really as far as it goes." Carmen lifted her third finger, "The third level is close friends. These are people you hang out with often, you are very close to each other, and you intentionally stay in communication with each other." Then Carmen lifted her fourth finger, "The highest level of friendship is core friends. These are the people who are closest to you. They're practically family. You spend a lot of time with them, you know everything about each other, and you can be yourself around them. They are the people who know you better than anyone else, they love you unconditionally, and are always there for you."

Carmen dropped her hand, "You need to have some core friends in your life."

Krystal didn't seem convinced, and looked like she was about to say something, but Carmen finished before she even began. Carmen leaned in closer, as if summarizing her whole speech in one sentence. She spoke solemnly and softly, staring directly at Krystal, no bull, and said, "*You want a close friend; be the close friend.*"

Krystal retorted, "But I have a hard time with that!" Krystal shook her head, "I tense up. I lose the words. My heart feels like I'm tangled in a bunch of ropes and its choking my heart to death. The words . . . they get lodged in my throat. And I can't do it! I just can't do it!"

Krystal expected Carmen to be offended or dumbstruck from her sudden outburst, but she was calm and unfazed like a tree in a storm. The outburst didn't frighten her at all. Carmen tilted her head slightly and said, "Alright then," she raised her index finger, "Whenever you are having a hard time talking to people, remember this verse . . . '*I can do all things through Christ who strengthens me*' (Philippians 4:13). Think about that when you're having difficulty doing something." Carmen leaned over the small table, "You do have a weakness, Krystal. Socializing and talking with others is hard." She leaned in closer, "But just because something is hard, does not mean it is impossible, for nothing is impossible with God." She spoke solemnly, "I wholeheartedly believe you can do this." And that was it. The conversation was over.

Krystal lowered her eyes back down to her lap, thinking over what she had just heard. Carmen's words struck her melting heart and glittered it with refreshing drops of water over her soul. Krystal felt a sense of confidence fostered within her. *Maybe I can do this?* Krystal raised her eyes, taking notice of Carmen's age. How much wiser she was, despite being only twenty-four. The wisdom she imparted to Krystal was just what she needed at this point and age.

For a moment, it felt like Carmen was the older sister Krystal never had. The kind of wisdom a child needed to get through the tough times in life. Krystal whispered, "Thank you. I needed that."

Carmen grinned, "You are very welcome." Carmen shifted and planted her elbow on the table, "Now let's talk . . . why did you want my brother's phone number?"

～

The phone lay faceup on the desk mocking Krystal. Taunting her with its mere presence. Krystal towered above the phone like a jackal ready to pounce on an early dinner. *I've never been so frustrated at my phone before.* After a quick talk with Carmen this afternoon Krystal regained some of her confidence and thought of trying again. She felt her face start to sweat as her hair dangled down in her vision, nearly touching the lifeless phone below her. She felt her heart tighten like a snake coiling around her. *Why is this so hard!* Krystal rocked back and forth debating what to do. She took her eyes off the phone and began pacing around the room again. This time with more intensity. Like a drummer boy marching off to war mindlessly. There was no wind tonight, not even the moon was out. Only the still air and mild hum of Krystal's air conditioning filled the room. Krystal exhaled. *This should not be that hard.* She was getting tired of this debate and wanted to just get this over with.

She walked over and picked the phone up with fury, tapped into Jaime's contact info and began typing,

"Hey are you okay?"

But fear gripped her, and she deleted the sentence. She bobbed her head back and forth, searching for ideas. *What should I say?* The fear gripped her heart again. She put down the phone and threw her fists in frustration. *Come on girl! This shouldn't be so hard! Just ask the guy if he's okay! Wouldn't you want that?*

Yes. Yes, I would. So do it.

Krystal grunted and gritted her teeth. She picked up the phone again, typed the phrase, *"Hey Jaime, It's me . . . are you okay?"*

Krystal deleted that entry. *NO! That's terrible!* Krystal's patience ran out and she put the phone down again. *Why can't I do it? It's like all the forces in the world don't want me to write it.*

That's because they don't. Maybe Satan doesn't want you to write that sentence and check in on Jaime?

Krystal hadn't thought about that before. She had no problem texting her mom before, but this was different. Krystal was going out of her way to check in on someone who was still a total stranger. So it was weird. *Huh. I hadn't thought about it like that.*

So, are you going to do it?

Krystal answered, *No. Not tonight. I'll do it another night.* She gave herself that same excuse the last time, and the night before.

Krystal put the phone down and covered herself with the cushions of her bed. The thought still ate at her.

So, when are you going to do it?

She answered, *Tomorrow. I'll do it tomorrow.*

Liar.

ॐ

Her mind snapped wide awake after sleeping for a couple hours. It was late in the night, too late for anyone to be up. But the thought was still eating at her. *When are you going to do it?* She didn't want to feel judgment from herself, but she did. She was both guilty and innocent, knowing that she was deliberately procrastinating but also was having legit difficulty. Krystal opened her eyes and threw her sheets off. She grunted and sat on the edge of her bed in her nightgown. This time, being honest with herself.

"I can't do it. I just can't."

I know. That's because you've been doing it on your own . . . This is not something you can do on your own. Remember, "I can do all things through Christ who strengthens me."

Krystal suddenly felt her mind clear, like the storm had finally calmed. Her eyes turned to the phone on her desk, she reached over and checked the time. 3:23am.

It's not a good time.

There's never a perfect time. Krystal hesitated as she pulled out the messaging app and typed in Jaime's contact info. The fear gripped her again and she wanted to put the phone down and go back to bed, but she remembered,

"I can do all things through Christ who strengthens me."

She reiterated those words in her mind, then looked up to the midnight sky and prayed, *God . . . I can't do this on my own. Will you please help me, like you did with my depression and sorrow? Please help me to reach out to Jaime. Please.*

Immediately Krystal felt peace rush over her shoulders and into her heart. She let out a relaxing breath, feeling every fiber of her body relax.

Realizing the fear was gone. Krystal looked at the phone and began typing with little resistance.

⌇

He heard the knock on his bedroom door. The muffled sound of his mom's voice, "Jaime, dinner's ready." Jaime didn't answer. He sat on the edge of his bed staring at the floor. The past coming back to haunt him once more. He felt his breathing intensify and tried to calm down. Jaime steadied himself and brought his attention back to the knocking on the door. "Jaime? Dinner's ready." His mom's voice softer this time. Jaime knew he had to go down at some point, but he shook his head, *I don't want to talk to them.* He felt repulsed by his family. He didn't want to feel that way, but he did. He loved them, but he also wanted to stay away from them. He heard his mom's footsteps fade away as she walked downstairs. Jaime waited a bit, knowing they would all be down there, expecting him to be there. One of their family attempts to get him back at the dinner table.

He lowered his head. *I can't be around them right now. Even if they are my family.* Jaime waited a couple more minutes and sighed. *It's time to go down.* He turned his heart to stone and clamped his mouth shut. He opened the door and stepped downstairs to find his whole family waiting for him, his dad at the head of the table, mom at the end, Carmen in the middle, and an empty chair across from her.

Knowing all eyes were on him, the whole room lay quiet. Neither of the parents said anything as Jaime picked up his plate of food and walked past them. He went outside to the backyard patio and closed the door behind him, trying to ignore their looks of concern. His heart tensed and began to crack. *I'm sorry . . . I can't.* He headed toward the back gate where an entrance to the community center lay. Jaime brushed past the entrance and walked over toward his usual destination. The firepit. He pulled forward a plastic chair, ignited the fire, and tried to relax with little success.

He eased himself into the seat, putting his plate aside, letting his gaze settle on the dancing flames. His eyes stared, unblinking, at the fire, a mixture of red orange and yellow, creating straight pillars until they merged into a blazing triangle. There was no wood, the pit was purely gas. But the sight brought a natural beauty even artists have a challenge achieving. Jaime sat there staring at the flames in complete silence, letting his thoughts drift, staring into nothing. It was the only time he felt he could relax.

One thought broke through his mind: *I wish I could go back.*

But he knew there was no going back, so he continued to stare into oblivion, holding back his demons until it was late in the night.

Hours went by and Jaime still hadn't moved. He hadn't eaten his dinner and it was long past his bedtime. Jaime checked his phone for the time, 3:23am, he sighed. "Another night with no sleep." Feeling the burden on his heart grow. He exhaled, "I should get to bed," stretching his stiff muscles and went back inside. Jaime entered the empty house, the darkness providing a new shade to the kitchen. The surrounding lack of activity mirrored the sadness within his own heart. *It used to be so much happier here . . .* He felt the tears surge, but he suppressed them. *Not here. Not now.* Jaime put his plate away then headed upstairs, knew his family was listening, but he didn't care.

Jaime reached the safety of his door and closed it gently behind him. He exhaled and lowered his defenses. Feeling the weight fall off his shoulders like shedding armor. Jaime walked over in the dark and fell on his bed. Leaving his phone on his desk next to him. Jaime lay in bed, staring at the ceiling, then shifted his attention to the sky out his window. Looking at the sky reminded him of all the times he used to look up. Of all the conversations he used to have. Jaime looked away. He didn't want to think about that right now. He just wanted to go to bed and call it a day. Tomorrow was going to suck anyway, going on about the day without sleep. Jaime closed his eyes in frustration and felt his body begin to drift. Then he heard a vibration on his desk.

Jaime opened his eyes and looked at his phone. He read a text from an unknown number, *"Hey . . . are you okay?"*

Jaime was suspicious, but in truth, he was relieved. The text sent a feeling of relief over his heart, melting away the bitterness. It had been a while since he'd felt this. He felt his heart melt and replied,

"No . . . I'm not."

"What's going on?" the number asked.

Jaime held the phone up and was surprised by this sudden act of caring. He didn't want to let himself get sucked in by whoever this was that was texting him, but he couldn't help but want to answer truthfully.

He thought about his reply, then his defenses kicked in. He texted, "Hang on, who is this?"

. . .

Jaime waited for the person to respond, "My name is Krystal. Krystal Henninger."

Jaime lowered his brow and cocked his head back in confusion. *Who the heck is Krystal Henninger?* He wrote back, "I've never met a Krystal Henninger." Send.

The person wrote back, "We've met. You just don't remember."

Jaime put his hand to his chin, *This is an odd conversation to have at three in the morning.* "What do you look like?"

"A regular girl."

Jaime wrote, "Don't lie to me."

"I don't lie." Jaime found that suspicious. He racked his memory but couldn't think of any girl that came to mind named Krystal. He doubted that was her real name. He typed, "How come I've never seen you?"

He waited, watching the gray text bubbles flicker as the person typed, "You have, but people don't tend to see me." That text made Jaime feel both bemused and suspicious. She wrote, "I'm sorry if I sound creepy, but that's the way things are. You don't really know me. You don't have a reason to know me. I'm not exactly a popular person at school..."

Jaime coiled back slightly. *That was a little ... admissive.*

He texted, "How will I find you?"

The text came back quicker than he'd expected, "Look for the girl dressed in all black sitting on the white bench during lunch."

Jaime closed his eyes and craned his head back, moaned, "Ohhh boy... this chick's a creep."

He texted back, "I look forward to seeing you then."

She texted back, "Uhh, okay ..." and that was that. The conversation ended and Jaime clicked his phone off and closed his eyes.

"Definitely one of the weirder conversations I've had," he said aloud. But as he closed his eyes, he remembered the initial relief from the text. How nice it made him feel that someone was reaching out. *It was touching though.*

Jaime leaned against the wall next to the lunch line, searching out among the courtyard for "the girl dressed in all black sitting on the white bench." He wasn't sitting with his normal group of friends, this time he was on the hunt. He couldn't help but feel a powerful sense of expectation. He wanted to find out who his mysterious texter was. The excitement boiled the lack of sleep away, but it was fueled by skepticism and suspicion. It was a little weird to get a text from somebody who claims to know you, but you don't know them. Either way, if it turned into a fight, he wouldn't be against that.

Jaime's eyes scanned the courtyard looking from left to right. He couldn't see anybody sitting on a white bench, so he began walking around, searching corners and friend groups he normally never paid attention to. Jaime looked from one clique to another but didn't seem to find a girl dressed in black sitting on a white bench. Jaime gave up and reached for his phone.

He texted, "Are you here?"

The reply was instant. "Yes."

Jaime frowned and wrote back, "Where are you?"

"Look to your right." Jaime lifted his head and looked right but couldn't find anyone sitting on a white bench. She texted back, "Can you see me?"

Jaime finished his scan and wrote, "No. I can't."

He was busy writing another text when she replied, "That doesn't surprise me."

Jaime held the phone in bemused suspicion. He started checking corners now, the paranoia beginning to settle on him. *Whoever this chick is, she has got some issues trying to stalk me.*

Jaime was about to send a forceful text when the girl wrote, "I'm waving."

Jaime's head snapped to attention and began looking for someone waving, but he was having some difficulty. Finally, his eyes scrolled past a white bench next to the teacher's lounge and saw a girl dressed in all black, waving timidly at him. It was such a weak wave that Jaime almost didn't register it as "waving." The girl was looking straight at him. Jaime felt his body pause as he saw her.

"Can you see me?" she wrote.

Jaime replied "Yes" and started walking over. His eyes locked on the girl in black, all the suspicion and doubt concentrated within his eyes, shooting daggers her way as he walked. The girl seemed unfazed by the hard stare. She looked even more deadpan than he was. Her face expressing a kind of innocent passivity, while apathetic to what other people thought of her. Jaime approached the girl as she sat on her white bench. Her impassive expression changed to slight surprise. Jaime wasn't sure what she was so "surprised" about, but either way he knew he'd found his target. He towered over her as her surprise faded. He held out his phone, "Are you the one who has been texting me?"

The girl nodded slightly.

Jaime frowned and spoke frankly, "How did you get my number?"

The girl took a moment to answer, "Carmen."

Jaime felt a fury build inside his chest. "What gave her the right to give you my phone number?" His voice was controlled but darkened with anger.

The girl, unfazed by Jaime's intimidation, said simply, "Older Sibling Rights."

Jaime felt his heart blaze in anger. "If Carmen put you up to this, I'm going to have a serious talk with her later."

"She . . ." the girl faltered her words, "She didn't . . . put me . . . up to this." She took her eyes away from him. That sudden lack of quality communication threw Jaime off. He watched the girl's body language and could tell she was embarrassed.

He got right to the point. "So why are you texting me? If Carmen didn't put you up to this, then who did?"

Jaime watched as the girl's eyes searched for an answer, "I—"

Jaime's patience ran out. He cut her off and shouted, "Know what? I DON'T CARE!" The anger contained in the lake of fire within him came rushing to the surface, "Don't butt into my life!" Jaime's figure towered over the girl, his shadow encompassing her. But the girl wasn't fazed in the slightest like his anger went right over her.

Jaime nearly started again, when the girl responded plainly, like he'd never even yelled at her, "I just . . . wanted to check if you were . . . okay." Jaime paused. Her response left him at a loss for words. He deflated, feeling the anger quickly vent from his system. He suddenly felt like the world's biggest idiot for raging at some girl he'd just met. He wanted to apologize the moment those words left his mouth. A feeling he experienced often after his verbal tirades.

The two of them watched each other for a few seconds, Jaime observing the girl's expression, making him feel more guilty at the sight. *That face . . . that expression . . . I don't see any malice in her eyes.* Jaime stared at her, observing her body language and facial expressions. The girl just looked at him with a saddened stare. One that said, *"I'm used to pain."*

Jaime thought, *I don't know why, but I feel like I know that look on her face. The eyes, her expression, all of it.* It only added to his growing sense of guilt weighing upon his weary heart. Jaime let out a sigh. *Shoot. I messed up.* He contemplated his next move; *I need to go apologize to her.*

Jaime opened his mouth, "I—"

But the girl got through first, "I'm sorry for bothering you," as she got up and vanished behind a corner. Jaime felt a sense of puzzlement rack his heart and mind. He didn't know what to say. The only thought playing on his mind was, *I'm sorry. I'm sorry.*

⌒

"God, I'm trying!" Krystal lifted her eyes to the sky, calling out to the Lord. "God I'm trying . . ." she broke down in tears. She lay on her knees, in her room, staring into the night sky with tears draping over her eyes. *What am I doing wrong? Why can't I do anything right? I can't even be nice to people without bothering them. What do I do? What do I do?!* But Krystal received no answer that night. Which was fine. She didn't expect one anyway. She put her hands together again and prayed, "God please give me a friend. Please give me a friend. I need a friend, just one, only one."

⌒

Jaime came home, wanting to lower his guard but he knew this, of all places, was where his guard was up the most. He closed the garage door behind him and entered the house. To his lack of surprise Carmen stood there with her arms crossed, shooting him daggers with cold blue eyes. "I heard you yelled at Krystal today," she said with cold anger.

For once, he answered his sister, "How'd you hear about that?" he said unenthusiastically.

"It got brought up in a conversation I had today with Krystal."

Jaime said, "Did she rat on me?" He wouldn't be surprised. If it were him, he would rat on someone if they yelled at him.

Carmen shook her head, arms crossed. "No, in fact she was reluctant to talk about it. She only told me because I slowly pried it out of her. And she was exceedingly kind when speaking about you. You should count yourself lucky you have such a friend."

Jaime was done with this conversation. He wasn't going to have this. Not now. In his annoyance he muttered something he shouldn't have. "Whatever." That sent Carmen soaring with anger.

"What is wrong with you!" Carmen yelled, emphasizing each word. The words echoing through the house. Carmen stood there glaring deeply at her younger brother, while Jaime stood there, ignoring Carmen's gaze, trying to get out of this reprimand, but Carmen wasn't going to let him off so easily. "You go out of your way to ignore your own family, you slam the door as you leave, and to top it off, you walk up to a girl and yell in her face!" Carmen planted her hands on her hips. Jaime was lucky Mom and Dad were out, but when they got home, they were going to have a serious chat.

Without answering, Jaime turned and started to walk toward the stairs. Carmen called after him, "NO NO NO! You don't walk away from this!"

Jaime stopped and yelled back, "I don't need to deal with this right now!"

Carmen pointed at Jaime, "You cannot dismiss the fact that you've been completely rude to everyone these last few years and for no reason!" Carmen cut Jaime off before he could make it to the stairwell. "You can ignore your own family! You can treat us like we are all dirt if you want!" Carmen pointed toward Krystal's house. "But you do NOT! Treat other people like that!" Jaime tried to weave around her, but Carmen was on her guard. "You're letting what happened spill out onto other people! And you DO NOT LET THAT SPILL OUT ON *HER*! DO YOU HEAR ME!"

Jaime said apathetically, "I'm done with this." This time he headed towards the front door.

Carmen let him walk out before following him, this time calling out in a more controlled voice, "That girl has no family." Jaime stopped in his tracks, listening to Carmen with his back turned to her. She knew her words were sinking deep. "She never had a *good dad* in her life. She never had the luxury of a loving mom always at home. She never had the benefit of siblings." Carmen braced herself for the kicker, "Or the love of an older brother."

Jaime turned, all the rage in his heart came raging out. He pointed a stern finger at Carmen, "You keep *her* out of this! This has nothing to do with that!" He lowered his finger, knowing his point had been made. (No pun intended.)

Carmen called back, "It has everything to do with it! Just look at you! You don't talk to your own family anymore! You don't even talk to your friends! And you're angry all the time! This hatred that you're harboring is ruining you." Carmen's voice gradually grew calmer with every passing second. "Look what it's doing right now," her voice now completely cooled off. "How it's tearing us apart." Carmen lowered her arms, allowing Jaime to hear the weakness in her voice. "And Jaime . . . You're not the only one suffering." Her voice was now drowned with tears. "And I want my brother back . . . I don't want to lose you too."

Jaime felt her words touch his hardened heart, but he staved off the tears and couldn't look Carmen in the eye. Holding himself together, trying to be the man he should. *Don't cry! Men don't cry!* Maintaining that bravado like it was the only thing he had left.

Then without looking, he walked off into the darkness. Hearing only the sound of whimpering and sorrow coming from the doorway of his own home. From the pain he'd inflicted, knowing that he couldn't take that back. It was done, and now he'd regret it.

❧

Once Jaime returned home later that night, he went straight up to his room and closed the door. He breathed and tried to relax, but it didn't last for long. He heard a knock against his door. He ignored it for a moment then heard, "It's Dad."

Jaime knew when to respect authority and when not to, so he opened the door partially. He saw his dad's massive frame in the slight crack of the open doorway and had to look up to meet his dad's piercing brown eyes. For a moment both of them said nothing, then Jaime's dad said, "I heard you yelled at Krystal today." His tone was not stern. At least not yet.

To his reluctance, Jaime nodded, letting his dad see his shame. Then his dad spoke in a stern tone, one that sparked tremendous fear inside Jaime. "The next time you yell at her, there will be consequences." Jaime almost went white. But for some reason, he wasn't as intimidated as he thought he should be.

So all he could say was, "Okay."

His dad cooled his voice and was back to his gracious self. "That's it. So good night."

"Good night."

❧

Jaime put his hand against his face, smushing his cheeks and lips. "Why is this so hard," he mumbled. His eyes searching boringly out among the crowds

187

of people flocking through the school courtyard. His eyes shifted from person to person in monotony as he tried to identify the girl. *I know her name is Krystal but come on, how hard could it be to find someone at this school?* The sight before him proved him wrong. The look of two thousand people roaming about the school created more disbelief in Jaime's heart. *Uggghh this is a pain.* He looked everywhere but couldn't find her. "Well, she isn't out here," Jaime said. Lowering his hand, readjusting his backpack. He started heading to his first class as the bell rang and all the high schoolers started scrambling to get to their first class of the day. Jaime sighed. "I wouldn't be searching for this girl if the guilt on my heart wasn't so strong," Jaime grunted and made it in time to his first class.

He entered the class and took a seat. His brain was already fried, and he wanted nothing more than to go home and get away from everything. Jaime placed his hand on his cheek, groaning from having to look for that girl. *Uggghh this is such a pain. I just want to get this over with.*

His eyes glanced lazily to his left then shot wide open as if he couldn't believe it. *No . . . freaking . . . way.* The girl sat across the room from him three rows down and yet Jaime never noticed her before. Never had a reason to, until now. *She's in my first period class?* Jaime still couldn't take his eyes off the surprise that this girl was in the same class. *How long has she been there?* The question left his heart unsatisfied, yearning for an answer.

A thought dropped in his mind, *You can apologize to her now, if you want.*

Jaime considered it, then backed off. *No. I'll do it later. It'll look weird if I just walked up to a girl I have never talked to before and apologized to her in the middle of the class.*

The voice answered back, *Class hasn't started yet.* The voice was gentle and calm. It wasn't malicious whatsoever.

Jaime thought about it, his body tensing from the discomfort and replied, *Uggghhhh not right now.* He settled the matter and leaned further over his desk. *I'll do it later.*

But the weight of guilt on his heart only began to grow. Weighing heavier and heavier with each passing moment. *Crap,* he thought. *This is only going to get worse. I'm gonna need to pull off the band aid at some point.* But his own comfort got in the way, and for the next two hours, he felt his heart grow heavier as he failed to apologize to her.

Jaime sat in his usual lunch spot, ready to go apologize to Krystal. He started shaking his feet out of nervous habit (you know, the habit of when people sit in their desk and start shaking their leg, that sort of thing). He groaned. *Mmmmphhh all I have to do, is walk over there, say I'm sorry and then walk back. Simple as that.* He felt the pressure against his heart grow, this time from another source. He could feel the atmosphere of the scene, walking away from his friends and going up to a complete stranger and saying he's sorry would look weird and cause people to notice. He started tapping his fingers fervently. *Uggghhhh if I don't do it now, then I won't get around to it. But if I do it now, then it'll look weird.* He groaned, feeling his heart stricken as he looked out across the courtyard at Krystal sitting by herself.

Doesn't she have somewhere to be? But the girl remained where she was and continued eating her lunch. This was the second time Jaime had seen her on that white bench. A bench he had never cared to think about before. He never bothered looking over in that direction because nothing happened over there. Now here he was, just sitting there, debating what to do while the guilt was eating away at him like maggots. He groaned for a final time, this time murmuring through his clenched mouth, "Mmmmm, I'll do it later, when the time is right." And so, the school day ended, and Jaime still hadn't apologized to her.

Carmen asked. He knew she would ask. Carmen sat there at the table, sipping on a fruit drink leftover in the fridge while Jaime walked down from his room to get a quick drink. The setting begged for a conversation, and with a conversation came the question Jaime knew she was going to ask. "So have you apologized yet?" Jaime pulled out a can of pineapple juice and poured himself a glass.

He took a sip. "Not yet. I couldn't get around to it." He knew it was a poor excuse, but Carmen allowed it. "I was going to text her and apologize that way."

Carmen shook her head slowly, speaking with gentle authority, "Don't apologize over the phone for this. You do it face to face." She went into the fridge and pulled out a plastic container of cookies their mom had made. "You take these cookies. You go to her door and give them to her. She lives down the street from us, and you apologize to her face to face. Alright?"

Jaime became defensive and was going to retort but Carmen held the container of cookies patiently in front of him. Jaime saw the cookies and knew Carmen was only trying to help. There would be no argument over this. Jaime scoffed. *Older Sibling Rights . . . great.* He took the cookies and said, "So where does she live?"

It took Jaime well over ten minutes to find this place, even though it only said eight minutes on his phone. The darkness of the winter season was already taking effect with daylight savings. Even though it wasn't 6pm, it was already dark out like 9pm. Jaime clutched the box of cookies, bobbing his head back and forth, thinking of what he was going to say. He knew he had to get this done before dinner, otherwise Carmen was going to ask him about it again and he would have to tell his family that he had procrastinated and hadn't apologized to her yet. He shook his head. "Nope. I'm not going through that discomfort."

So you're going to go through this discomfort instead?

Jaime said, "You know what. I've got to get this done anyway, otherwise this guilt will still be on my chest. So yeah, I'm going to do this. Plus, Carmen won't let me back in the house until it's done."

Jaime thought, *It's not like you want to go back and have dinner with them anyway.*

Jaime sighed; *I know. I don't want to have dinner with them.* He shook his head and focused on the task at hand. *Let's get this over with.*

Jaime checked the address on his phone and walked up the stairs, trying to find the right number. There was no car parked outside and the rest of the apartment complex seemed quiet for the night. Jaime stood before the door, confirming the number on the door. "Yup, this is the place." He put his phone away and held the cookies in hand. He reached over, knocked on the door and waited. The door opened and his nostrils were suddenly flooded with the scent of spices and delicious food. *Holy crap! That smells good!* His mouth began to salivate as he brought his attention to the girl standing in the doorway, wearing an apron with her black hair tied back in a ponytail. He expected the girl to be surprised but she wasn't, although Jaime could tell she didn't expect him to show up at her door either. She just gave him that blank stare she had mastered so well.

Jaime waited for the girl to say something, but she fell silent. Jaime could feel the ball landing in his court. *Dang it, why does everybody expect me to talk first?* He opened his mouth and said, "Hey . . . ummm. I'm sorry, you know, for yelling at you, the other day."

The girl nodded and lowered her eyes to her feet, half-whispering, "It's okay." Jaime expected it to end there, until she spoke up, "I'm sorry . . . for causing you . . . trouble." Jaime felt confused.

Why is she sorry?

Jaime tried to reassure her, "It's okay. Don't worry about it. It's really no big deal." He held out the container of cookies, "Here, my family made some cookies for you."

Krystal took the batch of cookies and looked confused. Jaime couldn't tell what was going on in her head. Her face was so passive it was completely unreadable. It was like she was wearing a mask without a mask. She raised her head and said, "Thank you," then glanced at the kitchen and then back at him. She paused for a moment and said, "You are welcome . . ." she shut her mouth, struggling to get the words out, "to stay . . . for dinner . . . if you want."

Now that was something I was not expecting. Jaime stood there like he had been hit by an imaginary bullet. *Is she really inviting me to dinner? Doesn't that seem like a date?* Jaime thought about it. *But then . . . if I have dinner here, then I can skip dinner with my own family.* The wheels started turning. He nodded to himself. *Yeah, that could work.* So he turned to the girl and said, "Alright sure, I'll stay for dinner." Jaime looked at the girl and saw her staring blankly back at him. Jaime was starting to feel uncomfortable. *Is she gonna say anything or is she gonna just stand there?*

Krystal's mouth opened halfway and said, "Okay," with a hint of surprise in her own voice.

Jaime said, "Cool," expecting something to happen. Krystal opened the door for him and let him inside. Jaime stepped into the apartment, taking in the sight of the bland white walls and the small living room, with a tan couch, a glass coffee table, and a tv. To the right was a dinner table and the kitchen where Krystal was busy cooking some food. Jaime stood there for a second, taking in the imagery of the apartment. It was small for a family, but for one to two people it was enough room. Jaime expected some younger siblings to come rushing out of one of the rooms or a parent to greet him, but no one came. The rest of the apartment was completely empty. Jaime checked around and saw there were two bedrooms, a kitchen, a bathroom, and a living room. The basics, but they got the job done. He looked around at the walls and grunted. *There aren't that many family pictures around here.* He stopped and tried to get a "feel" for the room. His heart could sense the mood of the apartment. *It feels so . . . lifeless.*

Krystal gestured toward the kitchen table, "You can take a seat . . . I'm almost done." Jaime followed the gesture and pulled a wooden chair from the table. The table itself could fit about four people. *Not very roomy either.* Jaime took the time to notice the wear of the table and the light shading of the wood. He noticed the thin frames of the legs and how off balance the table was. *Definitely need to be careful with sudden movements on this thing.* He glanced up at Krystal while she was busy making dinner.

"Your parents coming home soon?" Jaime asked.

Krystal stopped cold and stared at him. Her blank expression shifted a little. So miniscule that Jaime almost didn't notice it. Her blank stare and casual frown heightened.

"They're not around," she replied, frankly.

"What do you mean?"

She looked at him and answered simply, "They're not here anymore." She lowered her gaze back to her food but didn't continue working. Jaime instantly regretted the question.

Oh shoot, that's right! He put his hand to his face. *I should have remembered that she lost her parents from when she came over to our house. I completely forgot.* He felt like an idiot forgetting such an important detail.

Jaime replied with the only response he had, "I'm sorry."

The girl bucked up a bit and said, "It's okay," then resumed working. She brought Jaime a plate full of lasagna, mixed vegetables, and a glass of water.

Jaime grabbed one of the forks she laid out for him and said, "Thank you." He took a bite out of the lasagna and instantly his pupils dilated, and eyes flew open. He felt a presence wash over his body as the flavor enlightened him. Jaime swallowed. "Wow . . ." It was the best thing he'd ever tasted. Jaime glanced up at Krystal in awe, "You're an amazing cook!"

Krystal was stunned, like a computer trying to contemplate a foreign message. Krystal looked down at her cooking, not expecting a compliment like that. The words pinged off her soul like a ripple in a pond as Krystal said in embarrassment, "Thank you."

Jaime felt a twinge in his heart as she said that. He looked away for a second then back at her. Jaime was conscious not to stare for too long, but the smell of food brought his attention back to his plate and he began devouring his food again.

Krystal came over with her own plate, noticed Jaime's empty plate, and asked, "Want more?"

Jaime nodded his head eagerly, "Yeah."

Krystal swapped plates with him, handing him her own plate full of food. "You can have mine." Jaime was a bit surprised. He wanted to object, but Krystal was already heading back toward the kitchen. Jaime took the second plate and began his work. Even the vegetables were delicious, and he didn't even like to eat vegetables. He swallowed. *This is the most delicious food I've ever tasted.* He tried recounting all the restaurants he'd been to with his family or all the home cooked meals by his mom, which were in a league of their own, but here . . . this was something else. This girl . . . has a gift. *Oh dang, I want more.*

Krystal finished making another plate and sat down while Jaime was halfway done with his second plate. He looked up, his head hanging directly over his plate of food. He looked at Krystal and saw she looked tense. Like she was holding something in. Jaime looked at her a bit confused. "What?" he asked. Krystal relaxed and pointed to his face. Jaime touched his face and noticed red sauce on his cheek. He groaned and wiped his face with a napkin. If Krystal had laughed, then she kept it to herself.

Jaime finished wiping his face and asked, "How long did you know that was there?"

Krystal answered, "Long enough."

Jaime sighed and continued eating, checking every bite to see if there was food on his face.

Jaime pointed his knife around, asking with a mouth half-full, "So who takes care of you since your parents aren't here?"

Krystal took her first bite of food and swallowed, "My . . . Aunt Sarah. She works late nights . . . at the hospital."

Jaime paused, then swallowed, "You know, you don't talk much, do you?" Krystal stayed silent for a minute.

She looked down at the table, and whispered, "Sorry."

Jaime was a little puzzled. "There's nothing wrong with that."

Krystal's head lifted. Her purple eyes showing a hint of light. "So it's . . . okay?"

"Yeah." Jaime nodded. He didn't quite understand how much she needed to hear that. Krystal felt some appreciation for Jaime now. Whether it was him enjoying the food or the compliment. Either way she was beginning to see this boy in a new light. Meanwhile, Jaime had no idea what kind of effect he was having on a girl whose expression was unreadable.

They finished dinner and Krystal said, "Thank you . . . for the cookies."

Jaime replied, "You're welcome," then glanced at the clock on the microwave. "I think it's time for me to go." Krystal nodded.

Jaime cleaned out his plate in the kitchen and opened the front door. Before he could turn around and leave, Krystal said, "You're welcome . . . to come back anytime." Jaime considered that.

He said, "Sure."

Maybe I will, he thought, then went out the door. Leaving Krystal to her own devices.

Carmen sat there, waiting for him. Swaying the chair she had stolen from their dad's office, spinning around like a villain in expectation with her fingers perched together. "So . . . how did it go?"

Jaime closed the front door. "Were you waiting for me the whole time?" Carmen grinned and nodded profusely. Jaime wasn't in the mood for this. He walked past Carmen.

"Did you give her the cookies?" she asked.

Jaime called out, "Yeah."

But before he could get to the stairs Carmen said, "Hey . . . I'm sorry for yelling at you." Jaime stopped. Held his back to her. He said nothing but was willing to hear her out. Carmen's tone was soft and genuine as she looked at him. "I shouldn't have gotten that angry." She paused, "But I am glad you apologized to Krystal. That was a good thing you did." Jaime almost looked at his sister. He could tell in her tone she was being genuine. He wanted to look her way, to go over and hug her. He felt his body turn slightly, but he stopped himself. He thought for a moment, but he steered himself forward, vanishing up the stairwell.

CHAPTER 21

Growing Closer

"As iron sharpens iron, so a friend sharpens a friend."

—Proverbs 27:17 (NLT), King Solomon

Jaime stared out into the courtyard, sitting in his normal spot with his buddies. He couldn't look at his friends. None of them bothered to notice what was going on in his life. Jaime was starting to deteriorate, and he knew it. He was becoming less and less of himself every day. What frustrated him the most was that his friends didn't bother to ask him what was wrong. They all just smiled and assumed everything was normal. It's not like Jaime was trying to get attention. He was just surprised that not one of his friends has asked if he was okay when he was clearly not okay.

Jaime looked away. *Do they really care? I mean really. If we're good friends, wouldn't they reach out and ask me if I'm okay?* But Jaime hasn't received that question yet. No matter how he felt. It's not like he masks his emotions. Jaime raised his head and searched the courtyard for Krystal. *Why is it always so hard to find this girl? You know, it's not like she moves places every day.* Jaime searched, and to his luck found her sitting on her white bench. Yet something was different today. Jaime felt something different other than the common bitterness and anger he resented and held so dear.

No! I don't want to think of You! Jaime shook the thought off and refocused. Jaime watched as Krystal casually ate her lunch, then thought of last night. The dinner she'd made for him was so delicious. Then the question started burning within his chest. *Who is she?* He knew her name, but he still felt like he didn't know her.

Jaime patted his best friend Luiz on the shoulder. "Hey man."

Luiz looked his way, "Yo what's up?

Jaime nudged his head in Krystal's direction, "Hey. Have you ever seen that girl before?"

Luiz followed his gaze, "What girl?"

Jaime pointed, "The one sitting on the white bench over there."

Luiz peered hard for a moment then gave up, "I have no idea who you are talking about man."

"Are you serious? She's right over there, right in broad daylight. You can't see her? She's wearing all black." Jaime pointed harder, as if that would somehow help Luiz find her. Luiz looked harder, now squinting. Jaime found Krystal and pointed, "Right there."

"Are you talking about that girl?" Luiz had found his target.

Jaime nodded, "Yes! That's who I'm talking about."

Luiz leaned back, "Okay, what about her?"

"Do you know anything about her or have seen her before?"

Luiz looked embarrassed and answered, "Honestly man, I've never seen that girl before in my life."

That struck Jaime as odd. "Are you kidding me dude? She's in our first period class."

"What, really?" Luiz leaned his head forward, surprised. "I've never seen her before."

Jaime asked, "Why haven't you seen her before?"

Luiz shook his head, "I guess I've never paid attention to her." Jaime looked out, finding that curious. Luiz saw Jaime thinking. "Why the sudden interest in this girl?"

"I don't know, she just strikes me as peculiar."

Luiz rubbed his finger under his chin. "I don't know what's going on in your head man but that's strange to take an interest in a girl who's a nobody."

Jaime turned to face Luiz; he was slightly annoyed by what Luiz had said. "Are you implying something?"

Luiz didn't fall for it. He knew it was an intimidation tactic. "No. I'm only saying it's random that you're taking an interest in this girl all of a sudden."

Jaime let the conversation die, but one thought was starting to bug him. Why *was* he suddenly taking an interest in this random girl? A girl whom he'd never cared of or thought of before. So why now? His face turned to stone. *This girl . . . she's different. And I can't seem to put my finger on it.* That frustrated Jaime. What was her endgame? What was she trying to achieve by inviting him over last night? It irked him, and he wanted to know more. But how?

❧

Jaime walked through the garage door and hung the keys up on the key rack. He stormed through the doorway and immediately headed upstairs. His mom poked her head around the corner and asked, "How was your day, Jaime?" Jaime caught the tail end of the question and answered, "Fine" then closed his bedroom door behind him.

Jaime didn't even want to bother thinking about his homework today. In fact, he didn't want to leave his room at all because he knew his family was downstairs. He immediately wanted to get away from this house, wanted to go anywhere but here. Jaime lay on his bed, letting the cushions envelop him. He turned faceup and lay there for a minute. *Another tough day. Geeze. Why do I even bother going to school or coming home?* A few minutes later Jaime heard his phone go off. He picked up the phone and saw it was a text from Krystal. He opened it and read,

"Hey are you okay? You looked down today."

Jaime looked at the text. He felt that same sense of relief the last time Krystal texted him. To know there was someone out there who cared enough to write him a message. Normally Jaime wouldn't indulge in this kind of thing, but for once he decided to try something different. He texted back. "No, I'm not." Send.

The bubbles lit up. "What's wrong?"

Jaime held the phone. Contemplating what he was going to say. He felt the urge to open up and tell her everything. He didn't know why, he just did. Wanting that black lake of emotion to come rushing out, he held it back. He decided to go with a more general answer. He wrote, "Personal stuff."

Good answer, he thought. *It keeps it vague yet doesn't divulge too much information.*

"Do you wanna talk about it?"

Jaime saw the text and felt both angered and relieved. He did want to talk about it. But if he did, it would drudge up old emotions he was trying to ignore.

He replied, "No . . . not right now." Send.

The text came back. "Okay. If you ever need someone to talk to, I'm here." Jaime stared at his phone. He wanted to be mad, but he was too mesmerized by the message. He felt enormous relief flush over him, a feeling he was not expecting. His stone heart felt watered a bit from this invitation.

He texted back, "I appreciate that."

She wrote back, "No problem."

Jaime held the phone there, a little happy staring at the message. It was from a girl he didn't really know and yet she was reaching out to him to check if he was okay. An act that even his friends haven't done. He immediately felt a growing sense of respect for Krystal.

"She's caring," he said. It made him wonder why she was caring. He put the phone down. "But it is nice . . . to know someone out there cares for you."

〜

Krystal helped Carmen set the table while Carmen finished dicing up the rest of the vegetables for dinner. Krystal didn't have to help out, but she wanted to. It was nice to be outside the house and in the company of people she liked. At least, the Fishers that is. They were a good family, and Krystal enjoyed spending time at their home.

The garage door sounded, and the door slammed. Krystal and Carmen looked over to see Jaime walk past them and head straight up stairs.

Krystal looked at Carmen, could tell what she was thinking. She noticed Carmen's eyes. Her blue eyes were black underneath them and tired. Krystal knew those eyes. Eyes that showed someone who had been crying the night before. Krystal wanted to go over and hug her, but she held off. She didn't want to get in the way of Carmen when she was holding a big knife in her hands. Krystal had already had a bad enough experience with her own kitchen knife. (Imagine making dinner with the same weapon that tried to kill you.)

Krystal read Carmen's face, could tell what was going on but didn't have all the details. Her curiosity was eating at her. There was clearly some family drama going on that she didn't know about. But she also had questions. Real questions she wanted to ask.

They were alone. Carmen's parents wouldn't be home for another half hour so they had to house to themselves, except for Jaime being upstairs, but he wouldn't come down. Krystal roused up the courage, building up the words in her throat. "May I . . . ask a question?"

Carmen met her gaze, this time not hiding her disappointment. "What's your question?"

Krystal looked at Jaime's room then back at Carmen. "What's . . . wrong with Jaime? Why is he . . . so distant?"

Carmen put the knife down and sighed. She looked at Krystal and said, "He wasn't always like this." Carmen looked up, thinking of the memories of Jaime in the past. A smile curved in the corner of her lip, a slight giggle, contained laughter, a good boost to the low morale. Carmen spoke but continued to look up at the ceiling. "He uhh, he was kind of . . . a klutz. Very joyful, very playful. Good with kids. Always engaging."

Krystal thought of these characteristics but none of them matched the current Jaime. She showed no surprise but did find the information peculiar. *How does somebody go from engaging to giving everyone the cold shoulder?* She wanted to think she had an idea but that was only a guess.

Krystal said, "That's . . . different . . . than he is . . . now."

Carmen darkened, "He's in a rough spot right now." She nodded in Jaime's direction. "He isn't himself lately. But I think . . ." she paused, "once he gets out of this funk, I think you'll see the real Jaime."

Krystal just looked at Carmen. She wasn't feeling enthusiastic or hopeful. She just accepted the idea as is. *We'll see*, she thought.

⌒

"I can't believe I got sucked into this." Jaime groaned in the driver's seat as he merged the car onto the freeway.

"Aww come on Jaime! You know you're like going to have a fun time with three pretty girls," said Summer from the passenger seat.

Four girls, Krystal thought. Amber was sitting behind Jaime, Cassie in the middle seat, Summer in the passenger, and Krystal behind her. Krystal wondered whether Summer did that on purpose or not, either way Krystal said nothing. Cassie leaned forward to get in on their conversation. "Yeah yeah," shaking her head fervently, "we are going to have a great time. Right Amber?"

Amber was busy filing her nails, "Knock yourself out. I, personally, am ready to do some shopping. I could kill for a new wardrobe this year. I want to get some new clothes this season."

Summer squealed like a chipmunk, almost breaking Krystal's eardrum. "Me too! I totally like wanna get some like new clothes. I'm like dying to bust out my new credit card!"

Krystal wasn't feeling the intensity of uhhh . . . whatever "this" was and stayed silent. She wasn't too keen on going shopping, but Carmen had extended the invitation to all of them and it's not like Krystal had much to do these days, plus the idea of hanging out with friends outside of school secretly excited her. Just the idea of being invited to an event brightened her day. So she couldn't say no. It would have been too boring at home.

Jaime scoffed silently to himself. Krystal couldn't help but take notice. He looked forward and watched the road in what looked like contempt. *The guy clearly doesn't want to be here. Then again, I wouldn't want to be here either if I were the one who had to drive everybody in my free time. Jaime is the only one out of this group who has his license and Carmen is out busy today, so Jaime got delegated to be the designated driver for the group.*

Summer leaned over the middle console, trying to get as close to Jaime as possible. She leaned over and said, "So, like Jaime. Have you like ever heard of the story of the vicious coyotes on social media?"

Jaime glanced at Summer then returned his eyes to the road. "No," he said sternly.

Summer tried to lean in closer, nearly blocking Cassie's view of the front of the car. "Well, I like heard of this one story that coyotes could like grow to be the size of elk. And like those coyotes grow up to eat like both humans and their dogs too." Summer was speaking so fast it was hard to keep track of what she said.

Jaime pulled up to a red light, gave Summer a look and said, "Don't believe everything you hear," and turned his eyes back to the road.

Well, that was interesting, Krystal thought. *Why did he have to say that? He could have just said no.*

Jaime's answer created an awkward lull in the conversation. Summer paused for a second then resumed her ecstatic behavior. "What are you talking about I like totally heard this from like a friend of mi—"

"I heard of something different," Amber cut in.

Cassie chimed in too, "I heard about that too. It was like really freaky to read about!" Krystal took herself out of the conversation, as did Jaime, as they drove on toward the mall. Krystal stared out the window, feeling like an outsider in this group, like she didn't belong. *Why am I here?* She wondered but didn't have an answer, as usual. Krystal took in a breath and watched her breath cloud the window in front of her. She thought about drawing a smiley face, but she held back. The cloud faded and was back to its transparent self.

Hmm. My spiritual high is gone, so I'm back to my normal self again. Or at least, my new self. I wonder if it will last or will just fade? Krystal didn't have the answer and she didn't bother trying to. These days, it was easier to just go with the flow.

The car pulled to a stop as Jaime said, apathetically, "We're here."

Summer squealed, "YAAASSS!" and exited the car. Krystal tensed up, trying to keep her eardrums from bleeding. Cassie and Amber followed suit as they stepped out of the car and onto the blacktop parking lot. Krystal closed the door and was grateful to be outdoors where she could check her hearing. The rest of the group stepped out and were already on their way toward the entrance of the mall. Krystal did what she could to keep up, avoiding cars and weaving through the parking lot to catch up. Jaime led the way with Summer lingering next to him, while Cassie and Amber walked behind them. Krystal continued walking but she couldn't help but notice the distance between herself and the group. It was growing larger and larger, almost like they weren't even waiting for her.

The sight of all that struck Krystal. She didn't react, she just took the punch and continued on. The sense of distance and the sight of people's backs reminded her of school. *Is it really so different outside of school?* Regardless, Krystal had to stick with the group because they were her ride home. And they would leave when the group wanted to leave. *Or maybe just when Summer wants to leave.* That idea sent a chill down Krystal's spine when she caught up with the group and entered the mall. Summer took off immediately, charging to the nearest store like a child, showing more enthusiasm than Krystal had ever seen. Amber and Cassie followed suit, leaving Krystal behind. Krystal sighed. *This might take a while.*

Jaime stood in front of Krystal and watched Summer run off squealing toward the nearest clothing store. For a moment, Krystal thought Jaime was going to say something then turned and walked away, leaving Krystal to her own devices. Krystal wondered which direction she should go. *Should I go with Jaime or should I go with Summer and everyone else?* Krystal did want to talk to Jaime, but she did want to try and socialize with everyone in the group, so Krystal turned and followed Summer into the nearest store.

⟡

"This is totally my type!" Summer held a white and yellow dress with sunflowers, the kind of dress for a girl who would dress like a sunflower all the time. Summer held it up, "Like what do you guys think?"

Amber glanced over, "Definitely fits your personality, Summer. I'd take it." Summer turned to Cassie.

Cassie said, "I love it! It would look so great on you." Krystal was busy checking out some t-shirts with mild interest if none at all. She half-expected Summer to ask her as well, but Summer continued her shopping delight with all the joy in the world. Krystal let Summer power through her shopping experience and tried checking out some new clothes for herself. Krystal slid through multiple sets of t-shirts but none of them seemed to catch her eye. Krystal held up a red shirt to herself in the mirror. The shirt did look nice, but Krystal wasn't feeling it, so she hung the shirt back up.

She held another shirt in the mirror, sizing herself up and sighed. *I've never really been good at this.* Krystal lowered the shirt and put it back. *Shopping has never been my forte.* Krystal glanced over toward the group. Both Cassie and Amber were digging into whatever they were looking at, while Summer was busy changing in one of the dress rooms. Summer came out wearing the white sunflower dress looking amazing. Both Cassie and Amber were dazzled by the sight, even Krystal was mildly impressed by the sense of fashion.

Oh yeah, that definitely suits her. She couldn't help but agree.

Summer rushed on over, tripping and nearly falling on her face in the process. She ran up to Amber and asked, "So! How does it look?"

"You look dazzling," Amber said. Then turned her back to show Summer the new shirt she was wearing, "And what about m—"

Cassie cut Amber off. "Yeah, you look like a ray of sunshine Summer!" Krystal returned her gaze back to the shirt rack she was working on again. This time she found something of interest and held it up in the mirror.

This doesn't look too bad. Krystal held up a black ACDC shirt. It was just a plain black long-sleeve shirt with the ACDC letters in white, but Krystal liked it. Krystal's excitement faded as she glanced over at Summer shining in the corner of the room. Her enthusiasm for the shirt faded as she compared herself to Summer. *I'm not pretty. Not like her.* Despite her comparison, Krystal decided she would still buy the shirt. She had to at least get one thing while she was here.

She went to rejoin the group as Amber was finishing a rack when her phone vibrated. Amber took her phone out, checked it and smiled. Summer noticed and instantly threw her vision toward Amber's phone. "Who you talking to?" she asked.

Amber wasn't fazed by Summer entering her personal space. "Just some guy I'm texting."

Summer lit up, "OHHHHHH! Who's the guy?"

Amber chuckled and shifted to keep her phone to herself. "Just a guy I've been texting," then she lowered her voice, "and making out with."

"OHHHHH!" Summer squealed. "I've got to meet him some day!"

Amber tried to calm Summer down, enjoying her enthusiasm like an older sibling, "You will one day. You will."

"How'd you guys meet?" asked Cassie. Everyone followed Amber toward the checkout line.

"I met him online. He actually goes to our school. I've seen him, and he's *hot*!"

"Like how hot?" Summer intrigued.

Amber flicked her eyebrows up, "Like *hot hot*." Summer and Cassie careened with intrigue and attraction. That's a pretty high scale to give some guy, and both of them were racking their minds as to who the guy might be.

Summer asked, "Might we have a name?" keeping her voice low and intriguing.

Amber replied with the same intrigue, "No you may not. That's private."

Summer's intrigue vanished and she turned into an eight-year-old girl, "Aww but come on! I wanna know!"

Amber kept it to herself, smiling at her own little secret. "You'll find out later." They exited the store and went into the next one and the next one and the next one, checking out aisle after aisle, store after store of nothing but clothes for two hours. They exited Macy's, completing the entire top floor of the mall. The group broke away from the clothing stores and headed toward the food court. Krystal wasn't hungry. She didn't do much, so she hadn't earned an appetite just yet. She followed them from the top floor to the escalator, watching Summer and the rest of the group head on down, but Krystal stopped and wondered, *What would happen if I just didn't go with them?* Krystal decided to test it out and waited. Watching Summer and the rest follow slowly down the escalator until they were out of sight. Krystal felt the distance between them widen until they were gone. Krystal finally felt free to move around, not tied down by the decisions of the group. Krystal looked around, hoping to find out where she was and then decide where to go and what to do.

We should be done soon. It's not like we can be here much longer. Krystal checked the time on her phone. *Still only 12:30pm on a Saturday? We should be wrapping it up soon.* But that wasn't the case. Krystal walked along the second floor, observing Summer and the group head to the food court when the realization hit her. *Oh no, they're going to get their second wind after eating!* Krystal leaned against the railing and let the mall traffic flow behind her. She could hear a nearby fountain towards the center of the mall. The din of background music playing, as people passed by, avoiding eye contact with all the store clerks offering discounts outside if they showed any interest. Krystal took her eyes off the people and let her mind wander for a bit.

She felt a sense of disappointment envelop her. *This isn't as fun as I had hoped. I wish I was home right now.* She hung there for a while, watching people pass by beneath her. Krystal's eyes searching in boredom from person to person, until she suddenly found Jaime sitting in a chair across the way. He didn't seem to notice her; he had his focus down on his phone for most of the time. Krystal straightened for a bit.

Jaime sat there, holding his arm comfortably in front of him as he seemed to watch whatever was happening on his phone. Krystal noticed Jaime's expression. He looked a little mad, like he was frustrated with something, but he couldn't take his eyes away. Krystal leaned closer over the railing. *What's he looking at?* A part of her wanted to know, but a part of her didn't want to bother him either. He had that: *Don't bother me* look to him, but Krystal wasn't as fazed by the look as some people were.

Krystal felt her stomach start to growl as the hole inside her stomach widened and she suddenly had the taste for something sweet. Her eyes drifted down toward a nearby carmel apple shop and paused for a moment. Her eyes drifted back to Jaime, a part of her was fearful from approaching

Jaime from the last time. Krystal was about to abandon the idea when the thought popped into her head.

"Love your neighbor as yourself."

The idea clicked in Krystal's mind. Then she glanced from the carmel apple store to Jaime. The issue was settled. "Okay . . . I'll do it."

This was a lot harder than she thought. Krystal was now standing only a couple of feet from Jaime, clutching two carmel apples in her hands. Standing this close to Jaime, Krystal could sense there was something familiar about him. Krystal suddenly felt gravity intensify and the discomfort gripping her heart like a hostage. But Krystal held firm to the verse. *"Love your neighbor as yourself."* Picturing herself sitting there in that chair. Krystal was fearful that Jaime would lash out at her again once she gave him the apple if she gave it to him at all. It wasn't too late, she could back out now. But Krystal was filled with compassion at the sight of seeing herself in that chair. She knew she was going to bother Jaime, but if she were in his shoes, she would want someone to hand her a carmel apple when she was down. There was just something about him that Krystal knew was off.

Krystal stepped forward, feeling the grip on her heart tighten. If she didn't hand him the apple soon she was going to give up again. She took another step closer, now only a foot behind Jaime. She didn't worry about making a noise. People hadn't noticed Krystal her entire life, so she was naturally silent in her movements. Her left foot planted, and Krystal could almost see over Jaime's chair at what he was looking at. His phone slowly coming into view. The grip on Krystal's heart was so strong she felt she was about to have a heart attack. She started to turn, to back off and abort, but then her heart suddenly cleared. Replaced by a warm feeling within her chest. The feeling relaxed and steadied her. As if it were telling her, *"It's okay. You can do this."* Krystal suddenly felt no pressure on her heart and the power of gravity returned to normal. She felt the opportunity was at hand. She felt empowered, only slightly, but just enough to get through this uncomfortable experience.

Krystal took one last breath, finally feeling free to do what she wanted without any pressure. She gripped the apples tightly in her hands and leaned forward into Jaime's view. She stopped when she realized she was staring at a picture of a young blonde-haired girl, who looked no older than twelve years old. Jaime held the phone out, glimpsing at a picture of the girl. Krystal was left to wonder, *Who's that girl?* Krystal made the deduction that she couldn't be his girlfriend because she looked so young, so what was the correlation? Krystal looked further and realized there were some physical similarities between Jaime and the girl.

The dots connected and Krystal shifted her gaze towards Jaime in understanding. *I see . . .* Krystal was right at the threshold of Jaime's vision, and she found this to be the easiest part. There was no discomfort. No fear. It was all replaced by a sense of compassion and love. A love, Krystal knew, came from when she accepted Jesus into her heart. She felt her heart fill and then pour out. Yearning to share it with others. So Krystal lifted her arm into Jaime's view and waited for him to react.

Jaime noticed the apple and whipped around in surprise, jolting in his chair. "Whoah!" Krystal said nothing, she didn't even react. Jaime caught his breath, and she held the apple out in front of him. Jaime calmed down and pointed to himself, "For me?" Krystal nodded. Jaime took the apple, confused but grateful, and glanced down at his lap. He mumbled "Thanks." Krystal nodded once. Jaime realized he still had his phone out in his left hand, the picture still visible. Jaime glanced at Krystal, she met his eyes and then glanced at the picture. Jaime clicked the phone off and put it away. "Thank you . . . for the apple," he said. Krystal nodded and realized her business was concluded. She straightened up and began to walk away. Jaime looked over his chair in her general direction and called out, "Hey." Krystal stopped, as if struck by lightning, surprised that someone was calling out to her. Krystal turned and saw Jaime nudge his head for her to come back. Krystal headed over, feeling uncomfortable now that someone was actually looking at her. Krystal entered Jaime's view again as he gestured to the chair next to him. "Would you like to sit?" Krystal's feet suddenly began to ache. She had been walking for nearly two hours and was ready to sit down. She took the gesture of goodwill and sat down, resting her feet and knees from all the walking. The two of them sat there, unaware of how to properly initiate the conversation.

Jaime stared down at his feet. Krystal stared out at the mall, searching from figure to figure of people walking across the way or down below through the glass railing. Both of them avoiding each other's gaze out of fear of what awkwardness might come next.

Krystal suddenly felt embarrassed and wasn't sure of what to do. Jaime noticed her brief moment of confusion and lowered his brow with bemused curiosity. Krystal looked at Jaime, now curious of his bemusement. The word came through her lungs with ease when she asked, "What?" the word came out half-baked but still comprehensible. Krystal still wasn't used to talking to people, so her vocal cords were still coarse when she talked initially.

Jaime shook his head, "Nothing." Krystal wondered if he was about to smile. She turned away, cringing from the awkwardness. Krystal looked back to see if Jaime was looking at her, but she found him staring out towards the mall again, deep in thought. His expression returned to its sullen mood. What was going on in his mind, she wondered. The two of them remained quiet for a while as the mall continued with its usual activity.

Krystal glanced at Jaime, who didn't mind being looked at. Well . . . he hadn't told her to stop anyway. Krystal lingered for a minute until Jaime spoke, "You know when you're having a bad day, and you wished someone would ask you about how your day was going?" Krystal wasn't sure where that statement came from, but she didn't dare to answer. She sat there listening patiently as Jaime glared at her, half expecting an answer, while the other half was suspicious of Krystal's intentions. Jaime dangled the carmel apple between his fingers and looked at it. He took her silence as an answer and continued. He exhaled, "I don't want to be here. I don't want to be stuck babysitting a bunch of prima donnas while I have to play driver." Jaime glanced down through the glass railing and saw Summer, Cassie, and Amber all hanging out in the food court below. Jaime turned and half-faced Krystal, taking note of his mistake. "Sorry." But Krystal felt no offense to the comment. In fact, she was relieved. She wasn't the only one who thought that way. Jaime raised a hand and rubbed his forehead, "I know I've been mean to you the past couple days but . . ." he raised the apple into view, "Thank you, for this." Krystal nodded with good intent. The atmosphere between the two of them cleared a bit and Krystal felt she could rest easier now that the hard part was over.

Krystal grew more comfortable the more time went on. For once she enjoyed sitting down and allowing her feet to rest. Watching the people stroll about the mall seemed a bit more enjoyable without a reason as to why.

Krystal could tell Jaime seemed a bit more relaxed as well, but she didn't know why. He still looked deep in thought but for some reason he just looked more relaxed.

Krystal took note of Jaime's emotions and could tell that something was on his mind. Something haunted him. Jaime looked up, taking a breath, sounding like he was about to burst into tears. "I jus—" he caught himself, realizing he had given too much information. Remembering there was a stranger sitting next to him, hearing his darkest secrets spill out. He looked at Krystal with extreme skepticism. His softened tone turned to controlled anger. He lifted the carmel apple, asking, "Why did you give me this?" a tad bit short of demanding.

Krystal saw that it was her turn to speak. If she didn't, she sensed Jaime would only get mad, so she answered truthfully.

"Because . . ." her words blocking themselves in her throat like traffic on a freeway, "You looked . . . familiar."

That answer was certainly not what Jaime was expecting, but he kept up the skeptical bravado. "As in you know me?"

Krystal didn't have any other way to put it. She repeated "You looked *familiar*." Jaime deflated again, knowing he wouldn't get a different answer. He took a bite out of the carmel apple, feeling the sweet-tart of the apple mixed with the sugar of the carmel, flood his taste buds. Krystal took that as her cue and took a bite out of her own apple as well. The sweet-tart flooded her mouth. It was delicious. Jaime lightened a shade then returned to his calm, sulking demeanor, while Krystal sat there watching people pass by. They ate in silence for the next ten minutes until their apples were gone. Krystal looked at her finished popsicle stick and then glanced over at Jaime's. Krystal was frightened at first, but she held her hand out anyway. Jaime saw the gesture and refused, but Krystal was patiently persistent, so Jaime relinquished the popsicle stick to her. Krystal got up from her chair, her feet now rested and headed over to find the nearest trash can. She tossed the sticks away in a nearby trash bin and looked around. Her attention was drawn down to the fountain on the first floor. Krystal watched the water glimmer and flicker with tiny bits of coins shining at the bottom. She glanced over to where Jaime was, but he was already back on his phone. Krystal returned her gaze toward the fountain. She wanted to get a better look. To see it up close for herself. She didn't get out that much so why not.

Plus, Summer and everyone else were off on their own so it wouldn't make a difference.

Krystal did one last check on Jaime. Walking past him toward the escalators. She didn't bother to look where Jaime was as she went down the escalator. All that she focused now on was the fountain lying in the center of the mall.

Krystal came up toward the edge of the fountain and watched as the koi fish swam up toward the edge, poking their heads out of the water, gaping for food. The sunlight was flickering through the windows overhead into the pool of water, as the water flowed like droplets of glass and glimmered. Some fish swam through multiple pools of water, surrounding the central body of the fountain, with a turtle statue in the center spewing water. The sight was delightful. Childhood memories of wishes floated back as she felt a joy she hadn't felt in a while.

It reminded Krystal of her mom, and suddenly the memories of the recent past came flooding back. Krystal braced herself and held the memories back. She realized her eyes were closed and opened them, putting aside those painful memories. Krystal regained her sense of delight and continued staring at the fountain.

Krystal knew she was standing alone but she didn't mind it this time. In fact, she liked being by herself more than around people. The common label for that would be introvert and Krystal would not disagree. She enjoyed what she was doing more when she was by herself than when she was with other people sometimes. But even introverts still need to be social.

Krystal watched as the turtle spewed clear water throughout the fountain, watching the flickering of coins glimmer in the water. Krystal felt for her pocket, hoping to find some change but didn't find any. Then a hand held out a penny next to her, Krystal turned, and found Jaime was there standing beside her. He gestured to her to take it. Krystal didn't object, took the coin, and gave it a flip. Hearing the satisfying sound of a coin flipping, flicking it as high as she could before it splashed into the water.

"What'd you wish for?" Jaime asked.

Krystal stared into the fountain and answered honestly, "A friend." Jaime was unsure how to answer that. Which didn't surprise Krystal. She knew it was a big ball to drop on someone.

Jaime blinked a couple times and put his hands in his pockets. "You know, I don't really know you that well." For some reason Krystal felt her defenses lower.

Krystal's only reply was, "I know." She looked back at Jaime, then stared at the fountain in silence. Jaime followed suit, and they just stood there, silently basking in each other's company as the beautiful water flicked and flowed, washing away their pains. The two of them enjoying the benefit of having someone simply be *there*. Both healing from the benefit of the other's presence.

Krystal let her guard lower and whispered, "Thank you."

Jaime was caught off guard again. He decided to roll with it, accepting the gratitude, not wanting to ruin the moment, and replied, "You're very welcome." As the two of them stared off into the running water, wondering what tomorrow would bring.

CHAPTER 22

Fire and Pain

"Through honesty comes healing."

—JL

Krystal felt uneasy. The sight of Jaime sitting across the room wasn't what concerned her. It was how he looked. Jaime had a certain look on his face that drew her attention. Krystal watched him out of the corner of her eye in the classroom. The teacher was going on about his usual class lecture, the rest of the class was not paying attention, but today, Krystal had her attention fully on Jaime, and she could tell that something was wrong, very wrong.

Jaime's eyes were darkened, she could see the lines under his eyes from a night with no sleep. His energy was drained but Krystal could tell there was an ambiance of anger about him. That wasn't what concerned her. What concerned her was the determined look on his face. Not moving a single muscle. It was the look that showed he was deep in thought, like he was about to murder someone.

I feel like my mom right now. Is this how she felt when she dropped me off at school every day? Krystal couldn't help but feel that way. She snuck looks at Jaime throughout the entire class period, and Krystal never saw the guy move, not even an inch. Her concern only grew as the longer class went on, and Jaime never said a word to anyone or anything.

Krystal had never felt this concerned about anyone before, which was strange. Why did she care so much about this guy? Then again, when did she care about others to begin with? That thought struck her as curious.

When did I start caring about others? For once, she knew the answer to that. *When I started believing in Jesus.*

Krystal remembered her days looking just like Jaime's. The saddened look across her face, the strife of constant pain. It struck her as ironic and eye opening. *Weird. I remember most of my days moping about me, and now here I am worrying about someone else for a change. I can't tell if that's an improvement or not.*

The bell sounded; Jaime was up and in motion.

He got up fast. Krystal followed him outside toward the main courtyard. Jaime was ahead, walking with a determined anger in his step, his pace going faster than his classmates and Krystal. Krystal had never been a fast walker to begin with, but Jaime was physically fit and was able to outrun her if necessary. He quickly vanished among the crowd. Krystal tried to find him but was unsuccessful.

Krystal gave up on the search and decided to spend lunch on her bench again. Jaime would come back into view as he always did, right? Krystal's hunch proved to be correct. She quickly found Jaime walking towards his usual friend group, giving high-fives, and acting all cheery around them. *Something's wrong. Something is very wrong.* Then she watched as Jaime's cheerful attitude faded and he returned to his darkened stare. For the rest of lunch Jaime just sat against his concrete wall and didn't say anything to his friends. He just stared into nothing. Then his gaze shifted, and he looked in Krystal's direction. Krystal found his gaze and didn't move. Their eyes met and neither of them had anything to say. For only a second, Krystal could have thought his gaze weakened when he saw her. Jaime eventually took his eyes away and went back to sulking.

Krystal leaned forward on her bench and wondered, *What is he thinking right now?*

Krystal lay in her bed unable to fall asleep. It had been another long night, even though she had no issue with why she couldn't fall asleep. It reminded her of those long nights being unable to sleep from her depression. Long nights with nothing but her thoughts to drive her crazy, unable to sleep. The memories didn't haunt her as much, now she could face them with a more mature mind. She looked over and saw the empty wall next to her. The sign recording the number of days she tried not to kill herself was gone, and for good measure. Krystal did not miss the sign. It was better now that it was not there.

Krystal shifted her thoughts back to watching Jaime this morning. The determined look on his face gave her worry.

Not everyone goes through the same problems. Krystal didn't argue with that thought but given her own experiences she couldn't help but worry a little. *It was that look on his face. That determination, hiding whatever he was thinking.* Krystal pondered Jaime's dilemma a bit longer then gave up. She couldn't read people's thoughts.

Krystal took a breath and checked the time. 2:17am. She sighed. She hadn't fallen asleep since 10pm. Krystal was tired of doing nothing, so she felt the need to do something. An idea dropped into her head and her heart glowed.

What if you go for a walk?

Krystal didn't bother with thinking about this one. She was done with thinking, so she left the house quietly, aiming to not disturb Aunt Sarah sleeping. Krystal stepped out onto the street in her usual black clothing with no direction in mind. She went wherever her feelings took her. Habitually, she started walking toward the Fisher's house. The night was calm, the houses quiet. It had a nice feel to it. To know the entire world was taking a break. Krystal knew it was late at night, but she didn't feel tired. She'd feel that tomorrow though.

There was no moon, and the stars were blacked out, so it was just her and the nighttime sky. Krystal walked down the block and noticed an orange light coming from her left. Instinctually, Krystal followed the light. (We humans usually like to gravitate toward shiny things.)

Krystal approached the light, and saw it was a public community center. She saw there was a gate in front of her, but it was left open. She took caution entering, closing the gate behind her without making a sound. The community center had a firepit and tables where people could spend time together and eat.

She saw a figure sitting down on a red plastic chair in the firelight. Krystal approached the firepit and saw Jaime, sitting there, staring into the fire like it was a portal into oblivion. His eyes were burdened and cold. The firelight flickering, the mixture of light and dark revealing hidden features on Jaime's face. His back was facing toward her, but he was at an angle just enough for Krystal to see his face. Krystal approached casually, stepping closer. She squinted, trying to capture all the details of Jaime while he sat there. Jaime had his elbows on his lap and his hands hanging between him. But something stood out, an L shaped figure in his hands, dangling lightly between his fingers like it weighed nothing at all. Krystal's eyes widened. He was holding a gun.

"I know you're there," Jaime called out. Krystal wasn't surprised. She stepped closer, now only a few paces away from Jaime. She came to the right of him, peered down at Jaime and saw the result. He was broken. His eyes were dark and red from constant crying. Eyelids heavy from lack of sleep. The deterioration clear across his face. He was a young man who has had enough. Krystal showed no reaction, in fact she never felt so calm before in her life. It terrified her. How desensitized she had become over years of isolation and depression.

Krystal's eyes dropped to the gun, dangling in his hands. Jaime looked up. Tired eyes looking back at her. Krystal refocused on Jaime, tried to feel some kind of compassion, but for right now she felt nothing. She was a blank slate, but willing to listen. Jaime took his eyes off Krystal and looked back into the fire. "You're probably wondering why I have a gun in my hands," Krystal said nothing. Jaime held up the gun casually, "I just wanted to understand what people feel like when they try to do something like this." Krystal felt her heart leak with compassion, finally establishing a connection with this guy. Jaime held the handgun to his head, but Krystal saw he had no ill intent to harm himself, so she didn't try to stop him. He was simply reenacting a scenario, like an actor imagining a scene but with props. He pressed the gun against the corner of his forehead, looked at it, and then slowly let his hand fall, dropping the gun on the concrete. Jaime sagged forward, bringing his elbows onto his lap. "I wanted to know what it feels like, but I can't. I can't imagine what people are thinking of when they do something so horrible." Again, Krystal said nothing, but she felt it was the right call to stay silent.

Jaime stared into the fire for a bit, Krystal standing there patiently, not making a sound. Jaime spoke, "I just don't know . . . what she was thinking of when she did it." Jaime put his hand to his face, starting to sob. "Why she would do something so horrible." It was all coming out. Jaime held nothing back. He let the emotions come flooding to the surface from that black lake within him. "I simply can't bear to see her like that." He lowered his head, covering himself with his hand while he sobbed. Krystal stood there waiting, knowing there was more to come.

Without looking Jaime muffled, "You probably have no idea what I'm talking about so I'm going to tell you anyway. I don't care if you're a stranger, I just need someone to talk to right now." He straightened up, still sobbing, muttering short breaths. Jaime whimpered for a sec then regained control of himself. His voice was clear again. He put his hand to his forehead, and felt it was time to open up. Ready to pour his heart out.

Jaime let out a long and hard sigh, "I had a younger sister, named Carole." Jaime closed his eyes, fighting the tears itching to the surface. "She was the sweetest thing ever. She was only a few years younger than me. We did everything together. I don't think I loved anyone or anything more than my younger sister." Jaime put a hand to his mouth and took a watery gasp. "And then high school started. I was doing well. Had been doing well for a while. I was busy with sports and was popular, I still am popular."

Krystal nodded. *That part was true.*

Jaime continued, "But I was so caught up with what was happening in my life, and how good things were, that I neglected my younger sister." Jaime's words grew more difficult. He was near to breaking out in tears again, "I never paid attention to how difficult things were going for her. How hard middle school was for her." The anger came back to his eyes as he relived the bitter-sweet memories. "I remember Carole having to go to the counselor's office so much because kids were constantly bullying her." Jaime shook his head; the sorrow waving off him. "I never paid attention to it. I never bothered to ask her how things were going or to check in on her. My little sister was the most innocent thing I could think of. She never had a harmful bone in her body and all she wanted to do was be kind to everyone." Jaime's eyes stared into the fire. "I never cared or tried to go out of my way to comfort her. I was too busy living my awesome life that I neglected how hard hers was." Jaime gasped for breath. "I remember one day, she came home . . ." Jaime stopped, it was too hard to speak, but he had to get it out. The dam of emotions that had been building inside him needed to be released. He had to get it out.

Jaime took a sharp breath, "She came home, and she told me that she couldn't take it anymore. She had had enough. And you know what I did?" Jaime looked straight into Krystal's eyes, "I did *nothing*." He paused to let the words sink in. "I did . . . nothing. I brushed it off and didn't make a big deal out of it. I never stopped to care for her when she needed me." He took a breath, "I know she loved me more than anyone else in our family. Carole looked up to me as her older brother." Jaime began shaking, he couldn't hold the tears back any longer. His voice getting higher, raspy, whispering sharply with tears clogging his lungs. Jaime stopped. The pain was too much. He held an arm to his face to cry on, "And she's gone!" He said it. He finally got the words out. Jaime cringed forward, the sorrow weighing on him, letting out all the emotions. Jaime cried out, long and hard. Krystal had never seen him look so weak before. So exposed. He was showing her everything right now. Nothing held back. "I feel like I've failed her. I wasn't there for her when she needed me the most. What kind of older brother does that?!" Jaime lowered his head and wept. The fire was still dancing before him.

It brought back memories of Krystal's own suicide attempt. How she lay in a puddle of her own blood. How she could be lying in the ground, dead. Then she thought of middle school. Images came rushing back to her mind. The long days of isolation. The urge to kill herself taking root. Krystal's heart softened as she thought, *"What would Jesus do?"* So Krystal did the first thing that came to her mind. She stepped behind Jaime's chair, spread her arms wide, and slowly enwrapped Jaime in a hug. Krystal felt Jaime jolt from the presence enveloping him, but he didn't fight it. Jaime felt her warm presence encroach upon him, wrapping around him, giving him the warmest hug, he'd ever experienced. The mere presence of her touch brought a relief Jaime hadn't felt in a long time. The tears from Jaime came out in rivers. Krystal wrapped her arms completely around Jaime as she cried as well. Jaime found Krystal's hand on his shoulder and put his hand on top of hers, reciprocating the kindness.

There they held each other, two people, broken, finding comfort amidst each other's suffering. It was one of the happiest, saddest moments of Krystal's life and she felt another part of her, begin to feel whole once again.

CHAPTER 23

A Good Laugh

"Sometimes all you need is one friend.
One close friend who will stick by you."

—JL

"Alright. Is everybody ready?" Carmen called out.

"Yeah!" the group replied, everyone except Krystal, but that was becoming normal. Tonight, there were a few more people at the Bible study, more of Summer's friends from school coming down to the Fisher's house as an excuse to hang out. The group sat around the couches in the Fisher's living room. Krystal sat with her Bible ready in her hands, eager to flip to the first passage Carmen suggested, hoping to beat anybody from calling it first. Krystal normally didn't want to read the passages, but tonight she did. She wanted to try a little harder to get along with everyone.

Carmen spoke, "Alright, let's—" then her attention shifted suddenly toward the staircase as Jaime came casually down the stairs. Carmen followed Jaime in the corner of her eye, as Jaime finished stepping down the stairs and lay down on one of the open couches in the other room, but still within earshot. Carmen resumed, trying not to make a big scene out of it. "Let's start with Romans chapter five."

Krystal looked over and found that odd. Carmen saw it too. Jaime had never bothered to come downstairs during a Bible study or any time, but at least he was downstairs. Krystal watched as Jaime pulled out his phone and paid no attention to the group next to him. Carmen controlled her delight and focused on the group again. "Alright, can somebody read for me the first passage . . ."

Krystal snuck glances over at Jaime during the Bible study. He had never once looked in her direction or toward the group. Krystal couldn't tell if he was listening to the discussion or not. It was too hard to tell with his current expression. Jaime stared at his phone for the most part. His face looked so casually determined that Krystal felt he was either hearing everything or nothing.

The night ended and Summer stretched her arms high in the air, "Ahhhh good discussion gals. That was certainly very fulfilling indeed."

Krystal sat there braindead. *That wasn't a discussion. You were the only one talking the entire time.*

Carmen looked at her watch, "Wow guys, it looks like we finished early this evening. We have about twentyish minutes before your parents come up and get you, so we can hang out for the time being." Everyone eager to hear the "okay" was like a class eager to hear the go-ahead from their teacher to leave class early. The circle had formed even faster than Krystal could have anticipated, as all seven girls circled around Summer like she was a deity.

Meanwhile, Krystal felt totally excluded. The backs of the circle impeded her view and shouted back at her, *GO AWAY! YOU DON'T BELONG HERE!* Krystal felt her heart sting with betrayal. Carmen had left the room to get something while the rest of the group quickly divulged into another conversation with Summer leading the chat. Amber sat next to Summer and the two of them were the powerhouses of the conversation.

Summer stopped and turned toward Jaime, "Hey Jaime! Wanna join us?"

Jaime stared at his phone and spoke in monotone, "No thanks."

Summer made a cute frown, "Aww come on!"

"I said I'm fine," Jaime replied, looking back at his phone.

Summer pouted and went back to her conversation. Krystal wanted to close this distance between herself and the rest of the group, so she got up from her seat and found an open spot on the couch to listen in on the conversation.

"So, I was like busy one time with like my ex-boyfriend and we were like . . ."

Krystal craned her head back in boredom, *It's more of the same. She's always talking.* Krystal felt the gap between herself, and the rest of the group widen, making her feel self-conscious of her position in the social hierarchy.

And right now, she was on the lower end of the list. The "Untouchables" as they say.

Krystal gave up and decided to walk over to Jaime. Jaime shifted his attention from his phone as Krystal walked by and found a nearby seat next to him. Jaime turned and said, "Hey?"

"Hey," Krystal replied.

"How are you doing?" Jaime asked, still a bit bewildered.

"Bored."

Jaime looked back at his phone, said, "Yeah me too," in agreement.

Krystal leaned forward and tried to catch a glimpse at Jaime's phone. "What are you looking at?"

Surprisingly, Jaime showed Krystal the phone, showing more pictures of himself and his younger sister Carole, "More of the same I guess." Krystal realized he had a whole album of pictures, if not hundreds of pictures with him and his sister. Normally a person would feel a little creeped out with how many pictures a guy had, but it delighted Krystal at the sight, at least a little. Krystal saw a lot of love in those pictures. Jaime scrolled through the photos showing all kinds of backgrounds. Krystal pointed to one, Jaime stopped and elaborated, "Oh this one? This was when Carole and I went out and played in the mud." Jaime chuckled. Krystal noticed Jaime was a bit happier in his tone and it felt nice to see him chipper for once. "We were out in the rain, and she started throwing mud at me and I threw mud at her and eventually we were both so muddy that we had to capture the moment you know." Jaime lowered the phone and scrolled to another photo. He held it up for Krystal to see. "Oh, and this!" Jaime showed a picture of himself and Carole smiling as wide as they could with their faces covered with ice cream. "This was when we tried to see who could eat more ice cream in one go." Jaime chuckled, "I nearly vomited that night. Carole wasn't so lucky." Jaime flipped back to the muddy photo of the two of them and turned and looked at Krystal with a wholehearted smile on his face. Krystal, normally blank-faced and calm, was a bit taken aback by the sudden burst of positive energy. She could feel her guard lower, but it felt good to be open with someone for once. Deep down she enjoyed the sight of Jaime smiling at her and felt her heart pump with a little more enthusiasm than before.

Krystal's expression shifted by one percent, changing to a lighter shade than it had been before, as she peered closer at the picture of Jaime and his sister. Krystal saw how frazzled and messed up Jaime's face and hair was from all the mud, then she shifted her attention to Carole who was smiling and missing a few teeth, *Oh she looks cute in that photo.* Krystal felt a laugh build up in her chest when she saw how funny Jaime looked. *Oh boy, he looks so stupid.* She stifled her laugh, *but I can't tell him that.*

Jaime read her expression perfectly and said, "You think I look dumb, don't you?" Krystal stifled her laughter and gave a quick nod. Jaime didn't find any offense at all, "I know I look dumb. It was a fun time." Krystal for once felt comfortable seeing this warmer side to Jaime. She wasn't used to seeing him smile so often or much about anything. Sometimes she wished she would do the same. *One day*, she thought. *One day.*

Jaime flicked to another picture, showing himself in an orange bathing suit but wearing a long red cape tied around his neck, watching the cape flutter in the wind as Jaime clicked on the live photo and watched it play out. The laughter within Krystal was growing stronger now. She fought to contain this feeling within her chest. *Don't you dare laugh. Don't you dare laugh.*

Jaime saw her stifling expression and broke a crooked smile across his face, knowing he was finally getting to her. He held the phone closer, "You think it's funny, don't you?"

Krystal fought to keep herself contained but the stupid sight of Jaime looking so confident wearing that ridiculous cape made her want to burst out laughing. What made it worse was that Jaime saw her weakness and was now exploiting it. Krystal fought to keep her laughter in and squeaked, "No."

Jaime smiled even wider now and held the phone closer to her face. "Come on, laugh. I dare you!"

Krystal tried to keep her laughter controlled but it leaked through the cracks, "No."

"You wanna laugh so hard huh? HUH!"

Krystal froze up, trying not to look at the picture but Jaime kept holding it within her line of sight. His pressure made the laughter worse as her heart wanted to explode. Her lips widened as the smile broke through.

Jaime saw that victory was at hand. "Do it! I dare you!"

It was over. The laughter overtook her, and Krystal burst out laughing. It was a sound she hadn't heard in a while as her laughter filled the room. It was too good to miss, and Jaime started laughing himself. The whole room stopped as Krystal and Jaime's laughter filled the room. She was so busy laughing she had completely forgotten about everyone there.

Jaime looked straight at Carmen as she walked into the room holding drinks in her hand, raised his fist in the air, and shouted, "Victory!" Carmen froze. Completely dumbstruck at the sight of her younger brother looking at her, smiling.

Krystal's laughter died down and realized the whole room was staring at her. Her smile and joy vanished the moment she became self-conscious of everyone looking at her. She took the excuse of going to the bathroom to hide her embarrassment, leaving Jaime satisfied with the result.

Not a bad night.

CHAPTER 24

Explosion

*"Sometimes it's better to be alone than surrounded
by people who make you miserable."*

—JL

"Thanks for coming over, guys. I hope you all had a wonderful week," said Carmen. Krystal nodded. She took a seat around the couches and chairs in her usual spot. Carmen took a seat, even finding Jaime lying on a separate couch in the other room, staring at his phone. Carmen said, "Alright, let's get starte—,"

"—Oh my gosh," Summer cut in, stealing everyone's attention, "This reminds me of this one time of when I got this papercut on my pinkie and I totally thought it was going to get infected, so I made my brother go all the way up to Mayland and get me this special ointment that only gypsies use. It turns out the ointment he got me was just a bottle of toadstool softener and I totally believed it would heal my finger. I ended up going to the hospital because I did get an infection from using the toadstool softener, but anything could happen right?"

Everyone laughed while Krystal sat there glaring at Summer, uninterested.

Carmen recovered and said, "Let's read the passage and then discuss it after, 'kay Summer? Now open your Bibles to Matthew 21:12–13." They opened their Bibles and Carmen read,

*"Jesus entered the Temple and began to drive out all the
people buying and selling animals for sacrifice—"*
—MATTHEW 21:12A (NLT)

Summer looked up from her Bible, breaking the silence, "Oh my gosh! This reminds me of this one time of when I was on my period and so I totally charged into a grocery store looking for tampons, and to make matters worse I yelled out to everybody around me where the tampons were and the whole store pointed to the other end. I should have been more considerate of my clothing since my blood began seeping through and all the people could see as I was walking by them."

Krystal watched in silence, dumbstruck and not in a fun way, *Why on earth would you do that?* she thought.

Carmen was also dumbfounded by the sudden interruption and tried to regain the momentum of the passage, "Let's try to finish reading the passage, 'kay?" Everyone looked back down at their Bibles, the room suddenly grew quiet again.

Good, Krystal thought and resumed reading.

> *"He knocked over the tables of the money changers*
> *and the chairs of those selling doves."*
> —MATTHEW 21:12B (NLT)

Summer looked up, Krystal closed her eyes and braced herself, *Oh no.*

"Oh my gosh!" Summer's face lit up with all the excitement in the world, "This reminds me of this one time of when I thought I was asleep, and I almost drowned because—"

"Summer." Carmen interrupted.

"Yaaaaassss?" Summer replied, all innocent, like a puppy not realizing it just chewed up the couch.

"Let's finish the passage first before we start talking about it kay."

"Okayyy," Summer replied. They went back to their reading, but Krystal continued to stare at Summer. Krystal's defenses were up as she braced for another interruption. Like rhythmic noise in the middle of the night keeping you awake, expecting the sound after hearing it so often. Krystal felt her heart tense and the outer portions of her body emanating heat and frustration. *She's going to do it again. I just know it.* Krystal braced herself, but nothing came. So Krystal lowered her guard and went back to reading.

Carmen said, "In verse thirteen it says,"

He said to them, "The Scriptures declare, 'My
Temple will be called a house of prayer—'"
—MATTHEW 21:13A (NLT)

"Oh my gosh!" Summer cut in and Krystal tensed up like a rock, "This reminds me of another—"

"Summer!" Carmen raised her voice but kept it contained. "We aren't finished reading yet."

"Oh, you aren't?" Summer tilted her head sideways, acting all surprised, "I thought you were done."

Everyone went back to reading the final passages. Carmen read, "In verse thirteen it says,"

"but you have turned it into a den of thie—"
—MATTHEW 21:13B (NLT)

Summer cut in again, "Oh my gosh! This reminds me of this one time when I was twelve years old and—"

"Oh my gosh, will you just SHUT UP!" Krystal started low in a whisper, increasing in intensity with every word until it became a full shout at the end. Silence permeated the room. Everyone, especially Summer, was thunderstruck by Krystal's outburst. Mostly because Krystal never spoke that much, so to hear her shout was like experiencing thunder for the first time. Jaime sat upright like Dracula out of a coffin with a look of bewildered curiosity.

Krystal was laser focused on Summer and unleashed the firestorm of anger welled within her, "Will you, just, SHUT UP!" Krystal stood up from her chair, "You go round and round telling all these"—Krystal quoted her fingers—"*amazing* stories about yourself and how it was sooooooo awesome of you to do these ridiculous things. Or how about when you almost had a kidney failure because you tried to eat nothing but protein powder for a week, and all of the other 'impressive' stories that happened because you were too *stupid* to have some common sense! Do you know what, that doesn't make you look *cool*, that makes you look like an idiot! So pardon me if I'm sick of hearing your BS or about your ex-boyfriends or of how much you love to hear yourself talk for forty-five minutes straight. Why don't you let someone else talk? Do you ever give anyone else a chance to tell a story?

Do you realize Summer that in the entire time I've known you, you've never asked anyone a single question? You've never given anyone else the opportunity to speak because you're too insecure about yourself and because you just LOOOOVVEE to hear the sound of your own voice." Krystal took a deep breath and clasped her hands together and raised a deceitful smile, "So do us all a favor," then frowned, "and SHUT UP!" Silence . . .

Summer sat there horrified like she had just stared death in the face. Everyone stared at Krystal in shock, even Carmen. Krystal knew this but she didn't back down. She didn't care. She was tired of hearing Summer dominate the conversation in the group. Krystal stared Summer down with eyes of death for what felt like eternity, the glare piercing deep within Summer's soul, terrifying her to the bone. Krystal broke her stare from Summer and noticed the rest of the group, seeing everyone horrified, except for Jaime, who had his head sticking out from the couch in the other room.

Krystal started to laugh, gradually then maniacally, while everyone sat there terrified as to why she was suddenly laughing. Krystal laughed for a solid minute, faded off, then started up again. Everyone watched Krystal cautiously in terror. Krystal finally spoke up again, "You know it's kind of funny. You guys have never been this quiet for so long before, and I have *never* had the opportunity to speak in the group for this long." Krystal smirked, giving off that maniacal smile again, "I never once had a chance to speak . . . not once. And now, here you are, listening to me speak for *the very first time*. Staring at me like I'm a psychopath, and you know what, I don't care anymore . . . I really don't. I would rather spend my time alone, than be with you jerks who make me feel miserable." Krystal paused, scanning the room from person to person, "Judging from the looks on all of your faces, I think it's time for me to go. Not that you care too much about that. I could leave this room any time and you still wouldn't notice I was gone."

Krystal grabbed her Bible and walked to the front door in stride. She opened the front door halfway then turned around, formed the peace sign "V" with her fingers and smiled happily, "Peace out," then flipped her middle finger in the air with a frown, "and piss off!" slamming the door.

The room was silent. Not one person said a word, until Jaime stared in awe and said, "That . . . was awesome!" as the rest of the group lay bewildered as to what just happened. He looked at Carmen and the rest of the group and said, "Best Bible study ever!"

CHAPTER 25

Carmel Apples

"Sometimes friendship can come from the most random of places."

—JL

Krystal was busy getting dinner prepped for tonight. She was going to marinate some meat and had to get it done so it would taste better in a few hours. Krystal checked the time. *Still only 2:25pm, so I've got three hours before I can start cooking.* Krystal got to work, readying the food in her kitchen, opening drawers, and pulling out spices. Her phone vibrated on the table as she was painting the meat with the marination sauce. Krystal wiped her hands on her apron and picked up her phone.

Her head recoiled slowly when she saw she had a text from Jaime.

It read: "Hey . . . could I come over? I don't wanna be home right now."

Krystal held the phone frozen. She was both surprised and shocked by the request. It was a guy wanting to come over to her apartment. Someone was asking to hang out with her for once! Krystal was both overjoyed and terrified. She didn't know whether she should say yes or not. But it was Jaime, and Krystal felt pretty comfortable around him, so she texted "Sure?"

Jaime knocked on the door and waited. It took a few moments, but Krystal opened the door wearing an apron again. Jaime was relieved at the sight, it meant she was making more food. Food he hoped she would share. Jaime's mood only brightened so much. He was feeling a bit down and wanted to be out of the house.

"Hey." Krystal said. Jaime felt caught off guard with how casual it was for Krystal to speak first, but that was as far as it would go. Jaime could tell that Krystal's body tensed up from how shy she was. His heart leaped a little at that sight. Krystal stood aside and held the door open for him. Jaime entered and walked into the barren apartment once more. Jaime walked into the living room again, taking notice of the empty walls and lack of decoration around the apartment.

Jaime thought, *For a place run by two women I would have thought it would be more decorative.*

Jaime looked over the room from left to right and said, "You know, you need to get some decorations for this place. It feels too . . . barren."

Krystal was suddenly standing next to him, making Jaime jump. He hadn't even heard her come up to him. *Geeze this girl really knows how to sneak up on me.*

Krystal said, "I'm not . . . much of a decorator." Krystal headed back to the kitchen, "You can . . . leave your stuff there . . . on the kitchen table and . . . do homework . . . or something."

Jaime took a seat at the wooden table and said, "Thanks." He wasn't really here to do homework though. He just wanted to get out of his own house. Jaime sat at the wooden table, the round heads of the chairs placating the surrounding table. He looked around, looking for more decorations or some sort of memento that made this place feel more like home, but he couldn't find any. *It's so empty in here. It's so different from my own house you know. My house is filled with all sorts of pictures and decorations, mostly from my mom of course, but this . . . this is just sad.* But Jaime didn't come here to insult another person's home, he came to get away.

Jaime pulled out his phone, lifting his eyes to see what Krystal was doing. She was getting busy again preparing some sort of dinner for tonight. Jaime chuckled a bit, *Reminds me of my own mom.* Jaime clicked open the phone but felt boredom strike him instantly, so he put the phone away. He rocked the chair back and forth, looking for something to do while Krystal was busy getting dinner ready.

Jaime lowered his head, spoke honestly, "You know, that was the coolest thing I'd ever seen when you yelled at Summer the other day." Krystal stopped. She didn't say anything, but Jaime could tell she was embarrassed. She didn't show it much but deep down he knew she was embarrassed by what happened. Jaime lowered his voice, "I wanted to say that was really cool," looking down at the dinner table. Krystal unfroze and looked at Jaime. Seeing how open he was with her. It made her feel more comfortable around him, also she didn't know how to react to his compliment if she could call it that. She held a plate of uncooked chicken in her hands and hadn't moved for a full minute.

Jaime, eager to change the subject, said, "You know I never really learned how to cook." Krystal resumed her work and looked at him over the countertop that separated the kitchen from the dining room table. "My mom mostly does the cooking in the house." Krystal opened her mouth to say something but held back. Jaime looked over at Krystal's work and asked, "What are you making?"

Krystal answered, "Marinated chicken and potatoes." Jaime found that intriguing. She didn't stutter or slow in her speech that time. Is she becoming more comfortable around him?

Jaime leaned forward, "You know dinner's not in a couple hours, right?"

Krystal nodded, "I know."

Jaime shook his foot up and down, eager to do something. Then he said, "Do you wanna go get carmel apples?"

Krystal froze, "Now?"

"Yeah," Jaime's enthusiasm began to rise. He pointed behind him, "I can drive us since I have my license. We can do something and then come right back for dinner."

Krystal took a moment to contemplate the thought, Jaime waited for a full three seconds before she said, "Okay?" her calm, shy voice sounding so sweet.

"Cool," Jaime said. "I'll go get the keys and then we can go."

Krystal glanced at the kitchen, "The food?"

Jaime calmed her doubts, "You can cook it when we get back. We won't be gone for long." Jaime shook his head reassuringly, "In and out, then we'll come back."

"Okay," she half-whispered. Then before she knew it, she was in the car driving with Jaime.

Krystal sat in the passenger seat of the car, not knowing how to react to the situation. Without prompting, Krystal was on her way to get carmel apples with a guy. Her mind raced in a million directions while her overriding conscience tried to keep her thoughts stable, but it wasn't doing a decent job. Krystal couldn't help but feel warm. Noticing her heartbeat increasing with every passing second. She glanced at Jaime; *He must really not want to go home today. I mean, I don't blame him. He's not exactly on good terms with his family. But then why would he want to get carmel apples with* me?

Jaime sat in the driver's seat, completely unaware of the raging storm happening within Krystal's heart and mind. He looked so calm and resolute as he drove; his eyes focused completely on the road. Then they turned left and pulled into a large parking lot. Jaime and Krystal stepped out, Krystal taking notice of the sun still high enough in the air. It was still some time around three in the afternoon, so there was plenty of sunlight left in the day. Krystal's mind dragged back to her marinated meat she left back in the kitchen. She needed to get that stuff ready or there wouldn't be any dinner, but her mind jolted back to reality when Jaime called out, "Hey you coming?" Krystal's heart did a slam dunk. The words she always wanted to hear from someone. Her heart flushed with joy, then she became self-conscious, retreating back into her shell. Krystal grabbed her right elbow with her left hand and nodded timidly. Jaime said, "Let's go" and entered the mall.

It wasn't the fact that Krystal was hanging out with a guy on her own, it was the fact that she was hanging out with someone in general that surprised her. She hadn't even prompted this hangout and yet here she was, getting carmel apples with a guy she barely knew. Krystal made sure her left sleeve was down far enough to cover the scar on her wrist. She didn't want anyone to see it anytime soon.

Krystal entered the mall after Jaime and was surrounded by the Saturday afternoon masses. The mall was booming with activity, hundreds of people swarming around like ants all moving to their presupposed destination. Krystal immediately felt self-conscious. She always felt uncomfortable being around groups of people. But this time was different, and for some reason she felt more confident in herself. That had been a changing factor lately, she could even see it happening in her studies at school and in groups . . . especially after she yelled in Summer's face not too long ago. She was slowly becoming increasingly comfortable around people and in herself too.

Jaime looked back, "Something wrong?"

Krystal shook her head, "No."

"Let's go, the carmel apples are waiting for us." Krystal followed and they headed down the escalators through the swarms of people.

Krystal and Jaime stepped off the escalator and headed over to a candy shop called Schweet Tooth. The same shop Krystal bought those carmel apples for Jaime. Krystal stepped in line behind Jaime and looked down over the assorted options. There were apples covered with all sorts of toppings. Everything from almonds, Oreo bits, frosting, sprinkles, candy bar crumbles, and even some marshmallows. Some of the apples were customized to make faces like clowns and such. Jaime overlooked Krystal's gazing eyes, "Find anything you like?"

Krystal found one that piqued her interest and pointed, "That one."

Jaime spoke to the clerk, "Could we get the one with the clown face and one with the candy cane crumbles on them." The clerk handed them the apples and Jaime paid for the food.

Krystal saw Jaime hand over his card and objected, "Wait. I haven't paid."

Jaime shook his head, "It's fine."

Krystal retreated back into her shell, "Thank you," letting him pay for the apples. Jaime took the two apples and walked over to find a nearby table. Krystal said, "I thought . . . we were leaving?"

Jaime waved her off, "No need to be in a rush. Let's enjoy the moment. It's always better to eat these things fresh." Krystal didn't object but Jaime could tell she wasn't too comfortable with that response. Jaime handed Krystal her clown faced apple and was about to take a bite out of his own when Krystal clasped both her hands together and made a quick prayer with the apple between her hands. Jaime saw her prayer and felt his heart shut off. Krystal opened her eyes and immediately saw the cold look on his face.

"What?" she asked innocently.

Jaime's face was a stone-cold killer now. Krystal's curiosity was replaced by her blank expression again, ready to receive any harsh reaction. This time Jaime merely sighed and let it go. He didn't flame up like he did before. Krystal felt the atmosphere between the two of them lift and gradually return to normal. Krystal took a bite out of her own apple and felt the sweet sugar overload her taste buds. She bit too much and had to cover her mouth from the oozing sugar. Jaime took a bite from his apple too, his mood lifting from the taste of the candy corn and peppermint.

Krystal searched for something to say. Something to get the conversation started. It was hard to produce a topic. Something to say. She wasn't too well rehearsed in conversing with other people, so Krystal had no idea what to talk about. So, she said the first thing that came to her mind, "How's . . . the apple?"

Jaime had his mouth full, "It's really good." He smiled at her with a mouth full, letting some juice leak from his mouth. Krystal felt her mood brighten a shade. *At least he's enjoying the apple. It seems to relax him.* Krystal took another bite out of her own apple, this time more moderately. Jaime finished his food and asked, "I noticed you don't have that many pictures around your house."

Krystal took a moment to answer properly, "My mom . . . was usually the one to take photos. But she worked all the time, and it was hard . . . to spend time with her."

Jaime asked without thinking, "Do you miss her?"

Krystal fought the tears wishing to come forth behind her eyes. She blinked them back and answered, "Yeah."

"I'm sorry." Jaime said, realizing he'd stepped on a landmine again.

"It's fine." Krystal said. But then she had something to say, something to actually fuel the conversation. "She . . . was often too busy to take the pictures. So . . . we didn't have that many." It was strange, Krystal didn't feel as weird talking about her mom this time. Maybe she was finally moving on.

"Do you like to decorate?" Jaime asked, "You know, like design or fashion?"

Krystal looked down at her clothing, checking the all-black outfit she always wore. There was not a single piece of skin revealed on her body except for her neck and face. The only thing that was fashionable on her was the black ACDC symbol on her shirt. Krystal thought of her closet and the lack of decorum in her apartment and said, "No." She shook her head, "I've never been . . . good at that sort of stuff."

Jaime blinked and leaned back in his chair, "I can imagine. Every time I see you, you're always wearing black, you know."

Krystal asked honestly, "Is that bad?" lowering her head.

Jaime shook his head. "No. There's nothing wrong with that."

Krystal looked up, genuinely surprised with that sort of comment. She had never heard anyone tell her it was okay with how she looked, and yet this boy was saying it was alright. Then Jaime leaned in, getting awfully close to Krystal's face. Krystal saw his approach but chose not to move. She let him lean closer over the table, allowing him to enter her personal space, not because of a romantic interest but more out of defensive curiosity. He could hold a knife to her face, and she still wouldn't move. He paused for a moment, glaring deep at her, and said, "You know, you have really nice eyes. Although, they're not so much blue, as they are purple. Like the ocean at night." Jaime nodded, leaning back. "Definitely purple."

Krystal felt her heart and face blush. "Thank you." She looked down for a moment then said, "You . . . you have nice eyes too." Jaime felt his own heart jump and the two of them couldn't look each other in the eye. Without thinking Krystal looked up and said plainly, "Do you like me?"

Jaime recoiled a bit. He wasn't expecting that question, especially right now. His mind pondered the question, then answered calmly, "I don't know." His face looked as if it were searching for what the right answer would be but couldn't find an appropriate response for the time. "I mean you're easy to talk to, which doesn't happen too often with people, but at the same time, I don't know you that well and you're kinda weird sometimes."

Krystal showed no reaction. She felt she had received both an insult and a compliment within the same sentence. Jaime seemed to shut down. His mood dampened until it was back to that angered depressed state she was getting so used to seeing. He wanted to clear the air and he wanted to do it now and get it over with. "Look . . ." He raised his head and met her gaze with determination in his eyes. "I'm not looking for a *lover* right now. Okay? I'm looking for a *friend*. Cause I'm not in the right emotional state to want a girlfriend. I'm too emotionally wrecked, and I have some problems that I need to sort out, got it? So right now, I need a friend, not a lover."

Krystal understood him completely. That answer was better than she expected. She nodded in understanding then fell silent. She didn't know if she was particularly looking for something in the realm of romance either, at least not right now. But a friend, a friend with whom she could contend, that sounded nice.

"Alright," she said, "So . . . are we friends?"

Jaime was stymied a moment, his mouth half-open then said, "Yeah, I guess so."

Krystal said, "Cool."

Jaime replied, "Cool."

"No . . . way . . ." Amber held her boba straw an inch away from her gaping mouth dumbstruck. "Is that Jaime?" She could not believe her eyes.

Summer's head whipped around like a dog seeing a squirrel. Her vision went laser-focused to where Jaime was sitting. Then Summer's eyes shifted to the girl across from him. Her bright smile fell into a dangerous frown. Amber saw the look on Summer's face and knew this meant trouble. She had an idea what Summer was thinking but couldn't understand why the hatred.

Summer looked at Amber in jealous disbelief. "Is he with the girl who yelled at me?" Amber frowned, perplexed. "What are you talking about? Who yelled at you?"

Summer pointed in vile hatred at the girl dressed in black sitting with Jaime. "That girl! She's the one who yelled at me in front of everyone the other day! You weren't there but she freaking yelled at me!"

"What!" Amber suddenly flamed with anger. Her eyes locked on the girl with equal hatred. (Amber hadn't realized that she forgot entirely about Krystal.) Their position in the food court allowed them to hide in plain sight while getting a good view of Jaime and the girl. The two of them watched as Jaime and the girl sat at a table across the way. Summer asked, "Do you think like, they're on a date?"

Amber sipped from her straw. "Probably. You don't see guys and girls spending time together just to be friends now do we?"

Summer's head whipped around and stared with eyes of fire. Amber studied the girl in black, *This girl is gonna get it. That's a fact. No one yells at my best friend Summer and gets away with it.* Then she saw the look on Summer's face and before Amber knew it, Summer was up and walking over in their direction. Amber called out, "No Summer wait!" but Summer ignored her. Amber leaned back and put her hand to her forehead, *This isn't going to end well.*

Summer walked up toward the table where Jaime and Krystal were sitting and said, "Hey Jaime! It's so good to see you!" Summer threw her arms around Jaime without giving him time to prepare. Jaime let the unwelcome hug slide as Summer broke off.

"Oh, hey Summer," he replied. Feeling a bit awkward.

Summer glared down at him with a mixed look of happiness and hidden conceit. Jaime saw the look on her face and did not like where this was going. Summer asked, "What are you two doing?"

Jaime was not in the mood for the interruption and replied sternly, "Talking."

"About what?" Summer's eagerness crept into her words. It was a little intimidating, but Jaime gave her no ground.

"School."

Summer burst with energy, stretching her arms wide, "Oh I love school! It's the greatest! I have such an awesome time there with all the people I love! It's great!"

Jaime kept quiet. His silence mixed with Summer's unanswered question drove the atmosphere of the room down a whole level. Summer slid a secret glance in Krystal's direction. Allowing Krystal to see a glimpse of hatred in her eyes. Krystal met the glance with her own deadpan expression. Her defenses kicked in and she didn't allow Summer's arrows to reach her.

Summer looked at Jaime and then Krystal. "I didn't know you two were friends!" Jaime could hear the nuance in her voice. She was clearly not here to make them feel good. Jaime looked at Krystal.

"Yeah, we're friends. And we're hanging out. Enjoying our carmel apples." Jaime lifted the remainder of his carmel apple, seeing how it was almost finished. Summer froze for a split second, long enough to make her feel creepy even with a bright smile on her face.

Summer lit up, "Well that's great! And here I thought you two were on a date!"

Jaime shrugged. He looked over at Krystal and saw she was looking at Summer. Krystal was no fool, she knew what was going on. Neither of them said anything out of the awkwardness Summer imposed.

Summer quickly tried to regain the momentum. She looked at Jaime, ignoring Krystal, and pointed over her shoulder, "Hey Jaime, we're going to go get some ice cream if you want to come with us?" She pointed in Amber's direction behind her but never looked at Krystal.

Jaime said, "I'm good," his tone and expression uncharismatic.

Summer's eyes flickered for a quarter second at Krystal and then back at Jaime. She clasped her hands together and turned on the cute act. "Aww come on! We're like, going to have so much fun together!"

Jaime didn't share her enthusiasm and replied in the same tone, "I'm good." He shifted his gaze back toward Krystal, "You were saying?" But Krystal looked too uncomfortable to speak. Her eyes were too busy looking down at her lap to say much of anything.

Summer said, "Okay! If you change your mind, you know where to find us!" Then skipped back to Amber's side.

"That . . . was weird," Jaime said. Krystal nodded. Jaime noticed Krystal's demeanor had changed and she looked uncomfortable. "What's wrong?"

Krystal took a moment to answer, "I don't know." Jaime looked over his shoulder at Summer and Amber sitting across the way. Jaime said, "Either way that was weird." Krystal nodded.

Krystal said, "I think we should go."

Jaime was a bit surprised. "Alright, sure. Let's go." The two of them pulled out of their chairs and threw their apples away, walking out of the food court and heading out toward Jaime's car. Jaime could tell Summer was staring them down like a hawk as they walked out. Either way, Jaime got a bad feeling. He could only imagine what Krystal was feeling right now.

They got into the car and started driving. The first fifteen minutes of the drive were in total silence. Jaime didn't mind, but he was enjoying the conversation they were having up until the point where Summer budded in. Jaime snuck a glance at Krystal, finding her head lowered, looking down into her lap. Jaime brought his focus back to the road but was not content with doing nothing. *She looks gloomy again.*

"You look sad," he said. Bringing it out in the open. He looked at Krystal in the corner of his eye, hoping that would do something to jog her out of this funk. Jaime saw Krystal glance at him, but he couldn't see the whole expression. He stole another glance as Krystal settled down into her mute self again. Jaime lowered his driver's side window and stuck his head out into the wind, being careful of the cars around him. Krystal looked at him as Jaime screamed out into the windstream. The roaring wind filled the cabin and the air swirled like a maelstrom. Even Krystal's own hair flung up and danced around. Jaime brought himself back inside and looked at Krystal with his face and hair all windblown, like he'd been in a tornado.

"What was that?" Krystal asked.

Jaime lowered her passenger window, "Stick your head out."

"What?"

Jaime cracked a grin, nodding his head in encouragement, "Stick your head out the window."

"But I don—"

Jaime cut her off, "Don't think. Just do it."

Krystal stuck her head out and she was immediately overwhelmed with wind. Her hair flickering uncontrollably. The cool air was shaking everything around her. She was mostly taken aback by the sudden force and the complete lack of reasoning for this action, but her heart was exhilarated as she came back inside the car windblown. Jaime raised the windows up and the cabin fell silent with the roar of the wind muted behind the glass. Krystal looked a bit shaken but in a good way. Jaime started laughing at the sight of her. The dumbstruck look on her face was more than enough to send him over the edge. Krystal, still feeling on an adrenaline high, couldn't help but join him. The two of them laughed for a few minutes until their stomachs hurt. Jaime caught his breath and said, "There. Feel better?"

Krystal nodded, "Yeah."

Jaime could sense a hint of joy there. He looked forward and said, "Cool."

Krystal did the same, "Cool."

CHAPTER 26

Summer and the Party

"You can't expect people to just come up and talk to you. You have to initiate and go talk to people first. Otherwise, you'll just be sitting in a corner feeling miserable at an event."

—JL

Jaime was not hanging out with his normal group of friends during break like he usually did. He didn't want to be around them, so he decided to take a walk. He figured it would give him a chance to gather his thoughts. There was still time left during break, so he wasn't worried about walking around campus. He found himself in the outer portions of the school where there were fewer people around. He had hoped for some silence to think, to wonder how things were going, but his thoughts were interrupted when he heard footsteps behind him. Jaime turned and saw it was Summer, and she looked to be quite flustered.

"Hey," she said, sounding almost demanding . . . almost.

Jaime replied casually, "Hey?"

Summer simmered down, but still sounded direct. "I need to ask you a question."

Jaime lowered his brow, "Okay . . ." He certainly wasn't expecting this when he woke up this morning.

"I need to talk to you about Krystal." Summer's voice was beginning to rise. "I want to know what you see in her." Jaime could clearly hear the jealousy imbued in her speech. If he was being honest, it amused him slightly.

So that's what this is about huh. Jaime wasn't all too surprised. He had known Summer liked him, but he never felt that way towards her. He found her wildly unexciting.

"What is it you find so interesting about her?" she said. The question gave Jaime pause. His mind drifted to an area he had never thought of before.

"What do I think about her?" he mumbled. Jaime tried to think, and it wasn't that difficult, but his mind was in a quiet lull. Like feeling relaxed after taking a long nap. *You know, I don't think I've given much thought to anything else these past few years.* Jaime's mind was thinking of something other than his hatred for once. It all felt so new but not unwelcome. Something legitimate to think about, but also something he would deal with later.

"I need to think about that one," Jaime said. He was so calm that it surprised him. It was like all the anger had been drained out of him for the moment and he didn't have it in him to get mad.

"That's not an answer!" Summer yelled, sounding like a spoiled little girl, "I want to know what it is you *like* about her!" Summer gestured to herself. "I am a popular, pretty, and eccentric girl. I have friends, a great personality, and I think you're a great guy. But what I don't understand is like why you spend so much time with that loser, and not spend time with me and the people who matter." Jaime felt a portion of his anger return, but only a necessary 1%. Summer yelled at the top of her lungs, "WHAT THE HECK DO YOU SEE IN THAT GIRL!"

Jaime waited for Summer to finish her tantrum. A couple seconds dragged on before he could answer. He spoke with more resolve in his speech. "Unlike you, she knows how to *listen*."

Summer tilted her head defensively. It was not a jab she was expecting. "I listen to people!"

Jaime was too tired for this kind of argument. He kept his anger level low, and his voice controlled. "Summer, you don't know what it means to listen."

"What does this have to do with Krystal?"

Jaime couldn't believe he had to clarify this. "Unlike you, Krystal understands the value of listening to people. She cares more about others than she does herself. That's the value of listening. It's about putting aside what you were going to say and giving the person speaking your attention. Meaning, you actually understand what they are saying. You see Summer, you don't know how to listen because all you do is talk. You never give someone else the spotlight and you always interrupt people when they try to talk. You always have the spotlight on yourself. You love the fame. You love the popularity. You love being the center of attention. And most of all, you love to *talk*."

Jaime continued, "Well Krystal doesn't *talk*, she *listens*. Krystal is the kind of person who's always there for you when you're having the worst day of your life. She notices when people are suffering around her and cares for them regardless of the pain she's going through. Unlike you, who's always busy living like you're the center of the universe. Well, here's a newsflash for you Summer. It's not about you. When was the last time you asked someone in your group if they were okay? When was the last time you stopped talking for once and listened to someone having a bad day? If you even notice that."

"I have no idea what you're like talking about," she retorted.

Jaime stood firm, "Exactly. You have no idea because you've been so blinded by your own popularity that you can't even see the person crying next to you. Did you know that Krystal was suffering every time she hung out with you?"

Summer retorted defensively, "But she's always quiet! She like, never says anything!"

"Summer, she's tried to say things, you just never let her speak. How shallow are you?" he said sternly.

Summer's words were becoming more desperate. "But I always get uncomfortable when things get quiet. Plus, I don't know what to say around her!"

Jaime's voice angered slightly, "That gives you no right to ignore and ostracize someone. If someone is part of your group, you talk to them, you make them feel welcome. You ask them questions. You make them feel like they belong, not like they should be rejected. Because when you give someone your attention, you are loving on them. To be frank Summer, you haven't been loving towards anybody, only yourself. That's why I like Krystal a lot more than you. She has by far a greater sense of character and kindness than you ever would have. She understands that life is not about you. Now if you'll excuse me. I have a nice quiet walk to address."

Summer was dumbfounded hearing all this. Nobody had ever said this to her before. She assumed everything was fine, leaving people as is but that was not the case. And here, the guy she crushed on, was telling her how selfish she was for the first time in her life. It only enraged her. Summer cursed Jaime, "I don't care anymore! You go on with your little . . ."

But Jaime was already walking away, lifting his fingers into a "V" peace sign, and said, "Peace out," flipping his middle finger up, "and piss off." Summer was stunned as Jaime walked away, feeling slightly better. *What an interesting morning so far.*

~

Krystal had just finished cooking dinner and got herself all comfortable on her couch. She had her bowl of jambalaya ready and turned on the tv. Aunt Sarah had gone out to work for the night, so it was just Krystal at home. Being alone was growing on her, like she could sit down by herself and actually be okay, maybe not happy, or overjoyed, but okay.

Krystal checked the calendar app on her phone, staring at the empty sleet of the weekend ahead of her. It disappointed her. It was going to be another calm and boring weekend but at least she had some movies lined up to watch. Movies were always a good passtime for Krystal, it was all she did when she was alone, that and one other hobby.

Krystal saw the time on the tv, 9:36pm, just enough time for one movie before she went to bed. Krystal settled in, food in hand, blankets covering her. The ambience of the nighttime setting complimented the comfort, but it was only half-fulfilling. Krystal sighed. She had done this before, and her heart knew that. It was all part of the same boring routine she had always done every weekend, but she didn't know what else to do. It was so engrained in her routine that she didn't know how to do anything else.

Her phone buzzed and to her surprise, it was a text from Jaime. Krystal clicked open the text and read:

J: "Going to a party right now. You in?"

Krystal did not know how to react. She sat there stunned for a while. *What do I say?* she thought. While Krystal was elated from receiving an invitation, she couldn't help but feel conflicted. She took a mental check of her feelings and concluded that she did not want to go. It was hypocritical. On the one hand, Krystal wanted to do something different, while on the other hand, Krystal just got comfortable into her Friday night routine. It's not that she didn't want to go, it's that by going she would be changing up her routine and that would cause discomfort. It's the same as an animal getting comfortable with their cage. They were trapped for so long but at least the pain was predictable. It was something they were "comfortable" with, and that's how she felt. The door to the cage was open, but the fear of the unknown was strong enough to make her want to remain where she was. (Ironic, don't ya think?)

In her indecision, Krystal texted back, "That's okay but I'll pass. I'm tired and feel like staying home." Krystal clicked send and waited for a response. She saw the gray bubbles light up on Jaime's side and waited.

Her phone vibrated immediately. All Jaime said was, "I'm on my way." Krystal looked up from her phone in confusion. A minute later there was a knock on the door. Krystal got up from her couch and opened it. Jaime stood there and spoke in a slightly authoritative tone, the kind of voice that won't take no for an answer.

"We're going." And that was all he said. Krystal stood there bewildered. She wanted to say something but before she knew it, she was in a car driving off with Jaime.

∽

Krystal instantly regretted her decision. She stood behind Jaime, tense as a statue, on the porch of some stranger's house. Jaime looked at her and said, "Something wrong?" but Krystal said nothing. Jaime shrugged it off and knocked on the door. The door opened and Jaime's buddy Luiz saw him and said, "Aaaayyyy come on in!" and threw his arm over Jaime's shoulder as the two of them walked into the house like a bunch of bros. Krystal couldn't help but feel out of place watching. Luiz pushed the door fully open, the music flaring out from inside. Krystal subconsciously felt her left hand grip her right elbow as her whole body felt uncomfortable. Krystal took her time entering, watching Jaime and Luiz act all buddy buddy with each other.

Krystal thought, *I wish I could be like that. To have that connection with somebody.* Krystal took note of the house, the two-story building, multiple rooms inside, an office, nice carpeting upstairs, tiled flooring on the bottom. Growing chatter filled the kitchen as people swarmed around the countertop grabbing drinks and other "assortments." Krystal followed Jaime and Luiz into the kitchen where Jaime was greeted by an entire lot of them. There were about fifteen to twenty people crowding the kitchen and living room areas, all of them had red cups in their hands, some of them already looking a little tipsy. Krystal wanted to hang closer to Jaime, but he already threw himself into the crowd, acting all cheerful and wild. Krystal tilted her head, *Huh, I've never seen this side of him before. He's so active and sociable. It's different from the side of him I've been seeing.*

Krystal saw Jaime smiling and clapping hands with his guy friends while hugging other people as well. Krystal detected no trace of lying in his body language. *Huh. He isn't faking it.*

Krystal had hoped she would at least get to spend time with Jaime, given how he was the only person she knew at this party. The rest of the people were all faces she didn't know. She couldn't even recognize whether these people were from the same school or not. Krystal was beginning to feel bored, so she walked over into the kitchen, poured herself a cup of Sprite and watched the party go on.

She leaned against one of the walls hugging the kitchen and watched the groups of people engage in front of her. She had no idea what to do or how to have fun in these kinds of situations. So, Krystal sipped her Sprite, hoping that someone would be willing to come up and talk to her. Time went by and still no one had come up to her. Krystal lowered her head. *This isn't fun.* She went over and sat down on an open seat in the living room, taking in the sight of the party. More people flooded in as the night went on. Krystal was starting to feel like she was back at school. With all the groups around her talking with people they all knew, ignoring those they didn't. Krystal searched for Jaime a little while ago, but he was wrapped up in conversation with a bunch of people. In a way, she was happy for him. At least Jaime was having fun and expressing a joyful side of himself that he didn't share often with his own family.

I wonder if he is more relaxed when he's away from them? That might explain why he likes to come to my apartment so often.

Krystal sat on a chair in the living room. The couches surrounding the flatscreen tv were filled with people all drawing their attention to the football game. Krystal could hear what the people watching the game were saying:

"Do you remember that touchdown from Andre Jordan on the Packers last week? It was insane!"

"Yeah man, I heard he was going to get traded for Michael Dejourno from the Buccaneers."

"Duuuude! That's insane! It's just like the . . ."

Krystal sipped her Sprite and tried to follow along in the football game. It was the Miami Dolphins versus the Pittsburgh Steelers. It was only about the second quarter, but the game felt like it dragged on longer than it should have. Krystal watched the clock slowly tick down. Too slow for her count. Krystal had a tough time tracking the game because she barely knew the football teams, let alone any of the players' names. She would look up at the tv screen, but she never felt the same draw that it had on the rest of the people around her. Yet all the conversation around her was about the game. Krystal felt even more left out because she simply didn't understand the terminology. She had never bothered to watch sports or care about it really, so she was never interested in the things most people enjoyed.

Krystal crept away from the couches in search of Jaime, hoping he would be available, but Krystal saw he was busy entertaining another group of people. *Dang, he sure is popular with this crowd.* Krystal sipped her Sprite. *Maybe this is why he looks happier outside his home than at school? Here there are more of his friends where he can have a good time.*

But Krystal didn't feel the same. She walked over and stood against one of the corners to the kitchen and watched the party drag on. People were shuffling around her, talking, high-fiving, looking at the game, pouring drinks, playing beer-pong outside. None of them seemed to notice her. Krystal could feel herself becoming self-conscious again. Down in her heart she got the feeling that she was out of place. That she didn't belong here. That she wasn't accustomed to this setting. And she was right. It hurt her heart to watch everyone around her look so goody goody with each other while ignoring her. Krystal felt her mood dampen.

I wanna go home.

But she couldn't leave. Jaime was her driver, and he was having the time of his life. So the party went on. Krystal entertained the cup of Sprite and watched the party drag on for hours. Playing well into the evening and then the early morning, and all she could feel was how much she wanted to go home.

Jaime sat in the driver's seat. Krystal looked at him expressionless but enough for Jaime to tell what she was thinking. He said, "Don't worry, I'm not drunk. I didn't have a single drink tonight."

All Krystal said was, "Okay," and they drove on.

Jaime said, "That was a good party huh?" His enthusiasm was still glowing, even at this hour in the night.

"It was okay," Krystal said. Jaime could hear the depression in her voice.

"What's wrong? You didn't like the party?"

Krystal answered, "Not really." Jaime was a little taken back but when he thought about it, it made sense.

Jaime ticked his head to the side, "Did you talk to anyone?"

"No." Krystal said, "No one would come up to me." Krystal's voice was low and depressed, while on the other hand, he had the most fun he'd had in a while. But something from that last sentence irked him, and he couldn't help but be defensive about it.

"Krystal, you can't expect people to simply come up to you and start talking. It doesn't work like that." Jaime said bluntly.

Krystal raised her eyes to Jaime, "I'm not *you*." She was a little stern in her voice, and Jaime could feel the distance between them growing because of it.

He lowered an eyebrow, "What do you mean?"

Krystal shook her head, looking frustrated. "I can't do . . . that social stuff like you. I'm not good at it."

"Okay but no one is going to talk to you if you don't talk to them first. Just a word of advice." Krystal made a small grunt in the passenger seat. Jaime could see the look on her face, that she did not have a good time, but then again, she never bothered to go up and talk to a single person. It was partially her fault and not, at the same time. Jaime felt a sense of responsibility arise within him. A responsibility he did not want but had. Jaime made a low grunt and groaned. *We're going to need to work on this.* As they drove off into the night, eager to get the sleep they both desperately needed.

CHAPTER 27

The Sunrise Hike

*"Sometimes you have to do something outside of
your comfort zone in order to have fun."*

—Jaime Fisher

J aime lay in his bed, eyes half open. He wanted to drift off to sleep but couldn't. He couldn't manage to get his brain to shut off. He had awoken twenty minutes before his alarm would go off and was awake. His mind imagined sitting in class at zero period in one hour, how boring it will be. His heart felt repulsed by the idea, but he had to go to school because he had to be "responsible."

I feel like ditching, he thought. He wasn't opposed to the idea, actually it excited him. He wanted to do something different, to get out of his normal routine. Then he got an idea. He pulled out his phone and checked the time, *I wonder if she's up right now?* So he hit "Dial" on his phone and waited as the line rang.

✺

The phone vibrated over and over. The periodic and constant thrum slowly brought Krystal back into reality. Krystal sat up groggily and looked over at her phone with blurred vision. She tapped the screen a couple times, hoping it would turn off her alarm, but the thing kept on ringing. Krystal peered through her mucky eyelids and saw with just enough clarity that it wasn't her alarm. It was a phone call from Jaime. Krystal sobered up a little and put the phone to her ear.

"Hello," her voice was coarse and unprepared.

Jaime's voice seeped through the phone speaker, "Krystal hey. It's Jaime."

Krystal tried to sit upright, her eyes closing again yet still in the conversation with about a third of her usual brain capacity. "Yes?" rubbing her eyes.

Jaime said, "Listen, I'll get to the point. Do you want to skip school today?"

The thought didn't connect in Krystal's brain immediately. It took her a moment to realize what Jaime had just asked. "What?" she said, her body waking up more. "You want to what?"

Jaime lowered his voice into a whisper, "Want to skip school and go on a hike?"

Krystal wasn't even able to think clearly about this. She moaned, "Not really," falling back onto her bed, nearly falling asleep in the process.

It was silent for a few seconds, the phone just sitting on Krystal's bed as she drifted back to sleep. Until the words sounded so clearly, Krystal snapped wide awake from hearing them. Jaime spoke in all seriousness, like a professional assassin getting ready for an important meeting. "I'm coming over," he said. Krystal got up suddenly and quickly grabbed her phone, but Jaime had hung up already. Krystal's heart began to race as she was unclear as to what Jaime was planning. She held the phone in her hands, the empty screen staring back at her. *Is he . . . coming here? Now?* Her question was answered twenty minutes later when Jaime suddenly appeared at her front door.

Krystal opened the door and felt a blast of frigid winter air snap her wide awake. She found Jaime standing there, sweating and out of breath. The chilly air doing its job to keep him cool as he breathed clouds in front of her. Krystal stood in the doorway, stunned at the sight before her. "What are you doing here?" she whispered, grasping her pajamas tight with her hands.

Jaime grinned like a criminal, "We're going on a hike." He nodded, "Right now." Krystal was stunned by Jaime's enthusiasm, especially so early in the morning.

Krystal hesitated, "But . . . I'm not going to have any fun. There's nothing fun out there and we've got to get to school today."

Jaime nodded, expecting that answer, his enthusiasm not dropping a hint in level from her words, "Today we're ditching!"

Krystal was dumbfounded, searching for words to end Jaime's insane thinking. "I . . . I've never done that before. I typically take my studies very seriously."

Jaime pushed on, "You are. But today we're doing something different. So let's go on a hike while the sun is still down and watch the sunrise." Krystal had no words to respond. All she wanted to do was go back to bed and sleep in comfort for a few more minutes before going to school. She wasn't used to doing this sort of thing.

"What if we get caught?" she asked.

Jaime shrugged his shoulders, the idea still brimming in his head like he had the power of the sun inside him. "Then we get caught. But at least we are going to have some fun."

"I won't have fun," Krystal said somberly, as if she knew the outcome before it had even happened. Thinking of the party Jaime had recently taken her to.

Jaime said, "Let's make a bet. If you have fun, then I'll buy the next round of carmel apples at the mall. If you don't have fun, then I won't bother you again." Krystal stood there hesitant and unable to make a reply. Jaime stuck his hand out, "Put her there?" Krystal reluctantly took the hand and gave it a shake. Jaime smiled with glee, "Great! Now get ready and wear some clothes that will keep you warm, but you're going to need to shed a layer or two once the sun comes out."

Jaime ran down the stairs, quiet enough to not wake the neighbors, and all Krystal could think of in her tired state of mind was, *This guy is insane.*

Krystal sat in the passenger seat while Jaime sped the car in the darkness of the morning a little faster than she had wanted. Krystal could tell Jaime was excited, but she wondered if it was more than that. So she asked, "Why did you decide to do this all of a sudden?"

Jaime gave Krystal a quick look then returned to his focus on the road. "Because I was bored and wanted to do something different."

"You call this different?" Krystal said, like a bothered housewife annoyed with her husband.

Jaime ignored the tone and replied with his own charisma, "Yes! And we're going to have some fun!" He pulled the car off to the side of a dirt road Krystal had never seen before. Jaime threw his arm over the shoulder of the car seat and said, "Are you ready kids?"

Krystal got the reference, and spoke in slight monotone, "Aye aye captain."

Jaime smiled at the acknowledgment. He clenched his fist, channeling all the excitement into his hand, "Let's do this!" and threw himself out of the car. Krystal couldn't help but feel a slight sense of enjoyment at the sight of

Jaime looking so happy. Just watching him go off on his own was entertaining enough. The guy was oddly a goof ball other than his depressed angry side she usually saw. But when Jaime was not in his depressed state of grief, he was actually pretty enjoyable. He was fun and outgoing and a little bit of a pinball. Krystal stifled her emotions and stepped out into the cold dark air. Krystal bundled her arms close to her body, shivering. She looked around and was unable to see anything this dark in the surrounding countryside. "Are you . . . sure this is safe?"

Jaime said, "Don't worry, I've done this hike hundreds of times by myself, and every time I love it and come out even better than when I went in. Trust me, by the time we're done here, you are going to enjoy this sight I'm about to show you."

Krystal was doubtful of Jaime's comments and hugged herself tighter. Glancing around, unable to see anything in the dark. Jaime turned on a flashlight, gesturing over to an open trailhead, "Come on, this way. The trail begins here." Krystal followed, holding her own phone in her hands, turning the flashlight on and following behind Jaime. The flashlights didn't help too much, it was still too dark for that but at least Jaime knew where he was going. Krystal felt the gentle crunch of the gravel beneath her shoes, eyeing the ground for stray rocks that would give her the trip. The trail seemed to follow into the hillside and then curve upwards towards the top. It was a little hard to see with so little moonlight, but Jaime knew the trail like the back of his head.

As they walked, Krystal's mind was raging with thoughts.

I'm not going to have any fun! I just want to go home!

There's no point in doing something as nonsensical as this.

Even I just want to go home and be in bed for a few more minutes than to be out here in the cold hiking up some dumb hill with this psychotic boy I just met.

The sad reality was that Krystal agreed with the thoughts in her mind. She wanted nothing more than to go home, feeling her heart harden, and her hands and arms grip her body tighter, trying to keep warm in the cold. Even with her usual black outfit, she was still cold, feeling the cold whisp of air stab her face in the breeze. Krystal's shivering increased to a new level, and she wanted nothing more than to go home and get this dumb experience over with. The next half an hour the night sky brightened, the trailing dredge of the orange glow breaking over the horizon, shearing away the blue of the night and replacing it with the joy of a new day.

They reared to the edge of the hillside when Jaime ran forward and sprinted to the peak, throwing his arms up like Rocky and began jumping. Krystal drudged forward, wanting nothing more than to get warm again, as well as get back to school and back into her normal routine. *I'm going to get into so much trouble doing this,* she thought. Krystal had never been one to break the rules, and she took her academics very seriously. She was the daughter of a hardworking nurse after all, so it was part of her nature to work hard in academics.

Jaime squatted and waved Krystal on, "Hey hey come on!" Krystal was nearly out of breath, already mentally exerted from thinking the entire time. Krystal made it to the peak and joined Jaime standing there, noticing a nice wooden bench placed to the side of the dirt path, overlooking the surrounding area with the current sunrise. Krystal stood next to Jaime and the two of them watched as the rising glow of the sun erased the surrounding darkness of the sky and permeated the air with the hope of a new day. Krystal saw the mixture of the colors. The glow of orange mixed with neon pink across the clouds, the light blue of the morning sky complimenting the arrival of its best friend, as the sun broke the horizon, raising its gentle head slowly into the sky as its rays beamed down on Krystal, wiping away the cold on her face and greeting her with its warmth.

Krystal couldn't take her eyes off the sight, as the sun rose above the hills and took its rightful place in the sky, bringing life and light into the world. Krystal took a mental picture of the sight. It was the most beautiful sunrise she had ever seen. All her negative thoughts about the outrageous adventure were gone, encapsulated with the joy of waking up to see a new day rise. Krystal's heart melted and said a quick prayer to herself. *What a beautiful sight God. Thank you for making the sun.* She of course didn't say that out loud, but for right now, the moment was theirs and theirs alone.

Krystal looked over and was amazed at how quiet Jaime was, finally seeing the warm sunlight gleam off his face and she saw him smiling, smiling at something he genuinely enjoyed. *Wow. There really is a joyful side to this guy.* Krystal couldn't help but smile. It was not the biggest smile, but it was enough to brighten her day. What started as a dreadful morning turned into a warm and inviting day. And all Krystal could say was, "Thank you."

Jaime, never taking his eyes off the sun, said, "You're welcome."

Krystal took a breath, "I guess I owe you a carmel apple."

Jaime grinned at his victory, "I guess so."

PART FOUR

The Actress

CHAPTER 28

The Actress

"Who am I?"

—The Actress

Vomit swelled into the bottom of the toilet bin in currents. Hands grasped the sides of the bin as more and more vomit surged into the toilet, turning the clear water into a greenish yellow. The smell perforated her nostrils as the girl heaved the last of her dinner into the toilet. Fatigue gripped her body like an illness. Draining the energy from her body and leaving only weakness. The girl wiped her face with her hand and hit the drain on the toilet. The girl walked faintly over to her walled mirror and stood wobbly in front of the sink.

She turned on the light, not pleased with what she saw. Last night had been rough. Kristina could see the lines under her eyes from lack of sleep. Dark bags haunted her usually youthful and vibrant face. She checked her phone and saw she had only gotten two hours of sleep. Kristina lifted her head and tried to smile, but it killed her inside and sucked a majority of her energy just to smile. It had been getting harder and harder the past couple of weeks.

Kristina put both hands on the counter and stared at herself. Looking at the pale beauty in front of her, with her long black hair draping down her back. Staring at the stranger in front of her. The thoughts played on automatic in her mind. Her heart twisting from the pain as she looked in the mirror. *Who am I?* She tried to answer. *I am Kristina Walker, the Actress,* but it only made the pain in her heart worse. Loss and lack of direction swelled and spread to the surface, causing confusion to cloud her heart and mind.

Kristina looked again into her eyes, hoping to find an answer there. *I need . . . to keep up a good image. I can't let anyone see me weak.*

Kristina's self-esteem plummeted. She tried thinking about her day, planning it out minute by minute, but the idea of maintaining a false image the next twenty-four hours only drained her. She could feel it. She was running on fumes already.

Kristina smiled to herself and reached to grab her toothbrush but stopped. Her hand hovered over the brush and started shaking out of control. Kristina grabbed her wrist, trying to get it under her control, but the shaking spread until it permeated her entire body. Kristina looked back into the mirror, her arms like pillars of Jell-O as she looked at herself in horror from what was happening. All she saw was fear in her ocean blue eyes with the question, *Who are you?* settled in the center. Kristina shook violently, fearfully waiting for the episode to pass, until she finally calmed down and regained control of her body. Kristina gripped her hand, feeling the tightness in her chest from the anxiety racking her heart, causing her thoughts to run wild.

Oh my gosh! What am I going to do? What's going to happen today! How can I possibly keep this up!

Kristina took deep breaths to calm herself and managed to cool off. She steadied herself and looked in the mirror. Already out of breath she smiled wide, putting on her happy persona, "It's okay! Today's going to be great!" but the words stabbed her heart inside like an icicle, cold and sharp. She could already feel herself waning.

Can't let them see. Can't let them see.

⟡

"And . . . action!"

Kristina was dressed like a ragtag cowgirl for her new hit role, "Hill Riders." Wearing a dark brown cowboy hat, her lips laced with pure red lipstick, making her appear even more beautiful than before.

They were behind schedule in production, and it had become a necessity for Kristina to push aside some of her normal schoolwork so that she could be ready once on set. Kristina tipped her hat forward, all decked out in makeup, looking like a supermodel as she approached the character Billy

Van and spoke in a thick Southern accent, "My my Billy, it takes two to run a party, and three to run a show."

Billy Van, all tucked up in his beard and rag tag clothing said, "But Sis, we ain't got nothing on the Belkins! We can't never get up there an compete with them hoolies!"

Kristina paused. *Who am I?* interrupted her thoughts. She froze in place, the words just on the tip of her tongue yet they alluded her memory. The prompter revealed her next line, "We can do anything brother," but Kristina remained frozen. Kristina's head started vibrating, then her hands. Kristina tried with all her might to keep herself controlled but the shaking only grew. The director interrupted, "Say your line Kristina," but Kristina was caught up in her own world. The background faded out and she was alone facing her own thoughts.

Who am I? Who am I? Ambiguity and anxiety racked her brain drowning all sense of direction like a ship lost at sea. Kristina didn't know where she was. Couldn't tell who or where she was. Her sense of direction felt impeded, almost like everything was drifting into a haze. Words became muffled but Kristina managed to understand them.

"Kristina. Kristina? Are you okay?" People started giving looks of concern, until Kristina suddenly walked off set, ignoring the crowd of people flooding behind her. She closed the door to her personal makeup studio, locking it behind her. She put a hand against the wooden wall, finally alone, feeling weak and fatigued. Kristina lowered her head, barely able to stand. She turned, put her back against the wall, then slid down until she was on the floor. She was out of breath, breathing heavily, forgetting all about being dressed as a cowgirl and focused more on catching her breath. Kristina mumbled to herself, "Who am I?" the fear imbedded in the question.

Kristina managed to calm down after a couple minutes. There were a few knocks on the door, but she ignored them. She couldn't manage talking to people yet. All her energy was gone. Once she calmed down, Kristina felt her mood tank hard. She didn't even have the motivation to lift her hands. Kristina caught her breath; *It's getting harder to do this. My motivation is waning day by day. They might even recast me.* The fear of losing this role petrified her. She could not lose this role! It was too big to lose to some other low time actress. They needed her and she wanted to do this role, but it was getting harder and harder with every passing day. Kristina didn't even have the energy to stand up right now.

Another minute passed until there was a knock on the door. "Kristina? You in there? It's Carlo."

Kristina took a breath and called back happily, "I'm doing great Carlo! I only need a minute." It took all she had to sell the lie.

Carlo answered cautiously, "Okie dokie. Come back out when you're ready." Kristina knew she had to rally. She forced herself to get back up, putting what little energy she had into her arms and legs. They weren't done shooting and she had to get through the next couple hours. Kristina stood up and leaned against the wall, then felt a surge in her stomach and reached over and puked into a nearby trashcan. The stench was vile, a mixture of oats and eggs she had this morning. Kristina put the trashcan aside and cleaned herself up, wiping the vomit from her mouth, messing up the lipstick, then taking a shot of some mouthwash she had in her purse. Kristina forced herself to smile and put herself back together, even if she was held together by only willpower. She took a deep breath and steadied herself, putting on her happy persona. "We're going to have a great shoot!" opening the door for the flood of people waiting for her.

They completed shooting for the day, but Kristina had never been happier to finish. Her body was aching so much that she was itching for the final minute where the director yelled cut and stopped for the day. Kristina went to get her make up off and return the outfit, but while she was on her way, she overheard the director talking to her agent, Carlo, and heard the words, "recast" and "problems." That was enough to cause her to worry.

This wasn't the first time she had left mid-shoot and collapsed. This was at least the third time this week she had suffered an attack like this. She couldn't call it a panic attack because that was only half of it. It was a mixture of anxiety and depression followed by the question: "Who am I?" Kristina saw its effects more every time she looked in the mirror. She was starting to deteriorate, and people were starting to notice.

Kristina was driving home later that night when she received a phone call from her agent. She picked it up, putting on her happy persona, "Hey there Carlo! How you doing?!"

"Kristina, I have to tell you something." His voice was not cheerful or lighthearted as it usually was.

"What's going on Carlo?" Kristina said, but Carlo was not matching her enthusiasm.

"Tina, the director is worried about you and so am I. We've barely started shooting this new show and you haven't been yourself lately." Kristina wanted to object but she had no proper answer.

Carlo sighed, "Look, I'm worried about you. I know a lot has happened since your parents got divorced recently and you filed a motion to become an independent minor, so I know you have a lot on your mind. So please, make sure you're taking care of yourself. Go home and figure out your health. Or else you might lose the role." Kristina froze, still holding the phone to her ear. The effect of the words still hitting her like a truck. It felt as if steel wire wrapped around her heart, choking her from within.

Kristina held the phone up, killing her inside to hide her dismay, "Okay! Don't worry! I'll be back and ready to go!"

"Okay. Great. Take care. Rest up and I'll see you soon. Bye."

The phone hung up and Kristina didn't know what to think. She put the phone down, letting the silence fill the car. All she could say to herself was, "I might lose the role . . . I can't lose the role, and if I do . . . then what else am I?"

Kristina pulled up to her private apartment. She had bought it recently with Carlo's help and she now lived independently from both her parents. The recent divorce had left a major gap between Kristina and her parents. What made it worse were the scandals that followed once Kristina became a young movie star. She just couldn't trust them anymore. Kristina thumbed the door handle to her apartment door, letting it scan her thumbprint. She heard a latch flip within the metal frame and pulled the door free. She entered her four-bedroom apartment, complimented with a complete kitchen, living room, four bedrooms, a closet, and so much more. It was more than enough for a lone high schooler to live and get by. Kristina flicked the light and gazed at all the family photos, coloring of the walls, flags set up, posters of famous movie stars as well as her own, complimented with the smell of a coconut air freshener. Kristina inhaled and tried to relax but she felt both anxious and depressed. She missed the affection of having a family at home. Kristina headed toward her room and closed and locked the door, you never know who's watching through the windows of a famous actress. Kristina stepped onto the white carpet of her main bedroom. The bed frame fitted in the middle of the room like she was royalty, with all the red velvet drapes dangling from all sides. Kristina leaned back against the door and slid down into the fetal position.

She felt empty and without direction, letting those feelings stir questions in her mind. *Who am I?* Kristina leaned her head back and looked up at the ceiling, the white walls converging in the middle. *Who am I?* The questions left unanswered, causing more pain in her heart. Her mind felt more and more lost the longer she thought of it.

She was suddenly out of breath. "It's getting harder . . . Trying to keep up an image." She shook her head. "I can't do this forever." Kristina looked over at her bed, the velvet and gray sheets inviting her. "I guess I should try to get some sleep." But sleep would not come. She would often wake up at night and vomit in her bathroom because of her anxiety. Even breathing had become difficult lately, and with her current course, Kristina feared something was going to give, either her body or her insecurities. Her bet was on the former.

Getting out of the car was the worst. Kristina took a deep breath just before the door opened. Kristina put on the smile and happy persona, before she stepped out into the cold, feeling the chilly wind steal all sense of warmth on her face like a thousand needles. She walked on, ignoring the cold as best she could. The school was still drowsy in the early morning but that didn't matter. Drowsy or not, people lit up the moment they saw her.

Kristina rounded the corner and walked out in the open toward her first classroom. Almost immediately people began shooting looks of awe her way. Kristina raised her smile, trying to lift her spirits to the cute fun-loving actress she was. But it came at a cost. Kristina felt her heart tug downward like a rock. *You have to suck it up! Fake it till you make it!* But it killed her inside. Kristina made sure to keep the smile on and wave at them politely. They waved back. It wasn't long before people began to approach her.

A freshman boy with brown hair and a white t-shirt walked up to her and asked, "Hey! Oh man, can I get a picture with you, Kristina Walker?"

Kristina smiled wide, feeling the tug on her heart fall deeper, like a boulder underwater. "Why of course!"

The boy lifted his phone and together they took a picture. The boy walked away saying to his friends, "I got a picture with Kristina Walker!"

Kristina wanted to drop the smile, but she couldn't drop the act even if she wanted to. She was now Kristina Walker, the Actress. That's who she was. That's who she had to be. Kristina headed toward her first class, when more people began swarming her, asking for photos, what it's like to be an actress, all that stuff.

With each greeting, Kristina felt her heart pull downward, draining her energy like a parasite. It was alright for a time, but eventually Kristina was out of breath and needed to find cover before she passed out. Amidst the admiring crowd she finally said, "I'd love to satisfy all of your requests, but I need to get to class soon." The crowd aww'd in disappointment and dispersed. Kristina, finally having a moment to herself, walked toward her first class, out of breath. She tried her best to not pay attention to the crowd, but no matter how hard she tried, people kept sneaking looks in her direction. With every look, Kristina lifted her guard up even higher, smiling wider, acting more outgoing, but with it came fatigue and the tug on her heart yearning for honesty.

I can't let them see. I need to be who I am. Kristina Walker, the Actress.

And with that, she kept on the façade. Building invisible walls around herself as she went through the day, being someone she's not. Day after day, holding up the façade, wondering if anybody will ever truly know her. But now is not the time. Now is the time for first period. The draining torture would continue and all she could do was grin and bear it. Afterall, she had a persona to maintain. She couldn't even face math class without the prying eyes of the paparazzi sneaking up to the window, hoping to catch her mid sneeze or something equally embarrassing that they could sell to a tabloid for a quick buck. But still, school continued regardless.

"Ugghh" Kristina exhaled, trying to find a place of refuge from the paparazzi now that third period was over. She looked around the school, searching door to door, avoiding all the groups of people walking by, trying to find a place of refuge before she physically collapsed. The hallways packed with groups surrounding the lockers. Kristina found a classroom that appeared empty, and quickly and cautiously closed the door behind her. It was a rare opportunity to find an empty classroom during lunch, so she took it anyway. She put her back to the door and exhaled, lowering her guard.

"Alone at last," Kristina said, feeling a slight burst of energy return to her now that no one could see her. Kristina put her hand to her forehead and rolled it through her long black hair. Her perfectly ladled eyelashes and ear piercings set the tone for her beauty. She took a deep breath and exhaled, "I can't take it out there. Everyone coming up to me, trying to get a picture. Everyone! Trying to be my friend. It drives me crazy because I know they're all fake. They say they know me, but they don't really know me. They only know the image I put on. The image I must continue." Kristina threw her hands in the air and paced around the empty room. She was surprised the teacher wasn't there, but she didn't mind it. Any alone time was time well appreciated. The lights were off, but Kristina didn't bother to turn them on. She wanted some peace and quiet before she headed out into the world where people couldn't stop looking at her. Kristina did a mental check of her body and felt the fatigue weighing her down. Everything from her shoulders down to her toes was exhausted. It was hard even to stand. She was barely holding herself together and was ready to collapse at any moment.

But you can't let them know! You can't! You have to keep going. You have to sell the act!

Kristina said aloud, "I know, I can't let anyone see this part of me. It would ruin me."

Out of nowhere Kristina heard shuffling. She whipped around, and lying down on one of the desks was some dark figure sleeping quietly. The figure shifted but didn't wake up. Kristina's immediate instinct was to leave the room, but instead she stepped closer to get a better look. The darkness in the room hid any details, but she could tell it was a person sleeping. She closed in until she was right next to the sleeping figure.

It was a girl, dressed in all black, asleep with her face in her arms. Kristina thought she must have fallen asleep during class, and no one bothered to wake her up. The figure slowly stirred, and Kristina lifted up her happy persona again. The girl awoke and looked up at Kristina with dreary eyes. Kristina greeted her with a powerful, "Hey!" but the girl showed no reaction to the warm greeting. The lack of reaction stymied Kristina for a second but she didn't break character. Kristina asked, "What are you doing here? Are you lost? Did you fall asleep or something?"

The girl rubbed her eye and yawned. Kristina wanted to yawn too, but that would only blow her cover, so she fought the impulse gripping her face and lungs. The girl croaked, "Yeah," looking up at Kristina with her midnight purple eyes, looking more purple than blue.

Kristina said, "What are you doing in here?" Turning on the cute act, smiling as cheerfully as she could.

The girl in black answered frankly, "I fell asleep."

Kristina tilted her head, "Why'd you fall asleep?" Her voice forcibly raised to complete the act.

The girl answered, "Long night."

Kristina hummed in understanding. "Ah yes, I've had a lot of long nights. It comes with the job, you know." Kristina waited for the girl's explosive reaction, but it never came.

All she said was, "Yeah."

Kristina paused. *Okay . . . this girl is one for few words. I wonder if she knows who I am?*

Kristina gestured to herself, "You do know who I am right?" Kristina's heart pained asking the question. She never liked having to establish what was already so obvious to many people.

The girl's passive expression only said, "Yeah."

Yeah? Kristina thought. *That's it! No major reaction or anything?* Kristina wanted to react, but she kept her defenses up. She clapped her hands together and pointed to herself, "It's your friendly childhood star Kristina Walker, the Actress!"

Kristina imagined an audience clapping, spraying graffiti, but the girl said, "Okay," like it was no big deal.

"Aren't you excited? You do know I'm a big-time actor right?"

"I know."

Behind Kristina's smile she thought, *This girl throws me off. I can't get a read on her. And why doesn't she seem more surprised if she knows who I am?*

"Do you want an autograph?" Kristina asked.

The girl shook her head. "Not really." The girl picked up her things and got up to leave, but before she walked out the door, she stopped and said softly, "You can cut the act. You don't need it," then walked out.

Kristina turned pale, nearing panic. *What the heck was that?* Kristina worried. *Did she see right through me?*

CHAPTER 29

Two Truths and a Lie

*"Friendship is a two-way street. Sometimes you have to
sacrifice a little on your end in order to have fun."*

—Jaime Fisher

In the distance Krystal could hear the loud bustle of music and people chatting. This was unfamiliar territory for her. *Here we go.* She could feel
herself mentally drained already, wanting to be anywhere but here.

"Uggghhhhh" Krystal groaned.

"Come on," said Jaime, waving her on like a crossing guard.

"I don't want to," Krystal defied, "I'm not gonna have fun." They
approached a house with a tan colored front door, the walls were lined and
rough with a few vines growing on them. Krystal planted herself on the stone
porch as Jaime stood next to the door. A dull light hung next to the front
door adding an orange glow, complimenting the darkness of the night outside the house.

Jaime centered himself in front of Krystal like an older sibling, his taller
and broader physique made him look a few years older despite the fact that
they were both in the same grade. He looked down at Krystal and spoke
softly, "Krystal, you are not going to make any friends unless you get out of
your comfort zone."

Krystal grabbed her right elbow with her left hand, feeling her heart
tense with discomfort and grunted, "I know," she sighed, "It's just . . . I'm
not . . . comfortable with this scene and . . . I'm not gonna have fun." She was
certain of this.

Jaime sighed slightly and said, "You will have fun. There are times when you think you won't have fun, but then you do something different with people and you do have fun. That's what socializing is all about. You do something that someone else likes and try to have as much fun with that as you can."

Krystal didn't have a good argument, so she answered honestly, "I just don't want it to be like last time."

Jaime replied, "Good," as if he were expecting an answer like that. "It's up to you to make it a different experience. Friendship is a two-way street. Sometimes you have to sacrifice a little on your end in order to have fun. Besides, it'll be better than sitting at home by yourself doing nothing."

Krystal mumbled, "It's not that bad."

"What was that?" Jaime leaned down and looked at her with a sly, *"I want to know what you really think"* look.

Krystal didn't give him the satisfaction. "Okay fine."

Jaime grinned. "I want you to try to talk to people tonight. I know it may be hard, but hard does not mean impossible. I want you to try and talk to at least one person tonight." Then he paused and raised the corner of his lip in a wicked half-smile. "Or else I'm not driving you home."

Krystal lifted her gaze and read through his sarcasm. She was a little appalled by the gutsy action, but she could tell Jaime was not joking. She didn't have an argument on this one. She had to try and meet *somebody* at this party. Krystal controlled her voice emphasizing the one word coming from her mouth, "Fine."

Jaime put his hands pridefully on his hips, "Great! Now let's go in."

Why do you have to make it hard like that? she thought.

Jaime knocked on the door while Krystal waited behind him. If it wasn't for Jaime, then Krystal probably would never have come. That was the benefit of having a friend who was different from you. For Krystal, Jaime was the type of guy to push her outside her comfort zone and get her to try new things. That could be a blessing and a curse, but it did help Krystal experience life more. Krystal could now go and try new things because she had a friend who would go with her. If she were on her own, then she wouldn't have gone in a million years to a party like this, especially on her own.

A guy answered the door, "Oh, you must be here for Ritchie's party." His voice was deep and masculine. The guy was clearly in the best shape of his life, but he didn't look extremely old either. "I'm Hank," he said, "Come on in."

Krystal and Jaime followed, and Krystal was immediately overwhelmed with obnoxious chatter from the inside of the house. There had to be well over a hundred people at this party. People hanging out by the ping pong tables, some outside drinking like college students, others sitting around the couches chatting.

Krystal spotted a nice living room with fancy silverware on a red table-top that appeared relatively undisturbed. It was a place of quiet amidst the noise of the house. People were everywhere, standing and chatting, not doing much other than sipping from their red cups. (Ever hear of a fish out of water, well Krystal was one now.) The atmosphere of the crowd engulfed Krystal and she suddenly felt like a kite lost in a storm. Krystal and Jaime paused for a second, observing the party. Krystal glanced at Jaime and could tell he recognized a majority of the people. She could tell he wanted to go and hang out with them, but he held back a moment.

Jaime stood next to her and pointed to a group across the way. He had to yell in order to be heard. "You can go up to those people and try to say hi."

Krystal groaned, "Okay." She felt the discomfort attack her heart, urging her legs to run back to safety. Jaime had picked a group of people standing around the kitchen countertop, the area filled with snacks, drinks, and all kinds of "fun" material. (I'm not gonna tell you, you can figure it out.) It was the perfect place for people to hang out and talk over snacks. Krystal approached them with caution. She felt her mouth clamp down subconsciously, fighting just to speak. Even though no one was looking at her, Krystal felt self-conscious again. Her introverted side empowering itself, wishing to go back and hide in the corner. Her shyness screaming at her that this is wrong and that it wouldn't end well, but Krystal tried to ignore the voices and temptations, but it was difficult to block them out.

Just go back and sit down. It will be okay.

You're not going to have fun, so just stay where it's comfortable. Please.

They were very convincing. Krystal felt like she was at school again, remembering when she tried to simply text Jaime, how difficult that had been. Krystal was still having difficulty talking to people, but it was less so these days. Perhaps going to church had helped with that, she didn't know, but it was still hard for her to socialize with others. Merely going up to a group of strangers made Krystal turn white and feel like she was going to pass out, but she had to at least try.

She approached the countertop and stole a couple Dorito chips from the bowl, observing the group, waiting for an opportunity to speak. There was a guy standing right next to her, chatting with some guys in the process. Krystal tried to listen in to what he was saying but had no idea because of how loud the music was. She picked up a few things, something about a tractor and a cat. Krystal opened her mouth to say, *"Hey how's it going?"* but her mouth clamped shut. She turned around with her tail between her legs and walked back over to the corner where Jaime stood holding a red cup in a bourgeoise manner.

Jaime didn't look surprised. "Wow, you really can't talk to people, can you?"

Krystal's discomfort and dampened mood were not good places to start with that comment. Krystal glared at Jaime with a dark look in her eyes. "It's not easy," she said, speaking slow, stern words. She shook her head. "I hate talking to people. I don't do it well."

"You're talking to me," Jaime said, sipping his drink.

Krystal looked at Jaime, "You're different. You're a lot . . . easier to talk to."

Jaime sighed, "Same. You're pretty easy to talk to yourself." Krystal found encouragement in that compliment. A little team booster out of all of this. "Well, good luck," he said, as he pushed off the wall and joined the party. Krystal stared at him blankly. Jaime turned back at her, "And remember, I'm not taking you home unless you talk to someone."

"That's cruel," she said.

Jaime took his jacket off and tossed it aside, "But true." He then turned and was on his merry way, running straight into a group of guys while the rest of them greeted each other like a bunch of bros.

Krystal shook her head, both out of amusement and jealousy. *Dang, I wish I could be like that.* Suddenly, there she was, alone again. Like a lost child without a parent. The sight of all the people around her was intimidating. Krystal could sense the high school aroma in the party like blood in the air, but somehow it felt different. Most of these people Krystal had never met before, and they didn't know each other either. But that was only a guess. These people could all be close friends for all she knew. Like a horse drawn to water, Krystal found herself standing at the kitchen countertop pouring herself another cup of Sprite.

Krystal heard the sound of applause grow as the front door closed and people started cheering. Krystal glanced over the side of the kitchen wall to see what's happening.

Somebody called out, "Yo! It's Kristina Walker!" Everybody cheered and welcomed her in. Kristina Walker smiled and threw her arms in the air, "Let's do this!" The whole room erupted in applause. Someone came up and handed Kristina a drink while Krystal watched the scene unfold. Krystal saw Kristina wearing a fashionable blue colored dress and a nice red hat to accompany it. She looked like a 1920s celebrity. Kristina disappeared amongst the crowd and Krystal was left to plan her next move for the rest of the night.

The next couple of hours were more vain attempts by Krystal trying to talk to people, all of which ended poorly and without a single conversation being struck up. The night dragged on and Krystal was beginning to run out of Sprite to drink. Krystal found a hallway leading from the kitchen to the dining room with the red tablecloth. It was a small hallway, but one that provided some sense of security and quiet, at least the best kind of quiet you could get in a house roaring with both people and music. Krystal was amazed the cops hadn't been called yet. She leaned against the dark hallway and put her hand to her forehead, taking a breath.

It feels like the last party I went to. She shook her head. *I'm not having fun.* Krystal wanted to go over and try the other events such as beer pong, but she didn't know how to play, and all the places were packed with people. So all there was left to do was . . . talk. Krystal grimaced. She didn't like a party where there was nothing to do but talk. Because if talking didn't work, then the party was extremely boring. Krystal took a deep breath, trying to calm herself. She felt something nudge on her heart and she looked down the hall into the fancy dining room. Out of curiosity Krystal followed the impression and poked her head out, only to find Kristina Walker sitting in a chair by herself. Krystal read her expression, it was the same one she had, a face that echoed: *I'm not having a good time.* Kristina Walker sipped the beer in her hand then put it down, annoyed with the sight of it. She leaned back in her chair and was watching the crowd around the house. Krystal saw the look in Kristina's ocean blue eyes and thought she should do something.

What should I do?

I think this is an opportunity for you to say hi to her Krystal. Fear swarmed Krystal as the idea gripped her. Krystal looked back at Kristina;

her expression hadn't changed. Watching somebody who was clearly not having a good time, who was waiting for the night to be over. Krystal whipped around the corner and planted her back against the wall.

What should I do?

You should go up and talk to her. That's what you should do.

But how should I do it? I mean I can't just walk up to her and say, "Hey how are you doing?"

Yes, you can.

Well, it's not that easy! Krystal peeked again, no change.

Krystal looked up and prayed, *God . . . what should I do?* Her heart calmed and she suddenly felt at peace when she remembered God.

The words *"Love your neighbor as yourself"* played through her mind, and they seemed to settle her as she heard them. Krystal's arms and neck relaxed, and she sank back against the wall. She snuck one more peek at Kristina then came back into the hallway. Krystal glanced over into the kitchen, observing all the drinks being poured. The idea forming in her mind.

Krystal pulled her head back and gritted her teeth, *Aggghhh please don't make me go over there*, but an image of herself flashed in Kristina's place. Krystal remembered standing alone at a party like this. Sitting in the back of the room against some potted plant. Her left hand holding her right elbow as Krystal stood there, unsure of how to proceed, let alone how to interact with people. Krystal remembered how people walked right by her, not noticing her in the slightest. Krystal couldn't have been more obvious while at the same time more hidden. *Is there something wrong with me?* Krystal thought. *Was I doing something wrong that caused these people to ignore me? I could have sworn that some of them had noticed me, but they did nothing.*

Krystal remembered the silent call, *"Somebody please help me."* But no one did. The only person Krystal ever remembered showing her love was her mom and Jesus. Krystal pictured Jesus hanging on the cross for her, who called her worthy, forgave all her sins, and died for her. Krystal clambered back to reality and observed Kristina once more. There she sat, looking at her phone, like the most miserable person in the room while everyone around was having the time of their lives. Krystal took a breath and exhaled slowly. *I know this is going to be awkward, but if that girl is truly hurting, then I'm going to try.* This time she had the courage to step out, not of her own accord but out of the Holy Spirit's power. She got herself ready and headed over.

Krystal came up to Kristina, red cup in hand, and silently gestured to Kristina. Kristina caught sight of Krystal and nearly jumped. Krystal said nothing and held the cup out to her.

Kristina's saddened expression flipped like a switch. Turning into a bright smile as she suddenly became the happiest girl in the world. "Oh, for me? Thank you!" The sudden change of character would have made most people worry, but Krystal showed no change in expression. It was strange though for a person to go from zero to a hundred all of a sudden. Krystal put the cup on the table and turned around. Kristina noticed the gesture and asked, "Where you going?" Krystal remained silent and pointed to the kitchen. Kristina widened her smile, speaking more enthusiastically than before, "You don't want to stick around?" Krystal merely shook her head. Kristina paused for a long moment, but it felt like an eternity between the two of them. Kristina was frozen, smiling in place, the sudden lack of interest catching her off guard while Krystal showed no change. Her expression almost looked a bit merciless if you looked at it a certain way.

Kristina tried again, tapping the chair next to her. "Come on!" but Krystal didn't take the bait. Krystal thought, *For some reason, I get the feeling this girl is playing some kind of game.* But Krystal wouldn't bite. She shook her head again, then turned her back toward Kristina and headed into the kitchen hallway, but before she could enter the doorway, she heard, "Wait!" Krystal stopped. Surprised by how different the voice was from before. Krystal turned and saw the expression on Kristina's face. It looked entirely different than before. What was a beautiful example of youth revealed signs of exhaustion. Krystal saw the fatigue in Kristina's eyes, the lines beneath her eyelids, the obvious lack of sleep hidden through a masterpiece of makeup. Krystal could see it all. The pain, the helplessness, all coming together to create this look of desperation.

Kristina's eyes dragged downward, the exhaustion revealing itself. She seemed out of breath. Her eyes widened in horror, and she threw her smiley persona back on. What disarmed Krystal wasn't the smile, but the moment of weakness Kristina just showed. Almost like she had accidentally revealed herself, like she had let her guard down, and that seemed to relax Krystal and make her curious.

Krystal wasn't sure if this was another act, but she saw the expression drawn across the actresses' face. The act of the smile really meant: *"Help me."*

Krystal felt a tug on her heart and groaned inward. This was already getting out of her comfort zone, but she decided to take a risk because that's what Jesus would have done for her. Krystal faced Kristina, watching Kristina gesture to an open seat across from her.

Krystal stepped down and took a seat. Kristina brightened a bit and increased her positivity. She shouted, "Hooray!" raising her arms in the air like she was a childhood movie star. (Well . . . that's exactly what she was but you get the picture.) Krystal felt her defenses rise slightly as she sat in front of Kristina. This was an unusual occasion to be sitting across from a movie star that everyone is usually fawning over, but right now, it was just the two of them. Just Krystal and Kristina, sitting across from each other, like two players in a game of poker. Krystal stared down Kristina, and Kristina did the same. They were almost mirroring each other, despite one of them smiling and the other was not. (Guess which one Krystal was.)

Kristina reached for the red cup Krystal had placed down and said, "Thank you for the drink! I'm really glad you gave it to me."

Krystal made no change in expression. For a long time, the two of them didn't know how to interact with each other. For some reason, Krystal felt she resonated with Kristina despite not knowing a single thing about her. There was something . . . *familiar* about her, like what happened with Jaime.

Kristina's smile flickered, like a twitch, when she said, "What's your name?"

Krystal hesitated for a moment. For some reason, she had more confidence to speak now than earlier in the party. It was strange but not unwelcome. She said, "Krystal."

Kristina tilted her head sly-like, "Is there a last name in there?" Krystal said nothing. There was a part of her that was skeptical towards this type of person. Kristina was a popular person, no doubt, but it was the deliberate act she put on that made Krystal not want to be totally honest with her. It was like playing against a professional poker player. It's hard to tell who knows more about the other. When Krystal didn't say anything, Kristina seemed at a loss for words, "You do know I'm an actress right?"

Krystal spoke callously, "Yeah."

"Like from the movie?" Kristina affirmed. Krystal understood and nodded. She wasn't doing an excellent job coming across as Mrs. Charismatic.

But what Krystal found interesting was how Kristina didn't recognize her from the other day.

Krystal analyzed Kristina's smile. *I can't tell why,* Krystal thought, *but I feel like she's not who she says she is.* They stared each other down for a while, until suddenly Kristina's demeanor weakened, like her tower of charisma came crashing down bit by bit. This time the smile was gone. Now that detail Krystal found interesting, but she didn't show it. She had just seen a different side to Kristina a moment ago, like she shed her armor and let Krystal peer through the cracks for a second. Of course, Kristina was an actress, she was good at hiding things, but that moment of weakness made Krystal want to lower her defenses as well.

Krystal allowed herself to lighten her defenses a smidge and asked honestly, "Are you okay?" Now Kristina was surprised. They were the first words Krystal said, but it made Krystal feel a connection building between them.

Kristina brought her spirits back up and said, "That's very kind of you. But don't worry about me. I'm peachy."

Krystal wanted to raise an eyebrow but held it back. *Peachy huh. That's the perfect word for a lie.* Then a thought dropped in Krystal's head, and she asked, "Do you want to play a game?"

Kristina cheered. "Sure! I love games!" Her voice was so egotistical and cheery that the air waves around her emanated brightness. Krystal didn't let the feeling affect her one bit.

"It's called two truths and a lie. You heard of it?"

"Oh yes of course I have!" Kristina shriveled with excitement. Her smile widening so large Krystal felt she would go blind from staring at the sun. There was something about her that Krystal just couldn't nail down. *She's good at this. Incredibly good.*

Krystal said, "Okay then, you go first."

Kristina nodded ecstatically, her face brimming with excitement. Kristina searched the room, taking time to ready her answers. She turned and faced Krystal, "I'm ready. So the first one is, I've been bitten by a cat in the last week, I have a strong desire for peaches, and I'm allergic to dogs."

Krystal leaned her elbows on the table and stared at Kristina, reading her every expression, every muscle movement like a professional poker player. Kristina saw this and wasn't going to let Krystal in that easy.

Krystal glared hard at Kristina and said, "Allergic to dogs is the lie."

"That's correct," Kristina said, a bit surprised by Krystal's observation skills. "Your turn."

Krystal warned her, "I'm not particularly good at this. I can't lie."

Kristina waved off her modesty. "Just think of something, anything. I don't care."

"But I do," Krystal said in all seriousness. "I care a lot . . . about what I say." Krystal's mind searched the inner portions of her brain, but she couldn't think of anything fun. All she could think about was serious stuff. Krystal looked Kristina dead in the eyes and said, "Okay, I'm ready." Krystal's tone was all serious as she listed off the options, "I don't talk much, I sit by myself during lunch, and I'm an all-star athlete."

Kristina leaned forward like a seductive mistress and took a long hard look at Krystal, but Krystal never budged. Never showed a chink in her armor.

Kristina said, "All-star athlete is the lie."

"That's correct," said Krystal, not surprised at all by Kristina's guess. In fact, Krystal had expected Kristina to get it right. She had allowed Kristina an obvious answer. "Your turn."

Kristina pondered for a moment, listing off her fingers, "I went on a hike and befriended a bird along the way, I can sing every Disney song ever made, and third, I shaved my head at one point."

Krystal didn't hesitate, "Shaving your head is the lie." Kristina's happy expression shifted, the slight twinge in her smug grin showing a brief loss of control in the situation.

Kristina curved the corner of her mouth, playing the game, "You're two for two" she prompted, "Your turn."

This one Krystal was a little more prepared for, but she already knew Kristina would guess the answer correctly. "I have a hankering for pony princesses, I like to wear black, and I don't smile much."

It didn't take long for Kristina to figure this one out. She quickly looked at Krystal's black outfit and blank face and said, "Hankering for pony princesses is the lie."

"That's correct," Krystal said. Another easy one, but only because Krystal let her get the answer right.

"We are both two for two," Kristina said, her charismatic voice sounding a little more confident.

Krystal said, "Remember . . . I can't lie." Krystal had said it so casually that even Kristina couldn't tell whether that was a lie or not. Kristina was beginning to wonder who was playing who in this game of theirs. Regardless, it was Kristina's turn.

Kristina said, "I have a brother named Moses, I was born premature, and I almost died in a car crash when I was six." The two of them stared at each other like nothing else in the universe existed. Krystal glared back into Kristina's blue eyes, Kristina grinning at Krystal, silently telling her, *"You'll never get this one right."*

Krystal didn't even blink and said, "Trick question, they're all true." Krystal said it like a heartless detective describing a murder. Kristina didn't move, in fact, she didn't move for a whole minute. Kristina just sat there, frozen and smiling, unsure of how to react. Krystal didn't move either. The first person to move would lose this secondary game, but Krystal wouldn't budge. She was good at not moving and staring off into the distance. Kristina saw defeat was inevitable and lowered her shoulders and pulled her head back. Krystal had won. But something urged Krystal to continue speaking. Krystal saw Kristina's mask flicker. "And . . ." Krystal continued, "You don't trust people." Kristina's face slowly shifted from happiness, to hidden defense.

In an attempt to regain control of the conversation Kristina said happily, "That isn't part of the game."

Krystal glared back at her, "I told you I can't lie. But I do know when *you're* lying."

Kristina smiled wider, her energy kicked up a few levels and said, "What are you talking about?" like the sentence prior was from a normal conversation. "We are only having a good time here. Like good ole friends." Kristina smiled as wide as she could at Krystal. Revealing those pearly white teeth of hers. (Yup. Total supermodel actress right here.)

"Say what you want," Krystal said tonelessly, "You can convince other people you're not lying but you can't lie to me." Krystal stood up from the table and walked out the room. Krystal probably left Kristina bewildered beyond imagination but that was the goal. Krystal thought, *Making friends, huh, I sure am good at doing that.*

CHAPTER 30

Fake It Till You Make It

"Every day I put on a mask. Because I'm more terrified showing people who I truly am than lying to them."

—Kristina Walker, the Actress

"Brother Dairy, it's mighty fine of you to come today." It took every ounce of strength Kristina had to keep herself standing. She stared at the actor across from her, knowing all the cameras were looking her way.

Dairy spoke, "Sis, I don got it. I don got it right. That's right."

Kristina froze again, her thoughts beginning to run wild. Her heart tightened as insecurities attacked her heart and mind. *Who am I? Am I Kristina Walker? Am I this role, Kat Miller?* The world began to fade to black, losing her sense of direction. *Where am I? What am I supposed to be doing?* Her mind was lost in the storm as Kristina froze once more. On the outside she appeared perfectly normal, but on the inside, she was losing herself more and more. She could feel herself slowly slipping away from who she was; who she wanted to be, but was there anything she could do about it? It wasn't until a few seconds later the director yelled, "CUT!"

Everyone relaxed except for Kristina. The director looked in Carlo's direction and shook his head. Carlo tried his best not to look shaken, but he wasn't the actor here. The director called five and everyone dispersed trying to look uninterested. Kristina found herself and realized what happened. Carlo approached her and said, "Hey . . . the director and I had a chat . . . He told me if things don't improve soon, we're going to lose this role."

The words came as no surprise to Kristina. The surprising thing was that she didn't feel hurt by the ultimatum. Her motivation to keep acting waned with each passing day, and Kristina loved to act, she loved the career, she was good at it, but for some reason she was losing her motivation. Every day was getting harder and harder. She could feel the constant pressure weighing on her. The expectations of everyone, but also the struggle of finding herself. Her insecurities grew by the minute, and she could feel it impacting her health and motivation at work. Work that she used to love, now it was just work.

Kristina looked at her agent with sullen eyes, "Okay." And that was all she said. She didn't have the energy to press her case further. Then again, if she lost the role . . . would it be a bad thing?

She didn't even have time to breathe. First period finished and she had to find a class for tutorial. Kristina's usual "friends" joined her. They were comparable to the average paparazzi touring group for high schoolers. Kristina had never considered any of them to be "real friends" because a majority of them didn't even try to get to know her.

I can't let them see me weak. I have to be who I am. I am Kristina Walker, the Actress. Kristina walked out into the hallway, surrounded by her "friends," and chatted with them. Kristina and her group walked through the English hallway packed to the brim with people all shuffling to get to their next destination. Amidst the crowd Kristina thought she spotted a figure she recognized. It was a sly shadow that faded in and out. Kristina wanted to pay more attention to it, but by doing that, that would suck away energy she needed to entertain her "friends."

They won't like you for who you are, she thought. *So I have to keep this up.* Kristina pointed to Mr. Howard's classroom, "How about this room?" Everyone in the group agreed and they were soon taking their seats within the class. Mr. Howard was one of those teachers who didn't care what you did during his tutorial session so long as you cleaned up afterward. (And trust me, he had a vacuum and a brush.) Kristina and her friends sat down in some open seats, as Kristina got stuck in conversation. She was always the one everyone turned to when they wanted to hear something fascinating.

"I remember a time when . . ." She began with a story but thought: *They always want to hear what it's like to be a famous actor and how some of them want to be actors themselves. That's great an all, but do they really care?* Kristina could feel all the interesting looks glaring her way, all of them expecting to hear something fascinating. She didn't have much to offer, so she lied. It was easier to lie than to tell the truth. It all worked out once you got used to it. The group of four, sitting among the desks grew to eight, and then to twelve as more and more people came over, wanting to take pictures and see Kristina Walker, the Actress. Kristina did her best to entertain them, as they all wanted to be, lying a majority of the time about the stories she would tell them, but they never dared question her, because she's a famous actress. In the middle of one of her stories Kristina thought, *Happiness comes when you fake it hard enough to where you'll believe it. You'll see. They won't like you unless you lie to them.*

Kristina finished her story, and the crowd was already begging for another tale, so she indulged them with another. Before the tutorial session began, Kristina watched as more people funneled into the classroom. In walked the same girl from the party last weekend. Kristina wanted to say she felt dumbstruck, but she was too engrossed in her act to allow that. She watched in her peripherals as the young girl walked in. Observing her sense of clothing style and guessing her possible age. She might have been in the same grade as Kristina, maybe, maybe not. She wore a long black sweater covering up her arms as well as plain black pants and black shoes and socks. She watched curiously as the girl entered the room, Kristina noticed there was a certain eminence about the girl. Like there was something off about her. She quietly sat at an empty desk in the corner of the room. She didn't talk to anyone. She simply stared down at her desk for a while before pulling out her homework.

It was clearly the girl from the party last weekend, and Kristina couldn't help but be fearful of this Krystal girl. She had seen right through her act in a way that no one else had ever been able to. She saw the real Kristina Walker, and that terrified Kristina knowing there was someone out there who could read her. Yet, she couldn't help but feel a sense of comfort as well, knowing there was someone out there who could see Kristina's true self and not seek to take advantage of her. It was partially her own fault for letting her guard down but at the same time she felt the need to open up to someone at that party and that girl happened to be it.

Kristina observed the girl's behavior through some casual glimpses, but nothing seemed out of the ordinary. She seemed like just a regular girl. Kristina wanted to observe the girl more, but her "friends" begged her for another story. Kristina shifted her attention and raised her enthusiasm, feeling her heart sink lower the wider she smiled, "Of course! I'll tell you guys anything!"

The crowd cheered, "Hooray!" and they went on, listening to yet another lie. One after another the lies spewed out like sap slowly falling down from a tree, seemingly endless in its journey.

⤳

The class bell rang, and Kristina got up to leave from her group of "friends" from Mr. Howard's room. She stepped outside feeling the brisk air brush against her skin, waving her beautiful black hair in the breeze. She looked up, the gray clouds forming a barrier against any entry from the sun. She lowered her gaze and was on her way to her locker when a young freshman boy with blonde hair came up to her and asked, "Hey Kristina Walker! Could I take a picture with you?"

Kristina smiled with glee at the question and nearly jumped with excitement. She steadied herself and answered, "Of course you can!" in the cheerful voice of her persona, "You can always take a picture with me!" The freshman boy smiled and walked up beside her. Kristina stood towering over the young boy, easily two years younger than her and needing a growth spurt desperately at that, but for now, Kristina would settle with a picture for the boy.

The boy hesitantly handed Kristina his phone as she held it up selfie style. The two of them smiled, then Kristina took the picture and handed the boy his phone. The boy seemed genuinely happy and said, "Thanks so much!" then ran off into a distant hallway, most likely to brag to his friends that he got a picture with the esteemed Kristina Walker. Kristina thought about that small interaction, finding it somewhat enjoyable. *At least I enjoy that factor of fame. Finding some joy out of making that boy's day.*

Then suddenly, without a moment's hesitation, another person came up and wanted to take a picture with Kristina. Kristina wanted to say no, but that would go against her persona. So she reluctantly said yes while hiding her resentment, feeling the choking of her heart strengthen the longer she smiled. Kristina finished the picture and went on to the next one, and the next one and the next one, finally finding time to herself once the crowd dissipated. Kristina tried to let herself relax, checking over her shoulders to see if there was anyone else who wanted to take a picture, but for the moment, she was safe. Kristina took that as her cue to leave and rounded a corner to find some alone time. Taking a minute to feel she was truly by herself, and then planted her hand firmly against the ragged concrete wall.

She felt the fatigue hit her hard, her legs shuddered like jelly and her heart felt so tight she would've guessed she was about to go into cardiac arrest, but she couldn't stop. *I must keep going. I must sell the act. It's who I am.* She felt her stomach churn and wanted to vomit, then began coughing into her arm. She pulled her arm away to reveal a spatter of blood on it. Kristina was horrified at the sight, but the bell rang, and she had to get to class. She hefted her happy persona back on and told herself, *You've got to suck it up! It's the only way.* She felt her heart tighten but she had no choice. She had to move forward, no matter how painful it was.

Fake it till you make it right? That was Kristina's motto.

CHAPTER 31

An Unlikely Friendship

*"You can either sit there and be uncomfortable doing nothing
or you be uncomfortable making friends. Your choice."*

—Jaime Fisher

"Again, why?"

"Quit your whining you're gonna be fine," Jaime said, sounding more like an older brother than a friend. "You know my buddy Marcus has these great parties at his house. What better way to meet people than to go to a party."

The two of them approached the front porch of yet another unknown house Krystal had never been to. It was starting to feel like a repeated process now. (Déjà vu perhaps? Yeah, definitely déjà vu.)

Krystal craned her neck back, "Whyyyyyyy?" The idea of being surrounded by tons of strangers in an unknown house was not an amusing image to Krystal. She had played this game before, which only made her intentions of calling it quits and going home intensify. *I don't want to go to a party again. Let's just call it a night so I can go home and watch a movie or something.* Jaime could see the look on her face, reading her thoughts. He had gotten a little better at reading her, just like she had learned to read him too.

"Come on Krystal you've got to try new things if you're going to meet people," Krystal grunted. Jaime squared up to Krystal and said, "Hey. You can either sit there and be uncomfortable doing nothing or you be uncomfortable making friends. Your choice." His words were blunt but kind as usual. The sound of a loving mentor echoed to her. *I'll be uncomfortable either way?* Krystal let the thought churn in her mind and echo through her being. Jaime raised his index finger and leaned down at Krystal like an older brother and said, "Now I'm going to give you a goal today. Today I want you to try and meet one person, but this time actually form a friendship with them, at least to some degree. I want you to have a conversation with them that lasts longer than five minutes, get to know them, befriend them, and I want you to tell me what you talked about after the party, okay?" Krystal stared at him deadpan, Jaime reiterated, this time sterner, "Okay?"

"Okay," Krystal said reluctantly, trying not to offend him.

"Now what are you going to try and do?" Jaime reiterated.

"I'm going to try and meet one new person tonight . . . *make* one new friend tonight." Krystal corrected herself before continuing. "I'm going to try and have a conversation with them that will last longer than five minutes and then I'm going to tell you what we talked about after the party."

"No, I want you to *have* a conversation, not *try* to have a conversation. I want you to *be* social, not *try* to be social, okay?"

"Okay," Krystal replied. Jaime lightened.

And with one last look at her, Jaime spoke in a Yoda accent, "Do or do not, there is no try." Krystal held her smile in; it seemed to brighten her spirits despite her distaste for the joke.

"I hate your Yoda impressions." She admitted.

Jaime grunted in joy as Yoda, then ran off toward the door and opened it for Krystal. "Hmmm! Have fun we will HMMMPPPH!" Krystal could not help but chuckle even though she hated the impression. Jaime dropped the act, held out the door for her, and said, "Great! Now let's have some fun tonight." Then he charged in through the door and yelled, "WHAT'S UP FELLAS!"

Krystal heard a wholesome roar, "Yeeeaaaaaahhhh!" And then immediately realized the party had only football players inside.

Krystal stared, processing, *Uhhh . . . this is not what I expected.*

Jaime screamed, "Let's partayyyy!" Forty football guys erupted in shouts as a wrestling match erupted within the living room. Couches were flipped over, and a stage was set as all the guys stood in a circle, shouting for challengers to enter the pit. Two guys immediately started wrestling each other while the rest stood around shouting and chanting like an eighties fight club. Krystal spotted Jaime in the pit, wrestling some other dude. Jaime was able to cope with the strength of the football players because he was a water polo player himself, so he had some muscle to compensate. Krystal saw the excitement in his eyes. It was like he was a little boy happy to be playing with kids his own size.

Krystal stood there abandoned and helpless, watching the wrestling match take place. *There sure is a lot of testosterone at this party.* Then one thought began to play in her mind . . . *Do or do not, there is no try.* Krystal winced in annoyance. *Dang it Jaime you stuck that line in my head!* Krystal pictured Jaime's stupid face grinning at her in sly victory. That look, that stupid look drove her nuts. Krystal found a corner to lean her shoulder on and looked around, hoping to find another girl here but nope, there was not a single girl at this party. The lack of another girl made Krystal feel all the more left out.

Oh my gosh. It's a football afterparty. There's not a single person here who doesn't play football except me and Jaime, and Jaime's the exception because he is fit enough in water polo to hang out with these guys and not get killed. The front door opened and stepped in was none other than Kristina Walker. All the guys suddenly stopped, and the room fell silent. They all looked in Kristina's general direction like she was a supermodel. Like little boys who found a shiny new toy.

Kristina took in the sight of the room, lifted her arms wide, and shouted, "LET'S PARTY!" The room erupted in applause as all the guys cheered in unison. Some of them clapped while some of them broke formation like a pack of apes trying to secure their mate. Going up, asking for a picture, talking to Kristina, treating her like a goddess among men. Meanwhile, Krystal didn't want to get mixed up in the chaos, so she evaded the paparazzi and went into another room for shelter.

A full hour went by, and Krystal still hadn't built up the confidence to talk to anybody. Being surrounded by guys who were all a foot taller than her and were as thick as a tree, made Krystal feel extremely intimidated. Krystal wanted to talk to Kristina, but she was constantly surrounded by guys, so she was unapproachable for the time being. The same went for Jaime, who looked to be having the time of his life hanging with his bros. Krystal poured herself another drink of soda and backed off into a nearby guest room. She found some nice white seats and sat down. Krystal sipped her drink in silence, giving her ears a break from the constant roaring and raging testosterone from the other room. Krystal thought, *What was Jaime thinking bringing me to a party with all guys? Doesn't he know I don't like football?* Either way it didn't matter. She was here and there was no changing that.

Krystal leaned back in her chair, wishing she had her Bible or something to do. Kristina Walker stepped into the room, dashing away from her pursuers like a Disney princess. Without looking at Krystal, Kristina whispered, "Those boys in there, they're like animals." Kristina forgot Krystal was still there before she said that, so to correct herself she smiled like a cute girl and looked at Krystal, "I'm sorry. Did you hear that? Please just forget the whole thing happened, okay?"

Krystal said, "You don't have to put on an act." Then looked away, back to her observation of the male species. Kristina was bemused for a moment. She tried to catch her breath as if she had lowered some massive weight off her shoulders.

Kristina looked at Krystal and asked, "One of these chairs taken?" Krystal shook her head and Kristina sat down, exhaling a breath of relief. Krystal studied her, and could see lines under Kristina's blue eyes; fatigue wearing her down. Krystal could tell Kristina was barely holding herself together, looking like she was about to collapse at any time.

Kristina lowered her voice and asked, "Can I be real with you?" Krystal faced Kristina, giving her full attention. "I don't really know what to think of you." Kristina expected to have some reaction, but Krystal held her blank, passive stare and said nothing in return. Kristina became a bit frazzled and said, "It's not that I don't know how to react to you. I mean, uhhh," she tried to put it correctly, "I don't know you, so I don't know what your true intentions are." Kristina lowered her head and admitted, "Most people I meet tend to want to get to know me because I'm famous. But you, on the other hand, handed me that red cup and didn't want to get to know me."

Krystal's blank stare weakened as she looked down at the table. "It's not . . . that I didn't want to get to know you." Krystal raised her head and looked at Kristina, "I . . . I do want to get to know you."

"Then why did you give me that red water cup? Weren't you doing it because I'm an actress?"

Krystal shook her head, "I . . . I didn't do it because you were . . . an actress. I did it because . . . you looked sad."

Kristina felt like a bullet struck her, goosebumps rushing over her skin while maintaining a perfect actor's composure on the outside. Krystal wasn't sure what Kristina was thinking, but the next thing Kristina said was, "Oh . . ." Krystal watched as Kristina lowered her head and gazed down at her lap. A second passed and Krystal waited patiently for Kristina's next response. "Can I tell you something?"

"Sure," Krystal said.

"I think you're the first person in a while to notice I'm not doing well."

Usually, Krystal would have felt overjoyed hearing that statement, but Krystal lowered her head, reliving the memories of loneliness all over again. She whispered, "It takes one to know one."

Kristina tilted her head, "What was that?"

Krystal raised her head and met her gaze, "Nothing." Kristina saw a slight change in Krystal's demeanor. Like she had brightened a shade or two. For someone who wears only black, Krystal sure did look a bit happier. Krystal asked, "Could we . . . start over?"

Kristina raised her voice back to the cutesy actor's octave, "Yeah girl!" and stuck her hand out. "I'm Kristina, Kristina Walker, the Actress." Krystal wanted to object to the sudden change in character, but she let it slide. Besides, she just made good terms with this girl, so she didn't want to ruin it.

Krystal took the hand and shook it. "Krystal."

Kristina blinked a couple times, "Soooo, do you have a last name?"

Krystal nodded, turned off from the act, "Yes . . . I have a last name. You already asked me that." Kristina leaned closer on the table, raising her eyebrows. Krystal saw the question on her face and answered, "Henninger. Krystal Henninger."

Kristina sat up and threaded her hands together like a seductive woman, "Well it's nice to meet you, Krystal Henninger."

Krystal knew Kristina was putting on an act, but she couldn't help but relax a little. She felt a genuine connection with Kristina for some reason and was unsure how to proceed with it. Allowing her guard to drop a few levels, but still keeping her defenses up. Maybe the same could be said for Kristina.

Kristina turned her head slightly, elbows still on the table, "So, are you getting ready for the dance in the next couple weeks?"

Krystal gave no reaction. *A dance? What dance?*

Kristina leaned back in her chair, "It's not exactly a dance, per say, it's more a formal dress up party, or Black-Tie Event. You know, dresses and tuxedos. The fancy stuff people only wear once a year."

Krystal shook her head. "No, I'm not aware of it."

Kristina screamed like a valley girl, her excitement brimming like an overflowing cup. "It's a dance held by this guy who goes to our high school. He's a friend of mine and invites lots of people to come. We can even bring our friends if we'd like."

Krystal remembered all the parties Jaime dragged her too and pictured people in nice suits and dresses. *It sounds out of the ordinary but I'm not sure I would like to go.* Memories of the last time Krystal wore a dress flooded back to her mind. The sight of the blood-spattered car, the loss of a parent. Krystal turned to stone, so much so, that Kristina noticed.

"Did I say something that offended you? If so, I'm sorry."

Krystal recollected herself and waved Kristina off, "It's fine. Uhhh . . ." Krystal tried to think of something to say. But her first thought tracked back to Jaime's Yoda impression. *"Do or do not. There is no try. Hehehe."* Krystal shook her head. *No that's not it!* But the phrase kept repeating in her head. *Arrggghh dang it Jaime!* Krystal racked her mind for the right phrasing. Kristina sat there looking perplexed at what was going on inside Krystal's head as she searched for the right words.

Noise rattled in from the hallway door and in walked Jaime, holding a red cup looking a little "weary" (if you know what I mean). Jaime noticed the two of them talking and said, "What do we have here?" He pointed at them, his body weaving back and forth. "Are you guys talking?" He sounded surprised when he wasn't.

Krystal said nothing, a little bothered by Jaime turning loose tonight, mostly because he was her ride home, but Kristina stood up and extended her arms, "Haaaaayyy! What up Buck!"

Jaime smiled, "Hey Kristina! Good to see you," throwing an arm over her shoulder. Kristina did the same and the two of them half hugged like bros.

Krystal's eyes flicked back and forth between them, but Jaime pointed to Kristina and said, "We go way back." Jaime looked from Kristina to Krystal. "Am I interrupting?"

Kristina said, "Hey Buck, no we were just talking and smoothing things out between us. Like old friends an all, you know." Kristina's voice was different this time. Lower and tom-boyish than the cutesy girl act. Krystal found it interesting. How one person played different characters at the same time.

It was like Krystal never knew who the real one was. But that was Kristina's stick. She was an actor after all.

Jaime winked at her, "Oh I know," he turned to Krystal, "Listen, if you need a ride you're going to have to wait, but I will totally be there for you in like a couple hours, how's that sound?"

Krystal looked at Kristina and for once she didn't object, "That's fine."

Kristina looked to Jaime, "Hey Buck, how are the preparations for the Black-Tie Event coming up?"

Jaime grinned, "Things are going great! I've got the suit ready and everything." Krystal looked a little perplexed at the sight of Jaime looking so jovial over something she'd never heard of until now. I guess these two had more history than she thought.

Krystal looked at Jaime, "You know about the party?"

Jaime lowered his eyebrows, "I haven't told you? My family and I host an annual Black-Tie Event at my house every year. I'm in the loop with Kristina. I host the party; she brings the party." Jaime looked like he was about to fall over, having Kristina as a crutch helped. "She also tells me where the other parties are, and I go. It works out that way between us right Kristina?"

Kristina nodded, "That's right Buck. You and I are like peas and roosters." Jaime burst out laughing. He patted Kristina on the shoulder and walked back up the steps toward the sounds of the party. "Oh, you know how to kill me, Kristina. I'll see you two later." Jaime waved and headed into the hallway. Krystal could have sworn she'd heard a vomiting noise follow, but maybe it was her imagination.

Kristina shifted her demeanor, as if she had just put on some invisible coat as her voice lowered back to its normal octave. "Sorry about that," she said, "but I didn't know you were friends with Jaime!"

Krystal shied away, balling her arms and knees under the table. "I mean . . . we started to get to know each other . . . recently." Kristina tilted her head and grinned. Krystal read her expression perfectly and said nonchalant, "It's not like that."

Kristina grinned even wider and nodded, "Uh-huh." But Krystal was dead serious, causing seeds of doubt on Kristina's twisted face. She asked honestly, "You sure you don't like him?"

Krystal looked down at the table, "I don't know . . . I've never liked anyone before." It didn't take her long to answer but she felt it was the appropriate response. Kristina wanted more hints, but from how plainly Krystal said it, revealed she was being completely honest. That's how she felt, but it didn't sound jovial. Kristina glanced toward the hallway; Krystal watched the thoughts form in her mind, cresting the corner of her lip at the idea. Krystal showed no change in expression, proving she was almost as good of a poker player as Kristina was.

Kristina raised her hands and shoulders, "I don't know. Whatever you like." She stepped down and said, "But remember, the party is happening soon, so you have some time."

"Great," Krystal spoke in monotone. "I can't wait."

⌇

"And . . . action!"

Kristina tried to hold herself together, but she could feel herself slipping already. The workday had just begun, and she was already exhausted. Sleep wasn't providing her with any relief lately, and the times she did sleep she woke up feeling as though she hadn't rested at all. Kristina's heart felt so tight as if it was being held hostage by her insecurities. It took all she had just to stay standing, and even then, her legs started to buckle.

Looks were exchanged with the set members. They were all worried. The director did not look optimistic, only saddened. For a long moment everyone stared, watching Kristina intensely. Kristina felt all eyes on her and tried to speak her line, but the words would not come out. She tried again, tensing her stomach hard but nothing came out. Her fatigue began to show, her breathing increased, and her skin turned pale. Kristina began to shake, attempting to uphold the façade and finish out the scene, but doing so killed her inside. The more she faked it, the more it hurt. She was an actress, but this was getting harder and harder to hide. It was like having an anchor chained to her heart and the more she tried to fake it the more it pulled her down into the abyss. Pressure gathered deep within Kristina's throat, as she wanted to vomit. She felt dizzy, losing control of her sense of direction. Her legs gave out and she fell backwards.

Kristina tried to stop her fall but to no avail. She landed on her butt then crumpled down like a falling statue. The entire world muffled, losing all sense of sound, fading to black. Kristina tried to lift herself back up, but her body wouldn't respond to her. She was paralyzed in her own exhaustion, both mentally and physically. The set crew came rushing to her aid, but she knew they would not be able to help her. Kristina actually relaxed a bit, letting the façade drop given she had no energy to hold it up anymore. Only to look up at the director among the swarms of people and see the face of a man who had to make a hard decision.

The result was crushing, through fading eyes Kristina saw the decision was made, she had lost the role. Losing the only piece of her identity she had left.

CHAPTER 32

Breaking Point

"Even popular people can feel lonely."

—JL

Jaime was in his zero period, so Krystal arrived at school early with nothing to do. Well, early wasn't the right word. School started in ten minutes so the school yard was active but Krystal didn't have anyone to talk to but that was normal.

A blue Porsche pulled up into the student lot, and out stepped Kristina Walker. She was dressed in slim brown pants and a white top with sleek silver earrings and a hat that looked like it belonged to Sherlock Holmes. It still made her look extremely fashionable but everyone in school remembered her for her role in the Hampered Princess as the beautiful princess Mathilda who falls in love with the local prince, and they live happily ever after. The movie was a huge hit despite being the cheesiest of cheesy films, think sharp cheddar. (But hey if it ain't broke don't fix it.) There was something about Kristina that stuck with Krystal since the day she met her. Krystal couldn't put her finger on it exactly, but it felt . . . familiar. Like Jaime, Krystal felt called to get to know this girl. Krystal couldn't explain the how or why, she just felt like God was telling her to get to know this girl more. And so, Krystal watched her, like a hawk stalking its prey (minus the stalker.)

Krystal wished Jaime were here. He would know what to do, or even her Aunt Sarah, but that would have to wait. For now, Krystal watched Kristina as she exited her car, only to be surrounded by hordes of people all wanting to be her friend. Krystal felt a hint of jealousy. *I wish I were that popular.* Krystal tried to imagine what her life would look like if she were popular.

How different would I feel if I were the popular girl instead of the school outcast? Krystal tried to picture herself being outgoing and extravagant, but that image died as quickly as it birthed. Krystal shook her head. It was like ice trying to feel hot and fire cold. Krystal leaned against the concrete light pole, bored.

Huh. I can't really imagine myself as anyone else. I can't picture my life looking any different than it is now. It's not like I don't want to, that's simply how it is. It's like living as a fish your whole life and then walking on dry land for the first time. You have no idea how to do it or what it's like.

Krystal brought her thoughts back to Kristina. *What is it like to be so popular? To have everyone want to be you, having everyone around you know who you are and want to be friends with you. What's that like?* Thinking about it now, Krystal came to understand simply how different she and Kristina were. Krystal slugged harder against the pole and sighed. *I don't know. But I can't imagine what she's going through. She has a completely different story than me.*

Krystal stood there and continued to watch as people swarmed Kristina walking out, all wanting to take photos as she looked fabulous with her luscious, beautiful physique. *She certainly looks beautiful; I'll give her that.* Krystal watched the crowd surround Kristina as she disappeared around the corner. Krystal could hear Kristina from where she was standing. Her high-pitched voice and energy were sending waves of happiness and enthusiasm to the people around her. *Oh yeah, that's a real celebrity.* Krystal's interest in the sight vanished as she stood up and went to her first class. *Well God, it's about time for me to get to class anyway.*

Krystal gripped the strap of her backpack a little tighter, instantly searching for a room to sit in during tutorial. Krystal searched for an open door, a classroom she knew that she could join before the bell rang. She flashed a look at her phone.

Oh shoot! I have less than a minute to find a place. Krystal was mid-level in the middle of a breakdown. She didn't want to get caught out in the middle of school with a supervisor asking where she was going. Krystal panicked and grabbed the handle to the first door she could find. A few other students had just entered, and the teacher was busy looking at their phone, so no one minded Krystal joining the class a little late. Krystal quickly found a seat and blended in with little effort.

She exhaled relief. *I made it.* The door swung open, and a few other students walked in, but all attention was drawn toward the girl with long black hair and perfect figure.

Someone shouted, "Hey Kristina Walker!"

Kristina took her sunglasses off and said, "Hey everyone!" The whole class roared with applause as Kristina and a few of her friends entered the classroom. Krystal made no motion to make a scene, let alone to disturb uhh . . . whatever "this" was. She pulled out her notebook as Kristina and a few other people sat at the opposite end of the class. None of the seats were available, but without prompting, a few students gave up their seats in willing obedience for Kristina and her friends.

Krystal ignored the whole scene and went back to her work. She wanted to be done with this school day as soon as possible and working on homework made the day go by faster.

Just another boring day.

Krystal was working on an outline when something prompted her to look up. She put her pencil down and gazed around the room in boredom. The class seemed pretty normal overall. It wasn't too loud, some distant chatter now and then, a majority of the people were on their phones while a group of boys were busy playing a game in the corner. But for some reason Krystal's gaze was drawn like a subtle magnet toward Kristina. Krystal looked over to find Kristina talking amongst her friends. Just like Summer, everyone around seemed to be interested in what she had to say, and nobody dared cut her off. Krystal didn't know why she was intrigued watching them, but she felt it was the right thing to do, given the feeling. After a couple minutes Kristina stopped talking and the group split up into smaller conversations.

Krystal's attention on Kristina began to narrow when she thought she saw something. Krystal sat up straighter, taking her fist off her cheek to peer more closely. Kristina was talking a minute ago, but now she wasn't talking to anybody. Krystal felt her heart begin to beat a little faster. *What is it about this girl that's causing me to look at her?* It wasn't because Kristina was beautiful and a flat out ten, there was something about her that Krystal found . . . familiar.

Krystal watched closer, observing Kristina's actions, watching how she interacted with the people around her. What was it? What about her intrigued Krystal's curiosity? Then she saw it. Kristina looked down at her desk with a sullen, depressed look on her face. Her smile and enthusiasm faded as Krystal saw it all. There, in the midst of all those people, Kristina Walker was lonely, and nobody saw it but Krystal. She looked like she was about to fall apart. Krystal's mouth opened and gasped silently. She could not believe it. Someone so popular, so loved, was experiencing loneliness. It all made sense. Why Krystal felt a resonance with this girl. It's because even at the top of the social pyramid, people can still feel lonely.

This new revelation changed Krystal's perspective on everything. She leaned back in her chair and tried to recollect her thoughts. She had never imagined that popular people can feel loneliness too. It made her heart cry out with empathy and wanted to walk over there and give Kristina a hug. Krystal stayed planted in her seat, but she looked upon Kristina in a new light.

I need to do something, but what? Krystal contemplated the answer.

Krystal watched Kristina closely as they entered their third period class, ready to begin a test. Everyone took their seats. Krystal was a few seats behind and one row across from Kristina, but Krystal's focus wasn't on the test at all. She looked at Kristina with concern and knew something was up. Normally, Kristina was smiling and happy, but as the day progressed, Krystal could see Kristina faltering in her appearance. Her smile was gone, and Kristina had a mixed look of both depression and horror as she stared forward into oblivion. That was not a good sign and it worried Krystal. She thought back to when she saw Jaime looking so down in class back when she was still getting to know him, and how he revealed how much of a burden he was carrying. Krystal now wondered whether the same thing was happening to Kristina. She was carrying a burden alone and had no one there to support her, even when she was the most popular person around.

The teacher finished passing out the tests, but Krystal did not take her eyes off Kristina, and Kristina never bothered to look at the test. She looked defeated, completely defeated, yet whenever someone talked to her, she still put up the happy front to sell the idea that she was okay, but she was not okay, and Krystal knew it. She was hurting inside, Krystal could see Kristina's suffering clear as day and yet, no one was there to help her.

The teacher said, "Begin" and the class got to work, but both Krystal and Kristina did not look down. That only solidified the worry in Krystal's heart for Kristina. She saw Kristina try to pick up the pencil, slowly, like she was in a state of half sleep, and try to answer the first question. For a full minute Kristina froze and held the pencil over the paper. Krystal watched her closely, then saw Kristina's pencil hand start shaking. The shaking moved from her hand to her whole body in a matter of seconds. Kristina's eyes widened in horror, trying to control the shaking, but to no avail. Krystal could hear Kristina's breathing increase to quick and short muffled breaths, until Kristina could take no more of it. Kristina stood up from her chair and left the room a little too quickly. Krystal was the only one to notice her leaving the room and wondered what she should do next.

Should I follow her? Or do I stay and finish this test?

Krystal finally looked down at her paper and realized she hadn't done any work yet either. She was mortified for a second and remembered just how important this test was to her. Her work ethic drilled into her by her mom urged Krystal to get to work, because a bad grade was a bad mark on one's self-esteem. Krystal picked up her pencil and moved to answer the first question, but her hand stopped before she could answer. *But what about Kristina?* Krystal looked away from her test toward the door to her left. *Should I check to see if she's okay?* The thought repulsed her, but then she thought, *Love your neighbor as yourself.* Krystal sighed and felt cornered again. *If I was hurting, then I would want someone to go and check on me, even if it meant not doing well on this test.* So against all her instincts, Krystal got up and left the room.

Kristina stumbled out of the classroom, her state of mind a mess, left in chaos, unable to control itself. Kristina's breathing increased so fast she thought she was going to pass out. Her body felt so weak from the fatigue and stress on her mind. She ran as fast as she could, trying to get away, going from hallway to hallway, trying to find some place safe. Someplace where she could get away from everything. A place no one could see her. All she wanted in this moment was to disappear entirely. She dredged all over school, not caring that she had a test in the class she just left, she only wanted to heal herself, but how? *Who am I?* she shuddered, passing beyond a corner at the outskirts of school. Her mind spinning out of control like a whirlwind of thoughts.

Who am I?

I'm not Kristina Walker, the Actress anymore!

Then who am I?

Am I Kristina?

Kristina or Kristina Walker, the Actress?

Who am I!?

Kristina's tired eyes searched frantically for a safe haven. Somewhere to be alone. She had walked all across the school by now, desperate to get away, but now she needed somewhere to go. She spotted a bathroom across the courtyard and breathed heavily on her way over there. Her vision blurred and she felt queasy, her legs feeling like jelly as she entered the empty bathroom. She briefly spotted herself in the mirror but tried to ignore the stranger in the mirror. She entered the largest stall at the end and locked it behind her before she fell to the floor and passed out.

It was getting more and more difficult the longer she looked. Krystal could feel the tug in her heart to go back to her classroom and give up on the search for Kristina, but her compassion fueled her to keep looking. More than fifteen minutes had passed, and Krystal would need every second once she got back to finish the test. However, every passing second tempted Krystal to go back and finish or else she could fail the test. Krystal gritted her teeth and debated the idea but shook her head. *No. I'm going to find her and make sure she's okay.* So, against her wishes, she pressed on, searching hallway after hallway for the lost actress.

Where did she go? Krystal wondered. Checking left from right but only finding empty hallways. Krystal checked the bathrooms closest to their classroom but did not find Kristina in any of them. What started as fifteen minutes turned into thirty minutes, leaving Krystal with less and less time to go back and complete the test, but still she refused to give up because she knew Jesus wouldn't give up on her.

Krystal stood in the middle of the courtyard, hoping to avoid any supervisors on campus, scanning any and all ways Kristina could have gone. Krystal realized though that she was searching for a needle in a haystack. Krystal gave a frustrated sigh, having no idea where Kristina could have gone.

For all that I know she could have driven home. Which was not an implausible idea either, but from the way Kristina looked, Krystal doubted she had the ability to drive herself home. Krystal stopped and wanted to give up, knowing she would never find Kristina without help. Then a thought dropped in Krystal's mind, and she looked up at the overcast sky. She lowered her gaze and understood, then she threaded her hands together and prayed, *Father, if it's Your will, please let me find her.*

A warm presence developed within her chest, feeling the Holy Spirit within her, urging her to go towards the outdoor basketball courts. Krystal didn't question the feeling and followed. She found herself out by the basketball courts then paused, wondering what to do now. She searched around and there it was. A public restroom right in front of her.

This is the place.

Krystal opened the door and could feel the cool air inside vent outwards. Her skin developed goosebumps despite her all-black clothing as she walked inside. The checkered tile and black stalls made it feel slightly like she was in a horror film. The lime-colored lighting only added to the awkwardness of the scene. (See, this is why schools are weird. Even the bathrooms don't give it a good atmosphere.) Krystal stepped inside and slowly searched from stall to stall, until she found the largest stall at the end locked. Krystal knocked on the door, her chest tightening, not wishing to speak. She forced the words out, her voice coarse and low, "Are . . . are you okay in there?" No response. Krystal knocked again, no answer. Krystal knelt down and looked underneath the barrier and found Kristina lying on the tiled floor unconscious.

Immediately Krystal slid under the stall and inspected Kristina's condition. She tapped on Kristina's shoulder gently, "Hey, hey are you alright?" she whispered. "Kristina?" Her mom's nursing skills were coming into action as Krystal checked if she was still breathing, wondering if she'd have to call 911.

Kristina looked pale like she had just been struck with an illness of some sort. She didn't appear to have used the bathroom for long because she was still fully clothed, but she had passed out on the floor. Then Kristina started gagging. Krystal's eyes widened in horror. *She's choking on her own vomit.* Krystal knew she would have to shift Kristina's position or else she could die. Kristina could have been choking even before Krystal got here. She grabbed Kristina and helped her up, facing the toilet, as the vomit hurled out in torrents. Krystal showed no sign of reaction as Kristina emptied her tank. Krystal moved over and held Kristina's hair back while she worked her "magic" within the confines of the most pleasurable toilet the school had to offer.

After a few minutes the vomit fest was over and Kristina could breathe again, knowing the worst was over. Kristina tumbled over to the side of the toilet, slinking down onto her side, facing the wall. Krystal helped put her in the resting position then took some toilet paper and wiped Kristina's mouth with it. She still seemed too out of it to care, so Krystal did it anyway. Krystal saw Kristina looked pale and wondered if she should get some water. Krystal stood up, unlocked the stall to the door and said, "I'll be right back. Don't go anywhere."

Kristina lay in a resting position against the wall and let out a cough, and then another one and then another one. Her weakened body was unable to cope with the previous vomiting, and now with the blood oozing from her mouth. She thought she heard someone say, "Don't go anywhere."

If Kristina could laugh, she would. *"Don't go anywhere,"* she thought. *I couldn't go anywhere even if I tried.* She waited a few minutes, taking the time to breathe, delighted in being able to take in a full breath without heaving her guts out. A few minutes later a girl dressed in black came into her stall with a bag of chips and a bottle of water. Kristina wanted to freak out, but she was out of energy. She had nothing left to hide herself, but then she recognized the girl who walked in, the same girl from the parties she previously went to. Kristina mouthed, "It's you." She took one look at the chips and water and was repulsed with the idea of eating. Krystal offered the food and drink, but Kristina dismissed them with a wave. So Krystal placed the food down and took a seat beside Kristina. Kristina didn't want Krystal to see her like this, to see herself bare and weakened, not the joyful amenity people had come to enjoy and love.

Crap. I can't hide myself, Kristina thought.

Kristina took her eyes away from Krystal, still half-conscious and said faintly, "Don't look at me."

Krystal understood the comment and looked up at the ceiling, "Then I won't look at you," she answered plainly. Kristina was certainly not expecting that comment, stealing a glance at Krystal, making sure she was true to her word. Kristina grew faint again and closed her eyes, not enjoying that fact that someone was seeing her in this weakened state and yet . . . part of her enjoyed the presence of another. To know that she was not alone in this matter as Kristina passed out again.

∽

Kristina opened her eyes to find the presence of the bathroom the way it was when she fainted, then looked over and saw Krystal to her left. She wanted to freak out but to her surprise she didn't. Krystal too, had fallen asleep sitting next to Kristina, enjoying the well needed rest. Kristina took the moment to watch Krystal, finding it somewhat enjoyable to watch the girl sleep. Her breathing was deep and calm; peaceful and rhythmic. Krystal stirred awake, stretching her arms out then opened her eyes, "Good morning."

Kristina was more intrigued with the fact that Krystal had stayed with her. She looked over at Krystal and asked, "How long was I out?"

"Not sure. You were passed out even before I found you."

"How did you find me?" Kristina asked, anxious to find out if anyone else had seen her like this. She wanted to put on her mask but was too tired.

Krystal unscrewed the cap to a bottle of water and handed it to Kristina. "I had help."

Kristina took the water, her stomach more open to eating now. "Why didn't you call the nurse?"

Krystal opened a bag of chips and held it out to Kristina, "I wanted to, but I figured you wouldn't want to be seen like this, and plus you were stable, so I let you sleep."

"You're terrible at this saving thing," Kristina mocked, not able to maintain her cutesy act with her current condition.

Krystal mocked back, "At least I'm not as pale as a polar bear right now."

Kristina couldn't help but laugh a little. *So this girl does have a sense of humor*, Kristina thought. She drank from the water bottle, feeling more of her strength return to her, then worked on the chips, "How long were you there?"

Krystal answered without looking at Kristina, "Long enough." Krystal thought about her own time in the hospital, the fatigue that came after she had tried to kill herself, the snacks the Janitor brought her in the night, and how he listened to her. Krystal breathed through her nostrils, and chuckled, finding the mirror image of herself sitting in Kristina's position.

Kristina finished her water and chips and the two of them sat there, not knowing what to say as the conversation drifted into an unexpected silence. Krystal didn't find it too awkward though, she enjoyed the silence while Kristina regained her strength. Both of them lost track of time while Kristina figured out what she was going to say next.

The answer was simple, "Thank you," Kristina spoke gently.

Krystal widened her lips into a thin smile, "You're welcome."

Kristina found great comfort in someone being there for her. It wasn't like she didn't want to be seen, but it was nice to have someone simply be *there* for her. Kristina heard tapping coming out from outside the bathroom. The tapping grew stronger and larger in number until she recognized the sound. Rain. The sound relaxed Kristina as she closed her eyes and listened to the refreshing water tap against the surface outside. Krystal did the same, picturing herself in the rain, soaking in its very presence.

Kristina was too tired to put on her façade and spoke simply, "You like the rain?"

Krystal nodded, "I do," craning her head back, looking up. "It relaxes me."

Kristina broke a tiny smile, leaning her head back, looking up as well, "You and me both." Once she had her strength, Kristina attempted to stand up as Krystal watched her carefully. "I'm fine," Kristina reassured. Krystal nodded cautiously and watched as Kristina managed to stand on her own, looking a bit more like herself now after she had the food and water in her system, as well as a bit of rest. Kristina opened the stall door and said, "Thank you," one last time. Krystal nodded like a humble servant and watched as Kristina made her way outside, this time more worried about the rain than people seeing her.

Kristina made sure to keep it slow and casual, not wanting to push it after such a chaotic day. She managed to regain her energy, but the moment she put on her mask again, the weight upon her heart doubled and she was back to losing her energy again. Kristina faintly walked out from her final class of the day, eager to get back to her car and drive home as everyone in the school hurried out. She had almost made it past the final exit when Jaime intercepted her. Kristina relaxed a little but managed to keep the mask on for Jaime. "What up Buck!" throwing her arms around him like a long-lost friend. Jaime reciprocated the hug and was casual with it.

"It's good to see you too Tina."

Kristina almost called it there when Jaime asked, "Before you go, have you seen Krystal around?"

"Why? Is something wrong?"

"Nothing. I wanted to ask her how her test went." Kristina tilted her head, puzzled. Jaime read her admitted expression, "She was going on about it this whole week, and I wanted to check to see how she was doing with the results."

Kristina's mind raced. *Wait. I had a test today in Mr. Harkinson's class during third period.*

Kristina asked, "Was she supposed to take it today?"

Jaime nodded, "Yeah," he looked up remembering, "in Mr. Harkinson's class during third period," confirming what Kristina wished wasn't true. Kristina's thoughts ran wild with realization. *Oh my goodness. She missed her test because of me!* Guilt instantly bombarded Kristina's already fatigued heart, making her want to have a panic attack right here and now.

"Oh," Kristina said, "Well I wouldn't know anything about that," she lied.

Jaime shrugged, "Alright, I'm sure I'll ask her about it later. Bye."

"Bye," Kristina said, as Jaime passed her by, but all she could think about was how Krystal missed her test because of her passing out in the bathroom, but then reason and doubt accompanied her thoughts. *She came looking for me . . . she didn't have to miss the test, did she? I mean she didn't have to stay with me. She could have taken me to the nurse and made a whole big deal out of it, but she didn't. She kept it quiet and actually stayed with me during that time.* The thought of it brought a sense of joy to Kristina's harrowed heart. *Did she really do that . . . for me?* Kristina felt overjoyed with the heroism of it all, but the question still remained, *Why?*

Kristina closed her bedroom door behind her, feeling the usual fatigue slam into her like a freight train. The accumulating dust in the room added to the emptiness she felt. The curtains blocked the window, preventing any lighting, leaving the room bare in the dark. Kristina dropped her bag and fell face first onto her velvet king-sized bed, welcoming the silence of the room and the lack of activity for the rest of the day.

"What a day," she muffled into her pillow. Kristina turned and faced the ceiling, catching her breath after yet another exhausting day. She didn't tell anyone she had fainted at school. That would only cause problems, and even more so if it had gone public. But it wasn't a win either. At least one person saw her, and it was that girl Kristina had seen at parties and around school.

Kristina lay with her defenses down, pondering the events of today. *Why did that girl not go and tell everyone about me while I was in the bathroom? Better yet, why did she stay with me when she had a test to go to?* Kristina pondered the reason for that question. She didn't care that she herself failed to take the test, but it was different when someone else had to take it. She dared herself to wonder, *I guess it was because she was nice? But then why was she being nice when most people don't do that? I mean, sure it is okay to be nice and there are some people in this world who are but . . . there aren't that many people in this world who do that, I should know.* Kristina's mind raced back to all the times when people cheated her out of her money and fame, her parents included. One of the downfalls of being a famous actress is that people were constantly trying to use and abuse her, taking advantage of Kristina's need for love and companionship, and using her when she didn't realize it to take advantage of her perks.

I've lost a lot of friendships because of that, and now it's just . . . me. Kristina couldn't even trust her own parents because of her fame. Regardless, things had gotten cold between her parents, and no one showed Kristina what they honestly thought. It was all a lie. Their family and everything in it. A house full of liars. Even Kristina's younger brother Moses was starting to feel the effects of not having his sister around and it was tearing Kristina apart. Sure, Kristina received a lot of attention from the media, but on a personal level, she didn't have any friends she could trust. As the saying goes, "It's lonely at the top" well, Kristina was feeling pretty lonely as of now. And so, interactions with people became as cheap as ordering a hamburger from McDonalds (depending on inflation, but you get the point).

Kristina tried to shift her thoughts away from Krystal, but she couldn't. Something was lodged in her heart about that girl. *There is something about her that I can't put my finger on.* And that was saying something from a professional actor. *She stayed to help me when she didn't have to. Why? Why why why? It doesn't make any sense. It would have benefited her to simply go to her class and take her test, but she chose to stay with me when I needed comfort. And to be honest . . . I actually liked her being there.* Kristina fought the idea that the girl was just using her to get close to Kristina so she could be famous, but Kristina didn't get that impression from her. *I mean, she's refused my auto-graph before, so why would she want to care for me then?* Kristina didn't have the answer, she would have to go and ask Krystal when she saw her again. Kristina let out a breath, "I guess I'll go talk to her the next time I see her," as she closed her eyes, and fell asleep.

Okay Kristina it's time to go searching. Kristina got up and out of her desk and headed out toward the school courtyard. Kristina held out her phone while standing in the light of midday, reading the message Jaime had sent her.

"*She normally sits on a white bench on the edge of the school courtyard.*" Kristina closed the phone and mumbled to herself, "She sits at a white bench. Uhhh . . . white bench, white bench, white bench, courtyard," scanning the school grounds. The courtyard was brimming with life today, everybody in their assorted groups and cliques. It was hard to find people because there were so many groups around campus, but Kristina had a specific area to search and Jaime was a known source who knew of Krystal's location, so she hoped it wouldn't take long to find her. Kristina looked from left to right, searching for a white bench, scanning the whole courtyard. She finished her scan in disappointment. "I'm not seeing her." Kristina tried again, this time spotting Jaime and his group of friends, but she still didn't find a group of people sitting on a white bench. Kristina scanned from group to group, not finding a match. Kristina was beginning to lose hope. *Maybe she's not here today.* She doubted that. Jaime told her that Krystal didn't like to miss school, so it was likely she was here; Kristina just wasn't searching in the right places. Kristina did a third and final scan of the courtyard, ready to give up, until she spotted a lone girl dressed in black sitting on a white bench reading a book and eating a sandwich.

Kristina was a little surprised. *How come I didn't see her before? What is she a ghost?* Kristina suddenly realized her mistake, there was no group that sat around the white benches. Kristina was skimming over the groups of people in the courtyard but wasn't looking for the individual. Kristina leaned against the wall next to her. "She sits alone?" Kristina wondered if there was a group of people Krystal sat with but then remembered that in school, cliques were set in stone, so to not be in one means you never had one to begin with. Kristina felt her defenses lower a shade. *She looks sad, but also*—Kristina tried to find the right word for it—*hopeful*. Kristina watched as the girl casually read her book, trying to flip the pages with one hand while holding a sandwich in the other.

After a short while Kristina thought, *If I'm going to talk to her then now is the time.* So Kristina pushed herself from her corner and walked over. Kristina could feel eyes looking her way, but most of them were hidden from view, so she raised her invisible barrier and put on her energetic persona. Kristina approached Krystal with the sun shining behind her, causing Kristina's shadow to linger over Krystal. Krystal looked up passively, not reacting entirely, but not expecting a visitor either.

Kristina waved like a dandelion in the sun, "Hi!" Krystal widened her eyes slightly like a docile puppy in a corner, waving slowly back with her sandwich in hand, surprised Kristina was talking to her in the first place. "Do you remember me? I'm Kristina, Kristina Walker, the actress from yesterday." She knew the girl knew but couldn't think of any other way to greet the lonesome girl.

"I remember you," Krystal said, her demeanor more resolute than before. Kristina wanted to dance around the topic, but with this girl it felt better to simply get to the point.

Kristina clapped her hands together and acted all happy. "I wanted to ask you a few questions if that doesn't bother you?"

"Okay," Krystal replied plainly. She sounded neither happy nor excited with the fact that a famous actress was talking to her right now. That struck Kristina as peculiar, but she couldn't break character now.

Kristina leaned forward, "I only wanted to know if you had told anybody about our little *encounter* the other day?"

"No," she said, her impassive yet thoughtful expression looking back at Kristina. That struck Kristina as odd. *Why is she so unenthusiastic to talk to me?*

Kristina clapped her hands together, "Great! If you could keep that a secret that would be amazing. Okay thanks!"

"Sure," was all Krystal said. Kristina almost winced but kept that reaction contained. *Don't break character*, Kristina thought. *But this girl needs some better vocabulary.*

"One more question and then were done, okay?" Kristina had to brace herself because she was about to ask an honest question in front of someone, "Why did you stay with me when I was sick?"

Krystal paused before she spoke, "Because it's what God would have done." She looked at the floor, embarrassed.

God? Are you kidding me! That's this girl's reason for caring for me! What on earth kind of ridiculous answer is that! All of this never changed Kristina's expression as she learned long ago to keep her emotions and thoughts in check whenever encountering people, but she couldn't help but let her guard down when she was around this girl.

Kristina wanted to say, "God! Are you kidding me! That's your answer? Why should I care about God?" but she never did. Kristina simply smiled wider and said, "Okay great!" raising the pitch of her voice to the sound of a child, "That's all I needed to know. See you later!" and she was off. Leaving Krystal in the dust without a second thought. Except on her way out, Kristina couldn't help but lower her guard and look over her shoulder for a final glance. Krystal showed no sign of reaction to Kristina's visit, although there was a hint of slight discomfort, but overall the girl didn't seem too shaken. Kristina watched as the girl picked up her black hardcover book and continued reading. Kristina saw the book and said, "Huh, I wonder what she was reading?"

CHAPTER 33

Connection

"What do you place your identity in? Is it your job?
Is it your family? Your hobbies or your name?"

—JL

"Mango passionfruit huh?" Krystal held the testing tube awkwardly in her hand. Like it was an alien device she had never seen before. Krystal gave the testing kit a press. A short puff came out then died quickly. Krystal leaned over to sniff but accidentally pressed the trigger and sprayed more perfume into her face. Krystal coughed and put the mango perfume back. Krystal noticed how ridiculous she looked and hoped nobody noticed. Luckily, no one had. Krystal looked around the retail store in the mall, surrounded by white tiled flooring, makeup stations, perfume, hair accessories, and all other sorts of products.

It wasn't her original intention to go into this retail store, but Krystal decided to try the perfume station out of curiosity. It was a bit out of her character since she never wore perfume or makeup, let alone tried to make herself feel "pretty." For once she tried it, and she felt so out of place. Krystal looked at the series of containers, all containing a mash of colors, not knowing what any of this stuff is. Trying to figure out what products there were felt like reading a foreign language to Krystal. She had never been much of a "girly girl." She held up a new perfume with a clear liquid inside. Flaming Coconut powder.

Krystal frowned. *What kind of marketing is that? Who would want to buy flaming coconut powder? What does that even smell like?* But she laid the trap for herself. Now curious as to what it smelled like. Her curiosity got the better of her and she accidentally pulled the trigger again and sprayed herself with the most unpleasant scent of perfume she'd ever experienced. It smelled like a mixture of burnt rubber and coconuts. Krystal coughed away the awful scent. *I can't believe people pay at least sixty-five bucks for this sort of thing on a daily basis.*

"You seem to be blending in nicely." Krystal knew that voice. She suddenly felt self-conscious, knowing someone was looking at her. She turned her back and saw Kristina Walker standing there wearing a blue top, silver-gray pants, sunglasses, and red lipstick, carrying a brand-new lime-green gator scaled purse, all of it complimenting her beautiful pale skin. Krystal could tell she had just gotten her hair done too, with its recent sheen glowing in the light. Silky, smooth, and beautiful, as was the rest of Kristina's body.

It took Krystal a moment to realize someone was actually talking to her. Kristina watched her with glee as Krystal stood there like a deer in headlights. After their recent encounter in both the bathroom and when Kristina visited Krystal during lunch, Krystal wasn't sure how to react around her. Krystal put down the horrid sample and said . . . well . . . she actually didn't say anything. Kristina approached Krystal and looked over the samples she was trying. Kristina picked one up and looked both intrigued and confused, "Flaming Coconut powder?"

Krystal muttered, "That's what . . . I said."

Kristina put down the sample and surveyed the rest of the table. It was strange. Krystal observed Kristina's body language and she seemed more relaxed and down to earth right now than the other times they've spoken. Even her voice was lower and more casual. Kristina turned and leaned one hand on the sampling table like a guy trying to pick up a girl at a bar. "I don't see you hanging around this part of town now do I?" Busted. Krystal knew there was no way out. Kristina caught Krystal with her guard down and now she had to pay the price of admission.

Krystal lowered her head, "Yes . . . I was . . . trying new . . . perfumes out."

Kristina smiled, "There's nothing wrong with a girl trying to make herself more appealing." Krystal noticed Kristina's "act" wasn't on right now and found intrigue in that. *She seems more comfortable now than when I first met her.*

"Uhh . . . yeah" was all Krystal could say. She had no idea what to say in regard to that statement.

Kristina smoothed her finger over the containers one by one, "Might I ask, does this have anything to do with a certain someone?" Her voice was coy, asking a question she already knew the answer to.

Krystal thought it over. She didn't want to tell Kristina she was here at the mall with Jaime. The truth of the matter was Krystal had left to go to the bathroom and in the interim ended up here, so she answered honestly. "I don't know," she said, glancing at the containers, "Normally . . . I don't care to think about this kind of stuff but now . . . I don't know. I feel like something's different this time. Like something sparked within me that wasn't there before."

Kristina coiled her head back, impressed. "Well I'll be. That was a rather good answer. You kept it genuine and mysterious without making me feel uncomfortable. Well done."

Krystal wasn't sure whether to take that as a compliment or not, so she kept her emotions to herself. Then she paused, looking for the right response but nothing came to mind, so she asked the first thing that came to her mind. "What . . ." she stumbled, fumbling for the right words, "brings you . . . here?"

Kristina grinned and looked down the mall at the series of clothing stores before her. "I mean, I've got what you call an addiction. A shopping addiction." Kristina threaded her hands and grinned like an evil genius, "I love shopping and I've got the money to do it, so why not?"

"I don't find an objection there," Krystal said, looking down at the two bags of clothes next to Kristina.

Kristina inquired, "I mean, what brings you to the mall today, might I ask?" Krystal glanced out the entrance to see Jaime sitting at their usual table in front of Schweet Tooth. She didn't want to tell Kristina that she and Jaime usually got carmel apples together at least once a week.

Krystal returned her eyes back to Kristina, "Just . . . hanging out with friends . . . that's all."

Kristina nodded, "Fun fun, fun fun. You buy any new clothes?"

"No," Krystal replied, trying not to sound shy and disgraced. "I'm not much of a shopper."

"We can try right now," said Kristina, her voice sounding like an encouraging mentor. "Let's get you some stuff." She smacked Krystal on the shoulder a little harder than Krystal expected. Krystal flinched from the unusual physical comradery. It was like she was slapped on the shoulder by a boy, and Krystal had no idea how to react to it. Her eyes searched for the right emotion for it. *That was weird. There's really no other word for it.* Kristina grunted happily at the awkward reaction from Krystal. Krystal looked up at Kristina, now seeing her in a new light. *It's like she's . . . more of a tomboy than a cutesy girl right now.*

Krystal hesitated, "Maybe . . . next time."

Kristina nodded, completely unoffended. "No prob no prob. I totally get ya. You barely know me, and I barely know you, so it would be a little awkward." Kristina looked at her watch and said, "Hey I gotta go but it was great to see you again."

"You too," Krystal said.

Krystal almost turned away when Kristina came back in a rush, "Hey let me get your phone number! Then we can go shopping some other time." Krystal was dumbstruck. *Wait . . . is she . . . asking to hang out . . . with me?*

Bewildered, Krystal pulled out her phone, "Okay." Kristina entered her phone number into Krystal's and vice versa, then Kristina sent Krystal a text to her phone.

Krystal's phone lit up and Kristina said, "Text me when you want to hang out sometime."

Krystal replied, "Okay?" It was all she could say in the moment. Her mind was still comprehending what was happening like a computer from the eighties downloading a song.

"Cool cool, cool cool." Kristina headed off and called out, "I'll see ya around Krystal." Krystal felt a slight shockwave hit her from hearing her own name come from another person. Krystal awkwardly waved back, her mind in a tizzy, still comprehending what had just happened. Kristina gave a quick wave and ran off into the crowded mall. Krystal stood there, staring off in Kristina's direction, then looked down at the contact information displayed on her phone.

Did I just get Kristina Walker's phone number? Krystal looked up, blown away. *What in the world just happened?*

༄

Kristina walked out from the school courtyard wearing her new brown sunglasses, a white t-shirt, a hat, and blue pants. She was trying to go incognito when she was around school so as to not attract as much attention. It only worked half the time, but half is better than none. Kristina held her backpack over her shoulder, surveying the lunch crowd. All the cliques sitting together, friends eating and laughing over the stupidest things. As well as people she recognized, who she hoped didn't see through her disguise. Kristina walked through the courtyard glancing around, her anxieties ramping up again with the idea of people looking at her, seeing her true self.

You're a hypocrite you know. That caused Kristina to pause. She had been a hypocrite lately. The whole time she had been telling herself not to reveal her true self to anyone, but when she hung out around Krystal, she purposefully dropped her false persona and let her real self show. Kristina shrugged. *Hmm, I mean, you're not wrong. I have been more relaxed when I'm around Krystal lately. But it's not like it's a dreadful thing . . .*

Kristina raised her head and searched the courtyard. It was lunchtime and she was in the general area where Krystal's white bench was so maybe she'd find her. All Kristina had to do was look to her left and there Krystal was, sitting on her white bench, eating a sandwich, and reading the same book as always. It didn't surprise Kristina. All she thought was, *That is the fourth day in a row where I've seen her sit by herself. If she doesn't have friends now, then I'll doubt she ever will.* Kristina was blinded to it before but now she could see it clear as day. Krystal Henninger was a loner. Yet it was that same loner who came to her rescue in the bathroom and didn't tell anyone.

The thought of Krystal mentioning God to Kristina gave her pause. *Is that really why she did that? Why she gave up her test to check on me?* It wasn't exactly a huge conundrum. Missing a test isn't exactly like saving the world. Krystal was still the one person who was there for her in her time of trouble when no one else was. Kristina grunted, *Hmm, the girl is more caring than she looks.*

To not overstay her escape, Kristina took her eyes off Krystal and headed back to her car. Her anxieties weren't done with her yet, so she wanted to get away from everyone as soon as possible. Yet there was a part of her that missed Krystal. She wasn't sure if they had a real connection or if it was something else. Whatever it was, she had a feeling she would see Krystal again.

⁓

Krystal took in deep breaths, her hand hovering over the phone. The text was already written out. Now all she had to do was hit send. Fear gripped Krystal's heart. It was still awkward, and Krystal wasn't sure how it happened, but she felt it was the right thing to do. Krystal whispered, "I can do all things through Christ who strengthens me," then felt her body and soul relax at the reassurance from the words. She felt a slight boost rush over her and suddenly she felt more confident. She hit the send icon and watched the text go through, saying a tiny prayer that she wouldn't be rejected in the process.

Krystal immediately freaked out. *Oh my goodness! Oh my goodness! Oh my goodness!* Her thoughts shooting on rapid fire like a machine gun. *I can't believe I just sent it! Ohhh what's she going to say?!* The suspense was eating Krystal alive.

Almost immediately a response came through and Krystal read: "Heck yeah let's do it!"

Krystal looked up from her phone, "Okay . . . I guess we're doing it."

Kristina closed the door to her room again, taking in the sight of the dreary bedroom. She detested this view. She threw her backpack down when she noticed her right hand shaking. Kristina gripped her hand, but the shaking transferred over into her left hand until both hands were shaking rapidly. It spread up her body and Kristina's breathing increased into rapid short breaths. In the span of an instant, Kristina's body went from normal to fight or flight mode. Her heart pounded like a drum and her eyes searched the room for an answer.

WHO AM I?!

Kristina's legs gave out and she fell on her knees to the floor. The panic attack went into full power, bringing her mind to the brink of insanity. Kristina threw her hands to her head and curled up into a ball against her bedroom door. Fear shrouded her heart and mind, and she whispered in terror, "Who am I? Who am I?" The darkness of the room only masked her suffering to the outside world, as no one knew of her current suffering, not even her parents. Time passed for what felt like an eternity before Kristina's phone vibrated in her pocket. Kristina shakenly took her phone out and read a text. Miraculously, she somehow calmed down at the sight of the message. She instantly replied to the text, leaning her head back against the wall in exhaustion. Her body was sweaty, fearful of the shaking that would attack her again. It felt like Kristina had been hit by electricity and was now coming down from the fight or flight mode. She had no idea whether to feel tense or relaxed. The fatigue answered for her when her body slumped down, too tired to react, but awake enough to realize the horror that another attack could hit her any minute.

〰

Kristina stood at the door and glanced over her shoulder to make sure she wasn't being followed. Paparazzi were always butting into her life, trying to get a snapshot of what she was doing in her free time. She stood in front of the white door to Krystal's apartment complex. Kristina glanced around, noting the simplicity of the complex. There was a stairwell that led to the second floor where Krystal lived, along with an open parking lot where Kristina had parked nearby. Kristina grunted, *Hmm, so this is where Krystal lives.* She wasn't impressed nor disappointed, she just found it interesting to learn about a person's upbringing. What did surprise her, however, was how close this apartment complex was to Jaime's house. Kristina formed the bridge in her mind and knew it wouldn't be hard for Krystal and Jaime to hang out.

Kristina took a deep breath, trying to calm herself as her anxiety continued to attack her every second of the day. She held the shaking within and had built up enough energy to appear normal for the time. She knocked on Krystal's door and waited a few moments. Each second she waited felt like an eternity. The door finally opened, and Krystal stood in the doorway, wearing a black apron with her black hair tied back in a ponytail. Kristina relaxed a little at the sight of her. Feeling her defenses drop down from 120% to 80%, not a huge improvement but better than most. Krystal didn't show any signs of excitement, but she wasn't gloomy looking either. She just looked at Kristina with those passive, purple-colored eyes.

Krystal held the door open and said, "Come on in." Kristina flinched at that statement. Kristina remembered talking to Krystal before, and how she had a challenging time speaking, but this time her sentences were more resolute and words flowed easier, a definite improvement since the last few times they spoke. Maybe it was because she was in her home where she was most comfortable.

Kristina stepped inside and felt more relaxed once the door closed behind her. She lowered her defenses more, feeling her stress lower knowing she was out of reach from prying eyes, at least she hoped she did. She took her shoes off and entered Krystal's apartment. She looked around, taking in the sight of the kitchen and living room, trying to find any and every detail she could around the room. The floor was a nice amber wood, with a glass coffee table, a tan couch, and a tv in the living room to her left. Kristina immediately noticed how quiet the apartment was and how it reminded Kristina of her own apartment. While Kristina marveled at the silence, it quickly became quiet, too quiet. Kristina glanced around, noticing how empty the apartment felt. There were a few pictures, some of them even left stains on the walls from where a canvas used to be. The white walls and empty shelves all echoed a sense of emptiness and hallow living. It was like the room was dead and needed some life to it. It needed to feel more like home than just a place to stay. Kristina felt the dread sink into her heart as she centered her attention on Krystal, who was busy shuffling together some pasta.

Is this what you come home to everyday Krystal?

It felt like a library with no people in it. As though it was rude to make any noise at all. The feeling surrounded Kristina's heart and dampened her mood, lowering her charisma as when she walked in. "Do you live here by yourself?" she asked.

Krystal didn't look up from the active stovetop, "No. I live with my aunt. But she works the night shift at the hospital so she's rarely around."

Kristina grunted, "Hmph." Kristina was still trying to get a grasp of the way things worked within these walls. It felt so foreign that Kristina almost missed the noise in her family's house when they used to live together. Here, everything was so bare, like there were no secrets. "You can take a seat," Krystal said, "Dinner's almost ready."

Kristina remained standing. She wanted to take a seat but wanted to explore more of the apartment. She wanted to know what it was like to live this girl's life. Kristina walked over to a section of the apartment that split off into two doorways. Krystal noticed Kristina's intrigue and said, "My room is on the right in case you're wondering."

I was wondering. Thanks for asking.

Kristina didn't bother to look away, instead she stared at Krystal's door. Kristina turned the knob and opened the door. It was nothing special, the single room was barer than the apartment itself. The walls inside the bedroom were white with no decoration, not even a poster. There was a desk and a computer with some books but nothing else. Kristina did notice a guitar in the corner but was quickly engulfed with the sense of lifelessness echoing from the room. *This room feels even more dead than the living room and the kitchen.* The air inside was dry and dusty. Kristina glanced over and saw a single window to the right of the desk, beside the bed. The bed was a full sized mattress with two pillows, white sheets, and a comforter. Nothing special along with the rest of the room. Kristina looked from side to side, hoping to find some sort of decoration or flair from Krystal's hidden interests but found none. *This room has no class.* Kristina snuck a look at Krystal while she made dinner. *What kind of life do you live Krystal?* Kristina felt nothing but a sense of hopelessness echoing from this room. It had no sense of livelihood to it. No sense of home. Just a room, bare and empty. She wondered if it reflected Krystal's life. Feeling immense pity for the girl, she shrugged the thought away. Kristina managed to spot the same black and gold hardcover book Krystal was reading at school the other day. The golden rimmed pages calling out to her, almost magnetically. Kristina picked up the book and saw it was opened to a passage in the book of Mark. Some of the words were underlined in a certain passage. Kristina's eyes drew toward this marking and read:

"Daughter, your faith has made you well. Go in peace. Your suffering is over."

Kristina read the quote and caption, "Mark chapter five verse thirty-four." She closed the book and put it back where it belonged. Something about that verse spoke to her. *I can see why she underlined it, but I can't understand why she did it.* Then Kristina's gaze shifted over toward the closet. Kristina opened the closet door and found nothing but cobwebs and dust mustered all over the flooring. Kristina looked around, finding nothing on the hangers, but did find Krystal's wardrobe beneath. Kristina opened the wardrobe and made a mental list of everything she saw. *Long sleeve shirt, black, long sleeve pants, black, etc. etc. Does this girl wear anything other than black?* Although it wasn't the coloring of Krystal's wardrobe that made an impression on Kristina. It was how bare and empty the closet was compared to Kristina's own closet. Kristina's own closet was first of all, a lot bigger than this one. It was easily the size of Krystal's entire apartment. And second, that same closet was filled to the brim with multiple sets of shirts, hats, dresses, and at least a dozen or more pairs of shoes Kristina hadn't worn. Here, it was totally different. There was a single pair of shoes, black (not surprising), along with clothing and coloring that made only a homeless person feel impressed. This wasn't the problem though. The problem was that it lacked *attention*. Kristina assumed Krystal could have improved her wardrobe if she wanted to, but this was the result of someone who'd never paid much attention to it in the first place. The only interesting article of clothing she found was a plain black ACDC shirt but that was it.

What kind of person . . . no, what kind of girl, only wears one type of outfit? Just the closet itself makes me feel gloomy.

"Are you impressed with my room?" Krystal called out sarcastically, like a parent asking if their child had taken out the trash, when they knew full well, they didn't.

Kristina called out, "Yes it's very lovely." She lied. It made her feel horrible. Kristina was so bothered by the wardrobe she stormed out like an angry parent into the kitchen. She looked at Krystal, put her hand on her hip, and pointed to Krystal's room, "Listen up! This room and closet need a MAJOR makeover! And I mean MAJOR! Do you hear me?" Kristina pointed at Krystal. "You and I are going shopping. Right now!" Krystal just stood there bewildered, still holding a pot of pasta in her hands.

"Uhhh," Krystal said, clearly not sharing Kristina's enthusiasm. "Can we do it after dinner?"

Kristina shook her head. "No."

⸙

Kristina ran into the mall like a child while Krystal followed casually behind, as if they were on two separate deadlines. The mall was getting busy as it was the early evening on a Friday. Kristina took a couple steps then turned, "First of all," as she pointed at Krystal, "we need to get you a dress because Jaime's Black-Tie Event is coming up and I know you didn't get a dress yet." Krystal showed no sign of argument there. She just stared back at Kristina, not sharing her drive. "Second of all," Kristina elaborated, "we need to fix up your whole wardrobe. You can wear black, that's fine, but you need a little more"—Kristina waved her hand—"*class*, if you know what I mean?"

"Okay . . ." Krystal said obediently yet somewhat confused. Kristina sensed a tad bit of hesitation in there but ignored it. She was surprised Krystal wasn't sharing the same enthusiasm she was. *Doesn't she want to go shopping? Like to improve her wardrobe or something?* But the blank stare Krystal gave back was not the answer Kristina expected. Kristina shook her head, *No. I'm not giving up on her yet.* "We are going to find something for you today and we are going to buy it, and you are going to love it, ya hear?"

Krystal answered like a child who fully understands the obvious instructions a parent just gave them. "I hear," she said flatly. Dullness and boredom filling her tone.

Kristina clenched a fist in victory. "Great! Now let's get started."

"This is not what I expected."

"Aww come on. I mean, you look great!"

Krystal stood atop a podium wearing a pink dress, looking like she belonged to a mashed-up version of the Wizard of Oz. The clothing store Kristina picked out had khaki-colored walls and was relatively empty, giving the two girls the store to themselves.

Krystal looked down at Kristina, who glimmered at Krystal from her handiwork. Krystal frowned at Kristina, "You're having a lot of fun with this aren't you?" Normally Krystal would be more hesitant with her words, but lately since she's interacted with Kristina so much, it was getting easier to talk to her. Krystal felt herself start to come out of her shell whenever she was around Kristina.

Kristina smiled, her hands clapped together like a happy parent and nodded, "Oh I am, I am very much." Krystal rolled her eyes, but somewhat enjoyed Kristina's enthusiasm. Maybe it was rubbing off on Krystal, she couldn't tell. Krystal looked at herself in the mirror, the pink dress clung tightly to her body.

Krystal looked over her shoulder, "Are you sure this is a good look on me? I'm not really feeling it."

Kristina put a finger to her lips and acted like a detective, "Hmm, I see your deduction Watson, and I do believe you have an adequate response."

Krystal waited for a proper explanation but received none, "So . . . you agree it doesn't look good on me?"

Kristina answered plainly, spit firing the words, "Oh yeah it looks terrible on you."

Krystal felt embarrassed, happy, and relieved all at the same time. Krystal took one last look at herself in the pink dress in the mirror and shook her head. *No this doesn't suit me at all. I'm not the type of girl to wear pink dresses. It stands out too much.*

"What about this one!" Kristina handed Krystal another dress, Krystal looked back and forth between Kristina and the dress.

Krystal held the green dress and looked up, "Are you serious?"

"Yes," Kristina smiled eagerly, reaching over "and put this hat on while you're at it." Kristina handed Krystal a red beret.

Krystal squirmed, "Alright." Then went to change.

Krystal stepped out wearing a dark green dress with black gloves that covered her forearms, and a red beret. A part of Krystal believed Kristina had been planning this all along. Only time will tell.

Kristina was awed at the sight of her. A version of Krystal she had never seen before. And to be honest, before today she would have never imagined seeing this sight. The silk green dress didn't look too bad actually. Krystal felt like she was mimicking poison ivy from Batman a bit (minus the provocative dressing of course). Krystal stood atop the podium and let Kristina gaze at her with awed aspiration. Krystal could see Kristina's fingers jittering with excitement, giving off exhilaration and a few other emotions. Kristina made a twirling motion with her fingers and Krystal reluctantly obliged, twirling around, trying not to fall off the podium.

Krystal looked at herself in the twin mirrors on both sides and thought, *It doesn't look too bad on me, but I don't feel like this suits me.* Part of her thought of Winter Formal, but she brushed those memories off, not wanting to get sucked into a blackhole of depression. Krystal snuck a look at Kristina eye-balling her. Kristina clapped her hands and said in a dresser's accent, "Come on now ladies! Ve need to see zhe spice in zhe nice!" Krystal had never felt more self-conscious in her life. She wrapped her arms around her upper body, uncomfortable revealing this much skin around her shoulders.

Kristina shook her head, swerving her body like a wave, "No no! You need to express yourself darling! You need to show zhe vorld who you are!" Kristina snapped her fingers.

Krystal clenched her hands tighter around herself, shaking her head. *I've never felt so self-conscious wearing a dress in my life.*

Kristina stared at Krystal, her eyes nearly bulging out of their sockets from how much excitement she was having. "Yes, yes! Give me zhe spice!"

Krystal gripped herself like she was out in a snowstorm with no jacket, feeling naked without her long sleeve shirts on.

Krystal looked back at Kristina amidst her embarrassment, "You're having way too much fun with this you know that."

Kristina grinned, letting the comment bounce right off her. "Yes, but I bet you're having fun too, ya?"

Krystal held her emotions in but felt a sense of laughter build in her chest. As much as she hated it, she was having fun. She nodded her head up and down slowly, "Uhhhhh, a little bit," she admitted with defeat, sounding cheerier now than before.

"Zhen ve are perfect ya?"

Krystal made one last look at the green dress, "I . . . don't think so."

Kristina's arms and energy dropped to zero, "Don't be such a buzz kill darling."

Krystal still covered herself, "Well you asked me what I think, and I think no."

"Come on darling, you've got to show zhe confidence. You've got to show zhe vorld who you are!"

Krystal looked around. "I'm just not feeling it."

Kristina tapped her chin with her finger, dropping the accent. "Hmmm, I mean, maybe it's the gloves? Try taking the black gloves off."

Krystal looked down at her hands and back at Kristina in all seriousness. "I don't think that's a good idea."

Kristina stepped up to the podium, "Oh come now, what's the worst that will happen?"

Krystal defended again, "I really don't think it's such a good idea."

Kristina tilted her head, looking at Krystal more seriously, "Oh come on."

Krystal looked at Kristina cautiously as Kristina raised her hands to take off Krystal's gloves. She took the right one off, then the left. Kristina pulled the final glove off and said, "See. I mean, I don't know what the problem i—" She stared at the huge scar on Krystal's left wrist. Her mouth agape in shock. The sight of it made Kristina repulse with horror, yet she was unable to look away from the horrible wound. Eventually Kristina looked up and met Krystal's midnight purple eyes. Kristina stared at Krystal, not knowing what to say, while Krystal looked back at her with compassion.

After a long pause, Kristina finally said, "Oh . . ." then sought to change the subject. Her eyes browsed upon a new dress that piqued her interest and she held it up in front of Krystal and said, "I mean, what about this one?" Krystal stared at the dress with renewed intrigue. She held it in her hands and without a word, left to go put it on. Kristina was relieved with the change of subject and let out a long exhale. The mood returned to normal, and Kristina waited, feeling jazzed with excitement from how she would feel when she saw Krystal wearing this dress. "I can't wait to see how this one looks."

Krystal came out a few minutes later and immediately Kristina was in awe even more so than before. She pointed and said, "This is the one . . . it's . . . it's perfect."

∽

Kristina pulled up to Krystal's apartment and put the car in park. The two of them walked back up the stairs to Krystal's apartment. Krystal opened the doorway and said, "I had a really good time today. I want you to know that." Kristina was surprised. She didn't expect Krystal to be so kind with her words as of now. "It's been a while . . . since I've had fun shopping with someone." Krystal sounded embarrassed.

Kristina smiled, "It was fun for me too. Let's do it again sometime."

Krystal turned to Kristina and asked softly, "I know we didn't get around to it, but you are welcome to stay for dinner if you want."

Kristina was surprised but kept it to herself. She turned on the cute act and answered, "Of course I can stay! Who wouldn't want to!?" Lifting her arms in the air, Kristina closed her eyes with fake glee, hoping to sell the act to Krystal, but when she opened them, she almost saw Krystal smile.

Krystal looked a little red but happy, "Cool."

Kristina deflated a bit, "Cool" and the two of them walked into Krystal's apartment.

∽

"Here," Krystal offered Kristina a bowl of pasta. The two of them ate on opposite sides of Krystal's couch in her living room. It was just the two of them but the atmosphere in the apartment seemed livelier. Kristina munched on her pasta, enjoying the free food along with the delicious taste of every bite. Krystal saw her glee and tried to hide her own. Krystal asked, "Do you like it?"

Kristina almost said, "Oh I like it . . ." like a seductive man but kept that to herself. What Kristina actually said was, "Are you kidding! This is amazing!"

Either way, the reply was enough to make Krystal feel happy inside. Kristina looked down at the bowl between her hands. It was just simple pasta, and yet it was the most delicious thing she had ever tasted. Kristina looked up with glee, *Krystal's a really good cook! I wish I had more of this around when I was growing up.* It reminded Kristina of her own mom, her thoughts following a dark path in her mind, leading her toward a restricted area within her conscience. *No. Don't go there. You cannot go there.* Kristina pushed her thoughts aside and continued eating the delicious food in her hands.

As she ate, Kristina felt her defenses lower when she stared down at the bowl of pasta between her hands. She felt herself relaxing more and more. Kristina didn't notice her defenses drop completely until it was too late. "This is really good . . ." she whispered honestly. Krystal noticed and contained her joy as her lips curved into a slight smile. Kristina realized her mistake too late. Her eyes widened in horror. Her body immediately tensed up like a stone, the tightness around her heart increasing like someone was choking her from the inside. The weight and pressure placed upon Kristina's heart increased at the cost of her own willpower. Kristina felt her energy plummet, but she had to keep the façade going. She couldn't let anyone see her true self. No one. Kristina brushed her hand through her hair, hoping to allude to any awkward gestures from Krystal. Either way Kristina had no idea how Krystal would react.

But Krystal was the first to break. She lowered her bowl from her face and said, "You know . . . you have very nice hair . . ." Kristina was surprised. It was simply not what she expected to hear from Krystal. It had caught Kristina off guard, causing her defenses to lower again and just be honest. Kristina stroked her hand through her hair, feeling the soft silky texture between her fingers.

Kristina didn't know what to say, so she answered back, "You have nice hair too Krystal." Saying that came as a surprise to Kristina. It was the first honest thing she said in a while. The feel of the room, the silence of it all, the closed doors and emptiness, brought in all the factors of what seemed like a safe place. Kristina casually whipped her head around, checking they were alone. She had to always keep her head on a swivel, since there was always some paparazzi lurking around. Only this time it was different. This time, it was just the two of them in this apartment, with all the time in the world.

Krystal broke the ice again and looked at Kristina timidly, "I had a fun time today . . . It's . . . been a while since I . . . enjoyed dress shopping." By Krystal inadvertently lowering her guard, Kristina felt her own guard begin to drop again, like they were connected somehow. Like it was okay to come out and be honest. Kristina felt curiosity rack her heart and wanted to be herself for once. Kristina didn't try to alter her voice or ask anything smug. This time, she simply asked the question that was on her heart, "When was the last time you went dress shopping?"

Krystal expected that question but still seemed embarrassed to admit it. Kristina appeared empathetic towards her. Kristina could feel the fear in her own heart from opening up to another person. A person you don't fully know, but you trust them enough to tell them what you really think. Amidst the silence, Kristina felt the pressure in her own heart to open up. *What is happening? I mean, why am I feeling like this all of a sudden?*

But her thoughts were thrown out the window yet again when Krystal answered, "It was one year ago . . . when I went shopping with my mom." Kristina felt the scene click in her mind, then glanced around the room. It all made sense now. The empty apartment, why Krystal was so good at cooking, the lack of décor, her empty closet, and her choice of clothing. Everything clicked.

Fear gripped Kristina's heart, as if asking the question was the same as opening up. But Kristina asked anyway, feeling it was the appropriate thing to do. "What happened?"

"She got hit by a truck," Krystal spoke so casually about it that the mere honesty frightened Kristina. Her words were riddled with pain. Kristina couldn't tell whether to cry or feel horrified. But now she understood the whole picture.

Kristina asked, "So . . . that was the last time you went dress shopping huh?"

Krystal nodded. "It was for the Winter Formal dance last year." Krystal chuckled to herself but not in a joyful manner. "And to think I was having a good time . . ." Kristina could hear the contempt within her voice. Krystal trailed off and let the conversation die. There were a few cold seconds between them. Kristina was unsure how to answer, and yet, it seemed like being quiet was the right thing to do at the moment. Krystal looked like she was pondering something, and said, "So . . . the Black-Tie Event is coming up . . . and I . . . I still haven't decided . . . on what hair style to go with . . ." Krystal raised her eyes and met Kristina's gaze. "Could . . . could you help me?" Krystal pointed, "Braid my hair?" She seemed a bit embarrassed, but that comment allowed Kristina to relax.

Kristina nodded, "Sure," Unaware that she had dropped her act completely.

Krystal put the bowl aside and the two of them shifted position on the couch to where Krystal sat upright while Kristina stood behind her. After a painful session brushing the knots out of Krystal's hair, Kristina finally began braiding. Krystal sat on the lower portion of the couch, looking forward, so as not to disturb Kristina's work on her hair. Kristina threaded her hands through Krystal's hair. Krystal could feel the tug on her hair as Kristina gently pulled it back and got to work. Kristina straightened it out and took some strands from the back of Krystal's hair, putting them together into a single braid, flowing with the rest of Krystal's hair down her back. Kristina said, "Your hair could use some work. Do you use any products?"

"No," Krystal said, "I don't ... do anything." Kristina stopped midstride. Krystal sighed and lowered her head slightly, "I've never been good at this, not when it comes to fashion or connecting with girls about this sort of stuff. I don't even wear makeup." Krystal expected Kristina to say something but for once she was silent. So Krystal felt the urge to keep going. "Most girls spend so much time focusing on what they wear or what they are going to do this weekend or what fashion is trending right now but not me . . . not me." Krystal sighed and looked down at her feet. "I've just never been into it . . . even when I want to." Krystal shook her head, disappointed in herself. Krystal gestured her right sleeve for Kristina to see. "You've seen it with your own eyes. All I like to wear is black." Krystal paused, trying to find the right words to say. "But I . . . still . . . want to feel . . . pretty." Krystal may be unique in fashion, but she was still a girl nonetheless, and all girls want to feel beautiful.

Krystal let the words sink in. "I want to feel girly and beautiful. To enjoy myself, and let others enjoy me . . . you know?" Krystal paused. "And when I see you Kristina, I can't help but see how beautiful you look. With your gorgeous hair, your nice earrings, and your elegant resolve." Krystal looked down at the wooden floor, "I can't help but want that." Kristina said nothing. She wanted to think of something clever to say but nothing came up. The truth was, even Kristina didn't feel she was pretty at times, despite people constantly telling her she looked beautiful.

Krystal briefly chuckled to herself. "I know this is odd . . . but I like it when you're yourself. It's more . . . comfortable." Kristina stopped braiding all together. Krystal took a breath but continued to look forward, "I know you put on a mask for others, and I understand." Krystal spoke softly and with grace, "but you don't have to put on an act with me." There was a certain relief Kristina felt hearing those words. Krystal wasn't judging her, in fact, she was supporting her. Krystal was allowing Kristina to be herself without any judgment while keeping up the act around others. Krystal finished, "And for what it's worth . . . I'm glad it was you . . . who could do my hair and take me shopping." Kristina had finished the perfecting touches on Krystal's hair as Krystal turned around and looked up at Kristina. "I couldn't have done this without you."

Kristina's lips buckled as she fought the urge to cry. Her heart filled like a dam ready to burst. Kristina threw her hand to her mouth, trying to hide the quiver on her lip. The mask was crashing down, opening Kristina's soul to a world of healing. All she had to do was let it happen.

"I . . ." Kristina choked. "I . . ." her breathing grew more troubled, fractured. The realization hit her like a freight train. That it was okay for her to open up. A chance, to finally trust someone. "I don't know what to say," Kristina's voice fell apart. "I . . ." Kristina tried to find the right words as Krystal watched her patiently, her face unchanging, waiting. Kristina fought to find the right words; her mouth open yet unsure what to say.

Kristina's heart provided the words, words she had been begging to tell someone for an awfully long time. Through honesty came healing and relief, as the words formed slowly on Kristina's lips. "I . . . feel so . . . alone." Her voice was weak like a child, the vain attempt to find something to grasp onto. The dam began to buckle under the pressure that had been building for years. The words flowing faster now. The weight upon Kristina's heart beginning to lighten. "I've had to put on a mask . . . for so long . . . around everyone I know, even my parents." Kristina paused. "Acting . . . that's what I'm good at. Perhaps too good. For years I've lived a false life around everyone. Trying to act more cheerful. Acting like there's nothing in the world that bothers me. And with this work that I do, the fame that comes with it. I can't help but feel alone. Like there's no one who I can trust. There's no one at school I can relate to. Not even the other drama kids. They have no idea what it's like to feel this alone and out of touch with the rest of society."

Kristina felt the weight lift from her heart, could feel the healing enter her soul like lotion on an open wound. Being honest with someone for the first time was like shedding an enormous weight off her shoulders. Kristina's voice grew more frustrated, "Then I have all these people who come up to me, not because they want to get to know me, but because they want to be friends with *Kristina Walker, the Actress*." She said her name as if it were a title she despised.

Kristina suddenly shot Krystal a look of skepticism. "Was that why you tried to become friends with me?" Accusation flooded Kristina's tone as her defenses kicked in again, she actively sought to question Krystal for humiliating her. Krystal showed no reaction. It didn't surprise her at all.

"Kristina." Krystal's voice was calm and assuring, "When I saw you at that party and offered you that cup. I saw that same look on your face that I had. The look of loneliness. The look of someone who's hurting. The look of a person who's silently screaming for help, finding none. Wishing someone would just come over and save you." Krystal took a breath, watching as Kristina cooled off and settled into her seat again. "Because when I saw you at that party, sitting all alone, wishing for someone to save you . . . I saw myself. And I want to love people the way I want to be loved. The same way Jesus loved me." Krystal met Kristina's blue eyes. "That's why."

There it was. The truth. There was no changing that. Krystal said her piece. Now it was Kristina's turn. Kristina stared at Krystal for a hard moment, trying to decipher whether Krystal spoke the truth or not. But Kristina was having trouble reading Krystal's face. She couldn't tell whether it was an intended construction or if it was Krystal's natural face. Yet, there was a kind of innocence to it. A slight genre of honesty, yet it was honesty hidden in honesty. It threw Kristina off because she did the opposite. Kristina lied in everything she did, and yet here was a girl who spoke the truth, though it could be a lie. It seemed too real to be genuine, and Kristina couldn't decide which one to believe. Regardless of her thoughts, Kristina saw the look on Krystal's face, a look of true compassion, from a girl who had nothing to gain from being honest. She was simply someone who cared.

Kristina felt her defenses lower once more, despite her better judgment. "I think . . ." she paused, fearful of being honest again, "you're the first person . . . who's ever been honest with me." Kristina paused, finding there was more for her to say, "I feel . . . like I can be honest with you." Kristina shook her head, puzzled. "I don't know what it is, but for some reason, I feel more comfortable around you compared to other people. You have an . . . an innocence about you that I can't fathom. I feel like I can be myself around you. Because there's nothing malicious about you . . ." Kristina's voice picked up a little more spunk again, relaxing to her casual self, "I don't know. Maybe it's because you don't talk much that I feel like I can talk with you."

Krystal loosened her expression in agreement. "I'm not much of a talker."

Kristina chuckled, appreciative of the light-hearted comment. "That much is true." The conversation paused for a few seconds, but the air in the room lifted to a lighter tone. It was more casual and the awkwardness between them lifted.

Krystal asked without even thinking, "So . . . are we *friends* then?"

Kristina answered happily, "Yes."

Krystal nodded and looked away, "Cool."

Out of nowhere Kristina said, "Would you like to see how you look?"

"Sure."

Kristina pulled out her phone and held it out as a mirror for Krystal. Krystal saw herself in the reflection, observing the new hairstyle Kristina had done for her. It was a simple style, but it changed the way Krystal looked at herself. It was a simple braid down her back, using two strands of hair in the middle while the rest of her black hair draped down her back like a waterfall.

Kristina looked over Krystal and said, "You look pretty."

Krystal's eyes widened. Tears welled up, blurring her vision, as she put her hand to her face and silently cried. It was the first time in her life someone said she was pretty.

Kristina decided to take the more mature approach and let Krystal cry. She waited until Krystal wiped her face and was back to normal, then grabbed a whisp of Krystal's hair, making Krystal flinch, "You know . . . that hairstyle suits you. You should wear it like that more often."

Krystal was mystified by someone complimenting her on her hair. Krystal looked at herself in the reflection of her phone. "Okay . . . maybe I will."

CHAPTER 34

Who's That Girl?

"One's touch can be so powerful, that sometimes simply holding someone's hand can brighten one's day."

—JL

"Are you all buttoned up and ready Jaime?" Mrs. Fisher called out.

Mr. Fisher finished tightening Jaime's tie and called back, "He's almost done." Jaime stood there as his dad finished the final loop on his red tie, complimenting the black suit he wore, making him look very handsome. His broad shoulders stood out, making him look even more muscular. Definitely a result from water polo for sure. Mr. Fisher finished and clapped his son's shoulders, "There you go. All done." Then he sized Jaime up from head to toe. "You look very handsome son."

Jaime smiled but it didn't last long. It faded like the sun setting on the horizon until it was gone forever. Jaime didn't say anything, but he wished he did. The silent message stabbed his dad like a knife in the heart. Mr. Fisher didn't show his reaction, but it killed him inside to know his son was isolating himself. So he took the blow and left the room.

Jaime stepped down the stairs and heard the rumbling beneath him. A large group of people had formulated downstairs as Jaime walked halfway down the grand staircase, leaning over the railing, dressed like the great Gatsby. Jaime raised his hands and shouted. "Good evening, everybody!" Their heads looked his way and mouths hushed. Jaime clapped his hands together, "I would like to thank you all for coming to our annual Black-Tie Event, where we all dress our finest and show off our true beauty." He extended an arm toward the kitchen and said, "We have a fine assortment of drinks tonight, non-alcoholic I might add, as well as games, so eat, drink, and *party*!" The crowd cheered as Jaime soaked in the applause. Jaime stepped down and found his buddy Luiz dressed in a fine black and white tux.

"My man," Luiz said, jittering with enthusiasm, giving Jaime a massive bro hug, both of them broad in each other's arms. "That was quite the speech you had there."

Jaime met Luiz's enthusiasm with his own, "You know me, man, I'm always good with speeches."

"Yeah?" Luiz cocked an eyebrow, egging him on, "You gonna give a speech at the annual talent show coming up? I hear they need a couple slots filled."

Jaime shook his head, "Nah man, I've got too much on my plate right now." Jaime made a swift twirling gesture with his hand, "I've got this party to run, and that's enough."

"Fair enough." Luiz nodded, glad to see his friend back in action. He handed Jaime a much-needed drink and they both stood there watching the party unfold. Groups of people formed in various corners of the house, some playing pool while others chatted around the snack tables, munching down on several types of chips and dip. More people entered through the front door. Guys and girls, high schoolers, dressed in their finest. Beautiful dresses for girls, guys in amazing tuxedos and suits flowing into the house, looking more like a ballroom setting than a formal party. Jaime took delight in that. He loved the idea of the 1920s, the blues, the suits, and of course, the dancing. Everything about that era had such an allure and seemed so elegant to Jaime. They had cleared some of their sofas from the living room to make it a suitable dance floor, but the issue these days was that people didn't know how to dance, so Jaime knew he was going to have to step in and be an instructor for tonight. That didn't bother him though, he liked it when people were able to join in his passion, so much so his community had grown used to it.

Jaime and Luiz took turns checking out the girls arriving at the party. Every one of them looked amazing wearing their unique dresses. Jaime spotted one girl in a red Chinese dress with an embroidered dragon across the back, along with a white and red flower dangling from her black hair. The look of the dress astounded Jaime. More girls were coming in wearing dresses of all sorts, orange, blue, red, and silver. A group of them wore white dresses like they were ready to get married. *It's not too out of the ordinary,* Jaime thought. *I mean, everyone here has already dressed for the part, it would be funny to host a fake wedding here.* But Jaime dashed the thought. *No that's too creepy, even for me.* Extravagant hair styles were coming in as well. Girls folded up their hair into perfectly styled towers, some forming amazing bundles and some with lined pens in their hair to complete the look. All of it looked amazing to Jaime, (in a non-creepy fashion of course.)

Jaime took another sip from his drink, when the door opened, and Kristina Walker stepped in. She was wearing an oval hat, wearing a beautiful black silk dress, like a New York mistress. Kristina looked his way and greeted Jaime, "Hey Buck! Good to see you." Giving him a hug.

Jaime replied, "It's good to see you too Kristina. How are you?"

Kristina stepped to Jaime's side and threw her arm over his shoulder nonchalantly, "I'm peachy. Ready to start the party." Kristina seemed more light-hearted, yet softer in her energy. Jaime wasn't quite sure why, but she seemed different than the last time he saw her. More subtle and not over the top. Kristina looked around and said, "I see the party has already begun my friend."

Jaime felt relieved, *There's the Kristina I know.* Still seeing the spunk in Kristina. Luiz stepped in and said his greetings, and Kristina responded in kind. Jaime gestured a thumb toward the snack bar and said, "Do you guys want to get something to eat?"

Kristina waved them off, "No, I'll wait here. I want to be here when it happens."

"When what happens?" Luiz asked.

Kristina bent a devil-like smile, "You'll see," then took a drink from Luiz's cup. Jaime was both stunned and not. *Yup, that's Kristina for you.*

The front door opened slightly and in walked a girl wearing a beautifully laced purple silk dress. Her hair was curled slightly, falling down her back like a waterfall, with two small strands coming together into a single braid.

Jaime felt his heart leap within him. The world blurred as sparks flew at the sight of this beautiful girl. She was stunning and far more breathtaking than any girl he had ever seen before. Her midnight purple eyes looked back at him. The sight of it took his breath away. The girl was absolutely gorgeous. The dress encompassed her, looking like a beautiful peacock walking into a room as people began to stare at her. She seemed a bit uncomfortable with herself, but that was okay. It only made her look cuter.

The words flowed out of his mouth before he could even ask, "Who is that girl?" His voice in awe and wonder at the sight of something utterly amazing.

"You don't recognize her?" Kristina said coy-like. As if expecting Jaime's answer. She nodded her head in the girl's direction, "That's Krystal."

Jaime's heart fell. He could not believe his own eyes. *That's Krystal?! I didn't even recognize her.* Jaime took in the sight. Realizing Krystal was wearing makeup for once, as well as having her eyelashes done, adding a sprinkle of shine, making her look even more fluorescent than ever. Her black hair looked smooth and shiny flowing down her back. It was like she was a gem. Something hidden and beautiful to the eye, yet not easily seen. One that requires effort to see its true beauty.

"Jaime? Jaime?" Kristina asked, snapping her fingers. Jaime snapped back to reality. Kristina pointed, "Your jaw is open."

"It is?" Jaime was surprised by his own reaction. He cupped his hand to his jaw and tried to recollect himself. *You have got to get a grip on yourself, man!* He magnetically looked back at Krystal. Taking in the sight of her formal attire. Wearing black gloves over her hands and forearms with partial bits of her shoulders exposed, revealing portions of pale skin. Her body looked more beautiful than Jaime had ever seen. But it wasn't just that. There was something about her that seemed . . . different.

Images of Jaime seeing this girl sitting by herself at lunch flooded his mind. *There's no way this is the same girl!* Even Luiz seemed stunned at the sight of her. Kristina saw both their looks and laughed. She threw her arms around them and said, "Drink it in boys. That's the real deal."

Jaime felt hot. He loosened his tie and felt his armpits dampen. Soaking in sweat already. *Aww man, the party just began and I'm already soaking wet.*

Kristina took full advantage of the situation, leaning close to Jaime's ear, "You gonna ask her to dance?" Jaime and Kristina exchanged glances, and Jaime for some reason couldn't recognize Kristina. She seemed . . . happier for some reason. He couldn't put his mind to it, yet it evaded him. A voice whispered in his mind; *I wish I could feel that happy.* Jaime wanted to sit down and sulk for a minute but now was not the time. He glanced back over at Krystal who was looking a bit out of place among the party. Some people had already started dancing and Jaime could tell Krystal was studying their movements, trying to play it out in her mind and mimic them.

Kristina looked out at Krystal then back at Jaime, "Now's your chance buddy." Kristina pushed Jaime forward and said, "Go get her tiger." Jaime looked to Luiz for help, but Luiz raised his hands and gave him the *"This is on you"* look. Jaime took his first step forward, losing all sense of thought and consciousness as he walked closer and closer toward this rare beauty.

Krystal stood there holding her elbow looking uncomfortable as always. Jaime approached Krystal trying to do his normal routine. Talking to people was his specialty because he was an extrovert. But the moment he came up to this strange beauty, he suddenly lost all thought and couldn't find himself. He approached the girl as she looked up at him, waiting. Jaime was frozen in time and could not break out of the fog he found himself in. *What in the world is going on? This is the first time this has ever happened.*

Both Jaime and Krystal stood there looking at each other. Neither side knowing what to do. Krystal, to Jaime's surprise, waited patiently for him to make the first move. Giving Jaime the time and space he needed. A full minute passed by for what Jaime felt like an eternity. *Heck man, even planets move faster than this. Get on with it!* But the words never seemed to come out. Jaime started sweating. Krystal noticed immediately, but she wasn't repulsed by Jaime's embarrassing behavior. In fact, she seemed delighted because of it.

Finally, Jaime urged the words through his foggy brain, like a city in its pollution. Jaime let out a breath and said, "Can we start over?"

"We may," Krystal bowed, almost like they were meeting each other for the first time. Jaime couldn't get over the fact that Krystal looked even cuter up close. There was something new about her, the way she carried herself, that opened her up and made her more approachable. *Is this really the same girl? She's so open and kindhearted. It blows my mind away.*

Jaime took a breath and said, "Good evening, I am Jaime, Jaime Fisher," bowing like a courting gentleman.

Krystal lifted her dress and bowed. She seemed a bit embarrassed but reiterated in the same tone, "It's a pleasure, I am Krystal, Krystal Henninger."

Jaime extended his hand out, "Would you like to dance?" Krystal blushed. A rare sight that nobody, not even Jaime has seen. Her cute, round cheeks glowed red hot as Jaime patiently held his hand out. For a moment she hesitated, then obliged. She took her black gloves off, checking that her sleeve was covering up her left wrist, and laid her hand in his. Her head lowered and she looked at the ground beneath her, embarrassed but not unwelcome. Jaime felt his breath leave him when he felt how soft her skin was. *Oh wow. Her hand feels so nice.*

Jaime led Krystal over to the dance floor where they found multiple couples slowly dancing with each other, performing the simple two-step maneuver.

The music slowed down from the classic upbeat jazz to a more subtle slow song that everyone could enjoy. The speakers played, "Dear Mr. Fantasy" (You know, the soundtrack of Avengers Endgame with Captain America and Peggy.)

The speakers playing the gentle and lowly song, the sound of the rising trumpet playing in the background,

"Kiss me once then kiss me twice then kiss me once again, it's been a long, long, time."

Jaime turned and faced Krystal. She blushed even harder with him standing so close. Krystal lowered her hands and held them at her waist, as she stood there, waiting for instructions. The question that had to be asked flowed from Jaime's lips, "Have you ever danced before?"

Krystal couldn't look at Jaime for a moment, then raised her head and met his gaze with her beautiful midnight purple eyes. Her gaze distracted him and brought Jaime into a whole other world. He lost track of time. "Uhhh," he shook his head, jolting himself back to reality. "I'm sorry, what were we talking about?" Krystal stood there; head lowered.

"You were about to teach me how to dance," she whispered timidly, staring at the ground, her face red hot.

"Right." Jaime planted himself and prepared. *Okay good, this is something I can do with my eyes closed.* He said, "Alright, now what we need to do is get into position. Krystal, will you put your hand in mine." Krystal looked up at Jaime, then slowly grasped his left hand, locking her fingers with his, feeling the warmth of his hand in hers. "Alright, and now I will put my hand on your waist."

"What?" Krystal said, dumbfounded. That loosened her calm demeanor. Krystal suddenly felt extremely self-conscious, and Jaime noticed.

"Hey hey," he whispered. Krystal looked up, meeting his hazel-colored eyes. "It's going to be okay." Krystal exhaled and relaxed. That managed to calm her down as she allowed Jaime to place his hand on her waist and pull her close. Krystal jolted for a second, while Jaime kept his hand firmly placed and fought to keep his thoughts from running rampant. But the one thought that bounced around in his mind was one any guy could not ignore. *Should I kiss her?* Jaime felt how close Krystal was to his body. The presence of another human, no, not another human, the presence of a young *woman* standing so close to his body, brought out a deep natural desire having the opposite sex so close in proximity. There was something about it that made the experience unique. Something memorable.

Jaime tapped his feet against the ground to get Krystal's attention. "Now all we're going to do is swerve from side to side. Shifting our weight from our left foot to our right as we swerve, okay?"

"Okay," Krystal said, obediently.

Jaime saw Kristina and Luiz peering at him in the corner of the room, giggling like a bunch of girls. Luiz raised both his eyebrows in a smug, know-it-all sort of face, expressing, *"Bro, I've never seen you like this before,"* nodding. Jaime waved him off in sarcastic frustration when Krystal wasn't looking. Luiz and Kristina smiled and continued watching.

He brought his attention back to Krystal and said, "Good." There they held each other, hesitant of the other's presence but not rejecting it either. The music playing in the background, Jaime standing with the purple dressed beauty. Some people were starting to stare, wondering who it was that Jaime was dancing with. But Jaime pushed those people out of his thoughts. There was something . . . warm about Krystal's presence that relaxed him as the two of them swerved from side to side. The trumpet playing in the background, making it feel as if everyone were in slow motion. They swayed from left to right, bobbing with the flow of the music, holding each other close, not wanting to be any farther apart, yet not ready to fully embrace the other. It was as if all Jaime's fears and insecurities seemed to melt away when he held Krystal, and he knew she felt the same.

Jaime motioned his hand outwards, Krystal flowed with it, spinning as Jaime twirled her out and back, then brought her back into his arms. They both chuckled and laughed, forgetting about the party around them, only enjoying the company of each other. It was funny, the power of one's touch can be so powerful, that sometimes, simply holding someone's hand can brighten one's day.

Then Krystal looked at him, their eyes locking. Then in a moment of weakness, Jaime leaned his head forward and laid it gently on Krystal's shoulder. Krystal, being shorter, leaned her head against Jaime's chest. Fully embraced, they stood there swaying, eyes closed, holding each other, enjoying the comfort of the other's presence, more than just a simple romance. It was deeper than that. It was healing, for both of them. Krystal wrapped her arms around Jaime in a slow hug, Jaime did the same, embracing her, holding each other there, swaying with the music, feeling the comfort of each other in their arms, their touch, their warmth, their gentle presence, speaking to them in a language stronger than words, telling them that *everything will be okay*. Calmly, they held each other there and swayed, and swayed, and swayed. Giving each other a comfort that only the other could give. Healing poured over their souls, washing away all their sorrows, as they held each other there, taking their time, one step after the other.

PART FIVE

The Suck Up

CHAPTER 35

The Suck Up

"No matter what you do, you can't force people to like you."

—JL

I need to make some friends. *I need to make some friends. That's all I need.* The thought ran on repeat within Joanna Watson's head as she entered the school grounds once more. The dull gray melancholy sky in the morning made the day all the more awful, as every student entering the grounds wished for the day to already be over. The weather warmed up as spring drew near. Joanna's hazel green eyes flicked from place to place, watching for anyone looking in her direction. Her brunette-colored hair flowing down her back and her olive brown skin adding a beautiful sheen, mixed with her brown pants and a cute white shirt, allowing her to blend in safely with the scene. Joanna hurried at a faster pace through the school, trying not to be noticed by the surrounding groups of people already present.

Joanna turned the corner and there was Summer, Amber, Cassie, and the rest of the group, all standing there looking chummy in the morning. Joanna felt relieved, approaching the group from behind and finding her spot within the circle. Joanna felt safer knowing she was in the circle now, listening to the most recent gossip within the group.

Amber started it off . . . or continued it, depending on when you join the conversation, "Terese in the sophomore class was caught sleeping with a guy this last weekend, we should remember that."

Cassie twisted her puzzled head, her sleek blonde hair gleaming in the sun, "Amber, don't you sleep with your boyfriend all the time?"

Amber answered proudly, "Heck yeah but I keep it under wraps, and even when it is known I own up to it, so nobody cares."

"Shouldn't you be more careful about that?" Joanna added. Amber gave her a stern look draining all the confidence out of Joanna's body. Joanna backed off like a servant, having interrupted the king and fell silent.

Summer resumed speaking, "I heard Terese slept with that guy, Jordan, on the senior basketball team. He is such a pervert."

"Yeah!" Joanna cut in, sounding a little too desperate. "That guy is totally a creep!" She lied. Joanna actually knew Jordan and the guy was not a pervert whatsoever. Joanna's eyes made a quick search, checking everyone's faces to see where their focus lay. There was an awkward pause in the conversation, as everyone looked at Joanna like she was a weirdo, which Summer took as an opportunity to resume speaking again.

Summer continued, "Anyway, I like, heard he's a chump." The heads nodded from the girls in the group.

"And don't forget about Terese," Amber said, muttering an obscenity.

Cassie grinned hearing Amber curse, "Oh you and your big potty mouth Amber."

Amber glared at Cassie. Cassie backed off and went silent. The rest of the conversation went pretty much the same as it always did, Summer and Amber did most of the talking while the rest of the group listened and watched. Joanna felt fear constantly gripping her soul like she was held hostage to her own superstitions.

Joanna tried to chime in on the conversation when she could, always trying to find a loophole to jump in. Joanna found another opportunity and spoke, "I liked that perfume too, I never knew she was a runner . . . how could I know what she was thinking . . . no I don't like that brand of shampoo . . ." and every time she was greeted with silence from the group, as everyone stared at her like she was a psycho. Joanna fell silent again, but found her voice later, agreeing with everything Amber and Summer said, being the suck-up she was.

Summer was in the middle of a story when something caught her eye. Looking off in the distance like a dog spotting a squirrel. Everyone looked in response as Summer glared vilely at a girl with black hair passing by. Joanna took in the sight and thought about the way the girl dressed. *She likes to wear black. Not sure if I would go down that fashion route.*

Summer began muttering curses under her breath. Joanna looked over at Summer with horrific concern. She wasn't used to seeing Summer look so angry before. Before she could ask, Summer said, "Look at that girl over there. Her and her stupid outfit. Like, get some fashion sense please!" She stopped and stared menacingly toward the girl. "I'll get you back for what you did. I promise you that!" Summer was talking more to herself than to the group, which was listening to every word she said. Some of them gave her looks of concern, Joanna included, while others immediately joined her in her hatred.

Amber came next to Summer, sharing her hatred and said, "You want me to do something about her?" But Summer deflated. Rather than getting angrier, she looked insecure. Like she was all bark and no bite.

Summer mumbled, "Well, like, maybe, maybe not."

Amber saw Summer's faltering ego but continued looking at the girl in hatred, "You may not do anything, but trust me . . . I will." Suddenly Joanna's fear shifted from Summer to Amber, as she stared at the girl in black with eyes of fury.

They won't like you if you don't like what they like, Joanna thought. So she chimed in, "Yeah screw her! She's nothing but a loser!" but the group only stared at her. Deep down, Joanna felt something stab her. Regret, from saying something so awful to someone she didn't even know.

The bell rang and Joanna took this as her opportunity to back out. She waved, "Okay, I'll totally see you guys later," but got no response from the group as it dissipated.

Joanna walked around a corner and planted her back against the concrete wall. She paused, thinking about how that interaction went, how uncomfortable it was. Suddenly she felt the loneliness strike again.

No! Joanna cringed. But it was too late. Joanna felt more self-conscious with every passing second. Feeling as if the whole world were pushing down on her like a bug crushed by a boot. Joanna breathed and tried to control herself. "You're okay," she lied. "I'm okay, I'm totally okay." Joanna knew the truth though, and the truth was that she was far from okay.

✍

Joanna lay in her bed late at night, scrolling through her phone mindlessly. She wasn't ready to go to bed yet. It wasn't late enough to call it a night anyway. And so, she lay in her bed in the dark, staring at the brightness of her phone with squinted eyes as she scrolled through the latest postings on social media of the people she knew at school.

Joanna stopped on one photo. It was a picture of a girl named Trinity, showing off a picture of her and her boyfriend spending time together at some beach, both of them smiling. Joanna felt a stab in her heart. *I wish I had a boyfriend.* Feeling the emptiness strike at her heart like a snake. Joanna double tapped the picture and the heart icon flashed.

She scrolled to another photo; it was a picture of a blonde girl showing herself off in a cute brown sweater and jeans. Joanna noticed how beautiful the girl looked, how pretty her face was and how perfect it all seemed. *I wish I were that pretty.* Joanna felt her heart choke with pain. "I have to be likeable. I have to be likeable," she repeated.

Joanna scrolled to another photo, this time it was a picture of Summer and Amber hanging out on their recent trip to Hawaii. Joanna looked at their smiles and envied them. She envied every picture she saw. Joanna studied their faces, admiring their natural beauty, staring at their smiles. Looking at how perfect their lives looked. Jealousy pierced her heart, making Joanna feel all the more hideous, like a grotesque monster. She wasn't mad though, she was sad. She could feel the pain from the comparison yet couldn't stop it. She wanted more, hoping that one day she'll be pretty enough, hoping one day she'll have it all together like these people do, maybe even find a guy too.

That thought caused loneliness to strike Joanna's heart to its core. The pressure weighing down on her, like a rock at the bottom of the ocean, stuck and unchangeable. Joanna cringed into the fetal position. *I need to make friends.* The thought repeating in her mind, as the anxiety crept in. *I need to make friends. They won't like you unless you like what they like.* The fear of going out into this world alone dragged her down to a dark, bottomless pit, one she was too familiar with, and it scared her to death. Joanna started trembling. *I can't go back there. I can't go back there.* As she picked up her phone and started scrolling again. Torturing herself with her comparisons.

CHAPTER 36

Turning the Other Cheek

"No matter what you do, there will always be people who don't like you."

—JL

The shade from the building's overpass faded as Joanna stepped out into the main courtyard. Joanna took a moment to look over the entire courtyard, taking every detail of it in. Everyone sitting in their usual places, the lunch lines bustling with kids ready to eat the most artificial food on the planet, the sun gleaming down, both beautiful and hot on this awkward Wednesday afternoon. Nothing was out of its usual place.

It was the start of the lunch period, meaning everyone was sitting down with their respected groups, but for some reason, one individual stood out to Joanna. A piping hot individual marching somewhere. Joanna stopped and knew exactly who was marching. Her red hair in the sun now brighter than ever, stomping on the ground so loud it could be heard a mile away. Worry struck Joanna. *This can't be good.* She decided to follow, though she didn't have to travel far. Amber marched in an ongoing direction until she came up to a girl with black hair and slapped her. Joanna was shocked, as was everyone around watching.

The girl who got slapped was surprised at first, the first slap was powerful and unexpected, but she did nothing in return. Joanna's eyes widened in shock, gasping. She couldn't believe her eyes. Amber had stormed right up to this girl and slapped her in the face, hard. Joanna drew closer with the crowd but didn't intervene for fear of Amber turning on her. Amber struck the girl again, this time harder, the crack echoing through the school yard and leaving a red mark on the girl's face, but again the girl did nothing.

Joanna put her hands to her face in horror. Amber was slapping this girl and she hadn't the faintest clue what this girl did. Amber wailed on her repeatedly, this time with the back of her hand. Joanna could see no anger in the other girl's face. The pain seeping through her red cheeks, her eyes closed, and her arms held down. Joanna thought the girl would fight back, but she didn't. The girl just held her arms down and mumbled something only she could hear. Joanna, now fully indoctrinated with the crowd, peered closer and realized the girl was holding her fists down on purpose. *She's holding herself back?* Joanna was astounded. What in the world happened between these two? So many questions, too little time.

More people were beginning to surround the scene, but nobody dared to intervene. All people were doing was pulling out their phones, letting the drama unfold without a single person trying to stop it. Especially not with Amber swinging. Amber threw another blow and another blow and another blow; the girl's cheeks turning purple and beginning to swell. The sound of sharp slapping echoed across the courtyard like someone was making a rhythmic beat. Amber screamed in the girl's face, "WHY WON'T YOU FIGHT BACK HUH!?" Amber threw another blow, but the girl remained steadfast and halted any movement from her clenched fists. Amber landed another blow and then another blow and then another blow, increasing in speed, shouting, "YEAH! WHERE'S YOUR GOD? HUH! WHERE'S YOUR GOD RIGHT HERE! RIGHT NOW!"

The girl's cheeks were so swollen, Joanna thought the girl's face was a blueberry. The girl finally raised her eyes and met Amber's, quivering slightly but maintaining a strong resolve. The girl would not be beaten. Then she gave Amber a death stare so deep, so powerful, that even Joanna felt its effects. Joanna thought for a moment that the girl was gonna melt Amber with her gaze. Then the girl did the one thing Joanna never thought she would do. She raised her hand, and gestured to the other cheek, implying, *"You may hit me, but you won't break me."* Proving this girl was the stronger among the two.

"You want me to hit you again?" Amber coiled back, bewildered from the unnatural response, infuriated. Everyone else in the crowd was just as surprised with the amount of self-control this girl had. The girl closed her eyes and braced herself for another barrage. Amber raised her hand, putting all her anger in this blow, and turned it into a punch. Amber struck the girl's swollen cheek as the girl faltered back a couple steps, but the girl did not scream, she only spat blood from her swollen mouth.

Amber shouted, "I've had enough of you! Come on! Fight back!" squaring right up to the girl. Amber raised her own shirt up to expose her stomach and shouted at the girl, "Come on! I'll even give you a free shot! Hit me in the stomach, as hard as you can!"

The girl looked a bit dazed as she steadied herself and remembered where she was. Finding the excellent opportunity laid out before her, with Amber's shirt held up, stomach exposed, calling for her to strike Amber in the stomach as hard as she could. Amber simply did not care who saw what or what happened. "Come on!" Amber yelled. "Strike me!"

To Joanna's surprise the girl raised her arm high, her fist clenched. *Oh my, she's going to do it. She's going to hit Amber back!* Joanna couldn't believe the sight. Neither could the dozens of onlookers who were all recording the entire spectacle. You could tell the girl wanted to strike Amber; wanted to hurt her bad for all the pain she caused. But then the girl lowered her hand, and her expression changed. From insufferable pain to compassionate realization. The sight bewildered the whole crowd, especially Amber.

Then the girl whispered something only Amber could hear. Amber's eyes went wide with horror, and she suddenly turned pale, losing all her fire, and coiled back, legs trembling. Everyone watching was baffled by how the fight had suddenly turned around. And now it was Amber who was on the defensive, looking weak like a frightened animal. Amber's face was filled with horror. The girl just stood there, her stoic demeanor softened, now full of compassion, not for herself, but for Amber. That was the final blow, as Amber ran away in tears, charging through the crowd, not looking back.

Joanna blinked a couple of times, disbelief from what her eyes were telling her. Everything that had just happened, *really happened*. There was no denying that, not with everyone staring at the lonesome girl in horror. The question running through everyone's mind, *What did she say to her?* The girl lowered her gaze to the ground, ignoring everyone's stares, and slowly walked away. The crowd parted like she was a plague, as the girl in black walked forward, vanishing among the school before the teachers arrived.

∽

That was not how Krystal imagined her day would go. She held a tall plastic cup filled with ice to her cheek, mulling over whether she was going to have to see a doctor due to how bruised her cheeks were from the fight. Krystal looked at herself in the reflection of her phone and saw just how thick her cheeks had swelled. It looked as if Krystal had just gotten her wisdom teeth pulled out and her cheeks swelled like a chipmunk. Krystal exhaled through her nostrils and held the ice close. At least the ice helped reduce the swelling.

"Order for Jaime!"

Krystal's eyes shot towards the barista behind the counter holding a white Half & Half coffee cup. "Order for Jaime!" but no Jaime came forward. Krystal expected Jaime to come up out of nowhere, but he never showed. Maybe that was a good thing. Krystal didn't really want anyone to see her like this.

The entire Half & Half coffee shop was moderately calm. The type of white noise that conceals one's actions from the people around them. For once, Krystal welcomed the commotion. She wanted to hide and heal. Today had been a rough day. Krystal had iced her cheeks so much they felt like they were going to fall off. Krystal put the cup down and spit blood into it. The grinding of beans, and the shrilling sound of whip cream filled the air. At least Krystal felt hidden here. She couldn't drink anything, not with how bruised her cheeks were. She caressed her swollen cheeks with her fingertips hoping for a shed of relief.

Krystal stared at the cream-colored mahogany table beneath her. *I know I was the victor today, but I don't feel like it.* Her thoughts began to wander again. *I know I did the right thing, God. But why doesn't it feel like it?*

Krystal's phone buzzed and saw she was receiving a video call from Jaime. Distracting her from her previous thoughts, and without thinking she clicked Accept and Jaime's image came into view on her phone. Jaime's face was a mixture of astonishment and anger. "Hey," he said, "What happened?"

Krystal looked away from the screen, regretting the video call for this matter. "Nothing," she said timidly.

But Jaime spoke in a concerned tone, "Hey, Krystal. You can talk to me. What happened?"

Krystal exhaled, "Amber attacked me."

"What?!" Jaime glared at Krystal. She could see the anger building in his face, like a bull being taunted in its arena. There was a brief pause between them, then he said, "You want me to do something? Because I will."

Krystal built up the courage to look back into the screen, "No."

"No?"

Krystal regained her resolve, embedding her authority, "No."

Jaime leaned back in the frame, frustrated. "What do you expect me to do?"

Krystal spoke softly, "Let it go."

"What?"

Krystal spoke more firmly, "Let it go." Jaime stared at her in disbelief. She could tell he wanted to act, but she would not let him. She knew what God expected of her, and this was not it.

Jaime saw her stance and knew she would not back down. He crossed his arms in the picture, and let out a frustrated sigh, looking away for a moment, a feeble attempt to cool himself down. Eventually, he looked back at her, taking in the sight of her swollen purple cheeks. "Fine . . . but if anything, and I mean anything else happens, I'm doing something." Krystal did not answer that, only stared back at him with authority. Jaime deflated again, looking away then back at Krystal. "Well, I'll let my family know what happened and . . . we'll try and help you out with the school too."

Krystal wanted to smile but it hurt too much. "Thanks," she said, accidentally spitting out some blood. Jaime looked at her with honest concern.

"I'll bring you some ice packs later."

Krystal nodded. "Okay." Then she ended the video call and went back to icing her cheeks.

✍

The door opened and Joanna stepped into the Half & Half coffee shop, relieved to be out of school and away from all the people. Joanna took a survey of the room and to her horror saw the same girl from the fight today (if you could call it a fight). Joanna froze instantly, she didn't know what to do. Curiosity ate at her, but fear gripped her like a lion. If she went up and talked to this girl, Joanna feared someone she knew would see her and get the wrong idea. Joanna hadn't even considered who this girl was until this afternoon, and even then, she had never seen her before. Joanna's heart stirred with a nagging sense of curiosity, she felt compelled to walk over there and get the whole story as to why Amber suddenly railed on this random girl in front of her, and in front of everyone.

Joanna checked over her shoulder to see if anyone she knew was here, but no familiar faces came up. Joanna relaxed but only by five percent. Her heart and mind were still on alert as she approached this wounded character, who now had her head down on the table, her arms covering herself. Joanna approached the girl and thought, *Huh, this girl is wearing all black, interesting.* Joanna moved cautiously, like approaching a wild animal, not knowing whether it would attack her or accept her. "Hey," came out before Joanna could think of the words. The girl raised her head. Joanna could see now the wounds inflicted by Amber on this girl. Her cheeks were purple and very swollen. The beating clearly had its consequences. "Are you okay?" she asked.

Joanna expected the girl to say something but to Joanna's surprise she said nothing. Joanna was getting nervous and checked over her shoulder one more time. "Uhh," the girl's impassive face shooting down all ideas that came to Joanna's head. "Uhhh, you do understand me right?" The girl gave a nod. Joanna felt nervous, more from the girl's glare than from the possibility of people seeing them together. *I can tell why Amber backed off from this one.* "I saw you get in that fight today. It was totally crazy." The girl lowered her head. She grabbed the cup full of ice and spit blood into it. Coating the clear cubes in dark red liquid, then pressed the cup gently against her swollen cheek.

"I guess you could call that a fight." The girl said, finally speaking.

Joanna tilted her head curiously, "Are you going to get checked out?"

The girl didn't look up at her, "Nothing I can't fix at home."

"I'm totally sorry for what happened to you." Joanna said.

The girl looked at her; her midnight purple eyes echoing her emotions. "Thank you," she said. The sight of it made Joanna's heart warm. She wasn't sure why she was talking to this girl, but it felt right. She felt drawn to this mysterious girl with the swollen face. Then the fear crept in again and Joanna glanced over her shoulder, getting a feeling someone was looking at her for real. Joanna turned back to the girl and said, "It was nice meeting you. I hope you get better, but I totally have to go now."

The girl kept a passive look to her, "Okay, see ya." And before she knew it, Joanna was out the door without looking back.

The next day, Joanna finished walking down the school walkway and headed towards her group's usual spot after school while everyone was waiting for their parents to come and pick them up.

Joanna found Summer and the rest of the group present and accounted for, but she was shocked to see Amber there too. Surprisingly, the fight was not reported to the school and Amber received no punishment of the sort. That's what you get for a planned attack.

Joanna saw all of them standing together in a circle, their looks somber and dry. Joanna wondered why the long faces. Joanna approached the group with a casual and warm hello, but the group didn't turn her way immediately. She pressed again, "Hello? Helloooo?" Joanna called. All at once, as if they were attending a funeral, they turned and faced her. Joanna suddenly felt nervous. Her blood started racing, feeling like she had some spotlight on her or something. "What's going on?" she asked.

Amber stepped forward and spoke callously, "You were with that girl, weren't you?"

Joanna whitened with fear. She lied, "What no! I wasn't with her!"

"Darna saw you talking to her at Half & Half the other day."

"I don't know that girl! I promise!" Joanna pleaded, but Amber was unrelenting.

"Don't take the time to come back," Amber said, "cause you're out of the group." Joanna's eyes widened with horror. Her worst fear had just come to life. She could feel the adrenaline kick in like she had just suffered a jump scare from a horror movie.

"Please give me another chance!" she begged, "Please don't kick me out!"

"Let's go guys." Amber turned, and the rest of the group followed. Joanna tried to match Summer's eyes, to see what she truly felt, but Summer never gave Joanna a second thought. Joanna was now clique-less, and without friends. All of it was gone within a matter of seconds. How could this happen? The anxiety and fear attacked her, feeling totally helpless to the invading forces around her.

I'm without friends. I'm without friends! Joanna stared around the courtyard in horror, feeling as if all eyes were on her. She had to get away, to get out of sight, or else people would start talking about her. People would get the wrong idea. But it was too late. The deed was done, and the question lingered, what would she do now? Were all her friendships over? She didn't want to think about that right now, all she wanted to do is curl up into a ball and disappear forever.

CHAPTER 37

The Outcast

"If you live your life trying to please others, then you will always be a slave to their expectations."

—Krystal Henninger

Joanna gripped her backpack sling tighter than normal. Fear spread through her mind like wildfire, terrified of what might come next. High school can be brutal, Joanna knew that, but it can be the worst when you're on the other end of the stick. And now, Joanna was on the other end of the stick. Her friend group had just abandoned her, and she was on her own. Joanna stood in the middle of the school courtyard and felt very alone. It was as if all her friends in her life had vanished, and she was the only person left on earth. Everyone else had forgotten her. Joanna pondered on that. How long had she known Amber and Summer? A year? But to see them become so heartless to others was what dumbfounded her. Summer had always seemed to be such a confident and charismatic person that Joanna naturally felt drawn to that. The kind of high school confidence that most people want but don't obtain until years later if they ever do. So it was natural to draw towards a person's confidence like a moth to a flame. Only this time, the flame burned back.

Joanna stepped into her first class, the seating spread out into neat lines, but some students wanted to push their luck and put both of their tables together. The level of chatter in the room was high compared to the usual morning banter. Joanna sensed this was not a helpful sign. She took her seat and prepared for the class, the teacher still getting things ready while they waited for the bell to ring. Joanna leaned to her left and saw a guy named

340

Charles Signet. Joanna leaned over and whispered, "Hey, what's all the chatter about?" Charles coiled back a bit, as if Joanna had some lethal disease. Joanna seemed bewildered by his reaction and asked, "What's up? Why are you backing off?"

Charles seemed hesitant and said, "I'm uhh . . . It's . . ." he leaned forward and whispered, "It's not a good idea to be talking to you Joanna."

"What?" Joanna was surprised. "Why?" But Charles didn't answer. He shifted his attention toward the whiteboard and looked uncomfortable sitting next to her. The lack of attention was what drove the stake deeper into Joanna's heart. *Is this all because of what happened the other day?*

Joanna leaned in closer again and whispered, "At least tell me what everyone is talking about?"

Charles seemed terrified and reluctant to answer but he told her anyway. "They're talking about the rumored fight and the random girl who stood Amber up and sent her away crying." His head ticked like he was hiding something. There was more. "And . . . and they're talking about *you*. They say a few days ago you hurt Amber's feelings and stormed off. They're saying you're bad business and people shouldn't be around you." There, he said it. After that Charles shut off and didn't say another word.

Joanna was dumbfounded and leaned back into her seat. Her mind was in a daze like the morning fog. *This can't be happening. This cannot be happening. After one conversation they go behind my back and start spreading rumors about me?* Joanna checked the room, searching for the emotion in people's eyes. Some of the eyes were deliberately trying to avoid her, fearfully going about their business, while others shot her looks of condemnation. Joanna suddenly felt like an outcast. Joanna could hear the conversations happening around her:

"How could someone hurt Amber's feelings? Whoever that girl is I want to slug 'em.' "

"Yeah, they should have done something to her. What kind of person hurts Amber's feelings, let alone Summers?"

"I hear that girl Joanna Watson, over there started bullying Amber and Summer too. We should stay well clear of her guys."

Daggers flung about the room, all of them targeting Joanna and the girl from the fight, but apparently, no one knew who the girl in the fight was, so no one knew what to say about her.

Joanna scanned the room again, her eyes scrolling from one face full of fear to the other, but then her eyes stopped, finding her focus on the girl in black, who sat there minding her own business, not seeming to care what people were saying about her. But Joanna saw something in her eyes that seemed different from everyone else's. They weren't eyes of malice, but eyes of cold suffering. Eyes accustomed to pain, yet also gentle and mature. The girl wasn't trying to avoid Joanna the way everybody else was. She was just minding her own business, not letting the daggers reach her, even though it looked like the girl knew everyone was talking about her.

How is she able to do that? Joanna wondered. *To not let their words hurt her?*

Joanna didn't have that kind of resolve and pondered whether the girl had somehow learned not to care what other people think or if that was just part of her personality. Either way Joanna would never know; but a feeling from within her heart wanted to reach out toward this girl and connect with her. But Joanna's eyes saw the rest of the room, there were eyes everywhere and people would see and in turn post everything on social media. All her movements were being monitored by the crowd and were up to scrutiny.

Joanna felt her heart tighten. It was like she was being held prisoner by her fellow classmates, where the judge, jury, and executioner was the mindset of the majority around her. To do something out of the ordinary was to ask for criticism. The fear weighed Joanna down and she immediately dashed the thought of walking over toward that girl. *Not a chance!*

It wasn't hard to figure out; the whole room was talking about it. The fight with Amber the other day . . . if Krystal could even call it that. It felt more like a flogging than a fight. All Krystal did was tell Amber something and then she ran off crying. Maybe that's why Amber and Summer had been so hateful toward her lately. It wasn't implausible, Krystal figured it was likely to happen. They hated her, and in return for "winning the fight," they spread rumors about her hurting Amber's feelings, rather than telling the truth about how Amber beat Krystal's face to a pulp. It was kind of sickening.

Krystal wasn't surprised though. It's not like the crowd was ever on her side to begin with. She exhaled, *I wish Jaime were here, or Kristina.* They weren't though and Krystal was on her own again. Krystal felt like she had gone back to square one, although it wasn't exactly the same feeling. She could tell that things were different now. At least people were talking about her and weren't flat up ignoring her, but they still didn't know exactly who the girl in the fight was, so Krystal still maintained a sense of anonymity, even after the swelling in her cheeks had gone down.

Krystal sat in her desk and opened her eyes to find the classroom vibrant with jittering students and rumors spreading like wildfire. Krystal pretended not to hear them, but she heard it all. There was no point in trying to correct them. They didn't know it was her and it wouldn't change anything either way. So, what was she going to do? She was going to keep her mouth shut and if someone wanted to hear her side of the story then she would tell them, plain facts, nothing else.

Krystal felt a stirring in her heart cause her to look up and scan the room to her right. She noticed everyone in the room was deliberately trying not to look in a certain direction. There was fear in people's eyes, but it wasn't fear of her. The class hadn't started yet, but something was off. What was it that made everyone in the room avoid looking in a certain direction? Krystal's best guess was that these people all knew Amber and were hearing rumors spread about how some girl attacked Amber, making Amber the victim in the matter. School is tough, who can deny that? Krystal observed the room, her eyes scanning from person to person like a robot assessing everyone's condition before moving on. Krystal's eyes stopped on a girl named Joanna.

Joanna Watson was about Krystal's age, with lush brown hair streaming down her back. Her skin was of a darker tone, probably a mixture of Hispanic and Filipino, and very pretty. Krystal saw Joanna look confused and fearful. Whipping her head from side to side as if someone was gonna attack her out of nowhere. Krystal cocked an eyebrow. Joanna was emitting that kind of aura that said she was not in a good spot right now. Krystal's eyes rescanned the room and then back to Joanna. Connecting the dots. *These people aren't avoiding me. They're avoiding her. Why?*

Krystal found it interesting. She was already used to people avoiding her but why were they avoiding Joanna too? Wasn't Joanna a lot more likable than she is? Krystal could tell Joanna understood the situation and didn't like it in the slightest, but she also looked extremely uncomfortable, like a lost child. There was one undeniable fact, however, this girl was drowning and was looking for someone to save her. Maybe it was all just a fluke. What if it's something completely unrelated and Krystal ends up embarrassing herself again? Krystal doused those feelings. *Do you really think it would make things any worse than they already are?*

Yes, they would.

Well I don't care. Krystal looked over at Joanna and thought, *"Love your neighbor as yourself."* Then the image of Krystal flashed in Joanna's position, and she remembered all those days of waiting for someone to help her. For someone to check on her to see if she was alright. Remembering how Jesus loved on her and saved her from her depression, and to use that pain to help others. Now was the time to act.

The room quieted as the class neared to start. If Krystal made a move now, everyone in the room would see it. The chattering did not resume, and the room was still dead quiet, as more and more people began filtering into the classroom. Krystal felt the awkwardness stab her like an icicle. She had grown more used to getting outside of her comfort zone lately, but it still felt awkward. Like stepping out from safety and exposing herself to harmful chemicals in the room. There was blood in the water and people were ready to bite. But Krystal also remembered the pain of sitting by herself all those years and could not stand still.

Those memories were powerful, and Krystal was going to use them. *Please God, give me the strength to continue.* Then she got up from her desk, felt her legs weaken, yearning to sit back down, to enjoy her warm peaceful seat and not go anywhere or do anything that would get people to look at her. Krystal brushed those fears aside and continued forward. The awkwardness in the air was so thick, Krystal felt like she was going to vomit. But the love of God pushed her forward and she did not stop. Krystal could feel some eyes looking her way, but she brushed them off and thought, *Who cares what other people think. The only thing that matters is what God thinks of me.* Krystal came up to the side of Joanna, as she turned, revealing round brown eyes and a small nose that made her look adorable. Krystal leaned over and whispered, knowing full well that some people were looking at them, "Hey . . . are you okay?"

The look in Joanna's eyes was a mixture of horror and relief. Krystal knew Joanna was looking in her peripherals at all the other people in the room while her focus was on Krystal. For a moment, Krystal was freaking out inside too. *Was this the right move?* Krystal asked again, this time even softer, "Are you okay?" but Joanna didn't say anything. Krystal took the hint and went back to her seat. Krystal was fairly sure half of the class saw that, but she didn't care. It's not like her life was going to get any worse. Then the bell rang, and the lesson began. Krystal exhaled. *That was uncomfortable.* Brushing off the interaction.

∽

"I want you to get into groups and work on this sheet of paper," the teacher held up a piece of paper and began passing it out to the class. "This will be due by the end of the period, so I want you to finish this together. Don't forget to put your names on the paper and turn it in to me, okay?" The teacher looked at the class, doubtful they will follow his instructions, and clapped his hands, "Okay. Let's get started."

Desks and tables shuffled as the classroom was set in motion. Joanna looked from side to side to see if anyone wanted to join her, but all the desks pulled away faster than she could blink. All the groups were set, and people were already chatting it up. Smiles, laughter, giggles, all the kinds of social things that high schoolers love to do when their teacher isn't paying attention. Joanna felt the distance between herself, and the rest of her classmates widen. The betrayal setting into her heart. These people, whom she had known for years, had all of a sudden turned on her like she was a leper. It felt as if the entire world was against her, shooting her silent daggers saying, *"We don't want you!"*

Joanna thought, *Don't let them get to you, don't let them get to you.* But they were. And she could not stop the daggers from hurting. Joanna could hear the murmuring in the room, people sneaking looks in her direction.

Joanna heard footsteps, keeping her eyes and head low to not attract attention. The footsteps grew closer until a shadow towered next to her, "Hey."

Joanna looked up and saw it was the girl from the fight. Her mouth searched for the right words and cautiously said, "Hey," back. Joanna looked around, hoping someone else would be her partner but everyone deliberately looked away and pretended to go about their business.

"Do you want to be partners?" the girl asked calmly, as if she was willing to accept whatever decision Joanna would make. Her voice simple and soft, yet there was a certain glare about this girl. There was a depth in her midnight purple eyes that stared you down and made Joanna want to tell her the truth because you know she will figure it out eventually.

A mass of thoughts flurried through Joanna's mind like a blizzard. Joanna took another glimpse of everyone avoiding her and whispered, "Okay."

"Cool," the girl responded, sounding neither excited nor surprised, gesturing over toward her desk, "I'll pull my desk up to yours and we can work together."

Joanna could only manage, "Okay," then watched as the girl pulled up her desk in front of hers and got comfortable. Joanna could not take her eyes off how much black the girl wore. Her long sleeve shirt was black, her pants were black, plain, and not ripped. Joanna thought she was one of those goth looking girls, but this girl dressed more conservatively despite her lack of color coordination. Even though her hair was black, the only difference in color Joanna found was in her midnight purple eyes. It intimidated and awed Joanna at the same time. Joanna looked down and saw that even her shoes and socks were black. *What is with this girl and black?* Joanna's gaze went back to her eyes. They were icy, sharp, and deep. Like there was a world behind them she did not yet know.

The girl took out the assignment paper and began writing. Joanna sat there in silence across from her and watched. *Why did she ask me earlier if I was okay?* Joanna wanted to work, but she was too focused on watching this girl right in front of her. The girl started working on the paper and fell mute. The only sound between them was the scribbling of the girl's mechanical pencil. A few minutes passed and neither of them said anything. Joanna didn't move, waiting for this girl to say something, but she never did. The girl just kept on scribbling. Joanna thought the girl knew she was watching her but kept working anyway. For a moment, Joanna wanted to take advantage of this and be lazy, letting this girl do the work, but the thought occurred to her that that would be rude. Joanna stowed those lazy high schooler feelings and tried to get to work, but her pencil stopped before it could reach the paper.

Joanna held her pencil a millimeter above the paper then put it down and said, "You're working pretty hard there aren't you?"

The girl said nothing. Joanna coiled back a bit, uncertain but kept her composure. *Not what I was expecting.* Joanna tried again. "So . . . do you like working on homework?"

The girl continued working, mind focused, not bothering to look up and said, "When you want to ask the *real* question on your mind, then I'll talk to you." The girl clicked her mechanical pencil a few times, leaving Joanna dumbstruck, resuming her work. *Did she read my thoughts or something? How in the world did she know?*

Joanna decided to try a more upfront approach, "So ... why'd you do it?"

"Now we're moving along." The girl said, sarcastically. Still maintaining her deadpan expression.

Joanna blinked, "You were expecting that?"

The girl didn't look up, her pencil moving lightning quick, "It's the question that everyone in this room is asking each other so I figured it was gonna come up sooner or later."

Joanna crossed her fingers and said, "So what's your response?" still wondering the answer.

The girl didn't bother to look up and said, "I deserved every bit of it." Joanna was surprised.

"You don't deny it?"

"Nope." The girl said casually like it was old news. She clicked her pencil again and continued writing.

Joanna asked, "So what happened?"

The girl stopped writing and put her pencil down and crossed her arms on the table. "Here's what went down ..." She told Joanna about how she exploded on Summer and what she felt in the heat of the moment. Joanna just sat there in shock. Not hiding a single emotion. "And then I told her, 'Peace out and piss off!' And that's what happened. I guess Amber heard about it and wanted revenge for Summer, so she attacked me. Simple as that." The girl picked up her pencil and began writing again. Joanna was more surprised with how casual the girl was. She was clearly goal driven and she didn't miss a beat on her homework, that's for sure. But Joanna was also surprised with how upfront she was. This girl didn't sugarcoat anything, and that confused Joanna. Joanna was used to girls beating around the bush, but not this girl. Joanna realized she didn't even know the girl's name, but before she could ask that question, Joanna heard people gossiping.

"Look at those two hoodlums over there." One girl said.

"Yeah, I bet they're real chummy over there."

Another boy chimed in, "Almost too chummy."

"Hmmmm," all three of them hummed together.

Joanna stopped looking over her shoulder and covered herself a little. Feeling exposed.

The girl in black said, "Don't let them get to you. You can't please everyone."

Joanna brought her focus back on the girl. Her tone slightly accusatory, "How would you know?"

"Experience." Again, no hesitation in the girl's voice.

Joanna gestured a finger toward the group behind them and said, "You know they're talking about us, right?"

"I do," the girl said, still not looking up from her work.

"And you know that everybody in school is gossiping about some person who hurt Amber's feelings because of that rumored fight a few days ago. As well as rumors about me."

"I do."

"And do you know what happens to people like us who are ousted from the group and left alone?" Joanna egged her on.

"Yeah," the girl replied, unsurprised.

"Oh yeahhh?" Joanna egged her on even more now, pushing the line as far as she could.

The girl in black suddenly stopped her writing, put her pencil down and stared at Joanna for an icy second, like Joanna had offended her. Then she spoke in a stern voice, "*Yeah*, I do." The girl was clearly offended but contained her frustration, allowing portions to leak out in her voice under her permission. The girl's icy stare was more than enough to scare Joanna all the way back into the womb. She had clearly outdone Joanna in her rhetorical question, and made Joanna feel like she insulted her. Maybe she did? Joanna suddenly felt guilty, like she was trying to blend in with the class by making fun of the other outsider in the group. Joanna lowered her head in self-pity, when the girl lowered her tone, speaking softly like an offended parent who quickly forgave their child, "You don't have to feel guilty. It's okay. You just . . ." the girl paused, "touched a nerve."

"I'm sorry," Joanna said, feeling like she finally gained some ground. There was a thick silence between them, but this time it was the girl who looked up at Joanna, meaning to say something but stopped for some reason. Joanna's heart leapt, like she was expecting a jump scare in a movie. Joanna sensed the girl was going to tell her even if she asked her. Joanna decided to take a different approach. "I've got another one for you."

"Shoot," the girl's tone was lighter and not as heavy.

"Why did you come up to me a minute ago and ask me if I'm okay?"

The girl resumed her writing and said, "Because you looked sad and alone. And I didn't want you to feel alone."

Joanna paused because of that. No one has ever said that to her before. It was like the girl's very words had stopped her. Halting Joanna in her tracks with the idea that someone out there cared for her. "Oh . . ." Joanna said, "Uhh thank you."

"You're welcome," the girl's words were sweeter now. Joanna lightened a bit, feeling a little more comfortable now.

"What's your name?" Joanna asked. The girl's eyes widened. Something Joanna did not expect would break through the girl's impassive expression.

"You actually want to know my name?" she asked, not expecting the question.

"Yeah." Joanna nodded.

"It's Krystal. Krystal Henninger."

"It's nice to meet you, Krystal. I'm Joanna. Joanna Watson."

"Like in Sherlock Holmes." Krystal pointed.

"What?" Joanna said, puzzled.

Krystal blushed uncomfortably. "Oh, uhh your name . . . it's uhh from a movie . . ." whispering, "And a book series," trailing off.

Joanna almost laughed, but her eyes caught sight of people looking at her and the joy from the moment vanished. Joanna unconsciously backed away from Krystal, hoping she didn't see, but Krystal caught her movement.

"You don't have to sit with me if you don't want to." Krystal said.

Joanna blinked, "What?"

Krystal put down her pencil and looked at her. "I get the sense you don't want to be around me, because there are people in the room looking at you, isn't that right?" Joanna wasn't expecting Krystal to plunge right into the drama, but she never held anything back either. Joanna nodded sadly; it was all true. "Look," Krystal spoke softly, "If you don't want to be around me you don't have to. I don't want to make you feel uncomfortable. I just wanted to check if you were okay."

Joanna felt taken back. She was surprised with how caring this girl really was. It amazed Joanna but she also couldn't understand it. What was it about this girl that made her so different?

Joanna fumbled but told the truth. "Well . . . yeah, I guess . . . I guess I don't want to be seen with you." There, she said it. It had been on her mind, but it was also her own fault for entertaining the idea by sitting with Krystal. Joanna expected Krystal to be mad, but she didn't react. It was more like a knowing parent who's been hurt by their child, but they refuse to get mad at them.

Krystal handed Joanna a sheet of paper. "Here, you can turn this in as your part." Joanna took the completed paper and said nothing even though she wanted to. Joanna didn't even say thank you as she got up from her desk and went to hide in some corner of the room, away from Krystal and the gossip of the class, but there was no escape. The stage was set, and the truth was out.

⌁

It felt odd. Extremely odd to be sitting somewhere else during lunch. Joanna looked around, saw all the cliques, groups of people she had known for years, sitting with their friends around the school courtyard. Terror gripped Joanna as she observed all the cliques around her. *It's not like I can just walk up and ask to sit down with some group . . . all these people know each other. They totally wouldn't just let me sit with them. They would reject me.* Joanna looked around and saw a bench beside one of the school buildings and decided to pitch up there. Joanna sat there and opened her lunch, looking out into the school courtyard. It was quiet and lonely. Joanna sighed, feeling the pressure of the loneliness strike her heart. *I miss sitting with Amber and Summer. Those gals were totally nice company.*

"I heard she's been sleeping with Jimmy Hernandez." A girl said down the ways.

"Jimmy Hernandez! OHHHH that's gross! What was that girl thinking? I mean come on!" The conversation from the group a few feet from her caught Joanna's eye.

A girl with blonde hair and tied up locks said, "Yeah, what a shame. I would hate to be Joanna Watson right now. I don't know why anybody would be friends with that reject, whew! She's got a name for herself already."

Joanna's eyes grew livid. Betrayal and fear flushed through her body. Then the eyes of the group next to her shifted in her direction. Joanna saw the girls notice, so she picked up her lunch to find another place. *All this because I talked to Krystal? Really? One time?* Joanna couldn't contemplate the vast anger that was flowing from the rumors Amber and Summer had been spreading about her. Joanna knew that it was mostly Amber. Summer didn't have the evil in her to be spreading rumors around like this. Amber was just loyal to Summer, that's all. But sometimes Amber was too loyal to where she would do anything for Summer.

Joanna sat on another bench, and again more eyes looked her way. It was like she had some sort of disease. A disease that no one else wanted. Joanna pressed both of her hands to her ears, blocking out all sound. *What is happening? Why is this whole school suddenly targeting me for one thing?* It was only one discussion. A discussion with Krystal at the coffee shop.

Summer's relationship with Amber made them a power duo in school. The fight recently didn't help either. So many rumors were spreading around the school despite the staff trying to douse them, but that was like trying to stop a wildfire after it had already burned down the forest.

Joanna's eyes scrolled across the school grounds, feeling as if the whole school was sneaking looks at her when she wasn't looking. Joanna felt like the main attraction in a zoo as she walked around the campus. Gripping her backpack harder and continued walking. She headed past the front office and back into the main school yard. But her pace came to a sudden stop when she saw Krystal eating alone on a white bench covered in bird dung.

Joanna felt an urge in her heart to walk over there and apologize for earlier, but the thought and image of everyone staring at Joanna flooded her mind. Still, her feet began walking over there, wanting to say something. Krystal came closer into view and Joanna realized she couldn't stop. She was too close for Krystal not to notice her, but Krystal never raised her head from her book to notice Joanna coming by. Joanna came within a couple feet of Krystal, but the fear and temptation to walk away overruled her. Joanna twisted her feet and walked right in front of Krystal, watching her stare down at a black leather book with golden pages in her hands as Joanna walked right towards her. Joanna was now directly in front of Krystal, the lone girl gazing down at her book but still well within her line of sight. It was impossible not to notice Joanna standing right in front of her. But the fear inside Joanna overruled her, the pain of betrayal stabbed deeply into Joanna's heart. She cringed in shame as she walked away.

Joanna sped up, wanting this moment to be over with long before it even began. *I'm so sorry. I'm so sorry. I . . . I can't.* Joanna felt the urge to look over her shoulder. *Don't do it. Don't do it.* But she did. She had to. Joanna glanced over her shoulder and saw Krystal staring back at her, Joanna was riddled with disgust at herself. Watching all the pain and betrayal she cast onto this lonesome girl who was nothing but kind to her. *I'm sorry. I'm sorry. I . . . I can't,* Joanna walked away from Krystal's gaze, feeling the betrayal and guilt strike deep within her heart. *I'm sorry. I'm sorry.*

I know why she did it. I know why she walked away. It's because she fears being associated with me would make her a target for bullying. I understand, I mean, what person wouldn't do that when faced with those kinds of circumstances? But it still hurts, and she knows that. I saw her standing right in front of me. She knew that even as she walked away. I guess it hurt us both.

Krystal took a deep breath and inhaled, feeling disappointment linger within her body. She closed her eyes and nodded, trying to relax in the sun and negate the sense of betrayal in her heart. "It's okay. I don't hate her . . . I understand why." Krystal truly did. She didn't feel a deep sense of hatred towards Joanna, in fact it was the opposite. Compassion and pain struck Krystal's heart as she watched Joanna turn her head and walk away. Krystal leaned back in understanding. For some reason, the betrayal didn't strike her as deeply as she thought it would, but it still hurt. Krystal shrugged. *I get it. I really do. We do what we can to make friends right?*

CHAPTER 38

The Drinking Party

*"Sometimes you gotta make a thousand friends to
find the one person who you connect with."*

—Jaime Fisher

Jaime turned and faced Krystal with a crazy grin on his face and spoke in a Yoda accent. "Rhhheeehehehe, have fun, we, must, yes yes." Krystal glared at Jaime, annoyed while fighting to keep her laughter hidden. Jaime stared deeply into Krystal's walled expression, looking for any kind of crack in the foundation he could break into. He could see the pressure was working. "Hmmmm, have fun we will," bobbing his head up and down happily with that stupid smirk on his face. Krystal's heart was tense as steel wool, holding her laughter in.

She leaked out a smile, trying her best not to laugh, hitting the breaking point of her façade. Jaime knew he only needed one more push. He hummed so loud, "HMMMMMMHHHH!" as he broke Krystal's final stronghold and caused her to burst out laughing.

"I hate you so much," she laughed. Jaime raised a fist. Victory.

Jaime grinned. "You know you love it."

"I freaking hate you," Krystal grinned back as Jaime went to the door.

"Ready for another party?" as they stood before another large wooden door, containing inside the most complex of all creatures. High schoolers.

Krystal faced the door alongside him, "You know I'm not."

"Let's do this."

〜

Joanna entered the house to find the party in mid-swing. Laughter and shuffling permeated the house, people moving all over, getting drinks, and having a good time wherever they could. It was not her first party, far from it, but it was her first time going to an event alone, without a group of friends. It's not like Joanna didn't know people, in fact, she was pretty well rounded with the school community because of her cheerful personality. But here, at this high school party at somebody's house, Joanna had never felt more out of her comfort zone going without a friend group. She had nothing else to do on her weekend either, so going out was the classic option. She hoped Summer and Amber wouldn't be here, but secretly wished they were. There was still a part of her that wanted to be good friends with both of them despite how they treated her.

So Joanna poured herself another drink and raised her head to find someone she never expected.

Krystal finished pouring her own drink and looked across the room in boredom. She scanned all the faces, trying to identify anyone at the party she knew at school. Most of the faces were all new to her, which made it harder, until Krystal's eyes stopped on a figure across the room. There stood Joanna Watson, having drink after drink, trying to wash away the horrible week she had. Krystal locked eyes with her and for a moment, Krystal could see the fear enter Joanna's soul as she waved awkwardly. Krystal didn't smile with the wave, she could tell Joanna was just as uncomfortable being at this party by herself, so she wasn't in the best of moods either. Joanna came up to Krystal and asked, "What are you doing here?" having to yell due to the music.

Krystal replied, "Jaime's friend is hosting the party, so we came along."

"Jaime Fisher?" Joanna inquired. Her jaw nearly dropped at the name. "You know Jaime Fisher?"

Krystal nodded, "Yeah, he's my neighbor."

"You live close to Jaime Fisher?"

Krystal was hesitant to answer the obvious question, "Yeah," not seeing the big deal.

"What are you guys dating or something?"

Krystal shook her head, "No, we're just friends."

Joanna leaned in closer, "But do you want to date him?"

Krystal shrugged her shoulders, "I don't know." And that was the truth.

Krystal didn't know how to feel about Jaime. She knew of his dark side, so she was hesitant at times to get to know him better, while on the other hand, Krystal wondered what Jaime thought about her.

"So is he fair game?" Joanna asked.

Krystal felt it was an odd question and said, "I don't think you *want* to date him right now."

"Why is that?"

"He's going through some stuff, and trust me, you don't want to."

"Sounds all the more interesting. Maybe I'll attack him a time or two." Joanna got all coy-like and winked at her.

"Good luck," Krystal said with sullen sarcasm, wanting this subject to be over with, knowing full well how Jaime would react if a girl started hitting on him. Krystal took a sip from her Sprite and said, "You look more relaxed tonight."

Joanna hoisted up her red cup, the smell of alcohol strong in her breath, "I'm just a little drunk that's all."

"Clearly," Krystal said flatly.

Krystal thought, *That explains why she's talking to me. She's so drunk she forgot about everything that happened this week.*

Next to them, a guy in a light blue shirt entered the kitchen and started pouring himself a drink. He was taller than the two of them but seemed friendly enough. Not drunk, at least not yet, but he seemed sober enough to Krystal's standards. Then he came up to Joanna and said, "How are *you* doing?"

Krystal tensed up like a statue, while Joanna turned on the charm, tittering her drink with her fingers, "Oh you know . . . just having fun."

"I see I see," the guy said, "and what is your name?"

"I'm Joanna," sticking her hand out, the guy took it and gave it a shake.

"Nice to meet you, I'm Sean." Joanna looked in Krystal's direction and Sean took notice and looked Krystal's way. "Oh, I'm sorry," he said, "I didn't see you there." Krystal looked like she had something to say but stayed quiet. Joanna blinked, eager to hear what Krystal had to say. A few moments of awkward silence lingered between them when Sean finally turned back to Joanna, "So what do you like to do for fun?"

Joanna played along with his game, "Oh you know me, go to parties, and meet people. That's what I do . . ." The conversation didn't last long as the guy soon left to go play beer pong with some other people, leaving Krystal and Joanna. Joanna took another sip from her drink, observing the brown liquid swath in her cup. Krystal stood there looking as uncomfortable as ever. Joanna noticed Krystal's uncomfortable expression, and admired how open she was. Joanna took another sip from her drink and said, "That was awkward."

"You too?" Krystal inquired.

"Yep," Joanna said.

"Are you as uncomfortable as I am?"

"Yeup." Joanna raised her cup to her lips, taking another few gulps. "Do you have a problem talking to people or something?"

"Only with meeting new people. Once I've gotten familiar with someone, I am more comfortable around them."

"Is that why you're more comfortable around me here?"

"I'm not comfortable at all here," Krystal said. Glancing boredly towards the party, watching all the groups of people dancing around the house to some type of music she didn't understand while the rest of the party was busy getting drunk as quickly as possible.

"You been to a party before?" Joanna asked.

Krystal took a sip from her drink. "Only a few, I have a hard time making friends while there."

Joanna nodded. "Everyone does. Parties are just another place to meet people and even then, everyone is still uncomfortable. That's why we need this," tapping her red cup.

"I don't use that," Krystal said, looking gloomier than before. Almost like she was disappointed in herself. Joanna noticed that and wondered why. Krystal continued, "I don't have the kind of confidence Summer does at these kinds of events." Krystal lowered her head looking at the floor while Joanna took another swig from her drink, letting the liquid confidence guide her throughout the night.

Joanna stood in front of Krystal and raised her index finger. "Well, if you want to be social, then do this one thing. *Ask questions.*"

"What do you mean?" Krystal said, now more interested in Joanna's lesson.

Joanna clarified, "People like to talk about themselves. They particularly like it when people ask about *them*. So . . . try to get to know them. Ask people about who they are and what they do. Show them you are *interested*, not *interesting*. Because people don't like to listen to people who only talk about themselves. People like to be listened to. So, listen to people and see what happens."

To her surprise, Krystal felt Joanna's words ring true. She lifted her head thinking, *that actually was some good advice.* "That's a good idea," she said. "Can I try it?"

"Sure!" Joanna said cheerfully. Glad that someone was adhering to her advice.

"On you." Joanna's enthusiasm vanished.

"What?"

"Can I try it on you?"

"Uhh sure," Joanna replied, unsure how this would go.

"So . . . your name's Joanna?"

"Yes." Joanna nodded.

"What uhh . . . what uhh . . ."

"Ask me anything," Joanna encouraged.

Krystal quickly skimmed over Joanna's body, looking for some idea to latch onto, then said, "Do uhhh . . . do you, like your nails?"

Joanna stretched her hand out showing Krystal her freshly painted blue nails. "Yes, I do! I got my nails done at Stylus Salon the other day. They do an excellent job on . . ."

I guess it worked a little too well, Krystal thought. *At least that's a new trick. I'll remember that.*

Joanna continued, ". . . and I specifically remember asking her to do it in thirty minutes, but she totally got it done in fifteen. Isn't that crazy?"

"Yeahhhh . . ." Krystal nodded, clearly not following what Joanna was saying in the slightest. "Uhh, thanks for that."

Joanna put her hand to her chest, "It's always been my absolute and total"—Joanna vomited on the floor, nearly missing Krystal's shoe. Joanna stood up, wiping her mouth—"pleasure." Krystal stood there unfazed by the yellow vomit stain on the floor as Joanna ran toward the bathroom, finding it more of a surprise that no one cared about someone vomiting in the middle of the kitchen while the rest of the party went on business as usual. Krystal looked up from the stain and thought, *Definitely an unusual night, that's for sure.* Krystal went to check on Joanna, but Joanna had locked the door and wouldn't let anyone in. Krystal asked if she was alright, but Joanna was too busy hurling into the toilet with the latest draft of Jack Daniels. So, Krystal left Joanna to her own devices and rejoined the party. *Not much else I can do here.* She pondered while walking away.

Krystal went to refill her Sprite in the kitchen (after the stain was cleaned up of course), finding some new party members around the counter. Krystal remembered Joanna's saying (even if it is a saying from a drunk but whatever), *"Ask questions." It's not a bad quote from someone who was drunk at the time.* Krystal didn't want to linger on the fact that it came from a drunk but right now she was open to experimenting.

A girl in yellow-black pants passed her by and started snacking on the various chips available on the countertop. Krystal looked and tried to find something to break the ice. Something, anything, to get a conversation going. She thought of Joanna's advice, *"Ask questions"* then saw a silver ring on the girl's index finger and thought that was a good place to start. Krystal opened her mouth and pointed, "That's . . ." The girl stopped and looked over her shoulder, "A nice ring . . . you have there."

The girl looked at her hand then back at Krystal, "Oh, thank you." The girl turned fully to face Krystal, open to conversation. She wasn't drunk yet and seemed to have just joined the party. She held the ring out to Krystal, "Have you seen it before?"

"Uhh," Krystal wanted to say something, but her mind came up blank, so she had blurted out the first thing she thought of. "To be honest not really. I was just looking for . . . something to say to you." But Krystal's words grew increasingly robotic as she neared the end of her sentence.

Her answer made the girl uncomfortable. "Oh, uhh . . . I'm sorry if that bothered you." Then she turned and walked away.

Krystal closed her eyes and groaned. If there was a scale of discomfort, ranging from 1 to 100, Krystal was at a solid 85 right now.

"You were a little blunt," Krystal turned her shoulder and found Jaime standing there, drink in hand, happy as a snowball. "You need to watch what you say or else you could hurt people."

Krystal lowered her brow and retorted, "You're one to talk." Jaime grinned. Krystal lowered her head forward like a hunchback, "Give me a break, I'm new to this."

Jaime said encouragingly, "You're trying. I never said it would go well."

"Well you're a big support." Krystal said sarcastically.

Jaime raised his hands in a nonchalant defense, "Hey I'm only watching the show. I've been in this game a little longer than you."

Krystal didn't need Jaime's humor right now. She wasn't in the mood to hear from someone who was clearly more socially adequate than her tell her how to interact with others. "Thanks for the help," she said unapologetically.

Jaime still tried to charm Krystal with his satirical advice, "You need to learn to not take this place so seriously. You won't have fun if you don't." Krystal groaned but knew it to be true. It was all new to her and she *had* to get used to these kinds of situations. She had to stop being Debbie-downer all the time and start trying to relax or at least not take things so seriously. It was out of her nature, and normally she was quiet and collective, but none of those elements applied here in the party setting. It was all calm casual humor going around and people were trying to get past the discomfort and have some fun.

Krystal said, "Parties are hard."

Jaime nodded in agreement, "They really are." Jaime thought about it for a moment and added, "Honesty is good. But if you're so honest that it's rude, then it's not good. Try thinking of that the next time you talk to somebody."

"Okay." Krystal replied obediently. Still slightly confused.

Jaime leaned in closer, the alcohol driving him, "Think of it like this. Take the phrase, 'Love your neighbor as yourself' and apply it to conversation. Okay. Think of how you would want people to speak to you and then do that to others. If you want people to speak kindly to you, then speak kindly to others. Do you understand?"

Krystal raised her head in puzzled surprise, "Yeah." *It's actually some good advice, just like Joanna's.* Krystal raised an eyebrow, "You must be really drunk for you to tell me that."

Jaime raised his hands back in sarcastic defense. "What can I say, we let loose with a little liquid courage." Then Jaime felt his stomach grumble like a volcano and immediately ran to the bathroom. Krystal called after him, "No wait don't go to the"—but Jaime had already ran over to the bathroom door and jerked it open to find Joanna screaming, when he vomited on the ground in front of her, causing Joanna to vomit again—"bathroom." Krystal shook her head like a parent watching her kids do the very thing she told them not to do, laughing anyway, "I can't believe I'm taking advice from two drunks right now."

Krystal tried to look for a new person to talk to, anything to get her socializing skills better than they were. She had received somewhat helpful advice and was now ready to use it. *Speak to people the way I want to be spoken to and ask questions.* Krystal nearly smacked her forehead; *I can't believe I'm about to try this out.* Krystal searched the party for a potential target, watching people hurry all over the place either trying to find their friends or do something else in the party. Krystal checked her phone and realized it was getting late and more people were still joining the party. *Wow, I guess it's rush hour now.* Krystal managed to spot a group of girls standing in the corner underneath a painting of a medieval knight. Krystal saw an opening in the group's circle and started her approach.

Okay here we go. Let's try it out and see what happens. Krystal approached the group of girls, this time with more ease in her approach than before. *Huh, that was surprisingly easy.* At least walking up behind them was, getting to know them would be a whole other story. Krystal joined the conversation, finding an opening within the circle and hearing the group talking about spy warfare in the eighties and the late Cold War. *Well, that's something you don't expect to hear girls talking about these days,* Krystal thought.

One of the girls had nice brown hair and hazel-colored eyes, wearing a pink shirt and white pants. She turned and saw Krystal enter the circle. They locked eyes, as Krystal smiled slightly and said "Hi."

To Krystal's surprise, the girl cheerfully said, "Hi," back, opening herself to conversation.

Okay now that that part is over . . . Krystal tensed up and paused, feeling the lack of discussion begin to break between them. *Oh no, I'm forgetting what to say again!* Krystal tried not to panic and searched for anything to say to this girl to get the conversation rolling. Krystal tensed up like an elementary schooler in a spelling bee and said the first thing that came to her mind, "I'm Krystal," like she was holding her breath.

The girl found that introduction a bit odd but hey, everyone was drunk tonight. "I'm Sandra. Nice to meet you."

Krystal urgently tried to think of something else to say, any question to ask that wouldn't sound weird. So Krystal said, "What . . . school . . . do you . . . go to?"

"I go to McCander's High."

"Oh," Krystal said, "That's . . . the same . . . school as . . . me."

"That's nice," Sandra said. "What grade are you?"

"A junior," the words still sounding half-baked as they came out.

"Oh sweet. I'm a senior." Krystal nodded, running out of things to say, feeling the awkwardness settle between them like the morning dew on grass. A mixture of embarrassment, tension, bewilderment, and fear. All of it caused her to fall mute again. The two of them stood there awkwardly, waiting for the other to say something but neither of them did. So Krystal said, "I'm gonna go," and retreated.

Sandra smiled and said, "Okay, it was nice meeting you."

"You too," Krystal said.

Krystal returned to the kitchen, where she found Jaime leaning against the wall like a stud as he gleamed over at Krystal like an older brother. "You had a rough time there."

"Shut up," Krystal whispered, not having Jaime's satirical humor this evening. Jaime cackled. Krystal shook her head and poured herself another cup of Sprite. "I don't get it," Krystal nudged in Sandra's direction, "Why do I have a hard time talking with people?"

Jaime cocked his head and shrugged, "Eh don't beat yourself up. It's awkward for anybody to talk to strangers."

Krystal lifted her eye in contempt, "Not for you, you don't have a problem socializing."

Jaime stared in boredom at the crowd, "That's because I learned how to be social. It all comes with experience, which is what you're getting right now."

"This sucks."

"Yes, it should. If it were easy, then everybody would do it."

"But I don't understand," Krystal gestured to Jaime, "I have no problem with talking to you, but with other people I can't carry a conversation."

Jaime made the Shaka sign and gestured between the two of them, "That's because you and I 'connect' well."

"What does that mean?"

"It means that everyone is different. What I mean by that is, not everyone can be best friends with everyone. Some people 'connect' better with others than they do with each other. It's why people stay with their cliques so much because those are the people they already know or tend to 'connect' with better than others. What you just said proves my theory. You talked to that girl over there and had a tough time facilitating conversation, and yet with me, you speak so calmly, it comes *naturally*."

"So what do I do then?"

Jaime felt more like the older brother now than he'd felt in a long time. If it weren't for the alcohol in his system, he would have shut off and left the room, but for once, he indulged in answering Krystal's question. "You're going to have to meet a lot of people and see who you 'connect' with better. That's the rarity of friends you find among a crowd. It's why best friends and loved ones are so important." Jaime shrugged his shoulders and took a hard drink, "I can't explain it, but sometimes you just connect better with others. It's the difference between asking the typical things in life like: 'How's your weekend?' versus 'Do you remember my old cousin who liked to go drag racing?' or something like that." Jaime put his elbow against the drywall. "You gotta meet a thousand people to find the one person you connect with. Considering those people you meet are still going to be your friends, but only a rare few of them will be able to go on a deeper level with you than others. And you gotta make sacrifices for it because friendships and relationships are a two-way street. Both sides have to come forward and make sacrifices for the relationship to work. The bottom line is, it's not about you."

Krystal stood there amazed, finding Jaime's advice to be somewhat helpful. "That's actually some pretty solid advice."

Jaime felt good about that compliment and took a sip from his drink, feeling like the older brother he'd once been. *This brings back memories*, he thought.

"Okay," Krystal said, her demeanor appearing more confident. "I'm gonna do it. I'm gonna try and find people that I connect with."

Jaime reminded her, "Remember, one friend out of a thousand. That's all you need."

"Alright." Krystal said, trying to convince herself she could do this. Jaime didn't have a doubt that she couldn't. She'd shown some improvement so far, she was just getting used to the socializing game for the first time.

Jaime noticed his buddy Luiz entered the party with a gang of people and waved him over.

Jaime called out, "Hey! Where's my best friend?"

Luiz stopped in his tracks, threw his hands up, and said, "I'm right here!" then gave each other a bro hug. Krystal watched their interaction and wished she had a connection like that. Krystal was still getting used to the friend game, but to have a friend she was close with, that was something she lacked. She envied watching Jaime and Luiz, wishing she had a friendship like that. Jaime turned to the group and gestured to Krystal, "Guys, this is Krystal." The whole group looked at Krystal, causing her to shy up like a turtle in the heat. Krystal shot Jaime a fearful look, *"What are you doing?"*

Jaime read her description and said, "I'm doing the hard part for you. Now you take the lead." Krystal greeted everyone in the group, starting with all the guys and then with the girls. There were about seven of them total and they all seemed to take well to each other. Krystal fell silent as the group began talking.

Krystal stood next to one of the girls with short black hair down to her neck and asked, "What's . . . your name?"

The girl turned and said, "My name's Maya. What's yours?"

Krystal forced the words into her throat. "It's Krystal. Nice . . . to meet you." Krystal looked for something to start the conversation with but was having difficulty again. Krystal fought the engaging awkwardness settling between the two of them. Clearly, they weren't connecting well, at least not on this first encounter. Krystal thought of Joanna's advice, *Ask questions*, and said, "So . . . What . . . do you do . . . for fun?"

Maya seemed delighted by the question, "I like to play racquetball."

Okay, I'm doing well, I just gotta keep asking questions. "What's racquetball?"

"It's basically a game where you smack a ball in a room with four walls and try to beat your opponent. It's pretty fun. Basically, it's just running in a box while playing an advanced version of handball. But what's really interesting is . . ." Maya went on, engaging Krystal with all the interesting facts about racquetball and when it was invented and such.

Krystal thought, *Uhh . . . okay . . . it seems to have worked a little too well.* The conversation went on for another twenty minutes before Maya broke off and went to get something to drink.

Krystal took a breath and blew sharply through her lips. Jaime saw Krystal's fatigue, and asked, "How'd it go?"

"Pretty well," Krystal answered, sounding both brain dead from the nonstop information and surprised with the flow of the conversation. "I learned a lot about racquetball."

Jaime chuckled, "Yeah that happens when you ask Maya about that. It's one of her passions. You just happened to touch upon a likely topic of hers early on."

"Goodie for me, I guess," Krystal said flatly, not sure whether that was a compliment or not.

Jaime found another girl in his sights and pressured Krystal in her direction. "Try it again with that girl."

"Okay," Krystal groaned, not liking how awkward this night was going, yet growing more comfortable with this kind of setting. Krystal was at least able to talk to someone now, which was a major accomplishment for her since she wouldn't even talk to anybody beforehand, much less a stranger.

It happened again with a brown-haired girl named Misa. She raised her hands like a valley girl, "Oh my gosh that is totally up my alley! I love Half & Half coffee shop! Like crazy."

"Uh-huh," Krystal nodded cautiously, pretending to understand, as Misa talked about the various drinks she ordered at Half & Half, all of it flying over Krystal's head because she never ordered anything from Half & Half. The next fifteen minutes passed as Misa finished her speech.

Misa waved, "It was nice talking to you," and vanished among the crowd.

"You too," Krystal said, taking a mental check of her body. Feeling her mouth fall mute as she hadn't said more than ten words throughout that entire conversation. *Well . . . at least I'm talking to people. I guess.* It didn't feel that way though. People were talking *to* her, but it's not like she was talking to them exactly. Not exactly the accomplishment Krystal would have liked, but at least she was being social and that's a start.

Jaime came up and said, "You're improving. You talked to her at least," nudging his head in Misa's direction.

"It didn't feel like a conversation," Krystal spoke, trying not to offend Jaime, voicing her frustration. "It felt more like a podcast. I didn't really say much in the conversation."

"But at least you're talking to people," Jaime added, "and that's an improvement for you."

Krystal saw he had a point but brushed it off, "I'm not gonna argue with you there." It *was* an improvement, a noticeably big improvement on Krystal's part. But she had only learned half the equation. She was still getting used to the ins and outs of how to talk to people, how to socialize, and how to behave around others. All of it was brand new information that Krystal would have to deal with but had never learned before. All of it invaluable.

The night dragged on and the party continued.

> "If all your friends jumped off a cliff. Would you?"
> —JL

Meanwhile, Joanna was not having fun in the slightest. Aside from being drunk the whole night and spending much of her evening puking in the same toilet twelve other people had puked in, she was not having a good time. Joanna finished off the night lying down on one of the couches with a cup of water in her hand, trying to fight off the already developing hangover as the party fell into the later hours of the evening, or morning for all she knew. A brunette-haired girl wearing a nice green jacket stumbled around happily, the girl clearly had way too many drinks and before she knew it, she was passed out on a nearby couch. Joanna didn't mind the sight. The party was already dying down to less than twenty people and the music had been turned down due to a noise complaint a little while ago, and they did not want the cops involved.

Joanna paid no attention to the drunk brunette and tried drinking some water. *I think I'm going to stay the night. No way I'm driving home like this.* That was normal. Doug, the host of the party, knew Joanna and a few other people and allowed them to stay the night. His parents were very flexible with that kind of stuff.

She saw Krystal walk by the couch, looking to be on her way out with Jaime Fisher, when Joanna saw her stop and notice the brunette in the green jacket lying passed out on the couch beneath her. Krystal stared at the brunette for a while before Jaime called out tiredly, "Look Krystal, I know you had a good time, but we need to go. It's getting late."

"Hold on," Krystal called back, sounding worried. Everyone in the party had settled into their own nesting places, a majority of them passed out, some of them still talking. Almost all of them were drunk except Krystal. Krystal walked around the couch, leaned closer, checking the young girl's breathing. It was slow, and that worried Krystal. Krystal tapped on the girl's shoulder, "Hey, hey are you alright?"

Someone called out from the opposite couch, "Quit bothering her! Let her sleep."

"Are you sure she's alright?" Krystal asked. Her question was serious.

"She's fine," the guy called out, "Look at her."

Krystal looked at the brunette and asked, "Hey are you okay?" No answer. Krystal tapped the girl's shoulder and shook her a bit. No response. Krystal put her hand on the brunette's skin. It was cold, *very* cold. Krystal checked the girl's face, it looked pale. Krystal turned toward the same guy and asked him, "Do you know how much she had to drink tonight?"

A gal sitting on the couch with Joanna spoke up, "I can't remember the exact amount, but I know she's had at least ten shots."

"Ten shots!" Krystal quickly whipped her head around and checked the girl's breathing again, this time holding her head close to her mouth for a full sixty seconds.

People were starting to stare now, but Krystal ignored them. Joanna sat up right and asked, "What's happening?"

Krystal finished her sixty seconds as Jaime came over and said, "Come on Krystal, let's go." Krystal looked at Jaime quickly, with deep concern in her eyes, speaking faster than usual and in all seriousness. "We need to call 911." The very mention of that caused the room to fall silent.

A second later the same guy on the couch called out, "Come on, don't do that!" More people started to chime in on the criticism. Krystal turned and faced the guy, forgetting the developing crowd and spoke authoritatively, "My mom is a—" corrected herself, "was, a nurse. So I know the symptoms of alcohol poisoning." Krystal pointed, "And this girl is showing symptoms of alcohol poisoning."

Another person called out, "She'll be fine in the morn—"

"No!" Krystal interrupted, "If we don't call an ambulance right now, she is going to die!"

Jaime stepped in, still a little drunk himself, "Alright alright, let's take it easy."

Krystal looked at him and spoke in all seriousness, "Jaime . . . she is going to die."

Joanna was surprised by the matter altogether. How often is it that you find a person suffering from alcohol poisoning at a high school party? As well as there being someone willing to call the cops and ruin the whole party? Especially a party that had a lot of . . . "materials" floating around. Joanna saw this and wouldn't do that in a thousand lifetimes. It wasn't cool. When you want to fit in, you be quiet and go along with the crowd. But Joanna was fascinated with Krystal. Joanna doubted she would do it. It was too countercultural.

Krystal looked around at the growing number of faces, none of them seemed to give her any support as they grew louder and more hateful in their comments, but Krystal wouldn't back down. "I'm calling an ambulance," she said defiantly.

Another drunk called out, "Nahhhh! You'll ruin the party!"

Krystal retorted, "Is it worth someone *dying* over?" but all Krystal got was a series of objections and angry retorts. Regardless, Krystal pulled out her phone and dialed the rare number in contempt. It felt weird dialing 911, but she did it anyway and no one bothered to stop her.

"That girl was lucky," the police officer said. "If you guys hadn't called an ambulance when you did, she would have died for sure from alcohol poisoning." The police officer overlooked the group of twenty high schoolers outside the house, clearly a majority of them were hungover and barely standing. They were all lined up in the front yard, fearful of what the officer was going to do, but Officer Jordan wasn't going to spend the early morning of 2am arresting a bunch of high schoolers, so he would let them off with a warning . . . this time. "Who's the one who dialed the number?" he asked. Tired eyes shifted to a young girl, looking to be about seventeen, maybe eighteen, wearing all black and clearly sober, as she slowly raised a hand. Officer Jordan looked right at her and said, "Miss . . . you just saved that girl's life."

Joanna, barely standing amongst the group, looked over at Krystal, amazed at the compliment the police officer had given. They were all standing outside in the cold as the ambulance left and the police went away to manage business. The party was clearly over. Joanna looked at Krystal with a mixture of bitterness and admiration. *Wow. So she made the right choice after all.* Joanna couldn't believe it. She was still dead tired, ready to pass out, but she managed to sober up for this occasion and admire Krystal.

Krystal merely stared off in the police officer's direction, showing no sign of celebration whatsoever. She looked a bit embarrassed from the compliment. But what surprised Joanna the most was despite everyone telling this girl to back off, she withstood her ground and ended up making the right decision. *I could never do that,* Joanna thought. The mere idea of standing against the crowd scared her to death. *How in the world did she get the courage to do that?* The mere fact of it surprised Joanna even further. *Who is this girl?* She wondered, watching as the blue-red police lights flickered details on and off of Krystal's face in the night.

Joanna felt a pulse in her stomach and slumped over as she vomited on the front lawn. Everyone else standing saw the vomit and then vomited as well, all except Krystal of course, as nineteen high schoolers vomited together on the front lawn of Doug McClain's house. Officer Jordan shook his head, "Never seen nineteen people vomit at the same time before," he said, while Krystal stood there in the center, the only one smiling.

Jaime sat in Krystal's kitchen the next morning with his hand over his face. "So, did you have fun last night?" Krystal asked knowingly, as she made breakfast.

Jaime didn't even look at her, feeling like he got hit by a train from excessive drinking. He spoke slow and coarse, "I don't want to talk about it," as he heard her chuckle in the background.

"I still feel hungover," Joanna mumbled. It had been a full day since the party and Joanna still felt the effects of all the drinking that night. The noise of the coffee shop made Joanna want to crawl back into bed and die. Joanna put her hand to her face and took a sip from her macchiato. It helped, even just a little. But her mind, still in recovery, was drawn to thinking about Krystal. A girl she had barely known before was now at the center of everything. "I still can't believe she was willing to call 911. Even when everyone else told her not to." Joanna tried to put herself in Krystal's shoes, knowing full well she would put the phone down and continue business as usual.

Joanna asked herself, "How did she act with so much confidence? And why? Why is this girl suddenly sticking out so much." Joanna couldn't remember seeing Krystal before the start of this year. It was like she was a new figure to the game, and it boggled Joanna's mind every time she thought about it. "What is it that makes this girl so different? It's on the tip of my tongue." She sipped her drink, letting the blend of coffee drown out her thoughts.

CHAPTER 39

Coming Together

*"Everyone has an opinion about you. The only question
is, whose opinion matters? Theirs or God's?"*

—JL

Class ended and it was time to go to lunch, but before Krystal
could leave, Joanna followed her out. She had something she needed to ask.
Joanna walked out into the flow of students halfway, keeping track of Krystal
as she walked through the hallway. She didn't dare yell because that would
only draw attention. Joanna followed Krystal all the way outside until she
got to her locker when Joanna finally came up to Krystal and said, "Hey."
Krystal closed her locker. She wasn't surprised, but she wasn't expecting to
see Joanna standing there.

"Hi . . ." she replied.

"Can I ask you something?" Joanna leaned forward. "In private?" subconsciously looking over her shoulder.

"Sure," Krystal said. They took their business to the outskirts of the
school where there were fewer people and less of a likelihood of running
into Summer and her friends. Joanna still had reservations about talking to
Krystal, but after the party, she was now very curious.

Joanna anxiously looked around and then stared at Krystal for a long
moment.

Krystal, on the other hand, was able to receive all the staring from
Joanna like it wasn't even there. She didn't look uncomfortable with how
much Joanna looked at her, because Krystal frankly did not care. And even

that astounded Joanna. *I cannot get a read on this girl*, Joanna thought. It felt like a double feint to Joanna but to Krystal it was the truth, truth, and nothing but the truth, and that astounded Joanna, so much to where she didn't know what to think when it came to this girl standing right in front of her.

Sure, Joanna and Krystal were in the same grade and even the same age, but for some reason, Joanna felt Krystal was older. She had a certain sense of maturity that most high schoolers didn't have her age.

"Why did you do that?" Joanna said, getting down to business.

"Do what?"

"The party? Why did you go against the flow and call 911 when you could have done what everyone else was doing and blend in?"

Krystal lowered her head slightly, contemplating the question. Then she raised her eyes to Joanna's and said, "Because if I was that girl suffering from alcohol poisoning, then I would want someone to stop the party and save my life."

Joanna leaned closer, "But that doesn't make sense. I don't understand why someone would purposefully go against the flow when it doesn't benefit them at all?"

"It's simple really." Krystal said. Joanna tilted her head quizzically. Krystal looked at her and said, "Because I want to love my neighbor as myself." Joanna coiled back.

"But why? Where does that kindness come from?"

Krystal seemed prepared for that question too. "Because God loved me first." Silence.

It took a full minute before Joanna was even able to comprehend something to say. "Is that why you can speak up and act with confidence?"

Krystal nodded. She would have never been able to do the very things she did without God's help. She would still be sitting on that bench all alone or bleeding dead in her apartment if it hadn't been for God. Now, Krystal had grown in confidence so much that it was like she was a completely different person. Even Krystal didn't recognize the girl in the mirror anymore, she looked too joyful.

Krystal added, "Yes, that's exactly why. I used to not be able to talk as much and now I can. Before, I used to care a lot about how other people would look at me and what they would say . . . but now I don't care about what others think of me. I only care about what God thinks, and He calls me beautifully and wonderfully made. That's why."

This was a lot to take in, yet this was what Joanna had secretly been craving for all her life. Joanna's whole life had been nothing but trying to blend in. Trying to make friends, and to be who other people wanted her to be. But with this girl, it was the total opposite. Here, this girl, Krystal Henninger, didn't care about what others thought of her simply because she lived for an audience of one. It was . . . freeing. Joanna could tell Krystal was not like the other girls in their class. She seemed lighthearted and able to be comfortable with herself before she could be comfortable with others. She enjoyed being herself and not what other people wanted her to be. All of this was ringing true within Joanna's heart, as she lived her whole life trying to make friends, to fight the growing loneliness by killing who she was, and being the person everyone liked. But here, with Krystal, she didn't have to be anyone else. She could be herself and be happy. It didn't make any sense.

This girl . . . is special, was all Joanna could think; she felt nothing but awe of the character in front of her. And she wanted whatever it was that Krystal had. She wanted it so very much because Joanna could see a life possible with happiness sitting right in front of her. She just had to figure out how to get it.

Joanna tapped her shoe against the ground, "Krystal . . . you are something different."

Krystal smiled, "Thanks." Joanna meant to say something else, but Krystal's smile made Joanna forget. There was a healthy pause between them, then Krystal looked from left to right and said, "By the way . . . you don't have anywhere to sit during lunch, do you?"

Joanna remembered the reality of her current social status. "No," she said timidly.

"Do you want to have lunch together?"

Joanna looked up, amazed at the request. Joanna knew what would happen if the school saw the two of them sitting together, but she got the feeling Krystal already knew that, and was doing it anyway. "Not at that bench, right?"

Krystal shook her head, "No, in fact, I found a new table inside the cafeteria where we could sit."

And all Joanna said was, "Okay."

> "Pain has a way of bringing people together
> who had nothing in common before."
> —JL

Two minutes later . . .

"Are you sure it's a good idea? I'm not too comfortable with this."

Krystal walked ahead of Joanna toward the cafeteria, facing her before the entrance, "If you live your life trying to please others, then you will always be a slave to their expectations." Joanna knew if she went through with this, there was no going back. Krystal could tell Joanna was thinking about what everyone else would say if they saw the two of them eating together. Krystal was all on board for the idea, but Joanna was not. It was a public declaration of which side you were on and that didn't always have the best reaction to some people, Amber and Summer included. Krystal saw Joanna ache and shimmer in pain. Stuffing the powerful feelings deep into her heart. But Joanna had to grow from this. She had to move on, or else she would be bound by the opinions of others for the rest of her life.

"Remember," Krystal said. Joanna looked up, the fear parting, "The only opinion that matters is what God thinks of you." Then Krystal opened the door for her. Watching Joanna like she was about to walk into the lion's den.

Krystal walked in first and Joanna followed. Krystal held her backpack casually with one strap while Joanna walked behind her with both straps clamped anxiously in her hands. Krystal led the way, ignoring the people around the room, but Krystal was used to that. She made it halfway through the cafeteria when she stopped and realized Joanna wasn't with her. Looking back to find Joanna standing near the edge of the cafeteria. Krystal could read the fear on Joanna's face, paralyzing her. Yet Krystal waited for Joanna. After a couple brief moments, Krystal saw that Joanna wasn't going to budge. Krystal's heart sank.

Expectations betrayed once again. Krystal sighed. There was nothing she could do. This was Joanna's decision and hers alone. Krystal couldn't force Joanna to do anything she didn't want to do. So Krystal pulled out her phone and sent a text to Joanna.

Joanna's phone buzzed and she found a text from Krystal that said, "I won't force you to do anything you don't want to do. If you truly don't want to have anything to do with me, then I will accept your choice. I won't hold any judgment against you if you do."

Joanna looked across the room at Krystal displaying her passive stare. It was a look of neither conviction nor condemnation. It was just a look. One that Joanna wasn't sure how to react to. Joanna, on the other hand, was an open book. Krystal could see the guilt across her face as she met Krystal's eyes. Krystal knew she wasn't putting Joanna in an outstanding position if Joanna came with her, but she was also giving Joanna a choice in the matter. Either way, Krystal was still going to love Joanna however way she decided. But right now, this was Joanna's moment.

She lowered her head and reluctantly took a step forward. The bridge had been crossed. Joanna made her way toward Krystal, passing through all the crowded tables despite the looks she was getting. She made it all the way to where Krystal was standing and together the two of them took their seats at a nice clean table.

Krystal immediately noticed a shift in the room. Some people snuck glances at them, but Krystal didn't mind. No one knew who Krystal was, so she didn't care. But for some reason, Krystal's eyes weren't focused on Joanna sitting in front of her. Some warm, calming feeling drew Krystal's eyes upwards, and she began searching the room. Then she saw it. Jaime was standing there in line, waiting for his food. Krystal also looked over and saw Kristina engaging in the middle of a group. An idea popped into Krystal's mind. One that would truly rock the boat of the social norms in the school. There was no time for hesitation or self-doubt. It was time to act.

"One sec," said Krystal, leaving Joanna perplexed as she walked over to the lunch line. Krystal paced forward, her heart pounding, bracing herself for what she was about to do. *Oh man, this is going to be uncomfortable,* she thought. But Krystal also figured she had nothing to lose. So she walked right up to Jaime standing in line, and said, "Hey."

Jaime jumped in surprise and turned, "Hey." Krystal chuckled; she loved scaring Jaime. She always got the jump on him, even when she wasn't trying.

Krystal asked, "Would you . . . like to sit with us?" pointing her thumb toward the empty table with Joanna.

Jaime followed the finger, debated the idea, and said, "You know what, sure. I'd like that."

Krystal's heart glowed, flooding her chest with warmth. A feeling of hope was now flowing through her body. Krystal smiled, a rare occasion that not even Jaime got to see too often. Jaime blinked a couple of times at the sight, recoiling a bit, looking perplexed. "I'm sorry, did I offend you?" he asked kindly.

Krystal shook her head and let the smile grow a bit, "No, I'm just happy that's all." Then she turned around and walked away, leaving Jaime both perplexed and blushing red. He scratched his head and said to himself, "That girl is always a puzzle I can never figure out."

Two down. One more to go, Krystal thought. Now came the most challenging obstacle of all. Krystal walked forward toward a crowded table with Kristina at the center of it. Krystal could feel the power of the group's backs staring toward her. The fear of rejection clamped her heart, aching her to stop what she was doing and to go back to where she was sitting. *Why not stop here? You've already done enough.* But Krystal knew the answer to that question. Arguing back, *Kristina's hurting, we all are. I can't let people who are sharing that pain go on suffering the way I did.* The fear of rejection was overwhelmed with love. The love God was pouring from Krystal's heart. Krystal took a deep breath and prayed, *God, this is going to be awkward, but no matter what happens, please give me the strength to keep going.* Krystal suddenly found herself standing right in front of Kristina's group of friends. Their backs were like a wall to climb. No . . . a wall to break through. The only way to get in was through.

Krystal leaned over the person in front of her, looked at Kristina who was busy telling another false story and interrupted, "Hey Kristina." Krystal's tone had come out more positive than she'd intended. She didn't know whether that was simply a side effect, or if she truly meant it. Regardless, the whole group stopped and looked at Krystal. All eyes on her, and Krystal knew she was far outside her comfort zone now, but the discomfort felt less powerful this time and she was able to speak more naturally. The concerns about what other people thought of her were not as powerful. Like she was slowly becoming immune to poison by continuously injecting herself with it. The same thing was happening with her social skills.

Kristina was dumbstruck but that look only lasted half a second. Krystal knew Kristina wanted to say, *"What are you doing!"* but Kristina buried those feelings behind her mask and said, "Now what's this?" Kristina's voice sounding like a fairy tale princess trying to sound intrigued toward an unsuspected guest.

Krystal leaned in closer and pointed toward her table, "Would you like to come and sit with us?" Now Krystal's tone had diluted down a bit, but it was still positive. Krystal braced herself. She knew her request was unexpected, but she did it anyway. Kristina glanced toward the empty table with Joanna. Her eyes locking with Krystal, a secret conversation between them.

"Are you serious? I'm in the middle of a story."

"You don't need to come. I'm simply offering."

Kristina's eyes softened and looked over again. Her mind contemplating the decision as well as the ramifications. The idea would certainly rock the school, but Kristina met Krystal's gaze again and nodded. "Sure. I'll come along with you." Kristina stood up and picked up her things, people started to "aww" with disappointment, Kristina called back, "I know, I know, and I'm sorry, but I've already got plans." Kristina shot Krystal a coy look in the corner of her eye. That impression struck Krystal dead center in the heart and she suddenly felt she wanted to cry. It was a sign of loyalty. A sign of friendship. For the first time in Krystal's life, she was beginning to feel the love coming in from other people. To finally have friends. Friends who valued her, friends who cared about her and wanted to be with her for her and only her. Krystal could tell Kristina felt the same way.

Krystal smiled; *You have grown Kristina. You're not the same liar you once were. You're different now. More open. That's a good start and I hope it will only get better.* Kristina followed Krystal on their way back to the table. More eyes were now glancing at them. It was well enough that Krystal and Joanna were now sitting together, but all of a sudden, the famous figures of Jaime Fisher AND Kristina Walker were both making their ways to sit down at the same table with a girl no one knew or cared about, along with the main topic of gossip, Joanna Watson, now sitting with all four outcasts. Loners in their own world, coming together to find healing in each other's company. Strange how pain has a way of bringing people together who had nothing in common before.

⌇

They all sat around the table exchanging looks. Jaime asked cautiously to the three girls in front of him, "So . . . do you guys like movies?"

"Are you saying that because I'm *in* a movie?" Kristina chimed.

"Yes," Jaime responded simply. Krystal watched the three of them interact. Especially Jaime and Kristina. Both Jaime and Kristina were insanely popular around school; the mood of the entire room shifted dramatically as people snuck looks their way, contemplating the fact that Jaime Fisher, one of the most handsome and likeable guys in school, Joanna Watson, the talk of the town, and Kristina Walker, the world-famous actress, were all sitting at a table with some random girl none of them knew. Krystal felt the eyes of the whole school on them, but she didn't care. It was one of those things about loneliness that seemed to leave a lasting effect on her. It's not that she didn't care, it's just that she wasn't used to people looking at her, so she didn't feel anybody was looking at her. It was a strange side effect really. Some good things do come from being lonely. (hehe no.)

Jaime shifted to his side, turning to Joanna, and said, "I'm sorry, I'm not sure we've been acquainted," gesturing to himself, "I'm Jaime Fisher."

Joanna smiled, turning on the nice act, "I know who you are. You're friends with Summer and a bunch of other people."

Jaime leaned back, "Well . . . I wouldn't say we're friends but . . . it's complicated." Joanna nodded in understanding. "What's your name?" Jaime asked, "You apparently know mine already."

"Oh me? I'm Joanna Watson. I'm part of the Drama club here on campus. We work on sets and stuff."

"Isn't there a talent show coming up?" Kristina chimed in.

Joanna nodded with enthusiasm, forgetting a bit about the crowd, "Yes, there is. It's a mixture of performances from selected members. Some of the stuff requires a skit or background, so we prepare the stage for the contestants to better enhance their performance." Joanna ticked her head to the side now, gleeful. "It's also where scouts come to our school and evaluate the potential students on both their department as well as the school's future actors and performers."

Jaime nodded, "Oh so it's like football try outs but for performers."

"I've done so many of those, it can be a lot to bear," said Kristina.

"Exactly how many movies have you done Kristina?" Jaime inquired.

Kristina put her finger to her chin and looked up at the ceiling in a cutesy manner. "Too many to count."

Krystal tried to join in on the conversation. "I . . ." her voice cut off, but everyone stopped. All eyes were suddenly on Krystal, and she didn't know what to say. Krystal felt she wanted to say something cheerful, to have some story or something to tell them, but she couldn't think of one.

"What's up?" Jaime said. They all waited, something Krystal was not suited to just yet.

Krystal shut off her brain from the attention and just said what was on her mind. "I . . . I don't know. I'm not really sure of what to say right now to be honest."

Jaime gave a reassuring smile, "That's okay. You don't need to say much, just as long as you listen." Then Jaime pondered for a moment. "You know what, as I recall, we've all been doing all the talking and you've always been the one listening, so how about we flip it for once."

"Yeah," Kristina said. "I want to hear what you have to say for a change, Krystal." Krystal's heart tugged. All the blood in her body rushed to her cheeks as she turned bright red.

Jaime and Kristina stifled their laughter, when Joanna said, "Speaking of which," shifting their attention, "I don't know that much about you Krystal, only that you've been kind to me." Joanna brightened. An encouraging sight given her recent struggles.

"And me," said Kristina.

"And me," then Jaime.

Joanna finished off, "So, Krystal, if you'll tell us. What are you like? What makes you tick?"

Krystal said nothing. She retreated slightly into her expressionless face, but she didn't fully climb back into her shell. Her eyes stayed present, searching for an answer to the question. Searching for something to say, so . . . she said the first thing that came to her mind, "I don't know . . ." Pausing timidly, "I don't know myself that much."

Joanna looked from Jaime to Kristina, "Okay guys, I think it's time we dissect Krystal." They all nodded their heads and Krystal was suddenly in the spotlight. Joanna looked at Krystal and said, "Okay Krystal, let's start with this one . . ." Krystal braced herself, feeling uneasy in her stomach. The fear of opening up to them. Krystal suddenly wanted to go home and die, facing new problems with the coming friendships before her. "Krystal . . ." Joanna asked, "What's your favorite color?"

Krystal said nothing for a minute. The silence lingering so long that people felt tempted to check their phones, but they held off and waited for Krystal to speak.

"Purple," she said. "My favorite color is purple."

"Like your eyes?" Jaime asked.

Krystal livened a bit, nodding, "Yeah."

The next question followed, this time from Kristina. "What do you like to do for fun?"

"I don't know," she said. Sounding just as curious about the question as Kristina was.

"I mean, do you have any hobbies? Do you play music, videogames, sing, dance?"

"I play music," Krystal answered, looking away briefly out of embarrassment.

Both Joanna and Kristina leaned forward in curiosity. "Music! What kind? Do you play any instruments?"

"I play guitar," Krystal whispered.

"Do you sing?" Jaime asked.

"Not much."

Jaime leaned back in his seat, "Well I would love to hear you sing one day." Both Kristina and Joanna nodded.

"Maybe one day," Krystal said.

The conversation continued to grow, while Krystal was just grateful to have a group of people to call friends. It was a pivotal moment in Krystal's life. For this was the first time she'd ever had a group of people to sit with.

"Next thing you know, I'll be on America's Got Talent, playing the bagpipes." Jaime pointed to himself.

Kristina leaned over to Jaime, "Come on Buck, you and I both know that won't happen."

Jaime was both sarcastic and serious. "Hey! Have you seen those kilts and pipes? That is the dream my friend. The dream."

"Sounds like a nightmare," Krystal commented. Everyone paused and looked at her. Then Krystal couldn't help but chuckle, Jaime saw her and began laughing himself. The laughter spread to Kristina then Joanna as their laughter filled the indoor cafeteria with their joy.

Krystal wrote and rewrote the same question over and over again, preparing for a test coming up. She was busying herself late at night with studying and was trying not to worry about it when morning came. Krystal yawned, the ample desk light and nighttime appeal in her room made for a settling evening. Krystal leaned in her chair and stretched, enjoying the tranquility in her room. She liked studying, she liked being by herself, it was when she focused the most. She checked the time, 12:34pm. "Geeze, I really went overboard on the late-night cramming," but she didn't feel tired.

Krystal finished her stretch and got back to it. She picked up her pencil and looked down, finding wet streak marks dotting her paper. Krystal looked up and realized she was crying. Then sudden joy overflowed from her heart, letting the tears come down in two twin rivers. It was truly remarkable. The warmth and the joy flowing from her body with an overwhelming sense of peace and clarity. The taste of salt as the hot tears streaked down her face. Her heart and soul emanating and overflowing with nothing but joy. It was like she was a fountain of living joy, pouring out from her soul as Krystal smiled the most joyful smile she'd ever felt. She had never felt so happy before. She didn't stop it. Didn't want to. It was like she was enlightened. Every cell of her being was happy. Like her whole body was glowing with joy.

She relaxed and was remarkably calm. She never wiped the tears from her face, for these were tears of joy, not sadness. "Wow," she said. Krystal savored the feeling and relished the fact that she felt whole, and joyful. She didn't need to put her hand to her heart to feel it, that hole was filled; filled with the Holy Spirit, God living in her. It sounded silly, but Krystal knew it was true. She had never felt this happiness before in her life. Never. Krystal looked at the ceiling and whispered, "Thank you God, for saving me and giving me friends," expressing deep, heartfelt gratitude for this wonderful feeling. It was a gift from God. Nothing more, nothing less.

Krystal put her hand to her face, marveling at how far she'd come from over a year ago. "Gosh has it really been that long?" reliving the memories, finding they weren't as dark anymore. At least, not the recent ones. Krystal remembered all the people she'd met since she cut her own wrist, starting with the Janitor, the man who started it all. The first act of kindness that led to many. "Wherever that guy is, I want to thank him . . . Maybe one day, I'll see him again." Krystal put the pencil down. Studying was done. She would ace the test anyway.

PART SIX

The Loving Father

CHAPTER 40

A Father's Love

"Whether we realize it or not, everyone needs a loving father."

—JL

Mr. Fisher was busy cutting the tomatoes, getting tonight's meal ready. He held the knife over the tomato, ready to cut but lost all motivation. He sighed and lowered the knife. *What's the point of a family dinner if Jaime's not going to be here?* Mr. Fisher looked over at the mahogany dinner table, counting the number of seats. He knew two of those seats would be absent tonight. One of them Jaime, the other . . . Carole. A deep shred of pain rung in his heart. The loss of a child is enough to break a family. The loss of another child that's still alive? That is unbearable.

Mrs. Fisher noticed he wasn't cutting and asked, "Is something wrong?"

Mr. Fisher lowered his head, not hiding his sadness. "Yeah," then ignored his wife. Not wanting her to see him moping again. He tried to keep it in. In fact, he was ready to burst into tears. He continued cutting but knew he wasn't the same as before. A side effect that had started once Carole died, mirrored from Jaime. He knew he shouldn't button things up, especially from his wife, but he did it anyway, whether he liked it or not.

It was a hard state to live in. Ever since Carole died, his family had been on ice. Conversations were cold, looks weren't always happy. He was still trying to get through it. Jaime was only a product of the loss, the long-term effects it had on Mr. Fisher and his family were deep and thorough.

He heard a knock on the door and Carmen got up from reading her magazine on the couch to open it. Krystal entered the house with a gentle greeting and waved hello. Mr. Fisher cleaned his hands and said, "Welcome Krystal, glad to have you here." Krystal had been coming to their house for a while now, even after she left Carmen's Bible study, but Carmen managed to reach out and get Krystal to commit to a personal Bible study with just her and Carmen. It was a clever way to get Krystal to keep coming over to the Fisher's house once in a while.

"Thank you," Krystal answered, dropping her bag next to the dinner table, pulling out her homework. Every so often, Krystal would come by the Fisher's house early and work on her homework too. They didn't mind it, in fact, Carmen always appreciated more company inside the house.

The tv overhanging the living room was on, showing the news of the state festival coming up. Mrs. Fisher got all excited and said, "Ohhh! George, we have to go to that!"

"Maybe Jaime can drive us," Mr. Fisher snidely answered, "He did get his license recently, we should give him all the *practice* he can get," he winked. Mrs. Fisher laughed and then looked over at Krystal who was hard at work in her studies, when Mrs. Fisher said, "And what about you Krystal?"

Krystal jolted, startled by the question. "What?" she asked cautiously.

"The state festival," Mrs. Fisher nudged her head towards the tv announcement. "Have you ever gone?"

Krystal looked at the tv then took a second to find an answer, "No . . . but I want to."

Mrs. Fisher remembered something and waved her answer off, "Oh but you're young. You can drive yourself any time."

"No, I can't."

Mrs. Fisher blinked and tilted her head, "Why not?"

Krystal answered plainly, "I don't have a driver's license." Mr. Fisher exchanged a look with his wife.

Mrs. Fisher tried to recover, asking genuinely, "But you're seventeen?"

"Yes."

"But you've never driven a car before?" Krystal shook her head no. "Why not?"

"No one ever showed me."

Mr. Fisher gave Krystal his full attention, thinking about something. Mrs. Fisher said, "But your mom has surely shown you something?" Krystal shook her head dismissively.

Mr. Fisher looked at Krystal, the idea forming in his head, "Alright then," Mr. Fisher said. He stepped around the counter and grabbed the car keys from the key rack. He motioned for Krystal to follow, "I'll show you." Krystal's face changed from sullen expression to mute surprise.

"What?" she said.

Mr. Fisher looked at his wife, getting her nod of approval, then nudged his head toward the garage. "I'll teach you how to drive, then we can go and get your permit, and then your license."

"Are you serious?" her voice picking up hope.

Mr. Fisher smiled, "Come on," watching the hope glimmer in Krystal's eyes.

༄

He sat in the passenger seat of their white Audi looking at Krystal in the driver's seat. The black interior blended perfectly with Krystal's hair as she searched nervously for the right thing to do. "Okay, you ready?" he asked.

"No," she said simply. From the look on her face Mr. Fisher could tell she was nervous, and what high schooler wouldn't be when learning how to drive for the first time. It actually made Mr. Fisher smile for a bit, reminding him of when he had to teach both Carmen and Jaime how to drive. Oh, how much he laughed when Jaime struggled to drive for the first time.

"Alright so what's the first thing you're going to do?" he instructed.

Krystal shelled up, looking down at her feet. "I don't know."

"Your seatbelt."

"Oh, right," she said anxiously.

"Okay now get comfortable and adjust the mirrors, then we're going to go up and down the street for a bit. It's not that bad once you get to know it."

"Okay," Krystal obeyed. Putting her hands on the steering wheel.

She looks very frightened, thought Mr. Fisher, but he wasn't surprised at all by that reaction. It was her first time driving any vehicle, so anxiety was to be expected. No one ever felt comfortable their first time. Mr. Fisher instructed, "Okay now, turn the car on by turning the key," Krystal obeyed. The car whirred to life. "Now put the car in drive and take us off the driveway." Krystal obeyed, shifting the gear into drive, and pressing down on the gas pedal. The car pulled forward until Krystal suddenly panicked and accidentally slammed her foot on the brake. The car shuddered forward and came to a hard stop.

Krystal took her hands off the wheel in horror at what she'd done. Mr. Fisher saw her frightened expression and waved her off calmly, "Just relax. That's okay. Don't be afraid of that pedal." Mr. Fisher leveled out when he noticed her trembling. *She's terrified.*

Krystal breathed, "Okay," gripping the steering wheel. She tried again, this time putting more gas on the pedal. The car pushed forward, and Mr. Fisher could see Krystal was on the verge of panicking again. Before they got off the driveway, she took her foot off the pedal and slammed on the brake again. Krystal took her hands off the wheel and hid them painfully over her face. Mr. Fisher noticed how hard a time she was having with this and calmly whispered, "Hey hey, it's okay, you're learning. That's all there is to it. Now try again." Mr. Fisher could see her confidence plummet as she reached for the wheel again. She listened to Mr. Fisher's instructions, this time pressing down more on the gas as the car lurched forward onto the road then stabilized at a steady four miles an hour. They pulled forward and Krystal was even more freaked out despite her accomplishment.

"Well done," Mr. Fisher said. "Now go faster." Krystal pushed down on the gas pedal, pushing the white Audi forward. Krystal still looked shaken, but Mr. Fisher kept her going. "Now I want you to take us to the end of the street and back." Krystal obeyed and pushed gently on the gas pedal, still afraid of the power beneath her. "Good. Now take us back and then gently come to a stop." Krystal brought the car to the end of the cul-de-sac, turned the wheel then reared back toward the Fisher's house. They came up in front of the driveway when Mr. Fisher said, "Now slowly stop the car." Krystal obeyed, pressing down a little too hard on the brake, causing the car to jolt to a stop.

"I'm sorry! I'm sorry!" she said anxiously. Putting her hands to her head, shaking with fear.

"It's okay," Mr. Fisher said with fatherly patience. "Everybody has a challenging time on their first try. Don't be so hard on yourself." But he saw Krystal wasn't letting herself off the hook. He could see real terror on her face, her purple eyes searching frantically like she was about to have a panic attack. And then he remembered, *That's right. She lost her mom in a car accident, so she's fearful of cars.* She looked as if she was reliving the horrible memory. The fear and terror made her skin turn pale. Mr. Fisher said, "It's okay, next time we'll work more on your driving skills."

Krystal faced him with absolute fear and panic on her face, "Next time?"

∽

"Alright, now go on the freeway."

Krystal shot him a quick glance, returning her gaze to the road a millisecond later, "What?" Krystal drove the white Audi down the highway at forty-five miles per hour.

"Go onto the freeway." He said, his voice stoic and unyielding. Krystal obeyed and they sped up and pulled onto a nearby onramp toward the I-86 freeway. Cars were rushing home from work on the six-lane freeway, and Mr. Fisher saw Krystal whiten at the sight of them all. Coursing down the freeway like blood cells in a giant concrete artery. They pulled up to the end of the onramp and came neck to neck with the merging traffic. Krystal checked her blind spot and saw she was going too slow with the car next to her. "Pick up speed," Mr. Fisher said. She needed to merge soon, or they would get stuck in the onramp and hit someone. "Pick up speed," he said, this time slightly louder. Krystal hesitated, trying to keep calm despite her fears then sped up slightly. "Pick up speed," once more, this time slower and with more emphasis. Krystal tried to obey but her fear began to overwhelm her. Mr. Fisher saw her face lose color as she gripped the steering wheel so tight her hands were white.

Krystal sped up, putting her left-turn blinker on, passing the car next to them and stabilized safely in the lane. "Now get in the next lane," said Mr. Fisher. Krystal obeyed and merged safely into the next lane. "Good, now go a mile down and take us off on the next offramp." Krystal obeyed. Her entire body shivering like she had been through a traumatic experience. Mr. Fisher saw her expression but said nothing.

"Should I go behind or in front of the car next to me?" Krystal asked, sneaking a glance at Mr. Fisher, but he remained silent. "What should I do?" she asked frantically, but Mr. Fisher said nothing. Krystal took her attention back to the road, surrounded by dozens of cars on all sides, going seventy miles per hour, a speed she was not comfortable with, Krystal decided to brake and get behind the car next to her. Krystal began to shift over when a car in the next lane sped slowly forward, cutting Krystal off from entering the lane. Krystal didn't see it, but Mr. Fisher did. He spoke calmly, "Car, car," then raised his voice when the car was coming in too close, "Car, CAR!" Krystal finally saw the car and pulled left, saving the car from hitting them as the car cut them off and sped forward shifting lanes as it disappeared in the maze of vehicles. Mr. Fisher calmed himself and looked over at Krystal who was looking paler than usual.

"I need to pull over," she said frantically, Mr. Fisher said nothing. Krystal safely managed to pull off the freeway and stop in a parking lot at a Motel 6 on the offramp. Krystal put the car in park and sat there looking like she was about to have a panic attack. Her eyes whipped from side to side, her head and hands shaking treacherously. Mr. Fisher could see Krystal reliving the tragic memory. The fear, the pain, the loss, all of it so easy to happen again should she make a mistake on the road. Krystal's breathing increased to borderline hyperventilation. But Mr. Fisher spoke softly and with authority, "Get back out there." Krystal couldn't believe his words and stared at him, wide-eyed. Mr. Fisher showed no sign of backing down and waited.

Krystal put the car in gear, still trembling, wishing for this experience to be over and to be home safely where she wouldn't die from a simple mistake. Krystal improved her speed and merged again onto the freeway but got stuck once she was back in the second lane. She didn't know where to go and she didn't want to move anywhere. But Mr. Fisher said, "Get in the carpool lane." Krystal snatched a look as quick as a flash, watching the haze of cars fly by her like playing Froggy. Krystal hesitated, failing her first time to merge over. When she tried a second time and failed, Mr. Fisher spoke up, "Merge over." Krystal obeyed, shifting over, a little too desperately, nearly cutting off a car in the process (but let's be honest, we all have cut someone off whether it was intentional or not). Krystal merged again, with only one more lane to go, found her chance to merge and took it. Finally placing herself in the carpool lane. She was still shaking, and her breathing was frantic, but she had accomplished this much at least.

"Alright," said Mr. Fisher, "Now take us back and merge onto the next offramp. Krystal wanted to be anywhere but here, but she had to obey or else they wouldn't get out of this alive. She merged back into the following lanes once she had the chance. Having a couple of close encounters on the way but Mr. Fisher stayed calm like a cop the entire time, finally merging onto the next offramp, and pulling out onto Elmore street.

Krystal felt relieved, knowing the worst was over. She could feel her body weaken from the intense concentration. She wanted to stop but Mr. Fisher refused to let her. "One last stop," he said. Krystal's defenses went up and got back into driving mode.

"Where to?" Krystal asked hesitantly.

"Pull in here." Mr. Fisher pointed, and Krystal obeyed, turning the corner, and entering a nearby shopping center. Krystal slowed the car, but Mr. Fisher said, "Over there," he pointed again, and Krystal pulled up slowly to their destination, putting the car in park, finally relieved to be stable and at walking speed again. She sat there, trembling in terror from the near-death experience on the road. Mr. Fisher thought her heart must be pounding at a hundred miles an hour. (Driving is exhausting, let me tell ya.)

It took Krystal a couple minutes before she managed to calm herself down. Then Mr. Fisher glanced at Krystal and spoke softly, "I'm proud of you."

Krystal stopped breathing. He watched Krystal pass the final threshold as the seal on her heart broke and saw tears streak down her face. She didn't wipe them away nor hide her emotions. Then she slowly looked at Mr. Fisher, leaned over and suddenly hugged him.

Mr. Fisher was surprised and didn't know how to respond, unsure whether he should comfort her or not. He allowed her to hug him for as long as she needed, as he eventually lowered his left arm and placed it gently on Krystal's shoulder. For a moment he felt a ping of joy and sadness in his heart. Feeling his heart flush with warmth he had thought he'd forgotten. The memory of a playful child in his mind; warming his cold heart. He hadn't felt this way since losing his daughter.

Mr. Fisher let Krystal hug him for a few minutes before she pulled away and wiped her nose, "I'm sorry, it's just . . . I've never had a dad tell me that before."

Now it all made sense. Mr. Fisher remembered Krystal's first night in their home. How she mentioned she didn't have a dad. She never knew him or had the encouragement of a loving father in her life. She only had her mom, and even then, she lost her too. He said it once more, "I'm proud of you." Krystal tried to keep it together, trying to keep the tears inside. "You did a good job today." Mr. Fisher opened the door and stepped out, "Now come on, it's time for your reward."

"Reward?" Krystal looked confused then looked up, finding the ice cream shop "N-Ice Guys" in front of her. Krystal widened with aspiration and looked at Mr. Fisher through the windshield, motioning her forward. Krystal opened the door and was suddenly yanked backwards. Seatbelt. Krystal rolled her eyes and unbuckled it then rejoined Mr. Fisher.

He put his hands proudly on his hips, "Get anything you want. It's on me."

"Anything I want?" Krystal asked, her eyes filling with light.

Mr. Fisher smiled, "Anything you want." Krystal's face lit up as she ran inside, feeling for the first time in her life what it's like to have someone proud of her.

A few months later, Krystal burst out of the DMV, holding a paper in her hands. The day was sunny, with little clouds in the sky, and the Fishers all waited outside, even Jaime. Krystal ran towards them, paper in hand and shouted, "I passed! I did it! I did it! I got my license!" Krystal ran forward and threw her hands around Mr. Fisher, hugging him passionately and full of joy. "Thank you! Thank you so much! I couldn't have done it without you." Mr. Fisher felt a sense of loving pride flood over him. A feeling he hadn't felt since he'd lost Carole.

"Congratulations Krystal," he said, "You earned it," covering Krystal with his arms in a hug as the rest of the Fishers joined in. Krystal felt the love surrounding her. The warm embrace of people she loved surrounding her and supporting her. It was one of the happiest moments of her life.

A few days later, Mr. Fisher came through the garage door, carrying a bunch of groceries with his wife. Jaime did not come out to greet them, that wasn't new, but it still bothered Mr. Fisher. He wished his son would engage with the family more, especially since it's been all this time. Mr. Fisher checked the time and saw it was 6:38pm, *We still haven't made dinner yet*, he thought, trying not to let his frustration show. But Mr. Fisher was hungry, and he had had a long and unpleasant day at work. He was ready to eat some food and relax before he had to go to sleep and go back to work the next day. His heart grumbled in frustration like a boiling furnace. *I want to eat. I didn't want to spend my Wednesday evening going shopping.* He pulled the groceries inside with a grunt, his wife behind him, remaining silent, knowing he was in a bad mood. Mr. Fisher turned the doorknob and stepped inside, holding the doorway open for his wife.

The second he opened the door, the smell of cooked meat and spices filled his nostrils, activating his taste buds and salivatory glands. His stomach ached in response, and he was ready to eat. He was a big man, and "a man's gotta eat" as they say. Mr. Fisher picked up his pace, stepping into the kitchen, thinking Carmen had cooked something up, but to his surprise Krystal was working in the kitchen like a chef in a five-star restaurant, wearing an apron and getting the rest of the food ready. Mr. and Mrs. Fisher both stood there shocked but not unwelcome.

"What's all this?" Mr. Fisher asked, still surprised and ready to eat. Krystal finished the final touches on the food and answered, "Hi, sorry to intervene on your evening."

Mrs. Fisher stepped forward, always happy to see Krystal in their home, "Oh don't worry about it sweetie! You are always welcome in this home." Krystal relaxed after hearing that. Mr. Fisher saw the food and could not believe his eyes. There was prepped steak, properly sauteed with garlic bread and mixed vegetables, everything seasoned and ready to eat. He turned and saw the entire dinner table prepped and properly settled, clearly the girl had a knack for table etiquette. The dinner table had a red linen covering and had been set up properly for their arrival.

Mr. Fisher heard footsteps coming down the stairs, expecting to see Jaime, but found Carmen instead. Carmen read their faces and said, "Oh yes, Krystal came over while you were gone, and she offered to make dinner for us. I helped her out, but she was the one who did most of the work." Heads shifted back to Krystal, and she suddenly looked embarrassed from the unsolicited attention. Krystal gave an embarrassed smile and held her hands up in defense, "I didn't mean to intrude upon your evening."

Mr. Fisher stepped forward and said, "Please Krystal, you are always welcome in our home, and I thank you for making dinner for our family." Mr. Fisher motioned to grab a plate, but Krystal cut him off with her own hand.

"Please, allow us to serve you." Krystal offered. Carmen stepped down from the stairs and gestured for her parents to take their seats. She even called Jaime to come down, but he gave no answer. Mr. and Mrs. Fisher took their seats at the ends of the table while Krystal and Carmen, both served them water and plates of food. Mr. Fisher saw the massive plate of steak and was ready to dig in. All his frustration had gone out the window, as he witnessed the most delicious looking food he'd ever seen. After everyone had gotten their plates, Krystal filled a plate and quickly walked upstairs.

"Where are you going?" asked Mrs. Fisher.

Krystal replied, "I thought Jaime might want some," then vanished behind the corner, looking more cheerful than usual this evening. Both Mr. and Mrs. Fisher exchanged looks as Krystal returned moments later without the dish. Mrs. Fisher's eyes widened in surprise.

"He took the plate?"

Krystal nodded happily, "Yes he did."

"You mean, he opened the door?"

Krystal nodded, "Yeah."

Both Mr. and Mrs. Fisher exchanged glances once more. It came as a bit of a surprise but both of them were glad their son was connecting with *somebody*. Krystal then took her seat across from Carmen and the four of them put their hands together to pray. Mr. Fisher waited to see who would pray first as he was not in the praying mood this evening, but to his surprise it was Krystal who led the prayer, and with enthusiasm I'll bet.

She prayed, "God, thank you for this food. Thank you for the love you have given us even when we don't deserve it. Thank you for this time to eat together and thank you for all the kindness the Fishers have shown to me. Thank you."

They said, "Amen," and all dug in. Mr. Fisher took a bite out of the steak and immediately his eyes lit up. *This is some of the most delicious food I have ever tasted!* He looked up, awestruck as his wife had the same reaction. Carmen was there chewing her food with gleeful expectation of their reaction. Mr. Fisher took his eyes off Carmen and looked over at Krystal. She was happily eating the food she'd made, looked up and smiled at him. The sight came as a surprise to him; he had never seen the girl look so happy before.

Mr. Fisher remembered when Krystal first came to their house, how sad she looked. The girl could barely talk, let alone smile. But here was a completely different version of her, as if all the pain had somehow vanished and there was a new person sitting in that chair. Her deep purple eyes glanced up at him, and Mr. Fisher felt flustered for a moment then suddenly froze like he had seen a ghost. The sight of his younger daughter Carole flashed in his mind as the schema of Krystal sitting before him. Carole and Krystal both had the same look of joy when they were happy, which terrified and enlightened Mr. Fisher. But he couldn't express those emotions, not here. He kept it all in. Stifling the tears and keeping his emotions in check. His wife could tell something was wrong but said nothing. Mr. Fisher recollected himself and blinked a couple of times, bringing himself back to reality, remembering the pleasant food growing cold beneath him. He raised his fork and took a bite, breaking eye contact with Krystal. He couldn't tell whether she saw anything or not, but for the time being, he sat and enjoyed himself, as he ate one of the most delicious meals in his entire life.

CHAPTER 41

I Love You

"A man who cannot love his wife cannot be called a man."

—Mr. Fisher

A week later Mrs. Fisher turned the car into the familiar neighborhood with relief. It had been a long day and Mrs. Fisher had some business to take care of, so she wouldn't be able to make dinner tonight. Her husband would be out for a couple hours, so he wasn't able to make dinner either. Mrs. Fisher grunted but she understood the situation. She knew her husband couldn't come home any earlier. It was all too much for him to worry about, and he had a lot to worry about.

Mrs. Fisher pulled the car up to their driveway and put the car in park. She noticed there were no lights on in the house and found that curious. *Is anyone home?* She made a mental list of who could possibly be home, finding that at least Jaime should be home, maybe even Krystal. So, Mrs. Fisher concluded that maybe Jaime was up in his room with all the lights off and Carmen was out running errands. She locked the car as she stepped inside the house, finding a sweet aroma coming from the kitchen. It had the smell of egg rolls, sweet and sour sauce, and noodles, her favorite type of food. Mrs. Fisher strolled through the empty house and into the candle-lit kitchen, where she found her husband standing there with all sorts of food prepped across the dinner table. Mr. Fisher stood there like a gentleman with his hands behind his back. Mrs. Fisher stopped in her tracks. She gestured with her purse still hanging on her hand, "What's all this?" Mr. Fisher looked down, calmly gesturing to the nicely set up table, looking a bit embarrassed. Oh, how that made him look cute.

"I wanted to surprise you." He spoke.

Mrs. Fisher's eyes looked at the table, finding tall candles, the beautiful china, utensils, water cups, and even a bottle of wine, all set up perfectly in the candlelight.

Mrs. Fisher's love monitor jumped a couple levels. "Oh . . ."

Mr. Fisher lowered his hands and stood like a man weighed down by too much responsibility, "I wanted to make you happy." He shook his head, almost like he was troubled with himself. "It's been a while since I treated you, and I wanted to express my appreciation." He nodded, now more comfortable with his performance, but remained humble, "You've been an outstanding mother to our children, and I don't feel I've given you enough credit for that." He paused and took a breath. "What I want to say is . . . thank you, for being a loving mother to our children, and an even more loving wife to an undeserving husband."

Mrs. Fisher put her hand to her mouth as tears trickled down her face, and happily embraced the man she loved. The two of them held each other, letting all the pain, joy, and sorrow ebb onto the other, sharing their burdens.

Mrs. Fisher pulled apart from her husband and cupped her hand on his handsome bearded cheek. "Consider myself impressed," she said. Then smiled and gave him a wholesome kiss. "And that, is my appreciation and more," she whispered, his hands still holding her. "Shall we eat?"

Mr. Fisher held his wife close and smiled, "We shall my lady." They exchanged another kiss and took their seats. Mrs. Fisher sat down with her plate steaming, ready to dig into this wonderful meal prepared by her husband, but more appreciative of the action. It had been a while since George had done something like this for her, and it brought back some good memories. How they fell in love when they were young and stayed together despite all the strife and trouble. Cathy's mind drifted to recent events, *With what happened two years ago* . . . she thought. She caught herself. *Has it really been two years?* She felt her mood dampen and tried to hide it from George.

Cathy took her first bite and was instantly delighted. Her mood improving, feeling joyful. "This is good," she pointed with her fork, taking another bite. George seemed pleased with her answer and took a bite himself. Cathy was halfway done with her plate when she stopped, and felt the question linger on her mind. She raised her head amidst the silence and asked, "What made you want to do this?"

George stopped chewing. He looked down as if remembering something, then swallowed. "It was when Krystal decided to make dinner for our family," he said. Cathy remembered the meal Krystal had made recently, the smoking steak and the delicious vegetables, how could she forget.

"Yes, I remember," she said. "What about it?"

George lowered his head, "I was inspired when I saw the work she had done to be kind to our family, although that's not the entire reason."

"What is?"

George saddened, as if remembering the world he lived in, the difficulty and the strife just to get by. Cathy remembered George's experiences, not having a dad in his life while watching his mom struggle with her drug addiction, swearing to himself that he wouldn't wreck his family like they did. Eventually George spoke, "I remembered the kind of life that Krystal had, the problems she went through as a kid." George lifted his eyes to his wife. "That girl never had a dad. She never got to experience the joy of having a loving father. And then to lose her mom, the only person who ever loved her in a car accident. Yet despite that . . ." he breathed, catching his emotions before they leapt out beyond his control, "She still decided to care more about our family than herself." George nodded, agreeing with his own statement, yet staying humble. "And that meal she made, out of the kindness of her heart, made me appreciate what I have." He lifted his eyes to his loving wife, looking at her as if she was the treasure of his life. "It made me recognize that I haven't been grateful to you or to our family lately. I haven't been the good father I should be. Loving our kids as I must, but also loving my wife with all that I have." He paused, "A man who cannot love his wife cannot be called a man . . . And I thank God for putting someone as loving, and as kind, and as generous as you in my life, and I am deeply grateful that you are the mother of our children. Even if our family is broken, thank you for all that you've done. Both for me and our family. Thank you for the sacrifices you've made, all the times you denied yourself, all the times you hugged our children good night, and of all the times you prayed with our kids and watched them sleep soundly. Thank you for all the happy memories and thank you . . . for being my wife."

Cathy again put her hand to her mouth. Her eyes welling up with emotions she could not fathom. It was all so sudden. Where was this all coming from? This deep gratitude. But in a way she loved it. She loved it so much. Cathy gasped for air, trying not to bawl her eyes out as the tears streaked down the sides of her face. George watched her with somber observation, he had said his piece. It was done.

Cathy tried to hold herself together, weeping like a leaking dam, trying to hold it all in but utterly failing. She wiped her face with a napkin and said, "You sure know how to impress a lady." She paused, thinking of what to say but came up blank. The silence in the air growing thicker with every passing second. She threw her hands in the air, "I can't top that! I can't top that, George!" putting an elbow on the table, completely flustered with a mixture of sadness, joy, and glee. "What are you doing to me hon?" she whimpered happily. Then she sobered up like an actor switching characters for a role and spoke somberly, "I really did choose the right husband."

George got up, walked over, and stood behind his wife as she tried to calm herself. He put his hand on her shoulder; Cathy reciprocated, grabbing his hand with her own. Looking down, she whimpered, "Our family is so broken George . . ." she paused, knowing this was as fast as she could go without breaking down. "It's hard . . ." choking on her own words, "it's hard when . . . Carole's gone." George gripped her hand a little tighter. "I see her empty seat every night at this very table." Cathy let out a desperate breath, "I miss her so much."

"I miss her too," George whispered, wrapping his arms around his wife enveloping her in his warmth.

Cathy still couldn't look up, tear marks now staining her thighs. "You've been so good . . . this whole time. Keeping this family together." She nodded. "It's hard. I know it's hard on you, knowing you have to go and work, trying to keep this family together. I'm so sorry you have to go through that," she whimpered.

"It's okay." George's deep voice brought her comfort.

Cathy snorted and wiped her nose, "You've been a great and wonderful husband, don't let anybody tell you otherwise. Because I need you."

"And I need you, Cathy."

Cathy let out another desperate breath, "I miss her so much," the tears encompassed her again, as George held her there for as long as she needed.

"You've been the best husband and loving father to our children. Thank you. Thank you for being there, even when it's hard." George held Cathy closer now, reminding them of when they were young and in love. Those happy times to be lived again.

"I love you," George whispered.

Cathy broke down, "I love you too," putting her hands to her face as her husband comforted her and held her there for as long as she needed. Both of them finally feeling ready . . . to start a new chapter.

PART SEVEN

The Foreigner

CHAPTER 42

Sho

"A person can be lonely even in the presence of others."

—JL

"What is this?" Jaime held in his hand what looked like a wet napkin. He shot a look at Krystal, "What is that?"

Krystal stifled her laugh as much as she could, Jaime stared at her with an unsatisfied glare. His face crumpled with doubt and surprise as he held up the napkin and asked Krystal, "Did you do this?"

Busted. Krystal started laughing, like a scoundrel who laughed when they were intentionally caught in a crime. Jaime was more surprised by the mere act of the prank than by the prank itself. The thought never crossed his mind that Krystal had the gall to prank anyone. Jaime put the napkin down and said, "Wait a second." The thought dawned on him. He unzipped his backpack and opened it frantically.

"No, no, no no," his voice raising higher with each word, "No no no no no NO!" He threw his backpack on the lunch table. Out spilled hundreds of napkins, some of them wet, most of them dry, making his backpack look like a bag of garbage. All three of them, Kristina, Joanna, and Krystal, burst out laughing. They laughed in concert with each other. Jaime was still more surprised by the act itself than the result. He didn't care too much that his backpack was filled with paper towels; what he *did* care about was the fact that Krystal pulled a prank on someone when she was usually the most reserved person he knew. It was like ice taking a day off to go sunbathing or a cat playing fetch with its owner. It made no sense. In that moment Jaime discovered there was more to Krystal than meets the eye. So much so, that Jaime wondered if Krystal even knew that herself. And right now, he knew she liked to pull pranks.

Krystal took a mental picture of the scene. The three of them laughing as Jaime stood there holding his backpack up, intentionally looking dumbfounded. Without warning Jaime started laughing, laughing louder than the rest of them, more demanding, viler, until they all died down and Jaime was the only one laughing in the cafeteria. An evil grin streaked his lips, like a demented clown. "Alright . . . I'm game," he nodded, his voice low and cynical. His eyes filled with evil imagination. Krystal's eyes widened as the thought clicked in her brain. *What have we done?* Jaime grinned at the three of them and nodded, "You want a prank war . . . I'll give you a prank war." Then he sat down. "Enjoy today, you'll never know what might happen tomorrow."

Krystal still had some giggles in her, but now she was scared because she had just awoken a sleeping beast and given him terrible resolve. *Oh no . . .* They settled down and eventually changed the topic. But instead of focusing on the conversation in the center of the group, Krystal raised her head and did a casual scan across the room. It had become a new habit of hers, scanning for someone in the room who might look out of place. A person can be lonely even in the presence of others. They could be sitting right next to you but that doesn't mean they feel like they are part of a group.

Krystal's eyes scanned the cafeteria, from person to person. There had to be about a hundred or so people in the room. Lines of tables stretched down the hall; chatter and muffled conversation roaring throughout the room. The soaring ceilings echoing the sound, making it feel like Krystal was at a baseball game from all the surrounding chatter. Something drew her attention. Krystal prayed in her mind, *Okay Lord, who do you want me to go to now?* She closed her eyes and felt the Holy Spirit guide her attention to the right side of the cafeteria.

Krystal lowered her eyes upon a young freshman boy. He was short and young, so young in fact that it made Krystal wonder if he was truly in high school. He had a strong parting in the middle of his hairline with short black hair and had his head crumpled up into his arms. He wore a white collared shirt and plain black pants. It wasn't out of the ordinary, but he looked like a tiny man in that clothing. He couldn't have looked sadder even if he tried.

What bothered Krystal the most was that people were walking right by him and didn't notice him. The corner he sat in was closest to the boy's restroom, so people were constantly passing that corner; chatting while some of them went to use the restroom. Yet they all walked right past the boy. Not one of them giving him a single glance.

Krystal faded out of her own conversation, letting Jaime and the rest of them continue without her. Krystal stared toward the boy. Feeling her heart stir within her; an idea forming in her mind, and the fear that came along with it.

Jaime noticed Krystal's stare, "What's up?" but Krystal's attention was laser focused on the boy in front of her. Jaime followed her gaze, as did the rest of the group, until he asked, "What are you looking at?"

"Do you see that freshman over there?" she pointed. Everyone shook their heads.

"I don't know what you're talking about," said Kristina.

"I can't see anything either," replied Joanna.

"Don't you see him?" Krystal said, nudging her head in the boy's direction. "That boy, sitting alone by the bathrooms?"

It took Jaime a moment until he finally said, "Yeah I see him."

Krystal looked at Jaime and said, "Well don't you think there's something off with him?"

Jaime looked again, "I don't really know what you're talking about."

The idea slowly began forming the more Krystal looked at the boy. The final piece clicked; she knew what she had to do. Krystal stood up from the table, feeling the weight of the world crashing down upon her, making her legs weak and buckle like jelly. Jaime called out, "What are you doing?" but Krystal got up and began walking towards the boy. She knew if she stopped, she wouldn't make the trek. Satan was trying extra hard to get her to sit back down, the thoughts he planted in her mind roaring like a raging crowd begging for her to stop.

Please! Please! Please don't! You'll only make things worse! There's no greater pain than doing this! This is unbearable! It's uncomfortable! You could try again tomorrow! There's nothing wrong with the kid! You don't need any more heat on your back! Please stop!

But Krystal pushed on despite the temptations, not on her own power, but from the power of the Holy Spirit within her. It was uncomfortable,

Krystal knew that, but the possibility lingered in her mind. Krystal thought about the verse, *"Love your neighbor as yourself"* and put herself in the boy's shoes. *If I were that boy, then I would want someone to come over and invite me to sit down with them.* But again, Krystal wasn't sure if that was truly the boy's dilemma or not, but even if she was wrong, she would still offer the gesture. Be the one to offer help.

And so, Krystal walked up to the boy, and asked, "Are you alright?" The boy lifted his head and looked at her, almost shocked that someone was standing in front of him, but he didn't react, Krystal could tell because he was bracing himself for her to say something demeaning. His face was impassive and nearly unreadable. *That looks familiar,* Krystal thought, it reminded her of herself. But Krystal was able to read him just enough. She knelt down to the boy's level, speaking softly, "What's your name?"

The boy seemed hesitant to answer at first. After a brief ten seconds of silence he answered, "Sho."

Krystal gently put her hand to her chest, speaking softly, "My name's Krystal. Krystal Henninger."

"Henn-in-ger?"

"Krystal," she corrected.

"Kri-stal?"

She spoke slower, mouthing the syllables, "Kry-stal."

"Krystal-senpai?" he added.

"No, it's just Krystal," she said, not wanting to offend the boy.

But the boy said it again, "Krystal-senpai." Krystal tilted her head in confusion but let it go. There was no point in arguing with the boy. It would only belittle him.

"Sure," she said, allowing herself the title. Krystal tried to look the boy in the eyes, but he shied away. Krystal tried a different question. "Where are you from?"

"Where?" he asked. Krystal nodded. "Fah away."

"Wow, what brings you here?"

"Fahttah, work," he said in a thick accent. It was clear to Krystal that this boy did not speak particularly good English.

"How long have you been in America?"

The boy did not answer, nor did he change his facial expression. He simply shut off. Krystal wasn't sure if he understood the question.

"How long, you here?" she spoke slower for him to understand. The boy lifted his fingers. "Six? Six months?" Krystal asked. The boy nodded. Krystal looked at the boy's seating situation. Krystal reared herself to ask the question she had been waiting for. "Do you have someone to sit with?" The boy shook his head. Krystal asked, "Would you like to sit with us?" nudging toward her table. She could tell he was thinking about it, hiding his feelings that a girl came up to him and invited him to sit with her and her friends. It was so subtle even a regular person wouldn't be able to see it, but Krystal saw it briefly enough through his body language. The boy gave a timid nod. Krystal stood up and said, "Great. Let's go."

For some reason, both Krystal's tone and her demeanor felt happier than before. She wasn't sure she was doing this because she approached this boy or if she was truly feeling happier nowadays. The boy slowly stood up and followed Krystal. He was a head shorter than Krystal, which made her feel almost motherly toward him. He walked close behind her, afraid of the others towering over him. Krystal said, "Don't worry. There are good people at this table." The boy said nothing. Krystal approached the table and said, "Here, you can sit here with us."

Everyone at the table watched with observant eyes. They were all dumbfounded and awestruck with the fact that Krystal brought a total stranger to their table. None of them were entirely sure how to react. Krystal gestured to an open seat next to her own. The boy took the seat and said nothing. The whole group went silent, Krystal expected this. Read the same thought going through everyone's mind. *Who's the kid?* The whole group waited, but surprisingly Joanna chimed in and asked, "Who is this?" The boy said nothing.

Krystal then addressed the group as a whole, "Guys, this is Sho," she gestured toward the rest of the table. "Sho, this is Jaime, Joanna, and Kristina." The boy eyed them and still said nothing.

The air between Sho and the rest of the group went dry, except between himself and Krystal. Jaime decided to cut through and ask, "So what grade are you in?"

"Nynt grade." There was a thick accent on the boy. Given the boy's looks, they had to guess he was from some eastern Asian country.

"Where are you from?" Joanna asked. The boy hesitated for a minute and Krystal understood why. He went from no one seeing him to everyone seeing him. Putting him in the spotlight was like taking a pop quiz without studying.

"Japan." Everyone lit up.

Both Kristina and Joanna leaned closer and spoke in unison, "What's your country like?!" Sho gave no reaction.

"It, pretti," he said.

"Oh my gosh!" Kristina said. "He's so cute!" Both Kristina and Joanna were brimming with energy. At first, they were reluctant to talk to him but now they were hoarding over him, showing him pictures on their phones of his country. Sho reacted by crawling back into his metaphorical shell and staying close to Krystal. He stopped speaking all together but Krystal could tell he was happy inside, he just didn't show it. Maybe the girls were pouncing on him harder than Krystal intended but at least they were giving him attention, making him feel welcome.

"I'm home," Sho called, as he opened the door to his house. His mom was busy cooking dinner and filled the house with all sorts of foods and aromas. Sho stopped at the foot of the doorway and took off his shoes, placing them neatly next to his mom's.

Sho stepped into the kitchen where his mom greeted him, "Welcome home Sho." Quickly after, Sho heard the door close behind as his dad arrived also.

"I'm home," Sho's father said. They all spoke Japanese while at home. It was one of the only delights they had being foreigners in another country. Sho looked at his dad dressed finely in his suit. His father always looked good and was always on time, even for dinner. At least he paid attention to his family. They quickly dressed down and reconvened at the dinner table. Mrs. Kurosaki prepped their food and laid it out for them on the dinner table, but there was no furniture, only mats for their knees to lay on. It was a typical Japanese style dinner. Sho and everyone else paid their respects and began eating.

Mr. Kurosaki turned to his son, "So, how was school?" Sho didn't react, but he could feel his heart drag down. The gloom in his heart weighed him down. But he could not reveal that. He had to look resolute.

Sho straightened up and answered, "It was fine."

Mr. Kurosaki looked at his son with concern, this time speaking in English, "How is your English?"

Sho lowered his head. "It good."

"It's fine," Mr. Kurosaki corrected.

Sho didn't fight back, "It's fine," he pronounced, hiding his distaste for the language. Sho didn't like having to learn English, and so suddenly, be it that. His entire world was turned upside down when his dad moved to the United States for work, bringing his whole family with him. Coming to the United States without knowing the language was difficult, but getting used to the culture was a whole other matter, and Sho had never felt more like a foreigner than when he was here.

"Have you made any friends?" Mr. Kurosaki asked, reverting back to Japanese.

Sho answered respectfully to his father, "No." Mr. Kurosaki didn't react. Sho wondered what his dad's next move would be. "But," Sho's parents stopped and looked at him, "A girl did . . . come up to me and . . . invite me to sit with them."

"That sounds wonderful!" Sho's mom cheered. "Who is this girl?"

Sho didn't look up from the dinner table but continued, "I've never met her before, but her name is Krystal, Krystal Henninger."

Mrs. Kurosaki smiled, "She sounds nice."

"She is," Sho agreed. Wondering why that girl was so nice to him. Sho took his first bite from the dinner table and the conversation went on as normal. It was hard living in a foreign country, one with completely different values and ideals than his own. It made adjusting tough. Sho finished his food and said, "I'll be in my room," as he got up and went upstairs, closing the door behind him.

Sho stood there, gazing at his new room, still getting used to the scene. There was a bed, an actual bed, not a futon, and space, plenty of it. America was so different from Japan. He longed for home, feeling self-conscious despite the hardships he endured there as well. He did not miss *that* part of his home country. However, coming to America didn't help either, it was just more of the same. Sho found his typical corner in the room, hidden in the shadows cast by the moonlight and crouched.

Amidst the darkness in his room, he finally allowed himself to weep a single tear, holding the rest back with an iron will. He crouched in the fetal position. *I have no friends. I'm a foreigner in a foreign country.* He could feel the chronic discomfort. The yearning for home cried out from his heart.

I want to go home. I want to go home. But even home was not something he could have, for having that would not solve his problems. To be frank though, Sho didn't miss some aspects of home. He didn't miss the schools in Japan, for there his problems lay, and now here in America, his problems repeated themselves, again and again.

⌒

Getting out of class was a breath of fresh air. Sho held his emotions in, feeling them lump together like a ball of hot lead within his chest. At least he was out of that horrid classroom. Being in that "box" was pure torture. Aside from not knowing the language, Sho had to endure immature American students messing around while stuck in that "box" they call a classroom. *They have no windows in the buildings. At least we had windows in our classrooms back in Japan.* Sho headed to his locker, tired of carrying around heavy textbooks all day. At least they were on their break, and he could stretch his legs and get some fresh air.

Sho stood in the courtyard with lockers lined between class buildings, watching the swarms of students flow around him like a never-ending school of fish. The height difference was a problem. He felt like an ant compared to the skyscrapers around him. The encroaching presence of the crowd made Sho feel smaller, overwhelming him. All of them spoke perfect English and went about their normal lives. Sho wanted to get away, finding all the expressionism from the students too much to bear. He headed out toward the outskirts of the school but didn't feel any more relaxed. He quickly found dozens of couples making out in the corners of the school, not caring at all about who saw them, only caring about the face they were kissing. The public display of affection made Sho even more uncomfortable. Back in Japan, PDA was awkward, and yet here people were sucking face like their life depended on it. But this is not Japan, he remembered. Sho turned round and started walking, needing to get away, finding one side of the school barer than the others, suiting his needs perfectly as he caught his breath.

Sho felt the pressure encroach on all sides of his heart, dragging him down, draining all the happiness he had stored there. The darkness settled around him like snow, weighing him down as his vision drifted magnetically towards the black concrete.

He heard footsteps in front of him and looked up to find Krystal walking his way. Sho put on his self-reservation to hide his emotions, but Krystal was still a ways off and didn't seem to notice him yet. She looked preoccupied with something, looking upwards, thinking about something deep, yet still mindful of the present. Sho stopped and wondered for a moment. What was she thinking about? He read her expression. She didn't seem happy, but it wasn't sorrow either. It was a pondered acceptance. Like there was something on her mind that bothered her, but she didn't force herself to be happy either. It was a new light compared to the girl he saw the other day. The wind blew and brushed her black hair sideways, bringing out the girl's beauty. Sho felt hot blood rush to his heart.

Krystal lowered her gaze and did not appear surprised to see Sho. Krystal stopped and said, "Oh, it's you Sho." He could hear it in her voice. Something occupied her mind, but she didn't try to hide it. Why is that? Sho doused the thought. Americans were so expressive of their emotions. Sho didn't say anything. He didn't want to try to speak English with her. But Krystal asked him, "How is your day going?"

"Fine," he said. Krystal seemed satisfied with the answer, but Sho could tell she wasn't trying as hard to facilitate conversation right now.

Krystal nudged her head, "Are you heading to another class out here?"

"No." He thought about telling her, but he kept that information to himself, "Need . . . air."

"I see."

Sho wasn't sure if he was in the mood for conversation, but something about this girl seemed to relax him more than when he was around other people. "Why, here?"

"Why am I here?" Krystal asked. Sho nodded. Krystal lowered her head and answered honestly. "I don't like being around people too much." Sho was a little off put. He didn't like how direct Americans can be, but he was more surprised with the commonality between the two of them. *She can't handle crowds too?* That similarity struck Sho as odd, even for a girl like her. He showed no sign or expression of how he felt, mostly walling up his emotions like a dam deep within his soul. He wasn't going to express himself to her, not yet.

The bell rang with the five-minute warning. Krystal looked off, "Well, I have to get to class, but it was nice seeing you Sho." Krystal waved, another gesture he still wasn't used too but let it slide, and she was off. Sho raised his hand, imitating her wave back at her. He'd have to get used to that one.

CHAPTER 43

A Helping Hand

"There is a difference between loneliness and alone time."

—JL

He had done it again. Sho didn't show up at Krystal's table during lunch and found another spot around the school campus to sit by himself. He was still getting used to being around people and he didn't feel like he belonged in Krystal's group yet, which is why he stayed away, but at least lunch was the only place where he wouldn't be disturbed. People had surrounded him all morning and now he just wanted to be alone. Not that he wanted to be alone, he just needed some alone time (you see, there's a difference).

Living in a foreign country and to not be able to speak the language made socializing difficult. It was already hard enough that Sho was a shy person in general, but what made socializing in America nearly impossible was that Sho did not speak English that well. He had gone through some courses in Japan but that only took him so far. Here in America, it was the same way. Students would take a second language in high school for a few years and then forget about it once they graduated. Therefore, Sho's interactions with people were extremely limited, given the strong language barrier between them. As a result, Sho had little to no friends and could not hold a conversation except with his parents at home. It made him miss Japan, at least back there he could try to talk to someone; here he couldn't talk to anybody. He didn't want to learn the language, but he had to if he was going to live here. His parents knew the language fluently, but they didn't have time to give him lessons. He needed to go out and learn it on his own. Therefore, most of Sho's days were spent in self-exile during lunch because it was the only place where he could be alone. But with that brought loneliness as well.

Sho pulled out his bento box, (a Japanese lunch box), another memorandum of home, and ate his lunch in peace. It wasn't bad. He had found a nice grassy area around the outskirts of the school with few people where he could enjoy himself, but the enjoyment only lasted for so long. After being in the country for six months now, eating by himself had its consequences. He yearned deeply for conversation with someone other than his parents, and trying to talk with his classmates was proving more and more difficult.

Sho put his bento box aside and balled into the fetal position under a small tree. He was grateful for the shade but that was all he was grateful for. It was so different from Japan. He didn't enjoy living in America, but then again, he didn't have an enjoyable time growing up in Japan either. Some of the kids here were looking at him funny and talking about him behind his back. He could tell because he heard the word "Jap" every now and then. It didn't make things any easier when he couldn't speak the language because he was so different from everybody else. But over in Japan things were no different. His friends would constantly abandon him out of fear of being bullied. Therefore, Sho went through most of his childhood alone. It was hard, degrading, and his mental health suffered.

Sho started to tremble, but he contained it. He was waiting for someone to save him. Waiting for someone to make things better. But no one ever came, except for that one girl. Sho heard footsteps and lifted his arms covering his face to find Krystal standing there like a spirit in the wind.

"What are you doing here?" she asked, but Sho didn't hear the question. He was too encapsulated with her standing there. He looked away, avoiding direct eye contact but still saw her in his peripheral vision. Krystal waited a few more seconds before asking, "Are you sitting with anyone?" Sho shook his head. Secretly, Sho was amazed, but on the surface, he looked cool as ice. His heart was locked and overjoyed, because like the last time, someone *saw* him. He shied into the fetal position once more, like a snail retreating back into its shell. "May I sit with you?" she asked. The question did not register with Sho. He was so surprised by the action that he almost said no. Out of pure bewilderment, Sho nodded, still looking away from Krystal.

Krystal took a seat next to him, giving Sho the distance he needed. Physical contact might not have been a clever idea for the boy. He was still growing up and getting used to America after all. The two of them sat there in silence, under the shade of the tree. Krystal opened her lunch, admiring the nice weather while Sho sat there unable to comprehend the situation at all. How amazing it was that an upperclassman had said hi and had actually *seen* him. The mere action of it all gave Sho a happiness he hadn't felt in years.

Krystal took a bite of her sandwich and asked, "Can I ask you a question?" Sho looked her way but never looked her in the eyes. "Why do you come to sit here during lunch? You're always welcome to sit with us."

For ten long seconds Sho said nothing, enough to make the average person feel uncomfortable, but not Krystal. He tried his best to speak clearly, "No . . . Ing-ge-rishh."

"Oh," Krystal said, "Is that why you don't talk to people?" Sho nodded. Krystal looked up at the sky. "I see . . ." Sho brought his head down. Why was she so concerned?

Krystal glanced at him and said, "You know, I could help you learn the language . . . if you want." Sho's head lifted from his arms. Krystal saw the look of hope on his face, even though he still wouldn't look her in the eye. She could read his expression saying, *Would you really help me?* Krystal nodded happily, "Yeah." Krystal went into her backpack and pulled out a pen and paper. "How about this, every day at lunch we're going to practice your English and I'll help you get better until you can speak it. Deal?" Sho was amazed with the generous offer. No one has ever tried to do something so kind to him before. So why was she doing this for him now? What does she get out of this? He wondered. But he couldn't turn something like this down, especially from a pretty girl. So, Sho nodded.

Krystal saw the nod, "Great. Let's start right now." Sho gave no reaction but on the inside he went pale. *What?* he thought. Fear gripped Sho's heart and the discomfort of trying something he wasn't familiar with surrounded him. He wanted to avoid this sort of encounter but it was the very thing that caused him problems so he couldn't ignore it. Sho was reluctant but he followed suit. He squared up to Krystal and vice versa, still avoiding eye contact.

Krystal saw he was nervous but that was to be expected. "Try to introduce yourself." Sho looked confused. Krystal realized she had to give him an example. "Could you say, "Hello, my name is _____.""

Sho tried to perk up, but his shyness made him not as convincing. He tried to speak as best he could, "Hah-lo, my nammu isu Sho."

Krystal said, "That was really good, but let's try taking it a bit slower. Let's try saying the word, 'hello.' So say, 'hello' right now."

Sho understood and tried his best, "Hah-lo."

"Not bad, but this time, try to emphasize the 'E.' So try saying, 'Ehh.'"

"Ehh!" Sho repeated.

"Very good."

"Ehh?" Krystal forced herself not to laugh.

"Good, now put the 'H' in front of the 'Ehh' and add the 'lo.'"

Sho tried to speak slowly, knowing these actions were foreign to his tongue but that was how he would have to learn the language. "Hehh-lo."

Krystal pointed at Sho in happy accomplishment. "Yes! Now do it again." But Sho looked angered for a minute when Krystal realized she was pointing at him. She lowered her hand, "Oh sorry, pointing is rude. Sorry."

"Heh-lo."

"Good, now try saying it faster."

"Hehl-o," he said faster. His pronunciation was beginning to sound more coherent.

"Good, now try to make it flow better."

"Hel-lo."

"Yes! One more time."

"Hell-o."

"Almost there."

"Hello?"

Krystal nearly jumped. "Yes! That's perfect. Now do that again." Krystal tried not to sound so eager, but the accomplishment was almost too much to bear.

Sho tried it again, fearful of pronouncing it wrong. "Hello?"

Krystal was amazed. She pointed again, "Yes! That's perfect. Now say it like that every time." Sho saw the finger and frowned. Krystal realized her mistake and apologized. "I'm sorry. I didn't mean to do that I swear."

Sho tried again, "Hello."

Krystal erupted with glee, "Perfect! If we keep this up, then you'll be speaking English in no time." Sho wanted to smile but he kept that to himself. He looked aside and tried not to blush, but it was hard when a girl was praising him for such a small accomplishment. Sho covered his face again and Krystal smiled like a proud older sister.

The lunch bell rang, and Krystal stood up, "Well, I guess it's time for me to go. Take care Sho, I'll see you tomorrow." Sho tried to look up, but his shyness kept his eyes lowered to her feet, at least he nodded, acknowledging his gratitude. Krystal turned and said goodbye as Sho watched her walk off in the distance. Sho could not believe it. What immense kindness coming from a single person. Sho fought the urge to burst into tears. *No one has ever done that for me before* . . . Sho watched in awe as Krystal vanished around the corner like the setting sun. Then he remembered that was the first act of kindness anyone had ever done for him since he came to this country.

♫

"Good evening!" Sho called, as he took off his shoes and entered the kitchen where his mom stood making dinner.

Mrs. Kurosaki saw Sho's jovial expression, asked, "Hey Sho, did you have a good day at school?"

Sho replied with enthusiasm toward his mom, "Yes I did!"

Mr. Kurosaki entered the room and took a seat at the dinner table. "Did something happen at school today Sho?" he asked.

Sho clammed up as usual and took a seat, while his father waited patiently for a reply. He respectfully said, "Yes."

"What happened Sho?" his mom asked gently.

Sho took his time to answer, speaking in Japanese. "Krystal-senpai helped me with my English today."

"Really?" his dad said, raising his eyebrows. Sho nodded but never looked either of his parents in the eye. "What did she teach you?"

Sho knew his opportunity had come. He just hoped he wouldn't ruin it. He took a breath and said, "Hello," in English. Both of his parents were stunned. It was perfect. It came as a surprise to Sho's parents since they could both speak English fluently, but Sho had never shown any enthusiasm to learn English before. Usually, while he was at home, he spoke in Japanese because he was tired of being around English speakers all the time. But now there was an improvement, a step in the right direction.

Mr. Kurosaki smiled, said, "Well done," showing profound pride in his son. "That was excellent."

Sho didn't look up. He was still too hard on himself to feel accomplished about anything, but he did say, "Thank you, Papa."

Sho's mom chimed in. "Keep that up and you'll be speaking English in no time!"

Sho said, "That's what Krystal-senpai said too."

⌒

The next day was clear, and the sun was out. The tree providing an umbrella of shade as Krystal and Sho continue their daily English lessons.

Krystal spoke, "Okay try it this time."

Sho stuck his tongue out more to the front of his mouth. "Zzhank yuuu."

Krystal tilted her head in motherly kindness, "Almost. Try putting your tongue in-between your teeth like this." Krystal opened her mouth and stuck her tongue in between her teeth, and exhaled, making the "thh" sound. Sho tried to mimic her but failed to stick his tongue between his teeth, and instead was saying "zzz" like a bee. Krystal tried again, emphasizing the position of her tongue on her teeth. Sho adjusted and put his tongue in between his teeth more. "Now exhale." Sho exhaled, wheezing the air through his teeth. "Good. Now continue to exhale, but this time, say 'thank you."

Sho wheezed, "Thhhank yuu."

Krystal was impressed with Sho's improvement. "That was a lot better. Now shorten the 'th' and say it again."

Sho still felt uncomfortable, even though he understood how stupid he looked but how else was he going to learn. He felt like a baby learning to speak all over again. His tongue felt dry and tired, and his jaw was making motions to which he wasn't accustomed. At least the cool air around them made the setting more enjoyable as they sat on the green grass under the tree during lunch.

Sho tried again, this time slower, "Thhank yuu."

Krystal pinched her thumb and index finger together, ready for a breakthrough. "So close! Just a bit shorter."

Sho tried one more time, "Thank yuu."

"Now say 'you' but with the upper portion of your mouth."

Sho shriveled his face, "Thank, you?"

Krystal lit up like the sun. "Perfect!"

Sho was struck with joy from his accomplishment. Watching Krystal be happy made him feel happy. He tried it again, "Thank you?"

"Yes that's it! You said it perfectly!"

Sho could feel his confidence rising. "Thank you."

"Nice job!" Krystal raised a high five to Sho, but Sho looked at the hand like it was a strange object. Krystal understood and had to clarify, "Oh this is a high-five." She did a high-five with herself to demonstrate. Krystal held her right hand out, but Sho seemed a bit shy to come forward. "What's wrong?"

Sho cradled his right hand in his lap like a precious item. "No, touch."

"It's okay," Krystal reassured him, "This is a common gesture here in America." Krystal dropped her hand, killing her enthusiasm, lowering herself more to Sho's emotional level, speaking somberly, "We don't have to do it if you don't want to." Sho could see how genuine she was. It was more than enough for him to give in, so he lifted his hand. Krystal lifted hers, waiting for his hand to gently slap hers. Sho wasn't even looking, he was more afraid that he was about to touch hands with a girl. He extended his hand like a fearful child about to touch a puppy, slowly reaching his hand out until he gently tapped it against hers. Upon contact, Sho removed his hand as quickly as possible. Krystal saw the boy was embarrassed and raised a gentle smile. "Nice job," she said.

"Thank you," Sho mumbled. Krystal was surprised to hear the words come out so perfectly. He really was showing tremendous improvement.

Krystal nodded despite Sho avoiding her gaze. "You're welcome."

"Can you tell? Sho's English is getting better."

"I agree," Sho's father, Miyuno Kurosaki replied. "Nothing makes me happier than to see Sho fitting in."

His wife, Kimi Kurosaki happily answered, "It must be that girl he met. She's really helping him."

Miyuno smiled. "Either way I'm glad. I'm glad that our son finally has a friend here in America. Someone to teach him English."

Kimi replied, "How lucky we are. I'm just glad that Sho is finally fitting in. I know it's been hard on him, living here the past six months."

"It's been hard on all of us." Miyuno shifted over to comfort his wife on the side of the bed.

She whispered. "Yes. It has."

Somehow, he forgot how he got here. It was just the two of them. He and Krystal, walking side by side through the local mall. All he could remember was Krystal driving him here before he could understand what happened. *I*

think she asked me if I wanted to come with her? Sho wasn't sure if that was the case, but what mattered was that he was here. It was like a date but not. *Wait. Is it a date if she asked me? Does it work like that in this country? Do the girls ask the guys out on dates? Or is it the guys who only initiate? Or are we just friends?* Sho's mind was in a whirlwind, holding his hands close to his chest, not looking up, trying at all costs to avoid confrontation. He held his shaking hands like a prayer. He wanted to be home but would have to wait until their trip was over.

Sho looked around at all the hundreds of people walking by. His shyness was in full effect as he shriveled within himself like a turtle in its shell. He was in a whole new environment and did not feel comfortable at all. Krystal could tell Sho was nervous despite his saddened expression. She could tell he wasn't used to going out. It looked awfully familiar to her, almost too similar. Krystal could tell Sho was showing the same symptoms as her previous self. Not that it was a long time ago. They were still recent events in her life. Krystal was still shy and uncomfortable in a lot of situations; she had only grown up slightly and adjusted to it. She was still an introvert by heart, but she was an introvert learning how to be social. It was amazing what difference there was between her current self and Sho right now.

Krystal realized Sho had gone silent, so she decided to speak first. "Okay Sho, I've got some things to pick up, but before we do that, is there anything you like around here? Anything you want to do?" Sho didn't look up, shook his head. Krystal hummed in understanding. Krystal could tell Sho wanted to go home, but she had to try and get this kid to live a little or else he wouldn't do anything with his life. He will just continue to sit there underneath his tree alone and wallow in self-pity. She knew it because she had gone through it herself. So she couldn't stand there and let someone else go through that kind of pain.

Krystal said, "Let's stop over there first." Sho did not look up and followed. They went over to the candy store called Schweet Tooth and got in line. Krystal said to Sho, "Is there anything special you want?" Sho hesitated, but Krystal squatted down and encouraged him. "You can get whatever you want. It's on me." This time Krystal saw more reaction out of Sho. Could see the shyness diminish for a split second as he saw the line of sweets laid out before him. She hid her smile and watched Sho stare through the glass at all sorts of carmel apples sprinkled with various sweets. Carmel apples with tiny cookies on it, a green Frankenstein apple, and alphabet letters written in candy cane on another. Sho's eyes stared off in the direction of a Halloween-styled carmel apple, covered with small bats, and candied corn. "You want that one?" Krystal asked. Sho turned to her, still unable to look people in the eye, and shook his head. Krystal saw through his shyness, speaking softly, "It's okay if you want it." Sho looked at Krystal in his peripheral vision, wondering if it was okay. When he saw Krystal's look of approval, he turned toward the clerk and pointed.

"You want that one?" the clerk asked, pointing to a white icing apple covered with a rainbow. Sho shook his head, but Krystal said, "Sho . . . practice." Sho's eyes lit up and he suddenly realized why she brought him here. To help improve his English in real-life scenarios. It was smart thinking. He looked out among the display of apples, the intensity of the challenge intimidating him.

Sho pointed to the Halloween-style apple and said, "Can I that one, prease."

Krystal spoke over his shoulder, "Can I *get* that one, *please.*"

Sho corrected himself and tried again, "Can I . . . *get*, that one . . . *please.*" Speaking slower, knowing it was better to go slow and do it right than to go fast and learn bad habits.

"Coming right up," the clerk said.

"Very good Sho. Incredibly good." Krystal added.

Sho watched with contained excitement, lowering his guard, pressing his forehead against the class like a kid at a carnival as the clerk lifted the Halloween carmel apple over the register. Krystal paid for the apple and another for herself as the clerk handed them their apples. Krystal told Sho, "And what do we say?"

Sho turned toward the clerk, bowed, and said, "Thank you!"

The two of them left the carmel shop happy. Sho was still amazed by the carmel apple held in his hand. Sho looked at Krystal in his peripherals, while Krystal saw the look on his face and said, "Yes, you can have it." Sho lit up and chomped down, taking a huge bite, flooding his taste buds with delicious sour sugar. Sho dug into his apple, while Krystal took small bites out of hers, enjoying the sight of a happy Sho. It took Sho until they exited the mall to ask, "Don't you need . . . to get other thing?"

Krystal shook her head, "No." she smiled, "I just wanted an apple."

CHAPTER 44

Dinner

"Inviting someone into your home is a very kind gesture."

—JL

Kimi was busy prepping the noodles for tonight's dinner when Sho entered through the front door. "Hey mom!" he called. Kimi was still surprised to hear Sho sounding so jovial when he came home. He had been silent for months since they first moved to America but ever since he met that girl, he has been coming home a lot happier. Kimi finished stringing up the last bit of the noodles and said, "Did you have a good day?"

Sho nodded eagerly, "Yeah, I had a great day with Krystal!"

Kimi raised a devious smile, "I think it's time you invite her over."

Sho's smile vanished. "What?" Kimi tried not to chuckle but failed.

"You should invite her over. I would love to get to know her." Kimi watched Sho's eyes look away in contemplation. "In fact, she can come over tomorrow."

"Tomorrow?" Sho's face whitened with fear.

Kimi smiled; it was fun to get a rise out of her son. "I'll get everything ready. You won't have to worry."

Sho knew her mind was made up. There was no arguing. "Okay," he said with hesitation. "I'll text her."

Kimi smiled, "Great! Now wash your hands, dinner is almost ready."

She couldn't shake the discomfort she felt whenever she stood at a stranger's door. It was like worrying things were going to be awkward, and then things become awkward because you worry it'll become awkward. Krystal wasn't sure how this night was going to go but then again that's life, right? She held her specialized plate of brownies with care, struggling *not* to eat them. Brownies were her favorite dish and all, so Krystal couldn't help but crave her own creation. But they were not for her though, they were for Sho and his family. She didn't know whether she was supposed to bring a gift or not, especially when invited into the home of someone from another culture, so to her better judgment, she brought a gift. Better safe than sorry.

Krystal took a deep breath and exhaled, clicking the doorbell. She waited a second before a woman with short bangs and black hair, answered the door. She looked to be in her mid-thirties and spoke perfect English. "Hi! You must be Krystal." Krystal nodded but didn't say anything at first, old habits die hard. Mrs. Kurosaki recognized the same look in her son. She gestured inside, "Come in, my husband and Sho are waiting in the dining room."

Krystal opened her mouth, "I uhh . . . umm . . . made some brownies."

Mrs. Kurosaki brightened from the gesture. "That's very nice of you," taking the plate, "Please come in."

Krystal entered, finding a shoe rack at the foot of the door inside. She quickly observed that Mrs. Kurosaki did not have shoes on either and made the connection. Krystal took her shoes off and thought, *Oh gosh, I hope my socks aren't too smelly.* Krystal suddenly feared her feet would stink up the place but to her luck, they were perfectly fine.

Krystal followed Mrs. Kurosaki into the dining room but was stumped when she saw there was no furniture. Only a low table that was waist high. *Okay . . . this is new,* she thought. Krystal definitely felt she had jumped cultures now. Seeing there were no chairs and all the silverware had been replaced with chopsticks. Krystal worried, *Those chopsticks might give me trouble,* but she would make do. Krystal wanted to voice her opinion, but she did not want to be disrespectful to Sho or to his family.

Sho's father stood up from the table and stuck out a hand to Krystal, speaking in perfect English, "Hello, my name is Miyuno Kurosaki, call me whatever you like." He was a thin man, dressed in a nice white collared shirt, and had a very defined face. Krystal took the hand, but slowly, wondering if she should bow or not. She snuck a look at Sho, sitting at the end of the table. Luckily, he read her thought and shook his head, so Krystal shook the hand and didn't bow.

"It's nice to meet you, Mr. Kurosaki," she replied courteously.

Mr. Kurosaki smiled. "I hear you've been truly kind to my son. I am deeply grateful."

Krystal was a bit embarrassed; she was certainly not expecting to be complimented while in another person's home. "Oh, uhh it's nothing," she said, surreptitiously gripping her elbow with her hand.

Mrs. Kurosaki cut in, "Please wash your hands before eating." Krystal obeyed and the rest of them followed suit.

Mr. Kurosaki gestured to an open seat at the table with a pillow on the floor, "Please sit." Krystal sat in the gestured seat, trying to mimic both Mr. Kurosaki and Sho sitting at the table. Krystal saw how neatly everything was set up, the positioning of the chopsticks, the cups of tea and water, all in Japanese styling. Krystal took in the sight of the room, feeling more like a stranger in this house than in Jaime's. It certainly had a Japanese feel to it and Krystal did not want to screw anything up, especially in front of Sho's parents.

Sho seemed respectfully quiet, and Krystal could not determine whether it was rude to ask first or not. Mr. Kurosaki noticed Krystal's bewilderment as well as his son's current reticence. "You may relax Krystal. There is nothing to worry about here. Feel free to be yourself around us." Krystal exhaled and relaxed.

"So . . ." Krystal asked, hoping her question would not cause the family any trouble, "Where in Japan . . . are you guys from?"

Mrs. Kurosaki was the first to speak up from the kitchen, "We used to live in Tokyo. My husband worked there."

Krystal turned to Mr. Kurosaki, "And what do you do for work?"

"I work in one of the embassies here in America. I am part of diplomatic relations between America and Japan."

Krystal tried to hold herself together with the brevity of that statement. "Sounds heavy." Mr. Kurosaki tilted his head puzzled. Krystal saw her mistake, "Uhh, it sounds important."

Mr. Kurosaki chuckled. "It is. It takes quite a bit of work out of me. Doesn't it Sho?" All eyes were suddenly on Sho, but he simply nodded and kept his eyes on the table. Sho did his best to hide his feelings, especially since Krystal was here, but there was nothing he could do aside from go along with the dinner.

Mrs. Kurosaki brought out the food and laid it on the table. Krystal saw the deluxe platter before her: freshly cut shrimp, rice bowls, skewered fish, mixed fruit, along with clams and perfectly made miso soup. The rest of them took their seats. But before any of them could do anything, Krystal closed her eyes, put her hands together and made a quick prayer. "Thank you," she whispered.

Krystal opened her eyes to find they were all staring at her. Krystal suddenly felt embarrassed. Mrs. Kurosaki eased her discomfort, smiling, "You said thanks before we did."

Krystal's eyes widened, "Oh, I'm so sorry!" but Mr. Kurosaki raised a hand.

"Do not worry yourself." He put his hands together as if to pray and everyone else followed on cue. Krystal did the same out of respect and they all said their thanks and began eating. Krystal wasn't sure what kind of impression her prayer made but she could tell that Mr. Kurosaki was looking at her with curiosity.

Amidst eating, Mrs. Kurosaki spoke, "So tell us about yourself Krystal."

Krystal swallowed, checking if there was any food in her teeth. Definitely on high alert for table manners tonight. "Uhh," she said, struggling to find a suitable answer. "I was born and raised here. My life is not that exciting so . . ." she trailed off, her mind drifting elsewhere. Krystal caught herself and picked up where she left off, "I don't really have . . . a good answer to that."

"That's quite alright," said Mrs. Kurosaki.

Mr. Kurosaki chimed in, "My son tells me you've been very kind to him lately." Krystal was a little embarrassed. She wasn't used to being in the spotlight for doing a good deed.

Krystal said, "Oh, well, Sho is a pretty awesome person so . . ." she looked in Sho's direction, but she only made him blush.

Mr. Kurosaki recognized the friendship his son had made, and said, "I'm glad Sho has a friend like you." That compliment stunned Krystal. For a moment she didn't react, then she lowered her head, as if in shame, "Thank you."

Mr. Kurosaki looked a bit confused. Krystal recognized the confusion and raised her head, "I'm sorry. Uhh, I'm just . . . going through something right now." Her mood turned sullen as her mind drifted toward a dark corner.

Mr. Kurosaki nodded, "I understand completely."

"Thank you," Krystal said, bowing her head unintentionally, realizing she possibly offended the family with her gesture. But Mr. Kurosaki showed no sign of offense, in fact, he was more lighthearted than she thought, looking at her with a genuine smile. Krystal met his eyes to see if she had done wrong, but Mr. Kurosaki eased her fears, "You're okay, do not worry." Krystal breathed, unsure whether anything she did could be misinterpreted as an offense.

"Okay. Thank you."

The rest of the dinner went well. Sho did not talk much, he was too busy trying not to blush at the dinner table. When they finished, Mrs. Kurosaki got up and picked up some of the plates and Krystal began picking up plates too. Mrs. Kurosaki saw her and said, "Oh you don't have to."

But Krystal kindly replied, "It's no trouble," and lifted the remaining plates off the table. Both Sho and Mr. Kurosaki watched as the two women cleaned the dishes together, even sharing a laugh between them. Mr. Kurosaki watched the two of them and thought, *She has a good heart.*

Krystal finished helping with the dishes and realized it was time for her to leave. She slowly went and put her shoes on. "Thank you very much," she said, giving a nervous bow, making sure she wasn't offending anyone. But the Kurosakis showed no sign of offense, either letting the mishap slide or they were delighted by the girl's formality and respect. Most likely the latter. Krystal closed the door behind her, leaving the Kurosakis in the quiet air of the hallway.

"I like her," said Mr. Kurosaki.

"She seems lovely," his wife replied.

The two of them looked at their son and Mr. Kurosaki said, "You've got yourself a good friend," nodding, "She has my approval."

Sho could only blush as he stared forward.

Jaime watched with concern as Krystal waited in the lunch line. "Hey, have you noticed something's wrong with Krystal?" Jaime turned to Joanna. Neither Sho nor Kristina had shown up yet to the lunch table, so it was just Jaime and Joanna. "She seems a bit gloomy these days. I'm curious if something's happened."

"I don't know," Joanna said, "I can't tell what she's thinking sometimes. She's hard to read."

Jaime didn't say anything and returned his gaze toward Krystal waiting in line. He could see it there. That saddened expression. It was one that was hopeful yet sad. The sight of it worried Jaime. Krystal had been improving in her mood and attitude over time but recently she looked sad.

Jaime watched closer and wondered, *I hope she's okay.*

CHAPTER 45

Testimony

"For how can you possibly recognize a lonely person
when you have never been lonely?"

—Krystal Henninger

"How are you doing today?"

Sho answered slowly but more confidently, "I'm . . . doing good. How are you?"

Krystal put her backpack down. "I'm fine. Just a little tired." Krystal sagged down and leaned her backpack against the tree, looking up at the fine blue sky. For a moment neither of them said anything. The two of them just enjoyed the outdoors as the cool wind blew, watching the leaves fly by. Krystal closed her eyes and let the wind brush against her, feeling her long black hair flurry in the wind. She looked more tired than usual lately.

Sho twiddled his thumbs, his heart already racing. "Can I ask you . . . a question?"

Krystal kept her eyes closed, soaking in the nice weather. "Sure."

Sho built up his courage, bracing himself. "Why . . . are you so . . . nice to me?" Krystal slowly opened her eyes and noticed Sho was looking directly at her. The sight of his black eyes was mesmerizing, like ancient gemstones staring back at her. Actually seeing him face to face made all the difference. Krystal was finally able to see the emotions on his face laid bare. In those eyes, she could see the curiosity as well as all the other emotions he was carrying. In his heart, she could sense the yearning for value and the years of loneliness he carried, as well as the bullying, the constant bullying. It was the first time Sho had looked somebody directly in the eye.

Krystal leaned forward, meeting Sho's gaze with her own. She let out a breath and lowered the mood. "Because . . ." she paused, "you're just like me." Sho cocked his head back, bewildered. *Just like me?* he thought. *How in the world is she just like me? There is no feasible way we are the same.*

Krystal continued, "You may be wondering what I mean by that. To be honest, it's hard to explain. But if you saw me a few years ago you would've said we looked identical." Krystal broke her gaze and looked up into the sky. "Lonely people have a way of spotting lonely people. We all look the same. It's hard to explain but . . . when you're lonely, you can tell when someone else is too. It's like knowing what war is like. You don't know what it's like until you've been in combat. The same goes for loneliness. You don't know what it looks like until you've gone through it. For how can you possibly recognize a lonely person when you have never been lonely?"

"I don't understand." Sho was now giving Krystal his full attention. He had never looked directly at someone for so long. It was beginning to unnerve him.

Krystal made a circular gesture toward the school. "Growing up here was not easy. I remember every day, I would walk these hallways, because I had nowhere to go. Every day, I would eat my lunch on my white bench and watch all the groups and cliques around school talk with each other, watching them have the time of their lives." Krystal took in a painful breath, reliving the experience. Sho could tell it shook her, but she dived back into them anyway. "Trying to live wasn't easy. I would wake up every day feeling empty. I would go to school and feel ostracized and unwanted. I would hate every minute of being here simply because nobody wanted me here. I would go home, do my homework, and then go to bed hoping it would all get better. But it didn't get better. Years went by and I started to suffer from suicidal thoughts. I began to believe that I didn't matter, that I was invisible. That if I got up and left the room, nobody would notice."

Krystal took another painful breath but was more resolute this time. She turned and faced Sho, then pulled down the sleeve on her left arm, revealing a massive two-inch scar on her left wrist. Sho stared at the wound, his eyes wide, as she said, "A year ago, my mom got into a car accident, and I lost her . . ." Krystal paused. She took a breath and recollected herself. "She was the only one who loved me . . . and when I lost her . . . I took a kitchen knife and slit my wrist." Krystal waited long enough for Sho to get a good look at the horror laid out on her left wrist. She rolled up her sleeve. "I ended up in the hospital where I met a Janitor. And there he showed me kindness when no one else did. He said hi to me and listened to me. He gave me a brownie and told me about God and how he has great hope for someone like me . . . and because of that, he changed my life.

"After that I started going to church. I learned about God and how much He loves us. And because of that, I started to change. I started to breathe again. I began to wake up with hope for the first time, knowing I had purpose and value in life. One thing led to another and here I am today. So there. That's the answer to your question."

Krystal looked Sho directly in the eyes and awaited his answer. Sho stared intently, but he wasn't staring at her directly. He thought of all the memories of his life and compared it to hers. Remembering the days of sitting alone by himself in Japan. All the days of being bullied and ostracized. All the times when he felt worthless and didn't deserve to live. All the friends who abandoned him out of fear of being bullied. Every memory came flooding back to his consciousness. He understood exactly what she was saying, because he had gone through everything she had. It was too similar. And yet, what astounded him the most was how a girl like her was ostracized from her own society, yet she physically looked no different than anybody else in this school. The same thing happened with Sho. He didn't have anybody to care for him when at school, didn't have any friends who stuck around. No reason to be happy or to find value in his life. He remembered all the days when he just wanted to lay down and die. Yet . . . that's not the end of the story. Because here and now, Sho could tell this girl is truly and genuinely happy. She has something about her that brings her joy despite all the darkness in her past. It was like . . . no matter what life threw at her; it could not rob her of her joy. It was nothing short of remarkable.

No. It was an example. Not for her, but for him. Because if this girl can go from broken to beautiful, then maybe he could too?

Sho thought, *This girl is a living miracle. Having gone through the darkness early in life. After having been mistreated and outcast from her own society and told she doesn't matter, yet she still finds a reason to smile.* Just the mere sight of her brought Sho a new sense of hope.

"Do you think I can find hope like you did?" he asked, completing his sentence perfectly.

Krystal smiled and said, "You can. With Jesus Christ."

"How?" Sho didn't fully understand but he knew he trusted Krystal and that she had something that he wanted.

Krystal raised a soft smile, extending her hand out, palm up. "Give me your hands."

Sho blushed. "What?"

"Give me your hands," she said softly. Making sure to not pressure Sho in the slightest. Sho obeyed and offered Krystal his hands. She took them and Sho felt the warmth from her hands pour into him. It was like holding onto a light, allowing its heat to warm his cold hands and permeate his body with love and kindness he didn't think was there. "Close your eyes."

"What?"

Krystal held his hands tighter, making Sho blush even more. "Close your eyes," she whispered, closing her eyes. Sho obeyed. "Will you pray with me?" she asked.

"Hai." (That means yes)

Krystal bowed her head. "God, I believe that you are Lord of my life." Krystal waited while Sho repeated. "Jesus please come into my life and forgive me of my sins, and I will repent and follow you." Krystal opened her eyes to watch Sho finish the last sentence, and whispered, "That's how you find hope."

Sho looked up and for once, he didn't fear looking into Krystal's eyes. Krystal gave Sho a warm smile. Sho couldn't help but share in Krystal's enthusiasm as his lips widened and brought out the sweetest smile he had ever felt. The mere words were so simple, yet they penetrated the deepest portions of his heart. He couldn't explain it, but he could tell Krystal was glowing. And he could feel a warm presence flowing into him, permeating every part of his body and soul with healing from all the years of ostracism. In a moment, his life had changed, and he knew he would never be the same.

He sniffed and tried to hold back the tears, but it was too late. The words struck deeper than he ever imagined. Sho broke down crying while Krystal extended her arms and comforted him.

PART EIGHT

Awakening

CHAPTER 46

Dinner Time

*"It amazes me how far I've come in life. I'm surprised every time I realize
I'm still breathing. I was so close to death and yet here I am breathing
and happy. That makes me think that if I can change, so can others."*

—Krystal Henninger

Krystal finished putting away her books, closed her locker swiftly,
and gave the handle a quick spin. *It's odd,* she thought, contemplating the
fact that for once she had somewhere to go during lunch. It felt weird, like a
country that had been on the verge of starvation, now drastically going into
the most lucrative harvests they've ever seen. Krystal leaned her arm against
her locker, breathing deeply. *It's okay. It's okay. You'll get better at it. Don't
you worry.* She did worry though. Krystal finally had friends. *Real* friends,
unlike the last group where Summer and Amber simply ignored her. But
things were different now. Krystal was talking more. She was more active. Of
course, she wasn't the best at it but that would get better in time. Krystal was
still in high school after all. But the biggest difference of all was how she felt.

Krystal pushed away from her locker and headed towards her new spot
in the lunch cafeteria. It was strange. Different, but strange. It's like she had
stepped into the light and was being seen for who she was rather than the
loner she had built herself to be. Now, Krystal was no longer alone, and it
felt . . . strange. For some reason, a part of her missed being alone; she had
argued with herself over that but couldn't deny it. It's not that she didn't want
friends, in fact Krystal wanted that more than anything. But it was *new.*
It was uncomfortable. It wasn't predictable like the pain she understood. It
helped take away the ambiguity in her life because Krystal could see her boring, monotonous life played out in front of her by doing the exact same thing

every day. But in that same routine, lay her previous suffering. A routine and lifestyle that nearly killed her. Krystal had come dangerously close to death, and if she hadn't found God in her life, then she would be just another grave without a tombstone.

Krystal controlled her breathing, her heart pounding within her. Relishing in the fact that she was alive and well today because of the love of Jesus. And it felt . . . good. It was different and outside her comfort zone, but it was different in a better way. Her life was changing into healthier habits. Her attitude was becoming more pleasant and hopeful. She could feel her rude, no BS attitude lighten a bit. Like a coal miner finally seeing the sun after a long day in the shaft. She couldn't put her finger on it exactly, but her life was better. She could feel it. And she wanted to share these feelings with others. This hope, she had been given, she wanted to share it with everyone around her. She could feel it already happening with her friends, and Krystal didn't want it to stop. She wanted to grow with these people and help them, but that was God's job not hers.

For now, Krystal would settle and be content that she had friends, period. Friends she had prayed for for so long. Even years before she believed in God, she still wished for friends to come into her life. And now Krystal had found friends from the weirdest places. She knew they all had something in common, a pain that each of them shared. The struggle of loneliness. It boggled her mind, confusing her when she thought of the upbringings of some of these people. Something she wished she knew so much sooner in life. And the truth is . . . No matter what your upbringing or social life. Everyone suffers at some point.

Krystal found relief in that. It was a strange way to think of it, almost selfish to be glad someone is in your same boat, and she knew that but still . . . when she thought about Jaime, the most popular guy around school, who has a lot of friends and a great family; but when it came down to the hard points in life, he didn't have anyone close to him. He had "friends," but he didn't have any close *friends*. No one to be there when he was hurting. No one to text and check to see if he was okay. No one, except his family, but he's not exactly on the best terms with them right now.

And then there was Kristina. She was the same as Jaime. Although she is one of the most popular girls in school, Kristina Walker, the Actress, still suffered from loneliness. Krystal learned that Kristina doesn't trust anyone around her, and nobody cared for who she really was. Kristina keeps a mask on and lies to everyone around her out of fear of them seeing who she really is. Unlike Jaime who doesn't hide it, Kristina hides it behind a mask of energy and happiness. A mask that weighs on her until she eventually breaks down. Krystal felt empathy for Kristina. She knew Kristina only wished for someone to get to know *her* and not Kristina Walker the Actress, but things were getting better between the two of them.

And then there was Joanna Watson. A girl who used to be close friends with Amber and Summer McAdams but was later outcast from their group. In her desperate attempt to make friends, Joanna would hang out with whoever she needed to fit in. Joanna feared the expectations of others and suffered from the rumors spread around the school about her by Summer and Amber, a bridge Krystal knew she would have to cross soon. And so, Joanna feared being around Krystal sometimes, because Krystal was the loner girl Summer and Amber hated. Krystal could tell part of Joanna still wanted to be in Summer's group, but Joanna was beginning to warm up to Krystal and the rest of the group now, so things were generally okay.

And then there was Sho, the most recent addition to the group. A freshman year boy raised in Japan, having to live as a foreigner in another country. But Krystal could see a lot of potential in Sho. Like her, he struggles with shyness. Hopefully, that will change. All in good time. But at least Sho made the effort to come back to the group during lunch, having learned enough English to hold a conversation. It was a process, but Krystal hoped that all of them would grow in the future.

And so, Krystal walked out toward the lunch table; the mood of the school had shifted as a new group had formed. A group of popular kids, shy kids, loners, and actresses, all having one thing in common, loneliness.

"H—hey guys," Krystal said. Everyone stopped and looked at her. She suddenly seemed pale and sweaty. "Do . . . do you guys have any plans this weekend?"

Jaime said, "Let me check," pretending to flip through an imaginary booklet, "Nope." Jaime gestured to Kristina, "What about you Kristina?" he asked.

Kristina looked up at the ceiling, "I don't think I have anything. Nothing out of the ordinary of course."

Eyes shifted to Joanna, quickly checking her phone, "I don't think I have any plans. So I guess I'm free."

Kristina looked over at Sho, "Sho, you got anything planned?" Sho shook his head.

Krystal shriveled up a bit, hesitant to ask, "Would . . . would you guys like to come over to my house for dinner?"

"Like you make food for us, and we show up and eat it?" said Jaime eagerly. Krystal nodded shyly. Jaime shrugged his shoulders, "I'm in."

"Why not," said Kristina.

"Sounds fun!" Joanna added.

"Okay," Sho whispered.

Krystal suddenly felt very hopeful and surprised by how everyone was free for once. "Okay." she said, "I'll see you guys this Saturday at six?"

Everyone nodded, then finished eating. *Not a bad lunch*, Krystal thought.

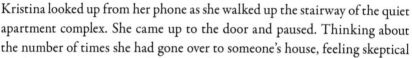

Kristina looked up from her phone as she walked up the stairway of the quiet apartment complex. She came up to the door and paused. Thinking about the number of times she had gone over to someone's house, feeling skeptical when she found that person only wanted to hang out with *Kristina Walker, the Actress*. She knocked on the door a few times and waited. Kristina was a couple minutes late but that was to be expected.

The door opened and Krystal welcomed her in, "Hey. Come on in." Kristina walked into the living room, taking in the sights. Sho was sitting at the dining room table waiting patiently while Jaime lay asleep, spread on the couch like he owned it. Sho even brought Krystal a gift, making everyone else wonder if they should have brought something too. Joanna walked in a moment later and everyone greeted one another. Kristina looked around the apartment and thought, *It's so clean.* She didn't know why she noticed that. She thought back to her own room, how spick and span it was when she left. A whiff of food caught Kristina's scent as she smelled something cooking in the air.

Krystal retreated behind the kitchen counter, tending to the curry and potatoes, while the smell of hot spices and curry powder loomed in the air. Krystal dropped a spatula while working, causing Joanna to ask, "Do you need help?"

"If you'd like that'd be great." Krystal invited.

Kristina stepped up too, "I mean, I'll help too. What do you need?"

Kristina saw Krystal pause a moment, more in awe as she watched both

Joanna and Kristina pull their hair up, getting ready to help her. Krystal said, "Here, Joanna, you can mash the potatoes, and Kristina, you can chop the vegetables. I'm sorry I'm late with dinner. Things took longer than I expected."

"That's okay," Kristina said. She wasn't sure why she was helping, but it felt like the right thing to do. They all got to work; the kitchen full of life while Jaime lay flat on the couch like a tired husband after a long day of work while Sho sat patiently like an orderly child awaiting instructions as the girls finished prepping dinner.

"You got the vegetables?" Krystal asked.

"Right here." Kristina said. She offered Krystal the vegetables and thought, *It's strange. Here, I feel like my guard is down. Like I'm more relaxed. Acting like myself for once.*

Joanna said eagerly, "I've finished with the potatoes."

Krystal turned and said, "Perfect, give them to me and I'll finish up." Joanna and Kristina waited there for a moment, but Krystal waved them away and said, "You guys can take your seats. I'll dish out the food soon." Kristina obeyed and followed Joanna over to the kitchen table.

Jaime got up like an old man from his slumber, while Sho was already seated, looking uncomfortable from the set up. Kristina took her seat and asked Sho across the way, "Do you ever miss home?"

Sho said, "Hai" but not as loud. He corrected, "Yes," thinking hard to translate, "I . . . miss . . . home."

Sho looked away as if hiding something. Kristina wanted to dive deeper, but Krystal interrupted, "Dinner's ready." Krystal handed out plates full of curry, mixed in with vegetables, seasoned chicken, along with mashed potatoes and peas. The food looked amazing. The powdery scent flooded the apartment building like a hot box of spices. Kristina relaxed from the smell and couldn't wait to dig in.

Krystal took her seat and a moment of silence settled. Everyone was unsure of how to proceed, but Krystal put her hands together and said, "Do you . . . do you guys want to say grace?"

Kristina hid her surprise. She looked around checking faces only to find Jaime sitting there, brooding at Krystal. Krystal recognized Jaime's expression and lightened her tone, not out of fear or intimidation but because she didn't want to cause a scene. Krystal looked straight at Jaime, "We don't have to if you don't want to." The comment defused Jaime and he relinquished his stare from the gentle comment.

Joanna spoke up, "I'm totally down for it if you guys are," sounding a little too eager.

Kristina could tell Joanna was feeling the room, trying to determine which side had the majority. Shoulders shrugged but it was Sho who said, "Let's do it." Krystal offered her hand to Joanna and the other to Kristina. Kristina hesitated but took it. In unison, they all took each other's hands and bowed their heads, except for Jaime.

Krystal led in prayer, saying, "Lord, thank you so much for this food. It truly brings joy to my heart to have these people here in my life. Thank you for getting us through the journey and bringing us all here together. In Jesus' name, amen."

Kristina opened her eyes. It was the first time she'd ever said grace before. It caused Kristina to think of her own family. The dinners they had together. *What are you talking about? What dinners?* That part was true. Kristina thought back to the many days of having dinner at home, where even her discussions with her parents were fake. Both of Kristina's parents were excellent liars. Honesty was not a shared commodity in Kristina's household, and so, opening up, and being yourself was not a common thing. That's why Kristina struggled to be open and honest with the people around her, it was hard to find people you trust. To find somebody you could be gut-level honest with and not feel judged or criticized. It became such an unhealthy lifestyle at home that Kristina couldn't be herself at all. It was one of the reasons why she goes out so much. But living a lie 24/7 caused her life to feel hallow, and she had no one to share it with, not even her parents.

So Kristina couldn't trust them. She couldn't trust anyone. She loved working as an actress and wanted to pursue it, but due to her recent panic attacks and high anxiety, she was unable to return to the profession. It sucked because she still didn't have an answer to her anxieties yet. She still didn't know who she was.

She glanced over at Krystal, watching her eat her food. Kristina thought back to when she first met Krystal, when she was asleep in the classroom, then later at the party. It was odd when Kristina met her, because for the first time Kristina found someone who didn't care about who she was as an actress. Krystal saw the loneliness inside Kristina and comforted her anyway, and Kristina would never forget that. Suddenly Kristina felt relieved to know Krystal. How underappreciated a person she truly is. And here she was, feeding them all dinner of her own accord. *She's more mature than anyone I know.* Kristina smiled at that remark.

Maybe . . . maybe I can be different too? she thought.

Krystal looked at Kristina, "Are you alright?"

"What?" Kristina didn't register the question. Kristina deflected the question and put on her cheerful persona. "Of course I am! I couldn't be happier." But Kristina could not fool Krystal, so Krystal didn't say anything to correct her. Krystal just looked at Kristina with concern and let it slide. Kristina felt a stab in her heart from that. Knowing Krystal liked Kristina more when she acted like herself.

The dinner table had grown eerily quiet. Kristina took her gaze away from Krystal and inadvertently found Jaime glaring heavily across the table like he was about to murder somebody. "Jaime . . . you doing okay?" Kristina asked cautiously.

"Fine," he replied, allowing everyone to hear the anger in his voice.

"Are you su—" but Krystal cut Kristina off.

"Just drop it. He doesn't want to talk." Kristina refocused on Krystal, surprised she had the ability to interrupt anyone at all. Everyone went back to eating in silence. Krystal took a bite from her food, feeling the mood in the air, but she said nothing, her mind elsewhere.

It was Joanna who first spoke up, wanting to change the conversation. "So, Krystal, this is where you live?"

"That's right," Krystal nodded.

"Where are your parents?"

Jaime stopped chewing and the room fell silent. Krystal didn't look up from her plate of food for a full minute. "I don't have parents," Krystal said. "These days I just live with my Aunt Sarah."

"What happened?"

Krystal didn't hesitate to answer, she spoke nonchalant, "I lost my mom in a car accident a year ago, and my dad . . . I never knew my dad," looking up from her food to meet Joanna's horrified gaze. Joanna's shock was more from Krystal's casual admittance of something so dark. Yet it was her past, and a recent one at that.

"I'm sorry."

Krystal lowered her head, "It's okay," the room feeling a little more open somehow. Kristina wondered what memories Krystal was reliving. Surprisingly, Krystal smiled and looked up and said, "You know . . . I really am grateful to you guys. You've been a huge help to my life recently."

Kristina coiled back slightly. *Thank us? For what?*

Krystal spoke up, trying to sound happy but everyone could hear the sorrow fill her voice, "It's . . . it's been hard lately. I know things have not gone well, but . . . I'm really glad you're all here," watching twin tears streak down Krystal's cheeks. Kristina felt her heart melt. Even Jaime seemed to relax a little but maintained his sulking demeanor. Kristina leaned forward, laying a hand on Krystal's shoulder. She wasn't sure why she was doing it, it just felt like the right thing to do. The scent of the warm curry, mixed in with powdered sauces and seasoning made the room feel even more welcoming. Putting her hand on Krystal's shoulder brought a warmth to Kristina's heart she hadn't felt before. It was like Krystal was glowing and Kristina could feel the warmth of the sun emanating from her. It felt so relaxing, so open, so free. And Kristina wanted it. Whatever *this* was. Watching Krystal be open made Kristina unconsciously feel more comfortable herself.

Kristina has gone through so much betrayal from people who all wanted to get close to her simply because she was a famous actress, but now, it was a change of pace watching another person show gratitude toward Kristina for being close to her. It made Kristina's defenses lower; *Can I be this open? Can I cry like that in front of other people and feel accepted?*

Sho got up from his chair and even Joanna came over to comfort Krystal. The three of them comforted her and put their hands on Krystal while Jaime watched from across the table. Krystal cooled off and wiped her nose. "Thank you," she whispered, regaining her composure. Smiles were exchanged and Joanna said, "It's alright Krystal. Don't worry about it. I totally know your mom is in a better place."

Krystal sighed in relief. "I'm sorry, I know I shouldn't have gotten like this it's just . . . there's been something on my mind lately. It's been coming up and I've known it was going to do this to me."

"What is it?" Kristina asked.

Krystal wiped her face and said, "Do you guys want to take a field trip?"

CHAPTER 47

Revelation

"Do you know what it's like to feel invisible?
To be treated like you don't exist?"

—Krystal Henninger

Jaime felt terrible because of earlier. Not because he had done anything wrong but because of his lack of empathy from the earlier situation. Krystal was crying at the dinner table, but Jaime felt anything but empathy. He felt completely disconnected, not because he wasn't empathetic, but because he was so focused on his own problems that he didn't care about who else was hurting around him. There was a war going on in his soul and mind against God.

God why? Why? Why?! How could you let something like that happen? He let his bitterness take over and distract him from the situation at hand. Jaime didn't even bother to comfort Krystal at the table as she cried. Jaime tried to listen to the situation, but his heart and mind were dragged elsewhere. Now they were in a car going to a place only Krystal knew.

Jaime didn't want to be like this. He didn't want to be that guy who didn't care about others' pain simply because he was dealing with his own. But he was, and he hated himself for that. *Come on man! Have a little empathy for those around you.* But he could feel it inside, his true self, arguing back, *"No,"* shaking his head in disapproval. Jaime was so caught up in his own anger that he was losing interest in others around him. It made him bitter and resentful, spiraling deeper into a pit of his own creation. *Why can't I just move on?*

They pulled up to a hospital and entered the waiting room, Krystal leading the way. She seemed to know where she was going. Jaime and the rest of the group followed. For Jaime, tearful memories flooded his mind being in the hospital. He hated hospitals. He hated them with a passion, not because they were places of healing but because they were places where people died. Where families would sometimes see their child get better, only to find them dead where they lay.

They went up to a nurse at the front desk. Krystal approached her and said casually, "Hey Darla."

Darla looked up and said, "Hey! Krystal. It's wonderful to see you again." Krystal returned the kind gesture. Darla nudged in the direction of a nearby hallway, her tone lowered, speaking somberly, "She's right where you left her."

Krystal said thank you, but Jaime and the others could tell Krystal's manner had grown more serious. They all backed off, giving Krystal space. Even Jaime was a little scared of her. He had never seen this side of Krystal before. He could tell you didn't want to be on her bad side. She was like a bomb waiting to go off.

Jaime was already running through simulations in his mind of what he was going to find. He had a fairly good idea, but guessing was only half the battle. Krystal stopped in front of a doorway labeled 2E and stared inside. The rest of the group watched as Krystal took a deep breath and walked in. The group followed at a distance, peering into the doorway. Jaime felt the bitterness rise within him, causing him to lose interest, but he never could prepare himself for what he saw.

Everyone looked in, horrified. Krystal stood there alone with her back turned toward them, looking down at a woman sleeping in a hospital bed. Jaime's first thought was the woman was dead; maybe she was.

After sixty seconds of pure silence, Krystal finally spoke up, "One year ago, my mom got hit by a pickup-truck and was put into a coma." Krystal turned and faced the group. What horrified Jaime was not the sight of Krystal's mom, but how stone-cold Krystal's expression was. He had seen her cry before but here was a Krystal more stoic than all of them combined. No, it wasn't stoic. It was hardened. It was Krystal hardening her heart right before them, etching itself onto her face. The iron glare, the cold midnight purple eyes, glaring back at them like she was staring death in the face and felt no fear. Krystal ended the death stare and exhaled, softening her heart and expression.

Krystal turned her back toward them and faced her mom again. "Shortly after that I tried to kill myself. I was in so much pain I wanted to end it all." She shook her head, "So I put a knife to my wrist and tried to take my own life. Surprisingly, I didn't die. Somehow, I did it wrong, and ended up in this very hospital." Jaime wanted to say something, but he knew it would be rude to interrupt. "It was shortly after I arrived here that I encountered a Janitor. A man very kind and caring, who brought me a brownie and listened to me while I lay in bed recovering from my injury." Krystal turned, half facing the group, letting her hair cover most of her face. "I know it may not sound important, but my life up to that moment was utter hell. Growing up I didn't have any friends. I was ostracized constantly. You may not understand, but just the act of someone *looking* at me was a miracle. I would sit alone at school every day, yearning for someone to come up and talk to me, for someone to welcome me into their group and to feel accepted . . . but I never received that. Every day people would pass by me like I was invisible. I questioned my own existence more times than I could count. I would ask, 'Would anybody even care if I disappeared?' And for years, no one saw me. I felt like a ghost. I felt invisible. Like I was a nobody. A loser, a loner, who didn't have any reason to live, let alone to hope. And I would go home, and my mom would ask me, 'How was your day?' and I would tell her, 'It was the same as yesterday' and try not to cry."

Krystal looked straight at Jaime, "Do you know what it's like to be *invisible*? To not be seen no matter how hard you try? To be excluded for no reason at all? To be treated like you don't exist? But then I can't put all the blame on others now, can I? Because it's not like I tried to be social either. I didn't go out of my way to make friends with others. I just expected everyone to be friends with me. I ignored other peoples' pain because I was too busy focusing on my own." That struck a chord in Jaime's heart.

Oh crap . . . she's the same as me! he thought.

Krystal slowly faced her mom, putting a hand on the bed railing. "So I went through the motions, trying my best to get through the day, but through it all I felt empty. And I had this hope that there was something more to life than this. And then I lost my mom . . . that's when I hit my breaking point." She shook her head. "I couldn't take it anymore. My one pillar of support . . . was taken from me."

Jaime's heart was struck again. *That's . . . just like me*, he thought in shocking wonder. He didn't want to feel a resemblance to Krystal, but he did. His heart made the connection without his permission, and Jaime could feel its effects hitting him right in his core.

Krystal faced them and pointed at the ground, "But then here, in this very hospital, that Janitor showed me kindness when I didn't deserve it. He didn't know me, he didn't understand my circumstances, and yet . . . he was kind to me. Simply because Jesus taught him how to love. He listened to my story and let me speak for as long as I wanted, even when his shift had long ended." Krystal's voice was beginning to falter. It was getting difficult to control her emotions. "Do you know what relief I felt when someone actually *saw* me?! Someone who took the time out of their day and listened to me? Allowing me to rant and go on about my story? To unload all my burdens and share my sufferings? Do you know what kind of relief that's like? I hadn't felt that good in years, and I still remember the feeling. Of God telling me, 'Krystal, *you matter*' through this man." She paused. "And that was it. That Janitor told me, 'I have great hope for someone like you,' and I instantly wanted to cry, because no one had ever said that to me before."

Krystal looked at them with a hard stare and gestured to herself. "You may believe that God doesn't exist but LOOK AT ME! Look at my story! Look at how different I've become and for the better. Look at me!" Jaime felt all this was directed at him. He could feel every word, every syllable reaching him, no matter how hard he fought against it. "You may not believe in God, but look at my story, look at the fact that I'm still *alive*! The very fact that I'm here is a miracle!" She paused and took a quick breath. "And now . . . I feel whole. I feel joy, and love. I have a purpose in life. A reason to live. A reason to breathe. A hope to get out of bed in the morning.

"Believe what you want, but this is what happened to me. And this is my story." Passion filled her voice, "You can argue all you want about God not existing, but I'm telling you, THERE IS A GOD!" Jaime coiled back and tried to hide it, but it was like Krystal was shouting directly at him, her words targeting his heart while the rest of the group looked at her with more compassion and empathy while Jaime was horrified and angry from how accurate her words were hitting him. "I swear, I'm telling you," Krystal's voice choked up from the tears flooding her face, "I wouldn't be alive if it wasn't for Jesus Christ!" She pointed to her heart, stabbing hard into her sternum, her voice so passionate that Jaime felt Krystal was going to break down and fall to her knees from how hard she was speaking. "I have felt that hole in my heart. I have felt the *emptiness* inside. I experienced guilt, guilt from taking my own life." Krystal pulled her sleeve down to reveal a two-inch-long scar across her wrist. The sight of it horrifying Jaime. "And because of that I have this scar on my wrist!"

Krystal turned and faced her mom again, her voice lowered now, more resolute and calmer, "And every day I've prayed for my mom to wake up, and to have a group of friends. That's all I want. A group of friends that I can hang out with, grow with, laugh with, and cry with. A group of people to share my soul and suffering with." Pause. "Now I see that God has answered at least one of my prayers. He has given me friends, even from the most inconvenient of places."

Krystal shook her head, her voice more somber, "I used to be unhappy, seeing life as dry and pointless . . . I was *lifeless*, but now I have hope. I have a reason to live, not a reason to die. And I will march on facing life because I, found, *Jesus*. There is nothing else in the world that can fill that emptiness in your heart except Jesus Christ. Nothing that can leave you fulfilled and hopeful. *Nothing!*" She pointed to herself, "And you can't take Jesus away from me, because He conquered death and rose again." Jaime could hear the frantic speaking in her voice, "So there, you've learned a little bit more about me! Why I'm so quiet and serious all the time." Jaime felt all his barriers come crashing down, as he realized how futile it was to hold them up. Krystal's words pierced every layer of armor he had. Then Krystal said, "So don't be mad at God, for He is a *good God*. No matter what happens, God has a plan, and He is doing everything in His power for our good." Jaime fought the building rage within him. He wanted to shout, to defend himself, to say something, but all of that evaporated earlier with Krystal's expression. Jaime was sure no one else in the group knew what Krystal was talking about, or at least got the better idea of Krystal's message. Still, he knew part of that speech was for him, Jaime knew that the rest of it was more general, but it was still meant for him whether she intended it or not.

Krystal took a deep breath and exhaled. All the passion in her body quickly evaporating. She calmed herself, wiping away the tears in her eyes, looking normal once again. Everyone stood there, hesitant about whether to comfort her or not. Krystal noticed, but she didn't hold it against them. She would be scared too if she were staring at herself from the hallway. She turned around facing her mom again and said, "I'm sorry, but . . . can I get a minute?" Her voice was steady and calm, like she hadn't cried at all. Everyone filed out, except for Jaime. Who stood there silently.

Jaime wanted to yell. To say something. To curse God for letting Krystal go through all this pain on her own, but Jaime couldn't deny the growth Krystal had experienced either. This girl had nothing, no family, no friends, no love, no hope, and yet she managed to find love in her life. She managed to grow from the pain, to go from the gloomy suicidal girl to the hopeful, loving person she is today. Krystal used to be so gloomy and dark, and had turned into this kind, caring individual who cared more about others than she did herself, even when the rest of the world treated her like dirt. The fact that she was able to care for others when she was on the verge of losing it all astounded Jaime. Krystal leaned over her sleeping mom while Jaime stayed and remained silent.

It was then Jaime finally understood Krystal. Why she was the way she was. He understood the world had never been kind to Krystal Henninger. There was never a moment in her life where she wasn't suffering, only getting worse as time progressed. Jaime's pain suddenly felt small and inconsiderate compared to Krystal's, and yet she never once complained about it. The world had been hard on Krystal Henninger from the moment she was born. In Jaime's eyes, Krystal had every right to be angry, especially at God.

Jaime stood there, breathing as quietly as he could, not moving a muscle as he watched Krystal kneel over the side of her mom's bed. Jaime thought Krystal knew he was still there. She usually did, but this time Jaime wasn't so sure. Maybe Krystal was too preoccupied with her mom to notice him, maybe she thought he had walked out with the rest of the group, or she simply didn't care if he was there or not. Regardless, Krystal never gave him any sign that she knew he was there, so Jaime couldn't tell whether she wanted him there or she was indirectly telling him to buzz off. Either way, she gave him no sign of leaving, so he stayed.

"I know you're here." Krystal said. Jaime tensed up. He was about to move when Krystal spoke "God, I've only asked for two things from you. One is friends and You answered that, and now I'm asking You. And I know it's crazy, but . . . but after You saved me, I know that anything is possible." Krystal paused. "I want my mom to wake up. I want her to come back to life and forgive me, but . . ." Krystal took a deep breath, Jaime watched a sense of relief flow over her like a gust of wind, relaxing her shoulders, almost as if it were the . . . the . . . Jaime paused. He finally realized what Krystal was doing. It brought back memories of his own. Too many memories he tried so desperately to forget.

For once Jaime felt something familiar, something he had in common with Krystal. His own feelings getting mixed in the process. Remembering all those days on his knees, praying to God, praying to the One he knew who had the power to save her yet didn't. Jaime never received an answer. Getting the constant silence for a prayer and the disappointment from that. The yearning in his heart to receive what he wanted but never getting it. And here, Jaime saw, was a girl going through the same thing. To watch her own mom lay in a coma, helplessly praying to God for a miracle. Krystal's pain didn't end, it only got worse. She didn't get what she wanted; she got something worse. Believing her mom lay in a coma because of her. Jaime imagined that for a moment, the pain of his younger sister Carole, lying in a grave. The sting in his heart was too great, so he shut the image down and opened his eyes. He hadn't realized he had closed them. Jaime looked to see if Krystal had noticed him, but she still gave no indication she knew he was there.

"God . . . God . . ." Krystal looked up, knees on the floor, leaning against the side of the hospital bed like a begging servant. The only sound was the heart monitor beeping. Krystal placed both her hands on the side of the bed, palms open and said, "God . . . I know it's much to ask but I want you to save my mom. To bring her back and wake her up." The next words blocked in Krystal's throat, etching out those final words like they were the hardest thing she's ever said.

Jaime's breathing intensified. His heart was under attack, and Jaime felt he was about to freak out and yell at her. He wanted to grab Krystal and shake some sense into her, to tell her that prayers don't get answered from a God who isn't there. He felt the same passion, the same love he had for his little sister Carole and wanted to shout it all out at Krystal. To tell her to get over this nonsense of God being a *good God!* But he held it in, for what came next would shake Jaime to his core.

Krystal spoke up, this time saying, "God, my Father, please heal my mom, please wake her up, I know you have the power to do so . . . so please heal her. Please, heal her in Jesus' name." She lowered her head slowly and eased it on the metal railing.

Jaime's heart pounded in anticipation. *Is her mom going to wake up?* Picturing the mirror image of himself in Krystal's position, bringing back all the memories he wished he could forget. They waited there for a solid ten minutes. Neither of them making a move. Jaime's feet were starting to ache, but he wanted to see this through. He wanted to see if something, anything would happen. To see if God would really heal this woman, to show Himself . . . but nothing happened. Jaime remembered the disappointment and felt like a fool for getting his hopes up. Even Jaime found himself wishing for Krystal's mom to wake up.

Another minute passed, and Jaime decided it was time to leave. He couldn't take this anymore. He walked out, revealing himself. Krystal never moved, but she didn't react either. She lay there, on her knees, having begged with all her intent, and all she could feel was . . . disappointment.

Jaime stormed out into the hallway. His anger at an all-time high. His breathing increased and he felt so hot he was ready to punch a wall. Then abruptly an intense pain struck his chest, and he was suddenly very weak and fell against the wall. He managed to catch himself, but he felt hazy, like he was going to pass out. His heart was a maelstrom inside. He couldn't make sense of what had just happened. All the memories came flooding back. The emotions he felt the day he lost Carole. The anger and the love. The bittersweet memories he'd held on to yet couldn't let go. His rage reaching its maximum threshold, feeling it directly impact his body. Jaime crumbled against the wall, trying to hold himself up, turning pale. "What the heck," he whispered, "is happening to me?" He felt light-headed, his mind dizzy, losing all sense of direction. His heart burned so bad he felt he was having a heart attack. The emptiness within screaming at him.

Kristina happened to be down the hallway and rushed over. "Hey Buck, you alright?" She grabbed him and tried to hold him up. "Are you good?" Kristina looked nervously at Jaime. "What's wrong?" He could sense the urgency in her voice, but Jaime could barely hear her. Jaime thought Kristina was going to freak out and scream. He sat down in an orange kiddie chair Kristina found, feeling totally humiliated. He chuckled.

That chuckle freaked Kristina out. His weak laugh died down and he grasped his heart. A sharp pain stabbed him. *I don't understand it*, he thought. Picturing Krystal kneeling in the room next to him. His face now pale white. Jaime's breathing accelerated faster and faster. His heart pounding rapidly like a drum, ready to explode.

Kristina shouted, "Nurse!" turning her attention back to Jaime, "Jaime. Jaime! Calm down. Nurse! Nurse!" Jaime's world faded into black as he fell off his chair. Kristina tried to catch him, but the guy fell face first, landing with his butt hanging in the air like a dung beetle. Kristina didn't know whether to laugh or freak out. Exasperated and confused, yet laughing from Jaime's position, Kristina threw her arms in the air, exclaimed, "What the—?" horridly laughing at the sight of Jaime splotched across the floor like a moron.

CHAPTER 48

Awakening

*"If I hadn't gone through that suffering,
I wouldn't be the person I am today."*

—Krystal Henninger

Jaime's eyes opened gradually, hearing a nearby heartbeat monitor. His eyes were fuzzy, slowly scanning the room. He felt weak. He wasn't sure how long he'd been out, realized it was nighttime and the hospital was quiet. The moonlight gleamed through the hospital window, shining down upon Krystal seated next to his bed. Jaime thought she was a spirit at first. A spirit encompassed in a purple aura with the moonlight showing her true beauty. Jaime saw why Krystal was different compared to most girls. Most girls wish themselves to be like flowers that bloom in the sun, but Krystal was a flower that bloomed in the night. That's why she's different. She's the rain when you need healing, the night when you need rest, the friend who will listen, and the one closest in your darkest moments, for she is an angel of the night.

Jaime gazed at Krystal. He had never seen her look so beautiful before. Her black hair gleamed and shined as it fell down her back. Her pale skin glowing in the moonlight. He felt she was a princess, a princess of the night. One not seen by many. One taken for granted.

Krystal was sound asleep, sitting upright on a stool with her head craned down. Jaime felt relief as he watched her sleep. She had probably been watching him a minute ago. He tried not to dwell on the fact that a girl watched him while he slept. It felt just like a scene from a movie. Jaime thought of all the people who had stayed with him and watched him while he slept and could think of none. He watched her breathe, sitting upright. *She must be tired*, he thought, so he let her sleep. He imagined her neck was going to kill her when she woke up, but he figured that would be the least of her pains when she awoke.

He could hear her breathing. The steady, raspy breathing as her body bobbed up and down slightly. Every time Jaime saw Krystal lean back, he thought she was going to topple over, but she would reverse direction like a pendant and wouldn't fall off. Jaime felt a sense of peace from watching her sleep. A peaceful bliss across her face made Jaime feel more relaxed, draining away the anger he felt earlier. He had almost forgotten about it, almost.

It was strange. Jaime was the one in the bed, yet he was the one watching Krystal sleep. It was late in the night, but Jaime didn't bother to check the time. He let out a long sigh and rolled over in bed, looking at how beautiful Krystal was. His heart, his aching heart, wanting to reach out and connect with hers. To take away all her pain, all her memories, and give her healing. The way she wanted to heal him. Maybe she was healing him, and he didn't know it yet.

A sharp ache pulsed in his heart as he grunted in pain. That seemed to wake Krystal, but it wasn't sudden. Her eyes slowly opened; the look of a person awakened from a long and much needed rest.

Krystal dragged open her cloudy eyes and whispered, "Hey."

"Hey." He whispered back. Jaime suddenly wanted to hug her. To hold her there and comfort her. His mind flashed back to Krystal holding the railing of her mom's hospital bed. The emotion, the ache, the desire to have her mom awake. Jaime suddenly felt guilty for not coming up and comforting her back then. Now, he wanted to hug her and tell her that everything would be alright, but he didn't. What surprised him was the smile she portrayed towards him. He thought, *How in the world can you be smiling right now when God didn't even answer your prayer?*

"How are you feeling?" she asked, relieved to see him. Always more concerned with others than with herself.

Jaime assessed his condition mentally, emotionally, and physically. Still feeling the sharp ache in his heart, the bitterness and rage boiling within. He answered honestly, "Not good." No that wasn't the right word for it. "Conflicted," he said. Yes, that was the right word for it. Conflicted.

"I'm sorry."

Jaime was surprised. "For what?"

Krystal's joyful demeanor vanished now. Replaced with saddened empathy. "I don't know. I just feel bad for you. You've been hurting a long time, and no one has seen it. Not even me." Jaime pushed himself up from his bed, leaning forward. His heart felt like it was on fire, but it felt more like physical heartburn than passion, and that worried him. He pushed it out of his mind for the moment. He wanted to object and say something, but he wasn't in the mood to get into an argument, but he did have questions.

Jaime looked away and spoke with a fatigued whisper, "I don't get it." His voice was so weak there was no energy to include malice within it. Jaime brought his attention back to Krystal. "Why . . . why would you pray when you know He won't answer."

"Because I know He's listening."

"How?" Jaime asked.

Krystal lowered her head in admission; Jaime got the sense she was trying to humble herself. Krystal let out a breath. "I've already told you my story. You know what I've gone through and how God filled the emptiness inside. And I always thought . . ." Krystal raised her head, looking at the moon through the window, "that if He can heal me, then He can bring back my mom." She paused. "So I prayed, and prayed and prayed so many days and nights for my mom to wake up. And today . . . today . . ." Krystal took a breath and exhaled, "Today I thought He would really do it . . . but He didn't." She paused. "I still think back to that night when I took my own life, how messed up I was back then. How I wished I hadn't gone through all that pain." She silently chuckled, "What a weird scenario." Jaime looked confused. Krystal took a breath and looked at him, "But now I look back, and I see just how much I've changed. I see how much I've grown because of my pain and how I can relate to others now, and you." Krystal took her eyes off Jaime and glanced at his feet on the bed. "If I hadn't gone through that suffering, I wouldn't be the person I am today. I wouldn't have met all of you. I wouldn't have been changed by you, or Kristina, or Joanna, or by Sho. I would still be my same depressed self."

Jaime whispered, "I still don't get it."

"Neither do I."

Jaime looked at Krystal in a new light. She seemed so different from the first time he met her. "You know," he said, "you're very wise."

Krystal lowered her head, partially blushing, but remained collected. "I'm alright."

Now Jaime looked away, "And I'm sorry for passing out and all. I just . . ." he looked at her. "Watching you pray brought up old memories."

"It's okay." Krystal whispered and then granted him a soft smile. Jaime stared stargazed. He was still getting used to that sight. Krystal got up from her stool, "Alright. Get some sleep. I'll see you in the morning."

"Good night."

"Good night," as she walked out the hallway. Jaime leaned back and felt sleep come to him again.

Thank you . . .

Jaime felt a little humiliated walking around in a hospital gown. Krystal found it very hilarious, as did the rest of the group when they visited the next day. Pictures were taken and Jaime's reputation had been ruined. The teasing was fine though. He could use a little humor after the past two days.

Jaime got dressed and walked out with the group, ready to depart. He stepped in the hallway, finding Krystal looking into her mom's room once more. Jaime motioned the rest of the group to move on then walked up to Krystal's side. He gave her a half hug, as they stood there soaking in each other's comfort at the sight of Krystal's mom lying peacefully in her bed. Steady breathing but no movement, only the up and down motion of her chest. Jaime gave a quick rub on Krystal's shoulder and whispered, "It's time to go."

"I know," she said with hardened understanding. Jaime didn't say anything. He knew nothing would help Krystal feel any better. But he allowed himself to know there was someone like him who shared his pain. Someone who knew the frustration and pain of receiving an unanswered prayer. Jaime treasured Krystal. He really did. There was truly no one like her on all the earth or ever will be. He lifted his arm off her shoulder, but Krystal stayed. She stepped forward and whispered, "I'm going to say goodbye." Jaime nodded and watched as Krystal approached her mom's bedside for the last time. Jaime felt remarkably calm watching this time. He felt relieved, and a little proud of Krystal for how much she'd grown. She seemed more resolute in her character. More like an adult compared to others her age. Regardless, Jaime was proud of her. Proud like the older brother he'd once been, watching his little sister grow.

Krystal approached the bedside of her mom for the final time. Knelt eye level with her mom, and spoke in a soft voice, "It's been a wonderful time with you mom. Thank you for all that you've done." Krystal held her tears back. She had had enough crying for the last couple of days and made one last prayer. "Jesus . . . I know I've prayed to You a lot. I know You hear all my prayers, even though sometimes I feel like You're not . . ." she stopped and took a breath, "God . . . whether You decide to answer my prayers or not . . . I'm still going to thank you." She stopped. Jaime's interest shot up.

"Thank you for giving me my mom. Thank you for the wonderful life I've had with her." She stopped once more, the words getting difficult. "But I'm surrendering her to You . . . I'm going to let her go. And if You decide not to bring her back," Krystal opened her eyes and looked up, "then I will still have faith in You. I give her up to You, knowing fully of Your power. Whether you choose to heal my mom or not . . . I will accept your decision." Jaime's previous frustration came back, and suddenly Krystal felt her heart warm, a powerful feeling glowing from within her chest like the morning sun. Krystal's heart wasn't beating faster, in fact she was cool as could be, yet she felt warm, very warm. A thought dropped into her mind, and she followed it. Krystal reached out and gently grasped her mom's hand. Krystal closed her eyes, thinking about the passage of the bleeding woman and the sleeping daughter, then whispered so low, Jaime almost didn't hear it, "God . . . I believe . . . thank you . . . for healing my mom."

Krystal kept her eyes closed and didn't move for what felt like an eternity. The whole world had stopped, and it was just Krystal there, waiting. She felt a healing presence flow out from her heart and up through her arm. Krystal's hand felt remarkably warm against her mom's cold skin. But she held it there. Something telling her to keep it there.

Jaime could sense something too, although he didn't want to. He was beginning to get suspicious, but he dared not to interrupt. He wondered if something was going to happen. But Krystal kept her eyes closed. Her mind blank, seeing nothing but black, as the whole world fell silent, until she felt a hand caress carefully against her face. The warm comfort of fingertips slowly holding Krystal's cheek. Krystal opened her eyes to see her mom looking up at her, smiling, as she said, "Krystal." Krystal felt the Holy Spirit flood her with relief as she let all her emotions out. Rivers of tears and joy poured out from her, drinking in the sight of her mom smiling back at her. The hope of a life restored, and a soul brought back to life.

Jaime couldn't believe it. He stood there, eyes wide in disbelief. He could not believe it, yet he could not deny what his eyes had just witnessed. God had just performed a miracle right in front of his very eyes. *I don't believe it . . .*

CHAPTER 49

Pain

*"Do You feel pain God? Do You cry when You watch
Your children die right in front of You?"*

—Jaime Fisher

Jaime hunched over on the side of his bed, arms on his knees. His mind in a whirlwind of thoughts, exhausted from the emotional fatigue of recent events.

He sat there, defeated. Not from anything but from himself. The images of the hospital playing in his mind. Of Krystal and the sight of her mom miraculously coming back to life. He hadn't been able to wrap his head around it.

Jaime leaned forward on the side of his bed, taking slow, deep breaths through his nostrils. He couldn't believe it. It just didn't seem possible. He thought back to his sister. Finding Carole with blood-soaked wrists on the floor. All the nights he had prayed for her to get better, begging with tears, heartfelt devotion, and the absolute belief that God would save her.

She was only twelve when he found her. Watching Carole's white, blonde hair stained with her own blood. He remembered holding her there, Carole's lifeless body not responding to any of his calls, to his tears and cries. Finding knife wounds on both her wrists. Remembering his prayers, prayers every morning and every night to God. Prayers to save his little sister. To stop her suffering. To save her from all her pain . . . He didn't ask God to watch her die.

Jaime thought, *Do You feel pain God? Do You cry when You watch Your children die right in front of You? You're supposed to be omnipresent right? So do You see everything that happens? Do You remember every act of evil and feel everyone's pain?* Jaime felt the denial cement as he held his sister's corpse, having known God failed him, a God who promised He would answer all prayers, who loved His children and would die for them. *But then why didn't He save her? If God is all powerful, then why did He do nothing?*

The memories began pulling Jaime back, back to the black casket where his young sister lay. All prettied up, ready to be buried. The funeral was especially difficult to get through. One of the hardest moments of his life. Jaime had read an article that families go through tough times when they lose a child. Parents drift apart, siblings isolate themselves. But the most frustrating fact about it all was that his family didn't seem that shaken up. It seemed to him that they simply brushed it off and told Jaime, "Thy will be done."

Thy will be done? Thy will be done . . . how could you possibly give me that answer?

While the rest of Jaime's family turned closer to God, Jaime had the opposite effect. He had placed all his hope, knowing, *believing* with all his heart that God would save her. And in that moment, when he held his sister's lifeless corpse, something shattered.

His heart grew cold and was filled with bitterness. He was angry at both his family and at God. Stuck with the question, *How could you let my younger sister die?* Jaime knew Carole believed in God, but she was too young, far too young to die. Having known God could have saved her. How God could have done something, with all His power, but instead chose to do nothing. How could he believe in a God like that? *It's His fault!* Jaime told himself. His anger flaring up and stirring his soul within. Jaime grasped the sides of his head, his fingers digging deep into his temples.

Then the images of Krystal began to float quietly into his mind. He remembered the firepit, remembering the feeling of Krystal's warm presence comforting him as he opened up about Carole for the first time in years. No one else had done that, not even his family who he loved so dearly. Remembering her warm arms slowly wrapping around him. The warmth of her soul and presence connected with his. Maybe that was the first time Jaime felt God begin to break through the cracks of his hardened heart.

Jaime brushed his forehead with his hand, "Gosh. Even their names are similar!" he yelled. "Krystal, Carole, Carole, Krystal. *Why?!*" Jaime screamed so loud the dogs next door began barking. No one was home. Everyone was out running errands or at work.

Why?! The thought began shouting itself inside his head, and pretty soon Jaime was shouting at the top of his lungs. "WHY?! WHY?! WHY?!" Jaime got up and nearly broke something. He screamed until he could scream no longer, feeling drained, sinking down to the floor like a defeated child. He put his hands to his face, his voice soggy and face full of tears, "I don't understand." But more images of Krystal began to play in his mind.

He thought, *The girl who had been a suicidal loner, who became a Christian, who became my friend. Having not saved herself from her own power, but from something else. I want to deny it but deep down I know . . .*

Then there was the recent event with Krystal's mom. A woman, stuck in a coma for a year after getting hit by a pickup-truck, to wake up miraculously when her own daughter prays to let her go. "IT DOESN'T MAKE SENSE!" he shouted with the last of his strength.

How could you give up your own mom? The person who loved you the most.

Every time Jaime thought of Krystal, he kept coming back to the *why*. The why. The why, why, why, why, why, why, why, the . . . *why*. And every time he came back to the *why*, he thought of Krystal. Thought of her journey and the level of growth that was not possible for a person of her own willpower.

How does a suicidal loner who doesn't talk much, go from killing herself to smiling? How does someone like her find hope? Why does she care about others and make friends when she has no reason to care about anybody? How does a person come by that? And every time he came to the end of that question, he knew the answer . . . the answer he didn't want to acknowledge but knew was the truth. The answer was God. God had truly come into this girl's life and changed her, changed her for the better. Even Jaime could feel the change happening inside him, whether he liked it or not.

Every time he came to that conclusion, he wanted to reject it, but every time he tried to reject it, it only hurt him more. It was beginning to tire him out. Jaime could feel himself reaching his limit. Having lived so long on nothing but fumes.

He had been living life as a hallow shell, filled with nothing but bitterness, emptiness, and hatred. To deal with the sadness weighing down on him. The grief of his dead sister still unaddressed. The hatred for a God whom Jaime refused to believe in. Yet, how can you hate someone who you believe doesn't exist?

"What are You doing to me?" he whispered.

CHAPTER 50

Jealousy

"Why is it that some people suffer more than others,
while some people are blessed more than others?"

—Jaime Fisher

Cups clanged together as soda flowed like the Nile River, spewing over the plastic edges. All the people closest to Krystal were at the Fisher's house celebrating. Everyone from Carmen, Mr. and Mrs. Fisher, Kristina, Joanna, Sho, and even Aunt Sarah were there to celebrate the awakening of Krystal's mom. The setting inside the Fisher's house was pleasant, warmhearted, and jovial. Everything Jaime did not feel.

Jaime sat in the corner of the room watching the celebration. Mrs. Fisher had gotten wind of what happened and threw together a quick celebration cake for Krystal's mom. Krystal's mom was still in the hospital, so it was really a celebration for Krystal, but it was a night of reckoning. Krystal had gotten her mom back and Jaime had never seen her so happy. The smile on her face was wide and genuine. Everyone gave her warm compliments and celebratory congratulations. He could tell Krystal was enjoying it.

But Jaime didn't share in the celebratory spirit at all. He wanted to, but his heart and feelings said otherwise. The condition of Jaime's heart was outrageous. He could feel the dark shadow encompassing him, his heart turning to stone, but most of all he felt jealous rage within him. There had never been anything like it; that miracle he'd personally witnessed in the hospital. And yet he couldn't shake this raging sense of jealousy inside him. He wanted to be happy. To share in Krystal's celebration, but he wasn't going to lie to himself. He was jealous and that was that. He was in such an emotional outrage that he wasn't thinking clearly. His mind shrouded with emotion. He could not make proper judgments and he did not care.

The celebratory congratulations around Krystal had dispersed and people were now spending time together in separate groups around the house and living room. Jaime saw his chance and stood up from his chair. He turned on his happy look and approached Krystal.

She hadn't taken a bite out of her cake and was busy staring at it. Oh how he wanted to know her thoughts. How wonderful it might have been to be in her position. Jaime leaned over and spoke calmly, "Hey, can I talk to you outside for a second?"

Krystal looked up and said, "Okay." Jaime couldn't tell if she was aware of his feelings or not. Either way, they needed to talk. Jaime headed out the front door and Krystal followed him out. The two of them took a walk down the street, the long evening allowing silence to settle as all the cars were home. Jaime walked on ahead, Krystal trailing casually behind. They walked a couple blocks before Jaime stopped in the middle of the street. Krystal hadn't said a word the entire time, feeling the quiet neighborhood surrounding them.

Jaime stood there, and without turning said, "I don't get it." He let the anger show in his voice. He wasn't going to hide it anymore. "I don't *get it*." He turned and faced her. As usual, Krystal watched him with passive, observing eyes. Unaware of what was coming yet undeterred as well. Jaime looked down and clenched his fists, his knuckles turning white. "Why?" raising his head. "Why did that happen?" Jaime expected an answer, but Krystal remained silent. Her lack of response drove Jaime to madness. He stepped closer, the anger finally showing. "Why did that happen?" but Krystal remained silent. Jaime's anger was flaming now. He could not accept an answer like that. He came even closer now, right up in Krystal's face. "Why!" he shouted. "I don't get it!" and for a third time, Krystal remained silent. That pushed Jaime past his breaking point.

Jaime towered over Krystal and yelled right in her face, "Tell me! Why did your mom come back, and my sister didn't?!" Krystal remained silent but she was not immune. She was starting to show signs of weakness yet did not answer. She slowly backed off but Jaime wasn't going to let her off so easily. He wanted an answer, and he wanted to hear it from her lips. "I don't get it! I don't get it! I prayed as hard as you did. I followed all God's commands, I read the Bible, I cared more about others than I did myself, and every night I prayed to Him just to save my little sister!" Jaime's voice weakened but his words shocked Krystal with every passing sentence. He pressed forward until Krystal was backed against a car with nowhere to go. Then he gathered up the rest of his voice and energy, all the years of grief and pain boiling to the surface, now coming out in full fits of rage aimed at Krystal. "NOW TELL ME! WHY DID GOD BRING YOUR MOM BACK AND NOT SAVE MY LITTLE SISTER!"

Krystal was so terrified she closed her eyes and looked away. Jaime waited for an answer. Then he saw her crying. Jaime was so caught up in his rage that he hadn't noticed her crying. But what he saw broke him completely.

Krystal opened her eyes and looked at him. Her purple eyes filled with sorrow. The tears came out slowly, as Krystal allowed the emotion to finally show. The weakness in her face, and utter helplessness to answer his question. "I don't know," she whispered. Now Krystal was shaking from her own sorrow. Her voice choked with tears. She looked Jaime dead in the eyes letting him see all the pain she carried, not a hint of joy she felt a few moments ago. "I don't know," she said helplessly. She shook her head as if ashamed, "I don't know why God saved my mom. I don't know why He didn't save your sister." She choked up, "I don't know why I'm still alive. I should have died that night when I slit my wrist." She nudged her chin at him, "Your sister should be here, not me. I don't deserve to live. I don't deserve to be happy. If it were my choice, I would bring her back, not me . . ." There it was. The answer.

Her words completely defused him, he didn't know what to say. It was not at all what he'd expected. He expected some religious secret about faith or an idea that she knew something he didn't, but it wasn't like that at all. It was open and honest, a simple 'I don't know.' How could you possibly get mad at someone for that?

With her eyes drenched in tears, Krystal raised her hands and slowly put them on Jaime's chest. Then she lowered her head and cried into his jacket. "I'm so sorry about Carole. I'm so sorry." She muffled. Crying for a full minute, her tears not stopping. "You were my first friend. You taught me so much and you're going through a lot." Krystal gripped his jacket harder. "But please . . . I don't want to lose you too."

Of all the times in his life, Jaime had never felt so ashamed. He had never felt so horrible and dismayed as he did now. He could feel the pick and patter of rain tap against him. All the anger, all the bitterness he felt toward God caused him to hurt the only person close to him, and it gained him nothing. He felt disgusted with himself, with his rage that drove him to perform this horrid action. His heart and mind were too mixed in chaos to determine how he felt in this very moment. Jaime looked at the concrete while Krystal held him close, letting her presence comfort him and drain away all the anger, the bitterness, and jealousy right out from his body. *What kind of feeling is this?* he wondered. It was too much for one person alone to display this attribute. And if Jaime were in Krystal's shoes, he would have punched himself long ago, but she didn't. Instead, she hugged him, and cried for him. *What are You doing to me?*

Tears fell from Jaime's eyes as his whole world came crashing down. The sadness built over the years was finally coming to the surface. His face wrinkled in sorrow as he leaned down and hugged Krystal, whispering, "I'm sorry, I'm so sorry." She wrapped her arms around him and let Jaime cry on her shoulder. All his strength amounted to nothing as he couldn't heal his own broken heart.

Krystal muffled beneath him, "I forgive you." His eyes shot wide open. The word causing all the anger to drain from his body as Krystal held him in the rain.

CHAPTER 51

Consequences

"We are most likely to change when we are at our lowest point."

—JL

They walked back. "Are you sure it's alright?"

"I'm sure," Krystal said, walking off Jaime's front lawn.

"I'll see you later?" he asked, hoping he wasn't sounding too eager.

Krystal gave him the courtesy of a thin smile. "Sure."

"Thanks," he said, and waved her goodbye. Jaime stood and faced the doorway to his house. It was incredibly quiet, and he was ready for a hot shower and a nice bed. He had let out all his emotions and now he was ready to sleep. Jaime pressed the front door open, only to be punched hard in the face. Jaime landed on the concrete walkway, too stunned to realize he'd been hit. There stood his lumberjack of a father in the doorway. His anger fitting that to the fires of hell itself. "I warned you." Jaime's dad said. The grim in his voice was no hidden feature. He towered over Jaime with stoic anger. "Carmen saw you yelling at Krystal. Is that true?"

Jaime took a second to recollect himself. He put his hand to his face, felt a river of warm blood gush from his nose while his dad showed remarkable patience despite putting on such a display of anger. Jaime was done hiding it. To his shame, he nodded, "Yeah. I did." Mr. Fisher stood up straight, wishing for it to not be true. Jaime could see the compassion in his eyes, as well as the pain of what his dad must do. Mr. Fisher struggled to keep his breath, and declared, "Don't come back. Until you've done some thinking about your life. But just know," Mr. Fisher faltered so heavily in his words Jaime thought he was about to burst into tears, "you're not the only one hurting." In his shame Jaime did not argue. He didn't have the energy to. Only held his bloody nose with his hand.

Both Carmen and his mom stood in the doorway, weeping. They wanted nothing more than for Jaime to come back, but he wasn't in the right frame of mind, so he could not come back yet, and he could tell that killed them inside. They wanted their brother and son back. They wanted their family together again, but in his rage, Jaime denied them that. He took advantage of the family he loved so dearly and forgot to appreciate them, disregarding the pain they were in because of his own.

Mr. Fisher towered, not saying anything, ready to slug his own son again if necessary. Jaime tried to stand up, felt disoriented. A wad of cash smacked against his chest. Three hundred dollars. Jaime looked up at his dad and could tell it killed the man inside to oust his own son. Jaime picked up the cash and didn't say anything. This was not the time for words. Jaime took the money and walked out into the rain, not sure where he was going, as his family, even Jaime's dad, watched him with tears in their eyes, waiting for the prodigal son to return.

◆

"What are you gonna do?"

Jaime sat on a bed, all showered, glad to finally be out of the rain. He held the phone to his ear, "I'm going to stay at my buddy Luiz's house for the time being. He was generous enough to let me stay for a little while."

"Okay," said Krystal. Jaime could hear the dismay in her voice. They both lulled on the phone for a minute before Jaime finally said, "Thank you . . . for being there tonight. I'm sorry I got jealous about your mom coming back, and I deserve everything that's coming to me."

"It's okay," Krystal said. Jaime lowered the phone and hung up. Feeling humbled now, unlike anything he'd ever felt before. He had lost his family, the family whom he loved so dear, yet he lost it because of himself.

PART NINE

The Mother

CHAPTER 52

The Failure

"Are we defined by our greatest achievements or our greatest mistakes?"

—JL

Her stomach was wide and bulging, it was now or never. She either would decide to keep it or end it now. Ashley was close to tears walking down the side of the street. The abortion clinic was only a block away. She deliberately parked far away so she would have more time to think about it, and the appointment was in ten minutes. She looked down at her bulging stomach; oh yes there was a baby in there. But the shame of it haunted her. That's the problem with going out drinking with Sarah for one night and sleeping with some guy she can't even remember. Only to find that he abandoned her the very next day and never returned, leaving Ashley with a baby in her stomach and a tough decision.

Ashley brushed her velvet brown hair from her face and looked down at her stomach. For weeks she debated the decision, whether to keep the baby or not, and now the deadline was arriving.

It will only be a burden, she thought. *I'm not financially ready to take care of a baby yet.* She was half right. Ashley was still in the middle of nursing school and was on her way to becoming a full-fledged nurse, something she'd dreamed about since she was a child. But now there was an actual child to worry about, and whether she was going to keep it or not.

I can't keep this baby, she told herself, resuming her stride towards the abortion clinic. She managed to take a couple of steps when her foot tripped on an open slab of concrete, sending her falling forward. In that very moment, the whole world drained away and slowed. Ashley saw the concrete and thought, *If I let myself fall, then it will all be over.* But Ashley's reflexes kicked in, throwing her arms out and catching herself before she hit the ground. It all happened so fast Ashley couldn't fathom what happened, then she looked down at her stomach in horror.

"I was willing to let this child die. A child . . . who had never done anything wrong to begin with, and I wanted this child dead." Guilt and shame overshadowed her, burdening her heart and soul with an enormous amount of judgment. "How can I live with myself for wanting this child dead?" Ashley knew she had to make a choice, yet it was already made for her. She rubbed her hand across her stomach, swallowing the bitter pill. "I'm going to keep this child, and I will raise it to the best of my abilities." It was a good line, but Ashley knew it was an attempt to relieve her newfound guilt. It will not be a birth out of love, but of guilt. She felt the baby kick and didn't know whether to be happy or remorseful. "Okay . . . let's go home."

Ms. Harker was no newbie to supervising kids on this playground. Elementary kids were always so active and lively it brought her a lot of joy watching them play. Kids needed to run and play and smile. It reminded her of the fun times she had when she was in elementary school. Kids playing on the blacktop, some doing handball, others running on the open grass field, some even playing basketball a couple courts down.

Ms. Harker smiled. All the kids seemed to be as active as the rest, having the time of their lives. Her gaze scanned the playground, watching a stray ball roll across the blacktop. Ms. Harker watched the ball roll until it stopped in front of a young girl with black hair. Ms. Harker saw nothing unusual about it, until she looked closer. The girl looked down at the ball with timid curiosity, as if she did not understand the ball or its purpose. Ms. Harker expected the girl to pick it up and run with it, but she just stood there and stared at it. It wasn't until a second later that Ms. Harker realized this was the only kid on the playground that wasn't doing something. She was so timid compared to the rest of her class she stood out like a tree in a desert.

A boy ran up and took the ball from the girl and ran back to his friends at the handball courts. Ms. Harker could tell the girl wanted to go play with them, but the girl remained where she was. Everyone else was busy playing some activity, but this girl just stood there, alone, not knowing what to do.

"You called me in? What's this about?" Ashley took a seat, worried about sitting in the school counselor's office at Krystal's middle school.

The counselor had her arms on her desk, hands threaded in the classic counselor style. "Mrs. Henninger," she said.

Ashley corrected her, "It's *Ms.* Henninger."

The counselor corrected herself, "*Ms.* Henninger, I've called you today to talk about your daughter."

Ashley looked at her more intensely. "What about my daughter?" The worry within her beginning to spread like a disease. Ashley waited for the counselor to say her part, but the woman seemed bemused. "I'm not sure where to begin, let alone know what the problem is?"

"What *is* the problem?" Ashley asked, her patience wearing thin.

The woman decided to come out and say it. "Your daughter Krystal is an unusual case. I've heard reports from her teachers that she's never once conversed with her classmates. They've never seen her participate in any activity at school and her teachers tell me that she usually sits alone and doesn't have any friends."

Ashley spoke up defensively, "Are you saying there's something wrong with my daughter?"

"No miss. I'm saying there's *nothing* wrong with your daughter. That's the problem."

Ashley's anger defused. She shook her head, puzzled. "I'm confused."

The counselor elaborated, "Well, if you look at it on paper, your daughter is a perfectly healthy, average individual, with no defects."

Defects. Did she have to say 'defects'?

Ashley was tired of this loose explanation. "What's your point counselor?"

"My point is I don't understand why she doesn't socialize with anyone. I've never once seen her talk to someone or answer a question in class. If she's a normal healthy girl, then why hasn't she made any friends or participated in any activities?" Ashley wondered that question herself and feared the worst. Elementary school had not been fun for Krystal and middle school was beginning to look that way too. "Mrs. Henninger—"

"It's *Ms.* Henninger," Ashley reinforced.

"Ms. Henninger, your daughter is a bright individual, but she is very shy and does not talk much."

Ashley looked at the counselor frustrated. "Is that why you brought me here, to tell me that my daughter doesn't talk that much?" Ashley was growing tired of this conversation.

"I don't know Ms. Henninger. I'm just worried about your daughter. Kids can be ruthless to those who don't fit in."

"Much appreciated," Ashley said apathetically, getting up from her seat.

She walked back to her car with Krystal in the passenger seat. Ashley stepped in and buckled her seatbelt.

"What did they say?" Krystal asked.

"Nothing sweetheart."

Ashley wanted to dodge the question, but Krystal asked, "Mom . . . is there something wrong with me?" Krystal kept her eyes on the car floor.

Ashley turned on the motherly charm, "No no sweetheart, you're perfectly normal. There is absolutely nothing wrong with you." Ashley paused and then said, "We just need to try a little harder that's all. You just need to try and talk to people more."

Krystal didn't look up. "I do try . . . but everyone avoids me." Ashley thought back to what the counselor said. Krystal read her thoughts and spoke, "The counselor may think I don't try, but I do . . ."

Ashley tried to soothe her way in, "Now sweetheart . . ."

But Krystal didn't fall for the sweetening words. She was too smart for that. "Why don't I fit in mom? Why do people avoid me?" Her questions were difficult for a Wednesday and Ashley wanted to get home and rest before her next shift began, but it was also her job as a mom to answer. These were the moments where being a parent was important in a child's life.

"I don't know sweetheart," she knew it was the wrong answer, but Ashley couldn't lie to her own daughter, Krystal would find out anyway. "Maybe they haven't seen the real you yet."

Krystal whispered "Okay," and that was all she said. Krystal went silent again and looked gloomfully out the passenger window. Ashley's heart pained with guilt as she turned the key to the car. *It'll be okay. It'll be okay.* But her mind lied to her, and her heart knew it.

Ashley sat at the dinner table unable to hide the concern from her face. Krystal stared down at the table, feeling the emptiness of the apartment surrounding them. The air was still, not even Ashley felt comfortable taking a bite. Krystal slurped her soup slowly as if she did not have the energy to go any faster. The fatigue and emotional drain weighed on her.

It had been another unfulfilling day in middle school for Krystal, and Ashley had to bear with the weight that she was failing as a parent. Krystal was looking worse and worse every day. The social isolation at school was beginning to show its effects. It's not like Krystal didn't want to make friends, but her classmates continued to avoid her. Every day was complete and utter hell from the isolation and ostracism.

Krystal was the first to break the silence, "Mom . . . where's my dad?"

A full minute passed but Ashley had no answer. She tried thinking of an excuse, but she knew she couldn't lie to her daughter about this. Another minute passed before Ashley gave up and answered honestly, "I don't know sweetheart." The shame in her voice came out. The regret stung her heart for not giving Krystal the gift of a good father and an untroubled home.

Ashley looked at Krystal for a response, but she gave no reaction, she only stopped eating. After another long pause, Krystal finally whispered, "Okay."

It was done. The question had been answered. Seconds ticked before Krystal opened up again, "Is that why you feel so guilty?" Ashley went pale.

She knew . . .

Ashley put her fork and knife down, and sighed, "I'm going to be honest with you Krystal . . . I never intended to have you." How odd it was for the words to come out so easily. She paused, "You were a mistake." Krystal showed no reaction, but Ashley could tell she just shattered her daughter to the core. Seconds ticked and Krystal didn't move.

She lowered her head, "I know . . ."

Ashley wanted to burst out and cry, but she held her composure like the nurse she was. It was one of the biggest regrets of her life. Not giving Krystal the dad she deserved, robbing Krystal of a wonderful life she could've had, and now Ashley had told her own daughter she was a mistake. All because she got drunk and met some random guy at a bar, oh the consequences from that night.

The guilt inside Ashley's heart increased to new levels. It was like having an elephant stand on her chest. *I'm the worst. I don't deserve to be a mom. Krystal deserves better than me.* Ashley covered her face. She could not look at Krystal. Did not want Krystal to see her like this. But Krystal was already staring at Ashley with a straight face. Krystal knew, she had known for a while. She wasn't stupid.

Ashley excused herself from the table and locked herself in her room. She felt alone with her troubles, left with a kid she did not want, and failed as a mother. All Ashley could do was give Krystal the truth and this empty home.

I haven't seen her smile once, she thought, crumbling to the ground against the door. Krystal approached the door and heard whimpering from the other side. She left her mom alone, knowing she wouldn't want Krystal to be around to remind her of the failure she was. So Krystal went back to her own room, and lay on her bed staring at the ceiling, trying not to cry from the truth she already knew.

～

"Everybody ready?" Ashley lifted her gloved hands, ready to start the procedure. All the other doctors nodded, and they got to work. Ashley was assisting one doctor when her heart and mind attacked her.

You don't deserve to have such a decent job as this.

Who do you think you are?

Do you still feel regret from the failure you are? Her inner thoughts made a wicked chuckle. *You tried to abort that baby on your own. What kind of person does that? You aren't a nurse! You're a murderer! You are supposed to save lives not take them!*

Ashley felt a ball of hot lead drop in her stomach. Her heart and stomach tensed, and she froze. The other doctors noticed. "Ashley, Ashley, what are you doing? We need to keep going," but Ashley was unresponsive. She felt queasy. Threw her hand to her mouth and the other to her stomach, calling out, "I'm sorry, someone take over for me!" Leaving the other doctors in a slight panic.

Ashley went to the nearest staff bathroom and locked herself quickly into the largest stall. She reared herself over the toilet and hurled so hard she turned white. After Ashley volunteered her breakfast, she hurled again, still feeling that ball of lead in her stomach. Her heart was in turmoil. The weight of her guilt suffocated her heart like an invisible and immovable boulder placed upon her chest. She knew what it was. It was her punishment for when she tried to fall on her stomach and kill Krystal. She kept the baby out of pure guilt, trying to atone for her mistakes. It had been twelve years since then, but every time she looked at Krystal, she was reminded of her biggest failure.

Her guilt was affecting her work now. Ever since Ashley had Krystal, she'd been going harder at work because the more she worked the more she forgot about the guilt, only to be reminded of it once the day was all over, draining what remaining energy she had left.

After a half an hour of lying next to the toilet, Ashley stepped out from the employee bathroom, only to run into her best friend Sarah who also worked as a nurse. Ashley didn't want to talk. She wanted to get back and finish the procedure, but Sarah held up a hand to stop her. "Ashley," she spoke softly, "What's going on? This is the third time this week you've had to leave in the middle of an operation. The staff is growing concerned and we don't want you making a mistake and hurting somebody or even yourself in the matter."

Ashley said faintly, "I'm fine." Not looking at her.

Sarah put her metaphorical foot down, "No you're not. Take a few days off and get yourself fixed up then come right back here okay." The argument was settled. All that was left for Ashley to do was to go home.

"No, no, I . . . I didn't mean it." Ashley writhed and turned on the couch as she slept. Her mind stuck in a hell of her own making. "No, I . . . I'm sorry. I'm so sorry. I wish I never did that. I wish I never did that." Ashley's breathing increased, her body starting to sweat. "I wish I never had her. I wish I never had Krystal." Ashley awoke from her dream to find Krystal standing there, watching her. Ashley held her mouth agape in horror. Krystal just watched her for a full minute and said nothing. Her passive gaze unreadable.

"Krystal I . . . I'm sorry I didn't mean it," Ashley called out desperately, but it was too late. The damage was done. Krystal just stared at her mom. There was no malice in her eyes, only sorrow and pure understanding. Krystal composed herself so well it was hard to tell if she was offended at all. "Krystal I . . ." but nothing she said would help this situation.

What have I done!

"What do you want for dinner?" Krystal asked somberly. Ashley was glad for a change of subject, but the regret was still there.

"Uhh spaghetti sounds good."

"Okay," Krystal replied deadpan. And she went over and started making dinner. As if nothing had happened. Ashley ached in pain from her guilt.

※

Another quiet dinner. The two of them sat on the opposite ends of the table, feeling the distance like it was a million miles. Ashley ate her food, knowing she had to get going soon to cover an overnight shift. Krystal had just started high school and Ashley hoped things would be different, that Krystal would grow up and start making some friends, but high school turned out to be just the same thing all over again. Ashley was halfway done with her food when Krystal spoke somberly, "Hey mom."

"What is it sweetie?"

Krystal said, "I think I want to kill myself . . ." It was so nonchalant it shocked Ashley pale white. Her worst nightmare was coming true.

"NO! Don't even think about it!" but her words didn't reach Krystal. It was like shooting arrows into the horizon hoping to hit the sun.

All Krystal said was, "Okay." Ashley's timer went off and she had to go to work now of all times. She'll call one of the neighbors to stay with Krystal. She was not leaving her alone tonight, not after that confession. Ashley picked up her bag and walked to the door. "I love you, sweetheart." Krystal didn't look up.

Krystal replied, "I love you too, Mom," but there was no warmth in her words. All Krystal could see was the sorrow that surrounded her mom. Ashley's heart ached again, and she nearly collapsed from the guilt. For Ashley, it had been growing harder and harder to cope the past few years. The guilt went down in elementary school but since Krystal just started high school, Ashley's guilt had only grown stronger. It weighed on her like a boulder. All she could do was hope for the best. This was her atonement. Her punishment for what she did back then. So Ashley opened the door and went to work.

※

Ashley had left Krystal for her Winter Formal dance and had just started her shift at the hospital when her phone went off.

Krystal was crying, "Mom . . ." more crying, "I want to go home." Ashley could hear the sorrow in her voice, the desperation. "I wanna die . . ."

Ashley responded instantly, "I'm on my way," her voice more resolute.

Ashley hung up the phone and found her supervisor. "Dave, I need to pick up my daughter. It's an emergency." The panic in her voice was all too real.

Dave nodded, "Go. I'll manage things." Ashley rushed out before she could thank him. She sped her car through a couple red lights until she was on the main road heading towards the Evergardens for Krystal's dance. Ashley could hear the fear in Krystal's voice. *Oh please no. I hope she doesn't kill herself. Please keep her safe.* Ashley gripped the steering wheel as her fingers went numb. "Please don't do anything. Please don't do anything, Krystal." The fear of Krystal's suicidal tendencies came roaring to the surface. Ashley feared immensely what Krystal would do. All the signs of suicidal depression had been showing lately, Ashley could see it all when Krystal came home. Ever since Krystal started high school, her depression had gotten worse and worse, until Ashley feared one day, Krystal would harm herself. Ashley had hired a therapist and prescribed Krystal anti-depressant medication, but both the therapist and medication were proving futile. Fear drove Ashley to speed there as fast as possible. She needed to save her daughter.

Ashley pulled up to the final intersection and could see Krystal across. The sight revealed a slight glimmer of hope in her midnight purple eyes, happy that she could see her mom coming to her rescue. Ashley waited impatiently at the red light, ready to cross the four-way intersection. Her foot hovered eagerly over the pedal. The light turned green, and Ashley drove the car forward. Ashley locked eyes with Krystal, mouthing, "It's going to be okay; it's going to be—" as the green pickup truck slammed into her side at sixty-five miles an hour.

CHAPTER 53

Change

"Time doesn't heal everything. Sometimes you have to properly address your wounds, or they will never heal."

—JL

*W*hat a failure. *What kind of person does that? You should feel awful about what you've done.*

A pregnant woman walked down a street, as the woman suddenly tumbled and fell out of sight. What happened to her? Where was she going?

You're horrible. What a failure.

Ashley opened her eyes slowly. Breath entered her lungs as she took in the surroundings of the hospital room. She had stayed a few nights in the hospital so the doctors could run a few tests to make sure she was okay, but they did diagnose she would have to do some physical therapy to learn how to walk again. Ashley looked to the side of the hospital bed and found Krystal sitting there peeling an orange. "Here," she said, offering a slice. Ashley lifted her hallowed arm and grabbed the piece. It felt so heavy she might drop it. Ashley held the orange slice, but her attention was not directed at the orange, it was on Krystal.

Krystal was humming something to herself like she didn't have a care in the world. The sight was so foreign, it terrified Ashley. *What happened while I was asleep?* she wondered. Watching Krystal act so differently was like looking at a total stranger. Krystal offered Ashley a glass of water and she drank it, feeling the cool refreshing liquid float down her throat, regaining some of her lost strength. Krystal smiled at the sight of her mom recovering. Krystal put down the cup while Ashley lay back in bed, bewildered from looking at

Krystal. The mere sight of Krystal's change in behavior was miraculous. It seemed too good to be true.

Ashley used up what little energy she had to move her lips. They felt heavy, the muscles weak and rusty, as if they hadn't been used in a while. "Krystal . . ." she croaked. Krystal turned and waited for her mom to speak. "What happened?" It was so low Krystal almost didn't hear it.

Krystal took a seat and figured it was time to tell her. Ashley still was wondering, *Is this really the same person? She's completely different.* It wasn't in Krystal's physical appearance so much, although she did look a bit older and did her hair differently, looking like a fine young woman now. But the real change was more in the way Krystal carried herself. There was something about how she moved, that made her seem more . . . *happy.* Krystal got comfortable in her chair and said, "It's going to be a little hard to take in, but mom you've been in a coma for more than a year."

Ashley didn't have the strength to react. The mere news of it caused her to faint, but only temporarily. Krystal looked worried standing over her, on the verge of shouting for a doctor. Ashley slowly came to, and Krystal offered another orange slice, "Here, you'll need this." Ashley livened up after eating the slice and looked to be better after a little rest.

Ashley asked the question she'd been waiting for, "What happened to *you?*" Krystal only looked at her, a mixture of pain, sorrow, and joy, all in the same look. Ashley had no idea how to react to that. "Krystal?"

Krystal stood up and spoke with wisdom, "I'll tell you when the time is right. For now, you need to rest. And then you'll be ready."

"Ready?"

"Yes. Ready. You're being discharged by the end of today. We're going home."

～

Sarah pushed the wheelchair through the doorway to Ashley's apartment. "Okay there, take it easy partner. No need to kick off running."

Ashley sneered from Sarah's tease. "I can open my own door thank you very much." Sarah smiled, enjoying the reaction of her best friend coming back to life. Krystal stood next to them, looking genuinely happy. Ashley could not get her mind off that. *Krystal . . . what happened since I last saw you?* she wondered, picturing the sight of her little girl from what felt like yesterday telling Ashley how she wanted to kill herself. But that had been a little more than a year ago, and now Krystal was totally different since they last spoke. Ashley tried to remember the car accident, how she was rushing to pick up Krystal, fearing her suicidal tendencies. Ashley had seen the results of suicide all the time. Kids being rushed into the hospital with self-inflicted wounds, overdoses, alcohol poisoning and others. Ashley had seen it all, the symptoms of suicidal depression all too conspicuous on Krystal as well. So what had happened to her daughter in the past year? What made her so jovial all of a sudden?

Sarah stopped in the apartment and said, "Oooohhhkay that's it. You're all set up. I'm going to leave now; I have to get back to the hospital."

"You do that," Ashley croaked, wanting to join her, but for now she was stuck in a wheelchair until she learned how to walk again.

Krystal pulled her hair back into a ponytail, "I'll get dinner ready, then maybe we can watch a movie?" looking at her mom, enjoying the sight of her mom alive again. Ashley wanted to say something but was stopped by her own curiosity. She was amazed at Krystal's change in demeanor, watching Krystal as she made dinner, looking like a healthy normal girl. The sight terrified Ashley, unsure how to react to this new girl who was supposed to be her daughter.

Ashley looked at her curiously and said, "Uhh sure . . . why not."

Three months passed and Ashley was still struggling with her physical therapy sessions. She knew relearning everything after being in a coma would be difficult, but she didn't expect it to be this difficult.

"Okay let's begin." The physical therapist stood there, ready to help Ashley should she need it. Ashley braced herself, staring down at her own two feet, feeling intimidated to the bone.

You can't do this. You don't deserve this! Ashley hid her feelings and stared down at her feet. Since she could not hold up a job while she was recovering, staying at home was torture for Ashley. She had no hobbies at home except to watch movies and when she was sick of that, Ashley yearned to be back in the operating room. So now she had all the time in the world to do nothing but think, and that was torture.

Ashley looked up at her physical therapist. Doubt etched on her face. The therapist smiled, "You can do this Ashley, you just have to believe in yourself."

Ashley snorted in contempt, *Heh, believe in myself? I don't believe in myself for a second.*

The therapist braced to catch Ashley should she fall, waiting for her to make the first move. Ashley stared at her toes for a minute longer before trying to lower her feet onto the ground. Touching her skin to the floor felt odd, like experiencing a cold shiver down your spine. Ashley leaned over, trying to put more weight on her feet, her heart and mind going into a frenzy. *I don't deserve this. I don't deserve this. What am I even doing? I should sit down and be in a wheelchair for the rest of my life.* Ashley tried to fight the thoughts off, but they were persistent.

Ashley stood atop her big toe and felt the pressure increase. She leaned forward but her heart wasn't committed at all. Ashley simply had no motivation to walk again. Ashley tumbled forward and the therapist caught her, helping her back onto the wheelchair. Ashley could tell the therapist was hiding her disappointment. *She's probably thinking, "It's been three months since she's woken up and she's made no improvement since the wheelchair."* Ashley tried not to look the woman in the eyes, catching a glimpse in her peripherals, finding them cheerful and supportive. *Liar.*

"Okay that seems to wrap up our session. We'll try again tomorrow."

"Sure," the doubt clear in Ashley's voice.

Ashley waited on the corner in front of the clinic as a car she didn't recognize pulled up. The passenger window lowered and revealed Krystal in the driver's seat. Ashley was amazed at the sight. *What the? When did she learn how to drive?!* Ashley was so absorbed in her surprise that her frustration from the session vanished.

Krystal waved and said, "Hey, Mom!"

Ashley did her best attempt to look cheery in her current condition. "Hey, sweetie." Krystal helped Ashley into the car and the two of them drove back to their apartment. They were quiet for a minute or two, as Ashley observed Krystal's driving. She looked calm and collective, like she had done this a thousand times before. The sight was so foreign to Ashley that she never imagined Krystal would drive a car.

Krystal noticed Ashley staring, "What?"

"Nothing, it's just . . . when did you learn how to drive?"

Krystal did a quick glance and returned her eyes to the road. "Mr. Fisher taught me."

"Mr. Fisher?"

"Jaime's dad."

"Who's *Jaime*?"

Krystal smiled for a moment, "You'll find out soon enough. They're our neighbors. I've spent a lot of time over there."

"Huh, it seems like you've done a lot without me." Krystal became quiet from that statement. Ashley did not mean for it to come across as snarky, but it did.

Krystal answered somberly, "A lot happened while you were asleep." Ashley couldn't tell if that struck a nerve with her or not. But she couldn't help but wonder, *Krystal . . . what happened to you while I was gone?*

> "Small things can have the biggest impact on others."
> —Krystal Henninger

"Thanks for helping out, Carmen."

Carmen stood at the doorway and saluted, "No problem. If you ever need any help, just come on by." Krystal was grateful. It wasn't easy getting a woman in a wheelchair up a flight of stairs without help.

"I appreciate that." Krystal closed the door and walked back to the kitchen. Ashley was sitting still in her wheelchair, pondering a good many things. Krystal strapped on an apron, "I'll get dinner started."

Ashley didn't look up, but she managed to raise her voice high enough for Krystal to hear. "Krystal . . ." Krystal stopped what she was doing and looked her mom's direction. "What . . . happened to you while I was gone?" Krystal lowered her head, it was time. "Because I need to know, what caused you to change?" Ashley looked up at her daughter. "Why are you so happy?" Krystal left the kitchen and knelt in front of her mom. It felt like the roles were reversed. Instead of the mom comforting the daughter it was the daughter comforting the mom.

Krystal said, "I'd tell you to sit down but you're already sitting."

Ashley couldn't help but chuckle at the snide remark. "I'll get you for that one," she replied smiling but got back to business.

Krystal could feel the pressure of her story bearing forth. "It's best I show you."

Ashley's eyes watched as Krystal pulled her left sleeve down, revealing the horrific sight before her. Terror and worry struck Ashley's body and she nearly went into a panic attack. Ashley had seen so many wounds like this one on thousands of hurting kids and even adults. People who had attempted to take their own lives but somehow survived. Ashley had seen it all. But it was worse when Ashley saw it on her own daughter. A victim of her own making. The sight of the two-inch-long knife wound across Krystal's left wrist was enough to send Ashley into shock. Ashley had never lost her cool when in a hospital but seeing it here was different.

"After I lost you in the car accident. I had lost all hope . . ." Krystal paused. The words were difficult to bring forth, but they needed to be said. It was a time for open honesty. "You were my only reason for living. My final pillar of support. And . . . when I lost you, I didn't think I could fall any deeper . . ." Krystal took a breath. "So, I took a knife, put it against my wrist, and sliced the radial artery. Remember, the one you taught me about." Ashley nodded. She had schooled Krystal on medical practice often, so it was not unusual for Krystal to know medical terminology. "And so . . . I sliced my wrist and bled out on the floor. And you know what I felt?" Ashley shook her head, "Empty . . ." Krystal looked down at the floor, "It wasn't the solution. It didn't provide me with the satisfaction I wanted. It didn't end the pain that I wanted to escape from. And so, I bled out on the floor until I passed out." Krystal looked back at her mom, "Remarkably, I didn't die. I woke up next morning and cleaned up my own suicide, as if it never happened." Krystal's joy was gone now, replaced by broken emotions and vivid memories. It was there Ashley was seeing the old Krystal again, but it was only a shadow, a glimpse of the past long dead. Maybe those memories will never leave Krystal. Maybe that part of her will remain like that for the rest of her life. You just can't forget when you tried to take your own life.

Krystal rolled her sleeve back up. "I ended up in the hospital just as dead as when I sliced my own wrist. But in that hospital, I met a Janitor . . . a Janitor who showed me kindness, a man who listened to me, a man who *saw* me." Krystal looked at her mom dead in the eyes, her words faltering. "The joy of being seen, of being acknowledged . . . I never felt that before." Krystal took a breath, "It was such a relief. That for the first time, someone cared for me. Who took time out of their day to listen to me for as long as I needed. It was like living water poured over my soul . . . and I had never felt that loved before in my life. I know it was a small thing, but small things can have the biggest impact on others." Krystal paused, lowering her head, a slight smile forming. "He gave me a brownie, and listened to me, and told me that he has great hope for someone like me." Krystal almost broke into tears after saying that aloud. "He cried for me and prayed that God would come and save me. I didn't take him seriously at first but the more I thought about it, the more I wondered whether there really was a God or not. And now, I know." Krystal raised her head, "Mom, I'm alive . . . because God saved me. I know it sounds crazy but once I prayed and received Jesus into my life, everything started to change. I started becoming more confident, I started caring about others, I started doing things I never did before. And because of that . . . I have *friends*."

"Friends?" Ashley asked, bewildered. The word seemed so foreign to hear coming from Krystal's lips.

Krystal nodded, "Yes that's right. I have friends. I don't feel empty anymore. I can wake up now and feel loved. I can wake up now and feel hopeful. I can wake up now and know that my pain will not last. That is what happened to me. That's how I am the way I am." Krystal paused, "I know it all sounds crazy, believing in a God you can't even see, but . . . if you seek God with all your heart, you will find Him."

Krystal watched as her mom lowered her gaze and said, "I'm not sure I'm there yet Krystal."

Krystal nodded in understanding. "That's okay," she whispered, "You take it at your own pace."

"I don't know what it is you're talking about, but I will tell you one thing Krystal . . . I can see a tremendous change in you."

Krystal smiled, "Thanks, Mom."

༄

Ashley stared at her feet, the dreadful perspective of facing a giant. She gripped the arms of her wheelchair, straining the leather beneath her fingertips. Ashley breathed nervously, shaking. It was time.

Ashley sent messages for her legs to move. Her right toe twitched then her foot responded, but faintly. She had to put a little more effort into moving her legs after being in bed for a year. Ashley put all her effort into lifting her foot. She successfully lifted her right foot up and planted it onto the ground, then did the same with her left foot. She already felt exhausted, gripping her chair harder. The floor stared at her and enlarged itself. The fear perpetuated her. Ashley kept telling herself, *It's time. It's time.* But her heart and soul disagreed with her.

Ashley tried to lift herself off the chair, but her guilt came back and weighed her down. Ashley felt herself sink into her chair despite struggling to stay up. Her thoughts were in turmoil.

Get up. You can do this!

I don't deserve this. I'm still guilty!

Come on! Let it go!

I can't do this!

I don't deserve to walk again. I don't deserve to be brought back.

The guilt sapped all her strength and Ashley fell back hard in her chair. "I still can't walk." Catching her breath, having failed to show any improvement.

CHAPTER 54

Guilt

"How do you get rid of guilt?"

—JL

Ashley awoke to the scent of bacon and eggs. Her mouth instantly salivated as she got herself ready and headed toward the dinner table. Ashley had nothing to do these days, so she did a fair amount of sleeping when she was at home, and it felt good to sleep in this Sunday. It was all new to her. Different from her prior schedule, because for the first time in years Ashley had not been working. It was a completely different change compared to her previous schedule and habits. Ashley was usually ready to be out the door and off to work, then come home at the end of the day completely exhausted and crash on the couch. But now the clock was limitless, and Ashley had all the time in the world to do nothing. It was starting to drive her nuts.

Ashley ate the breakfast Krystal had prepared; Krystal's cooking was always the best and had been since she was little. Krystal always had a gift for cooking, which made Ashley eager to come home to have a delicious meal.

Ashley finished her plate then saw Krystal getting ready to leave. "You going somewhere sweetie?"

Krystal walked to the door, "Yes I am, I'm going to church at the 10:30am service."

"Church?" Ashley said. The word felt so foreign to Ashley. She had never considered going to church before and wondered why. "You go to church?"

Krystal answered happily, "Yeah."

"Oh uhh, okay."

Krystal tilted her head, "Do you wanna come?"

Ashley thought about it. She didn't have anything else to do in this apartment, so she said, "Sure?"

"Cool."

Cool? Ashley raised an eyebrow, *Since when does Krystal say 'cool'? What else have I missed since I was asleep?* Ashley wondered about that question quite often. It was a whole new experience to wake up in a new world one year later. Although some things stayed the same, the majority of the world was different. Especially Krystal. And to that, Ashley was surprised with the changes that have occurred.

Krystal grabbed the keys and said, "I'll get the car ready."

Krystal pulled the car up to the church and opened the passenger door. She set up Ashley's wheelchair and helped her into it. She pushed Ashley forward; Ashley, not knowing what would come next, was hesitant to what kind of church Krystal had brought her to.

Ashley had never given church any thought. She always thought that was for people who choose to believe in whatever they wanted to believe in or had at least grown up in the church because their parents made them go. She had never entertained the thought for herself. But she was Krystal's mom and so she would be there for Krystal as she went to church, at least this time. If Ashley didn't like it, she wouldn't go the next time. Besides, Ashley had nothing to do today except mope around the apartment, so it was better to get out and try something new than to sit at home and do nothing.

Krystal pushed Ashley through a set of doors, receiving a quick greeting from the people standing outside. Krystal did her best to greet them while Ashley just watched. Krystal pushed her inside and they took their seats in the far back of the auditorium. After a couple of songs of worship, a man wearing a checkered shirt and glasses stepped onto the stage.

Ashley had no feelings when the man stepped out. She had never been to church before and knew relatively nothing about it, so she had neither malice nor joy towards it whatsoever.

The Preacher set his mug of coffee on the podium and placed a book down in the center. He glanced at the audience and said, "Good morning my friends. How are we all doing this fine Sunday morning?" The audience was somewhat lively and responded with quiet murmurs. The Preacher creased the corner of his lip, "You all seem pretty awake this morning." The audience chuckled. Ashley didn't see the joke. The Preacher looked out at the crowd and said, "Normally I start with a question but this morning I want to do things a little different." He paused. "First I want to thank everyone for coming this morning, and I want to welcome all our new members for joining us." The crowd applauded and Ashley felt this was for her somehow.

After the applause settled the Preacher said, "Now, I'd like to start off with a question . . . how do we find forgiveness?" The Preacher looked out at the audience; his tone dead serious. "Because I know that some of you today are still struggling with something you've done in the past. You can't seem to move on, or you don't know how to be forgiven for something so horrible. In fact, you've been struggling for years now, carrying this guilt, but you never seem to get this immense weight off your chest no matter what you do." Ashley sat up in her wheelchair, eyes wide. The Preacher lifted his hands in exaggerated curiosity, "So what then? How do we get rid of this guilt? Where does it come from?"

The Preacher pushed up his glasses, "The reason we experience guilt is because in each one of us, there is a built-in sense of morality. We don't give it to ourselves, it is a part of life. It is the very reason we know it is wrong to murder someone or to rape a woman. We feel guilty because we know we have done wrong. But then who sets the standard for right and wrong? If there is a Moral Law, then there must be a Moral Law Giver, and that Law Giver is God. For He set that moral law inside of us as proof of His existence. He defined what is right and what is wrong.

"You see, guilt is a direct result of sin. We don't feel guilty when we do the right thing. We only feel guilty when we do something morally wrong. And we experience this guilt because deep down we know that we have sinned." The Preacher raised his arms, "So how do we get rid of sin? Well, the Bible says that God loves us and that He sent His Son Jesus Christ, to die for our sins." The Preacher returned to the podium and said, "In the book of Romans 5:8–11, the Bible says,

> *"But God showed his great love for us by sending Christ to die*
> *for us while we were still sinners. And since we have been made*
> *right in God's sight by the blood of Christ, he will certainly save*

us from God's condemnation. For since our friendship with
God was restored by the death of his Son while we were still his
enemies, we will certainly be saved through the life of his Son. So
now we can rejoice in our wonderful new relationship with God
because our Lord Jesus Christ has made us friends with God."
—ROMANS 5:8–11 (NLT)

The Preacher looked up and said, "While we were still sinners, God sent His Son Jesus Christ to die on the cross for us, and three days later, Jesus was resurrected to cleanse us from our sins so that we may live with God in Heaven." The Preacher held his hands out in parallel. "You see, God took the first step and forgave us while we were still sinners. We didn't deserve God's forgiveness; in fact, we deserved judgment because we sinned against God. God could have condemned us, but that's not what God did. Instead, God forgave us." The Preacher pushed his glasses up, "But then how far does God's forgiveness go? The Bible says in Luke 23:34, when Jesus was hung on the cross, He said to His enemies,

"Father, forgive them, for they don't know what they are doing."
—LUKE 23:34A (NLT)

The Preacher said, "Even when Jesus was hanging on the cross, being mocked by His enemies, He asked God to forgive them." The Preacher looked at the audience, "You can be an enemy of God and He will still forgive you. Do you know what this means? It means that no matter what you've done, no matter how horrible the sins you've committed, God will still forgive you."

The words hit Ashley like a shockwave. Her heart pulsed and ached from the guilt inside. She allowed herself to think, *Can . . . can God really forgive me for what I've done?* She felt her heart pound within, thumping hard as she leaned forward and listened.

The Preacher pushed up his glasses, "But you may be telling yourself, 'It's too late. I can't be forgiven for what I've done.' But I say to you, as long as you're breathing it's never too late. Let's look at the example of the Thief on the cross. In the book of Luke, it says there were two criminals that were nailed on crosses to the left and right of Jesus, and in Luke 23:39–43, it says,

One of the criminals hanging beside him scoffed, "So you're the Messiah, are you? Prove it by saving yourself—and us, too, while you're at it! But the other criminal protested, "Don't you fear God even when you have been sentenced to die? We deserve to die for our crimes, but this man hasn't done anything wrong." Then he said, "Jesus, remember me when you come into your Kingdom." And Jesus replied, "I assure you, today you will be with me in paradise."
—LUKE 23:39–43 (NLT)

The Preacher lifted his eyes slowly and looked solemnly at the audience. "'Jesus, remember me.' That has to be the shortest confession in the entire Bible." He paused. "This criminal understood that we deserve to die for our sins. He understood that he could not save himself. But in his last moments he repented and believed in Jesus when he said, 'Jesus remember me.'" The Preacher paused and studied the audience. "That means that as long as you're breathing, it's never too late. This criminal was in his dying moments, and he repented, and what did Jesus say? He said, 'I assure you, today you will be with me in paradise.'" The Preacher raised his head and closed his eyes for a moment as if receiving something. Ashley was so focused that she would wait an eternity until he spoke again. Then he opened his eyes and said, "God wants to have you with him in Heaven. That is the sole purpose of why Jesus came and died for you. He died because He loves you and because He wants you to be with Him in paradise."

Ashley sat there in awe, completely entranced by this man's words. It's uncanny how authoritative this man's words were. It was as if he was speaking to her directly, telling her the answer she's been waiting to hear. Ashley could feel the words calling to her heart, receiving them, wanting to accept them as the truth. She felt a sense of elation from hearing this man speak. She was on the edge of her seat, wanting to hear more.

The Preacher pushed his glasses up and said, "So how do we receive this forgiveness from God? How do we repent from our sins and be free from our guilt and past? Well, the Bible says in 1 John 1:9,

"But if we confess our sins to him, he is faithful and just to forgive us our sins and to cleanse us from all wickedness."
—1 JOHN 1:9 (NLT)

"And in Romans 10:9, it says,

> *"If you openly declare that Jesus is Lord and believe in your*
> *heart that God raised him from the dead, you will be saved."*
> —ROMANS 10:9 (NLT)

The Preacher looked up, "If we confess and repent from our sins, declare with our mouths that Jesus is Lord, and believe in our hearts that God raised Jesus from the dead, then God will cleanse you of all your sins, and you will be saved."

Ashley felt her soul cry out. Ready to spill everything building within her. She looked at Krystal and wondered if Krystal could ever forgive her for the horrible things she's done. Ashley felt the weight of her guilt pile on her, dragging her down to a deep pit of depression and self-pity.

The Preacher put both his arms on the podium and spoke softly, "My friends, I do not want you to be living a life of shame. I do not want you to be stuck in the past hurting, unable to experience the joys that God has for us. I want you to be free. And so does God." The Preacher paused. "If you want to take that first step into forgiveness, then will you pray this with me." The whole audience put their hands together. The Preacher threaded his hands and lowered his head. "Jesus, I am a sinner. I have done wrong. I know I don't deserve your forgiveness, but Jesus, I believe that You are the Messiah. Jesus, will you come into my life and forgive me for all my sins. I want to follow Your will from now on. In Jesus' name I pray, amen."

Ashley opened her eyes. She didn't say the prayer, but she pretended to. Ashley wanted to say the prayer but held herself back. The guilt keeping a strong grip on her, preventing her from coming forward. The Preacher said, "If you prayed that prayer today can we give you a round of applause." The entire congregation applauded, and Ashley couldn't help but feel the enthusiasm in the air. Almost like it was meant for her. But her hope dissipated as she was reminded of her past.

You think a simple sermon will forgive you? No. You don't deserve to be forgiven!

Ashley hung her head forward, clinging to the message but could feel its power slipping away. The guilt ached in her heart, the pressure crushing her, until she felt a hand brush against her back. Ashley turned and saw Krystal looking at her with a soft smile. Ashley met her eyes, *Can . . . can you forgive me?* But Krystal looked at her like she had already answered the question. Her expression said it all.

Yes, I forgive you.

> "You cannot will yourself to be happy."
> —Ashley Henninger

Ashley sat in her wheelchair in the center of her room. The darkness of her room hiding all sense of weakness, allowing Ashley to be completely open with herself.

After what happened at the church, Ashley had no idea what to think. Too stunned for words to even fathom . . . Could she really be forgiven for what she's done? Was there really a God out there who could forgive her? Ashley contemplated the thought, but she wanted to refuse.

No! That can't be. It's impossible for something like that to happen . . . I could never be forgiven for what I've done.

But then, what about Krystal? Ashley paused. The thought of Krystal smiling popped in her mind.

How could one possibly explain the drastic changes in Krystal's life? As a medical doctor Ashley had no credible explanation. Krystal went from a depressed lonely girl to a kind and cheerful person. How could she explain that?

Ashley didn't have an answer. But one thing was for sure . . . Krystal was a lot happier than she was before. Ashley simply could not explain the reason for why such a dramatic change could exist. Krystal said it was because she encountered a Janitor and he introduced her to God, but Ashley didn't believe in God, but then . . . how could such a change happen if it wasn't for a God? Even when Krystal was in elementary school she suffered from depression, and every time Krystal came home from a therapy session, she showed no sign of improvement. Ashley had tried and tried but she could not make her daughter feel happy. But now, Krystal was happy. Why?

If Ashley couldn't think of a material answer, then perhaps it's an immaterial answer. A God perhaps.

But so . . . does that mean what Krystal said is true?

Ashley cupped her chin. *Krystal is not a liar. She can't lie, it goes against her very nature. And . . . if she tells me that God saved her then . . .* Ashley stopped herself there, shaking her head. *No, no you're just imagining things Ashley. God could never bring someone out of depression . . . can He?* Ashley was not one to believe in miracles, but that would be hypocritical given that Ashley herself was in a coma for the past year, and had miraculously awakened when quote on quote, "Krystal prayed for her." It was a detail Ashley couldn't factor into the equation because she didn't understand it.

How does a prayer bring someone back to life? But then again, Ashley thought, *Krystal is no longer her old self.* Ashley couldn't deny the positive changes she's seen in Krystal's life. No counselor, therapist, or pill could ever give Krystal hope. Yet this random Janitor comes by, and she suddenly finds a reason to live? Ashley shook her head denying it, but she also couldn't come up with an answer to refute it.

Then there were Ashley's own issues. The guilt she had been suffering for years and still is to this day. But that sermon from church hit home. And Ashley wondered for the first time, if it was possible for someone like her to be forgiven. If it was okay to admit her faults and not be judged for what she's done or deserves. She whispered, "Is it possible . . . to be forgiven? Is it true someone like me can find forgiveness?" Ashley doubted that but then she remembered the look on Krystal's face, how there was hope. All of it she could not understand yet couldn't deny.

Ashley shook her head. "I don't get it. I simply don't understand." Then Ashley remembered one of the Preacher's verses, *"If you openly declare that Jesus is Lord and believe in your heart that God raised him from the dead, you will be saved."*

Ashley paused for a moment. As if the doubt were beginning to fade. *Maybe . . . maybe I can be saved . . . maybe.*

CHAPTER 55

Choices

*"We are free to make our own choices, but we
are not free from the consequences."*

—JL

Amber stepped out of the car and stuffed her skirt under her coat. She now wore a coat every day, despite it being eighty degrees outside. The summer heat was certainly in full swing and well on its way. The moment she stepped out of the car, she headed as quickly as she could toward her locker, avoiding eye contact with anyone on her way. She made it through a school hallway and then peered out into the courtyard where her locker was located. Locker 298, standing high above the others. But in her way was an ocean of students going about their business. The cliques had formed in the morning already, ten minutes before the school bell was supposed to ring. Amber struggled with the dilemma she was facing. There was no way to get to her locker without being seen.

People were passing by like a river, so Amber figured she had no choice. She took a chance and that step proved to be lethal. Amber stepped out and got stuck with the flow of the crowd, being swept away like an ocean current. Amber could feel the eyeballs looking her way like she was a magnet for attention, or a diseased leper people should avoid. People began parting their ways for Amber. Amber saw all eyes on her and pushed forward anyways. Steam billowing from her anger. There was no hiding it now.

Don't peek, don't look at them. But Amber gave into the temptation and looked over her shoulder to see what people were looking at, then heard the whispering. The girls huddled around their lockers, the guys talking as

Amber passed. She was less than a foot away, passing through the crowds and cliques filling the courtyard like cholesterol in blood vessels. Amber wanted nothing more than to leave.

Amber made it to her locker and got the books she needed, and by that, she meant none of them. Amber emptied her backpack and slammed her locker, trying her best to ignore the glares shooting her way. Amber saw Summer and her group of friends and felt relieved as she walked over to join them.

But the moment Amber approached the group, they all reared back like she was a rattlesnake. Amber's eyes examined the distance between herself and them. "What's the deal?" she asked, as they all glared at her like she carried a disease.

Cassie came up and said, "Amber are you actually pregnant?"

Amber looked away and started grumbling. Then faced them and said slow and angry, "Yesss," with a sharp hiss in the "S." Amber glared at them. She wasn't doing a particularly good job maintaining her composure, in fact she was shaking like a wet dog. Cassie, Summer, and the rest of the group stood there, speechless.

Another girl stepped forward from the circle and said, "We're not really sure how to react to this Amber, so maybe it's best you hang out somewhere else?"

Amber could not believe her ears. "Are you kicking me out of my own group of friends?" Her own group was rejecting her, all because she got pregnant! Amber waited for a response but got none. Summer stood there ashamed as Amber met her eyes. "Summer!" she called, "Summer come on! Don't throw me away like I'm a piece of trash." Amber could see the difficult decision on Summer's face, but Summer did nothing. Amber could tell Summer wanted to, but looked away in shame. Amber saw the betrayal. Her heart was in uproar and her voice thick with tears. "SCREW ALL OF YOU!" she yelled, as she turned and went running to the bathroom. Locking herself away into the stall. Waiting there, long after the first bell rang.

An hour later Amber heard a knock on the door. "Amber?" It was Summer's voice. Amber felt a sense of relief and anger.

Amber shriveled and sneered behind the bathroom stall, "Go away you traitor."

"You put me in a difficult situation Amber," Summer replied, "It was like, a lot to drop on someone, especially us. We didn't know how to react to something like that. We also like, didn't think this would happen to you."

Amber muffled through the stall, "Yeah well it did. Now what do I do?"

Summer leaned against the door, "Amber are you really pregnant?"

Amber yelled, "Yes. I already told you!"

"Let me see."

"No."

"Let me see," Summer persisted. Amber, annoyed and out of patience, slid the lock open and let Summer into the bathroom stall. What Summer had witnessed was neither the Amber she knew or loved, but a broken person laid before her. Amber stood up and lifted the clothing over her stomach, revealing the bulging belly before Summer. Summer's eyes widened as she felt Amber's open stomach. "How far along are you?"

"Twenty-four weeks."

"Oh Amber." Summer said, her voice soft and anxious. Amber had lost the fiery temper she had earlier and now needed a shoulder to cry on. Summer held Amber at arms distance and said, "I can't be there for you one hundred percent. There's a lot of people looking at you at school. So we can't see each other during school, but after school, feel free to come by." Amber found both relief and frustration in that. Summer was helping her but was also keeping her at a distance. Amber hugged Summer for a while. Summer broke away and left Amber in the bathroom. Amber wished Summer stayed longer. She could only wish . . .

⟲

Krystal walked through the automatic doors into the department store. The classic ding dong, as she rolled in with a goal in mind. Krystal wanted to be in and out, nothing more nothing less. Plus . . . she didn't want anyone to see her buying what she was going to buy. Krystal headed toward the makeup aisle and standing before her, were hundreds of different items. At first glance, Krystal was totally lost. The sheer size and quantity of makeup overwhelmed her. Krystal felt her mind slowly lose its sanity the longer she stared.

"Coriander, Antima, Morose, Coriander, Antima, Morose, Coriander, Antima, Morose," Krystal's eyes skimmed through the same items over and over. A whirlwind spinning in her mind causing her to lose focus. Her vision darkened. Krystal took her gaze off the makeup selection and put her hand to her head. She backed out of the makeup aisle feeling dizzy and overwhelmed.

Krystal leaned against a perfume rack, carefully placing her hand down to not push any off.

Krystal took a couple deep breaths and gazed across the store. A man was busy checking out while the rest of the store loomed in silence. Krystal could feel it too. It didn't bother her, she actually felt at home in the silence. Only the sound of the air conditioning filled the store. Krystal tried to listen for any ugly music playing through the store speakers but there was none. It felt nice. It made her feel not as rushed and enjoy the moment. *Thank you, God, for this time of silence,* she prayed. She opened her eyes and felt a tug in her heart. Like the Holy Spirit was pointing her in some direction. Krystal followed it as she passed through the aisles and stopped, peering into the baby items aisle. Only to find Amber Cutthrose standing there, holding a basket in one hand, comparing baby items in the other. It didn't take long for Krystal to realize what she was doing here. *So, she really was pregnant.* After all, Krystal was the one who told Amber she was pregnant during the fight, but that was a while ago, so it wasn't like it mattered back then anyways.

Krystal felt a sense of fear erupt at the sight of Amber. Krystal remembered the fight, her cheeks purple and swollen in memory of Amber slapping her over and over. Krystal wanted to back away but was compelled to stay. Krystal looked up at the ceiling, *Is there something you want me to do God?* But the Holy Spirit inside her did nothing. Krystal stayed put and continued to watch Amber from a distance. Amber gave no indication she knew Krystal was there. She seemed to be in her own sad little world as she slowly picked up and examined each item.

What was interesting was how she pondered whether to buy something, only to put it back on the shelf. She already had a few things in her basket, but she never added anything. She repeated this over and over, but it wasn't the items that interested Krystal, it was how Amber looked that intrigued her. It took Krystal a moment to realize what she saw.

Amber lowered both her arms and looked up, nearly dropping her basket. Krystal's jaw slowly opened, and her heart melted within her. The memory of the fight melted away with mercy and compassion as she finally understood what Amber was thinking.

Pregnant at seventeen, deciding whether to keep the baby or not. Krystal hoped Amber would. Either way, Amber looked miserable. A misery that would last the next twenty years of her life. It was strange to see Amber look this way. To go from the fiery, hot-tempered chick wailing on her (although Krystal *let* Amber rail on her), now to a sad broken teenage mom who had to grow up way too fast. It was strange to see Amber look so . . . defeated. Krystal wanted to walk over there and give her a hug but there was nothing she could do to make the problem go away. Even if she went up and hugged Amber right now it would be awkward. Besides, Amber was giving off the vibe that she didn't want to be disturbed right now, so Krystal inched back and made her way toward the checkout.

Krystal stepped in line, finding two people in front of her. Then Amber stepped in line behind her; Krystal's eyes widened. Her heart began pumping a little faster, wondering what she would say if Amber recognized her. Krystal tried to keep her cool, which was normally an easy thing to do, but this time it felt like the most terrifying thing in the world to do. But Amber stood there and said nothing. Krystal wanted to look over her shoulder and sneak a glimpse of Amber's face but that would reveal Krystal's hand and Amber would recognize her. *How could you not recognize the person you beat in the face over and over in that fight?* But Amber said nothing, making Krystal change her line of thinking. *Maybe she does recognize me, but she chooses to do nothing?*

The line moved forward, now only one person in front of Krystal. Compassion filled Krystal's heart and she wondered if she should do something for Amber. *But what should I do? Also . . . WHY WOULD I HELP THE VERY PERSON WHO HURT ME SO BAD?!* The uproar in her mind felt so loud she almost yelped.

A verse Krystal had heard recently flashed through her head, *"love your enemies."* Krystal sighed and remembered the forgiveness God gave her when she was suffering from her own depression. So, Krystal took the chance. A substantial portion of Krystal was in uproar from the decision. It felt like her heart was at war with itself, split between two sides. Her old nature vs her new nature. Her old-self vs her new Christian self. And her old self was fighting hard. Krystal felt the temptation to turn around and slap Amber and say, *"That's what was coming to you! You deserve everything about this!"* But the image of Amber looking miserable flashed in her mind again. This time, Krystal placed herself in Amber's shoes.

Imagine if that was you, standing there, pregnant, not wanting anyone to know, awkwardness floating between you and your friends. Not wanting any of this, and knowing your future is ruined. To have to live each day in a hell of your own creation. And to deal with the guilt of it all.

Krystal cringed for a moment, drinking it all in. *Well, when you put it that way . . . I would want some mercy.* The world slowed down, though only for a few seconds. Krystal stepped up to the checkout, placing her razors and makeup on the countertop. The cashier scanned it, no conversation between the two of them. Krystal was too wrapped in thought to be thinking about that. Krystal pulled out her new credit card and stared at it. *Should I?*

"Miss? Miss?" the cashier said, with a look of worry and concern on her face.

Krystal blinked back into reality and said, "I'm sorry. Here," offering the card. Krystal could feel the pressure, what she was about to do was both uncomfortable and uncommon. It made no sense, and her old self was screaming in her heart against it.

Don't you dare! She deserves this! Amber deserves the judgment that's coming to her.

But Krystal retorted. *Like the judgment we deserve? . . .* no answer. *That's what I thought.*

Krystal chuckled. *It's funny how I can stymie myself.* It felt as if all the hatred melted off Krystal, leaving only compassion, no matter how hurt Krystal was from the fight. Krystal finished her payment, took her card back and gestured to Amber, "And I'll pay for whatever she's ordering."

The cashier was surprised and said, "Oh, okay. I can do that." The cashier looked over Krystal's shoulder and called out to Amber, "Is that all right miss?"

Amber blinked back to reality, "What?"

The cashier pointed to Krystal and said, "This girl is willing to pay for your groceries, is that fine with you?"

Amber shifted her attention to Krystal. Krystal faced Amber. Part of Krystal still screamed inside, but it was drowned out with compassion and forgiveness. Amber looked at Krystal dumbstruck and ferocious, unable to believe what had just happened. Ready to pick a fight without understanding why. Her eyes flicked back from Krystal to the cashier, Krystal still holding her credit card out. Krystal felt the anticipation building up in her heart like a giant air bubble ready to burst. Wondering whether Amber was going to accept the gesture or not. Amber finally said, "Yeah sure, that would be fine."

Krystal found relief in that. Part of Krystal imagined Amber being too prideful to accept help from the likes of her, but this time she didn't. Amber strode forward, placed her items on the countertop and the cashier scanned them.

Amber peeked at the items Krystal was holding, "Tamburlaine huh?" Krystal turned in confusion. Amber gestured to the makeup. "Tamburlaine. That's an okay brand but I'd recommend Violet's Gaze for you." Krystal blushed a bit. Unsure of what to say. Krystal handed the cashier her credit card and finished the transaction. The cashier handed Amber her items and the two of them strode out the store together.

Krystal didn't understand why she walked with Amber, it just seemed right at the time. It was quiet between the two of them, until Amber whispered, "Thank you." There was defeat in Amber's voice as well as gratitude, and that was enough to make Krystal not regret her decision. Then Amber straightened up and said, "Can I ask you a question?" A glint of anger returning in Amber's voice. Krystal braced herself but followed Amber around the corner. When they were alone, Amber turned, anger now flaring through her voice, "Why did you do that?" Krystal was not surprised. Her impassive gaze resumed as Amber got mad at her. This was a different girl than the quiet sulking girl Krystal had seen a minute ago. *We really should stop repeating this scenario*, Krystal thought.

Amber repeated her question, "Why did you do that?"

Krystal answered, "Because I saw you were hurting, so I put myself in your shoes and I wanted to do a kind gesture for you." There was no sarcasm in Krystal's voice. She spoke honestly to Amber because that was the tone Amber wanted.

Amber measured her, trying to figure out some hidden motive, but Krystal stood there expressionless and innocent. After a long pause, Amber lowered her death stare and rubbed her head so hard Krystal thought she was going to rip some hair out. Amber raised her voice, "Aghhh I can't figure you out! You always seem to do something out of the blue and I can never seem to understand why."

Krystal wasn't sure what the right thing to say was, so she spoke plainly, "I—"

Amber interrupted, "You see, most people don't do that!" Amber rubbed her head one more time then pointed in Krystal's face. Krystal didn't react.

She didn't even flinch. She just stared back at Amber with an iron resolve as the finger pointed right in her face.

"Do what?" Krystal responded calmly. Her face bland and defensive. Uncaring and unmoved, like she had better things to do than get railed on again. Krystal expected Amber to react differently, but she shouldn't have gotten her hopes up.

Amber pointed back to the store, "That! That right there." Amber shook her head in exasperation, "No one does that. Let alone buy the items for the person behind them. That's not something normal people do, so why did you do it?"

"Because" Krystal answered again, "you looked sad and I felt bad for you, so I decided to do something nice for you." Krystal's tone was getting more and more defensive. She tried to keep her voice calm, but she knew it wasn't helping the situation.

"But, *why!*" Amber persisted, throwing into a fit of rage. She wasn't leaving until she got a proper answer. But Krystal shot her a look that forced all the anger out of her body. That icy glare of Krystal's forced Amber to shut up the minute she saw those eyes. Eyes filled with a reservoir of anger. Eyes that carried the pain of being forgotten and rejected. Eyes that knew what it was like to be hated for no reason. Amber silenced and Krystal spoke frankly, "Because Jesus says to love my enemies." Her tone was stark and thorough. Enough for a calm drill instructor to dive into your deepest thoughts and rip out who you really are. "That's why. So I put up with your crap and went against my own inclinations, and I bought you those things because I know you're going through a hard time." Krystal didn't dare to mention the pregnancy, seeing the bulge in her peripheral vision.

Amber seemed to regain some of her flare after calming down a bit, "I don't get it. I don't deserve your kindness."

Krystal quelled her rebellion, "It doesn't matter whether you deserve it or not. I'm giving it to you regardless. That's what *grace* is." Krystal gestured to Amber then back to herself, "You harm me, I help you regardless, that's what it means. It means that no matter what you've done, I'm still going to love you the way I would want to be loved. So there, that's your answer." Krystal did not sound cheerful in saying this. In fact, she sounded frustrated, but she said it anyway because that was the ground Amber was setting.

Amber looked up at Krystal, curious and skeptical. Amber shook her head, "Seriously, I don't get you at all." Krystal squelched her anger and glared back with an expressionless look. Again, Amber found that both curious and unsettling.

"A lot of people don't."

※

Amber sat in a red chair at the Half & Half coffee shop and asked, "What do you know about that girl named Krystal?"

Summer finished sipping her Half & Half coffee drink. "What, about the fact that she stole the guy I have a crush on? How she's a two-faced witch! Oh, like that one time—"

"—Yeah yeah yeah." Amber interrupted. Summer did not like the interruption, but Amber knew if she let Summer speak, Summer wouldn't stop.

Summer planted her hands down on the table and said defensively, "Is there a problem?"

"Nope, there's no problem," Amber said, "Unless you consider how wrong we've been about her." Summer grew defensive and glared at Amber.

"Is there something you want to say Amber? And be careful, I'm still the only friend you have left."

Amber met Summer's frown with her own, "Don't start that. You're nothing without me."

Summer tilted her head defensively, "I thought we were like, talking about Krystal."

"We are."

"Then why aren't we talking about her?" Summer asked.

"Because you won't let me start," Amber said.

Summer waved her hand in exaggeration, "Well start then."

Amber paused, waiting to see if Summer would say anymore but for the first time ever, Summer was silent. Amber cooled off and spoke plainly, "I just feel all conflicted about this."

"Did anything happen?" Summer frowned, her curiosity turning into suspicion.

Amber met Summer's gaze, leaned forward on the table, and said softly, "The other day, I ran into her at the department store. I was out there deciding whether I was going to keep the baby or not. I couldn't decide on what I was going to do so I decided to call it and head toward the checkout. I didn't know she was there in front of me, until she turned around and said she would pay for my groceries." Amber sat back disappointed, "I can't seem to figure out why Krystal, the girl whom I slapped until her face was purple, would treat me with such kindness. It was the same when I was fighting her, and she didn't fight back. I knew she *could* fight back, in fact I wanted her too, but instead she chose to turn the other cheek. And then she goes and buys me groceries? That doesn't make any sense!" Amber slammed her arms on the table. "I don't get it! What causes somebody to do that?"

Summer gave a wicked smile, "I know what she's doing."

"What?"

"She's playing with you. Trying to get your defenses down so she could like, hurt you more."

Amber wanted to believe that, but Krystal's words flashed through her mind for some reason, *"It doesn't matter whether you deserve it or not. I'm giving it to you regardless. That's what grace is."* Those words rung through her mind like an echo in a castle. Amber didn't want to believe it, but there was something in Krystal's words that resonated with her. Summer kept trying to weed Amber out of it, to try and get Amber to believe that Krystal was simply some loner who manipulates people and does what she wants, but that's not the impression Amber got from talking to her.

"Amber? Amber?" Amber drifted her gaze back to Summer. "Like, are you listening?" Summer asked impatiently.

"Yes, I'm listening!" she exclaimed, slamming her hands on the table, standing up from her seat, glaring down at Summer like an interrogator for the FBI. "I *heard* you!" Summer coiled back, frightened. Amber continued, "And I don't believe you!" Amber looked off toward the freeway next to the Half & Half coffee shop, the cars flowing by like blood cells in a vein. Amber lowered her voice and spoke honestly, "I don't know anymore," looking down at the table, "I used to think she was some manipulative cold-hearted witch, but now I wonder if I see her in a different light." Amber let out a long sigh. "It's like she's different from other people."

Summer chimed in, but not in the way Amber wanted her to, "Yeah, like she calls people out and like, hurts their feelings, and that like didn't sit wel—"

"That's not what I mean!" Amber said. "Gosh, why can't you just shut up and listen for once."

Summer gestured to herself, "I'm trying to like, listen but you're not like, listening to *my* help!"

Amber gestured her hands toward Summer, "Do you even hear yourself right now?" Amber pointed to herself, "You just said that *I'm* not listening to what you have to say? Are you trying to help me or insult me? Cause I can't tell the difference. Are you trying to listen to me by offering me *advice*? That doesn't make sense. You can't listen and give advice at the same time. You either speak or you don't, and right now Summer, you aren't listening."

"But like, you're not listening to my help. And I know what's better for you."

"Summer!" Amber cringed her hands into fists. Amber was so tense she felt like she was a balloon ready to explode. "I'm not asking you to give me advice, I'm asking you to *listen!*"

"And you're like, not listening to me!" Summer retorted, acting all smart.

Amber felt an odd sense of betrayal. This inclination that she owed something to Summer simply because she was Summer. Amber backed away, shaking her head in disappointment. "You're on your own because I'm not dealing with this!"

Summer was now just as fired up as Amber, "Where are you going to go? Huh? Like, no one wants to be like friends with you! Go raise that baby on your own. Or get an abortion for all I care!"

Amber waved Summer off and started walking, then called back, "Hey Summer!" raising her middle finger, "Have a nice day!" That look on Summer was more than enough to bring a smile to Amber's face.

> "What is grace? Why is it so important?"
> —Amber Cutthrose

Amber let out a sigh, "Ahhh a nice hot shower really calms the nerves." Amber sat in her pajamas, lying on her bed scrolling through photos on her social media. Amber flipped through her phone for the next thirty-five minutes then put the phone down and stared at the ceiling. Amber looked back down at her stomach, seeing the bulge growing within her. Amber sighed in disappointment and guilt. The pain she was about to inflict on this child struck a deep wound in her heart. One that would not go away easily.

Amber continued to stroke the growing belly beneath her. "I've done a lot of things wrong." She sighed. Expecting to feel relief but found none. "There are things that I most likely should not have done." She inhaled, thinking of her past mistakes, "I shouldn't have gotten pregnant . . . I shouldn't have started that fight." The thought of Krystal streamed through her mind. *Why am I thinking of her right now?*

Amber felt remorse over the fight, "I shouldn't have hurt that girl. She took a beating from me and still won the fight. Even so, she was the one who warned me I was pregnant. She knew even when I didn't know, and that still boggles my mind." Amber pushed herself up off the bed and leaned over the side, feet dangling. "I've done plenty of things wrong. I've hurt people and I hurt Krystal." Amber looked down on her stomach, "Now I'm going to hurt you too." The shame of it stabbed Amber deep in the heart. Amber cringed at the thought of getting an abortion. Her thoughts drifting back toward Krystal.

"Heh, there's something off about that girl, but off in a clever way. I can't put my finger on it but maybe I never will." Amber stroked her stomach again. "It's strange the way people react when they hurt each other. But what she said about grace, how it's not about whether I deserve it or not. But then . . . what is grace?"

Amber lay back on her bed, "I should apologize to Krystal." Amber nodded. Agreeing with her own idea. "I need to end this. Because that girl . . . that girl, Krystal Henninger . . . she's something else." Amber leaned back in her bed, "I should apologize to her tomorrow."

> "Grace: favor or kindness shown without regard to the worth or merit of the one who receives it and in spite of what that person deserves."
> —Youngblood, Ronald F., F. F. Bruce, and R. K. Harrison, eds. Nelson's Illustrated Bible Dictionary. Thomas Nelson, 1995, pp. 468.

Krystal was busy closing her locker when she heard, "Hey." Krystal was both surprised and not when she turned and saw Amber standing there.

Krystal looked at Amber and said, "Hey," in return. Krystal's plain face stared back at Amber. Amber craned her head, gathering the words, reluctant to proceed. Krystal didn't react but her heart filled with anticipation. Krystal's eyes dropped to Amber's stomach, Amber saw the motion and covered herself.

"I know," Amber said, placing her hands on her lower stomach. "This part is hard."

"Are you going to keep it?" Krystal asked.

Amber tensed and clenched her teeth, "No."

Krystal felt a stab of pain, although she didn't dare express it to Amber. Yet, Krystal couldn't help but let her emotions filter onto her face. Amber saw Krystal's reaction and said, "I didn't come here to talk about my future abortion."

"Okay." Krystal said, her voice bland and toneless like a robot. Killing her emotions.

Amber let out an annoyed exhale and placed an arm on the locker next to Krystal. "I came here . . . to apologize."

"For what?"

"You know the answer to that question," Amber said, the fire returning in her eyes.

Krystal paused, part of her did not want to forgive Amber, but she knew better. *It's time to let the past be past.* Krystal looked up at Amber and said, "I forgive you." Her tone was genuine and calm. Amber looked at Krystal in the corner of her eye, suspicious. But from the look on Krystal's face Amber could tell Krystal meant it. Krystal recognized this and said, "So . . . are we friends?"

Amber didn't know how to take that, "Uhh sure, I guess. If you can call us that."

Krystal cocked her head to the side and shrugged her shoulders, "Eh, close enough." The bell rang. Krystal looked at Amber, "I'll see you later Amber."

Amber replied, "Yeah, uhh see you later."

PART TEN

Redemption

CHAPTER 56

The Talent Show

*"One of the hardest things you could ever do, is
stand in the light and be who you are."*

—JL

Jaime was bored with the usual conversation at the lunch table and asked aloud, "Hey is anybody going to that talent show this Friday?" All eyes looked at him in curiosity. Jaime wasn't satisfied with their reaction. "It's not that big a deal. I mean, is anyone going?"

Krystal said, "Is that really this Friday?"

"Yeah it is," Kristina chimed in, "They have it once a year. It's not much to show but they do bring in a lot of people if you win it."

"Like how many people?" Krystal asked, her interest somewhat growing.

Kristina said, "Enough to fill an auditorium full of people." Krystal turned white. An auditorium full of people looking at you on stage while you are expected to perform some amazing talent. The mere presence of that idea terrified her to her bones.

"So, is anybody going to join?" Jaime asked.

Krystal replied, "I don't know. I don't really have a skill I could show off."

Jaime put his hand to his chin and said, "Well that's a shame. I've always wondered what your hidden talents might be Krystal."

"She knows how to listen well," Kristina said.

Jaime agreed, "That she does." Nobody else seemed to have an answer, so the conversation grew quiet. The din of the cafeteria background made it hard to think sometimes. Jaime waited a couple seconds before asking again, "So does anybody want to go?"

Joanna was the first to speak up, "I'll do whatever you guys want!" masking the eagerness in her voice.

Kristina shrugged her shoulders, "Eh I got nothing better to do."

They looked over at Sho, who simply nodded, and then came down to Krystal. Krystal shied up and said, "I guess I could go."

Jaime said, "Cool! I'll see you guys on Friday."

Jaime walked through the metal doors with his ticket in hand and looked around the auditorium, finding the grandeur of it all mesmerizing. He nodded his head, *Yup, this is where stars are born.* (And no, that's not a joke relating to the movie: A Star is Born.) Jaime walked in first, followed by Joanna, Kristina, Sho, Krystal's mom, and then Krystal. Krystal was busy pushing her mom's wheelchair while Jaime kept the rest of the group preoccupied. Jaime took his seat and the rest of the group followed. At least one of the perks of having Krystal's mom be in a wheelchair meant they could sit up close to the stage, so they could see all the contestants clearly. Jaime didn't know why he wanted to go to this event, he simply got the impression that he should be here. A funny feeling though, something he hadn't felt before. It wasn't a nagging impression. It was a subtle, more gentle feeling. The sort of thing that gave you the option to back out yet allowed you to continue if you chose to. He didn't know how to respond to it, so he went along with it, looking to see what was happening.

The whole group took their seats, Jaime sitting next to Krystal and Krystal sitting on the end next to her mom. The rest of the audience followed in and took their seats inside the massive auditorium. The din of the crowd filled the auditorium until an announcer called out, "Alllright can everybody please take their seats. The annual talent show will begin shortly." The crowd quieted and the lighting dimmed. The announcer spoke, "And now, for our first contestant we have . . ."

They went through a majority of the acts, most of them impressive, others were just a performance for parents to be proud of their children. Even Summer went on stage and did a dance performance to the Bruno Mars song, "Just the Way You Are". Jaime didn't really care about any of the performances, he just sat back and enjoyed the show.

The announcer called out, "Thank you very much Summer for that wonderful performance. All right, ladies and gentlemen we are going to have a short break and will reconvene in about fifteen minutes."

⌇

When they returned Jaime glanced around and realized Krystal wasn't in her seat. He had his palms up, looking around in confusion. He leaned forward and asked, "Guys, where's Krystal?" Kristina and Joanna shook their heads. Sho, as usual, didn't react much. Jaime turned his gaze toward Krystal's mom, but she was just as confused as he was. Jaime looked from left to right and said, "No one knows where Krystal is? The show is about to start."

The announcer spoke, "Ladies and gentlemen, please take your seats."

The audience quieted and the lights dimmed. Jaime looked forward and sighed, *Of course it starts when I say that. I had to go and jinx it.* But his fear of Krystal's whereabouts was starting to grow. He was about to get up and start looking for her when the announcer said, "Now on the stage, we have, Krystal Henninger." Jaime looked up and felt his heart drop.

Stepping out on stage, Krystal came out wearing a beautiful purple silk dress followed by a cellist. (You know, those big violins.) Everyone in the group was thunderstruck at the sight of Krystal looking so beautiful that they had forgotten where they were. Even Ashley could hardly fathom the sight of her own daughter. She'd never seen Krystal willingly wear a dress before and one where she looked so pretty. Joanna and Kristina were slightly envious, but Jaime was wowed by the sight. And Sho . . . well he was lacking the vocabulary for the moment.

Jaime looked at the group and asked, "Did you guys know about this?" They all shook their heads. Jaime looked at Krystal's mom, but she was the same. Jaime looked back onstage, "So she didn't tell us."

⌇

Krystal's steps echoed across the platform. Loud and thick, her heels smacking against the wooden stage, drawing the attention of the crowd. Krystal felt all eyes shift toward her, the fear in her heart raging as she felt everyone looking at her. Krystal had never felt more self-conscious in her life. The chatter among the crowd had grown to a low mumble. Pressure surrounded Krystal's heart. Her body was beginning to sweat with so many eyes looking at her. Krystal's heart tightened so hard it felt as though there were a black hole in the center of her chest.

Krystal walked toward the front of the stage, where an acoustic guitar, a microphone, and a chair for the cellist awaited them. Krystal's anxiety warped in her heart. Her hands were already shaking. Just stepping out into the spotlight was hard enough, but now she had to deal with the hundreds of people looking her way, expecting her to do something amazing.

For a moment, Krystal froze. Her heart was thumping deeply, butterflies in her stomach. Adrenaline coursing through her body as she went into Fight or Flight mode. The eyes of the crowd were overwhelming. Krystal tried to reassure herself. *Just stay calm. Just stay calm.* But no reassurance came with those words. *Just stay calm. Just stay calm.* The intensity of the pressure growing worse.

Then, she heard a voice. A voice so gentle, it was only found within the back of her mind. The voice spoke in a gentle whisper, *"I'm with you."* With that, Krystal felt a peace fall upon her, taking away all her insecurities. It was enough to get Krystal to refocus on God until she was completely at peace.

For thirty seconds Krystal said nothing, and the entire crowd was staring at her. Jaime was starting to wonder if he should do something, until Krystal picked up the guitar, threw the strap over her, and spoke into the mic, "Tonight I'm going to show you a side of myself that no one else has seen. I'm going to be playing a song for you." Krystal strummed the guitar. "I know that times can be hard for all of us. This world can bring us to our knees at some point or another. Sometimes we feel we can't hold under the pressure. But I want to say this . . . that although life may be hard sometimes, the pain will not last. There is hope in this world, no matter how dark it may seem. And there is a reason to keep on breathing. So I want to sing a song for you. I hope you enjoy it." She paused one final time, "My name is Krystal Henninger, and this is my life-song."

Krystal let out a breath and was suddenly calm. Every cell in her body was completely at rest. There were no thoughts running wild in her mind. Everything felt so clear. Krystal closed her eyes and prayed, *I believe,* then her hands moved on their own, moving with a purpose as she slowly strummed the guitar. The cellist saw her cue and the two of them played in sync.

The crowd could feel the effects of the guitar hit them. The soft notes being played from Krystal's fingers were like living water poured over their souls. Krystal's playing filled the air with beauty and harmony. Her hands worked automatically as the cellist played behind her. Krystal closed her eyes, the notes naturally flowing from her fingers, the beautiful music echoing from the guitar. The cellist followed along perfectly with Krystal's playing. Strumming the cello with such grace, finishing a long, beautiful stretch before Krystal came up to the microphone, took a sharp breath, and sang softly,

> *"Didn't I tell you I hear what you say?*
> *Never look back as you're walking away*
> *Carry the music, the memories and keep them inside*
> *You*
> *Laugh every day*
> *Don't stop those tears from falling*
> *Down"*

The words flowed like honey. It was strange. Nothing had ever felt more natural, beauty flowing freely from Krystal's voice like a famous actor in a musical. Krystal felt the power within her lungs surge, the sweat, the passion flowing through her fingers into the guitar. The cellist paused, Krystal did the same, then kicked back up again, this time stronger in note.

> *"This is who I am inside!*
> *This is who I am, I'm not gonna hide*
> *Cause the greatest risk we'll ever take is by far*
> *To stand in the light and be seen as we are*
> *To stand in the light and be seen as we are"*

Krystal's voice permeated the room like a perfectly tuned instrument. A voice, that of an angel, controlled and beautiful. Slow and contained, yet smooth in every syllable. The cellist filling Krystal's pauses with her own melody. Calm, smooth and steady, as the song builds and builds. Krystal slowed again, catching her breath, singing softly.

> *"With courage and kindness hold on to your faith*
> *You get what you give and it's never too late*
> *To reach for the branch and climb up leaving sadness behind*
> *You*
> *Fight hard for love"*

The cellist began to build in tempo. Krystal took a breath, quickly building her voice,

"We can never get enough!"

The cellist followed along with her. Perfectly in sync. Reaching the top of her build just before Krystal sang,

"This is who I am inside!
This is who I am, I'm not gonna hide!
Cause the greatest risk we'll ever take is by far!
To stand in the light and be seen as we are"

Krystal raised her voice even higher now.

"To stand in the light and be seen as we are!"

The world slowly spun into a blur, yet the only thing that truly existed was Krystal standing there with the mic in front of her and the guitar playing perfectly within her hands. Krystal braced herself, filling her heart and lungs, raising her voice even higher now, higher than she ever thought possible. Her soul and passion flowing through her into the music.

"Riding the storms that come raging towards us we dive!
Holding our breath as we break through the surface
With arms open wide
With arms open wide"

Krystal paused, letting the cellist build the momentum behind her, feeling the world play out before her. And it felt AMAZING. Terrifying yet amazing. The cellist built up and up and up, the time coming for Krystal's cue. Her voice, singing with passion louder and louder in each verse.

"This is who I am inside!
This is who I am, I'm not gonna hide!
Cause the greatest risk we'll ever take is by far!
To stand in the light and be seen as we are!"

Krystal raised her voice, so loud in fact, she jumped a whole octave in a voice that was not her own yet belonged to her all the same and felt all the words and the passion flow out in perfect harmony as if it were God himself singing through her. Krystal braced herself for one last stretch, singing as loud and as powerful as she could.

"To stand in the light and be seen as we ARRRREEEEE!"

Krystal sang as loud as she could, feeling the passion, the pain, the memories, the love pouring out from her, echoing through her voice toward the audience. Hearts were changing. Love was flowing. Souls were healing. One final stretch. One more time.

"Cause the greatest risk we'll ever take is by FAR!
To stand in the light and be seen as we are
To stand in the light and be seen as we are!"

Krystal lowered her voice and sang the words softly, finishing strong and smooth like an airplane on a runway. Finishing with a gentle touch.

"To stand in the light and be seen as we are."
("Stand in the Light" by Jordan Smith)

When Krystal strummed the first notes on the guitar, Jaime's perspective immediately changed. The sound was perfect, almost too perfect. Then Krystal started singing. Her voice was unlike anything Jaime had ever heard. It was so heavenly he couldn't believe it was coming from Krystal's lips. It had never sounded so perfect. It was like a shockwave struck the crowd, silencing all doubt, leaving only awe and wonder at the spectacle before them.

The music and voice that flowed from that girl was unheard of. It was like Jaime was staring at a completely different person. Jaime could feel the emotion in Krystal's voice flowing over him. Creating goosebumps all over his body. The notes and the chords playing from the guitar, the beauty of the cello following along with Krystal perfectly, caused a change inside Jaime he had never expected. He could feel colors floating through the air, passion and love filling the room, joining with every heart. It was as if Jaime was witnessing a living painting. Vibrant with all sorts of colors and life with every note Krystal played.

The entire world slowed, freezing Jaime in this moment. Amidst Krystal's melody, amidst the delight and glamour, Jaime's whole world came crashing down. He forgot all about his anger against God, and in that moment, he felt a gentle peace course through his body and surround his heart and soul. Permeating his entire being with comfort and relief, allowing the song to wash over him like living water. Inviting Jaime to come forward, to come back. Jaime imagined himself standing on a battlefield before God, defeated. Then he exhaled, "Alright God . . . You win." And in that moment, Jaime knew he was finally ready to move on.

"Is . . . is that Krystal?" Kristina whispered. Both Joanna and Kristina exchanged looks. Unable to believe their own eyes. They held their breath, covering their mouths with their hands, the air in the room falling silent as the song came to an end. Kristina, who was acquainted with the guitar, found it immaculate that Krystal struck all the major chords perfectly and sang at the same time. Multi-tasking both singing and playing reflected a level of mastery that most musicians achieved after a good deal of practice. Kristina could not dispute it; Krystal's voice was that of an angel.

Kristina felt it in her heart, almost like the words were calling to her. Like the lyrics were speaking directly to her. For Kristina to come out and let people see who she really was. That it was okay, to be yourself.

Joanna couldn't believe it either. After the first verse, all Joanna's doubts eroded away and suddenly she was staring at something new. Something she had never seen before. The words were flowing over them like soft cherry blossoms in the wind. Ringing true within Joanna's heart; bringing comfort and warmth, but most of all . . . healing.

Joanna was no different from Kristina. The words were like a healing ointment pressed over an open wound. Telling Joanna that it was okay to step out. That it was okay to let others in. That it was okay for people to see who she really was, and not be what others thought she should be. It was like the music sent healing through the air. Seeking those whose hearts were truly broken. To the losers and the loners of the world. Telling them, *it will be all right.*

Ashley could not believe her own eyes. It was like she lived in an alternate reality because she had never heard Krystal sing before. Krystal by definition was shy, so shy in fact that she could not even talk in front of a group of people. But here and now, Krystal was singing in front of a crowd of hundreds of people, all without a shred of doubt in her mind. The scene of it all was overwhelming as Ashley could not fathom how much her daughter had changed in the past year. It was unbelievable. Krystal had gone from a shy, practically mute girl to a singing, confident, and loving individual. Ashley simply could not comprehend the tremendous amount of change that had happened to Krystal while she was in a coma. It was there, in that moment, that Ashley gave up her own assumptions, and allowed herself to accept the truth. That there is a God. A God who loves and cares about us, as if there were only one of us.

Ashley let out a sigh of happy defeat, "I guess You *are* real, God."

If Sho had to pick a moment where he'd officially fallen in love with someone, it would be now. Never before had he admired such a person. Sho felt a sense of hope gleam within him, like a ray of sunshine breaking through the clouds, from hearing this girl sing. Sho could feel a change strike him, like a rock dropped into a pond, adding color to his life that was previously stuck in black and white. The words poured over him, raising his spirits, telling him, if this girl can do something remarkable, then he can too. That it was possible for someone like him to change. That maybe . . . he could like himself.

Joanna was the first to break down, then Kristina, then Jaime, Ashley, and Sho. All five of them, experiencing the same thing. One simple message, whispered in their hearts, *It's okay, to not be okay.* As they all broke down in tears from the soft, heavenly voice flowing through Krystal's lips.

Krystal took a final breath, as the world resumed its normal pace, finding she was covered in sweat, her voice spent, and felt a final wave of relief wash over her. It is finished. Krystal lowered her eyes and was greeted by the universal praise of the crowd, as they stood up and cheered. The sound of the applause, people standing, clapping, clapping for her. The moment was almost too much to bear. Krystal's heart was fully at peace, soaking in the cheers of joy and love flowing back from the crowd. All the people cheering for that wonderful performance. Krystal did not come to win this competition; she had achieved what she came for. But Krystal knew it was not her own accomplishment. And through the cheers of the crowd, she praised God, "This was all you God."

All of Krystal's senses heightened as her eyes moved from person to person, taking in the awe and wonder of everyone in the crowd. Searching through the crowd, Krystal picked out Kristina and Joanna, who were both bawling their eyes out, cheering and hugging each other. Krystal looked at Jaime, watching tears gleam down his awestruck face. Then she saw Sho, who cheered silently and happily with a wide smile. Her gaze turned toward her mom, who was clapping with all her heart. The sight of her mom happy brought Krystal a new sense of elation. Knowing her mom was *proud* of her. Krystal had never felt happier.

The cheers raised, and Krystal felt like some soap opera singer who had just sung the greatest performance of her life. Krystal drank in the sight, grateful for what God had given her. *I will never forget this moment God. Thank you. Thank you for turning a loser like me into something beautiful. Thank you for taking me from broken to beautiful.* And she was right. She would remember this moment for the rest of her life.

She looked up to the front row, looking at all of her friends. Jaime, Joanna, Kristina, Sho, her mom, all their faces in astounding wonder, then her gaze shifted towards the center of the front row, where she saw a man dressed in white, with holes in his hands, clapping with immense pride and joy.

The world froze; Krystal forgot about the audience . . . and there she could see Him smiling at her, as He said, "Well done."

And that was enough. Enough for Krystal to feel all the love in the world flow into her heart and know that she *mattered.*

Tears flowed down her cheeks endlessly as she gave the most joyful smile she had ever felt in her entire life. It was here, in this moment, that Krystal had come completely out of the darkness. That although her past was filled with pain and sorrow, she could hold her head up high and know that a new chapter has begun.

CHAPTER 57

Recommitment

"You can box toe to toe with God but let me tell ya.
You're gonna lose."

—JL

Jaime leaned over the side of the bed defeated. He took a long, deep breath, and exhaled slowly. He leaned on the side of his bed in Luiz's guest room, allowing his head to sag down as far as he could. Defeated. Knowing he had been bested by a foe he refused to believe existed.

It's time . . .

Jaime took another breath, "It's been a while . . . since I talked to You . . . How long has it been? Two? Two years?" He remembered it like it were yesterday. The scene where his sister lay on the floor bleeding from her wrists. Jaime wanted to flare up with anger but there was nothing left. No fire to burn, only ashes and embers.

Jaime sat there, letting time slip by. He did not know whether he was sitting there for two minutes or two hours. But the time did not matter. Patience did.

"God . . . I know I've done a lot of wrong since then. I'm not the person I once was. Maybe I never will be." Jaime felt the emotions buried deep come rising to the surface. He wanted to fight it, but this time chose not to. Instead, he let them come forward.

Jaime exhaled, "She's dead . . ." Accepting the truth he fought so hard to deny. "Carole is dead." What was held back for so long was finally brought to light. "My little sister is gone, and there's no bringing her back." Jaime felt a weight like an anchor slide off his shoulders.

Jaime kept his head down in defeat, "I know . . . I've hated You all this time . . . I've tried to block You out and forget about You. After having my heart broken, I could not accept it. I could not accept that you were a good God after You let my sister die . . ." Jaime paused and took another painful breath. It needed to be said. He had to be honest. "Before, I thought You were a good God. I believed You performed miracles. I believed that if I just had faith, then You would give me a miracle, like all the rest of the characters in the Bible . . ." He paused. "I never could imagine I would lose the one person I hold most dear . . ." Jaime closed his eyes and pictured Carole. Her short blonde hair, her smiling face. What a delicate creature she was. The sight brought Jaime pain. Accepting the reality.

"For so long I didn't want to believe in You. I refused to believe You were real, but while I did that, my heart suffered." Yes, he could see it now. The result of what he had become. Of what he had chosen to become. "I became bitter. I had forgotten happiness, replaced only with emptiness and hatred." He shook his head. "How disappointing I must be huh? What a broken piece of work I am." Shame stepped in. Speaking the following words felt like passing a kidney stone. But it had to be said. He would not move on until he did. "I hurt my family by distancing myself. I didn't want to be around them, to share in their prayers that I believed would go unanswered. I just couldn't bring myself to share my pain with them because of how they reacted. How calm they were about the whole incident. But I think . . . I had mistaken their calm . . . I know my family was hurting, but maybe they were hurting in their own way. I'm sure a death like this would rock any family. I'm sure, at some point or another, my parents cried because of the loss of their child, and my sister Carmen holds her tears back to be the older sibling, the rock to lean on . . ."

Jaime took a breath, "Out of anyone else in our family, I loved Carole the most. Loved her more than anything else." Jaime chuckled, "I had such good times with her . . ." His words began to choke, the smile faded, "and my heart was torn when I lost her." The sight of Krystal in her purple dress played softly in his mind, remembering the knife wound across Krystal's wrist. How similar the two were, Krystal and Carole, how they both struggled with suicidal thoughts and loneliness for most of their lives.

Jaime's thoughts drifted more towards Krystal. "But Krystal never had a family. Never had an older brother to look after her. Never had a loving sister to give her advice. Never had a loving mom who was always home to make dinner, or a loving dad to give her wisdom and encouragement." Jaime straightened up, "I think back on that often. How a girl like that, just the same as Carole, managed to find hope in a world of suffering. After having lost it all, literally. Krystal found hope." Jaime laughed but it was not a happy laugh. "It did cost her her life though. Putting a knife to her wrist after she lost her mom," Jaime paused, "literally the one person she had in her life who loved her, and yet was taken away . . ." Jaime took a breath. "I know the feeling." He paused.

"I wanted to be mad at You for the rest of my life . . . to remain bitter and refuse to accept You, but . . ." Jaime thought back to all the time he spent with Krystal. Watching this shy girl, who never smiled or talked, turn into a beautiful princess of the night. The times he spent getting carmel apples with her, the time they spent at the firepit, where her warm presence comforted him when the fire could not warm the coldness in his heart. And then the hospital visit. Watching her mom get resurrected on the spot. How a miracle like that really did happen. And then . . . there was the talent show, the last bastion.

Jaime took another breath, "I want to deny You with all my heart but . . ." he choked, "I can't deny the changes You've made in this girl . . . How You took a loser, who attempted suicide, and You made her into something more beautiful than I could ever describe . . ." Jaime chuckled, now understanding the satire of it all. "Maybe that's why You put her in my life. Maybe that's why she went through all that, just so she could comfort a loser like me . . ." He trailed off. Took another breath, "God, I've done many things wrong. I didn't hurt just my family. I hurt the person who cared for me the most, Krystal. I got angry at her out of my own jealousy. I wanted the miracle that she had, yet I got mad at her for it, and I ended up hurting her." Jaime shook his head, "That girl has been through enough. I can see the suffering etched in her eyes. All the years of loneliness played out. I can read it all. Every day. Like lines drawn on a painting, the picture forming Krystal Henninger."

Jaime lowered his head, "What I'm saying is . . ." He took a breath, taking as long as he needed, ". . . I'm ready . . . to come back to You." Silence.

"I'm tired, God. I'm tired of being tired. I want to let go. I want to move on. I want to be with my family again. I want to be with Krystal. Even though I don't deserve her kindness. For she is a gem. Even if I should be sent to Hell for what I've done, don't forget her. Please don't forget her. For my suffering is nothing compared to hers. And yet she smiles anyway. How?" Jaime scoffed, "Well . . . I guess I already know the answer."

Jaime got on his knees before the Lord and looked up for the first time, "Father . . . I have done wrong . . . I have done plenty of wrong, and I deserve punishment. I don't deserve to go to Heaven. I don't deserve Your mercy. God . . . please forgive me for the sins I've done. Please forgive me for getting mad at Krystal and making her cry. Please forgive me for the pain I've caused my family. I deserved every bit of it when my dad punched me and kicked me out of the house. I deserve it all."

Jaime lifted his hands in surrender as if he were offering up an invisible sword, "God, I surrender both myself and my sister to You. It's time to let go. Please forgive me for all the wrong I've done." Jaime felt the final weight fall from his shoulders. Immediately Jaime felt his burden lighten and he could breathe again. He felt the Holy Spirit come into his heart and fill his soul where the emptiness remained. He felt the anger and bitterness replaced with mercy, letting the tears flow from the bottom of his heart. And he cried, knowing it was over.

CHAPTER 58

The Prodigal Son

"Even a smile can be a gift."

—JL

Does it feel weird?

Yes, it does.

Jaime had forgotten the feeling of waking up and going to church in the morning. Still feeling a bit sluggish after waking up at 10am and then rushing over to church. Jaime observed the church from a distance behind some trees across the street. The sight brought back memories, most of them happy, most of them included Carole. Jaime wanted to fight them but this time he let the memories come back. He let the grief hit him. Sure, it kept him from looking jovial but at least he was trying to come back. Jaime watched as people parked their cars and crowded the entrance. He quickly spotted Krystal, walking in, pushing her mom's wheelchair through the door. The sight brought Jaime a little joy for some reason. He wasn't sure why.

Then he spotted his own family, parking in their usual spot, heading in, greeted by everyone there. His family had gone to this church for a good ten years now, so they were well acquainted with all the members. It wasn't a large church, roughly two hundred people max, but they didn't come to all the services, so there was an average of about a hundred people at the service. Jaime looked up at the building, the metal cross standing up in the sky for all to see. Jaime felt uncomfortable looking at it. He was never sure whether that thing was judging him or trying to comfort him. He had gotten the two mixed up over the years, so it was hard to tell these days. Jaime waited ten more minutes before finally heading in. He was a good twenty minutes late, which was exactly as he planned. He didn't want anybody to see him, and once everybody saw him, he knew they would all greet him. He was an active member a couple years ago; he even strived to become a deacon at some point. (A deacon is like a member of the clergy along with priests and bishops.) And for a long time, Jaime had wanted to become a pastor. He felt he had a knack for it. But all that was put on halt ever since his sister died and he lost faith. Well, maybe things are different now.

Jaime entered the double doors and heard music coming from the auditorium. He checked the hallways, making sure no one was around and then slid inside the auditorium. The room was packed, and music was blasting with worship, but luckily people didn't look behind them when the service started. That was Jaime's plan, to hang out in the back while the service went on. That's all he really wanted. He didn't want his family to see him yet and he didn't want to be noticed by anybody. So, he stood in the back and listened to the worship, feeling his childhood come flooding back to his conscience as he soaked in the feeling of being at church again. And it felt . . . weird.

I knew I shouldn't have drunk all that juice this morning. Krystal quivered in her chair. Carmen noticed her squirming and whispered, "Are you alright?"

"Yeah, I'm fine," Krystal said, "I just went crazy on the apple juice this morning." Before Carmen could laugh Krystal was out of her seat, rushing past the entrance and into the nearest bathroom. She came out a few minutes later with a look of pure satisfaction on her face. Krystal opened the door to the auditorium and surprisingly found Jaime leaning against the wall to her left. Krystal was shocked, "Jaime?"

Jaime didn't look surprised to see her, "What's up?"

What's up? That's a new one, Krystal thought. The weird thing about it was Jaime's tone of voice. He didn't have any anger imbued with his speech. So it sounded weird to hear him speak so casually. "What are you doing here?" she asked.

"Isn't it obvious? I'm coming to church."

Krystal studied him. *Does he mean it?* she thought. Debating whether this was a ruse, but Jaime would not come to church if he didn't have a good reason. For all Krystal's time coming here, Jaime had not come to service once. So what happened? What changed?

"Oh," she said, nodding. Krystal let the news strike her with moderate delight. She knew how to manage her emotions when around people who were less happy than she was, so she kept it moderate for his sake. Krystal gave Jaime a soft smile as his reward.

Jaime was surprised by the smile. He knew he would run into Krystal here; I mean, he ran into her everywhere, but that smile was not like the others. It was a smile meant for him. It was Krystal showing him he had truly made her feel happy, and in return, it made him feel happy. Even a smile can be a gift. The two of them hung around awkwardly for a few more seconds, before Krystal asked, "Do you have somewhere to sit?"

Jaime replied, "Nah, I was going to hang out here. I'm trying not to be noticed today." Krystal nodded. Then she walked over and leaned against the wall next to him. Jaime asked, "What are you doing?"

"I'm going to stand with you. Is that okay?"

For once Jaime didn't object. He liked having Krystal around, so he decided to open up and let her in for a change. "Yeah. That would be nice." Smiling at her. The smile struck Krystal's heart. She had never seen Jaime give that kind of smile before. It was like seeing a whole new side of him, one that she kinda . . . enjoyed. It wasn't angry, it was open. And that brought relief to her. So the two of them stood there and watched the sermon go on, neither of them talking. Okay that's a lie. They did trade a comment or two, in fact they even made each other laugh. By the end of the sermon, they had no idea what it was about, and Jaime had to leave before his family found out he was there. But Krystal was certain of one thing. She had just witnessed a small, but monumental change in Jaime Fisher.

Jaime's hand hovered over the door. He lowered his hand and thought, *Maybe I shouldn't do this.* But Jaime shook the thought away. "It's time," he whispered. The mahogany brown door glared at him, menacing. But Jaime was too tired for this. His exhaustion from the weekend's events had drained him, leaving only honesty and truth. There was no energy to beat around the bush. It was time to come forward.

He knocked on the door three times. Carmen opened the door and stood in the doorway. Jaime's parents were behind her, saying nothing. Jaime felt the air thicken between them, but they wouldn't say anything unless he said something first. Jaime hung his head in humble admission, "Hey," he said.

"Hey," Carmen replied. There were no looks of joy.

Jaime built up the words he planned and exhaled, "I know I've been . . . distant lately. Very distant . . . and," he paused, his parents and Carmen saying nothing, "It's been really hard for me in my relationship with God since Carole died." Jaime expected looks of judgment but found none. Jaime took a breath, not as deeply as he had hoped, and continued. "And . . . I've been making things hard on you guys too. But . . ." Jaime exhaled, "I've finally come back. And I am so sorry for all the pain I've caused you."

Immediately Carmen threw her arms around her younger brother and cried. Jaime took his sister in his arms as his parents joined in. Carmen muffled, "I've been praying so long to hear that," as the message had finally gone through. Jaime held his sister there, held his family there, finding healing in each other's presence, knowing finally, their son had come home.

Jaime opened the door and called, "Hello? Krystal, are you in there?" Krystal came into the hallway wiping her hands with a towel. She was wearing a black t-shirt and a black apron, with her hair tied back in a ponytail. The sight always took Jaime's breath away.

"Hey Jaime," she said, "Come on in." Jaime entered the apartment and took off his shoes. Without looking up Krystal said, "You're early."

Jaime exhaled, "Yeah, I know. I thought I'd come by and hang out before everyone showed up." Krystal nodded and looked up at him.

"Well, feel free to hang out if you want. I know your favorite spot on the couch is waiting for you." Jaime followed the gesture and saw the couch did look comfortable, but this time he remained standing. Jaime looked at Krystal working, paused for a moment, then stepped towards the kitchen. Krystal saw him coming and asked, "What are you doing?"

Jaime rolled his sleeves up, "Do you need help?"

The action stymied Krystal. She certainly was not expecting such kindness from Jaime. Usually, he would go and lay on the couch while she made dinner until the guests arrived and then eat. So this was the first time Jaime offered to help her make dinner. "Okay," she said, searching her brain for a task, "You can help me peel the potatoes."

Jaime shrugged his shoulders, "Alright." He moved towards the sink to wash his hands while Krystal eyed him with curiosity. *He feels different*, she thought. And she wasn't sure what that meant. Krystal did an emotional check, feeling the room, checking Jaime's body language, and thought, *Hmm, he seems calm. Almost like he's lost his fire.*

Krystal made sure to watch Jaime carefully, remembering all the times when his anger flared up when she mentioned God or his family. Yet, the more she spent time with him, the more comfortable she felt. Jaime washed his hands and looked at Krystal in confusion. Krystal offered him a towel and then gestured toward the bowl of uncooked potatoes. She handed him a spare peeler and stood by him as the two of them peeled potatoes together. For a while, neither of them spoke. The silence of the apartment didn't feel uncomfortable for once. In fact, it complimented the mood. There were no distractions and Krystal could feel relaxed. She could sense it in Jaime too. The guy just seemed different somehow.

"So, how are things going?" she asked, breaking the silence.

"Good," Jaime said, allowing Krystal to hear a sense of optimism in his voice. Krystal immediately noticed and felt a little cautious from that, but it was quickly replaced with a growing sense of comfort. It felt as if the walls between the two of them were finally coming down.

Krystal got right to the point but still kept it casual, "Did anything happen lately?"

Jaime nodded, humbled but with a small glimmer of optimism. "Yeah," he said, as if it was a relief to say. He flicked the skin off a potato, "I reconnected with my family recently."

Krystal stopped. "Really? That's good news!"

"Yeah. It is." Jaime didn't look Krystal's way, but she could tell he was trying to be honest. That allowed her to feel more comfortable with him, knowing he wouldn't explode anymore. The comfort of no barriers between them. Like it was okay for him to be open for once and not get angry. Jaime finished peeling his potatoes and asked, "So what's next?"

Krystal was caught off guard once again, "Oh, uhh." She looked around, "Could you help me add garlic, and butter the toast?"

Jaime nodded, "Sure." He got to work immediately. He appeared more willing to help than normal. Actually, Jaime had never helped at all, so to see him eager to help surprised Krystal.

While Jaime buttered the bread, Krystal worked on the rest of the potatoes. But for some reason, her focus was not on the potatoes. She could feel her gaze drawing more towards Jaime the longer she worked. She whipped her head back and tried to focus on the matter at hand, but she just couldn't shake the feeling that something was different about Jaime. Krystal's head shifted once more, her hands moving on automatic with the peeler as she stared at Jaime's back, noticing for the first time how muscular he was. He had the water polo build around his chest and shoulders, which he normally hid underneath his clothing. Krystal felt something she'd never felt before and wasn't sure how she was supposed to react to it. Krystal's hands moved automatically until she flicked the peeler the wrong way and cut her hand.

"Ahh shoot," Krystal said, holding her hand. Jaime turned around and saw she was bleeding. It wasn't a deep cut or life threatening, but it was noticeable.

"Are you alright?" Jaime asked, stepping closer.

Krystal was still holding her hand, "Yeah, I'm okay." She stepped over and opened the medicine cabinet to grab some bandages. She raised her uncut hand to grab them but was interrupted by Jaime's arm reaching higher than hers. Krystal didn't expect Jaime to reach for the bandages so fast.

He pulled out a bandage and asked, "May I see it?"

Krystal said, "I can do it."

But Jaime politely asked again, "May I?" Krystal said nothing and nodded. Jaime reached and took her hand. The warmth of his smooth skin made Krystal's blood run. She wasn't used to being touched. Jaime held the wound up, "Aww man, we're going to have to amputate this." Krystal chuckled. Jaime pulled out a bottle of rubbing alcohol and cleaned the wound with a cotton swab. Krystal knew she could do this herself, but she let Jaime do it. She smiled within her conscience, *You . . . clever fox Jaime*, she thought. Jaime finished cleaning the wound and gently put the bandage on. He didn't seem disturbed at all from grabbing her hand.

Jaime said, "You should be alright. You are trained by a nurse." Krystal couldn't explain it, but her heart did a backflip. Jaime looked at her, all stoic and calm, "Let's finish making dinner."

"Okay," she said obediently.

The short rib came out perfectly, and the mashed potatoes complimented the peas and buttered garlic bread. It was almost too beautiful to take in. Krystal and Jaime finished their work and the two of them looked at each other and high fived. A job well done. The two of them stood in the kitchen, the food all prepped and ready, while the dining room stared at them with empty seats.

Jaime turned toward Krystal, "Everyone is coming right?"

Krystal checked her phone, "I don't know." Finding a couple messages from Kristina, Joanna, and even Sho. She frowned. Krystal lowered her phone and looked at Jaime, "They all couldn't make it."

Jaime asked, "Is your mom going to join us?"

"She's at physical therapy but she'll be home soon."

Jaime looked out at the empty dining room, "Huh . . . so I guess it's just you and me."

"I guess so." As the two of them stared out into the empty apartment, both of them clearly not expecting this.

They waited a few more seconds, until Jaime said, "I guess we should eat then."

"I guess so." Krystal added. They got their food and sat down. Krystal was feeling auspiciously nervous for some reason. The silence in the room only added to her growing curiosity.

For a while they said nothing. They just ate their food and tried not to feel awkward. The whole time Krystal was watching Jaime, while Jaime had his head down pretending to look at his food. Jaime took a bite and was amazed, "This food is delicious."

"Thanks," Krystal replied, always happy when someone enjoys her food. She sensed Jaime wasn't done, and she was right.

Jaime swallowed his food and said, "Hey . . ." his voice somber yet admissive. "I'm sorry . . ." Jaime looked up into Krystal's awaiting eyes. "I'm sorry for . . . being jealous of you, and hurting you, and yelling at you."

"It's okay," Krystal replied. Jaime sniffed. Holding back his tears.

"You give me more grace than I deserve." He looked down at the table, "But I want you to know . . ." he paused, "It's over." Krystal said nothing and watched patiently. Jaime searched for the right words, "I was going through a very dark period in my life, but I want you to know . . . it's over." His words and their reassurance caused Krystal's heart to wash with relief. "I'm not that kind of guy anymore." Jaime took another bite from his food then chuckled. Krystal gave no reaction. Jaime lifted his eyes once again, took a breath and said, "Thank you . . . for sticking by me through it all." He paused. "I gave you good reason not to be friends with me, and all the more to stay away from me . . ." He looked straight into her eyes; into her soul, "So thank you for still being kind to me, and forgiving me, even though I don't deserve your forgiveness. Thank you."

It was like the rift between the two of them had finally healed. Krystal exhaled; the relief of a new beginning overwhelmed her. Rushing over her body and soul like water. On the outside Krystal said nothing. She merely looked at Jaime and nodded.

Jaime pushed from his chair and took his finished plate. Krystal expected him to go straight toward the kitchen for seconds but instead he came towards her and asked, "Are you done with your food?" Krystal allowed Jaime to see her surprise. Jaime performed the courtesy of taking her finished plate from the table. And the thought of it made Krystal feel valued. It showed he was thinking about others more than himself. Krystal wanted to cry from the unexpected kindness. Krystal handed Jaime her plate as he headed toward the kitchen. Jaime turned his head, noticing how messy the kitchen was after preparing the meal. Krystal hadn't gotten up yet when Jaime started washing the dishes.

"Oh, you don't have to do that!" Krystal said.

Jaime turned, speaking kindly, "I know, but I want to." Krystal decided it was best not to argue and complied. She picked up a rag herself and dried off the dishes once Jaime finished them. Krystal could not explain it, but she enjoyed this moment. The open atmosphere between the two of them. It was like all the barriers were finally down and they could relish in the presence of each other's company. It also felt like Jaime was a different person now, and Krystal enjoyed washing dishes with him. It made things a lot quicker. But it also felt nice to have a friend. A true and devoted friend.

Krystal closed her eyes and made a quick prayer. "Thank you," she whispered aloud. Knowing it was for both Jaime and God. For she knew today, a heart had been restored.

CHAPTER 59

Mother and Daughter

*"There is no such thing as an accidental child. Your parents
may not have planned to have you, but God did."*

—JL

Sarah helped Ashley out of the car and into her chair. Ashley
wasn't too keen on being taken care of by her best friend and fellow nurse,
but she could tell Sarah was getting a kick out of it. Ashley was not in the
best of moods. Another physical therapy session had been wasted. She still
couldn't get herself to walk. It had been months since she had woken up,
but she had shown no improvement. Ashley was starting to fear she would
never walk again, even with the reassurances from the doctors saying she was
healthy enough to walk. But she wasn't walking. If she could walk, then she'd
be walking. Ashley stuffed her frustration inside and ignored it. Sarah pulled
her wheelchair up the stairs until they were at the front door to Ashley's
apartment.

Sarah caught her breath, "There you go."

Ashley looked over her shoulder, "Thank you Sarah." Sarah gave a
thumbs up and walked back down the stairs.

"I'll see you tomorrow, Ash."

"Bye Sarah." Ashley looked at the door and grimaced. She did not like
coming home in the same condition as before. Ashley's happiness and joy
drained out of her. Her feelings of guilt sneaked in and permeated her soul
until all that was left was unhappiness and despair. Her frustration grew but
she held it in. She didn't have the energy to be angry right now. She needed

to focus on walking again. But that would wait for the next day when she would try again and fail.

Ashley opened the door, holding her anger in, and saw candles lit and a table full of warm food. There stood Krystal, rubbing her hands with nervous expectation. Ashley's anger vented and replaced it with surprise. Ashley rolled into the apartment, "What's all this?"

Krystal gestured toward the food. "This, uhhh," she looked embarrassed, "This is a thank you."

Ashley tilted her head quizzically. "A thank you?"

Krystal nodded, "Yeah."

Ashley rolled forward. "What brought this on?" eyeing the delicious food. Krystal had made all of Ashley's favorite foods: seasoned calamari along with linguini spaghetti mixed with pesto sauce. The sight of it all made Ashley's mouth salivate, and the smell of the food made her stomach growl.

Krystal leaned back against the table, bobbing her head from side to side. "Well . . . given how you were asleep for so long and now you're awake . . ." Krystal looked at her mom. "I just wanted to say . . . thank you . . . for being my mom."

Ashley felt a surge inside her heart soar upwards and trigger her tear ducts. It came so sudden she had no control over it. The words struck her dead in the heart. Ashley exhaled in disbelief, "What?"

Krystal looked to the floor then back up, speaking somberly but still sounding hopeful, "I know you've had a rough time raising me, but this, this is a thank you for all the times you supported me. Even though you didn't want me, you still had me, and you supported me and tried to give me the best life I could have. So for all that. Thank you, Mom."

The sobs were uncontrollable. Ashley had no way to cover herself or hide what she was feeling. It was just too strong. Still, she had mixed feelings about it. Her heart was both overjoyed and sad.

I don't deserve this, Ashley thought. Feeling all the guilt and regret come soaring to the surface. Krystal knelt down beside her. Ashley soaked in the feeling of what it felt to be loved. To be appreciated. She had never felt anything amazing for being a parent until this very moment. Now, it felt as if her whole perspective had changed. Krystal let her mom cry it out. It felt good, felt healthy. Ashley wiped her face and put herself back together.

"Krystal . . ." Ashley said. Krystal stopped and looked at her mom, oblivious of what was about to happen. Ashley gestured for Krystal to take her hands. Krystal obeyed, a little perplexed by the action. Ashley took a breath, she was ready.

She spoke softly, "Krystal . . . when I had you, I didn't know what to do. I wasn't sure whether my actions were right or not." She shook her head, "All these years, I thought I deserved punishment for what I had done. I robbed you of the happy family you deserve and jumped the gun. And because of that, I didn't give you the father figure you needed . . ." Ashley looked down at her lap then back up, "I don't know where your dad is sweetie. I never knew who he was. It was just a drunk encounter, nothing more." Ashley gripped Krystal's hands, knowing that if she stopped, she wouldn't finish what she needed to say. "But then I had you come into my life, and for all those years I thought you were a mistake, *my* mistake . . ." Ashley paused, feeling disgusted with herself, yet it was the truth, how she really felt. "I regretted seeing you, because every time I did, it reminded me of my past actions. I didn't want to bestow that guilt on you, but I did. And so, I would work to keep my mind off of things, to try and forget my guilt. I would try my best to support you and be the happy mother when I was around, but it was all a lie. I was never happy during your childhood," Ashley admitted, pausing to take a difficult breath. It felt like a huge weight was sliding off her the more she spoke.

"It was especially hard when I would come home and see how terrible school was on you, how I couldn't do anything about it. I just left you alone to suffer all those years, trying at times to comfort you, but that's no excuse." Ashley gripped her daughter's hands tighter, "But Krystal . . ." Ashley took a deep breath, the heaviest breath she'd ever taken, about to cross the point of no return. It frightened her to her bones. It was the most difficult thing she'd ever done. Ashley looked into her daughter's eyes, "I can't deny the changes I've seen in you. I've watched you from a young age, and I know that before I went into that coma, you struggled just to get out of bed in the morning. You struggled to make friends. You struggled to find happiness and hope in the world, when you had all the reason not to." Ashley held dearly onto Krystal's hands, "But then I saw you *smile*. I actually saw you *smile*. I'm going to be honest; I've never seen you smile before." Ashley looked away but kept talking, "I watched as you made friends and cared for others. But more than that . . . I watched you find *hope*." She paused. "A hope that I could not understand. I asked myself, 'What is it that Krystal has that makes her joyful when she has no reason to be joyful?' Literally, I laid it all out." Ashley released one hand and counted off her fingers, "You were nearly aborted, your mom only half loved you, you never had a dad, you were treated like you were invisible by your classmates, and you struggled with suicidal thoughts and depression. Yet, here you are, scarred but smiling. Really smiling." Ashley reclaimed her grip on Krystal's soft hands, "I know it is something I cannot understand, but Krystal, simply watching you gives me hope." Ashley shook her head. "I don't deserve to be forgiven. I don't deserve grace for what I've done. And yet watching you makes me hope that I could be forgiven one day for all the horrible things I've done. So the question is . . . can I? Can someone like me be forgiven? For all the horrible things I've done and all the things I should have done better? Can you forgive me?"

Ashley expected tears from Krystal, but she found only warm compassion. It was the news Krystal wanted to hear for so long. Krystal gave a light smile and said, "You've already been forgiven Mom. What's done, is done. Now, you can start over."

Ashley asked, "How do I do that?"

A look of gentle hope spread across Krystal's face, "We can start now, by praying . . ."

"Okay," Ashley nodded cautiously. She didn't fully understand, but she knew it was the right decision, perhaps the first in her life. Ashley and Krystal threaded hands together in prayer, bowed their heads, and closed their eyes. Krystal spoke first, "I'll start, then you can say something after me."

"Okay." Ashley felt worried because she was about to embark on a whole new journey, a whole new life.

Krystal closed her eyes and said, "God . . . thank You for giving me my mom. She is the best thing You could have ever given me, and I want to thank You for all the years of support she's given me, even if her heart was mixed in the process, she still took the time to raise me and care for me. Thank You for that." Ashley waited, having opened her eyes, unsure how the process worked, but Krystal kept her eyes closed and said, "Now you go."

"Uhh," Ashley hesitated. "What do I say?"

"Say what's on your heart and we'll follow from there. I'll help you when you need it."

"Okay." Ashley's hands were shaking. She had never been so terrified before. Ashley closed her eyes and tried to mimic Krystal. "Uhh . . ." quickly losing track. It was difficult trying to pray to someone you've never talked to before, let alone seen. "God I uhh . . ." Ashley mumbled off, "God . . . I've . . . gone through a lot of pain." She started off slowly, then picked up in pace. "I . . . I'm not sure how to do this. I don't know what the procedure is." She stopped, then picked up somewhere she knew she could speak about. "God . . . I can't deny the changes I've seen you make in my daughter, Krystal. Every time I think about it, I come back to you. And I want what Krystal has. I want to be free."

Krystal gave a nudge of guidance, "Now repeat after me." Ashley followed and the two of them prayed together.

"Jesus . . . I believe that You came back from the dead. I believe You died for my sins. Jesus, please forgive me for the wrong I've done in my life. Please come into my life and change me. In Jesus' name, amen."

"Amen," Ashley opened her eyes, and instantly felt a weight fall off her. The guilt in her heart was gone and her conscience was clear, like a vanishing fog. It was like being able to breathe again. Ashley basked in having a clear conscience, oh it had been so long. A wave of relief flowed over Ashley, making her skin crawl with a warm and inviting presence. It washed away all the guilt from Ashley's heart, allowing her to relax, knowing she had been fully and completely forgiven. It was the first time in eighteen years that Ashley felt free.

Ashley and Krystal opened their eyes and looked at each other. The darkness was gone. Now was a time for change. A time for hope. Ashley looked at her daughter in relief. Her greatest mistake, yet her greatest blessing. Ashley wiped away the remaining tears, and for the first time she said, "Krystal . . . Thank you. Thank you, for being born."

It was like a gunshot had hit Krystal in the center of her soul. The world faded away and her heart overflowed with a love she had not experienced before. The love of a parent. Krystal fell apart and hugged her mom. The tears overflowing. It was the first time her mom said that to her. The first time Krystal felt grateful to be born.

Ashley felt the same, feeling for the first time she was a good parent. A parent who was appreciated. There the two of them held each other, feeling yet another wall break down between them. Amidst their tears and embrace, Ashley wondered, *Maybe this was the reason why I had her? Maybe I wasn't the one to save Krystal, but Krystal was the one to save me.*

Then, still gripping her mom's hands, Krystal stood up and said, "Are you ready?"

"What?"

Krystal said, "Little girl, get up."

Ashley failed to grasp the concept when Krystal reassured her. Then, helping her mom up, Ashley felt a surge flow from Krystal's arms into Ashley's legs. Ashley's eyes widened. Then, looking down at her feet, took her first step from the wheelchair, planting her feet firmly on the ground, then took one step, then another and another, walking perfectly as if the car accident had never happened. Ashley looked up amazed, Krystal sharing the same reaction.

"I can walk." She couldn't believe it. "I can walk!"

Krystal yelled, "You can walk!" Ashley stood on her two legs, feeling brand new. The sight brought a joy the two of them could not contain as they held each other in their arms.

Suddenly, the front door opened, and Jaime barged in, "Hey Krystal, sorry to drop in on you but—" He froze at the sight of Ms. Henninger and Krystal both *standing*, when he had only seen her yesterday in the wheelchair. At first Jaime was amazed, then it quickly faded. He looked to Krystal, lowered his brow, and said, "Did you have *another* miracle?"

CHAPTER 60

Identity

"Who are you?"

—JL

Kristina walked to school wearing a black outfit, trying to blend in more without announcing her arrival to the whole school. She managed to sneak past anybody who might have been looking. Once she was clear, she relaxed. There weren't that many people at school yet, so she could rest easy. Kristina thought about Krystal once again as she walked to her locker, thinking of her performance at the talent show.

Something changed once Krystal sang at that talent show. Something . . . within me. Kristina thought of Krystal's performance and how confident she was. *The thing is . . . I want what she has. I don't know what it is, but I want it.* Kristina looked up and wondered if Krystal was around. Both to her surprise and lack of surprise there was Krystal walking across the hallway.

"Speak of the devil," Kristina whispered.

Krystal walked up to Kristina and said, "Good morning!"

Kristina extended the greetings back, "Good morning my dude!"

Krystal chuckled, "You really are a tom-boy you know that."

"Nahhhh that's only a part of me. There are many different facets," Kristina smiled. Then her sarcasm faded, "Hey, can I ask you a question?"

Krystal gave Kristina her full attention, "What's your question?"

"What's the name of the church you go to?"

"Hill Crest church," she replied.

Hill Crest church, Kristina thought. "Okay, umm do they have like multiple service times?"

Krystal nodded, "Yeah, they have one on Saturday at 6pm, and then one service on Sunday at 10:30am. You thinking of going?"

Kristina shook her head, lying, "No no, I was just curious that's all."

Krystal shrugged her shoulders. "Okay. Suit yourself. You're always welcome to come," then walked away, leaving Kristina alone with the two service times playing in her head. *10:30am or 6pm, which do I choose?*

> "How do you find peace when your heart and mind are racked with anxiety? Where does it come from?"
>
> —JL

Kristina got out of her car and locked it. The sun was beginning to set but the sky still illuminated an indigo blue on top of a curl of orange on the horizon. Kristina looked ahead, observing people parking their cars and heading into the little church. The hard part was how new it all was. Kristina was starting to wish Krystal was here with her, to guide her at least. Kristina had never been to church before and was really wishing she had a friend right now.

Kristina saw the greeters at the doorway and knew they were going to see her. Kristina halted in the parking lot when she heard, "Kristina?" Terror swept Kristina, fearing she had been seen by somebody who knew who she was. Kristina whipped around only to find Joanna. Kristina relaxed, turning on her cute act, "Hey Joe! It's wonderful to see you!"

Joanna saw the enthusiasm and tried to match it, "Oh hey Kristina! It's good to see you too!"

Kristina simmered down a bit but still kept up the act, even when it killed her inside. "What are you doing here?"

Joanna looked over her shoulder, "Oh after what happened at the talent show . . . I kinda wanted to check out Krystal's church so . . ." Joanna trailed off. Now Kristina understood, she wasn't the only one impacted by the talent show. But for the most part Kristina was relieved she had someone she knew here with her. She regretted not asking Krystal, but this was something

Kristina wanted to do on her own. She knew it was selfish but that's how it was.

Kristina gestured to the door, "Shall we go in?"

Joanna nodded, "Yes," heading in first. Kristina trailed behind, dropping the act when Joe wasn't looking. Luckily the greeters at the door didn't recognize Joe or Kristina so they entered without a problem. Fatigue struck Kristina, and she held out her arm against a wall to catch her breath, nearly fainting in the process. Kristina thought, *Dang it. I still can't put on an act for very long.* Kristina knew she was pushing it. She was still racked with anxiety every moment of every day. The constant struggle to keep herself together drained her of all her energy. It felt like she was a ship caught in a never-ending storm. Anxious and jittery at all times.

Kristina did her best to hide with the crowd, but Joanna seemed to blend with the crowd pretty well. Kristina was surprised and thought, *She'd make a good actor one day.* Together they walked into the auditorium and found some open seats in the back. Kristina was more curious now than uncomfortable. The building wasn't anything special, the church felt more like a log cabin, but it was a nice log cabin. It was a new side of the world Kristina had never explored before, and Kristina liked that somehow. It would be good material for her next acting job, if she got another acting job. She was still trying to recover her health before she could get back in the industry. Kristina did her best to stay hidden and avoid people; she didn't want paparazzi bothering her inside a church. The auditorium darkened, and Kristina and Joanna took their seats and exchanged a glimpse of discomfort as the service began.

After the singing, the Preacher stepped out onto the stage with his checkered collared shirt, glasses, plain jeans, and short hair. For a man in his early thirties, he looked surprisingly good for his age. He finished walking up the stage and congratulated the worship team as he stood in front of the podium in the center. He put his coffee mug down and opened his Bible. He looked at the crowd and said, "Good evening, friends. So wonderful to see you here on this beautiful Saturday evening."

He waited for the crowd to settle then straightened his back, "I want to start us off with a question." He waited for the room to become totally quiet then said, "Who are you?" The room fell dead silent. The question sent an invisible shockwave striking Kristina's being. Every muscle in her body stopped moving and paid close attention to this man on stage.

No way . . . Kristina thought. Her focus zeroed in on this speaker.

"It's a simple question to ask but it can be difficult to answer." He put his hand to his chest, speaking softly, "Personally there have been times when I struggled to answer this question. Times when I've felt lost and don't know who I am."

He took a step away from the podium, putting his hands together as if making a plea, "My friends, I do not want you to live your lives in confusion and neither does God." The Preacher pushed up his glasses and said, "But to understand our identity we have to understand something about the one who created us, God. First, we must understand that God is omniscient, meaning God is all knowing. Well, what does that mean? It means that God knows your heart and your mind. He knows every thought you've had and are going to have."

The Preacher flipped his Bible to a marked portion and read, "In the Bible, it says in 1 Chronicles 28:9,

"For the Lord sees every heart and knows every plan and thought."
—1 CHRONICLES 28:9C (NLT)

The Preacher said, "So you see, God is *omniscient*, meaning He is all-knowing. He knows everything about you. You are fully *known*." The Preacher squared up to the audience, "You may be asking yourselves, 'Well gee that's great and all but what does that have to do with me?' It means there are no secrets from God. God knows you fully and completely, there is nothing hidden from him. Because of that, we can come openly to Him in His merciful arms. For even though God knows everything about us and knows all our wrongdoings and all the sins we've done, He still loves us to send His only Son to die for us and give us the gift of eternal life in Heaven. He does that so that He can adopt us into His family and call us children of God." The Preacher looked at his Bible again, "In John 1:12–13, it says,

"But to all who believed him and accepted him, he gave the right to become children of God. They are

reborn—not with a physical birth resulting from human
passion or plan, but a birth that comes from God."
—JOHN 1:12–13 (NLT)

"And in 1 John 3:1 it says,

"See how very much our Father loves us, for he calls
us his children, and that is what we are!"
—1 JOHN 3:1 (NLT)

The Preacher looked up and passively observed the crowd, the words reverberating off the walls. Allowing the silence to settle his words in their hearts. The Preacher lowered his voice like a loving father speaking to his children, "My friends do you know what this means? It means we have an *identity*; it means that if we believe in Jesus Christ as our Savior, then we are forever part of God's family. If you are asking the question, 'Who am I?' Well, I'll tell you. If you believe in Jesus Christ, then *you . . . are a child of God*. That is your identity, and nothing in all of creation can take that away from you."

The Preacher lowered his voice and spoke softly, "My friends, you can put your identity in your job, but you can lose your job. You can put your identity in your name, but what happens when someone else has the same name? You can lose your name. You can put your identity in your country, but even your country will not last forever. The only thing that lasts forever is the Kingdom of God.

The Preacher put his hand on his heart, "I'll bet that some of you have struggled trying to be like somebody else. Trying to be more like the popular kids in school or if our parents tell us, 'You should be more like your brother.'" The Preacher lowered his hand and leaned on the podium, "But do you know what God wants you to be? He wants *you* to be *you*. God doesn't want you to be anyone else. When you get to Heaven, God is not going to say, 'Oh why weren't you more like your brother or sister.' No, God is going to say, 'Why weren't you more like *you?'*"

The Preacher pushed up his glasses, "Have you ever tried to please someone? Has it ever worked out the way you intended? The Bible says in Philippians 2:3,

"Don't be selfish; don't try to impress others. Be humble,
thinking of others as better than yourselves."
—Philippians 2:3 (NLT)

"You see, even God can't please everybody so why should we worry about trying to please other people, it's foolish. God wants *you* to be *you*. To come as you are and know that you are fully and deeply loved. For there is only one *you*."

Kristina was lost for words. She had to admit, the guy was impressive. Everything this guy had said was hitting home. She had come here today not knowing what to expect, but she had gotten something she never could have imagined. Kristina turned her head, remembering Joanna was with her, and all Kristina could see was Joanna's face staring up at the Preacher like a mannequin. Kristina couldn't tell what Joanna was thinking, "You good?" Kristina whispered.

"Fine," Joanna replied, the word hanging with unintended weakness. Kristina decided not to pry and merely lifted her hand and patted Joanna's back gently. Joanna winced a moment then allowed it. Joanna regained herself, "Quite the sermon."

"Yeah," Kristina answered, shifting her gaze to the stage, watching the Preacher finish out with prayer.

The Preacher stood center on his podium, "Friends, if you have been feeling lost. If you've been feeling empty and want to live a life full of love and fulfillment, knowing who you are, then will you pray this with me?" Kristina paused. This was her moment. Her time to come forward and take a leap of faith.

She thought, *It's time . . . for me to discover, who I am.*

Just then terror struck Kristina as all her anxious thoughts and worries came rushing to the surface. Kristina's whole body began shaking violently. She was having the strongest panic attack she's ever had. Her heart was choking inside her. Pounding intensely as her body went into Fight or Flight mode. She legit thought she was going to die.

The Preacher threaded his hands together and closed his eyes. The rest of the crowd did the same. Kristina wanted to run out and hide, but she kept her hands threaded together and intentionally prayed with the Preacher, speaking word for word his prayer, "Father, without You I do not know who I am. I'm tired of living this life in obscurity. I feel lost God. I need direction. Jesus, will You come into my heart and free me from my chains. Please forgive me for the sins I've done. When I ask myself the question, 'Who am I,' I will answer, 'I . . . am a child of God.' Father, I want to be accepted into Your family and follow You for the rest of my life. In Jesus name I pray, amen."

"Amen," Kristina said. Kristina prayed the Preacher's prayer, meaning every word. Then, like a boat exiting a storm, everything was calm. Kristina's whole being suddenly felt tranquil like a lake. The entire world went mute, and Kristina slowly came to terms with the truth.

I know who I am. The statement sounded foreign yet true. Kristina felt it in her heart when she prayed those words. *I know who I am.* It was amazing. Kristina could feel everything was different. The pit in her soul was filled and the insecurity was gone. Kristina did a mental and emotional check of her body and could tell both her body and soul were calm. It had been so long since she had felt unified in thought. Her heart, soul, body, and mind were all at peace. She realized she no longer felt lost, for she had been found.

The Preacher looked among the crowd like a proud parent. "To those of you who said that prayer today I'd like to congratulate you and welcome you into the family of God." The whole crowd applauded, and Kristina could feel their cheers were directed toward her. It must have been like this for Krystal on the stage. Finally able to move on and start the next chapter. The Preacher gave a loving smile to his audience, "I'm so proud of all of you."

Kristina looked over at Joanna frozen with thought. It was surprising to see Joanna look so somber, but church was a place where emotions came out and feelings were challenged.

The choir came back on stage and began singing Amazing Grace. This time, Kristina stood with the crowd, raised her head high and said proudly, "I know who I am."

The next morning Kristina opened her eyes and searched for the storm inside her, but it was no longer there. She lifted from her bed sheets and felt odd for a moment. She didn't feel lost anymore. She didn't feel anxious or worried or fatigued. In fact, she felt energized, ready to run a marathon.

Kristina looked at her hands then at her feet. She could sense in her heart the insecurity was gone. Her question had been answered and she had never felt happier. Kristina threw on her running clothes and ran out the door.

Kristina had her phone in hand and ran down the street, sprinting as fast as she could, testing how much energy she now had. It was like she was plugged into an electric generator after running on low power for years. She never felt more energized in her life. Kristina ran out into the rain, not caring if she got wet, feeling the joy flow through her being and letting the water wash away her past. Kristina ran and put her phone to her ear.

"Carlo! I'm ready to get back to business!"

Krystal remarked at how annoyed she was that her backpack strap broke. Now she was wearing a backpack with one workable strap and would have to get another one. Krystal decided to let it go and put her books in her locker. She turned and saw Kristina walking toward her, but Krystal noticed something was different about Kristina. There was something in Kristina's step that told her something was different. Krystal did a quick analysis and saw that Kristina looked happier, but also, it wasn't an act. Her defenses were down. Kristina was out in the open.

Kristina saw Krystal and waved, "Good morning, Krystal!"

Krystal waved back hesitantly, "Hey," feeling an odd sense of joy emanating from Kristina. She didn't have the high-pitched girly voice and she was particularly happy for a regular Tuesday morning. Kristina came up to Krystal and threw her arm around her like she did to Jaime.

"So . . ." she looked at Krystal, "How you doing?"

Krystal wasn't sure whether to feel happy or suspicious, but she went with the first option. "I'm fine," she said cautiously. Still a bit uncomfortable with whatever *this* was. "How are you?"

Kristina spoke more casually, like her tone was more ground level, "I feel great! In fact, I haven't felt this good in a long time!" Kristina took her arm off Krystal and did a twirl in the walkway.

Krystal cocked a concerned eyebrow, "Did something happen?"

Kristina turned around, "Yeah. I accepted Jesus into my life."

The reveal stunned Krystal. It was certainly out of the blue and not something she expected this Tuesday morning. "Wow uhh, okay great." She couldn't seem to find a proper response. "Uhh, that explains why you seem so cheerful."

Kristina smiled. Krystal watched her and thought, *You know, she does seem different. I can tell she's not putting on an act, so this must be the real Kristina.*

Kristina leaned one arm against the locker and nudged her head toward the school courtyard, "Come on, let's go get a snack from the cafeteria." Her personality was calmer and more controlled rather than her usual ditsy enthusiasm.

Krystal decided to roll with it and followed Kristina toward the cafeteria. As they walked, Krystal could tell Kristina's spirit seemed happier and her mind was more grounded. Her confidence had risen but most of all she seemed relaxed. She wasn't putting on the act anymore and was simply being herself. It made Krystal feel calmer too, knowing Kristina wasn't playing any games.

They walked out into the main school courtyard and Krystal knew what was coming. The paparazzi. Immediately a group of freshman boys saw Kristina and came up to her.

"Oh my gosh! Oh my gosh! It's Kristina Walker, the Actress! May we take a photo with you?" Asked a young freshman boy with all his friends.

Krystal expected Kristina to light up with enthusiasm but instead she remained calm and cheerful. "Sure," Kristina replied sweetly. Now that surprised Krystal. Normally Kristina would have exploded with excitement, but she was more mature this time. They all got in the picture together as Kristina held the camera high and said, "Smiles guys!" They all smiled, even Kristina, and Krystal could tell that it was a real smile. Kristina handed the phone back to the boy.

The boy held the picture like he had received the best present ever. His eyes lit up and said, "Thank you so much!"

"No problem," said Kristina, gesturing her hand in the air, "High five!" The boy gave her a high five, then Kristina shared the high five with all the boys in the group. She even came up to Krystal, surprising her. Krystal hesitated but eventually gave in and gave Kristina a high five.

One of the boys looked at the two of them and asked, "Is that your friend?"

Kristina casually threw her arm around Krystal, "No. This is my *best* friend. Krystal Henninger."

The boys in the group all went, "WHOAH!"

All of them looked at Krystal as one boy asked, "So you're friends with Kristina Walker?" The spotlight suddenly fell on Krystal. She felt embarrassed by the immediate audience. She still wasn't used to crowds like Kristina was. (Despite how she just sang a song in front of hundreds of people? Give me a break man.)

Krystal snuck Kristina a snide look, *You're enjoying this aren't you?* Kristina's coy face said it all. Krystal stuck out her chin, steering a sly look back at her. *Oh, I'll get you for this.*

Krystal returned her focus to the group of freshman boys and said, "Uhh, I guess I am." The discomfort did not fade. Kristina saw it and laughed. Krystal was still uncomfortable with groups, and maybe that wouldn't go away but at least Kristina found it cute to watch.

A boy with light brown hair asked, "So what's it like to be best friends with Kristina Walker?"

Krystal wasn't ready for a questionnaire, but she tried to answer as best she could. "Well . . ." looking at Kristina. Then she looked at the boy and answered honestly, "She's a good friend. And loyal. She's helped me a lot. Especially with my wardrobe, but also in helping me feel pretty." Krystal nodded, glancing at Kristina. "I couldn't have asked for a better friend." For a moment, Kristina was taken back. Then she smiled, threw her arm around Krystal, and pointed at her, nearly putting Krystal in a headlock.

"You see that! That's why she's my best friend! Because she's honest. And I couldn't have asked for someone better than her." Kristina looked out at the boys, "Okay no more questions, we've gotta go. We've got business to address." Kristina looked to Krystal, "Shall we?"

Krystal saw the gesture and nodded, "Let's shall." Then Kristina and Krystal both left like they were walking away from an explosion in a movie. Together the two of them walked off to the glorious cafeteria, where expensive artificial food awaited them.

CHAPTER 61

A Friend in Need

"Even giving someone your attention can lift their spirits."

—JL

Sho was on one of his usual walks around the outskirts of school during break. It had been a hectic few weeks so he was glad for the peace and quiet of the morning. He rounded his usual corner and came up to one of the hallway exits on the outside of school when his eyes lifted and saw a girl about his age with brown hair sitting alone on a bench next to a hallway entrance. For some reason, Sho couldn't take his eyes off her. There was something about her that intrigued him. The girl was a freshman like himself but after looking at her, Sho realized something. *She has that same look as I do.* It was so obvious yet so inconspicuous. People walked by the girl like it was normal, but to someone who struggled with loneliness, Sho knew the look all too well.

The way she hunched over and lowered her head. No reason to lift her head high and believe things will be alright. Eyes that were shallow and empty, yearning for hope. Only when the girl looked up at people passing by did he see the disappointment on her face as they ignored her. It broke Sho's heart. Why hadn't he seen it before? He didn't know if the girl was waiting for friends or not, but they were in the final minutes of break, therefore if anyone wasn't there already, they were never there at all.

The girl turned in his direction and Sho immediately looked down. He continued walking, pretending everything was normal. You don't want to stand out and look weird or else you won't have any friends. Isn't that the unspoken rule of high school? So Sho kept his head down and walked forward. But a part of him wanted to look in the girl's direction, part of him wanted to go up and ask her how she was doing. *I should say something. Ask her if she's okay.* But fear and discomfort gripped his heart.

Sho stepped forward, now in direct view of the girl. This was his moment. Time to lift his head and look her in the eyes. Even giving someone your attention can lift their spirits. To let them know you see them and that they matter. Because you don't look at things that don't matter, and people feel the same way. When you fail to look at someone, it's indirectly telling someone they aren't important to you. Now imagine you were treated like that by everyone. Not one person giving you the time of day. Not even bothering to share a look with you. How depressing is that.

Sho kept his hands tucked in his pockets, head down, staring intently at the concrete beneath him. He could sense her looking at him, the girl wanted to be seen, even when she looked like she didn't. But Sho kept his head down and hands tucked. Passing by like nothing happened. Shame instantly burdened his heart as he rounded the corner, passing out of eye's view. Even though he never saw her face, he could tell he let her down. *What have I done?* Sho thought. But Sho also felt the fear paralyze him. The fear of standing out and doing something different was all too real. He didn't want to face it, so he kept walking like nothing happened. But in doing that, he did the same thing everyone else did. He ignored her, and he never felt more shame before in his life.

Sho gripped both straps of his backpack, and with his head lowered, approached the cowling beast that was high school. It was another chilly morning like all the others. Sho looked around hoping to get some satisfaction out of the scenery of this place but there was not much nature to look at. All of it was brown shrub with a little green mixed in. Take the green away and the place would look like a total desert. That was one of the things he missed about Japan, the nature and greenery of the land always blew his mind away with how beautiful things were. Here in this state in America everything was dry, dull brown, and it barely rained. He wished it would rain more here.

Sho brought his eyes down and kept walking. He was in no rush to get to his locker. All his books were already there and there was no need to get anything from it anyway. He had time to kill before school started, so he spent his morning walking around the outskirts of school. Sho was not pleased with what he saw. He found multiple couples making out in their specified corners while also finding many people sitting in their self-designated areas. His eyes were drawn towards the ground and his legs moved on autopilot, until he came up around a corner and saw the same lone girl from the other day sitting on her bench. Sho hid behind the corner and watched her, hoping she didn't see him. The shame from last time struck his heart like a gong.

She was sitting on her bench as usual, reading a book of some sorts, but he was too far away to see the title. Sho saw all the same signs as last time. Someone begging for a person to talk to them. Sho's heart shriveled up and tightened. He peered around the corner, debating whether he should go up and talk to her, when he heard, "What are we looking at?"

Sho nearly jumped out of his skin, "Aghh!" and turned around to see Krystal standing behind him. He caught his breath, "Uhhh Krystal-senpai! What are . . . you doing here?" His English was still a bit of a challenge, but he was getting the hang of it.

Krystal said in a devious manner, "I was wondering the same thing about you." Krystal looked past him at the girl and put two and two together. She smiled, "I see." She looked at Sho. "Are you gonna talk to her?"

"No." Sho wrapped his arms around his chest and tried to act tough. "I wasn't planning on doing that."

Krystal didn't buy into Sho's tough guy act. In fact, she found it to be quite cute. Maybe that was one of the reasons why Sho liked her so much, because he could always be honest with her and she could always see right through him, no matter how hard he tried to hide it. Krystal looked over at the girl, "She looks like a nice person." Sho looked back at the girl and could see how miserable she looked. It was obvious, but only to him and Krystal. Everyone else walking by the girl didn't seem to notice how awful she looked. That angered Sho. He remembered months sitting by himself waiting for someone to walk by and talk to him. It wasn't until Krystal came by that his wish had come true, but the trauma lingered. You can't simply forget the tough times in your life that easily. With that kind of experience, Sho, like Krystal, was able to recognize people who were lonely. Only lonely people tend to notice lonely people.

Krystal shrugged her shoulders and spoke nonchalant, "Well if you won't do it, then I will." Walking over without a moment's hesitation. Sho watched in complete shock as Krystal walked right over to where the girl was sitting and asked what she was reading. Sho watched how the conversation played out. He couldn't tell what they were saying but Sho noticed the girl seemed a bit surprised from an older classman coming up and talking to her. But what Sho also saw was how happy the girl was from someone talking to her. The two of them shook hands and Sho thought he heard Krystal introduce herself and ask the girl her name. The conversation ended and Krystal waved goodbye. Sho could tell Krystal had made that girl's day as she returned back to safety behind the corner.

Sho asked her, "Doesn't that feel . . . awkward?"

Krystal spoke candidly, "Yes. Every time."

"So why . . . do it?"

"Because," Krystal said, humbling herself, "It's what Jesus would do."

Sho remembered their previous session when she told Sho about her past, how Krystal used to be a loser like he was, but how God loved her and brought her out from the darkness. To love our neighbors as ourselves. Sho took his eyes off Krystal and looked back at the girl sitting alone by herself, "Do you think I could go up and talk to people like you do?"

Krystal answered, "For nothing is impossible with God. Luke 1:37." Sho looked up at her, amazed. Krystal was wise as she was beautiful. How remarkable he had met someone so kind here in the United States. He wished she were Japanese and would come live with him in Japan. She would have made a fantastic wife. Sho stood there in wonder, his face blushing and his mind racked with questions. But he could not connect the fact that someone so happy used to be someone as low and depressing as himself. He simply could not imagine it. And so, before he could try again, the bell rang and Krystal was off, waving him goodbye.

A week later, Sho approached the corner where he knew the girl would be and stopped. He took a few deep breaths before peering around the corner, finding the girl right where she usually sat. It came as no surprise to him. People who get settled in their schedule rarely tend to stray from it. People can sit in the same spot for years and never bother to think about changing it.

Sho lingered around the corner, having difficulty getting started. Until he heard, "What are we doing?"

Sho jumped, this time looking Krystal in the eye and showing a little more emotion before answering, "I was planning on talking to that girl over there."

Krystal peered past Sho, "Ohhh I see, that's the same girl as before huh. Well then, I guess I should let you get to it."

Sho was bemused a moment, "You're not going to stop me?"

Krystal straightened her back and crossed her arms, "Nope, this is only something you can do. Besides, it's good for you to make friends who are your own age. I understand it can be difficult for you to hang out with juniors and seniors all the time since you're a freshman." Sho had no argument there. Krystal gave him a pat on the back, an action which was unnecessary and so unlike her. Sho received the pat awkwardly, "Go get 'em tiger." He didn't know what that phrase meant but it sounded encouraging.

Sho stepped out, walking towards the girl sitting on the bench. He gripped the straps on his backpack, the fear of trying something new clutching his heart. *Is this what Krystal feels like every time she talks to a person?* He felt the weighing pressure and discomfort grip his heart. *This is awful. Why does she go through this so often?* Then he remembered how Krystal used to be the girl sitting on the bench, and then he understood. Because to Krystal, you can either sit there and be uncomfortable doing nothing or you be uncomfortable making friends. Either way it was painful, but only one of those would make things better. It was the same with Sho. He could either choose to avoid people and hope that someone kind enough will come by and say hi or he can get out there and introduce himself and make some friends of his own.

Sho's heart tightened so much he felt he was going to drop dead from a heart attack. The closer he got to the girl the harder it became. It was trial by fire, only the fire was all in your head, but you still felt the burn. Sho stepped closer and closer, feeling the temptation to walk away increase, to ignore the girl and move on, but when he pictured that future, he realized he would be the same as all the people he resented by choosing *not* to help her. It was there, Sho realized the power of compassion, how necessary it was to care for others. You need to have compassion to care more about others than you do yourself. But how do you get compassion? Where does it come from? Maybe we get compassion from seeing someone go through the same suffering we've gone through. Maybe we get compassion from God, or maybe compassion is something we learn, not are born with.

Sho took a few more steps and faced the girl. His face was pale white, and he was ready to pass out, but the girl lifted her eyes from her book to see her new visitor. The two of them didn't say anything. They just looked at each other for a moment, grasping the fact that they were looking at each other on purpose and not just by chance. The girl spoke first, "Hi." Her voice was sad but sweet.

"Hi," Sho replied, lost for words, but he could tell the girl didn't know what to say either. The two of them were rusty in their social skills. Sho looked for anything to start the conversation, so he looked for any detail, anything at all that would prompt a question. He looked at the title of the book she was reading and pointed, "What are you reading?"

The girl said, "Oh . . . this is just one of my English textbooks. I have an assignment due today." The girl herself looked pale white. Krystal observed from behind the corner and did her best not to intervene. This was all on Sho. He was the one who had to prove himself, and he succeeded, because now, he was looking someone in the eye and talking to a stranger. It was a beautiful first step for him.

Sho's fear was starting to show, "Who . . . is your English teacher?" He strained to get the pronunciation right.

"Mrs. Scythe. I have her in third period."

Sho tried not to look surprised, but he couldn't help but reveal a little on his face. "I have Mrs. Scythe in third period as well."

The girl's face lit up, "Really!"

Krystal watched from a distance knowing her work here was finished. Of course, she had no control over the circumstances. She was simply happy to see Sho finally making some friends. Of course, socializing doesn't always go smoothly. There will be some awkward moments but remember that everyone is uncomfortable and wants to connect. We humans constantly strive for community in any situation, so even if you think your neighbor doesn't want to connect with anybody, deep down we all have the need for community. So when you see someone sitting alone, why not invite them to lunch and sit with them for a change. You never know, it might spark something amazing.

Krystal smiled, watching the two freshmen talk. She didn't know what they were talking about, but she was happy that Sho had made a friend his age. Krystal nodded in approval, like an older sibling acknowledging a younger sibling's accomplishment. "He's going to be just fine," she said, knowing that Sho was now in better hands. In a way Krystal felt proud, but it wasn't her accomplishment. It was Jesus working in Sho that made her feel proud. Krystal looked up to the sky and prayed, "Thank you God, for taking care of Sho."

Krystal watched them talk for the entirety of the break until the bell sounded and the two of them departed. Sho walked back to Krystal and Krystal stood there feeling tall as he approached. Sho came up and said, "I did it." It wasn't a boastful comment. It was more out of humility.

Krystal knelt to Sho's eye level and said, "I'm proud of you Sho. You took a big step today."

Sho looked into Krystal's eyes and said, "Thank you." His English was perfect. That brought relief to Krystal, knowing that this boy would be all right. Krystal lifted the corner of her smile, feeling like an older sister right now. It was a rare feeling, causing her to wonder if this is how Jaime felt with Carole. Krystal straightened up, looked Sho in the eyes and said, "Now I know you're gonna be alright. And that makes me incredibly happy." Krystal took a breath, enjoying the moment. "Keep making friends Sho. Keep being yourself. And I know that things will get better."

Miraculously, Sho appeared very mature. He smiled wide, looking into Krystal's eyes and said, "Thank you, Krystal-senpai."

Krystal smiled, "It's my pleasure."

Krystal stretched her arms high in the air, everyone at the lunch table joining the discussion about whether churros or pecan pie were the greatest inventions in all of history. Krystal lowered her arms and listened in on the conversation. Jaime was leading and getting into a bit of a heated debate with Kristina. "No no no, have you ever had churros with ice cream? They are the greatest thing on the planet!"

Kristina retorted, "But have you ever had pecan pie from the South, that stuff is like the greatest thing ever!"

Krystal leaned back and watched the show. She noticed Joanna still hadn't shown up. She had recently gone back to Summer's group, so she didn't show up to the lunch table anymore. It bothered Krystal a little, but she didn't fight Joanna's decision to leave. It was Joanna's choice and Krystal would respect that. At least things had died down between Krystal and Summer, but there was still drama. Krystal put it out of her mind and noticed Sho sitting next to her. He seemed more interested in the conversation, looking more confident in himself. It was plain to see. Sho was even looking up for once.

Sho cut in, "But have you—" Everyone stopped and looked at him, surprised. Both from the clear pronunciation of his English but also because he rarely engaged in conversation. Sho saw all eyes on him, but he didn't ignore them. This time he looked everyone in the eye, even Krystal. Krystal was amazed at this sudden growth and let the boy speak. Sho felt pressured to stop but he continued—"have you ever had mochi before?" The clear pronunciation amazed everyone at the table.

Kristina was the first to break the ice, "No, I've never had mochi before. Is it good?"

Sho put his hands on the table, "You guys . . . are gonna like it. It's a chewy bun made of rice. You can fill it with ice cream. It's good." Everyone was amazed at Sho's perfect pronunciation. Jaime, Kristina, and Krystal all had their jaws open. Not only that, but he also sounded confident saying it. Sho seemed to be growing more and more comfortable with both himself and with the culture around him.

Jaime spoke, "Maybe you should bring it along some time."

Sho shied up a little like a sea anemone. "Okay," he said. "One day I'll bring some."

"That'd be nice," Kristina said. Then they all went back into conversation, this time with Sho joining in on the fun. Krystal leaned back, taking in the sight of a new change that occurred. She watched the group as Jaime, Kristina, and Sho all seemed to be in much higher spirits than when she first met them. Krystal took a mental picture of the scene and smiled to herself. *They've really come a long way. All of them.* And so, she listened in on the conversation, now with Sho advocating his mochi while Jaime and Kristina argued over their favorite desserts. Krystal just leaned back and watched the whole scene play out. Feeling content with the sight of everyone looking so happy. Where life was more than just pain, but of fun and laughter too.

CHAPTER 62

Disappointment

"The sad reality of life is that everybody disappoints."

—JL

It wasn't always like this. It wasn't always hard to make friends. Joanna sat on the edge of her bed and remembered elementary school, having the time of her life with her friends, playing, and having fun. It was bliss, no problems, no nothing, just enjoyment. But things changed once middle school rolled in. The days of middle school grew stagnant. Every day was the same, but the social differences were becoming more and more distant from the happy days of elementary school. Joanna could see it clearly. Soon enough Joanna found herself without friends for no likely reason. She hadn't offended anyone, she hadn't done anything wrong, people just drifted apart. Joanna couldn't tell if it was growing up or because of the dramatic differences in middle school. Very soon cliques started to form and no one dared leave them. And that . . . is when the loneliness came.

The long days of bitter torture. Joanna sat outside alone, for most of middle school, with no group, and no friends to stick by her. It was hard. People rarely talked to her despite Joanna's attempts to make friends, and all Joanna could do was endure it . . . That's when the bullying started. Boys were mean, girls were worse. Nobody wanted to see "Gloomy Joe," the nickname further isolating her. It was nothing but pure darkness for years.

To cope, Joanna figured she had to "re-invent" herself or else she would continue to suffer. So, she killed her true self and created a lie. She smiled more, not because she was happy, but because she discovered people liked her more when she smiled. And so, she smiled all the time, putting on a new face and personality, quickly swooning some of the boys who had bullied her, joining the cliques of the girls who hated her. But that lie, came with a cost. Joanna was empty inside, living a constant lie, but it was living the lie that kept her going. She couldn't be who she was, so she sucked up to others to survive. Anything to be noticed, out of fear of being ostracized again. Anything to survive.

By the time high school started Joanna joined a group rather quickly, Summer's group. Every day she kept up the charade. Living to please others, out of fear of being rejected.

Joanna started trembling in her bed, shaking uncontrollably, trying to hold herself together with sheer willpower. But willpower only lasts so long. Eventually, we all break under pressure, and Joanna was at her breaking point.

She looked at her phone, trying to divert her attention. Checking to see who her friends were on social media. But she knew the truth. None of them were *actually* her friends. They were just people she knew, no one she actually connected with. No one to call a "true friend." They were just people who enjoyed the life she was living. Acquaintances, that's a better term for it. They couldn't accept her for who she was. Despite being surrounded by tons of people, she was alone. It was a bit of an oxymoron, but people feel the most alone when they are surrounded by others, not when they're away from them.

"But there's one thing I don't understand," she said. Joanna's thoughts drifted back to Krystal. "How can that girl be herself and still seem happy?" The girl wasn't exactly the most optimistic of people, but at least she didn't lie to herself, and Joanna found that admirable about her because it was something she herself could not do. *How can Krystal be herself and not have any problems with it?* Joanna searched her past experiences but came up blank. "She seems so confident," Joanna whispered, "Walking tall despite what people throw at her," Joanna remembered the talent show and couldn't help but admire the girl. "And whatever she has, I want it. I totally want it, because . . ." she trailed off, picking up a moment later, "It's hard to live like this."

> "No matter how hard we try, it is impossible to please everybody."
> —JL

Joanna was relatively excited to go to the State Fair. Joanna waited up at the entrance after she was dropped off by her mom. The chatter and din of the fair brought Joanna excitement like a little schoolgirl. Hundreds of people were filing in line, parents and children alike. The sky was mostly clear, with a couple beautiful clouds. It was bright outside, and the weather was good. "I totally can't wait for this awesome event!" Joanna gripped her ticket and waited for Summer and everyone else to arrive. Summer had told Joanna they were all going to arrive together, and she even promised to give Joanna a ride home, so Joanna didn't have to worry about asking her mom to drive her home. Summer and her friends would do that for her. Joanna got there a few minutes early, but she was sure Summer and everyone else would arrive shortly.

An hour passed until Summer and the rest of the group finally showed up. Joanna noticed Amber wasn't with them, which came as a surprise, but she was relieved they finally came. Joanna wasn't angry. She was too infatuated with Summer to mind. Although she would have liked Summer to answer her texts or at least call her back and not show up an hour late to the original time.

They entered the fair and were instantly surrounded by game stands and overpriced food. Joanna felt the excitement with the rest of the group. Joanna rushed to the front of the group, next to Summer and eagerly asked, "What do you want to do first Summer?"

Summer looked around, "Let's, like play some games first." Summer turned to the rest of the group, "Is that like good with you guys?" Everyone agreed and nodded. Nobody wanting to disagree with the Sunflower Beauty. Summer quickly found a dart throwing booth with some balloons. Summer went first and came close to popping one but no one else could pop a single balloon at the stand.

Joanna was last. She stepped forward and picked up a dart, feeling the pressure. *You got this. Summer is watching so don't make a fool of yourself. I need to impress Summer!* Joanna felt pressure in her heart as she knew Summer was watching. Joanna held the dart up and threw the first dart. Miss. That was to be expected. Joanna had two more darts left. Joanna picked up the second dart. *Take two, I totally got this.* Joanna had played darts at home with her family before, so she was naturally pretty good at this, it would be a piece of cake.

Joanna threw the second dart and missed. She grunted in frustration, trying to keep her cool. *It's fine. You have one more try.* She could feel the slight pressure to impress Summer was throwing her off her game, literally. Joanna picked up the third dart, taking a slow breath and exhaled. Feeling the pressure of everyone looking at her. Joanna threw her final dart and nailed a balloon, winning a stuffed animal as a prize. Joanna cringed in victory, "Yessss!" She turned, "Did you see that? Did you see me hit it?" But her joy turned to disappointment as everyone in the group had left. Not one of them had stuck around to see her hit the balloon. Joanna received a stuffed whale as a prize with dissatisfaction and went after the group.

Joanna followed along, trying to catch up. She could smell deep-fried foods and all sorts of baked desserts around the fair. It was a joyous time as families were smiling and enjoying themselves. Meanwhile Joanna's insecurities quickly oozed to the surface. Joanna was freaking out. *No no, it can't be this way! I have friends. I have friends!* But the more she tried to convince herself, the less she believed it. She looked around for Summer and the rest of the group until she found them in a batting cage. Joanna met up with the group and wanted to say something about them leaving her, but the moment they saw her, she instantly forgot what she was going to say and felt overjoyed to find them. "There you guys are!" she said. "I was totally looking for you."

One of the guys said, "Oh hey. We were over here."

Joanna smiled and turned on the cutesy charm, "That's totally fine. It's no problem at all." *Good, incredibly good. Lie to yourself. It's the only way you'll have friends.* Joanna felt her heart tense like it was wrapped in steel wool. She stepped through the group until she came to the front and watched Summer swinging the bat in frustration. Summer threw the bat down and walked out of the cage.

The worker at the stand said, "Next!"

Joanna stepped forward and took the bat. She did a double take to make sure the group, especially Summer, was watching. Summer was there, looking like a sore loser. Joanna turned and looked straight forward, waiting for the ball to shoot from the machine. She waited for the right moment and swung hard. The ball flew by her, and she felt like an idiot. Joanna felt the pressure of everyone watching and felt the need to please Summer increase. It affected her gameplay because she tried to go for a homerun. Joanna swung two more times before her turn was up. She didn't hit a single ball, and, on every swing, she swung so far off that she looked ridiculous. She left the cage disappointed as the whole group observed her failure. Joanna avoided their gaze, knowing their eyes were all on her.

They went to another game stand, this time with the classic milk bottles stacked like a house. But these milk bottles were really sturdy and had some heft to them. The whole group had tried their luck but no one, not even Summer, had been able to knock them all down. Finally, Joanna stepped up and took her try at it, and on the first two throws she managed to knock all the bottles down. "I got it! I got it! Summer, I got it!" Joanna whipped around in frantic joy only to find the whole group had left her once again. Joanna was given another prize, but disappointment was her only reward. The group was already off in another direction with Summer leading the way. They wouldn't have left if Summer had not wanted to. That part stabbed Joanna the deepest.

Joanna tried to catch up with the group, but her stomach growled, and she immediately had to go to the bathroom. Joanna yelled to Summer and the rest of the group, "I totally have to go to the bathroom! I'll be right back!" Then left to find the nearest port-a-potty.

Joanna finished her business and came out to find that Summer and the rest of the group were gone. Joanna dialed Summer's number, but it went to voicemail. Joanna searched for them but could not find the group. Fear and insecurity attacked Joanna's heart and mind, feeling alone in a place swarming with people. Joanna texted Summer but she never replied to any of her texts.

Joanna looked up and tried to find them but realized she had lost them. She panicked, *No, not again! Not this time!* Joanna searched harder, even asking some people questions but no one could help her. Eventually Joanna waited near the entrance for them to come back, but an hour went by, then two hours and still no one showed up. Joanna had texted Summer to say where she was, but no one came. So, she waited at the gate a little longer until she came to the realization. "No one's coming," she said. The truth was hard to bear. Finally coming to terms with the fact that the day had ended in disaster. Therefore, Joanna walked out of the State Fair and called her mom to pick her up.

> "Even God can't please everybody."
> —JL

Joanna waited at the front of school, this time with a little anger. She hated how the group had ditched her at the State Fair the other day, and she wanted to say something about it. Joanna waited in their usual morning spot before school started as people began to trickle in. Joanna wondered why Amber wasn't at the fair with the group but maybe that was a good thing. Joanna felt less intimidated when Amber wasn't around.

This time Summer was the first to show up before anyone else arrived in the group, and Joanna was glad because she would have a few minutes alone with Summer. "Good morning, Summer!" Joanna waved joyfully, complimenting Summer with a wide smile. A nice touch to the greeting. Summer did not reciprocate, which struck Joanna as odd, really odd.

Summer only replied, "Hey," like it was a chore.

Without thinking, Joanna felt anger build inside her and leaked out her feelings, "Where were you guys yesterday?"

"Huh?" Summer seemed perplexed. "I don't know what you mean?"

Joanna was surprised by Summer's confusion. So she spoke candidly, "You guys totally left me yesterday after I went to the bathroom. Where were you?"

Summer shrugged her shoulders, "Oh sorry, I guess we like, forgot about you." The way Summer said it was so casual and dismissive, it only seemed to make Joanna angrier.

"You just forgot?" Joanna said, unable to comprehend Summer's answer.

Summer pulled up her phone and started scrolling, "Yeah, we did. I'm sorry."

But Joanna wasn't going to let her off the hook that easy, her anger growing, "Did you forget the fact that you were supposed to be my ride home?"

Summer looked up for a moment, "Huh? Oh yeah, I guess we were. Sorry." But her tone didn't sound apologetic. It sounded annoyed.

Joanna wanted to clarify what she was hearing. "You just *forgot* to give me a ride home and left me at a public event all alone?"

Summer shrugged her shoulders. "Ehh, you'll get over it." Joanna could not believe what she was hearing. Now she felt offended, intentionally offended. *Is she serious?* Joanna thought. *Does she have no sympathy for what she did?*

Joanna picked the next question without much thought, allowing her emotions to drive her words, "So what do you say about that?"

Summer looked down at her phone, "Sorry," her voice completely unapologetic. Joanna wanted to say something, to throw a fit of rage, but instead she kept her mouth shut and watched as the rest of the group entered the conversation. Killing herself inside and smiling, continuing as if it was business as usual while Joanna stood there feeling abused.

Lunch started and Joanna sat with Summer's group again. She regretted not being with Krystal and her group but a part of her still wanted to be friends with Summer, even if Summer treated her poorly sometimes. They all took their seats at Summer's new lunch table and started eating. Summer was in the middle of a story when she saw Krystal pass by on her way to sit with her table group. Joanna saw Summer sneer with vile anger, "I can't believe that witch won the talent show." Joanna coiled back a bit. Summer was steaming. "I mean like, what were the judges thinking! They were bought off, that's for sure. Yeah, yeah that's it. She bought them off!" Summer was seething. Joanna could finally see the wicked side of Summer she refused to believe. Joanna checked the group, but nobody was looking at Summer or pretended to ignore the conversation. "I mean like, what where they even thinking," Summer put her fists to her hips, smirking her face and lowering her voice, "'Oh we believe that she is the rightful winner.' I mean come on! That witch doesn't deserve to win! I do!"

A tiny fire was born inside Joanna's heart. She remembered Summer's skit at the talent show. It was, quote unquote, "terrible" but Summer didn't know that. She believed she was the best performer, when in reality, she got eighth place. *Talk about a sore loser.* Joanna kept her mouth shut, the fear in the group getting stronger the more Summer went on. "I mean like what the heck! Doesn't that girl know how to play a guitar? I could play the guitar far better than she ever could!" Joanna felt the fire rise within her. She had loved

Krystal's song and thought it was the rightful winner of the competition. But Joanna killed that side of herself. Commanding herself, *Don't stick out! Don't stick out or you'll get ostracized again! They won't love you if they reject you!*

Joanna's heart raced. All the fears from her past came etching to the surface. Joanna started to tremble, but the fire inside was powerful and growing. Joanna remembered the constant bullying in middle school, all the girls in her class criticizing her for the kinds of clothes she wore and how she acted. Joanna's anxiety defenses kicked in, *kill who you are, blend with the group, don't stick out.* But accompanied by that pressure, was an emptiness that lingered in her heart like poison. Joanna put on a smile and said, "Yeah, you're totally right Summer! That witch doesn't deserve to win at all!" but saying that killed Joanna inside. It was hard enough leaving Krystal's group again to join Summer's, but this betrayal was worse. Gossiping about Krystal felt like a knife stabbing deeper in Joanna's heart like never before. Joanna liked Krystal. She admired her stoicism and determination to be herself. But most of all . . . after seeing Krystal perform at that talent show, showing how she could be herself *and* be happy, made Joanna think she could too. It caused Joanna to wonder for many nights how Krystal was able to sing in front of an entire crowd of people, when Joanna could not bear to be herself in front of anybody.

Summer looked at Joanna, "Thank you Joe, I appreciate that. You're like a loyal friend," patting Joanna's shoulder. Joanna smiled, getting the admiration from Summer that she'd always wanted, but it wasn't what she thought it was. All she felt was empty inside. By getting the admiration she wanted from Summer, Joanna also stabbed Krystal in the back. The pain of that betrayal had only grown deeper in the weeks to come. Joanna never wanted to hurt Krystal, but her actions to gain Summer's approval hurt one of the few people she cared about. Summer wrapped her arm around Joanna and the two of them looked in the direction of Krystal. Summer said, "Don't you hate her? How gloomy she looks. How she only wears black. Hehe, I bet she's a prostitute too."

Joanna tried to hold the smile, the words painful to say, like she was ingesting shards of glass, "Yeah . . . she is." Gritting her teeth, Joanna felt the pain kill her inside, leaving her only emptiness and sorrow. It was not the fulfillment she wanted. Joanna had gotten Summer's approval, but it wasn't enough, it wasn't worth it. She couldn't take it anymore.

Joanna smacked Summer's hand off her shoulder, "No . . ."

Summer turned in bewildered surprise. The rest of the group followed suit. The spotlight landed on Joanna. Summer was slow to understand, "What do you mean *no?*"

"No." Joanna said, shaking. Joanna felt a surge in her stomach begin to rise. The words she always wanted to say leaked to the top.

Summer caught on, "You mean, I'm *right* in the matter?" Summer etched the wickedness in her words, speaking slowly, allowing Joanna to understand the threat.

Joanna was shaking terribly, knowing the whole group of ten people were now all staring at her like she was a freak. A feeling she was all too familiar with. Joanna's trauma came rushing forth, the memories all flooding back from middle school. *It was just like this . . . back in middle school.* Joanna knew she had a choice to make, and one that would decide her fate. Summer pressed on, "You do agree with me, *right* Joanna?" the cold anger in Summer's voice prevalent for all to hear.

Joanna wanted to say, *Yes, I agree with you. I agree that Krystal Henninger should have never won that competition.* But she couldn't say it. She couldn't betray both herself and Krystal again. Even if it meant losing all her friends and suffering loneliness all over again. Sometimes, it's better to be alone than to be in the company of bad people.

"No." Joanna said, sealing her fate.

Summer was amazed at the newfound defiance. She quickly tried to regain control. Turning on the cute act, "You don't have to lie to me. I forgive you."

"No." Joanna said, still shaking.

Summer grit her teeth, everyone was watching in terror. Summer killed the cute act and spoke solemnly, "You trying to say something?"

Joanna lifted her head to face her persecutor. The words she wanted to say came bubbling to the surface. *Don't say it. You'll ruin yourself.*

I can't betray myself and Krystal anymore. I'm not worthy of having friends. My heart can't take this anymore.

Joanna looked fearfully up into Summer's evil blue eyes and said, "Yes. Yes, I am." The words coming out slow and fearful but gaining traction as they went. "I believe . . . that Krystal Henninger is a good person and is kind and caring and deserved to win that competition." Joanna shook her head, letting the fire inside fuel her words, "You never deserved to win it Summer."

Summer grit her teeth so hard she almost chipped a tooth, "Oh yeah! What does *she* have that I *don't*!"

Joanna simply said, "Character."

Summer stared at Joanna with avid anger and bewilderment. "Get out!"

Joanna stood up, feeling the power of her defiance, looking out among the group of people in Summer's clique then left the lunch table. It was strange. Joanna didn't feel doubtful about her actions this time. Joanna left Summer's table and headed on over to the last place she could go, Krystal's table. Feeling resolute in her actions for the first time. Maybe Joanna had finally grown and she just didn't realize it until now.

Joanna came up to Krystal's table, finding just her and Jaime. Krystal looked up, giving Joanna her typical blank-faced expression. Joanna looked over her shoulder, could tell Summer and the rest of her group was shooting daggers at her, then turned back to Krystal and asked, "Could I . . . could I sit here?" Krystal showed no surprise then was filled with compassion.

"Yes, you can." Krystal scooted over making room for Joanna to sit. Joanna realized she'd left her lunch back at Summer's table. She looked over, only to see Summer throw the lunch in the trash. Joanna shied away into her shell, staring down at the table phasing everything out of existence, until Krystal offered the other half of her sandwich. Joanna took the sandwich and asked, "Won't you be hungry?"

Krystal shook her head, "That's alright. I have everything I need." Joanna felt a wave of relief wash over her as she munched down on the sandwich, knowing for the first time she'd made the right decision. It was time to make amends. It was time to move on.

Joanna sat on her bed with her hair down. She had just taken a shower but was not letting it dry in a towel. She sat alone in her room, trying to ponder but for some reason her mind wouldn't let her. She was only allowed to think blank thoughts. It wasn't bad but it wasn't going anywhere either. Joanna sat in her room, letting the silence filter into her. Filling her, letting the pause give her healing.

After a while, Joanna was finally able to think again. Her thoughts drifting to recent events. Events of the talent show, of Summer abandoning her at the fair, and how Joanna left Summer's group again, this time of her own accord.

She couldn't take it anymore. She couldn't lie to herself. It was too painful. Joanna knew she made the right decision going back to Krystal's group and was glad she did it. But she knew she needed a fresh start. Because to keep living her life as a lie would only kill her.

"I'm done," Joanna said. "I'm done . . ." She fell silent. Her pink room surrounded her. Eventually, she found her voice again. "What is it that makes Krystal so confident? Why is she so proud being herself and not being anything else?" Joanna's mind thought back to the church service she went to with Kristina. Then she remembered a saying the Preacher said, *"God wants you to be you."*

Joanna contemplated the thought, *Maybe I should give this God thing a try?*

Joanna got down on her knees, threading her hands together and prayed, "God . . . I'm tired of living for peoples' expectations. I'm tired of living a lie. I want to come as I am and be accepted for who I am, not as what other people expect me to be. I pray that I will live for your expectations alone. So please, help me." And just then she felt peace flood her body. Joanna's eyes widened as her desire for others approval shrank within her and she was filled with something she did not understand, yet she welcomed it anyway. Just then she knew it was over. Her need for approval and the lie to uphold it was over. She knew, finally, that she could be herself. That you can come as you are.

CHAPTER 63

The Decision

"What if it was you in the womb? Would you want to be aborted?"

—JL

"Hey, how's the gut workout Amber!"

"Yeah, have you been working on core lately?"

"Ahahahahaha, I bet she's secretly a prostitute and forgot to wear her condom."

The guys laughed as Amber passed by. The pregnancy known to everyone now. Amber steamed past them, trying to avoid their gaze, but she couldn't help but see their faces in her peripherals. All their mockery and comments about her struck like arrows to a target. Amber tried to have thick skin about it, to not let the insults get to her, but the words still hurt. More people were looking in her general direction as she made her way towards her locker. She could feel everyone looking at her, gossiping behind her back as she found her locker. Amber put her hand against the metal frame, trying to hold herself together. Her body tense like a wire, fighting the tears that so eagerly wanted to come out. Amber balled her hand into a fist and slammed it against her locker.

How did it come to this . . . how did I suddenly find myself as the school loser. A short while ago Amber was at the top of the world, now she was pregnant and an outcast. Amber's anger flared up and she started kicking any locker she found. She didn't care whose it was, she just needed to hit something right now. She looked to her left, found an open locker, and kicked it as hard as she can. The locker slammed shut, only to find Krystal standing there with her hand frozen midair.

"Uhh . . ." she pointed cautiously, "That was my locker." Amber shot her an angry look and walked away, kicking any other lockers she found. She didn't care . . . (okay, that's a lie, she did care, she just didn't want to admit it right now). As she walked off into the nearest hallway and vanished.

⌒

The lunch bell rang and everyone in class sprinted to the door. Amber tried to be one of the first ones out, but she got caught in a bottleneck with everyone else. She scrambled through the door and into the long hallway, but instead of going towards the main courtyard, Amber went the opposite direction, toward the outskirts of school. Amber had picked out a secluded corner for herself so no one would see her and her . . . "problem."

Amber threw her backpack down against the concrete corner and sat down in contempt. She looked down at her lap, the growing bulge in her stomach becoming more and more noticeable. Amber lowered her head, letting her amber colored hair cover her face, hiding herself in her own little world. The pain seeping through the cracks of her bravado, the tears fighting to come forth. Amber cringed and trembled. *How did it come to this . . . my entire world changed in the span of an instant.* She wanted her old life back. She wanted this nightmare to be over.

She heard footsteps, and tried to hide her weakness, so she looked up in anger at whoever was coming by. Her anger quickly defused into confusion when she saw it was only Krystal, wondering what she was doing here.

At first, Amber thought Krystal was merely passing by, but Krystal had stopped and looked at her quizzically. Amber met her gaze, "What do you want?" Krystal's curiosity changed into compassion, almost pity. Amber broke their eye contact, "Don't look at me like that."

"Sorry," Krystal whispered.

"Why are you here?" Amber said, avoiding Krystal's gaze.

"I wanted to see you."

Amber looked at Krystal now. "And do I meet your expectations?" Krystal didn't answer. Amber sighed, "Look if you want to say something just say it. I'm running pretty short on patience these days."

Krystal put her hand gently on the concrete wall, "Do you have a table to sit with?"

Amber paused, looking aside. "No, I don't have a table to sit at. Given my,"—Amber looked down at her belly—"condition."

"Do you want to sit with my table?"

Amber glanced at Krystal with suspicion but gradually heeded her offer. "Fine."

"Okay then. Let's go."

"Right now?"

"Yeah."

Maybe I should have thought about this more. Krystal looked back and forth from Amber to Joanna. Clear animosity between the two figures. Krystal had completely forgotten that both of them were part of Summer's group, and Amber had been the one who had kicked Joanna out of Summer's group in the first place.

Jaime saw it too, and Krystal could tell he felt just as uncomfortable as she was. "So . . ." he said, "how about this weather?"

Surprisingly, Amber broke her hardened stare at Joanna and softened her expression. "The weather's fine."

Joanna was sitting there, looking terrified of Amber. No doubt Joanna was thinking of the fight with Amber and Krystal. The fear of that attack had scared her, as she had always been afraid of Amber back in Summer's group. Jaime and Krystal's eyes met, Jaime saw the signal and went to comfort Joanna, saying, "Hey, hey, it's alright," while Krystal comforted Amber.

"Are you going to be . . . okay?" Krystal asked.

Surprisingly, Amber was more mellow in her response, "I'll be alright." With that, the tension in the air cooled. Both Jaime and Krystal relaxed, at least things wouldn't get heated today.

"So . . ." Jaime asked hesitantly, "Do you like puppies Amber?"

Amber looked at him and said, "I do like puppies."

"What kind?"

Luckily the discussion never turned sour. Amber avoided eye contact, but at least she wasn't picking a fight. Amber seemed to have lost most of her fire and was quite mellow. The lunch break went on, Amber commenting a time or two in the conversation, but for the most part it was relatively calm between everyone in the group, even with Joanna.

Lunch ended and everyone parted ways. Somehow Amber followed Krystal until they were out of sight of the others and said, "Thank you . . . for inviting me to sit with you."

Krystal was surprised with the gratitude. She turned and said, "No problem."

∽

"And don't come back!" The door slammed and Amber stood there shaking in the rain. Perfect timing for her to be kicked out of her family's house. Amber's parents had not taken the news well. It wasn't all that much of a surprise. Amber's parents had both been young when they got pregnant with Amber, but the fear that their children would repeat their mistakes was there, and now it was a reality. Amber expected her parents to understand. To show her some form of kindness, but there was none. Amber's parents had sternly warned their children not to have sex before marriage, especially because of the hardships it had caused them when they were young and dumb. It had caused a lot of pain for Amber's parents, but they had stayed together and raised a family. Amber would never forget the look of complete sadness on her dad's face. How his one and only daughter got herself knocked up, like he did to Amber's mom, and in her dad's rage, he kicked her out of the house, metaphorically speaking.

∽

Krystal could not fall asleep tonight so taking a drive out in the rain seemed like a promising idea. She didn't mind it. The rain wouldn't bother her. In fact, she was happy to see it. The rain always brought a change of scenery around here, and Krystal welcomed it every time. Krystal inhaled through her nose and relished the wonderful feeling of fresh breath in her lungs. The patter of the rain filled the silence as she drove into town. Krystal had no destination in mind. She just needed to get out.

She drove into an urban area and slowed the car to a stop, getting a taste of the late-night activity in the city. She rested her free hand against her cheek and leaned against the car door, glancing in boredom at people walking by.

Her concentration focused when she saw a girl with amber-colored hair walking in the rain with no umbrella. Krystal took her hand off her face and tried to get a better look. Right next to her, walking like a zombie, was Amber Cutthrose. If Krystal had ever seen the cliché look of hitting rock bottom, she was looking at it right now. Amber was drenched, her eyes dead and her movements sloppy, walking ahead with no destination in mind. The sight broke Krystal's heart. Krystal remembered the fight but only for a moment. It didn't cause her any hatred. She had moved on from that long ago.

The light turned green, and Krystal knew she had a decision to make. So she pulled to the sidewalk and lowered the passenger window. "Hey! Hey Amber!" she called out, but Amber paid her no attention and kept walking. Krystal parked the car in an open spot and got out. She stepped in front of Amber, getting drenched in the process. "Amber," but Amber didn't notice. Krystal bent down, trying to get within Amber's line of sight, "Amber." Amber slowly raised her head, staring back at Krystal with dead eyes. Krystal took this as her opportunity, "Are you okay?" but she didn't appear to understand the question.

Krystal looked down at Amber's stomach. It was bulging and ready to pop. Krystal looked up, and could understand a little more of what Amber was going through. The girl looked completely broken. What was once a bright flare of life was now a hallowed shell. "What are you doing out here?" she asked, but Amber didn't answer. She only lowered her eyes, allowing the rain to soak through her hair and clothes.

"Do you need a place to stay?" Krystal asked. This time, Amber looked up in response to the question. Krystal nudged her head, "Come on, let's get you out of the rain." Krystal took Amber by the hand and helped her into the car. Amber made no attempt to fight back as Krystal could tell by the look on her face that she just didn't care anymore.

> "You never know what your child might grow up to be. Or who they might save."
> —Ashley Henninger

Krystal laid a warm cup of tea on the dining table. The orange liquid offering a comforting warmth from the freezing world outside. Amber sat there in Krystal's nightgown with a towel wrapped around her head. Krystal pushed the saucer closer to Amber, who stared at it with little interest.

Eventually, Amber took the cup of tea in her hands, enjoying the warmth it brought her. The silence of the room and constant rain provided a relaxing atmosphere. It was late at night and only the two of them, so there was no rush to do anything. Krystal sat in her chair and waited patiently.

"Thank you," Amber whispered.

Krystal took that as the opening of the conversation. "So why were you out there?"

Amber held the teacup close, "I got kicked out of my house."

Krystal lowered her head, "I'm sorry."

"Whatever." For a moment they both said nothing. Letting the storm rage outside as they sat in silence.

Then Amber spoke, "It's hard . . ." shaking her head, "It's really hard." Krystal said nothing. "I'm stuck between a rock and a hard place." Amber looked down and stroked her stomach. "What do I do?" Amber stared forward, stuck in her own little world.

Amber looked down at her teacup, "The hard part about all this is that . . . I can't really blame anyone. It would be lame to say this was someone else's fault. Because it's not like I was raped or anything. Everything that happened was consensual, although maybe I can blame the guy a little bit, for at least half the problem but . . . I still allowed him." Amber paused. She tightened her grip around the teacup. "I hate this . . . all of it." Krystal noticed Amber was starting to shiver again. "This whole thing sucks! And I can't blame anyone about it!" Amber put her tea down and put her hand to her head, "I ruined my own life."

For a whole minute, neither of them moved. Krystal gave Amber all the time she needed. Amber breathed harder, "And I don't know whether I should keep it," she gasped. "My instinct tells me to end it, but if I keep it then I'll have ruined my life." Amber whimpered, "I just don't know . . . I just don't know." She gestured to Krystal, "Then you come along, and you invite me into your home, and I don't know how to thank you and all." She shook her head. Her eyes were red with warm tears. "I deserve all of this. I deserve all of this, but I never knew how bad it would be!" She broke down and put her hands to her face. "And now, I don't have anywhere else to go! I don't have a home."

Krystal got up and comforted Amber, shushing her and rubbing her back. "It's okay," she whispered, "It's okay."

Amber sobbed for a few more minutes before she managed to calm down and wipe her face. "You know . . . I still don't understand why you are so kind to me." Amber looked up, allowing Krystal to see her face. This time, Amber was looking for an answer.

Krystal saw her look and spoke gently, "Because God gave me grace when I didn't deserve it." Krystal could see Amber processing her response. She could tell Amber was actually listening to her advice.

"Do you think God could have grace on me?"

Krystal nodded, "Yeah."

Amber looked down and put her hand to her head, "Thank you for being so gracious to me."

Krystal whispered, "You're welcome," keeping it humble. She stood up and said, "I'm going to get you some blankets and a pillow. Then you can sleep on the couch tonight. Does that sound fine?"

"That's fine," Amber replied.

Good, Krystal thought. *Some sleep will do her some good.*

> "Every child is precious, even those not born yet."
> —JL

"So tell me. Why are we doing this?" asked Amber.

Jaime hefted a box, "Redecorating."

"I know but, still. I really don't see the big deal. Why did Krystal order so many nickknacks and homey stuff?"

Jaime put a box down and pointed his thumb behind him to Krystal's apartment, "If you've seen the inside of Krystal's apartment, you would know it needs a little . . . life to it." Amber glared at him. Jaime attempted a smile, "A change of scenery."

Amber was not sharing the enthusiasm. "Sometimes I can't stand your humor."

"But I really like it," Krystal chimed in. She gave Jaime a bump with her elbow. Amber lowered her brow. Krystal said, "You didn't have to come Jaime. I can do this myself."

"Please," Jaime said, hoisting up a large box, "It's the least I could do."

Amber said sarcastically, "Yeah, for waking up early on a Saturday morning to come and help move boxes."

Jaime walked by Krystal and said, "I think Amber's a little cranky."

Krystal smiled and matched Jaime's sarcasm, "I think she is." Amber rolled her eyes. She was only here because she stayed the night at Krystal's apartment. Apparently, Jaime had come in the morning and was helping Krystal redecorate. Amber helped out when she could, but it was still hard to lift anything when she was pregnant. She didn't want to be a burden on the people taking care of her, so she had to pay her rent somehow.

Krystal straightened up and asked, "Hey Amber, could you check inside the apartment for a small box? I think I left it in the kitchen."

Amber shrugged her shoulders, "Sure." Amber went inside and closed the door behind her. The morning sun vanished as she entered the cool apartment.

You know you have to decide soon. Amber tensed. The thought haunted her day and night. She knew the deadline was coming up.

Amber smelled breakfast being prepared and followed the scent into the kitchen. There stood a slender woman with brown-velvet hair and brown eyes, making pancakes. She appeared to be in her late thirties and was incredibly good-looking. The woman hummed as she flipped the pancakes and added chocolate chips to them.

She turned and noticed Amber, "Oh hello. You must be Amber."

This must be Krystal's mom, Amber thought, when she saw Ms. Henninger check Amber's stomach and pause. "Something wrong?" Amber said defensively.

Ms. Henninger said, "I'm sorry. I didn't mean to look at you that way." Amber's temper cooled.

"I've been getting that look a lot these days. The only people who haven't given me that look have been . . ." Amber trailed off and pondered. *Who hasn't looked at me that way?* Amber went through a list of people in her head and then thought, *Only . . . Krystal, I guess. Wait what? Krystal? Really? No one else? That's not possible.* But Amber double-checked but found the same answer.

Ms. Henninger said, "I actually wanted to talk to you."

"About what?" Amber asked.

"Getting pregnant too young." Amber felt the mood drop. The conversation was going to get serious and emotionally exhausting, so Amber braced herself. *Here we go . . .*

Ms. Henninger said, "I know what it's like to get pregnant at a young age." Ms. Henninger gestured toward the door and said, "All it took for me was one night."

Amber was taken aback. Her perspective of this woman suddenly changed, not as someone who shared that look of accusation and pity, but as someone relatable. Someone Amber could talk to about this problem.

"What happened?" Amber asked, knowing she would regret it.

Ms. Henninger took a deep breath and let out a long sigh. "Long story short, I'm a workaholic, I took a night off and let loose, I met a guy, went home with him, and nine months later, I have Krystal sitting on my lap with no child support when I was still in the middle of nursing school."

"Didn't sound like you were that young if you were in nursing school."

"True, but I was still unprepared, and it left me in a pretty undesirable situation right after college with a lot of student debt."

"Why didn't you abort?" Amber asked, curious to see Ms. Henninger's reaction.

Ms. Henninger looked at the floor, "I did have thoughts of getting an abortion. I debated them a lot. They were always running wild in my mind, even when I was on my way to the abortion clinic."

"What stopped you?"

"On my way to the clinic, I tripped over some concrete, and as I fell, I could have fallen flat on my stomach and killed this baby by accident. My body just reacted, and I extended my hands and caught myself." Ms. Henninger put her hand to her forehead, shame creeping in from old memories. "I sat down and took one look at myself and witnessed the atrocity I nearly committed. I could have killed this child, and the horror about it was . . . I wanted to. I wanted a way out. An easy escape from my actions. A way out from my own mistake. But then I realized, there was no way out. The moment I got pregnant I knew there was no escaping this. I could get an abortion sure, that would solve my financial trouble, but it wouldn't stop the guilt I felt because of it. I knew it would haunt me forever, knowing I had an abortion. And so, in order to curb my own shame, I kept the baby. A baby born out of guilt and shame, nothing more." Ms. Henninger looked at Amber with sadness and compassion. "There was no love in this birth. There was no agreement or joy. Only pain. A child born without loving parents is doomed to suffer a long and hard life, no matter how many riches that child may have."

Amber stood there, unsure of how to respond. Ms. Henninger resumed, "So I kept the child, and hoped I wouldn't regret my decision. I hoped I wasn't damning this child to a life of suffering because of my previous mistakes, because of one stupid night!" Ms. Henninger caught her breath, "But . . . I learned very recently that I made the right choice."

Amber tilted her head, puzzled, "What do you mean?"

Ms. Henninger gestured toward the open door, "I watched Krystal grow up, and for her entire life she was not happy. That girl, out there, my precious girl, was depressed, lonely, and an outsider, who did nothing but suffer. You see, Krystal doesn't function like most girls do. She didn't understand how to socialize back then, especially with all the social media happening today. So school was hard because she couldn't fit in. And for the longest time I feared that she was going to kill herself. I had seen the symptoms early on." Ms. Henninger gestured to herself, "I'm a nurse, and I've seen so many instances of children trying to kill themselves, asking what their symptoms were, both from themselves and their parents, and to my horror I saw all the same symptoms in my own daughter." Ms. Henninger nudged her head toward the door again, "If Krystal tried to kill herself, I knew I wouldn't be able to live with myself either. I probably would have killed myself out of shame too." Ms. Henninger shook her head with disappointment in herself.

"But when I awoke from my coma, I saw a completely different person in my daughter. I looked into Krystal's face, and I saw *hope*. I saw happiness. Something I never thought my daughter would have. And I still wonder . . . what happened to my daughter while I was asleep? I thought she would despair, but the exact opposite happened. She found hope instead. A reason for living. It's almost as if the darkness was just an empty shadow, and whatever it was that haunted Krystal is gone." Ms. Henninger made an explosive gesture with her hands. "Poof . . . Now when I look back, I'm glad that I kept that baby. I'm glad I didn't abort because she was the one who saved me." Ms. Henninger put her hand to her heart, "For all those years I was crippled by my guilt, but Krystal was the one who told me about God. And because of that, I was forgiven, and my guilt is gone." Ms. Henninger gently took Amber's hand, "Life is precious my dear. The road may be hard, but you have no idea what amazing things that child will do. For all that we know"—Ms. Henninger gestured to Amber's stomach—"that child might discover the cure for cancer one day or save somebody's life." Ms. Henninger let go of Amber's hand. "But know this . . . with whatever decision you make, we will always welcome you with open arms, because you don't deserve to suffer all this pain on your own."

Amber had no idea how to process this. The love this woman was giving her when she didn't deserve it was astounding. Amber deserved punishment for what she'd done, especially since she attacked Krystal, but instead, she was shown grace. The thought of Amber's child becoming something better, something greater, working to change something in someone's life, resonated with her. The fear and insecurity of what would happen still frightened her, but it was helpful to have some reassurance. To know that it's not the end of the world.

Amber looked at Ms. Henninger and thought, *This woman didn't have any support when she got pregnant. Plus, it was an extremely difficult journey for her too. But now things are different, things are starting to change both for her and for Krystal.*

Amber took a moment to look at Krystal. She didn't know Krystal was an unplanned pregnancy or that she struggled with suicidal thoughts. It made Amber look at Krystal in a whole new light. But it also reminded Amber of her own dilemma. *Can I really do it? Can I abort this child?*

Her thoughts retorted, *What if it was you in the womb? Would you want to be aborted?*

Amber paused. *No.*

She saw Jaime and Krystal laughing outside, could see the cheer on Krystal's face. Hope shining from her demeanor, like she was glowing somehow. That amazed Amber for a moment. *That girl has gone through so much. Been through so much change, I can't even imagine it. I still remember a time when I didn't notice her . . . now I'm sitting at her lunch table, talking with her daily. It's funny.*

Amber thought what her life would look like if she had never met Krystal. If Krystal's mom really did have an abortion. What would it look like? Amber thought back to the department store incident. How Krystal would have never shown her kindness. Or when Krystal invited Amber to sit with her group at lunch the other day. That wouldn't have happened either. Or even last night, when Amber had lost everything, who was there for her? Krystal . . .

Amber thought, *Could I abort Krystal if it was her in the womb?*

No. The answer was clear.

Amber placed her hand on her stomach and stroked it. *Maybe this child in me does have a future. No matter how hard it may be, a child can still grow and become something beautiful, regardless of their birthing circumstances.* Amber felt sad for a moment, her guard down completely. *You in there, you might be the only one who understands me. Like Ms. Henninger and her daughter. Maybe that will happen with you and me? What do you think?* The baby kicked. Amber jerked in surprise. *Wow. You really are a part of me.*

⟳

I know I was kicked out the night before but . . . Amber lowered her head and humbled her heart. She knew she had no right to be back here, especially after such a hectic night but still . . . she wanted to see her family again. The door opened and Amber's brother Lue stood there. He seemed surprised then shouted, "Dad she's back!"

Fear shot through Amber's body like lightning. Memories of the prior night came flooding back. It took everything Amber had to keep herself from running off. She stayed put, watching her brother Mack come to the door, followed by her mom, and then finally, her dad came. Amber expected anger, expected fury, but her dad was none of those things. He stood at the door, took one look at Amber, and threw his arms around her.

"I'm so sorry Amber," he whispered. "I should have never yelled at you last night." Amber's dad hugged her tighter. Amber embraced the hug. They came apart, but Amber's dad still kept his hands on her shoulders, "Amber I'm so sorry. The other night . . . caught me off guard. It shocked me because this same thing happened to your mom and I." Mr. Cutthrose looked at his two sons, his wife, then back at his daughter. He put another hand on her shoulder, squaring up to her, "You are welcome back home. I should have never kicked you out." Mr. Cutthrose shook his head in shame, not for Amber but for himself. He hugged her again and whispered, "Welcome home," the rest of the family taking the hint and slowly surrounding Amber with hugs.

Amber couldn't take it. It was all too much to bear. Why did she receive such kindness? Right there she had made her decision. They broke apart, Amber looked at her dad and said, "I'm going to keep it." Relief showered over her with clarity, as she looked down at her stomach, "And I think I know just what to name it."

CHAPTER 64

Compromise

"You can't be friends with everybody. But you can at least try to live with them."

—Amber Cutthrose

"Come on."

"No."

"Come on."

"I said I don't want to."

"You're coming," Amber said, as she yanked Krystal's arm forward. Krystal tugged back but allowed Amber to pull her along. "You're coming to my cousin's party whether you like it or not."

"Ugghhh" Krystal said reluctantly, letting Amber pull her once more. It was more comical than a debate. Amber found some satisfaction in that.

"You won't regret this," Amber said, pulling Krystal to the front door.

Krystal spoke, "I get the feeling I will." Amber rolled her eyes and knocked on the door. A girl with dirty blonde hair, opened the door and gleamed at Amber. She threw her arms around Amber and said, "Amber! It's good to see you!"

Amber returned the favor, "It's good to see you Ida" (pronunciation: "ee-da"). "I haven't seen you since Christmas last year."

Ida said, "You mean before you got yourself knocked up?"

Amber wasn't expecting that one, but Ida laughed and said, "I'm just messing with you. You know I love you either way. No matter how . . ." she glanced at Amber's stomach, "*round* you are."

Amber grinned, "Ohh you are gonna get it."

Ida braced herself like a football player, "Oh I welcome it." The two of them grinned at each other, ready to pounce. Krystal stood there expressionless. Watching them ready to attack. Ida turned her attention toward Krystal and said, "And who is this here? Your friend?"

Amber nodded and introduced Krystal, "This is Krystal Henninger, she goes to the same school as I do."

Ida creased a smile and turned her head microscopically. "Say . . . were you the person who got in that fight with Amber a while back?"

Amber hung her head, embarrassed and ashamed. *That's right. We did fight*, Amber thought. Krystal didn't seem bothered and said, "Fighting is a loose term, but yeah. That was me."

Amber was surprised to see how casual Krystal was about everything. At least, it felt good to let the past be past. "Water under the bridge," Amber said, "As they say," inclining her chin.

Ida nodded. "Water under the bridge," she confirmed like it was a religious greeting, then held the door open.

They both stepped in and were greeted with a loud, "YAAASSSS! The party has started!" Both Amber and Krystal stared as Summer was standing on top of a couch playing air guitar with a crowd of people celebrating around her like a rock star. Both Amber and Krystal looked at each other then back at Summer.

Oh . . . my . . . gosh. You have got to be kidding me, thought Amber. Amber felt a stirring within her but that was expected. She looked over at Krystal and was surprised to find her stirred as well, if not more. That worried Amber. She watched Krystal observe Summer, the anger visible on her face. *She's just as pissed as I am. If not more. But why?* Amber remembered when Summer told the story of how Krystal yelled at her, but after everything that's happened Amber wasn't sure how Krystal would react when she saw Summer again.

Ida stepped forward and Amber made a sharp gesture toward Summer, "Why is *she* here?"

Ida jerked a thumb in Summer's direction, "She's friends with practically everyone I know. So they invited her without telling me. It's not like it's a terrible thing." Amber and Krystal's eyes met. They exchanged the same thought. *Yeah right.*

Summer broke off her applause when she noticed Amber and Krystal standing at the entrance. She hopped off her podium and beamed at them with a wicked smile. *Oh boy*, Amber thought. *This won't end well.* Part of Amber welcomed seeing Summer again. She missed her and Amber wanted to make amends like she had with Krystal.

Summer charged at them like an over eccentric fairy tale princess. Summer threw her arms around Amber, catching her by surprise. "It's so good to see you, Amber!" Then Summer leaned back and wobbled a bit. "I was dooingg greeatt without you."

Amber lowered an eyebrow, *That clears up why she's so eccentric.* But from the looks of her, Summer appeared to be more sober than the rest of the crowd. Amber remembered the number of times when she and Summer would try to out drink each other at parties, and Summer would always beat her. Somehow Summer was a heavy weight even when she was as skinny as a sardine. But Amber couldn't drink tonight, or for another few months.

Amber simmered off; reluctant to watch Summer go crazy, but Amber saw Summer glaring at Krystal and Krystal was fuming. That unnerved Amber. She had never seen Krystal get mad before, and if Krystal was able to hold her own when Amber was smacking her face, then Amber could only imagine the amount of rage it took to get Krystal mad just by looking at Summer.

For a moment, Krystal deflated and exhaled. Amber relaxed too. Krystal opened her mouth and said, "I—"

Summer cut her off, "It's been a while huh missus muf-fah. Huh. I remember you pointing at me and calling me out for all my . . . what was it, *bull-something."*

Krystal looked like a stone-cold killer. Amber didn't like where this conversation was going. This interaction only made her more nervous. At least Krystal was *trying* to calm herself down in front of Summer. Krystal opened her mouth again and said, "I'm—"

"A piece of—" Summer cut in, "Oh I know that. You've told me that before too." Summer tapped her finger to her chin, "What was it? You told me to stop all my *ridiculous, stories, right?"* Summer jabbed a finger in Krystal's face. Normally Krystal wouldn't care whose finger was in her face, but Amber could tell Krystal was on the verge of starting a fight. Krystal wasn't the only one either, Amber wanted to beat Summer down for the way she was acting.

Amber said coldly, "You're drunk."

"Am I trunk?" Summer retorted. The response driving Amber to the brim of madness. Amber wanted to yell at Summer, but in the corner of her eye, she saw that Krystal was vibrating with rage.

Amber was more scared now of Krystal, so she lowered her voice and said "Yes," sternly. "You're *drunk*."

"Well then I'm having a goooood tiiiiimmme." Summer twirled around like a ballerina. She drew her attention back to Krystal. Waiting to stick the knife in deeper.

Summer lifted a palm to Krystal in mockery, "You were sssaying."

Krystal stopped vibrating and spoke, keeping her voice slow and controlled. "I wanted to say that I'm—"

Summer cut in. "A loner piece of—"

"SUMMER!" Amber shouted.

Summer glared toward Amber, anger flaring in her eyes. It was like Summer had sobered up completely, or maybe she played being drunk just to annoy them. "Don't look at me like that Amber, we both knew this was coming." Summer turned toward Krystal, acting like a fancy mistress, holding her red cup like it was a glass of wine and gestured to Krystal, "Continue."

Krystal ebbed the words slowly and said, "I wanted, to say, I'm—"

Summer cut her off again, "Nothing more than a—"

"SORRY!" The whole room fell silent. Krystal shouted as loud as she could. A level of speech even Amber didn't know. "I'm sorry, *okay*! So could you please stop cutting me off so I could finish what I wanted to say!" Krystal stormed off, slamming the door behind her.

Amber looked at Summer, "You're a real piece of work Summer, you know that." And walked out after Krystal.

The cold did not help, but Krystal walked out anyway. It was better out in the cold than burning with fury in front of Summer. Amber found Krystal sitting on a rock a little way from Ida's house. Amber treaded carefully and cautioned her approach toward Krystal. Krystal saw Amber and said, "The sheer gall of that girl always amazes me!" Amber was surprised. She had never seen Krystal so angry before. And thank goodness Amber didn't see it when she was fighting her. Amber lowered herself next to Krystal and listened while Krystal ranted.

Krystal said, "I cannot stand that girl and her constant talking. Was there ever a moment in her life when she wasn't talking? And the thing that frustrates me the most about Summer is how popular she is. How on earth is she so popular?" Amber opened her mouth but closed it. Krystal quickly glanced at her, "Don't answer that, I already know." Krystal rubbed her head so hard Amber thought she was going to lose some hair. "I don't understand why I automatically clash with Summer." Krystal shook her head in disappointment. "I can make friends with other people but not her. There's something about her that just conflicts with me. What is it?" Amber waited for a minute, a long minute, and then Krystal looked at her and spoke more calmly, "You can answer now if you want. I honestly want to hear what you have to say."

Amber was surprised how for once she was the one comforting Krystal. Krystal knew the right answer, but she needed someone to confirm it with her. Because if no one did, then Krystal would doubt herself and spin into a whirlwind of confusion. Amber bent down to Krystal's level and said, "I think you're learning that you can't be friends with everyone." Amber waved toward the night sky, "Not everyone connects the same with others." Krystal looked Amber in her amber-colored eyes. Amber broke away, stood up and said, "You two are like oil and water; polar opposites."

Amber held her hands out like a Greek weighing scale, "On one hand we have Krystal Henninger: you're quiet, resolute, but great at asking questions and one-on-one conversation. On the other hand, we have Summer McAdams, who is active, loud, charismatic, and great with crowds. One of you is an introvert, the other an extrovert, and we all know that society today values extroverts more than introverts." Krystal nodded. "So don't get mad when you find you don't connect well with Summer. You can't be friends with everybody. But you can at least try to live with them. Also . . . she's kind of being a jerk right now and that's her choice, but . . . I do want you to make amends with her. I want you two to be on good ground with each other, okay?"

Krystal breathed sharply through her nose, "Okay." That seemed to diminish the anger dwelling inside her.

Amber helped her up, "But do it in the morning. I know Summer will be a little calmer by then."

"What do you mean?" Krystal asked dubiously.

Amber grinned, "You'll see."

Her hand hovered reluctantly above the door then dropped. Of all the things Krystal wanted to be doing, this was the last on her list. But she had to forgive her enemies, even if they treated her like trash. "Amber's right," Krystal said. "I can't be friends with everyone, but at least I can try to live with them." Krystal balled her hand into a fist and knocked on the door a couple times. A full minute went by, and nothing happened. Krystal knocked again and still nothing. Krystal looked back at Amber in the car, as she waved in the passenger window to keep going. Krystal got the idea. *She's in there alright. Whether it's quiet or not.* Krystal knocked on the door again. No answer, she kept knocking and knocking, until the door slowly opened and there stood a hung-over Summer with her hair messed up and no makeup on. Her blue eyes squinted from the sun as Krystal could see dark lines under her eyelids.

Summer managed a dry and difficult moan, "Hello." Krystal felt a little better, not because Summer looked awful, but because Summer was so out of it that Krystal would have a chance to talk without Summer cutting her off.

"Hey," Krystal said softly, "I just wanted to say I'm sorry. I know I shouldn't have yelled at you last night, or for exploding on you a while ago." Krystal could feel the anger build up inside her, this was her chance, the time to rail on Summer when she couldn't fight back, but Krystal prayed to God, *Father, please give me the strength and self-control to not rail on her. Please forgive her as you forgave me.*

Summer stepped out from behind her door and faced Krystal. Hungover as she was, she still had the manner to stand on her feet and face Krystal. Summer looked at her with sleep deprived eyes and said, "Whatever." The grim was noticeable in her tone.

Krystal felt her emotions well up and felt a bit of anger dwell on her tongue, but she held it in and made sure her speech was apologetic and genuine. Krystal waited a moment, clearly getting the stink eye from Summer, and asked in honest curiosity, "Do you hate me?"

Summer seemed to sober up and said, "Yes," Without hesitation.

Krystal kept her tone level, "Why? What's your problem with me?"

"You wanna know what my problem is?" Summer squared up to Krystal, as if she were never hungover in the first place, getting all up in her face, but Krystal remained steadfast, not moving an inch. "I'll tell you what my problem is." Summer stuck her finger and jabbed it in Krystal's chest. *"You."*

"Why?"

Summer stepped back and shook her head, "I don't know why, but when I'm around you, I don't know how to react. You're always so quiet and that makes me feel uncomfortable."

Krystal asked the obvious question, "Why does that make you feel uncomfortable?"

"Like, I don't deal well with silence. Whenever I'm around people I need to fill the void with conversation. So when someone doesn't say anything for ten seconds, I get anxious and fill the void. That's why I talk all the time. Because silence bothers me."

Krystal found that curious. She had never thought about how other people felt about silence. Krystal had always felt comfortable when things were quiet. It helped her think more clearly. But with Summer it was the exact opposite, which explained why they clashed so much.

Summer continued, "So I ignored you, because I don't know how to interact with you."

Krystal lowered her head, "That's okay. You don't have to blame yourself."

Summer tilted her head. "Why is that?"

Krystal remained humble and meek, "It's partially my fault too. I didn't try my best to socialize with people as much as I should have."

Summer got back on track. "Yeah, well, we're both vastly different people. You're quiet, I'm loud, that's how it works. The two of us, we're on opposite ends of the spectrum, that's why I have a tough time being around you."

Krystal looked at Summer, slightly irritated but ready to move on and forgive. Krystal said, "Hey. I don't want there to be any hard feelings between us. I only want the two of us to get along. So how about we let bygones be bygones and go about our normal lives? We agree to live with each other, but we don't have to hate each other."

Summer took a slow, long breath and said reluctantly, "Okayyy."

Is it really that hard for her to get along with me? Krystal thought. Krystal raised her hand, "Shake on it?"

Summer rolled her eyes, "Sure. Fine. Whatever," and gave it a quick shake.

Krystal felt relieved, knowing she had made the final patch to the relationship. Now she could move on with her life with no hard feelings. It was finally over.

PART ELEVEN

Conclusion

CHAPTER 65

Church Camp

"Sometimes pain can be a blessing in disguise."

—JL

"You ready?"

"I guess so." Jaime looked out at the buses lined up in front of the church, ready to take the students to their annual summer camp. Jaime extended his arms and stretched his back, enjoying the warmth of the sun on his skin. He exhaled, *The annual church summer camp. This brings back memories.* Jaime opened his eyes and saw Krystal getting things ready by the bus.

Krystal put her bags down and looked at him, "Have you done this before?"

"Oh yeah, many times."

"Did you do it last year?"

"No, I didn't. I wasn't in the right mindset."

Krystal nodded, "So why are you doing it this year?" Jaime clamped shut. The only reason he agreed to come was because he was super bored on the weekend, and . . . because Krystal was going to be here. But he wasn't about to let that detail slip. Krystal looked at him, raising an eyebrow, "Did you come here just because I was going?" asking as if she already knew the answer.

Jaime was dumbfounded for a second, but he answered with as much dignity as he could, "Yes." To his surprise, Krystal smiled. It wasn't a strong smile, but soft and sweet. It made Jaime's heart skip a beat since he still wasn't used to Krystal smiling yet. It was a new sight and one growing more common by the day. Jaime knew it was time to switch topics, "And why is she here?" Pointing toward Kristina, who was helping load some bags onto the bus.

Krystal shrugged her shoulders, "I asked her if she wanted to come and help out, so she came."

Jaime asked curiously, "And why did my sister ask you to help out with this?"

Krystal lowered her head, "They needed leaders, specifically high school leaders, so I said yes. Plus, I signed up because I wanted to." Jaime found that curious. It was a bold thing on Krystal's part to try and be a leader on a church camp. But Jaime couldn't help but feel proud of her for trying something new on her own.

Carmen rounded the bus, "Alright, everybody ready?" Then looked at Jaime in surprise. "Jaime?"

Jaime gave a light-hearted wave, "Hey sis."

Carmen forgot about the bus and approached him, "What are you doing here?"

"What does it look like. I'm here to help."

Carmen was at a loss for words. "Oh . . ." Jaime's lips widened into a kind smile.

That answer was enough to satisfy Carmen. She smiled, "That's good enough for me" and walked toward the bus, looking more cheerful than before.

Krystal glanced at Jaime, "You warming up to your family again?"

"Yeah, I am actually," he said. His tone warm and cheery.

"I'm happy for you."

He glanced at her, "Thanks."

"You didn't have to come on this trip," she said. "I don't want you feeling uncomfortable."

"Nah, I want to be here." He looked at Krystal, "I'll help out wherever I can."

Krystal reciprocated Jaime's cheeriness, "Thanks. It always makes me more comfortable when you're around."

"Same," Jaime replied, looking at the bus filling up with students. "Same."

Krystal walked up to the growing crowd of middle schoolers surrounding the main bus. Over to the right she could see some commotion as Summer arrived and already began swooning some of the students to her liking. Krystal had to admit, Summer would be great with the kids, so she didn't mind Summer taking the glory for once. Krystal shifted her attention toward Carmen who stood on the stairwell to one of the buses and called, "Welcome one and all!" the crowd of middle schoolers quieted. "Thank you for coming on this fine trip! We are going to have loads of fun together and hopefully get to know Jesus a little more!" There were some cheers, some of the students clapping. Krystal enjoyed the sight but wasn't that enthusiastic about the event. She wanted to help Carmen out, but being in a leadership role was completely different than her normal lifestyle. Krystal never considered herself a leader in any way, and now for the next couple of days, she was going to be in charge of a group of middle schoolers. A role she felt wasn't suited for her. But she said yes to Carmen's request and couldn't turn her down; besides Krystal wanted to try and discover a new part to herself. *Maybe this trip will do me some good?* she thought hopefully, and part of her believed it. There was a remnant of her that was doubtful of the whole experience, and Krystal made sure to be wary of that feeling and try not to let it get her down. But deep down in her sinking gut, there was a sense that something was off about this trip. That somehow, something bad was going to happen.

Regardless, she put her feelings aside and went along with the group, loading onto the bus where it would take them to their remote location for the weekend. It was all new to Krystal. She might not be much better than these middle schoolers, but it was strange to remember that she was older than these kids. I mean, she was seventeen after all.

"Allllllllrrrrrriiiiiiiiiigggggggghhhhhhhtt!!!!" Carmen shouted, "Let's line up!" The kids all got off the bus and lined up on the basketball court. They were still in middle school, but they all seemed to remember listening to their proctors from elementary school. It made things easier on Carmen's part. Carmen called out, "Alright we are going to announce the leaders for the trip!" Carmen held out a hand. In line were Kristina, Summer, Krystal, and Carmen as leaders. Carmen turned to the other leaders, "Leaders why don't you introduce yourselves?"

Kristina was first, and you could already tell the crowd had warmed up to her. A majority of the kids already knew Kristina and were eager to be part of her group. Kristina addressed the crowd with a wholehearted greeting, not as high pitched with energy as Kristina's celebrity persona, but this time one that was more real yet still exciting. "Hello everyone! My name is Kristina! It's nice to meet you!" Already there were shouts and claps from the middle schoolers. A warm applause greeted Kristina as she finished her speech and stepped back.

Krystal looked aside and tried not to feel nervous, she wasn't expecting there to be introductions in front of the whole group. Krystal immediately felt self-conscious. She may have performed at the talent show but even then, it was still uncomfortable for her to stand in front of crowds.

Summer stepped forward and gave just as much a greeting as Kristina did, winning over a lot of cheers from the audience as well. Some of the boys were even staring a little too long. Krystal studied the mood of all the faces. Aside from a majority of smiles and giggles, some of the kids didn't look all that happy to be here. *I could guess that much. Who wants to spend their weekend learning about church when they could be playing or having fun?* Krystal thought. It wasn't too illogical. Part of Krystal wanted to simply have fun rather than lead a Bible study this weekend, but she stifled those thoughts and pushed past them. *No, I need to try new things. Maybe something will happen from this trip?* She knew it was a gamble, but it was like that whenever you tried something new. You never know when you are going to have fun or not.

Amidst the crowd Krystal noticed one girl who looked gloomy compared to the others. She had an innocent face and long black hair, but Krystal got the impression that something was wrong. Krystal made note of that girl and allowed Carmen to finish her speech.

Krystal's turn came and immediately all eyes beamed at her. Krystal felt her heart tighten and her hands sweat. *Crap. I've got nothing good to say.* Krystal raised a weak hand, embarrassed already, clearly not exuding as much excitement as Kristina and Summer. "Hey . . . I'm Krystal," she said awkwardly, "I uhh . . . I hope to have fun with you." She trailed off and the rest of the crowd stood there in silence. Krystal wanted to have a heart attack and die. *That was awful.* Krystal spotted Jaime out in the corner, as he gave a thumbs up. Krystal felt a mixture of relief and embarrassment with that.

Carmen stepped in, "Alright! Those are your leaders." She pointed to herself, "I will be one of your leaders as well, if you have anything to ask, then please come to me about it, kay great! Now let's assign groups to their leaders and then go to our assigned cabins." Carmen called out a handful of names as the kids lined up in front of each leader. Krystal saw the kids all standing before her, looking up to her like she was some kind of parent. Krystal wasn't used to being taller than people, despite being five foot six herself but still, she felt like she was some older character to these kids for some reason. The kids in her group looked at her with curiosity, while the kids in Carmen, Kristina, and Summer's groups all leaped with joy at the sight of their leaders. Krystal didn't know what to do, so she raised a weak hand and waved, "Uhh hi." Silence. *Oh boy*, Krystal thought. *This is going to be difficult.* "Uhh let's uhh check out the . . . cabin," Krystal led the way awkwardly, and the kids followed, as the four groups split up and went to their individual cabins.

∾

"Okay, so uhh . . . uhh . . ." Krystal held the sheet of paper out, relaying her instructions while her group sat around the cabin, looking at her with mild expectation, waiting for her to tell them what to do while showing no enthusiasm for it. "We are going to start off reading a portion of the book of Luke." Krystal raised her head, and the kids all went to Luke in their Bibles. Krystal said, "We uhh are going to uhh . . . uhhh." A kid raised her hand. "Yes?" Krystal said.

The girl lowered her hand, "Have you done this before?"

Krystal shook her head slightly, "No," she said, lacking the enthusiasm. Krystal watched as all the kids exchanged looks with each other and began whispering. It was late in the night so whispering was required in all the cabins. The darkness outside the cabin made the inside a good place for chit chat and gossip. The girls immediately started chatting with each other and Krystal had to get them back on track. "Okay, uhh let's . . . start . . . reading."

∾

Carmen frowned, "What do you mean they won't go?"

Jaime didn't like playing ambassador, but the news had to be relayed. "They won't go," he said plainly, shrugging his shoulders and shaking his head. "None of them want Krystal to be their leader. They've all requested to be transferred to another group. Either yours, Kristina's, or Summer's."

"What?" Carmen said in frustrated disbelief. She could not believe the tact of these kids. "It's only been one night and they're already asking to change groups?"

Jaime raised his hands in defense, "Hey I'm on your side. I find it ridiculous too. But they all called their parents, saying their leader was too gloomy, and the parents agree."

"What!" Carmen lowered her brow. This was ridiculous. She turned aside and crossed her arms; *These kids got some real nerve*, thought Carmen.

Jaime went on, "We've tried to get them to cooperate, but they all refuse to do the lesson with Krystal. They want to do it with someone else."

Carmen turned and faced her brother, angry beyond her imagination. "I'm going to have a talk with some of these parents." Raising her phone and stepping out.

⌒

Well, that was not what I expected, Krystal thought. In just one night, her group had all vouched to transfer, some of them even calling their parents to switch, and now Krystal had been reduced to a regular volunteer by the staff, not even able to lead one of the groups. Krystal raised her eyes to the morning blue sky, *You have a funny sense of humor God, you know that,* lowering her eyes to a fuming Carmen.

"Unbelievable," Carmen said. "They all just up and ditched you," Krystal said nothing, letting Carmen vent. Carmen paced around the cabin. "I can't believe they just left your group and went to join the others. I mean that blows me away. And I can't convince their parents to say otherwise, so now the staff demoted you to a regular volunteer, and there's nothing I can do about it."

Krystal answered logically, "Their friends were in other groups, and they all liked the other leaders more than me."

Carmen objected, "You were their leader for one night, and now you're not even a leader anymore and I can't do anything." Carmen grunted in frustration and craned her head back. "What a bunch of baloney."

"Maybe it's better this way," Krystal offered, a part of her glad to be out of the leadership role. To her surprise it didn't bother her that much.

"Well, you don't need to hang around if you don't want to, but if you want to help out in other areas, let me know," Carmen said.

Krystal asked, "What do you have in mind?"

⌒

This is not what I had in mind, thought Krystal as she gave a scoopful of mac and cheese to a nearby eighth grader. Being the school lunch lady wasn't what Krystal pictured for a relaxing weekend of service. Since they didn't have a need for another leader, Krystal was reduced to the school lunch lady, handing out the food, watching all the groups eat together.

Krystal handed another plate full of food to a lofty middle schooler and took in the sight of the dining hall. It was a lot more packed than she thought. The boys and girls had mixed with another camp, so two camps were eating together at large tables within the hall. In a sense, Krystal didn't mind being the lunch lady. Part of her was relieved because she didn't have to worry about leading a bunch of kids she didn't know; and besides, she was never good at getting to know them and leading a charismatic team to victory, which was more Summer's job, and serving the kids food wasn't that bad. It brought a sense of service to Krystal's heart she had never felt before. *You know what? I kinda like this.*

Krystal lifted her gaze and stared amongst the crowd, searching all the faces, watching the conversation and chit chat going about. Summer's table was crowded as always, they even stole some chairs from another table to make room for the extras. What was once a table for seven was now a table for thirteen, and even then, more people wanted to join. *Summer's got a gift, I'll give her that*, she thought. Krystal shifted her gaze back to the kids in front of her, all of them just grabbing their food and going to their tables. Krystal studied their moods. A majority of them seemed pretty happy, although she could tell that some of them did not want to be here. Regardless, they were here and did not complain . . . much.

Krystal reached down for another scoop when she saw a young girl with black hair, wearing a white shirt and black overalls. Krystal recognized it was the same gloomy girl from the basketball court. For some unknown reason, Krystal found her to be quite interesting. She could tell something was off about this girl. Krystal watched as the girl departed with her food and headed toward her group leader, which so happened to be Summer's group and tried to find a seat.

Krystal's gaze followed the girl, watching her every step as she sat on the outskirts of Summer's clustered table. Krystal stopped all motion and watched the girl with curiosity, finding a similarity with the young girl. Krystal noticed the girl's attention was focused on Summer. Trying to look past all the people in Summer's group, in fact most of the people weren't even part of Summer's group to begin with. Krystal even noticed her original group was sitting at Summer's table, chatting like nothing happened.

Krystal kept her eyes on the girl as she sat on the outside of the group and ate her turkey and mac and cheese. *Hmmm, that is interesting*, Krystal thought, returning to her duties as the main lunch lady.

Krystal watched from afar as the kids played dodgeball in the gym. The two teams were going at it and let me tell ya it was a bloodbath for both sides. The boys on each team were power hungry, some even hiding behind the girls to protect themselves while the balls were being thrown. It was Summer's team against Kristina's and neither of them wanted to lose. Kristina was at the head of the group, throwing balls like crazy, enjoying every moment of this game. Summer was at the head too, but her team was taking losses. Krystal didn't care much for who won, only that she had to clean up afterwards.

Krystal's eyes again found that same girl from the cafeteria, standing in the corner on Summer's team. Krystal observed further and could tell the girl looked miserable. She wasn't even trying to play.

Eventually the girl got out, mostly because she didn't try to dodge the ball coming at her. The match ended and the Weekend Olympics were over for the day. Summer ran out front in good spirits and said, "Let's take a team picture!" The rest of the group agreed, and the group handed Krystal the phone to take the picture. Krystal smirked, *Huh, taking a picture for Summer again, that's ironic*, as she snapped the photo and the group dispersed. Another event was over.

Krystal leaned against a potted tree watching the late-night dance party. Well . . . it wasn't so much a dance party; half the people weren't dancing and were busy going to the other tables to hang out and eat some food while the other half danced away to some rap music. Krystal watched the scene from afar with her arms crossed, not interested in joining. She was more content remaining where she was. Jaime came up behind her and said, "Wow, this looks like a roaring party." His sarcasm was briefly shared with Krystal as she grunted in agreement.

"It sure is," she said.

Jaime shrugged and took a breath, stretching his body as he asked, "So what have you guys been doing?"

Krystal glanced at Jaime, "Just cleaning a bunch of events, nothing serious."

Jaime leaned against the potted plant next to her, crossing his arms. "Yeah," he gestured toward the room, "they all kinda look like this. We have breakfast, have a sermon in the morning, have some quiet time, do some recreational activities, have dinner, another sermon and then more Bible study and then do it again the next day. That's typically what a church camp is like. I know because my family and I have gone on so many church retreats I've lost count." Krystal chuckled. She took her attention off Jaime and looked back at the crowd.

"This is my first," she said, not knowing whether she should feel happy or disappointed.

"Well, I hope you're enjoying yourself."

"Thanks." Krystal was focused on the crowd, somewhat enjoying watching the scene from afar. It had become a habit of hers over the years; she somehow found it entertaining to watch others interact. You never know what people will do. There was a group playing cards at one table, another playing Jenga, while others were dancing, hanging around the corners of the ballroom. Krystal's attention focused on the same girl from earlier. She didn't know why, this girl just stood out to her. The girl appeared to be roaming around in a black dress, unsure where to go or what to do. Krystal tilted her head and asked Jaime, "Do you see that girl over there?"

Jaime peered closer, as if that would help his eyes see the distance better, "What girl?"

"The girl with black hair in the black dress." Krystal pointed. Jaime looked closely and said, "I don't know who you're talking about. There's a lot of people at this camp and I don't see anybody who fits that description."

"She's right there," Krystal pointed harder, but Jaime gave no confirmation as to who she was talking about. Jaime gave one last look and shook his head, "I don't know who you're talking about." Krystal lowered her arm, disappointed.

"How come you can see her?" Jaime asked, wondering if Krystal was seeing a ghost or something.

Krystal watched the girl sit down at an empty table, but for whatever reason, Krystal felt the urge to go up to her. *Love your neighbor as yourself,* came to mind and Krystal felt a need to apply that verse right now. So she pushed herself off the potted plant and said, "I don't know," in reply to Jaime's earlier question. Krystal didn't look back, but Jaime didn't object to her sudden departure, waiting to see what Krystal would do next.

Krystal approached the girl sitting alone at the table, looking completely unhappy, and asked, "Hey, is this seat taken?" The girl looked up, and seemed a bit shocked. Like a frightened puppy not knowing whether it should run from a stranger or not. The girl shook her head slowly, Krystal pulled up a seat, realizing she didn't feel awkward meeting a new person for once. Krystal gestured to the girl, "What's your name?" Krystal observed the subtle surprise on the girl's face as she couldn't believe someone was talking to her.

"My name's . . . Secilia." Her voice was shy. She lowered her head and fiddled her thumbs. The girl could not look Krystal's way, either out of embarrassment or because she was too shy. It didn't seem like the girl was embarrassed though, it felt more open yet closed between them. Like the girl wanted Krystal to ask and not.

Krystal couldn't put her thumb on it, but she felt very calm right now. It was strange to feel older for once, actually seeing someone younger than you go through an experience you understand. Secilia looked up and watched the evolving party. Krystal followed Secilia's gaze and saw her looking toward Summer's group, all of them busy playing cards, having the time of their lives. Krystal read Secilia's expression and had a fairly good idea what the girl was thinking of right now. *She wants to be part of their group.* Krystal gave a small chuckle. *That feels familiar.*

Krystal wanted to say something to Secilia, but she felt something was preventing her from speaking. It wasn't her normal problem with speaking to strangers. This time it felt almost healthy to say nothing, watching the scene play out as Secilia watched Summer's group with yearning.

Secilia spoke, "Do you . . . do you feel like you don't belong anywhere?"

Krystal wanted to say, *I do . . . I know exactly what you're talking about,* but she held her response back. She didn't even nod but felt somehow it was best to just listen.

Secilia continued. "It hurts me. It . . . it hurts me a lot . . . because I want to have friends, but I don't. I try, but no one wants to be friends with me." Secilia looked up at Krystal, allowing Krystal to look into Secilia's eyes and see all the years of suffering behind her blue eyes. The sight reached down and touched Krystal's heart. Solidifying the connection between them. Krystal returned the gaze with a mature look of her own past sorrow. Secilia's eyes widened a bit, receiving something she didn't expect to find. Without words exchanged, the two of them understood one another's pain. Glimpsing into Secilia's life, showing her she was not alone in her struggle.

Secilia broke eye contact and looked down at the table, then shifted her attention toward Summer's table. Krystal could see the yearning for affection. The lack of community in this girl's life. The suffering clear as day. So Krystal reached her arm over and held Secilia in a half-hug, rubbing her shoulder. Secilia jolted upright but she didn't reject the hug. Secilia's shock turned to saddened relief as she allowed Krystal to hold her, comforting Secilia for as long as she needed.

Secilia was not one to mope but tonight she did. After returning back to the cabins and having the late-night Bible study session with her group, Secilia was lying on her bunk bed while the rest of the girls in her cabin chatted about the most recent gossip. Secilia had been listening to their conversation for forty-five minutes and she hadn't said a word. Summer was leading it, telling yet another one of her esteemed stories to her group, which every girl couldn't get enough of.

Secilia shifted her attention and stared up at the ceiling, recounting the thousands of days of ostracism, bullying, and loneliness at school. All the pain aching from her very heart, ready to cry out. Ready to pop. She was ready to burst during dinner tonight but that high school girl who comforted her stifled that feeling. It was a brief reprieve, Secilia almost forgot it. But pain was like a blister, it clung to you and always reminded you of its presence, no matter how hard you tried to forget it. Secilia lifted herself up on the edge of her bed, catching glimpses of the conversation about rock climbing or some sport while Summer was still at the center of attention. But Secilia needed to go. She needed to get out. Out of this sucky situation of being purposefully ignored by her peers. She helped herself down from the bunkbed and left the room, not a soul noticed she was gone. She thought. *It's like I'm a ghost.* And Secilia walked, going nowhere, yet going somewhere.

"What do you mean she's missing?" Carmen exclaimed. She was tired of this wonderful trip turning into a ridiculous nightmare. Carmen glared at

Summer, utterly disappointed and somewhat betrayed. Carmen's voice was stern and powerful yet controlled, "She was part of your group, and you didn't notice she was gone until hours later?" Carmen couldn't believe the explanation Summer had given her. She went through the entire night without noticing a member of her group was missing.

Summer couldn't rise to meet Carmen's face. Carmen didn't want her to. "We need to go looking for her *now*!" Summer flinched from Carmen's wrath. Keeping her head down like a puppy that knew it did something wrong. Carmen raised her head and looked at the other leaders in the room. "Everyone start looking. We have a missing member, and we need to find her. Move out now!"

Normally, Krystal wasn't one to go hiking in the middle of the night but tonight she couldn't sleep. She didn't mind it though; the air was a nice temperature and she wanted to get away from things. It was relatively peaceful outdoors, away from all the craziness of society. Krystal liked it. How quiet it was and the stillness of her surroundings. She soaked it in while moving up the trail around the hillside. Near the top of the hill was a cross planted for all to see. It would take her a solid half an hour before she was able to make it up there. But she didn't mind. After going on that morning hike with Jaime long ago, this was a cakewalk. Even the trail itself could easily be seen at night. Krystal looked up and for once noticed the immense sight of all the stars reaching out through the night. *That's lovely*, Krystal thought. Taking in the view that God had created for her.

Krystal reared up the side of the hill after another twenty minutes of walking. She wished Jaime were here for some reason, he would add an element of fun to the equation. She was glad things were going well for Jaime. He definitely came a long way and has experienced a positive change in his behavior lately. Krystal looked forward to spending more time with him, but for now it was just Krystal and herself.

Krystal neared the crest of the hill, high enough to see the surrounding areas all hidden in darkness. In a steep drop down lay the glowing light of the church camp below acting as a safe haven from all the surrounding darkness. The wind kicked up and Krystal felt her hair flutter and dance. It had grown recently and was now stretching farther down her back. After Jaime's Black

Tie Event Krystal paid more attention to her hair. In fact, she liked it more this way. It really brought out her cute side.

Krystal reached the crest of the hill, finding a tall cross off to her left, with a concrete ledge hanging on the hillside. And standing on the edge, was Secilia. Krystal wanted to feel surprised, but she wasn't. From the way things were looking earlier, Krystal suspected something like this might have happened. That bad feeling from earlier coming to fruition. Secilia hadn't seemed to notice her. Her focus was drawn more toward her feet on the ledge, standing on the wrong side of the safety railing that would most certainly end in her downfall (no pun intended). If Secilia leaned an inch closer, she would fall off the ledge. Krystal gazed down at the steep hillside. Anyone who fell from here would most likely die, hence the safety railing.

Krystal made an intentional step on some gravel and watched Secilia whip around in surprise, the wind blowing harder now, revealing Secilia's crying face. Desperation and fear painted her soul for what she was about to do. "Don't come any closer!" she shrieked. Her words and voice were like nervous bullets in a gun. Krystal paid no heed to the warning and casually walked forward, her hands still in the pockets of her jacket. Secilia cried out again, "Didn't you hear what I said? I said don't come any closer!" But Krystal paid no heed to the warning. Secilia was more terrified of Krystal walking toward her than when she was looking down the cliff. Thinking Krystal might grab her, Secilia almost nudged herself forward, but caution and fear stopped her.

What surprised Krystal was how peaceful she felt as she approached Secilia. She was completely calm, like there was no danger whatsoever. It was strange, Krystal didn't feel any fear or terror in these types of situations. For some reason Krystal felt more relaxed in stressful times and couldn't explain why.

Krystal lowered herself under the railing onto Secilia's side, came right up to Secilia, and stopped. Secilia didn't know what to do. Her body was petrified. Curious to see what Krystal would do. Part of her suspected Krystal was going to grab her and drag her back down with her. But Krystal made no sudden movement.

For a moment, Krystal and Secilia stood there staring at each other. Secilia's face ridden with tears and terror, Krystal's face as calm as can be, as the wind flicked and flowed around them. Krystal looked out toward the landscape then back at Secilia. She knelt down onto the ledge and said, "Scooch over," nudging Secilia's feet.

Secilia was so surprised that it looked like she forgot she was standing on the edge of a cliff. Krystal sat there on the edge staring out into the horizon while Secilia stood there perplexed beyond imagination. The wind pulled at Krystal's hair, picking up gentle strands, dangling them in the air in front of her. But Krystal paid no attention. Her attention aimed toward the horizon. For a while they stayed there, neither side making a move, letting the silence and the wind fill the space. Krystal could hear Secilia breathing slowly when she sat down. Krystal didn't even mind that there was a massive drop beneath her. She was so used to death now that she didn't care.

"What's wrong?" Krystal asked compassionately, glancing up at Secilia's standing figure. Secilia still had a look of shock on her face, still taking in the sight of a high schooler casually walking in on her attempted suicide. Krystal continued to wait for her to speak, nothing in the world daring to interrupt their moment.

Secilia was at a loss for words. It was surprising to her that this girl was miraculously here, and now she was sitting next to her on the edge of a cliff, putting herself in harm's way. A full minute lapsed before Secilia got used to the moment, finding this girl was not going to say anything until Secilia answered her question.

"Aren't . . ." Secilia ebbed, "Aren't you going to . . . take me back?"

The girl took her eyes off Secilia and stared into the surrounding hillside. She shook her head, "No," then brought her attention back to Secilia.

Secilia felt calmer now for some unknown reason. The calm of this girl made Secilia feel more relaxed despite the intense moment. "What's wrong?" she asked again, this time with the same patience and compassion as before.

Secilia saw that the girl was not going to speak unless she spoke first. For once, Secilia was grateful that someone was willing to listen. Someone who wanted to hear what she had to say rather than tell her what to do. It was odd but Secilia felt more comfortable with this older girl than with anyone she knew. Maybe there was something about her that appeared nonthreatening. Secilia looked at her frozen feet on the ledge, wondering where to start. She returned her gaze to the girl in black and said, "I . . . I can't take it anymore. I just can't." The girl nodded and listened patiently with compassion and understanding. Secilia saw the girl's response and felt she could keep going. It was strange to be speaking for once. Secilia looked out among the hills and the darkness, and said, "I'm just done," her voice wavered. "I can't take it anymore. All the bullying, the gossip, the *loneliness*, all of it." Secilia looked at the girl, but she showed no change. Secilia took in a quick breath but didn't exhale, "I'm at the end of my rope," more tears fell down her eyes, "I can't keep going. I can't take it anymore." Secilia shook her head, "No more. I'm done." The girl nodded while Secilia went on, "So I think I'm just going to kill myself now and be done with it," Secilia nodded, "Yup, that sounds good," but her voice faltered.

Secilia looked down at the girl in black next to her, eager for an answer, but all the girl said was, "Okay."

Secilia wanted to scream, "That's it?! You're not going to do anything to stop me?"

The girl looked up wisely at Secilia, her voice calm as ever, "Not unless you want me to."

I do want you too. Please, Secilia thought, but she didn't say it, yet she felt the girl understood her. Could even read the expression on her face and tell what she was thinking. Secilia wished she had a gift like that. To know what people were thinking. For some reason Secilia shifted the question back on the girl next to her. "And what about you? What are you doing here?"

The girl took her eyes off Secilia and craned her head back, staring up at the stars while she thought of an answer. "I don't know," her legs dangling off the ledge. "I was having a bad time on this trip, then I couldn't sleep, and now here I am." She breathed, "I don't know why I'm here." She glanced at Secilia and asked courteously, "Does that suit your answer?"

"Not really." Secilia had to admit she was disappointed. But it disarmed her without her knowing.

The girl made a crooked smile and chuckled, "Yeah I'm not good at that stuff."

"At what?"

"Talking. Meeting people. All that stuff."

"You're talking now."

The girl met Secilia's gaze, speaking honestly, "That's because we're one-on-one, I don't do well in group settings. So . . . I have a tough time meeting people."

Secilia felt a stroke of resemblance between herself and this girl sitting next to her. *Is . . . is she like me?* Secilia thought. Feeling her heartbeat slow and her body relax. "Did . . . did you have a hard time in . . . in school?"

The girl nodded, "Yeah."

Now Secilia felt the question begging her to ask, "What happened?"

The girl looked up at Secilia then down, contemplating. The girl read-justed her seating and pulled the sleeve down on her left arm, revealing a two-inch-long scar across her wrist. Secilia's eyes widened in horror. Even in this lighting, Secilia could see the scar clear as day. This girl had tried to kill herself, but she's happy somehow. Why?

The girl pulled her sleeve back up and Secilia felt her legs getting tired, so she sat down on the ledge next to her, completely forgetting she was on the edge of a cliff. "I'm sorry," Secilia said, completely bewildered from this whole experience.

"Don't be." The girl said, surprising Secilia. "If this hadn't happened, I wouldn't have found God."

"And what did happen?" Secilia asked.

The girl took a breath, staring out into the landscape. "For the longest time . . . I didn't have any hope in the world. I . . . didn't know how to live. I was living but I was never *alive*. And for years I struggled with loneliness. I struggled with making friends. I struggled with ostracism. I struggled with suicidal thoughts. And I struggled with depression. I thought that was all there was for me . . . pain. And then at Winter Formal, a little more than a year ago, my mom got hit by a pickup truck." Secilia gasped.

"And where was your dad?"

The girl glanced at Secilia, "I never knew my dad." Silencing any further interruptions. The girl looked down at her dangling feet. "After I lost my mom, I didn't think I could sink any lower." She shook her head. "I couldn't take it anymore. I just wanted the pain to stop. And so . . . I took a kitchen knife, cut my left wrist, and bled out on the floor." Secilia's eyes widened. The breath stuck in her lungs. "But somehow, I didn't die. It was like . . ." The girl looked at Secilia, "like it was a miracle that I didn't die." The girl took her gaze off Secilia. "I ended up in the hospital, and it was there I met a

Janitor who showed me kindness. He cared for me when no one else did and listened to me when I was at my lowest. And because of his kindness, I found God, and because of that, I found hope. I found the reason to living." The girl raised her wounded hand and put it on her chest. "I accepted Jesus into my heart, and for the first time in my life, I felt joy. I felt like everything was going to be alright. I felt *whole*."

It was so horrid and beautiful, yet the girl said it with such calm Secilia didn't know how to process it. Secilia compared her own pain to this girl and couldn't help but feel outclassed. *This girl had gone through what I'm going through, and she didn't even have her parents to help her along.* Secilia thought back to her own family. The happy memory of her parents at home, waiting for her return, made Secilia want to cry again. The girl saw Secilia's tears, reached her arm over and hugged her. The hug permeating Secilia's body with warmth and encouragement she didn't think was possible. It was like this girl was the sun, emanating hope. Then Secilia looked up and saw the girl was crying too.

Why are you . . . The tears came rushing forth. As the two of them embraced, broken souls being found.

They sat there for ten minutes, but it felt like an eternity as the stars flew across the sky, bringing forward the hope of a new day.

Secilia reached the end of her session and muffled into the girl's shoulder, "Thank you." They broke apart and Secilia wiped her eyes. "I think we should go back."

"Alright," The girl replied. And with the same reassuring manner, said, "Let's go back."

Krystal and Secilia returned from the hillside that night. Carmen was relieved to see the two of them alright. The situation calmed down and Secilia was returned to her group. Krystal never mentioned what truly happened on top of the hill at the camp, but luckily there was no investigation. The camp ended the following day and all the students and leaders returned home. Despite the setbacks Krystal thought it was actually a pretty good trip, thinking about Secilia as she hopped on the bus back home.

CHAPTER 66

Bonding

"Life is not all pain and suffering. It is filled with love and joy as well. There may be hardships ahead, but there is also joy."

—Krystal Henninger

Krystal waited out front, tapping her foot anxiously. Ashley saw Krystal's tapping and smiled. *She looks so cute when she's eager,* Ashley thought. The rest of the cars pulled up and found their parking spaces in front of the amusement park. Krystal stood next to Ashley and looked at her. Ashley, enjoying the fact she was standing on her two feet without a wheelchair, looked back at Krystal and said, "It's going to be fine Krystal."

"Okay," Krystal said, expressing the eagerness in her voice as she watched the rest of the group show up. Ashley found it adorable to watch her daughter look worried about an event such as this. It was kinda cute to watch Krystal fret over something so trivial yet important.

The entire Fisher family stepped out of their car and waved. Everyone from Mr. Fisher to even Jaime waved at Krystal and Ashley. Ashley wasn't used to receiving such a warm greeting but welcomed it all the same. Another car pulled up, this time with Kristina in the driver's seat with Joanna, Sho and even Amber stepping out. Only Amber did not look so round anymore, she had given birth to a healthy girl some time ago and found someone to take care of her child for the day.

Kristina, Sho, Joanna, and Amber waved at them. Ashley was surprised with the greeting from all of Krystal's friends. She could tell Krystal felt a little uncomfortable from all the warm greetings but received it humbly. The Fishers came forward and greeted Ashley and Krystal. Mr. Fisher extended a hand toward Ashley, "You must be Krystal's mom. It's a pleasure to meet you."

Ashley shook the massive hand, sizing up the hunk of a man he was. "It's a pleasure to meet the people who took care of my baby girl while I was gone."

Mrs. Fisher stepped forward and gave Ashley a warm hug, then pulled apart and held Ashley at arm's length, "It's so lovely to finally meet you!"

Ashley enjoyed the warm greeting, "Thank you. You've shown Krystal a lot of hospitality while I was asleep." Ashley looked over Mrs. Fisher's shoulder, "And who's this?"

Carmen raised her arms wide and gave Ashley a hug. They pulled apart and Carmen said, "Hi I'm Carmen. The oldest in the family."

Ashley gave a warm smile, "I see, so you've been the one watching over Krystal."

Carmen nodded, "Sure am. I'm her personal Bible study leader and have been for a while now."

"That's wonderful to hear," Ashley said. She watched as all Krystal's friends greeted her and formed their own little talking circle. Exchanging greetings and hugs, talking casually like high schoolers should. It made Ashley's heart warm to see her little girl have friends. People she could trust and hang out with. It brought joy to Ashley's heart.

"I know that look," said Mrs. Fisher. Ashley turned. "You did a fine job raising that girl," nodding, "she's definitely a gift. I'm glad we got to know her, and to meet the woman who raised her."

Ashley blushed a bit, "Oh uhh . . ."

Mr. Fisher cut in, "Don't worry about it. You don't have to say anything. Just look at the kids and watch how much they've all grown. Both in health and in character." Ashley turned and watched the sight of Krystal's group of friends, looking all cheery and happy. Laughing without a worry in the world. It was a sight Ashley doubted she would ever see, but here she was seeing it firsthand. Oh how wonderful life can be.

"We should get going," Ashley said, as they entered the park.

⌒

Everyone WHOAH'd when they entered the new amusement park. It was a park filled with all sorts of rides and food stands, mini golf, an arcade, roller buggies and all sorts of attractions. Kristina felt her excitement grow being surrounded by it all. There was so much to do and so little time. She felt her excitement rise to new levels as she turned around and said, "Alright guys! Let's go have some fun!" Most of the group cheered and they walked together into the park.

Kristina reveled in the sight of not being noticed for once. She knew she was surrounded by people, but for once she didn't have to worry about anyone coming up to her because she blended with the crowd. Kristina could breathe clearly and feel herself be at peace. Her anxiety was gone, and she was no longer confused about who she was anymore. She hadn't had a panic attack since she went to that church service, and it took a massive weight off her shoulders.

As they walked, the conversation between the group was light-hearted and happy. A lot different than when they first met. Kristina came up to Krystal and said, "Yo. I gotta tell you something."

"What is it?"

Kristina threw her arm around Krystal and said, "I got back into acting and I landed a new role in a huge movie coming up. Even better than the one I lost before."

"Wow, are you serious?"

Kristina nodded, "Yeah. We are going places!"

Kristina let go as Krystal said, "I'm so happy for you Kristina! You came a long way." Kristina paused and let the excitement fade. She fell behind the group and thought, *No Krystal, you've come a long way.*

Kristina rejoined the group and took a breath, feeling the weight of the world fall off her. Enjoying the fact that she could be herself and still feel loved. There were no more lies, no more masks. Kristina could finally be herself, even around other people. And for the first time in her life Kristina didn't feel lost. She looked up to the sky and prayed, *Thank you God, for putting Krystal in my life.*

Joanna felt the same way. Stepping into the batting cage, staring hard at the machine ready to spew a high-speed baseball. For once she didn't have to put on a mask or kill who she was to blend in. She wasn't worrying about what the group was thinking. Here in this group everyone was open with each other. Joanna could talk freely and be herself and not feel any judgment. It was wonderful, absolutely wonderful. Joanna felt her heart was free as well. Knowing she didn't have to impress anyone took a lot of burden off her shoulders. It was all too much to take. It made her want to burst into tears just thinking about it. Reveling in the fact that she didn't feel stressed or anxious about blending in with the group made all the difference. Joanna could talk about what she liked and share it with others without worrying about what they would think. It was wonderful. It was freeing. It was liberating, to live life without chains. To live without having the need to impress anybody. To feel loved as she is, not as others want her to be, but as God made her to be. There's no greater feeling in the world.

Joanna tightened her grip on the bat and waited. Not once did she think about what the group behind her was thinking, instead, she memorized one of the verses she heard in church.

> *"Don't be selfish; don't try to impress others. Be humble,*
> *thinking of others as better than yourselves."*
> —PHILIPPIANS 2:3 (NLT)

Joanna humbled herself. *Who cares what other people think. The only thing that matters is what God thinks of me.* Joanna felt her body relax yet strengthen, as she got into position. The ball shot, Joanna swung, hearing a clear DING as the ball soared out of the batting cage. Everyone cheered as the ball flew out of the park as Joanna never felt more humbled and freer in her life.

✌

They left the batting cage, everyone congratulating Joanna with her home-run. They were on their way toward another ride when Sho rushed in front of Krystal and said, "Ooh ooh, there's an arcade over there. We should go to the arcade!"

"Okay," Krystal said happily. "Let's ask the group first." She turned to the group and asked, "Do you guys want to go to the arcade?"

Amber said, "No thanks, I don't want to go to the arcade, I'm more down for the go-karts over there. I want to give those a try before lunch time."

Joanna agreed. "I totally want to go try the go-karts too."

Kristina said, "Me too, I'll go with them."

Krystal said, "Okay, you guys can go do that. We'll meet up with you later." The whole group agreed and split up. Sho led the way to the arcade, letting his excitement begin to show.

"Come on! Come on! Let's go inside!" Sho quickly ran in like a little kid and found a game called Raptor killer, with a plastic M4 assault rifle hung on the side. Sho didn't hide his excitement any longer and said, "I want to do that one!" Krystal and Jaime followed along like parents watching an excited child.

The parents in the group had let the kids go off and do their own thing while they were busy playing mini golf. Krystal could picture Carmen getting frustrated over mini golf. She was by far the most competitive out of her whole family. The thought made Krystal smile when Jaime said, "It's nice to see Sho so active. To see him express his own desires and do what he wants to do. Especially since his English has improved so much."

Krystal stood next to Jaime, the two of them watching Sho play the shooter videogame. Krystal said, "Yeah. He certainly has learned to express himself more and he seems more confident." Krystal nodded, "He's definitely come out of his shell since we first met him."

Jaime chuckled. "You're right about that. He reminds me a bit of you."

Krystal cocked her head sideways looking at Jaime. "You got a point there." They watched Sho go on for ten straight minutes playing that Raptor killer videogame. He was so good at it, he scared Krystal and Jaime with his skills. The final part was when Sho completed the game, turned around and smiled. Krystal saw the joy from his smile, knowing that Sho was finally outgrowing his shyness and gaining confidence. He was finally able to look people in the eye more and smile casually. He could express his own desires without shying away from things. *He's grown so much*, Krystal thought. The sight brought relief to her heart, knowing that Sho would be okay. That he would make friends and be alright on his own now that he's got God in his life. Krystal no longer had to worry. Plus, she could enjoy how someone like her could learn to be happy and feel loved. To see someone depressed find happiness was all the reward Krystal wanted, knowing there is everlasting hope in the world with Jesus Christ. A hope that can change people and bring them out of their darkest times.

Amber steered the buggy with the tenacity of a professional driver. Crazy and determined, letting all the excitement out through her buggy going twenty miles an hour down the speed way. Amber too felt her entire world had changed. The lump in her belly was now gone and had birthed a healthy, growing baby. Amber was glad to have kept the child. The road would be hard, but she knew everything would be all right.

Joanna was in the passenger seat, hanging with a death grip on the side rails. Amber pulled the buggy in line and waited for the next race to begin. Amber wanted to get it off her chest, turning to Joanna who was still white with terror and said, "Hey . . . I'm sorry for spreading rumors about you and scaring you in Summer's group. Summer and I had no right to treat you that way."

Joanna didn't comprehend the question at first and looked pale. The color briefly recovered in her face as Joanna said, "That's totally fine."

Amber needed to confirm, "We good?"

Joanna nodded, "Yes, yes we are totally good."

Amber grinned, "Great," The light turned green. She stepped on the pedal and sped the go-kart forward, laughing maniacally as Joanna screamed in the fading distance.

‹ঌ›

"Where did Sho run off to?" Jaime looked high and low for Sho but he couldn't see him anywhere in the arcade.

"He could have stepped outside," Krystal suggested. Both Jaime and Krystal headed outside, when Krystal got a text from Sho. Krystal clicked her phone off and said, "He's with our parents. He apparently got so excited about his victory that he ran off and had to tell everybody."

Jaime snickered, "He sure likes to win, that's for sure."

Krystal shrugged her shoulders, "Well what do we do now?" She then realized they were alone. Her perspective suddenly shifted, and she felt her body temperature increase.

Krystal looked up at Jaime, but Jaime was already looking at her for some reason. "What's wrong?" she asked.

Jaime spoke quickly, "Nothing." Jaime looked over and saw mini golf nearby, "You wanna play some mini golf?"

Krystal said, "Sure." They rented their putting clubs and began to play. The first course had three rocks surrounding the hole. Krystal went first while Jaime stood back and watched. Krystal struck the ball and watched it sink as a hole in one. Krystal rushed with excitement, turning to Jaime, "Look did you see! Did you see! I got a hole in one!"

Jaime stood there with his mouth agape. "How did you . . ."

Krystal shrugged her shoulders, "Beginners luck?"

Jaime said, "Very lucky," then took his turn. The next nine swings were followed by frustration and a small break as Jaime knelt down in defeat.

Krystal leaned over, "Are you okay?"

Jaime finished his overexaggerated spout and looked up, "Yeah I'm fine," his tone completely casual. Apparently, it didn't bother him at all. Krystal even found he looked happier than he'd ever been before. *Is he having fun?* Krystal thought. Krystal helped Jaime up and they went on to the next hole.

Krystal took her approach, and ten swings later Krystal was on the ground in defeat. "Mini golf is hard . . ." she said.

"Tell me about it," replied Jaime.

Krystal got up to try again, but before she putted the ball she turned and looked at Jaime, "How about we make this interesting?"

Jaime cocked an eyebrow, "Interesting how?"

"How about we go as fast as we can to try and clear as many holes as possible?"

Jaime gave an evil smile. "Alright. Whoever finishes all the holes first wins."

"Deal." The game was on. Krystal went first while Jaime hit right after her. She managed to get one hole ahead of Jaime, but Jaime was improving his game. Krystal swung shot after shot, trying to speed through the course as fast as she could. Jaime took his shot on the hole behind her and managed to sink a hole in one. Jaime threw his arm in the air and ran toward Krystal.

Jaime called, "I did it! I did i—" tripping on a concrete step and falling out of view.

Krystal winced. "Ooooo, I felt that."

Jaime dusted himself off casually and called out, "I'm good. I'm good." He didn't seem angry at all. In fact, he laughed more than Krystal had ever seen him laugh, and because of that she started laughing too. Jaime was truly having a good time, and because of that, so was she.

When the laughter died down, Krystal called out, "Are you alright?"

"Yeah, I'm good. Took a tumble that's all."

"You don't look that upset."

Jaime shrugged it off, smiling wide, "Nah why would I be?" The sight amazed Krystal. It was truly a genuine smile coming from the guy. She relaxed more, feeling more comfortable with this new side of Jaime she'd never seen before.

Jaime rejoined Krystal at the next hole, panting and out of breath but shaking off the embarrassment like it was nothing. Krystal resumed her speed run, but before she could hit the ball Jaime wrapped his arms around her and lifted her off the ground, "I'm not letting you get ahead this time!"

Krystal laughed as loud as she could, playfully trying to break out of his grip. "Put me down," she laughed.

But Jaime hoisted Krystal higher in the air, "I won't let you go." He said. Krystal could not stop laughing as he twirled her around.

"Hahaha stop it. Put me down." Jaime finally put her down and Krystal gave Jaime a little shove out of playful fun. The two of them grinned at each other. Preparing eagerly for the other party to strike. Krystal was mostly hiding her surprise with Jaime's attitude. He was normally so cold and uninterested, but now he was warm and playful. *Who would have thought that Jaime was such a sweet guy.* It was not unwelcome, in fact, Krystal enjoyed it more than the previous times she hung out with Jaime. Watching him always be so serious grieving over his sister, but now he was laughing, truly laughing. It was like the darkness around Jaime was gone and he could finally live his life with the happiness he deserved.

Krystal paused to capture the moment in her mind, looking up at the sight of a joyful Jaime.

༄

"Dang it! I can't believe you beat me."

"Eh don't beat yourself up. Mini golf can be frustrating." Jaime said, returning the clubs.

The two of them sat down on a bench, needing a break from all the walking. Krystal leaned back and felt her stomach growl. "Oh wow. I didn't realize how hungry I was."

Jaime looked at Krystal then looked around for possible food options. He lifted his head and got an idea. He turned to Krystal and said, "I'll be right back." And before Krystal could say anything, he was off.

Jaime came back a few minutes later with five carmel apples in his hand, each one sprinkled with different variations of candy. Krystal felt her heart warm at the sight and smiled. "Huh, carmel apples. That's nostalgic. But why'd you get five?"

Jaime said, "It's part of a game. You ready?"

Krystal didn't question it and said, "Yeah."

Jaime sat down and explained the rules, "The way this works is we are going to take turns and close our eyes, then the other is going to feed a carmel apple to the guesser, and the guesser has to figure out which carmel apple it is. You ready?"

Krystal stopped him right there, "Hold on, so you are going to feed me an apple, and I'm supposed to guess what it is?"

Jaime nodded, "Yes!"

"And I'm going to do the same to you?"

Jaime nodded, "Yes! You ready?"

Krystal decided to go along with it, "Okay, let's start." Then she thought for a moment, "Wait. Is there a prize?"

Jaime nodded, "There's a prize."

"Okay, let's do it."

There were five carmel apples in his hand. One with candied corn, one with Oreo bits, one with graham crackers, one with brownie bites, and one with roasted marshmallows. Jaime said, "Now I'll feed one to you and you'll have to guess."

Krystal peered at Jaime suspiciously, "Okay," closing her eyes.

Jaime then took the apple and held it up to Krystal's lips. Krystal opened her mouth and felt her teeth sink into the apple. She chewed it for a moment then said, "Oreo."

"Correct! Now it's my turn." Jaime handed Krystal the apples and they repeated the process.

Jaime took a bite and said, "This one is . . . marshmallows."

"You're right," Krystal said, handing the apples back to Jaime. Krystal closed her eyes and waited a moment. She heard the shuffling of plastic and waited for the apple to reach her lips, but a few seconds passed, and it never came. Krystal was ready to open her eyes, until Jaime leaned in and kissed her.

Krystal's eyes shot open. The warm comfort on her lips, the gift he had given her, drained away all sense of shock, filling Krystal's world with bliss. Krystal closed her eyes, embracing the gift wholeheartedly, feeling Jaime's hand caress her cheek, holding her close.

They held their lips together for what felt like an eternity, until Jaime broke apart yet maintaining a close distance from Krystal's face. Jaime looked aside and said, "Sorry if that was rushed." He paused, "But I wanted to tell you how amazing you are. How the change in your life has affected me so much. And to see you grow is more than a miracle. So . . . thank you, for being *you*."

"You don't need to worry anymore," Krystal spoke. "You don't need to be so hard on yourself. It's over. It's all over." Krystal threaded her arms around Jaime's neck, pulling him closer, looking in his hazel-colored eyes. "Thank you, for being my best friend. Through all the pain and the turmoil. You helped me grow and get out of my comfort zone and try new things. Because of that, I got to see a new side of life I didn't know was possible. So . . . thank you, and I'm so glad I met you."

Then Krystal put her hands on his cheeks, "And I've wanted to do this too," pulling Jaime close and giving him a kiss on the lips. Jaime's eyes went wide, and life fell into bliss again as the warmth of their two bodies shot up a few degrees. Jaime embraced the kiss and wrapped his arms around Krystal, pulling her close. Krystal allowed Jaime to pull her in, basking in the comfort of being wrapped in Jaime's arms. Krystal wrapped her arms around Jaime, and they held each other there for as long as they wanted.

Krystal and Jaime pulled apart, slowly, then started to chuckle. The comfort of the other bringing a harmony neither of them had ever experienced. (Don't think anything else happened you sickos! It was only a kiss . . . a very, passionate kiss.)

Krystal thought, *Is this what it's like to experience life? To find love and friendship, to care for others and to feel loved?* Krystal wasn't doing much thinking, but the thought remained. *Life is not all pain and suffering. It is filled with love and joy as well. There may be hardships ahead, but there is also joy.*

As they held each other there until the orange glow of the sun vanished and the indigo sky lit up with stars.

↶⏝↷

"When did that happen?" Ashley stared, her jaw open at Krystal and Jaime holding each other like a couple in the distance.

Carmen put her hand on Ashley's shoulder, "Well it's as they say, young love. Whereas I'll say, 'It's about time!'"

Ashley stared dumbfounded yet happy, "What happened when I was asleep?"

Carmen answered simply, "A lot."

✎

The day ended with a group photo in front of the amusement park. Everyone packed together as Krystal, Jaime, Sho, Kristina, Joanna, Amber, Ashley, Carmen, and Mr. and Mrs. Fisher posed for the photo. All of them giving the widest smiles they could at the camera, especially Krystal, feeling the happiest she's ever felt in her entire life. The bystander took the photo for them and handed them the phone. Krystal was the first to see the picture and could not believe her eyes. She saw herself, smiling, enjoying herself with a bunch of people she called *friends*, along with her mom and the Fishers. The sight of it all sent a jolt to Krystal's eyes, triggering her tear ducts, but she held them back and looked at the photo. A permanent memory of all the people she loved and held dear, none of which she knew or met before her suicidal incident. Oh, how life had changed since then.

"That's a good picture," she said, wavering in her speech, trying to hold back the dam of emotions. *Yup*, Krystal thought, *definitely the best picture I've ever taken.*

CHAPTER 67

Thank You

"There is a purpose to your pain."

—JL

The all pulled up to Jaime's house and looked at each other in question. The parents looked at each other and retreated back to their homes, but the kids still had energy. Amber was the first to say it, now holding her child after picking up her baby from home, "You guys still want to do something?"

Jaime said, "There's a firepit nearby we can all hang at."

Kristina chimed in, "That's a pretty dank idea."

Krystal tilted her head, *Dank?* she thought.

Joanna said, "We should do it."

Sho said, "I'm in."

Jaime said, "Alright then let's go."

Krystal smiled and leaned back in her chair, dangling a soda between her fingers, watching the conversation progress through the night. The firepit before her spewing pillars of fire, flowing like the gentle wind around them. It didn't smell of the nice wooden fire you're thinking of, but of natural gas, but hey, at least it was nice to have a firepit nearby.

The conversation grew quiet. Joanna and Kristina sat across from Krystal, waiting for something to happen. Sipping their soda like they were little trinkets but didn't know what to do with them. Kristina leaned back in her makeshift chair, the fire creating shadow and light off her face, making her look even more beautiful. The kind of nighttime mystique that made women look more attractive when given only half the visual, making Kristina look like a supermodel in a magazine (but not the kind you guys are thinking of).

Jaime sat next to Krystal and the two of them stared into the fire. Letting the warmth flicker and dance, mixing with the frigid air around them. Krystal didn't move. She enjoyed watching the flame dance in front of her. Amber sat on the other side of the pit from Krystal with her child tucked closely in her arms. The baby, cradled in a blanket under her shirt. Looking like a tightly packed teddy bear pressed against her body. On Krystal's right sat Sho. Quiet as always but appearing happier than normal.

The six of them stared into the fire brimming with life. The fire shifted position in the wind, swishing like a flag, raising vertically like a twisted pillar. No one said a word, all attention poised on the fire.

Kristina was the first to break the silence, "You know, sometimes I wonder how we got here. How life turned out the way it did for all of us?"

"Totally," added Joanna, then she paused in thought. "How is it that we all know each other?" The question struck everyone in the group, eyes shifted around, minds wondering about the same question.

Sho pointed to Joanna and Amber, "Well, how do you two know each other?"

Amber spoke up for both of them, "Oh we we're part of the same friend group the first couple years of high school. What about you Sho? How do you know everybody here?"

Sho pointed at Krystal, "Krystal introduced me to everyone. How do you know Krystal?"

Amber looked embarrassed and rubbed her head, "Uhh we went to the same Bible study but I uhhh . . . kinda got into a fight with her. That's mainly how we met."

Joanna hopped in, "I remember seeing that. Shortly after, I started noticing you Krystal, like back at the coffee shop, and when we spoke in class."

Krystal chuckled and pondered, "Huh, I almost forgot about that."

Joanna pointed between Krystal and Jaime, "How do you two know each other?" Jaime and Krystal exchanged glances.

Jaime looked at Joanna, "I met Krystal when she came to my house roughly a year ago and joined Carmen's Bible study. That's when I recall first meeting you," he said, turning to Krystal.

Amber pointed at Krystal and Kristina. "Okay, but how does that explain you two?"

Kristina happily defended her position. "Oh, I met Krystal when she fell asleep in class during a lunch period, but we later met at a party that Jaime took her to. That's mainly how I remember meeting Krystal."

Amber said, "Huh," and fell silent. The whipping of the flames filled the air.

After a long minute Jaime said, "You know. I can't imagine where I would be if I hadn't met you, Krystal." Krystal glanced at Jaime. Surprised by the sudden compliment, causing her to blush. Everyone slowly shifted their attention to Jaime as he stared into the fire. "I can remember that night when you came to me. It was in this same exact spot, on the anniversary of my sister Carole's death. A date, I will never forget . . ." Jaime paused, exhaled, reliving the painful memories, "I remember the exact way I felt, sitting right here, in this very chair, gazing into this fire. Wanting to lose myself. To forget everything. The memories and pain that came with it . . ." Jaime took a breath. "I remember sitting here, feeling alone in my grief. Yearning for my friends to call me, to ask me how I was doing, to notice if something was off. To send me a text and check to see if I was doing alright . . . but no one did. No one ever asked me once how I was doing when my sister died. It made me realize how little of a community of close friends I had." Jaime took a deep breath and slowly exhaled through his nostrils; his gaze still focused on the fire. He blinked, "And then I heard you coming behind me. Listening to me as I explained my grief. Being that one person who was there for me when no one else was." Jaime closed his eyes. He put his fist to his forehead, then glanced at Krystal gratefully, "I can't thank you enough for that."

Krystal put one hand on Jaime's shoulder and the other to cover her mouth, holding back the tears. Jaime let out a single pair of tears but maintained his competent posture. He exhaled and casually wiped the tears from his face, still gazing forward at the fire as if the fire was slowly purifying him. Burning away all the impurities and pain, leaving only the golden core of Jaime's existence, beautiful and pure.

Jaime nodded, as if answering a question in his own head, "I was lost for a long time . . . My relationship with God was not on good terms. I was so full of hatred towards God. Asking myself, 'How could there be a God if He let my innocent little sister kill herself?'" Jaime took a deep breath and cooled for a moment, keeping himself level. "I was alone and hurt with no one to lean on. And it killed me inside and I wasn't happy, even when I was at school and looked like I was happy, I wasn't. I distanced myself from my family. I could feel how far I was drifting from my family and from God. The further I drifted away from God, the further I drifted away from my family." Jaime chuckled but it was one of pain and hinted with shame, "I can't imagine what the pain was like for my parents when they lost one child, only to lose a second child quickly after." Jaime put his hands to his face in shame, "How could I ever forgive myself for what I've put them through?"

Krystal wanted to object but she didn't because there was still more Jaime had to say. Jaime looked at Krystal now, eyes sincere and open, "But after seeing you . . . and your dramatic change of character. After seeing you go from the gloomy girl sitting in the back, to the singing rockstar in the front. After seeing you care for others when you yourself were hurting. After seeing God perform miracles through you and change others through you, I know, and maybe I've always known . . ." Jaime glanced down at the concrete floor beneath his feet then back at Krystal, "You were the one to bring me back to God. You were the one that I needed when I was down. You were the one who was there in my darkest moment, even when no one was there in your darkest moment." Jaime took a breath, "I know I already said this, but Krystal . . . thank you. Thank you for being you. Thank you for being born. Thank you . . . for bringing me back." Tears welled up in Krystal's eyes as she fought to contain them, her heart flooding with joy. "It's all because God put you in my life that I'm here, restored, and alive with God. That my family is restored, and that I, Jaime Fisher, have finally come back to God . . . It's all because of you Krystal."

Krystal was bellowing with tears, wanting to unleash the tears like a dam ready to burst.

Kristina chimed in, "I've got something to say too."

Oh no, Krystal thought. *I can't take another round like that.*

The spotlight shifted toward Kristina; the wind flapping against her beautiful black hair. "For the longest time, I've been alone. And I know that is shocking to everyone given how I'm a"—Kristina made air quotes—"*famous actress* but . . ." Kristina let out a sigh, "I don't know. Being famous doesn't exactly mean that everybody loves you." She stared into the fire with inward darkness. "You see, being an actress, and especially a famous *young* actress, changes your childhood. You're automatically thrust into a world where people are judging you for every action you do.

"People look at you differently once they realize who you are and what you've done." There was a hint of sorrow mixed in Kristina's words that Krystal picked up on. "Growing up, being famous, being successful with money you've made. It's great and all but . . . it's not everything. You see, for the longest time, I've felt alone because there was no one I could truly open up to. No one shares the same problem with me. Because when you're famous, people look at you differently." Kristina pointed in the direction of their school. "You see, I may show up to school and look like I have lots of friends cradling around me, but those people are not my real friends. Remember, people look at you differently when you're famous, people act differently around you and they want to try and be your friend because you're an *actress* and not because they want to get to know *me* personally. And so, I learned not to trust anybody. I even had issues with my parents because they were siphoning the money I was making, so I couldn't trust them either, and as a result, I filed to become an 'independent minor.' It's legal, look it up."

Krystal and everyone chuckled. Kristina pressed on, "So, going all through elementary school and middle school, and then up into high school, I've never had any *real* friends. Friends who call to check on you and see how you are doing. Friends who you can be real with and totally open about everything. Friends whom you can laugh and cry and experience life together . . . I didn't have that. I haven't had that for the longest time.

"Then, my parents unfortunately got a divorce." Kristina paused, catching herself. "I had to choose my name, and because of that, I started to lose myself." Kristina shook her head, "I was lost. I didn't know who I was." She shrugged her shoulders, "I mean, sure I'm Kristina Walker, but was I Kristina Walker the Actress? Or Kristina Walker? Who was I?" Kristina paused, "When you change names, the value of a name becomes less. Then I thrust myself into my work and I started taking on all these differing roles and characters, all with different names and personalities." Kristina continued to stare into the fire, "That's when the anxiety hit, and my health declined . . . I started getting panic attacks on a daily basis. To the point where I couldn't act anymore." Kristina's shoulders sagged, "I didn't know what my identity was. And when I lost my acting job, I lost the only identity I had left."

Kristina looked at Krystal, "But then I met you . . . and saw you go from the non-talkative, shy girl, to the hopeful best friend I see today. Also, to see you walk onto that stage and sing that song with total confidence. It blew my mind." Krystal smiled at the remark. "But seriously . . . I have never seen anything like that. And I thought to myself, 'What is it about this girl that makes her so different? Why is she acting the way she does when she has every right to be sorrowful and bitter towards the world?' And for the first time in my life, I met someone who actually cared about me. Someone who would listen to my problems and not offer a solution but would give me the time of day." Krystal met Kristina's ocean blue eyes, both of them staring at each other over the fire, "Krystal, you showed me how to find my identity by being a living example. And you taught me to trust people again. You were my first *real* friend. You listened to me and didn't try to befriend me just because I was an actress but because you saw I was hurting, and I will never forget that. Thank you."

Krystal's cheeks were beaming as red as the sun. Krystal lowered her head in humble flattery. She had calmed down slightly after Jaime's spiel, but the emotions were fighting to the surface again.

"I too," Joanna cleared her throat, "have something to say." She paused, taking a breath. "Growing up, I had a lot of friends in elementary school. Things were great and I didn't have a care in the world. But then middle school rolled in, and things were not so great. Things changed and I totally should have seen it coming but . . . it didn't make it any easier. Very slowly, my friends started abandoning me, and that's when the bullying started. I sat alone and was picked on every day. 'Gloomy Joe' they called me and spread rumors about me causing no one to want to be my friend. Anyone who associated with me quickly abandoned me out of fear of being bullied.

"As a result, I would do anything it took to make friends. Which meant, trying to impress people, sometimes even the wrong people." Joanna shook her head as if debating something in her mind, "For years I would try to impress people. I would do anything people wanted me to do, I would suck up to them just to be close with them. They would take advantage of me, and I would know they were doing it, but I would let it happen because I didn't want to be ostracized again . . . The fear of being clique-less, of not having a group of friends to sit with is unbearable. The kind of silent hell I lamented and wanted nothing to do with. And so, I clung as hard as I could to every friend group I could find." Joanna took a breath, "But none of them tried to accept me for who I was, so I tried a different tactic to fit in. I killed who I was inside and became whatever people wanted me to be. I would agree with everything they said and changed myself to be more appealing to their needs and not my own . . . but with that lie came a cost.

"Every day was brutal. It killed me inside to be someone I wasn't. I was smiling but I wasn't happy, and that took a toll on my heart. It broke me every time to be someone I wasn't. But I needed friends, and I didn't want to go back to being bullied, so I kept up the lie. Pretty soon I was in high school, and that's when I joined Summer and Amber's group." Joanna looked at Amber, Amber lowered her head in mild shame, expressing *"I'm sorry."*

Joanna took a breath, "I thought I could keep it up forever, but after the fight things started to change. I began to notice you Krystal and see your change of character. How you were confident and caring even when people didn't like you. You never sought to gain people's approval and that astounded me. So, I thought, 'Why does this girl not care what other people think of her? What does she have that I don't?' It caused me to wonder why you were so different. Because Krystal, there was something about you that I couldn't explain, but I knew I wanted it too. I want the joy that you have, and I want to be like you. Because you showed me that it's not worth it trying to please others and that it's possible for people to be themselves and be loved. Which is why your performance at the talent show was so remarkable. It profoundly changed me. And so, because of that, I found God, and can finally be who I am. So, thank you."

Krystal raised her arm to cover her face as she cried. She could not keep the tears back any longer. They seeped down her eyes in clumps as Krystal did her best to keep herself from wailing at the top of her lungs. Jaime put his hand on Krystal's shoulder as she could feel the warmth even through her jacket.

"Now it's my turn," Amber said.

Oh gosh, Krystal thought. *I beg of you please. No more.* Bracing herself for another tearjerker, but Krystal knew she'd lost the battle before it had already begun. Krystal put her hand to her face and tried to wipe away the never-ending flow of tears. There were looks of relief spreading from one face after the other. Everyone who opened up looked happier. The bond between them strengthened because they were open with each other. Holding nothing back.

Amber's baby murmured as she gently rocked her baby and hushed it to sleep. Amber continued rocking her baby up and down and said, "I don't have much to say, but I want to say this." Amber looked down at her baby, her beautiful baby and said, "I saw a girl who was gracious enough to take a beating from the likes of me and have the strength to hold back; but not only that, you forgave me. When you did, things began to change. It made me wonder, 'How in the world can this girl, who I beat to a pulp, learn to forgive the likes of me?' A scumbag of a person who spreads rumors about others and used to not care about the people around me." Amber bobbed her child carefully up and down, rearing her child to sleep. "To me, it doesn't make sense, there had to be some ulterior motive. Some reason why you were doing things the way you were. Because I could never understand why someone would do that. But then you started talking about God and how Jesus taught you how to love your enemies the way He loved you. And it made me wonder, 'Can Jesus ever love somebody like me? Can He ever forgive me? Someone who deserves to be a single mom for the wrong I've done.'" Amber stopped and looked at Krystal. "But you forgave me Krystal." Amber's words were more genuine than anything Krystal had ever heard. Amber's eyes gleamed in the firelight. "You showed me mercy when I didn't deserve it, and it was because of that kindness, I felt loved. I began to believe that maybe I *could* raise this child." Amber looked down to the side of her chair, "Then I learned of your upbringing. How you were a single child with only your mom to be there for you. How your mom didn't intend to have you because she got drunk and had sex with some man you don't even know."

"Wait what?" Jaime interjected. He looked at Krystal and said, "Your mom didn't intend to have you?"

Krystal nodded, "I was an unplanned pregnancy." There was no shame in her statement. In fact, it sounded as if Krystal accepted it with dignity. Krystal understood that she wasn't an accident and was something worthwhile. For she was a child of God.

Amber resumed once Jaime calmed down, "I pictured this child's future being nothing but grim and full of darkness. But I watched your journey, and I learned that just because a child doesn't appear to have a promising future, doesn't mean they won't have one. A child can grow up in the most horrible of conditions, but they can still become a great and wonderful person. You can grow up in the ghetto for all I care, and you could still end up a wonderful person as long as you *choose* to be. For I learned that every child's life is precious, even the ones who aren't born yet. Because this child might one day save me or somebody else."

Amber gestured to her baby, "This child is alive because of you. Because I saw a girl give me grace when I deserved none. Which is why I've decided to name my girl Grace. A tribute to her name, for you. So, thank you Krystal. For showing me grace."

Krystal was surprised, she had no idea what kind of impact she'd left on Amber. The realization was amazing. Krystal felt a resemblance to Amber's child, and because of one small act of kindness, a life was saved. You really never know what a small act of kindness can do.

"You were the one to comfort me when I was at my lowest." Everyone shifted their attention toward Sho. He lifted his head and spoke up, "Growing up in Japan I was ostracized for being different. I was bullied and my friends abandoned me." Sho lowered his head, "I wanted to kill myself. But before I could do it, my parents and I moved to America." Sho raised his head and looked at Krystal, "But when you walked up to me that day and asked me to come sit with you. That was the first time anyone had ever done that for me. It made me feel valued. It made me feel loved. Because of that I found Jesus and I didn't want to kill myself anymore. I want to thank you for that Krystal. Thank you for caring for others and being yourself."

Krystal couldn't hold it back. The tears were flowing in steady rivers. Krystal had never been complimented like this before. And it was such a contrast from a couple years ago from how grim her life looked back then. Kristina stood up and walked over toward Krystal and put her hand on Krystal's shoulder. Jaime stood up as well and put his hand on Krystal's other shoulder. Joanna saw this as an opportunity and walked over to comfort her as well. Then Sho stood up, then Amber. Krystal cried in her arms, feeling the hands of Jaime, Joanna, Kristina, Amber, and Sho, all comforting her. The dark times were over. The Great Sadness was gone. A time Krystal will never forget.

Krystal wiped her nose, her voice thick with tears. "I . . . I just feel so joyful right now." They all gave Krystal gentle, caring smiles. Krystal looked down at the fire, "I don't deserve this. I don't deserve any of this. But I want to thank you guys anyway." Krystal turned and faced Jaime, "It was because of you Jaime, that I was able to get out of my comfort zone and try new things," Krystal shifted to Joanna, "It was because of you that I was able to ask the right questions and be able to talk to people." Then toward Kristina, "It was because of you that I was able to feel pretty." Then Amber, "It was because of you that I learned the power of forgiveness." And Krystal finally looked at Sho, "And it was because of you that I learned how to use my pain to comfort others." Then Krystal turned and looked ahead into the fire with hope shining in her eyes, "It was all because of that Janitor's kindness that I was able to feel loved." Then Krystal looked up at the sky, now glistening with a thousand stars like no one could've ever imagined, and spoke to God directly, "It was because of You God, that I was able to find hope. And it was because of You that I met that Janitor. Thank you, Jesus for putting that man in my life and for all the things You've done for me." Then Krystal lowered her head and looked from side to side at all the people around her, "And I thank all of you for teaching me and helping me grow into who I am today. Thank you."

Krystal closed her eyes and soaked in the feeling of community. Knowing the feeling of being loved filled her heart. Krystal bowed her head and prayed silently to God,

God . . . I thank You for what You've done. None of this would have happened if You hadn't saved me in the hospital through that Janitor. I wouldn't have learned to find hope in Jesus, and I wouldn't have learned to value others more importantly than myself. Thank You for giving me value. Thank You for calling me Your masterpiece. Thank You for calling me loved. Thank You for valuing my life and calling me wonderfully made. Thank You for putting each and every one of these people in my life, so that we can share life with each other. Thank You for being the one to love us first when You died on the cross for each and every one of us. I thank You for the journey and the growth that I've experienced from my pain, and for teaching me to use my pain to comfort others. Thank You for all that You've done Jesus. In Your name I pray, amen.

Krystal opened her eyes, looked up and took in the sight of all five of her friends, holding their hands on her, letting her know the dark times were over.

"You leaving?" Jaime asked, packing up his stuff from the firepit.

"No," Krystal said. "I wanna stay for a little longer."

"Alright," Jaime said, "I'll see you around then."

"See ya," Krystal replied.

Krystal stared into the fire for a long moment, basking in the feeling of what had just happened. She took a deep, long breath, feeling the rich and satisfying oxygen enter her lungs and fill her body with life. She couldn't remember the last time she *enjoyed* anything so much. But here, she felt happy just being here, being alive, and rejoicing in that. *Thank you, God. I really needed that.*

Krystal heard footsteps behind her. She turned around and a girl who looked to be about thirteen to fourteen years old stood there. The girl looked at Krystal expressionless, although Krystal could see the hardened gloom on her face. *That looks familiar*, Krystal thought. The girl had short brunette-blonde hair and was dressed in a red dance shirt. Krystal said nothing. The two of them stared at each other, yet there was no malice between them. Krystal, still feeling joyful, raised a soft smile.

"My name is Chloe, and I need to say something," The girl said frankly.

Krystal spread her hands, "I'm here to listen."

Chloe looked toward the fire, as if a bit embarrassed. Krystal wasn't fazed in the slightest. She just learned to embrace what happened and move on. A moment of pause occurred between them, but Krystal didn't dare to interrupt. Krystal bit her tongue and waited for Chloe to speak. Chloe raised her head again, looking straight at Krystal and said, "I was planning to kill myself that night, the night of the talent show. My life was hell and I've struggled with suicide for as long as I can remember. But I felt like something was telling me to go to that talent show. Like something was calling me to go there that night." Krystal nodded, listening quietly. Chloe took another breath and continued. "I thought to myself, 'When the talent show is over, I'll go home and kill myself.'" Chloe paused, "I wanted a way out. To find peace when there was none."

Krystal nodded, "I know the feeling."

Chloe went on, "It felt like I was stuck and there was no way out. I couldn't dig myself out of this pit I was in, and it seemed like everything I did just made things worse." Chloe watched Krystal for a reaction, but Krystal stood there with the patience of a statue. "So, when I went to that talent show, I was not expecting anything. I didn't know what was going on or who would be in it, but then I saw a girl with black hair in a purple dress step out on stage, and it reminded me of a girl I had met in the hospital a few years back who had also tried to commit suicide." Krystal stared at Chloe with no surprise. Chloe took a breath, "But when you sang that song and played that guitar, I could tell . . . you were calling out to *me*. Those lyrics rang true in my heart, and it was like the lyrics you sang brought healing to my heart when nothing else would. Then I thought, 'If this person can find hope, then I can too' and after watching your performance, I felt God calling out to me. Reaching into my heart through your words and telling me 'It will be okay.' And because of that I found Christ."

Chloe sniffed, Krystal was too emotionally exhausted to cry for this, so she looked back at Chloe with as much compassion as she could muster. Remembering Chloe as the brunette-blonde girl in the hospital.

Chloe put her hand to her heart and said, "What I'm saying is . . . my life was changed because of your story. So . . . thank you. Thank you for showing me Jesus and giving me hope." Then Chloe looked at Krystal and said, "I'm going to be in heaven, because of *you*." Krystal didn't feel any accomplishment. No celebration. She only felt like a regular person who hadn't done much. She wasn't a hero, but she did feel content looking back at her own story. All the pain she had gone through had been for a purpose. To save, at least, this one life. That her pain had not been for nothing but had been *for* something.

Krystal stood there and whispered, "Thank you." Feeling her heart swell with the Holy Spirit. The feeling was similar to finishing a marathon. That through all the pain and suffering, her life mattered and actually made a difference. That if she died today, she would have lived a full life. Krystal said humbly, "It wasn't me. It was all God."

"I know," Chloe nodded, looking up. "I know."

CHAPTER 68

Baptism

"Your pain is not only for you."

—JL

"Ughhh it's cold outside!" Kristina moaned.

"It's not cold," Jaime said, "You're just underdressed."

Krystal saw Kristina gripping her arms, covering the open diamonds weaved through the sleeves. Krystal thought the outfit genuinely looked good on Kristina, but she had to agree with Jaime. Kristina looked cold.

"Should I put on a jacket?" Kristina asked.

The whole group spoke in unison, "Yes." Kristina tightened her lips and frowned like a child. They all laughed at Kristina's desperate attempt to cover her own humiliation.

Krystal chuckled, "Here you can have my jacket."

Kristina took it and said, "You do realize I have like thirty jackets at home?"

"And where are your thirty jackets now?" Krystal said, raising her eyebrow in mockery.

Kristina shook her head, mumbling, "Fine. You win." Everyone smiled and shook their heads.

Krystal's mom stood in front of the whole group like their chaperone and said, "Alright everybody let's get inside. The rest of the church is heading in too." She overlooked Krystal, Kristina, Joanna, Amber, Jaime, and Sho all standing there. They had taken two cars to get there, and luckily had gotten there around the same time.

Krystal took in the sight of her mom and all her friends standing around her. When Krystal had asked them to come with her to church, she was surprised that all of them were more than eager to say yes. Krystal looked from her right to her left, surprised that all her friends were standing beside her. Aside from her mom, Jaime was the tallest next to Kristina while Joanna and Amber were all basically the same height as Krystal, while Sho was the shortest.

The doors opened and people were beginning to crowd the entrance, flowing in like a bunch of tuna into a can. The group went in and took their seats.

They all sat in a lengthy line together, the plush black and blue seats beneath them offering more comfort than they could have imagined. Krystal sat down, remembering the radical change in her life that happened over a year ago. How her life had changed from the suicidal loner to the now social Krystal Henninger. Krystal looked from side to side, taking in the sight of all the people she'd helped, but not of her own accord. If God hadn't been guiding her, then Krystal would never have seen these people hurting around her. She would have never met Jaime, or Joanna, or Kristina, or Amber, or Sho, and loved on them the way Jesus loved her. Amber and Joanna were sitting to her left, Jaime and Kristina on her right next to Sho, and then Krystal's mom sat on the end of the row. Krystal gave the widest smile she'd ever had. Krystal brought her eyes forward and thought, *It's all because of You God. You took me. A suicidal loner and gave me hope. Because of that, You were able to help others through me. Now I see the beauty of Your plan and how You can use broken people like me to help others. So, I just wanted to say, thank You.*

The Preacher walked on stage and said, "I'm going to start off with a question today."

Krystal nodded, *As you normally do.*

"What does your pain mean to you?" The Preacher paused to let the crowd decide amongst themselves before answering his own question.

The Preacher began his normal pacing on stage, "Pain is a remarkably interesting thing. We want to live our lives without pain but in reality, it is something we all go through. There is not a single person out there today that has not or will not experience pain at some point in their life. Even Jesus Christ experienced pain, and He was perfect. We look at ourselves and think, 'Well, there's one more thing we must bear as we live in this dreadful existence.' But that is not the case. Pain can be a blessing if you look at it a certain way." The Preacher returned to his podium and spoke solemnly, "There will be a unique pain in your life. Your experiences and the lessons you go through will shape you for the rest of your life, and one of the biggest ways to learn those lessons is through pain."

The Preacher started walking around the stage again. "What is your unique pain? What struggles have you gone through? It's interesting to ask because we have all gone through different types of pain in our lives. Some of us may experience the pain of loneliness while others have experienced the pain of an abusive family. Some of us experience the pain of anxiety while others experience the pain of a physical disease." The Preacher held his hands parallel to each other. "You see, we all have our own experiences, and it is those painful experiences that shape us the most. It is like forging a sword in a fire. You have to turn up the heat in order to craft a better sword."

The Preacher pushed up his glasses, "I hate to tell you but sometimes you won't do something unless the pain of staying where you are is greater than the pain of change." The Preacher raised his arms and let them fall. "So, what then? What is the point of our pain?" He paused, letting the words sit with the audience. The Preacher turned to his podium, leaned over, and lowered his voice, "My friends, God does not want you to waste your pain. He wants you to *use* it." Pause. "If you learn nothing from your pain then it is a wasted experience. But if you *use* your pain and learn from it, then you will grow in character." The Preacher held out his hand, "Sometimes pain can unify a people. Sometimes pain can teach you a valuable lesson. And sometimes, pain can give you a friend because you've both gone through the same experience."

Krystal's eyes widened as she took her eyes off the Preacher and looked at all her friends sitting around her. People who had all suffered loneliness in one way, shape, or form. They may have all come from diverse backgrounds and families, but the struggle was all the same. Krystal felt a strong resemblance to that. It was a sad reality but sometimes it feels better to know that you're not alone when going through a problem. And the reason why Krystal was able to connect with all her friends was because she went through that painful process.

But to find people who welcome you and are glad when you are around, simply for you being you, brought more relief than Krystal could have possibly imagined. To have people to cry with you when you are down and to have people rejoice with you when you succeed. You learn that *you are not alone.* (I'm speaking to you reader.) Krystal learned that people may think they are the only person on the planet going through this type of problem, but there will always be someone like you going through the same problem. The nights may be long, but the dawn will come. Those feelings you are experiencing right now will not last forever. The night will pass, and the sun *will* rise.

Krystal took a breath, feeling the center of her soul, now filled with the Holy Spirit and the satisfaction that she knew down to her core that *she, is, loved!* A loner suicidal girl gone from loser to hopeful, from suicidal to living, from a wreck to a masterpiece, from broken to beautiful.

"Remember," the Preacher said, "God is with you in all your pain. God knows your pain and He doesn't want you to go through that pain alone." The Preacher pointed toward the ceiling, "God cares so much about you that He even sent His one and only Son, Jesus Christ to come and die for us. You see, Jesus is God in human flesh, which means that Jesus got tired and hungry and experienced pain and temptation like the rest of us. Jesus set the perfect example for how we should live our lives. And yet, one of the most beautiful things about Jesus becoming human is that God can relate to us. Have you ever heard of a religion where the god chooses to live among the lowly humans they created and to go through the same pains and struggles we humans go through? What kind of God does that?" The Preacher paused, "I'll tell you, a God who loves you."

The Preacher pushed up his glasses, "And so, because Jesus went through life as we did. He lived, He breathed, He suffered, He died, and He was raised from the dead. He went through all the trials and temptations and pains we do. Not because He had to, God could have chosen to condemn us to hell for the rest of eternity, but He didn't. Why? Because God loves us, and He wanted to bring us with Him into Heaven. Therefore, Jesus used His pain. He used the most painful death in all of history, a *crucifixion*, to bring hope and joy and peace to humanity for all time!"

The Preacher lowered his voice and spoke solemnly, "My friends, there is nothing greater than the power of the Resurrection. I urge you to use your pain to benefit others. For pain can sometimes be a blessing in disguise if you learn to look for it. It can be a lesson to learn from and improve yourself and allow you to help others you never thought you would care for." The

Preacher pushed up his glasses. "Do you think a person would start a charity for children suffering from cancer if they didn't struggle with the loss of a child to cancer? Do you think a soldier coming home from war would start a therapeutic ministry helping other soldiers with PTSD if that soldier did not suffer from PTSD?" The Preacher lowered his voice, "The same way works for you and what you have been gifted and struggled with in your life. So, *go*. Go and help your neighbor. Go and help the weak and the abandoned. Go and love others the way God loves you."

The Preacher looked down and said, "I'm going to finish now with a prayer, and then I am going to be accepting baptisms at the end of the service today outside. If you don't know what baptism is, it is a public declaration of you accepting Jesus Christ into your life. If you are ready to dedicate your life to Christ, will you pray this prayer with me?" Everyone bowed their heads. "Father I'm done with living my old life. I'm done with living this empty life I have chosen to live. Jesus I am broken, I am a sinner. Will You please come into my life, and I promise to follow You with all my heart. Please forgive me for all I've done wrong and give me a new life in You. I pray all this in Jesus' name, amen."

"Amen," the whole crowd repeated.

The Preacher held his hands together and said, "If you want to be baptized and publicly declare that you have accepted Jesus into your life, will you stand with me?"

Krystal snuck a glance at the baptism pool. She thought back to when she prayed for Jesus to come into her life long ago; the dramatic change that erupted because of it. Krystal felt a strong tug in her heart. A call to action. She knew this was her moment, a decision that would change the rest of her life. And so, with confidence, she pushed herself up from her chair and stood up among the crowd for all to see. Krystal heard shuffling nearby and could tell that someone else around her stood up.

Krystal then looked to her left and right, finding Jaime, Joanna, Kristina, Amber, her mom, and Sho all standing with her. Krystal's heart leapt with joy.

The Preacher said, "For those of you who are standing, can we give them a round of applause." The whole auditorium filled with cheers. Krystal felt just like she did when she sang at the talent show. The cheer filled her heart with joy. The Preacher said, "Now, will you please join me outside in the baptism pool. We will provide clothing and towels for you once you are there."

Krystal glanced over at her mom and locked eyes with her. *You too?* A secret message sent between them. Krystal's mom only smiled, and the sight of her mom looking so happy made Krystal feel so happy. To know her mom was stepping in the right direction.

They made their way toward the baptism pool and stood outside. The warm sun gleamed down on them, replacing the morning chill, like it was destiny for them to be there, to stand in the light and be seen as they are. Krystal and the others quickly put on their designated baptism shirts. Krystal was the first to step into the pool, imagining the water to be freezing but in reality, it was warm like a jacuzzi. Krystal felt the warm water rise up to her stomach as she stood in the center of the pool. The warm steam rising from the water. Then Jaime, Joanna, Kristina, Sho, Amber, and Krystal's mom soon followed. "Let's do it all together," Joanna said, "at the same time."

Jaime nodded, "That's a great idea." They all nodded in concert and Krystal agreed.

They all looked toward the Preacher, who stood there smiling. More leaders stepped into the pool and strode up next to them, holding everyone by their side, the pool now filled to its max with people for its baptism. The Preacher came up to Krystal and held her by her side and said, "What's your name?"

"Krystal, Krystal Henninger," she said.

The Preacher spoke softly and with deep love in his voice, "Krystal, do you accept Jesus Christ as your Lord and Savior?"

"I do."

The Preacher looked toward the rest of Krystal's friends, "Do all of you accept Jesus Christ as your Lord and Savior?" They all said yes. The Preacher held Krystal by the side as did the rest of the leaders and said, "I baptize you in the name of the Father, the Son, and the Holy Spirit," then lowered Krystal into the water.

Krystal closed her eyes, her arms crossed in an X across her chest as she dipped backward. The world slowed; Krystal found it so peaceful as she was lowered into the warm water. *It's funny*, she thought. *It feels nice to fall like this.* The water slowly enveloped her, engulfing her in its warmth. Krystal stalled underwater for a moment, then felt whatever darkness that lay in her past fall off and vanish, leaving only a pure soul.

Krystal came splashing out of the water to be greeted with cheers and applause from everyone around, wiping her face as the Preacher smiled at her. Krystal hugged him with all her might. It was over. It was finally over. The darkness in her life was washed away completely, all signs of suffering and despair were replaced with this overwhelming sense of hope and joy. The dark times were over, the sun had finally dawned. And there was hope, hope for the rest of her life unto eternity through the amazing mercy of God.

"Thank you," she muffled into the Preacher's shoulder, "Thank you." Krystal turned to see Jaime, Joanna, Kristina, Amber, Sho, and her mom all standing there with joyous smiles on their faces. Krystal went towards them, raising her arms for a group hug. Knowing the dark times were over and hope had finally begun. Krystal hugged them as hard as she could, feeling joy and tears rush from her face as she held her arms around the people who all shared her pain, the pain that linked them all together. Knowing that love has won.

Parting Poem

Lonely days are long ahead
Days of plenty and full of dread
And though I ask, why are it I
I cry for help but alone I die
Come at last, come fill what may
Please at last end my day
Though I seek the light, and not the dark
My soul be empty, from You apart
Though not within me, though not of my way
Through Yours alone, through healing I say
Come fill me now, now with Your joy
Teach me true, my old destroy
The dark is gone, the day is bright
The spring is here, Your truth is light

My Testimony

Thank you for reading my story. Remember, this story is not for everyone. This story is for the losers. For the hurting. If you are reading this story right now, then ask yourself, "Was this book for me?" And if the answer is "No" then why the heck did you read the whole thing? (I'm only joking.)

If you are hurting and feel like you are stuck in a pit. If you feel trapped and wish for someone to rescue you from the darkness, then let me give a helpful piece of advice. *I've been there. I know exactly how you feel.* From personal experience, I have been in the darkness. That's one of the reasons why I am writing this. To express my heartfelt desire to reach out to each and every one of you and grasp you within my arms and tell you . . . **"It's going to be okay."**

I have known sorrow and depression. I have suffered from loneliness for a long portion of my life and to be honest, it sucks! It's horrible, and I'm surprised every day that I have made it this far. But I didn't make it this far on my own accord. I would have killed myself long ago if I didn't have God in my life.

Around fifth and sixth grade, I found God and accepted Jesus into my life. He fulfilled me and took away that emptiness in my heart and gave me purpose and a reason to live.

Throughout middle school I did not have that many friends, and I can testify that that was partially my own fault. I was not as sociable as I should have been. I was, for full disclosure, a gamer, and all I wanted to do was go home and play videogames, and perhaps that was the largest contributing factor to my own loneliness. (But there were a lot of great videogames coming out when I was young, I mean come on.)

High school started, and I'm not going to lie, it sucked! (That's putting it lightly.) I remember so many days where I would sit by myself during lunch, yearning for friends and having no one to sit with. And so, what did I do during that time? I walked. I walked nowhere and everywhere. I would walk circles and circles around the school because I had nowhere to go and no one to sit with. For nearly six months I remembered spending my time during lunch, looking magnetically at the pavement, watching everyone around me sit with their groups of friends, looking happy and having the best time of their lives.

Built into the human heart is the need for community; to belong. And when that need is not fulfilled, it causes negative feelings to erupt in our hearts and minds. For me, I felt worthless. I felt invisible. I could stand among a crowd and feel like I wasn't even there. I didn't start healing until years later when I grew more mature, but kids are ruthless man, remember that.

To be brief, I was ostracized in high school. I would show up to social events like eating lunch outside by the benches, only to have people shift to the bench opposite of me the second they got there. Or events such as Winter Formal where everyone would take pictures with each other, and no one would take pictures with me. I felt invisible. Feeling like I could leave, and no one would care. And that hurt. It hurt for a long time.

Little did I know that those two years of hell would shape the core of my being for the rest of my life. I found out what it was like to be unwanted. To feel worthless and invisible. I joined an invisible crowd of people that populated in the thousands. An invisible crowd that can only be seen by those who have been invisible themselves. It's a problem that continues to ruin kids growing up in school in our country. I wish I could be friends with everyone, to be able to come up to each and every one of you and tell you, "It's going to be okay."

My story continues into my first year of college. (Take into account, I started making really good friends by the time my junior and senior year of high school started.) I didn't know where I wanted to go, all that I wanted was to get out of the high school bubble and go make friends somewhere, and enjoy the college experience. My endeavors took me to Salt Lake City, Utah, where I went and studied Business Management for three and a half years. But the first year of college was by far the hardest for me.

Moving to a brand-new state, with no friends and no family was hard. It was a first-time experience for me to get to know people and learn how to live by myself. After my unpleasant time in high school, I was determined to make some friends. I learned in college that **you are only as sociable as you choose to be.** And so, I went out. I planned long in advance to go to social events and hang out with people. I tried ridiculously hard to be social. But things didn't work out immediately. A word of advice, **you won't see the fruit of your labor until later.** So, for four to five months, my very first semester of college, I had never felt more alone in my life. Every day got harder and harder to get out of bed.

Gradually, I found myself in a state of depression. There were some dark days, like going to a dance around Halloween and not having a single person to hang out with. Another time was during Fall Break, when I went to go see a movie and no one was able to come because everyone went home for break while I had to remain in the state to gain residency. And so, I watched a movie in an empty theater by myself. That's when the reality sunk in, and it got harder after that. Having all the time in the world and no one to spend it with was painful. Despite all my efforts to be social, I still hadn't found a friend whom I could connect with. I was being social and trying to meet people, and people were trying to meet me. (College is awesome like that because nobody knows each other, and everyone needs friends, so new friend groups can easily form.) But things were taking a lot longer than I expected.

Now that I was in a state of depression, I could not get myself out of it. It felt like everything in the world was gray. I could feel it every moment of every day as constant as the air around me. I was fighting to convince myself that I was going to be alright but no matter how much I tried, I could not reassure myself. And that was when the suicidal thoughts began to roll in.

I began to struggle with suicidal thoughts in my mind often. No matter how much I tried to fight them off, they kept coming back. I tried over and over again to reassure myself, and I eventually opened up to my parents that I was struggling with suicidal thoughts. (Just the kind of thing a parent wants to hear when their kid is out of state and all alone.)

I then went to counseling for a couple of sessions, but the sessions didn't really help. It was more centered on calming my thoughts through certain mental exercises rather than how to cure my actual depression, so I didn't find it all that helpful. The depression was still there.

I am a Christian and have been my whole life. But even Christians struggle with suicidal thoughts and depression. (But having God in your life dramatically increases your ability to fight depression and suicidal thoughts.) There were constant nights when I begged God to cure me of my suicidal thoughts. *"Please take them away! Please!"* I didn't want to think suicidal thoughts, but they kept entering my mind. I didn't want to feel down and depressed, but I did. It was like I could not convince myself that things would get better. And all it did was drain me.

I remember riding my Penny board on the way to the food court early in the morning. And I mean, WAY before the sun was even up, okay. I was a college student that had 7:30am classes my first semester. (I know, what was I thinking!) But as I skated to the food court for breakfast, I randomly started singing some Christian worship songs. The first one I was familiar with, but then I started singing another song that I didn't fully know, I had heard the song before, but I didn't know all the lyrics. For some reason, the lyrics of the second song felt appealing to what I was going through. I wanted to finish the song, so I sat down in the food court, put on my headphones, and listened to the rest of the song. The song is called, "Tell Your Heart to Beat Again" by Danny Gokey, a Christian singer who lost his wife before he went on American Idol. I listened to the rest of the song, and I felt the words flow over me, showering my heart, soul, and mind with relief and healing. I felt the change in my heart immediately once the song finished, and in that moment, I knew, *it was over.* (That song remains today as one of my favorite songs.)

And you're probably asking yourself, 'Jake, how is that important? I mean you just listened to a random song, and it made you feel better.' But here's the thing. That song was not random. I had heard that song from the Air1 radio station at least two years before my state of depression. The song was planted in my mind long ago by God, knowing that in two years, God would use that song to cure me of my depression and suicidal thoughts. I didn't even know the name of the song when I started randomly singing it. It was God who planted that song in my mind so that I could sing it at the right place at the right time. Because, at that point in my struggle, I had completely given up. I had surrendered myself to God, knowing I could not save myself, no matter how hard I tried. And trust me. I tried. I tried extremely hard.

If you don't believe in God, let me tell you this, God had directly intervened in my life there. I went from suicidal—where I had to get rid of my own flip-blade knife out of fear for my own safety—to hopeful. I felt the dramatic change in my heart and from that moment on, I was healed. I was able to feel happy again, knowing that I was truly loved and taken care of. If you don't believe God exists, then I ask you to look at my story. Because I would not be alive if it weren't for God. I would have killed myself long ago, even though I had a good family and a healthy upbringing.

Why I Authored This Book

And so, I come back to my reason for writing this story. My history as an ostracized loner was one reason. My other reason is because God called me to write it.

For more background, I was in my sophomore year of college and had finished the most stressful semester of my life. After going from super stressed to having all the time in the world, I had never felt more at peace in my life. For a couple of weeks, I remembered having this idea in my mind, saying, "What if I write a story about a Janitor? Where he is a gentleman-like character and where this man would help people with their problems." The idea was not too out of the ordinary as I remembered meeting a Janitor on a train one day in Utah after getting my bike fixed. He said to me, "I have great hope for your generation." And through those words, I wanted to cry. I don't know why, but he had this glow around him, like I was sitting close to the sun and his words brought me so much joy in my day. I'll never forget that man. I think his name was Curry, and he lived in Salt Lake City. (I think he also worked at a church.)

And so, for weeks I had this idea remain in my head. It came to the point where I said, "I need to pray about this." At the time, I was reading the book of Isaiah in the Bible, and consider, I was originally reading in the New Testament prior to that (Isaiah is in the Old Testament). I wasn't reading anywhere close to Isaiah, but for some reason, I got the impression that I should read the book of Isaiah a month or two prior. I don't know why, I just did. I stopped where I was reading in the New Testament and started reading the book of Isaiah. Nothing happened at first, but the surprise came later.

So, when I was sitting in my room, after being home in California for

Winter Break, I decided to pray about it. I took a quiet time (a time where you just be quiet with God, meaning you don't have your phone with you and you sit in silence for a period of time with no distractions, and you pray and read the Bible until God speaks to you). At the time, I remembered hearing Rick Warren, the pastor of Saddleback Church in Southern California, talk about how I should stop looking for God to speak to me in a *voice* and start looking for Him to speak to me in a *verse*, meaning I should look for God to speak to me through the Bible instead of Him speaking to me verbally. (Like reading a letter from someone.) And I asked God, "God, do you want me to write a book about a Janitor?" I flipped my Bible open to where I was reading and the *first* thing, I read was Isaiah 30:8, which read,

> *"Now go and write down these words.*
> *Write them in a book."*
> —ISAIAH 30:8A (NLT)
> (That's literally what it says.)

I looked up from my Bible, and at that moment, I had my answer. I said, "Okay God, I think You want me to write a book." And so, that's what I did. I started writing in the winter of 2018 back when I was 19 years old. And that's how I started writing this story. Question it if you want, but I know what I felt and I know what I read. What are the odds I flip to that exact verse out of the *entire* Bible, telling me to write a book? The Bible is made up of 66 books man, IT'S LONG, and to flip to the right page on the right day, in a book I wasn't even reading at the time, is all too much for me to count as coincidence.

So, for all that it's worth, I'm glad I made this book. I'm glad I got to write this, because since I wrote this, God has changed me in more ways than I could possibly imagine. I hope you enjoyed the story and I wish you the best.

But just remember (seriously remember): That although life is hard and you feel like giving up, **the dark days will not last.** The dawn will come. For there is hope in Jesus Christ. For nothing is impossible with God. (And trust me, life is a lot easier when you have God in your life than without.) And I want you to know, from the bottom of my heart, that *you matter!* You are not worthless. You are a masterpiece. There is a reason to get out of bed in the morning. There is a reason to have hope in this world, and that hope is Jesus Christ.

I thank you for taking the time to read my story, and I hope it has changed you just as much as it has changed me. Thank you.

Written by: Jake Lynch

Acknowledgments

Dad, thank you for giving me all the support I could ask for. You have always been a role model for me in your drive for justice and doing the right thing. Thank you for being the loving father I needed and for supporting me every step of the way.

Mom, I couldn't have asked for a better mom. Thank you for always caring for me and for giving me the support to pursue my dream.

To my older brother Troy. As the great Sylvester Stallone once said in Rocky II, "Yo Adrian! I did it!" I could not have gotten this far without your support in reading my work and your honesty. I'm so glad you love my work and I can't wait to get more of it out there for you. It was your feedback that revealed to me what kind of writer I am, and one that I hope to be one day. Thank you for being the best older brother ever.

To my younger brother Colby, thank you for being there and reading my work when you can, as you strive for your dream in the Air Force.

To my pastor and friend, Robert, who took the time to read my work and check that it was Scripturally sound with the doctrine of the Bible, as well as provide me with material on how to publish a book. You have been a big help in ways you don't even know. Thank you for your support.

To my cover designer on 99designs, ZeppelinDG, your work has been absolutely fantastic! Thank you for capturing the vision I could have never dreamed of.

To a janitor that I met on a train in Utah long ago. You may not know it, but you directly influenced my life. There was something about you that just seemed to "shine" as your kind actions played a part in a major crossroad in my life. I hope that you keep striving to make the world a better place with one act of kindness at a time.

And finally, to my Lord and Savior, Jesus Christ. This book wouldn't have been created if it wasn't for you. Writing this book has been one of the most difficult and frustrating journeys I could possibly have embarked on. Yet, if you called me to do it again, I would do it in a heartbeat. Through this journey, I have learned and grown in more ways that I didn't imagine possible. Thank you for creating me into a better man, and for using my pain to help others. So, thank you, for all the blessings you have showered me with, and for giving me an amazing life. Thank you for saving my life and for teaching me the truth. Thank you, God.

About the Author

Jake Lynch is an author specializing in contemporary religious fiction and action-adventure novels. Having grown up under the teachings of Rick Warren, he has a strong devotion to God and actively seeks to love on others. After receiving his Bachelor's Degree in Business Management at the University of Utah, Jake returned home to Orange County, Southern California in 2020 and worked various jobs until he decided to pursue writing full-time.

While writing stories is entertaining, his main mission is to help spread the Gospel of Jesus Christ and to bring hope and healing into the world.

When he's not writing he is usually surfing, doing Brazilian Jiu-Jitsu, and watching anime. Some of his favorite anime are Naruto, Rise of the Shield Hero, and 86. As a local of Southern California the call of the ocean is never far as his love for surfing constantly brings him back to the water.

 www.AuthorJakeLynch.com

 @authorjakelynch

 AuthorJakeLynch

 @AuthorJakeLynch

Helpful Links

Saddleback church url link (**www.saddleback.com**)
Pastor Rick's Daily Hope Podcast

Suicide Prevention hotlines

Call 988 for the National Suicide Prevention Hotline

Speak to a pastor

I urge you to find a local church and call the local pastor and
ask them about any questions you might have.

Amazon Review

Please leave me a review on Amazon
to let me know what you thought of the book!